COLD HIT

ALSO BY STEPHEN J. CANNELL

Vertical Coffin

Runaway Heart

Hollywood Tough

The Viking Funeral

The Tin Collectors

King Con

Riding the Snake

The Devil's Workshop

Final Victim

The Plan

COLD HIT

STEPHEN J. CANNELL

ST. MARTIN'S PRESS NEW YORK

For information, address St. Martin's Press,
175 Fifth Avenue, New York, N.Y. 10010.

www.stmartins.com

Library of Congress Cataloging-in-Publication Data

Cannell, Stephen J.
Cold hit / Stephen J. Cannell.—1st ed.
p. cm.
ISBN 0-312-34730-8
EAN 978-0-312-34730-7
1. Scully, Shane (Fictitious character)—Fiction. 2. Vietnamese Conflict, 1961–1975—Veterans—Crimes against—Fiction. 3. Police—California—Los Angeles—Fiction. 4. Homeless men—Crimes against—Fiction. 5. Undercover operations—Fiction. 6. Los Angeles (Calif.)—Fiction. 7. Police murders—Fiction. 8. Serial murders—Fiction. I. Title.

PS3553.A4995C65 2005
813'.54–dc22

2005046097

First Edition: August 2005

10 9 8 7 6 5 4 3 2 1

For my son, Cody
You have made your dad very proud

COLD HIT: Police terminology referring to a ballistics match tying one crime or weapon to another.

They that can give up essential liberty to obtain a little temporary safety deserve neither liberty nor safety.

—*Benjamin Franklin*

COLD HIT

1

2:30 A.M.

The phone jack-hammered me up out of a tangled dream.

"Detective Scully?" a woman's voice said. "This is Homicide Dispatch. You just caught a fresh one-eighty-seven. The DB is on Forest Lawn Drive one block east of Barham Boulevard, under the bridge.

"In the L.A. River again?" I sat up and grabbed my pants.

"Yes sir. The patrol unit is there with the respondents. The blues say it looks like another homeless man so the duty desk at Homicide Special told us to give you the roll out."

"Isn't that in Burbank? Have you notified BPD?"

"According to the site map, it's just inside L.A., so there's no jurisdictional problem. I need to give patrol an ETA."

"It's gonna take me forty-five minutes." I started to hang up, but hesitated, and added, "Have you notified my partner, Detective Farrell?"

"We've been trying," she replied carefully, then paused and said, "He's not picking up."

There was doubt and concern in her tone. *Damn,* I thought. *Did even the civilian dispatchers in the Communications Division know Zack Farrell had become a lush?*

"Keep trying," I said, and hung up.

I rolled out of bed, trying not to wake my wife, dressed quickly in fresh clothes, and went into the bathroom where I did my speed groom: head in the faucet, towel dry, hair comb with fingers, Lavoris rinse, no shave. I checked myself for flaws. There were plenty. I'm in my late-thirties and look like a club fighter who's stayed in the ring a few years too long.

I snapped off the bathroom light, crossed to the bed, and kissed Alexa. Aside from being my wife, she's also my boss and heads the Detective Services Group at LAPD.

"Wazzzzit?" she mumbled, rolling toward me and squinting up through tousled, black hair.

"We got another one."

Coming up to a sitting position immediately alert, she said, "Son of a bitch is six days early."

Even in the half-light, Alexa took my breath away. Dark-eyed, with glossy hair and the high cheekbones of a model, she could have easily made a living on the covers of fashion magazines. Instead, she was down at Parker Center, in the biggest boys club on earth. Alexa was the only staff rank female officer on the sixth floor of the Glass House. She was an excellent commander, and deft at politics, while managing to avoid becoming a politician.

"The L.A. River?" she asked.

"Yeah, another homeless guy dumped in the wash near Barham just inside our jurisdiction. I don't know if the fingertips have been clipped off like the other two, but since it's almost a week off his timeline, I'm praying it's not our unsub."

Unsub stood for *Unknown Subject,* what law enforcement called perpetrators who hadn't been identified. We used to use words like *him* or *his,* but with more and more female perps, it no longer made sense to use a pronoun that eliminated half the population.

"If the vic's homeless and is dumped in the river, then it's our unsub," she said. "I better get downtown. Did dispatch call Tony?"

Police Chief Tony Filosiani was known affectionately by the troops as the Day-Glo Dago, a term earned because he was a kinetic fireplug from Brooklyn. The chief was a fair, hard-nosed leader who was also a pretty good guy when he wasn't causing havoc by reorganizing your division.

"You better check Tony yourself. I'll let Chooch know." I said.

We'd converted our two-car garage into a bedroom for my son when his girlfriend, Delfina, lost her family and came to live with us last year. I stopped there before leaving the house.

Chooch was asleep with our adopted, marmalade cat Franco curled up at his feet. At six-foot-three-and-a-half, my son was almost too long to fit his standard-sized bed. When I sat on the edge, he rolled over and squinted up at me.

"I'm heading out," I said.

He was used to these late-night callouts and nodded.

Then his eyes focused as he gained consciousness and his look changed to concern. "What about tonight?"

Chooch was being heavily recruited by three Division-One schools for a football scholarship. Pete Carroll from USC was coming over for a coach's visit at six this evening.

"Don't worry, I'll be here. No way I'll miss that. Gimme a hug." I put my arms around him and squeezed. I felt him return the embrace, pulling me close. A warmth and sense of peace spread through me.

I jumped in my new gray Acura and pulled out, wondering where the hell Zack was. I prayed my partner wasn't drunk, propped against a wall in some after-hours joint with his cell phone off. I owed Zack Farrell a lot. He was my partner for a rough two years when I was still in patrol. I was completely disillusioned and close to ending it back then, tick-tocking along, heading toward a dark future. After work I'd fall into my big recliner in front of the tube, swig Stoli in a house littered with empty bottles and pizza boxes, and stare numbly at my flickering TV. By midnight I'd be nibbling my gun barrel, looking for the courage to do the deed.

In the morning my crotch was usually wet with spilled booze, my gun poking a hole in my ass somewhere beneath me. I'd dig it out, stumble to my car, and stagger back to work for another bloodshot tour. I was disheartened and circling the drain.

After two years working X-cars in the West Valley together, Zack left patrol and we hadn't seen much of each other in the years that followed. When Chooch and Alexa entered my orbit they gave new meaning to my life. But the reason the lights were still on when they arrived, was because Zack Farrell had watched my back and carried my water for those depressing two years. He refused to let our bosses take me down. All I had back then was the job, and if I had lost that, I know one night I would have found the strength to end it. It was a debt I'd never be able to square.

I pulled my life together after that and was now a Detective III assigned to Homicide Special on the fourth floor of Parker Center. This was Mecca for the Detective Division because all unusual or high-profile murders picked up on the street were turned over to this elite squad of handpicked detectives.

When I was assigned there, I found to my surprise, that Zack was also in the division. He told me he didn't have a partner at the time so we went to the captain and asked to team up again.

But I hadn't paid enough attention to some troubling clues. I didn't ask why Zack's last two partners had demanded reassignments, or why he'd been in two near-fatal car accidents in six months. I hadn't wondered why he only made it to Detective II, one grade below me, despite two years of job seniority. I looked past these very obvious warning signs, as well as his red eyes and the burst capillaries in his cheeks. I never asked him why he'd gained seventy pounds and couldn't take even one flight of stairs without wheezing like a busted windbag. I soon came to realize that I didn't really know him at all.

Two weeks ago I looked up one of his recent partners, an African American named Antoine Jewel. After almost twenty minutes of trying to duck me, Jewel finally leaned forward.

"The man is a ticking bomb," he said. "Stressed out and completely unreliable. Been so drunk since his wife threw him out, he actually backed over his own dog in the driveway. Killed him."

I certainly knew about his messy divorce, but Zack hadn't told me about the dog, which surprised me. Although by then, most of his behavior was hard to explain.

I made a detour so I could shoot up Brand Boulevard through Glendale to the apartment Zack moved into after his wife, Fran, threw him out.

Like so many buildings in Los Angeles, the Californian Apartments were ersatz Mexican. Two stories of tan stucco with arched windows and a red-tiled roof—Olé. I could see Zack's maroon department-issued Crown Victoria in the garage, but his personal car, a white, windowless Econoline van, was drunk-parked, blocking most of the driveway, which would make it impossible for his neighbors to leave in the morning.

I walked toward his downstairs unit and found the front door ajar, stepped inside and called his name loudly, afraid he would come out of an alcoholic stupor, pull the oversized square-barreled cannon he recently started packing, and park a hollow point in my hollow head.

"Zack? Hold your fire. It's Shane."

Nothing.

The place had the odor of neglect. A musty mildew stench tinged with the acrid smell of vomit. The rooms were littered with empty bottles and fast-food wrappers. Faded snapshot memories of my old life flickered on a screen in the back of my head.

I found him in the kitchen, out cold, sprawled on the floor. Zack was almost six-three and well over three hundred pounds, with a round Irish face and huge, gelatinous forearms shaped like oversized bowling pins.

He was face down on the linoleum. It looked as if he'd been sitting at the dinette table, knocked down one too many scotch shooters, passed out, then hit the table, tipping it as he rolled.

How did I deduce this? Crime scenes are my thing and this was definitely a crime. There were condiments scattered on the floor and blood under Zack's right cheek, courtesy of a dead-drunk bounce when he hit.

"Hey, Zack." I removed his gun and rolled him over. His nose was broken, laying half-against his right cheek. Blood dripped from both nostrils. I got a dishtowel, went to the sink, wet it, then knelt down and started mopping his face, trying to clean him up, bring him out of it.

"Fuck you doing here?" he said, opening his eyes.

"We got a fresh one. Vic's in the L.A. wash just like the other three. Dispatch couldn't raise you."

I helped him sit up. He put both catcher's mitt–sized hands up to his face and started polishing his eye sockets.

"Let's go," I said.

"Isn't our guy. Too early."

Our unsub was on a two-week clock and this was only day eight. But sometimes a serial killer will go through a period of high stress and that pressure will cause them to change the timetable.

Zack winced in pain as he discovered his nose was bent sideways and in the wrong place. "Who broke my goddamn nose?"

"You did."

He touched it gingerly and winced again.

"You want me to straighten it? I've done mine four times."

"Okay, I guess." He turned toward me and I studied it. Then I put a hand on each side of his busted beak, and without warning, pushed it sharply to the left toward the center of his face.

I heard cartilage snap and he let out a gasp. I leaned closer to check it.

"Perfect. Gonna hafta send you a bill for my standard rhinoplasty, but at least you qualify for the partner's discount." I helped him up. "Now let's go. We gotta make tracks."

"It's fuckin' killin' me," he whined, then started with half a dozen other complaints. "I ain't all together yet. My eyes are watering. Can't see. Gotta get another coat. This one's got puke on it." He looked around the kitchen like he was seeing it for the first time. "How'd I get here? You bring me home?"

"Stop asking dumb-ass questions," I snapped. "We gotta go. The press is gonna be all over this. I'm twenty minutes late already." Okay, I *was* pissed.

While he changed his coat and tried to stem his nose bleed, I moved his van. Ten minutes later he was in the front seat of my Acura leaning against the passenger door. He had twisted some Kleenex and stuffed a plug up each nostril. The dangling ends were turning pink with fresh blood.

"The Kleenex thing is a great look for you, Zack," I said sourly.

"Eat me," he snarled back.

I stopped at an all-night Denny's on Colorado Boulevard and got him some hot coffee, then we went Code Two the rest of the way to Forest Lawn Drive.

When we finally arrived at the location there were more satellite news trucks there than at the O. J. trial. This was the first big serial murder case in Los Angeles since the Night Stalker. The press had dubbed our unsub "The Fingertip Killer," and that catchy title put us in a nightly media windstorm.

Two overmatched uniforms were trying to keep fifteen Newsies bottled up across the street away from the concrete culvert that frames the river. Occasionally, a cameraman would flank the cops, break free, and run across the street to try and get shots of the body.

"Damn," Zack said, looking at the press. "They appear outta nowhere just like fucking cockroaches."

We parked at the curb and ducked under the police barricade. Camera crews started photographing us as Zack and I signed the crime scene attendance log, which was in the hands of a young patrolman. A damp wind was blowing in from the coast, chilling the night, ruffling everybody's hair and vigorously snapping the yellow crime scene tape.

"Detective Scully," a pretty Hispanic reporter named Carmen Rodriguez called out as she and her cameraman broke free and ran across the street, charging me like hungry coyotes after a poodle. They ducked under the tape uninvited.

"Is this another Fingertip murder?" she asked.

"How would I know that yet, Carmen? I just got here. Would you please move behind the tape? We put that up to keep you guys back."

"Come on, Shane. Don't be a hard-ass. I thought we were friends." She was trying to keep me occupied while her cameraman pivoted, subtly manuevering to get a shot of the body in the culvert forty feet below. I moved up and blocked his lens.

"You shoot that body, Gary, and I'll bust you for interfering with a homicide investigation."

"Everybody calls me Gar now," he said.

"Unless you turn that thing off, I'm gonna call you the arrestee. Now get behind the tape. Move back or you're headed downtown." Reluctantly they did as I instructed.

From where I was, I could just make out the vic, lying half in and half out of the flowing Los Angeles River.

2

ZACK WATCHED CARMEN and Gar head sullenly back across the street to the news vans parked in front of the sloping hills of Forest Lawn. The cemetery stretched along the lip of the river running for almost three miles, fronted by Forest Lawn Drive.

"Least they won't have to carry the stiff far to bury him," Zack noted dryly.

"Quality observation," I growled as I looked down into the culvert at three cops and paramedics standing a few yards from the body.

Zack and I started along the lip of the hill, looking for the crime scene egress that I hoped the uniforms had been smart enough to lay out and mark for us.

As soon as we started walking, the pack of video predators

across the street got active. They switched on their lights and moved parallel to us, gunning off shots as we headed toward Barham, looking for a pre-marked path.

"We're gonna have to start wearing makeup," Zack grumbled, sipping at the last of his coffee.

"Homicide Special," I called out to the group of uniforms standing down on the levee. "You guys mark a footpath?"

"Go further left. It's all flagged," one of the Blues yelled back.

Zack and I picked our way along the ridge, being careful not to step on anything that might later qualify as evidence. We found the trail marked by little orange flags on the ends of metal spikes. Everybody coming and going from now on would use this path down to the levee. The idea was, by using a remote trail to the crime scene we would limit unnecessary contamination of the site.

If this followed the pattern set by the three previous homicides, our unsub had shot this victim at some other location, then moved the body, dropping it in the river. That meant this wasn't the murder scene, it was a dump site.

Since getting this serial murder case seven weeks ago, I had been reading everything I could find on serial crime. It was a condition deeply rooted in aberrant psychology.

The FBI Behavioral Science Unit at Quantico has classified serial criminals into two basic categories: Organized and Disorganized. The organized killer is usually older, more sophisticated, and has a higher IQ. The crimes are often sexually motivated and the killer has managed to complete some form of a sexual act. Organized killers tend to scope out victims carefully, usually selecting low-risk, high-opportunity targets. The need for control is a major aspect of the organized killer's MO. That need extends right down to the crime scenes, which are usually neat and clean. Some organized killers have been known to actually wash their victims and scrub down the crime scene surfaces with cleaning aids to eliminate trace evidence. After the murder, the victim is sometimes moved and often hidden. There is no standard motive for the crime such as love, money, or revenge. For all of these reasons, organized killers are extremely difficult to apprehend.

The disorganized killer is a much less developed personality. Generally, he is younger, has low social skills, and is sexually inadequate. Disorganized killers are screwups who aren't able to hold jobs. If they do work, it's menial labor. The crime scenes are a direct extension of all of this—bloody, often dangerously close to the unsub's own residence. They tend to kill inside a comfort zone. The body is often left out in the open or right where it fell with no attempt to clean up or conceal it. The attack is often what is known as a blitz attack: an overpowering charge, usually from the front, using sheer force. There is little sophistication in a disorganized murder act and the unsub is generally much easier to apprehend.

There is a third type of serial killer who exhibits traits from both of the previous examples. This category, which is labeled *mixed,* happens for a variety of psychological and sociological reasons too numerous to list.

I had started both a preliminary criminal profile of the unsub and a victimology profile on the dead, homeless men, in an attempt to narrow down who my unsub was, and why he was choosing these particular targets. So far under victimology, all the dead men were unidentified John Does with no fingertips. They were of different physical proportions, all Caucasian, and all mid-fifties to mid-sixties. I believed they were victims of choice because we had found the bodies all over the city, which lead me to speculate that the unsub was searching for a particular kind of person who shared some trait I had not yet been able to isolate. Because of the mutilation, I felt there was a high degree of rage involved in the killings.

My criminal profile identified the unsub as male. All of our victims were white. Because most serial murderers did not kill outside their own ethnic or racial group, I also thought he was Caucasian.

The average age of all known serial killers is about twenty-five. Since this unsub was taking a lot of precautions, such as moving the body into a flowing river to obscure trace evidence, I thought this indicated a higher level of sophistication. For that reason, I had classified him as an organized killer. This pushed my age estimate up over thirty.

Further, the killer was not sexually abusing the victims, so while there was rage, he was not leaving semen behind, making me wonder if these homeless men were possibly father substitutes. The killer always covered the eyes of his victims with a piece of their clothing after he killed them. I reasoned if these were acts of patricide, then maybe he did this because he didn't want these "fathers" staring at him after death.

Still, after three murders, everything I had seemed perilously close to nothing. I didn't see how either profile was contributing very much. All I could hope was for the killer to screw up and make a mistake that would finally point us in a more promising direction.

When we got down to the concrete levee, I saw that the uniformed sergeant in charge was an old-time street monster. At least six-feet-four and two-fifty, he was one of those gray-haired grizzlies who are becoming scarce in today's new police departments. Civil lawsuits have changed height and weight requirements and opened the job up to women and smaller men. I once had a Vietnamese partner who didn't weigh a hundred pounds soaking wet including his uniform, shoes, and gun harness.

The old street bulls complained that cornered felons are tempted to attack small officers. The argument was that they were getting into dustups just because they had hundred-pound partners who looked vulnerable. Old-timers bitched constantly about the new academy graduating classes, full of "cunts and runts."

It's my opinion that the opposite may actually be true. Women don't have to deal with testosterone overload, so instead of feeling challenged they employ reason. Small men tend to choose discourse over a fistfight. It's a useless argument because there is no reverse gear on this issue. We're never going back to the way it was.

The big sergeant approached. He had a weightlifter's shoulders, a twenty-inch neck, and a face like a torn softball. There were seven duty stripes on the left sleeve of his uniform under a three-chevron rocker. Each hash mark represented three years in service, so I had a twenty-year veteran standing in front of me.

"Mike Thrasher," he said, his voice sandpaper on steel.

"I'm Shane Scully and this is Zack Farrell, Homicide Special. You set this up good, Mike. Thanks."

His frown said, *What'd you expect, asshole*?

I glanced around. "Has anybody heard from the ME or CSI?" noticing they weren't there yet.

"Apparently, the Rolling Sixties and the Eighteenth Street Suranos got into a turf war in Southwest," Thrasher rasped. "A regular tomato festival. High body count. Last I checked, CSI was wrapping that up. Should be along any time."

Usually, when you found an old guy like Thrasher with two decades of field experience still in the harness, it was because he loved patrol and didn't want to give up the street. He told us he had roped off a staging area for our forensic and tech vans around the corner near Barham, cordoned off the lip of the riverbank, and asked dispatch for three additional patrol teams to help contain the angry news crews. Because of the bloodbath in Southwest, the night watch was stretched thin and the backup hadn't shown yet. He'd also picked the route down to the body and flagged it. All of this while I'd been pushing

Zack's potato nose back into the center of his bloated, Irish face.

Just then, two more squad cars raced across the Barham Bridge, turned left on Forest Lawn Drive and parked, leaving their flashers on.

Sergeant Thrasher had separated the two teenagers who found the body. The girl was perched on a rock thirty yards to my right. She was a twitchy bag bride, speed-thin with pink and blonde hair and half a dozen glinting metal face ornaments. Her boyfriend was parked under a tree fifty feet from her. With his black Mohawk and milk-white skin, he looked like an extra in an Anne Rice movie. Even from where I stood I could see the white face powder. He was slouched against the tree trunk defiantly. His body language screamed, *Get me outta here.*

"Run it down," I said to Thrasher, as I took out my mini-tape recorder and turned it on.

"These two found the body. They're heavy blasters. I confirmed all their vitals. Addresses and licenses check out. Both are seventeen. Casper, over there has an extensive juvie yellow sheet. Drugs, mostly. He went down behind two dealing beefs in oh-two and did half a year at County Rancho. Name is Scott Dutton. The girl is Sandy Rodello—two Ls. No record. They say they were down here looking for her raincoat that blew out of the back of his pickup, but since the Barham overpass is the space paste capital of Burbank, I think it's beyond obvious, they were under that bridge slamming veins.

"Sandy's the reason they called it in. She can hardly wait to get up there and do some TV interviews."

"Ain't no business like show business," Zack contributed, slurring his words. Mike Thrasher looked over and sharply reevaluated him.

"Anything else?" I said.

"Putting the drugs and the bullshit about the raincoat aside, their story kinda checks. I made sure none of our guys touched the victim, and these two claimed they didn't either. Except when they found him his jacket was pulled up over his eyes, same as the other three vics. They pulled it down to see if he was alive. They claim, other than that, they didn't touch the body. But the corpse is still damp so somebody musta dragged him out of the water."

"Not necessarily. The river's been dropping fast the last two days. It could have receded almost a foot in the last six hours, and with this marine layer, the vic could still be wet, depending on when he got dumped."

I spent a few minutes with Sandy Rodello and Scott Dutton. Drug Klingons, both in the Diamond Lane to an overdose. Sandy was in charge, Scott amped to overload. Along with the vampire face powder, he also had some kind of black, Gene-Simmons-eye-makeup-thing happening.

"You think we'll get to be on the news?" Sandy suddenly blurted after they had confirmed the facts Mike gave me.

"Greta Van Susteren at the very least," Zack quipped. "You might wanta think about hiring a media consultant." Then without warning, my partner pulled the Kleenex twists out of his nose, spit some bloody phlegm into the bushes, and then wandered away without telling me where he was going.

Truth was, I would just as soon work alone. I was getting weary of Zack's sarcastic lack of interest.

"A media consultant?" Sandy Rodello said, earnestly searching my face for a put-on. "No shit?"

"Let's push on," I said. "Do your parents know where you are?"

"Of course," Sandy said defiantly. "They're cool."

"It's okay with them you're both down here doing drugs under that bridge at two-thirty in the morning?"

"Who says we're doing drugs?" Scott challenged angrily.

"Twenty years of hookin' up tweeksters, pal. I got a nose for it."

"Well, your nose must be as broken as your partner's," Sandy said, and Scott giggled.

"You two need to go home," I said. "I'm sending somebody from our juvie drug enforcement team over to talk to your parents tomorrow."

"Big fucking deal," Scott glowered and looked at Sandy for approval.

"We're done. Get going." I waved one of the Blues over. "Show Ms. Rodello and Mr. Dutton to their chariot. And make sure my prime witnesses don't talk to the press. I see you guys doing interviews, and I'll be forced to swing by your houses tomorrow and start taking urine samples. Let's do each other a favor and just keep everything on the DL."

"That's so fucking lame," Sandy whined. But I could see I had her worried.

After we got them out of there, Zack reappeared and we half-slid, half-duckwalked down the forty-five-degree concrete slope of the culvert until we arrived at the river. Then we worked our way back forty yards past the two cops and one paramedic to the body.

3

THE VICTIM WAS lying on his back at the water's edge, his light cloth jacket pulled high under his armpits, but no longer covering his face as Thrasher indicated. The victim's eyes were wide open and rolled back into his head. He'd been shot in the right temple, but there was no exit wound. The bullet was still lodged inside his head.

On the previous murders the head shots had all been through and through. Since we didn't know where any of the killings had originally taken place, we'd never recovered a bullet before. Retrieving this slug might be the first break we'd had since Zack and I caught this case seven weeks ago. After we pulled on our latex gloves, I shined my light over the body, working down from the head, pausing to study his ten fingers. Each one was neatly cut off at the first knuckle.

"He's in the club," Zack said softly.

"Yep." I didn't want to move the body before CSI and the crime photographer got here, but I kneeled down and reached under the corpse, being careful not to shift his position. I felt his back pocket for a wallet, but already knew I wouldn't find one. Unless we turned up a witness who knew him, he was going to go into the books as Fingertip John Doe Number Four.

I snapped on my recorder and spoke. "Jan ten, oh-five. Four-ten A.M. Shane Scully and Zack Farrell. Victim is in the L.A. River, one block east of Barham and appears to be a homeless man in his mid-to-late fifties, no current address or ID available. All ten fingers have been amputated at the distal phalanx in exactly the same fashion as the three previous corpses. Cause of death appears to be a gunshot wound to the right temporal region of the head, but there is no exit wound. Respondents who found the body said his jacket was covering his face, same as the other three John Does." I shut off the tape and motioned toward the dead man's chest. "Let's see if he's got the thing under there."

Zack knelt down across the body from me and we unbuttoned the victim's damp shirt and pulled it open. Carved on his chest was the same design we'd found on the other three victims. A crude figure eight opened at the top, inside an oval, with two parallel lines running horizontally and one vertically.

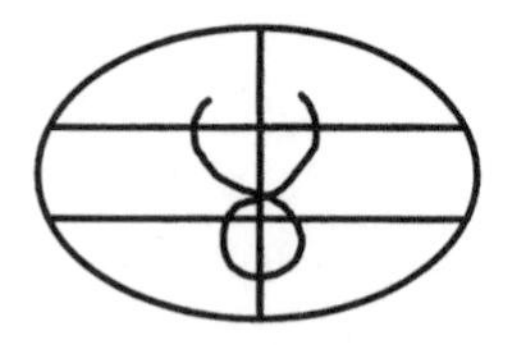

In homicide there is a simple formula. *How* plus *Why* equals *Who*. The modus operandi of an organized kill is part of the *how*. It tells us how the unsub did the murder. But MOs are dynamic, meaning they can be learned and are subject to change.

They are basically methodology and evolve as a killer gets better at his crime and attempts to avoid detection or capture. But this symbol on the chest was not MO, not part of the *how*. It was what is known as a signature element and was part of the *why*. Signatures have psychological reasons. In this case, I thought the unsub was labeling his victims and the symbol was part of the ritual and rage of the crime. If we could decode it, we'd gain insight into the why of these murders. So far the cryptologists at Symbols and Hieroglyphics downtown had not been able to identify it. We quickly rebuttoned the shirt, covering the mutilation.

Zack and I had kept this signature away from the press. On high-profile media crimes, there was never any shortage of mentally deranged people who step up to take credit for murders they didn't commit, wasting hours of police time. Zack called them "Droolin' Just Foolin's." By holding back this symbol, we were able to easily screen them out.

Zack informed me that he had to go tap a kidney and went back up to the road in search of a tree to water.

While we waited for the ME and crime scene techs to arrive, I took a second careful visual inventory of the body. This victim had bad teeth. Dental matching was a good way to identify John Does except when it came to homeless people who obviously didn't spend much time at the dentist.

I knew from all the books I'd been reading that the homeless were low-risk targets and high-risk victims. A fancy way of saying they were vulnerable and easy to attack and kill. I shined my light over the body, trying to see past the carnage into the killer's psyche. John Douglas, one of the fathers of criminal profiling at the FBI Behavioral Science Unit at Quantico, once said that you can't understand the artist without appreciating his art. So I studied the mutilated corpse trying to step into the killer's mind-set.

Then I noticed something on the victim's eyelids. I knelt further down and shined my light onto his face. His eyes were half open so I slowly reached out and closed them. Four strange symbols were tattooed on each lid.

The coroner's wagon pulled in just as the sun was beginning to lighten the sky. A slight man made his way down the flagged trail toward me. As he neared, I recognized Ray Tsu, a mild-mannered, extremely quiet, Asian ME known widely in the department as Fey Ray. He was so hollow-chested and skinny, his upper body resembled a sport coat draped on a hanger. Straight black hair was parted in the middle and pushed behind both his ears.

"Who's the guest of honor, Shane?" Ray whispered in his distinct, undernourished way as he knelt beside me.

"No wallet. Unless you can find me something that puts the hat on, he's John Doe Number Four." We both looked at the clipped fingers. I pointed out the symbols tattooed on the victim's eyelids.

"How the hell do you tattoo an eyelid without puncturing the eye?" I asked, thumbing the lids back to their original position.

Ray shook his head. "Beats me." He opened the shirt and studied the chest mutilation. "Sure wish we knew what this was." His gentle voice was almost lost in the sharp wind.

"I need this guy to go to the head of the line, Ray."

Normally, in L.A., there's almost a two-week wait on autopsies due to the huge influx of violent murder. But our Fingertip case was drawing so much media attention we had acquired the treasured, DO NOT PASS GO autopsy card.

Tsu looked at his watch. "I'll squeeze him in first up," he said. "Doctor Comancho will want to do the Y-cut, but I oughta be able to get everything done here and have him back to the canoe factory by eight." The ME's facility was dubbed the canoe factory because during an autopsy, the examiners hollowed out corpses, removing organs and turning their customers into what they darkly referred to as body canoes.

"Thanks Ray, I owe ya."

Just before I stood to go, I shined my light one more time over my new client. I wanted to remember him this way. Shot, mutilated, then dumped in the river like human trash.

I named him Forrest, for Forest Lawn Drive.

Homicide cops see way too much death, so lately, to fight a case of overriding cynicism, I've been naming my John Does, who are generally referred to as "its" and thought of as "things" with no gender or humanity. By giving them names, it helped me remember that they were once alive, walking around with treasured hopes and dark fears just like all the rest of us. Life is God's most precious gift, and nobody, no matter where they are on the social spectrum, should end up like this.

I looked at Forrest, taking on emotional fuel as the beam from my light played across his face. Then something caught my attention. I moved closer and leaned down. The top of his right eyelid refracted light slightly differently than the left.

"Hey, Ray. Come take a look at this."

The ME moved over and while I shined my light, he looked down into Forrest's eyes, then took forceps out of a leather case and carefully lifted the lid.

"What's that look like?" I asked.

"Contact lens pushed up in the eye socket. Right one only," he said, leaning closer, studying it.

"So where's the other lens, I wonder?"

"I'll have CSI look around down here, see if they can find it," he answered. "Probably washed out when he was underwater."

The crime scene van was just pulling in as I got back up to the road and spotted Zack talking to some cops over by our car. As I started toward him he laughed loudly at one of his own jokes.

Some of the cops near him shifted awkwardly and frowned. The crime scene is the temple of every investigation. Zack was drunk, defiling our temple.

I was starting across the street when I felt a hand on my arm. I turned and found Mike Thrasher staring at me.

"Your partner's loaded," he said flatly.

"He may have had a few," I defended. "We were off duty when we caught this squeal."

"This is your murder. There's no excuse. You're senior man and you need to take action, Scully. He's been stumbling around up here pissing on the bushes in front of the press, breathing whiskey on everybody. If you're not going to take care of it, I'll be forced to file a one-eighty-one. With all the bad shit this department has been through since Rodney King, O. J., and Rampart, none of us need this."

Of course, he was right. But I felt my heart pounding in anger, my cheeks turning red with frustration.

"It's not your problem, Sarge. You don't know what he's been going through. He's in a messy divorce. He just lost his moonlighting job at the Galleria. He's having big problems. Why don't you just be a good guy and stay outta his business?" Thrasher glared at me, so I said, "And if you file that one-eighty-one, I'll have to look you up and do something about it."

After a moment, he turned and walked away.

I'd won. But I'd also lost because I'd been forced to watch all the respect drain out of his cool gray eyes.

4

I DROPPED ZACK at the main entrance of Parker Center and watched as my partner trudged up to the large glass double doors, dragging anchor. Zack was in charge of keeping the murder book, so he was heading to Homicide Special to update the case file. While I attended the autopsy, it was his job to start a new file for John Doe Number Four, copy in the names and addresses of our two teenage respondents, Xerox the diagrams I made of the position of the body in the river, then paste them all into the book. Once we got the photographs of the eyelid tattoos, we'd copy them and send the originals to Symbols and Hieroglyphics for analysis. We'd paste in the crime scene photos after we got them, and tomorrow the coroner's report and autopsy photos would be added along with all the other details of the investigation. Little bits and pieces, some of it seemingly worthless, all of it carefully logged, dated, and placed in the murder book along with a detailed time line, until finally we hit some mystical investigatory critical mass and someone yelled, *I know who did it!* That was the theory, anyway.

The problem with John Doe murders is until you have the victim's ID, it's almost impossible to solve them. Without a name, you can't even make up a preliminary suspect list or question any witnesses. If we'd known who the first three victims were, maybe we could have begun to define the unsub's kill zone and set up a patrol dragnet. As it was, the case was going nowhere.

In an attempt to identify one of my John Does, I had the coroner retouch their faces and had a sketch artist do charcoal portraits. I ran them in the local papers and on TV under a heading DO YOU KNOW THIS MAN? Nada. Of course, most of the people who might have known them lived in doorways or cardboard boxes and didn't watch much TV or read the newspapers.

Now, for the first time in seven weeks, I was feeling hopeful. Forrest might deliver some useful clues. He still had the bullet inside him. The tool marks lab in ballistics would magnify it and graph the striations. Since every gun leaves its own specific rifling marks, maybe we could match the bullet to one used in another crime. He also had those unusual tattoos on his eyelids, which might tie him to some club or gang. Then there was the contact lens. If I could work that backwards, find the lab that made it, and use their records to locate the eye doctor who wrote the prescription, I might find out who the victim was.

These possibilities were spinning my spirits into a more optimistic orbit as I pulled into the stark, ten-story County Medical Examiner's building on North Mission Road. It was 7:45 A.M. when I got off the elevator on the seventh floor where autopsies were performed and walked past the losers from last night's gang war. This group of departed karmas was lying on metal gurneys; a collection of shrunken memories.

I checked the scheduling board and saw that Forrest had already picked up a city homicide number. He was now HM 58-05, which stood for Homicide—Male. The twenty-eighth murder in the city of L.A. for the year 2005. It was only the tenth of January, so not even counting the traffic jam of gang-bangers parked in the hallway, '05 was getting off to an energetic start.

As Ray indicated, Dr. Rico Comancho was doing the autopsy. Rico was raised in a blighted neighborhood in Southwest called Pico Rivera. But he'd been blessed with a high IQ and received a full academic scholarship to UCLA. He went on to med school, and a year after graduation, joined the ME's office, where he made a rapid ascent, eventually reaching the lofty position of Chief Medical Examiner. An exciting success story if your thing is sawing up dead people.

Dr. Comancho rarely did autopsies anymore, unless a press conference was scheduled to follow.

The cut was taking place in Room Four, the big operating theater, which had a twenty-seat balcony for those who enjoyed sipping machine coffee while watching corpse carving. L.A.'s Theater of the Absurd.

I don't generally get along with city administrators, and Rico from Pico was a well-known municipal assassin, but I couldn't help myself, I sort of liked him. He was devilishly handsome, with his full share of Latin charm. His teeth were as square and white as a line of bathroom tile and when he wasn't smocked, he wore expensive suits on a lean, athletic body. An oversized gold watch always rode his slender wrist like a tailor's pincushion. He also had a sunny disposition, which was an asset not often seen among those who perform the last act of desecration.

The autopsy was already in progress when I walked through the door. The center of Forrest's chest was cut from breast bone to crotch and clamped open. Dr. Comancho, in goggles, gloves, and smock, was leaning over the body peering inside like a man inspecting diamonds in a Tiffany jewel case.

"Pull that light down, Ray. Let's give Shane a look at the goods."

Ray Tsu reached up and lowered a large operating theater lamp over the body. The rib cage was already clipped and lifted. The stomach had been removed. Rico pointed at Forrest's internal organs.

"Kidneys are good. Nice and pink. Most of these homeless guys' kidneys look like old army boots."

I grabbed a chair and placed it where I wouldn't get splattered by the bone saw when Comancho got around to widening the Y-cut.

"If I find anything edible, how would you like it done? I'm told my liver flambé is exquisite."

"That's good kitch, Rico, very humorous."

"Guest of honor ain't gonna be needing any of this stuff no more. Might as well get your order in, amigo."

"You find my bullet yet?"

"Fished it out with needle forceps about twenty minutes ago. It's in pretty good shape. Small caliber. I sent it over to ballistics. They'll weigh it and let us know."

"Anything else?"

"Some deep-tissue trauma to the left side in the lateral pectoral region and a totally ruptured spleen."

"That sounds like a left hook to the ribs."

"The guest of honor could've caught a couple a sledgehammer lefts before he winged on outta here. But for all this bruising to occur, the trauma had to be pre-mortem, or at the very least anti-mortem."

"You saying he was beaten to death and *then* shot?"

He nodded. "Without the heart pumping blood, you don't get bruises. Also, in my opinion, this guy would've eventually bled to death from internal injuries without the head shot. An alternate theory is he could have been shot and thrown down into the wash with his heart still beating and maybe got the three smashed ribs and the deep-tissue trauma when he hit the concrete levee. Then once he hit, he croaked."

"Threw him down? Somebody threw him? How much does he weigh?"

"In kilograms or pounds?"

"In candy kisses, asshole."

" 'Bout two-twenty."

"So the unsub picks up two-hundred-plus pounds of dead weight and shot-puts this guy thirty or forty feet over the ledge into the river. You kidding me?"

"Not entirely impossible," Rico said. "You been down to Gold's Gym lately?" Then he looked up from the body. "Ray says there's no trace evidence, so how else would the killer get him down there without leaving drag marks or footprints?"

I had to admit it was a pretty good question. "Our unsub would have to be Godzilla," I said softly.

"Godzilla, Rodan . . . pick your favorite Japanese lizard. But hey, it's just a theory. Medical forensics isn't an exact science, especially when it's bein' done by some border-jumping cholo."

The mask covered his mouth, but I was getting some crinkling around the eyes, the residue of a grin.

"Anything else you want me to fish outta this guy, Shane?"

"I want you to get the contact lens from his right eye traced."

"Already sent it out."

"And I'd like a standard stomach content analysis."

"This guy eats out of trash cans. Don't put me through that."

I started to frown, when he waved a hand at me.

"Come on, lighten up, Homes. Stomach's already out." He pointed to a plastic container with a grayish-brown organ in it. "You think I wouldn't do a standard content analysis? This is Autopsy Central, dude. We serve the dead here. Speaking of which, sure you don't want something to go?"

Some jobs get black as coffin air.

I moved my metal chair further back as Rico took the Striker electric bone saw off a peg and extended the cut. The blade screamed as he opened Forrest the rest of the way up, widening the Y from sternum to crotch. He scooped out the organs, making one more body canoe, then weighed the heart, liver, and kidneys on a hanging scale, read their weights in milligrams into a mic hanging over the table, and dumped them all back into the body cavity like scrapings from a Christmas goose. Ray closed Forrest up with crude stitches reminiscent of the laces on a football. They ended with a standard toxicology panel and complete blood scan. Rico asked Ray to finish and do the stomach content analysis as the phone rang.

The ME stripped off his mask, goggles, and surgical gloves, then crossed the room to answer it.

"Yeah, he's right here." Rico turned the phone over to me and worked his eyebrows. "Some *chavala* named Darlene Hamilton from ballistics, wants your honkey ass. Cha-cha-cha."

"This is Detective Scully," I said.

"Are you the primary on HM fifty-eight-oh-five?" She had a high nasally voice.

"Yeah, only his name is Forrest now."

"Did we get an identification already?"

"No, but I can't deal with the numbers so he's Forrest 'til I can ID him. I was going to call him Barney after Barham Boulevard, but Barney's a comedy name, so it's Forrest."

She was silent for a minute. "Is this Rico? Is this a put-on?"

"It's Detective Scully. Tell me what you've got."

After a pause she said, "We just weighed the bullet Doctor Comancho sent over. It's a strange, off-sized caliber. Rare, actually."

"What is it?"

"A five point four-five millimeter, which makes it a little smaller than your standard twenty-two."

"That's from some kind of foreign automatic, right?"

"The most common gun still using that caliber is a PSM automatic. They were originally issued to KGB officers and Russian

Secret Police during the Cold War and were very popular for execution-type slayings behind the Iron Curtain in the mid-eighties."

I hung up and pondered this strange new fact while I waited for Fey Ray to finish the stomach analysis. When he finally gave me the results, the case got even more confusing.

5

I RETURNED TO my cluttered desk at Parker Center. Zack wasn't there, but Captain Calloway had left a SEE ME FORTHWITH note propped on my phone. I picked it up and headed through the teeming, linoleum-floored squad room packed with cubicles and old desks. Thirty detectives answered phones and worked at computers. We had taken over a space once occupied by the expanding Crimes Against People section. Assaults in L.A. were so high that CAPS had been forced to move to larger quarters on the second floor. We inherited their old area and some of their furniture. The squad room was divided into different criminal sections by colored wall partitions stolen from other floors. No effort had been wasted on decor and no two pieces of office furniture seemed to match, but a lot of good police work was done here. I walked toward Cal's corner office, the only enclosed room on our section of the floor. After I knocked, he yelled for me to come in.

I stepped inside and he barked, "Shut the fuckin' door."

Trouble.

An angry scowl dominated his massive face. Jeb Calloway was short, about five-eight; but he weighed two hundred fifty pounds, all of it muscle. He was an African American who always looked to me like he should be working event security at a rap concert. He had a shaved, torpedo-shaped head, coal-black skin and the ripped build of a comic-book hero. Intimidating under normal circumstances, when he was pissed it was major pucker factor.

"Here," he said. "This is yours."

He handed me a thick blue LAPD binder. I instantly recognized it as our Fingertip murder book. It was supposed to be locked up in Zack's desk.

"One of the guys found that in the Xerox room," he glowered, answering my silent question.

"Come on . . . no way. How'd it get left in there?"

But I already knew how. Zack was copying the crime scene drawings and had just walked off without it.

"You know how much somebody could get for this at one of the local news stations?" Cal growled. "The whole case is in there—crime scene pictures, wit lists, pictures of the chest symbol. The entire fucking investigation could a been compromised. And even though I know it was Zack who left it in there, I'm holding you responsible 'cause you're the lead man. Anything that goes wrong on this case is on you." He took a deep breath. "What the hell is going on with that guy anyway? Since he got back from visiting his mother in Florida, he's been a total fuck-up."

"He's . . . he's just . . . going through some rough water, Cap. The divorce and all. He'll sail out the other end."

He frowned. My sailing metaphor didn't seem to cut it for him.

"When you came in six months ago and asked to partner up with him, I was getting set to throw him outta here. I figured you guys were partners once before so maybe you knew how to straighten him out. This is an elite unit. We're supposed to be the best of the best, but this guy's spent the last two months flying up his own asshole."

"It's just things in his life are piling up."

"You're on the Fingertip murders 'cause the chief and the head of DSG both wanted it. I don't know if I would'a made that assignment because a homicide team has to work as a team, and as far as I'm concerned, you're working alone. This is the biggest red ball we've had around here in ten years. If you muff it, we all go back to traffic."

"Captain, I'll talk to him. I'll get him straightened out."

"Yesterday, I heard a rumor that the sixth floor is thinking about setting up a Fingertip task force. When that happens, this case turns into a cheese fart. Every cop working it will be dreaming of book and movie deals. They'll all start hoarding information. Worse still, a bunch of blow-dries from media relations will get assigned down here to arrange news conferences and press interviews and we'll be up to our asshole in assholes, not to mention the platoon of narrow-shouldered FBI agents who're bound to show up. The head of DSG needs to be told not to form a fucking task force, 'cause they never work."

In my presence, Calloway always referred to Alexa as the head of DSG.

His eyes strayed to the TV hanging on a bracket in the corner of his office. It was tuned to Channel Four with the volume muted. On the screen, Alexa was standing next to Tony Filosiani behind a podium displaying the LAPD seal. They were holding a news conference to officially notify the press about the discovery of the fourth Fingertip victim. The media room looked packed. Every news station in town was there plus one or two people from each of the networks. This could only be viewed as a bad development. Intense network coverage would amp up the pressure on all of us because no division commander wanted to get his balls busted coast-to-coast by Brian Williams or Wolf Blitzer. Cal glanced at his watch, grabbed the remote off his desk and turned up the volume. Tony was in midsentence speaking with his trademark Brooklynese accent.

". . . the facts are known, but as of this moment, we're listing this as the fourth Fingertip Killing. I'll take two more questions." Tony shifted his weight. He was bowling-ball round, short, pink, and bald. Humpty-Dumpty in pinstripes.

"Chief Filosiani, it's only been eight days since the last body was found. Is this killer shortening his time frame, and what does that indicate?" It was the field reporter from Channel Five.

"It would be foolish of me to seize on that one fact, Stan, and say that because the time frame is shortened from two weeks to eight days, this murderer is degenerating or becoming more unstable. I don't want to jump to any conclusions."

"Lieutenant Scully, isn't it about time you set up a Fingertip task force?" Carmen Rodriguez asked Alexa.

Both Cal and I groaned.

"We are not contemplating an organizational change in the investigation at this time," Alexa said. "We'll take that into consideration if, and when, circumstances become substantially altered."

"Thank you," Tony said, anxious to end it.

They both turned and walked off the stage. Alexa was almost two inches taller than the chief even wearing the flats she kept in her office for news conferences so she wouldn't tower over him.

"We're fucked," Cal said. He turned off the set angrily. "Once they start asking about a task force, it's only a matter of time. You got anything promising from this new kill to head that off?"

I looked out into the room full of detectives, then hesitated. I was reluctant to give him my suspicions and he picked up on it.

"*I* ain't gonna go blabbin' it to anybody. I'm your boss, asshole. You got somethin', put the shit down."

"I think there's a chance that this last kill might not be the work of our original unsub."

"When am I gonna catch a break here?"

"Lotta things seem off, Cap. For one, the vic had a contact lens in his right eye. How many homeless guys you ever met who wear contacts? I'm trying to trace it back. We'll see where that takes us. But I'm betting he's not homeless."

Cal furrowed his brow. "Maybe the vic used to have dough, became a wino but still wears his contacts."

"Maybe," I said. "But when Rico opened the stomach, his last meal, consumed less than an hour before he died, included eggplant, parsley, and caviar. So unless he was dumpster diving behind a gourmet restaurant, this is not what we generally refer to as homeless guy food. Also, he doesn't look like a wino on the inside. His liver and kidneys were pink and healthy."

"Maybe this one time our unsub killed outside of his normal victim profile," Cal countered. "Bundy killed a few girls who weren't college kids. Son of Sam didn't just do long-haired girls with their hair parted in the middle. All of the Green River hits weren't runaways or prostitutes."

"We also recovered the bullet," I went on. "That fact in itself is unusual, but there's something else. It turns out to be a five point four-five millimeter, which is a caliber mostly used in a PSM automatic."

"A what?"

"It's a small-caliber gun issued to KGB officers behind the Iron Curtain in the eighties."

"But it could also be the same murder weapon used on the other three 'cause this is the first bullet we've recovered." Cal's voice was getting shrill. He was frustrated with me.

"Except Rico says this guy might have been beat to death before he was shot. There's blunt force trauma and bruising on the right side of the ribs and a busted spleen. The coroner listed the other three victims as death by gunshot, so the methodology surrounding the death looks different."

"So maybe it just means the unsub is degenerating," Cal argued. "Beating his victims first, becoming more violent."

But his tone seemed desperate now. After seven weeks of nothing, he certainly didn't want the first body found that had any worthwhile clues to be classified as a copycat. Neither did I, but that's where the evidence seemed to be pointing.

"Any one of these things alone, I could live with. But all together, they make me think—"

"It's another shooter." Cal finished my sentence. Then after a long pause, he added, "But Zack said the vic had the figure-eight symbol on his chest. The oval thing. So how could it be a copycat? Nobody but a few people in the department and a few in the ME's office know about that."

"Maybe the symbol leaked somehow," I said.

Suddenly the murder book Zack had left unattended seemed a few pounds heavier in my hands. *How careless had he really been with it?* I wondered.

"Maybes and hunches don't cut it, Shane." Cal interrupted my thoughts. "You need to give me a theory that holds your suppositions together."

"You telling me not to work this case the way I see it?"

One of Cal's strengths was he let his detectives run their own investigations. "Okay, it's your case. If that's your take, separate J.D. Number Four out from the Fingertip case and work it separately so it won't contaminate the other murders. But keep this strictly between us. Tell nobody because you could be wrong."

"Yes sir," I said, wondering if nobody included Zack and Alexa. I turned to go.

"Scully, from now on, you keep the murder book."

"Yes sir."

I knew from the look on his face he wasn't finished, so I stood in the door and waited for the rest of it.

"And Shane . . . get your partner straight today. Don't force me to come in here tomorrow and make him piss in a bottle. If I think he's drunk on duty again, I'll sink him. One more misstep and I'm sending him to a Board of Rights."

"I'll straighten him out."

I walked out and started asking around on the floor for anybody who'd seen my missing partner. In the lobby, I finally ran into two auto-theft dicks heading into the elevator on their way back from lunch.

"He was over at Morrie's," one of them said.

Morrie's was a favorite hangout two blocks away on Spring Street. A dark, cozy, Irish pub restaurant with warm green walls and red leather booths. There were always a lot of cops there. Morrie's was well liked because they poured generous drinks.

That's where I found him, sitting at the huge mahogany bar, knocking back shooters.

MY BOYS THINK I'm an asshole," Zack said without looking over. He had three full shot glasses lined up in front of him as I slid onto the next barstool. "All they see are anger and divorce lawyers. They've tuned me out, turned on me." He picked up a shot glass, studying the amber liquid, holding it so the light shone through. "Zack Junior," he finally said in some kind of sardonic toast to his oldest son then downed it.

"It's only twelve-thirty," I lectured. "We're on duty. This place is full of Glass House brass. You're makin' us look bad." Hating the judgmental, kiss-ass words as they came out of me.

Zack didn't look over, but frowned.

"Okay," I said. "Look . . . at least let's move to a corner booth."

I grabbed the remaining two full shot glasses and moved toward an empty booth furthest away from the bar in the dark room.

Wheezing loudly, Zack followed and slid into the booth after me. His eyes were unfocused in sockets that were beginning to turn saffron yellow from this morning's broken nose. He looked old and used up. As soon as he was settled, he pulled one of the shot glasses toward him. He didn't drink, but instead, stuck a big, sausage-sized finger into it, then put the finger into his mouth, tasting the single malt scotch. For a moment I didn't think he would say anything, but then he leaned his head against the wooden back of the booth.

"Everybody's reading me wrong," he sighed. "Even you. I'm in a damn echo chamber. Whatever I say, it comes out sounding louder. People only hear what they already think. It's hard to get anybody to understand when nobody listens."

I decided to stay quiet. I wasn't sure where he was headed.

"It's not enough that Fran and I are getting divorced, or that those pricks at the Galleria fired me and I can't afford her attorney or Zack Junior's college next fall. Now Fran says she wants to know my feelings about it. She says she's worried about me, but she won't take me back either. How do you explain your feelings when you don't have any? Mostly I'm just fucking tired. I think if I could just . . ."

Then he stopped, and put the heel of his hand up to his forehead and rubbed so hard that when his big mitt came away, he left an angry red mark.

"Zack?" He wasn't looking at me. "Zack," I said again, louder, and watched as he turned his head and focused on me. "Lemme help you, man."

"How you gonna help me, Shane?" He stopped studying the shot glass, and downed it. "Just don't throw me overboard. I need the job . . . this case. We'll find some proof."

"Not in here, buddy. The only proof in here is eighty proof."

I watched him scowl.

"I've been where you are, Zack. I've been on the bottom, looking up. I know what it feels like to be out of options."

He was suddenly furious, his face a tight mask of silent rage. I don't know what I said to piss him off, but this is the way he was now. Sudden heart-stopping anger that would appear out of nowhere, turning his eyes into deadly lasers. Maybe he had come to despise himself so much he couldn't take friendship or sympathy. I realized as I sat there and watched a vein in his forehead pulse, that he was much closer to the edge than I had imagined. Then he saw the blue binder on my lap.

"Whatta ya doin' with the murder book? It's supposed to be in my desk," he snapped.

"You left it in the Xerox room."

He sat, dumbfounded. His expression softened. "Naw. Come on . . ."

"They found it in there. Cal gave it to me half an hour ago."

The anger left as quickly as it came, disappearing like smoke out a window. I wished I hadn't told him.

"How could I have left it in Xerox?" he said in wonder. "Shit. Really?"

I didn't answer.

He leaned his head back against the wall. "I am so fucked," he said softly.

"Listen, Zack. It's okay. I squared it with Cal, but I'm taking over the book for a while. I'm taking it home to upgrade it, okay?"

He didn't respond.

"And something else, Zack. Cal thinks Tony is about to form a task force to keep the press off his back. I've been on two task forces and both times it was a disaster. The more blue they throw at a big case, the more selfish and political everybody gets. We need to put this down fast. I need your help, buddy. Will you straighten up and help me?"

"What you really want is to get me outta your way," he said

sadly. "It's in your eyes. You wish you'd never partnered up with me again."

"That's not true," I lied. But it was so true it was laughable.

"Okay, I'm on the case," he said. "Finish this shot and I'm on the wagon."

"Good. Now you're talkin'."

"This new vic is crawling with clues," he grumbled. "The contact lens, the bullet, the eyelid tats. We'll have the unsub hooked and booked in no time. We gotta concentrate on this last kill. Forget the others. Solve this one and we solve them all." Then he picked up the last shot glass and drained it.

7

THE TROJAN TRADITION is a lot more than a bunch of brass in the trophy case at Heritage Hall," Pete Carroll said.

He was sitting in the living room; our cat Franco was at his feet, looking up, not wanting to miss a word. Alexa, Delfina, and I were sitting across from him on the sofa. Chooch was in the club chair leaning forward attentively.

"USC is going to expose you to one of the best academic educations you can get anywhere in the country. It's important to me and to our program to graduate our players. Sixty-one percent of our incoming freshman end up with degrees."

Pete Carroll was in his early fifties; youthful, with sandy blond-gray hair and a friendly, engaging smile. His nose had been broken and not set properly, which I thought added character to an already handsome face. The coach had been in our house for forty minutes and hadn't once talked about football or the two national championships he'd already won. Mostly, he was stressing teamwork and the academic and cultural advantages of the university.

Chooch was beginning to work his way up to a question, and finally asked, "Would there be any chance for me to play as a freshman, Coach?"

"I wouldn't be here if you weren't an outstanding quarterback, Chooch. Lane Kiffen went to several of your games and says you have what it takes. I've seen your tapes and talked to your coach at Harvard Westlake. He tells me you're a team leader and an honors student. I like everything I'm hearing. But my job is about more than who gets on the field or just winning football games. What we're really about is building our young men.

"I play freshmen when they're the best at their position, both physically and emotionally. You won't have to stand in line to get playing time at USC, but I also don't make promises I can't keep." Then he leaned back and smiled at Chooch. "Strange as it seems, your character is more important to me than your time in the forty, because I know a man with good work ethics, a sense of team, and a big heart is going to go out and take care of business not only on the field, but in life. The most gifted athlete isn't always the best man for the job. Heart, teamwork, and integrity count. A lot of what we do at USC is work on building what's inside."

This was my kind of coach. One of the other things I liked about Coach Carroll: he was talking to Chooch, not to Alexa or me. On visits from other coaches, Chooch was just furniture in the room, while the coach was selling the two of us on what their program would do.

"It's important to me that you get what you want if you become a Trojan, Chooch. But the way to get the things you want in life is to grow as an individual. Inner strength always creates opportunity."

Just then, my cell phone rang. It was the third call I'd gotten since Coach Carroll arrived and I could see the frustration in Chooch's eyes as I fished the phone out of my pocket. He wanted my complete attention on this visit and unfortunately, he wasn't quite getting it. But a fresh homicide had hit our table at two-thirty this morning and I couldn't let the first twenty-four hours of Forrest's investigation go stagnant.

The other calls had been from the coroner's office and forensics. No additional material was found at the crime scene. The blood work showed nothing special . . . a low alcohol count and no drugs. They were still trying to trace the contact lens.

I opened my cell phone as I left the living room, and went into the den. "Scully," I said.

It was a cryptologist who identified herself as Cindy Clark from Symbols and Hieroglyphics. We'd met once previously and I recognized her heavy Southern accent.

"I've translated the tattoo on the vic's eyelids," she said.

"Great! Let's hear."

"The figures are Cyrillic symbols from the old Russian alphabet. They date all the way back to Peter the Great."

"Russian?"

"Yes, sir. It's a warning."

"Go on."

"Roughly translated, it means, 'Don't wake up.' "

I started writing that on a slip of paper. "A warning or a statement of fact?"

"In the book where I found it, it just says that life is bad and it's better to sleep. But since this John Doe had it on his eyelids, maybe it just refers to him being asleep when his eyes are closed. I don't know."

"Listen Cindy, I really appreciate this, but what I need most right now is to decode that figure eight inside the oval. The case is starting to fall in on me. Can you keep working on that? If you're at a dead end, maybe you could send it out to experts in other departments?"

"We already did that. Everything we got back so far doesn't help much. I have a few possibilities, but we've eliminated most of them because they aren't exact matches and they don't seem relevant. I think you know Mike Menninger, our head cryptologist. He's gone over everything. He thinks what we have so far is pretty low-yield stuff and might just produce confusion for y'all."

"Let's hear, anyway."

I heard paper rustling, then: "One is a sailing club in Vancouver, Washington, called Pieces of Eight. Their flag is kind of like your symbol, but it's more just an eight in a circle with no cross-hatching. So we don't think it's anything."

I agreed, but wrote it down anyway. "Go on."

"There's a symbol from the ancient Greek that looks a little like it, only the eight is sideways, not perpendicular, and it's closed, not open at the top."

"What's it mean?"

"It was an academic symbol for a college of philosophers in Athens."

"Not very damn likely," I agreed, but wrote that down, too.

"Then, just some logos of businesses. A bike shop in the Valley, Eight Mile Bikes, a chicken franchise called Eight Pieces, stuff like that. None of it is close enough to take seriously. Since the perp carved the exact same symbol each time, we think it's probably a close representation of what he wants. It may be lacking detail, but none of this stuff seems right to us."

"Okay, Cindy, I agree. But turn up the heat, will you? I need a break."

"Yes, sir."

She hung up and I opened the murder book so I could stick the slip of paper inside to enter later. When I looked at the index page for John Doe Number Two, who I'd named "Van" because we found him in the L.A. River at Van Alden Avenue, I saw at a glance that some pictures were missing and the material was not organized correctly. I felt a flash of anger at Zack. What had he been doing instead of taking care of this? I closed the binder and walked back into the living room.

"A good pre-law major is political science," Pete Carroll was saying. "We have academic advisors who help our players with their majors. They also help our athletes register for the right courses. We have mandatory study halls, and tutors on standby if you need help on a subject."

Chooch was leaning forward. "Coach, can we talk just a little more about the program, because I have some questions."

"Sure," the coach said. "Fire away."

"Is Coach Sarkisian gonna stay at USC?" Chooch was asking about SC's brilliant quarterback coach who had recently been promoted to assistant head coach.

"So far that's the plan, but one of my jobs, Chooch, is to support my players and my coaches. If people in our system know that there's opportunity, they flourish. If that means one day Steve Sarkisian takes off to be a head coach somewhere, I'm never gonna stand in his way. In fact, I'll make some calls and try to help."

It went on for another thirty minutes, until Coach Carroll said it was time for him to leave. Franco was still sitting at his feet and before he could stand, our marmalade cat jumped up and landed in the coach's lap. Obviously, Franco's mind was made up. He wanted Chooch to wear cardinal and gold.

We still hadn't had our visit from Joe Paterno at Penn State, or Karl Dorrell from UCLA. Both visits were scheduled for the following week. But I liked Coach Carroll. After he left, we sat in the living room and talked it through.

"What a cool guy," Chooch said.

"He's good-looking, too," Delfina teased, her long black hair and dark eyes shining. She had brought more than I could have imagined into our family since she came to live with us.

"He sounds like a player's coach," Alexa added.

I nodded, but didn't want to put in too strong an opinion in or use my influence to help Chooch decide.

"What do you think, Dad?"

"He's obviously a quality person. But in the long run, it's got to be your decision."

"I wish he'd talked more about football."

"I liked that he didn't," Alexa said. "Anybody can come in here and make promises. What he was saying is he wants to build in you a sense of teamwork and inner strength. Let's face it, if you want success in life, it's inner strength that counts."

8

AFTER DINNER THAT evening, Alexa and I got into a rare, but somewhat heated, argument.

It ended up being about Zack.

We were sitting in our backyard looking out at the shimmering canals of Venice, California. The development was a Disney-esque version of Venice, Italy, designed by a romantic dreamer named Abbot Kinney, back in the thirties. The five-block area was spanned by narrow bridges that arched over three-foot-deep canals. Several of our neighbors had added rowboat-sized gondolas that bobbed like plastic ornaments on the shiny, moonlit water.

Alexa and I had just popped open two Heinekens, and agreed that Pete Carroll and USC would be a good fit for Chooch, when I decided to get something off my chest. I'm not good at keeping secrets from Alexa, so I launched into my theory on why I thought John Doe Number Four might be a copycat murder, running all the evidence past her.

She greeted the information in typical Alexa fashion. Her analytical mind dissected and examined what I was saying. When I finished, she nodded in agreement, realizing that there was good reason for my suspicion. But like Jeb Calloway, she wondered how a copycat would know about the symbol carved on Forrest's chest.

"It's something I can't explain. Maybe it leaked."

"Damn," she said softly. "I was counting on this one to give us something. We already told the press about finding the bullet. If you're right, and this is a copycat, I'll have to figure out how to downplay their expectations."

"Why tell those assholes anything?" I said, my anger flaring.

"Grow up, Shane. It's a media case in a media town. Once this stuff gets into the news, we can't stonewall. If we try, all they do is start putting pressure on politicians, who in turn, threaten us. The trick is to find the right balance. Give the press just enough to keep them cool."

"And when you can't hold 'em off anymore, you form a bullshit task force."

It sounded accusatory, and she turned to study me more carefully, those big, beautiful eyes suddenly hard and speculative. "You have something more to tell me, don't you?"

"Yeah. If you form a task force it's a vote of no confidence in me and Zack. You put me on this and I want some damn protection."

She remained silent, so I argued my case. "You know task forces are bullshit. They obstruct the sharing of information. The feds always show up and you know what happens when we invite the big feet from the Eye into our tent. They end up running the show."

9

IT POURED DOWN rain during the night. I heard it hitting the roof of our house around 3 A.M. banging loudly in the downspouts. By morning the storm had passed and L.A. was reborn and washed clean. The air had a brisk crispness, all too rare in this city of fumes.

As I drove from Venice across town to the Glass House, I decided to take a detour and stop by the city forensic facility on Ramirez Street. The crime lab is a very busy place, and even though I was working a red ball that should be afforded top priority, sometimes people make strange choices. One of my jobs as primary investigator was to make sure my Fingertip murder got the proper attention. Sometimes, by just showing up with a box of Krispy Kremes, you can work wonders.

I stopped at a mini-market just before getting on the I-10 free-

"Shane, in the long run, it's not going to be my call. It's Tony's."

"You're the head of the Detective Bureau. I've seen you go up against Tony and win. Don't hide behind him."

"He's the one the press is gonna skin, not me. If we set up a task force, it gives the news people something to write about. It looks proactive. While we're setting it up and getting it organized, it buys a week."

"And in the meantime, the case gets trashed."

"Then solve the thing, Shane. You've been on it for almost two months. Solve it and take us both out of this jackpot."

It was heating up. Our voices were rising in the cold night air, floating across the Venice canals. Our neighbors were probably rolling over in bed and muttering, "Those damn Scullys are at it again."

"Even Cal doesn't want you to form a task force. He says it's gonna bitch up the investigation."

"So I'm hiding behind Tony and you're hiding behind Cal."

"I'm not hiding behind anybody, because I completely agree. We can solve it ourselves."

"Okay. Then as long as we're on the subject of solving the case, maybe we ought to review it from an operational standpoint."

"Operational?" I was lost. "Okay, what's wrong operationally?"

"I'm hearing rumors that your partner is a problem."

"Look, Alexa, my partner is my business."

"You're sitting here giving me grief about setting up a task force while you're investigating the biggest case we've had in ten years with a fall-down drunk. Maybe that's why we're not getting anywhere."

"Too many lies and loose bullshit gets passed around your floor at Parker Center," I shot back. "My partner's problems are his and mine. We'll deal with it."

"Okay, then just look me in the eye and tell me he's not fucking up."

She was angry. But she was also right and she was under a lot of pressure from Tony. She had recommended me for this case and after seven weeks I was nowhere. Since my position on Zack was untenable, I did what most outflanked husbands do. I got pissed off.

"People go through tough periods," I almost shouted. "God knows I did, and Zack was the one who . . ."

"I don't want to hear about how Zack saved you back in the day! I'm talking about now. Four men are dead and if this fourth John Doe is a copycat, then the only clues we have on this damn serial murder case in seven weeks just evaporated." She threw her empty beer into the trash can next to the barbeque. "So tell me, Shane, is this guy the problem?"

"No, dammit! He's *not* the problem. *You're* the problem! You and all the other backstabbers at Parker Center."

I got up and stalked into the house, immediately feeling like a total ass. She wasn't the problem. Zack was. And I was, for protecting him.

I went into the den, picked up the murder book and angrily flipped it open. Proving Alexa's point, the binder was a complete mess. Things were filed wrong. The initial victim, whom I had named Woody after finding him in the wash at the Woodman Avenue overpass, had one of John Doe Number Three's crime scene photos pasted in his section by mistake. The section on John Doe Number Three, dubbed Cole for Colfax Avenue, was also a mess. Alexa and Cal were right. Zack was just going through the motions. He didn't give a damn. In fact, he was screwing up evidence.

I sat in the den and worked for almost two hours, reorganizing and bringing the murder book up to date. Some of it I had to do from memory because the transcriptions of our original crime

scene audio tapes were missing. Fortunately, I'd held on to the cassettes. If Zack couldn't produce the transcripts, I'd have to get them redone. When I finished, I thought it was about 90 percent accurate. There was still paperwork missing that I'd have to look for in the morning.

I closed the book and went down the hall to our bedroom. Alexa was already in bed. I took off my clothes and lay down beside her. It was dark, but I knew she was awake.

After a long moment, she spoke softly. "I'll do the best I can to hold off the task force. And I'll leave Zack up to you unless it becomes impossible."

What more could I ask?

Then she rolled over and took me into her arms. "Because I know a man with good work ethics and a sense of the team is going to take care of business." Using Pete Carroll's words.

What do you say to a woman like that?

I guess you say, I'm sorry, I was wrong. So after a short internal struggle, that's what I did.

I lay in the warmth of my wife's arms and thought about that. Pete Carroll said you win by depending on your teammates. But how could I depend on Zack?

Before I fell asleep, I remembered Cindy's translation of the old Cyrillic warning.

Don't wake up, the tattoos cautioned.

way and bought two dozen, then drove up the ramp and joined a long line of angry freeway commuters who were bumper-to-bumpering their way to work. My lane mates were holding their steering wheels in death grips, their faces scowling masks of anger. The frustration all of us accumulated on the 10 would be dutifully passed along to our coworkers, who would take it out on their subordinates. This domino effect of bad traffic karma would kill working environments all over town until noon.

I inched along past Wilshire Boulevard, and tried to stifle my frustration by running through a list of more pressing problems. Alexa, Cal, and Tony didn't want Forrest to be a copycat because that body gave everyone hope. The department could slip into wait-and-see mode and pray Zack and I would turn something. But since I was pretty sure Forrest was not part of the Fingertip case, it was just a head feint for the press. Eventually, we'd have to own up to that fact, and when we did, we'd undoubtedly get a task force, including a contingent from the FBI. The feebs like to bill themselves as experts in serial crime. After all, they have an Academy Award–winning movie starring Anthony Hopkins and Jodie Foster to prove it.

All of this made me hate the driver of the blue Corvette in front of me. These assholes in my lane didn't know who they were dealing with. I was pissed off and I was packing.

At 9:40 I finally made it to Ramirez Street and parked in the underground garage at the municipal crime lab. I took the elevator to the third floor and asked the girl on the desk if either Cindy Clark or Mike Menninger were in. A minute later Cindy came out. She was a sweet-faced, slightly round girl with the thick Texas accent I remembered. She smiled and looked down at the box of donuts I held out to her, selecting one carefully.

"Y'all really know how to tempt a girl."

"If that's all it takes, then I've been wasting a lot of money on jewelry and concert tickets," I joked.

"What can I do for you, Detective?"

"I was wondering if we're getting anywhere on my contact lens."

"I was just fixin' t'check with Brandon on that. Come on."

I followed her down a narrow corridor lined with tiny rooms that were the approximate size of walk-in closets. Each one contained a computer, a desk, and a geek. We entered a slightly larger room at the end of the hall dominated by a very skinny, young, black guy with a receding hairline. He wore no jewelry, not even a watch, but he had on a T-shirt that said "Crime Unit" with an arrow pointing down to his shorts. We're really going to have to do something about the quality of humor in law enforcement. Cindy made the introduction.

"Brandon Washington, Detective Shane Scully. Shane has HM fifty-eight oh-five."

"Grab a seat," Brandon said. "Lemme check my e-mails on that lens." When he smiled I saw that his two front teeth were box-outlined in gold. Not my favorite look, but hey, guys do what they think will get them laid in this town. He turned on his computer, and brought up his e-mail.

"I've got a shitload of correspondence here. Hang on a second. Let me shoot through them." As he started scrolling, he brought me up to date. "I examined that contact when it first came in yesterday. It's a rigid gas-permeable lens."

"Is that normal?" I asked.

"Gas perms with this kind of correction are pretty expensive and are used for special eye problems. I checked it under a microscope for a manufacturer's edge mark, but it wasn't made by any of the labs here in the U.S., so I sent it out to an eye clinic we use that buys from manufacturers in Europe to see if they can trace the country of origin. Ahhh, here we go." He leaned forward and read the screen. "Okay, the guy I sent it to says that he can tell from the way the lens was made, that it is from Europe, but they don't know where yet. It could take him a while to run it down because he says there are any number of countries with labs that might be able to do this kind of lens."

"Why don't you start with Russia?" I said.

He leaned back from his computer, looked at me and frowned. "Why Russia?"

"Hunch. Cops get hunches, it's how we solve cases."

"Okay, I'll start with Russia."

"You also might try all of the countries in the old Soviet Union," I suggested. "Georgia. The Ukraine."

"Okay." He picked up a sheet of paper from his out basket and handed to me. "I scanned your lens last night," he said. "That's the condition it was correcting."

I studied the sheet. Bell graphs and squiggly line drawings with a column of numbers.

"That prescription corrects an eye disease called Keratoconus, or KC. It only occurs in a fraction of one percent of the world population, so it's extremely rare. It usually occurs when a person's in their mid-twenties and can progress for ten to twenty years. The name refers to a condition in which the cornea grows into a cone shape and bulges forward. To correct KC, you need one of these rigid gas-permeable lenses."

"This is good," I said. "Anything else?"

"Historically, degeneration of an eye with KC slows around age forty or fifty. According to this prescription, the dead man in the wash was significantly sight-impaired and probably past middle age. Without his contacts, it would have been impossible for him to even drive."

"How expensive are these to get made?"

"My eye expert says hundreds of dollars. They have to be fitted several times to make them wearable."

I sat for a minute holding the printout, thinking not many bums are walking around with expensive contact lenses. "Since this is a rare eye condition, if we can find the lab in Europe that made the lens, we've got a damn good chance of finding out who he is."

"Yep," Brandon said. " 'Bout the way the donut crumbles." Then he took another Krispy Kreme.

10

YOU HAVE THE transcripts from the cassettes we made at the first three murder scenes?" I asked Zack. "They aren't in the murder book."

He was wearing yesterday's clothes and was slumped in his wooden swivel chair across from me in our cubicle, scowling down at the reorganized murder book, thumbing through the pages. He must have gone to a doctor because his nose was now encased in a metal splint and heavily bandaged. He seemed sober, but then it was only 10 A.M.

"I put them in there. In the flap leaf," he said, pointing at the binder. "Somebody musta removed 'em." Since I was the only other person with access to the book, the implication was that I had done it, forgetting for the moment, that he'd left the damn thing unattended in the Xerox room. But so what? I stand accused. Our troubled partnership wallowed on.

Then a look of momentary clarity spread across his discolored face and he snapped his fingers, tilted forward, and started rummaging around in his bottom desk drawer. After a minute, he sat up with an apologetic grin and handed me some Xeroxed pages.

Accused and exonerated. Swift justice.

"I threw 'em in there," he explained. "Was gonna put 'em in the book later . . . forgot." He shrugged as if to say, *hey, I'm only human.*

I took the blue LAPD murder book out of his hand and started to tape the Xeroxed transcripts for Woody, Van, and Cole onto a fresh page in each of their sections.

"You really wanta take this dumb-ass, new theory of yours to Calloway?" Zack said, leaning back and looking down his nose, studying me across a pound of medical adhesive.

Since Cal had demanded a theory that tied all the unaligned facts together on Forrest's murder, I'd been trying to find one. I'd come up with a promising idea this morning. The more I'd thought about it, the more I liked it. I bounced my copycat theory off Zack as soon as I got in to see how it played. It had been met with stony silence. Now I ran down my new idea. After I finished, Zack glowered at me.

"The skipper's gonna say two things," he complained. "He's gonna call this a hunch and tell us that Homicide Special dicks operate on evidence, not hunches. Then he's gonna say, you ain't got nothin' but bullshit here. Which of course, is exactly what it is."

"He'll listen to reason."

"If you're five and a half feet tall and shave your head every morning, you don't need reason." He leaned forward in the wood swivel. It squeaked loudly. "So, after he hears your dumb-ass idea, he's gonna call us morons and broom us both off the fucking case. No way he's gonna let us separate out John Doe-Four 'cause it's not a copycat, and that's the only murder in this chain a hits that we got a halfway decent shot at. Besides, he's also getting his nuts roasted over a slow fire every other Tuesday morning in the COMSTAT meeting." He was referring to the chief's bi-monthly meeting with all the division commanders to review computer crime statistics.

"We gotta tell him anyway," I persisted. "Because regardless of what you think, I believe I'm right."

Then, as if he had been waiting outside, listening for his cue, Captain Calloway stuck his shaved head inside our cubicle.

"You guys asked for a meeting?"

"Yeah."

"Let's do it."

He turned and walked across the squad room toward his office.

"You tell him," Zack said as I stood. "I ain't up to being screamed at by Mighty Mouse this morning."

"Fine," I said. "Just hold my back."

"Only reason I still come in is so I can hold your back and watch you work." Sarcasm.

On our way out, we collided in the doorway. I caught a gamey whiff of him.

"Since you've given up showering, how 'bout investing in some cologne?" I muttered.

"This is cologne. Eau de Werewolf. I send to Transylvania for this shit."

"Go ahead and joke it off. You got half the Glass House circling you. Maybe if you didn't come in smelling like Big Foot, it would help."

"Lemme get back to you on that," he snarled.

We walked into Cal's office.

"What's up?" Cal said. He removed his jacket, exposing huge arms in a short-sleeved shirt. His bi's and tri's bulged the white cotton.

"Cap, did you read the update I e-mailed you this morning?"

"On the hard gas lens? Looks promising."

"I think when we find out where it was made, it's gonna come back as being from a lab in one of the old Soviet Union countries."

"Are we having hunches again?" Cal said, half-smiling.

Zack shot me a dangerous look.

"Hunches based on shrewd observations," I corrected.

"Such as?"

"The tattoos in the vic's eyelids turn out to be Russian Cyrillic symbols. They translate: 'Don't wake up.' "

"How do you get tattoos done on your eyelids?" Cal asked. "Don't they have to press the needle down too hard?"

"I called a tattoo artist, Big Payaso, at the Electric Dragon in Venice. He told me this kind of eyelid art is mostly done in prison. They slide a spoon under the lid to make a work table." Both Cal and Zack winced. "Also, the bullet came from a Russian automatic so I think the vic is maybe a Russian immigrant and the lens is gonna trace back to somewhere in the Soviet Union."

"Okay, so John Doe-Four is a homeless Russian who did time. That's why you wanted to see me?"

"As I told you yesterday, I think this last hit is a copycat. I think I may also have the thread that ties it together."

Cal got up and closed the door. Then he turned back and motioned for me to continue.

"I think this last guy might have done time in a Russian prison and John Doe Number Four might be an ROC hit."

"Russian Organized Crime?" Cal said, raising an eyebrow. His expression told me I better make this good.

"The Odessa mob is aggressive and proactive. They've been trying to infiltrate the department for at least fifteen years, ever since Little Japanese came over here from the Ukraine in the late eighties."

Little Japanese was a violent Russian gangster named Vyatcheslav Ivankov who got his street handle because he was short and had squinty eyes. He brought several members of the Odessa Mafia with him. They had started small, but now there were more than five thousand members listed in our gang book, with large concentrations of Armenian Odessa mobsters in Glendale, Burbank, and Hollywood. I didn't have to remind Cal that we found Forrest right on the Burbank city line.

"The Odessa mob has tried to infiltrate the LAPD two or three times before," I said. "Maybe they put a mole in the ME's office and somehow found out about the symbol carved on the victim's chest. With that piece of info, they could duplicate these killings and use the Fingertip case to hide a high-profile mob execution."

Cal looked over at Zack. "How 'bout you? Whatta you think?"

"I completely disagree. I think John Doe-Four is part of the Fingertip case," Zack said, not looking at me. "Besides, if we isolate the case out on weak shit like this, we got a lotta explaining to do. There's more at stake here for all of us, than just who's killing a few bums."

He was obviously talking about our careers. So, despite his promise to the contrary, Zack had left me hanging. Maybe I should call that the last straw.

Cal thought for a moment, and then leaned forward on the edge of his desk. "I agree. We're not gonna take this last kill out of the Fingertip case because no matter how we rig it, it's still only a theory with nothing to back it up. But I also agree with you that all this background is starting to make this last kill look shaky, so I'll put a little weight on the Russian angle. Hibbs and DeMarco are freed up right now. I'll send them down to Russian Town with the dead guy's photo. Have them show it around, see if anybody knows him. But until something tells us for sure, like a positive ID or a witness, this last guy stays in the Fingertip case." He got up and opened his office door. "Stay in touch with DeMarco and Hibbs, but keep this on the DL. It leaks and you two humps will be workin' Saturday traffic at the Coliseum."

"Yes, sir," I muttered.

Zack and I turned and started out of the office. But Cal stopped us.

"And one more thing. If this investigation doesn't get a whole lot better before the next body drops, I'm gonna have to make a move."

"What's that mean?" I asked him.

"It means you guys better hurry up and clear these murders."

We nodded and exited the office.

"Thanks for the backup," I muttered.

"Motherfucker's about to replace us," Zack growled.

11

TERRELL BELL HAS lousy footwork," Chooch said. "He doesn't set up good at all. Remember the Montebello game? Three picks. If he goes to USC, I'll smoke him. I can't believe Coach Carroll would be recruiting that guy."

Chooch had been going on like that since we all arrived at Toritos, our favorite Mexican restaurant near the Pier in Venice. It was 6:30 and Alexa, Delfina, and I had barely been able to find an opening in his wall of braggadocio.

"Okay, you want to know who's pretty good?" he conceded. "Andre Davis from Servite. He's not what you'd exactly call overpowering as a runner, but the guy has an okay gun. His problem is he's slow. You gotta be able to run the naked bootleg and have enough mobility so when Coach Sarkisian wants to move the pocket, you can get out there. Davis probably can't break five flat in the forty."

"Anybody want to order?" Alexa said, shooting me a hooded look that said, *what's gotten into this boy*?

"Maybe you ought to wait and see if they even offer you a scholarship before you do all this brilliant hatchet work on the competition," I said.

"Sí, Querido," Delfina agreed. "It is not good to criticize others to make yourself strong."

"I'm just saying . . . if Coach Kiffen saw two of my games, then he's gotta know I have great mobility. That's a big plus running the USC offense." Then, without taking a breath: "If I can get rid of my last Spanish language requirement, which I should be able to test out of, maybe I can graduate early, get out of spring term at Harvard Westlake and enroll at SC for spring football. If I got a jump on those two guys, I know I'd be ahead on the depth chart by fall. Whatta ya think, Dad?"

I didn't know what I thought beyond being put off by his attitude.

Our waitress came to the table and everybody ordered the combination plate.

"Anything for dessert?" our waitress asked. "If you want the Mexican pie, I have to put the order in now."

"The Mexican pie is good," I said. "But what we could really use at this table is some humble pie."

The waitress smiled and left.

"Come on, Dad, I'm just saying . . ."

"You sound like a blowhard, Chooch. We taught you better than this. Del's right. You need to concentrate on your own game, and stop running everybody else down. Want my opinion? We were lucky to beat Montebello. That wasn't your best performance either."

"Sometimes I think you guys don't have a clue what it takes to win in football. You have to be confrontational and believe in yourself to win."

"Might be right," I said. "But you don't sound much like a winner tonight."

Right in the middle of this awkward moment, my cell phone rang. I pulled it out and pried it open.

"Detective Scully?" a woman's voice asked.

"Yeah."

"Homicide Special Dispatch. You've got a one-eighty-seven in the L.A. River at De Soto Avenue in Canoga Park, near John Quimby."

My heart sank. This was it. Five bodies and no clearances. I was about to get the hook. "Okay. Notify patrol that I'm on my way. Should be about twenty to thirty minutes, depending on traffic." I hung up without even asking if they'd been able to reach Zack. Deep in my heart I was hoping they couldn't find him.

"Another one?" Alexa said, concerned.

I nodded and stood. "Gotta roll. It's in Canoga Park."

I kissed Alexa, squeezed Delfina's hand, and was about to hug Chooch, when my son stood up with me.

"Can I walk you out?" he asked.

"Sure."

We walked through the crowded two-room restaurant without speaking. Outside, I gave the valet the ticket for my car. Since joining Homicide Special, I'd begun following Alexa on family outings so I'd have a car if I got called out. The wind off the water was still cold, and was energetically flapping the red awning over us.

"Listen, Dad, I know you think I was spouting off in there, but I wasn't," Chooch said.

"It's okay to be frightened," I said, finally picking the way I wanted to deal with this.

"I'm not frightened. Whatta you talking about, frightened? Who says I'm frightened?"

"In police work, courage is a career commodity. You learn pretty quick that the loudest talkers on the job are usually the last ones through the door. You see a cop with a big bore magnum in some fancy quick-draw holster, you're probably looking at a wuss. I hear a guy going on like you were in there, it just tells me one thing. He doesn't believe a word he's saying and he's scared to death somebody's gonna find out he's a fraud. I was only with Coach Carroll for an hour, but that was long enough for me to know he's a guy who understands what motivates people. You go running off at the mouth like that around him, and he's gonna know you don't think you're very good. I wouldn't let him see that if I were you."

I could see from the look on his face that I had read him right. He was scared to death, looking down at his feet.

"It's a big step, a Division One school like USC," he finally said.

"I know it is. But whether you go there, UCLA, or Penn State; or whether you go and sell clothes at The Gap, you gotta be yourself. The way to impress people is through actions, not words. You want Coach to play you, work on your game and be a good teammate. Help the other guy, even if it means he plays and you don't. Somewhere down the road it's going to bring success."

I could see that Chooch wanted to keep talking, but my car was delivered to the curb and I tipped the valet. It always amazes me how life chooses times when you can't linger to deliver up defining moments.

"We gotta pick this up later, son. I've got somebody important waiting for me."

I gave Chooch a hug, climbed into the Acura, and pulled out seeing my son in the rearview mirror, looking after me.

As I got on the freeway I tried to get my mind off Chooch and what I needed to tell him. I ran the case again in my head. It had been six days since we found Forrest. However, if you removed him from the Fingertip case, it put the killings back on a two-week clock.

I exited the 101 at Desoto. Old haunts beckoned me—bars and liquor stores where I'd once tried to eliminate the hollow feeling inside myself by drowning the ache with booze.

Being back in this part of the West Valley put me emotionally closer to Zack. I had a weird flashback Zack and I were on the mid-watch and had just heard a SHOTS FIRED OFFICER NEEDS ASSISTANCE call on the scanner. We raced to the scene, breaking red lights, going Code Two. Zack always chased adrenaline rides, always made a tire-smoking run at any Shots Fired situation. I was drunk in the passenger seat and the wild ride made me sick.

We hit the call ahead of the designated unit and Zack took off running into the apartment, leaving me sitting in our unit, still nauseous and dizzy. I remembered hearing gunfire inside the apartment and stumbled out of the patrol car, fumbling for my weapon. I dropped it in the flowing gutter water and fell in face first after it. While I fished for my pistol in the sewer drain, Zack was in a deadly shootout, dropped two assholes, both with long yellow sheets, and saved a wounded officer. He also kept me away from our watch commander, sending me back to the station with another officer before our field supervisor arrived on the scene. At the time, I'd been grateful. But now I was confused. Were these rages I was witnessing now, a new development, or had Zack always had them? Was I the perfect partner for a cop prone to violence—too useless to even be a witness? I didn't know. My memory of that period was an alcoholic haze.

By the time I arrived at the address in Canoga Park, the crime scene was already filling up with news teams and looky-loos. Zack was not on the scene. This time I decided not to wait for him. I had a hunch he would be a no-show. A lot of civilians and neighborhood kids were milling around near the edge of the concrete levee. Fortunately, there were enough cops this time to hold them back.

I located the officer in charge; a forty-year-old sergeant with blond hair, a Wyatt Earp stash, and three service stripes—nine years on the job. His nameplate read: P. RUCKER.

"Come on, we got a trail marked over here," Rucker said.

I followed him along the lip of the embankment while news crews tracked us from across the street and shot our progress. Rucker led me down through tangled sage, old McDonald's cups and Burger King boxes, into the concrete riverbed. There were three young cops standing near the body. Ray Tsu was already leaning over the guest of honor looking at the wounds, but was waiting to move him until I got there. A ratty old blanket, which probably belonged to the victim, covered the corpse's face.

"Thanks for waiting," I said.

Ray nodded and lifted the blanket. This vic, like all the others, was mid-fifties to mid-sixties, and had been shot in the temple. The bullet was gone—another through and through. I kneeled down and studied the body. He was bald, sun-weathered, and dressed in rags. His teeth were a tobacco-stained mess. I named him Quimby—a comedy name, but I was getting frustrated.

"John Doe Number Five," Ray said, looking up at me. "No wallet. Somebody in those apartments probably called it in. Anonymous call, so we don't have a respondent."

"Let's clear this crowd of uniforms out," I said to Rucker, not wanting any of the cops to see the symbol if there was one. Rucker moved the officers away while Ray and I kneeled down on opposite sides of the body and pulled up his ratty shirt.

The now-familiar emblem was carved crudely on his chest.

An hour later we were ready to carry the deceased up to the coroner's wagon. I was up on the street wondering where my partner was, when I heard a voice behind me.

"Detective?"

I turned to see a young patrolman whose nameplate read: OFFICER F. MELLON.

"Yes?"

"I think I might know this guy."

I pulled him away from the swarming press and walked him fifty yards up to my car, opened the door, and sat him inside. Then I got behind the wheel, turned on my tape recorder, and set it on the dash in front of him.

"Where do you know him from?" I asked.

"Well, not know him, exactly. I mean, I never talked to him or anything, but if it's the same guy, I used to see him all the time, a couple of miles from here, standing by the freeway off-ramp at De Soto holding a sign."

"Panhandling."

"Yeah. His sign read: HELP ME. VIETNAM VET. CORPSMAN. Or something like that. I remember thinking I'd never before seen a sign where the vet put down what he did in Nam. Maybe he figured vets who'd been hit and saved by a corpsman would stop and give him money."

"Officer Mellon, I want you to go back to the station and get some guys together. I'll get a picture of this victim over there in an hour. I want you to start talking to homeless people near that off-ramp. Show 'em the picture. I'll square it with your watch commander. Get me a name to go with this guy. Can you do that?"

"I can try."

I handed him my card and took his numbers.

After he got out of the car, I put it in gear, and drove Code Two down to the lab on Ramirez Street. On the way, I called the WC in Canoga Park and told him I needed everybody he could spare to go out and show the new vic's picture around.

Twenty minutes later, I pulled into the basement garage at the crime lab and ran for the elevator. I had just remembered where

I'd seen that symbol before. It was when I was in the Marines. The carving was so crude and lacking in detail that everyone, including me, had missed it.

When I got to Symbols and Hieroglyphics, everybody was gone. I found a secretary to help me. She took me to the stacks where I pulled out a book on military emblems. I started flipping pages until I found it.

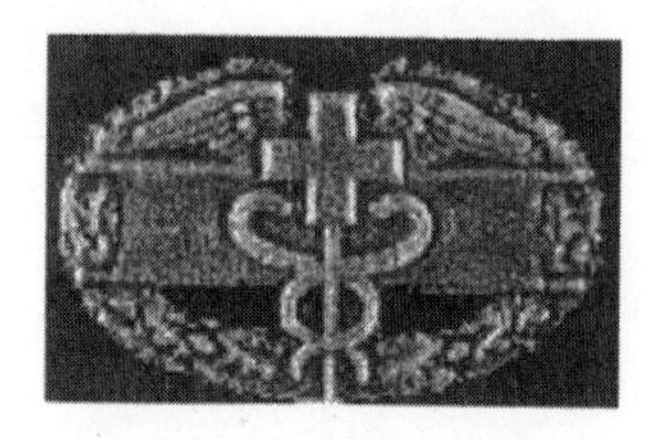

The badge for the Combat Medical Corps.

12

IT WAS ALMOST 10 P.M. when I arrived at the Glass House. I had to fight my way through a downstairs corridor crowded with news crews, staff rank officers, and press relations. A network news team had actually brought in their own coffee trolley. On the way into the elevator, Carmen Rodriguez of Channel Whatever found me and nodded to her cameraman, Gar. With no preamble, it was all Lights, Camera, Action. No *Hello*. No *How's it going?* Just shove the old mike under my nose and start asking questions. I'm not good at this. When I see myself on TV, I always look pissed and dangerous. My annoyance with the press comes across.

"What do you think of the Fingertip task force being formed?" was her opening question.

"Carmen, do you think it's possible that you and I might ever have even one conversation without that damn camera in my face?"

"Cut, Gar," she said to her cameraman who turned off the sun-gun that was mounted on the nose of his state-of-the-art HD 24 camera.

"Much better," I said. "What task force?"

"Chief Filosiani is naming a Fingertip task force. The news conference is in a few minutes."

"A task force ought to be a big help." I smiled. "Nice chatting."

I turned and ducked into a closing elevator before she could stop me and headed straight for six. The sea-foam green carpet and light-wood paneling on the command floor were a stark contrast to the overpopulated steel desk clutter of my space on four. I found Alexa in her office going over some notes. She had changed into a tailored suit since leaving the restaurant, and was putting on her flats with one hand while holding up a protesting palm with the other.

"Don't start up with me," she said as I came busting through the door.

"You've gotta stop this. Shut this task force down. I finally have something. One of the Blues thinks he remembers this last guy in Canoga Park holding up a panhandling sign at De Soto and the One-Oh-One."

"It's too late, Shane. Tony contacted the FBI two days ago and since all the homicide detectives in HS have full, high-priority caseloads, the manpower assignments are coming from the five city Homicide Divisions and have already been made. He was all set yesterday and pulled the trigger two hours ago when the new body was found. I told you this was about to happen. All that's left is to announce."

"But I've finally got a lead—a good one." I handed her a Xerox of the Combat Medical Badge I'd made from the book.

"What's this?"

"Combat Medic's insignia. That's what the unsub's been carving on all the vics."

She picked it up and looked at it, then reached into her top desk drawer for a photo of the carved symbol. She compared the two. "It's not very exact."

"Hey, it's a very intricate badge. To get it exact, he'd have to use a tattoo needle or a pen, not a knife. It's close enough," I said. "If I'm right, this sets up a course for our investigation."

"Look, Shane, I—"

"Lemme run it for you." She hesitated, but then nodded.

"Somebody is killing vics who are fifty to sixty years old. That makes all our DB's Vietnam vintage guys. They're homeless and they all have this medic's symbol carved on their chests."

"So you think the unsub was in Nam?" She leaned back in her swivel and studied me skeptically. "The mean age of serial killers is twenty-five. If you're right and the killer was in Nam, that makes this guy way over the target age."

She was right about the mean age. But that was just a computer-generated statistic achieved by taking all of the serial killers ever caught, adding their ages and dividing that by their total number. But serial murder, like bad fashion, often defies rationale, and when dealing with aberrant psychology, it's a mistake to marry computer generated facts.

"Maybe the unsub is a slow starter," I said. "Or maybe he's the son of a medic, was abused by his father and is killing him over and over. Maybe he's a current vet who was screwed up by a medic. Maybe all the victims were medics. Maybe he's a medic himself. Shit, come on . . . I don't know what the connection is, but this mutilation is a part of his signature, and it damn sure means something. This medic thing is the first angle I've had in seven weeks that I can work.

"I've got all the Blues the watch commander in Canoga can spare, showing this new vic's picture to homeless people around the De Soto off-ramp. If I get a name, I've got my first real foothold. I can start assembling possible motives, look for witnesses." I leaned toward her. "Give me and Zack another day."

"It's done. The FBI is sending us a profiling expert. Some ASAC from the local office named Judd Underwood. We're wheels up, babe. It's airborne."

"Shit." I turned and headed out of the office.

"Don't go away mad," she called after me.

I looked back at her.

"I tried to stop this," she said softly. "I really did. And Tony almost bit my head off for it. Wanta see the teeth marks?" She started to pull down her turtleneck. "Look." She exposed her beautiful neck. There were no tooth marks on her ivory skin, but hey, every defense can't be bulletproof.

"Maybe with more people on this, we can run down your Vietnam angle quicker," she said hopefully. "You know it's gonna be a huge job going through a military hospital V.A. check."

"I don't want any help. Zack and I should have been able to do this ourselves." Then I felt the cold breath of political anticipation. "By the way, who did Tony put in charge of this cluster-fuck?"

"Deputy Chief Michael Ramsey," she said softly, knowing I'd hate it.

"Great White Mike?" My jaw dropped. He was the biggest asshole on the sixth floor. The guy actually kept makeup in his briefcase because he loved being on TV. "Guess we'll be having lots and lots of news conferences," I said.

"Give the guy a chance, Shane."

"White Mike will run this task force like a Vegas lounge act. At least, don't bullshit me."

"Okay, no bullshit?"

I waited.

"You've had seven weeks. Nothing's happened. Now we're trying this."

I left her office and headed down to Homicide Special. Crossing the squad room to my cubicle was a little like being the losing pitcher in the locker room after the seventh game of the World Series. I heard way too many *Good try*s and *Not your fault*s.

When I got to my desk, I had a message waiting: Call Fran 555-6890. I picked up the phone and dialed.

When Fran Farrell answered, her voice sounded quiet, almost subdued.

"It's Shane," I said. "You called?"

"It's about Zack."

"You have any idea where he is?"

"He's here. You better come over."

"I can't come now, Fran. I've got my hands full. Our Fingertip case just went postal."

"You better come anyway."

"Why?"

"He tried to commit suicide. I came home and found him bleeding in my bathtub with his wrists cut. Get over here, Shane. He wants to see you."

13

THE HOUSE WAS a ranch-style, cream-colored bungalow with green trim in the Valley just off Rossmore. I parked the Acura at the curb and walked up the drive toward the front door. It was 11 P.M. I rang the bell, not sure of how I was going to handle this.

The door was opened by a red-haired boy about Chooch's age. It had been a while since I'd seen him, but I guessed this was Zack Junior. He was rawboned, with Zack's rugged Irish looks and blue-green eyes.

"I'm Shane. Zack Junior, right?" He nodded. "We haven't seen each other in a while," I added.

"Mom's in the living room," he said without expression.

I moved into the house and met Fran coming into the foyer.

Young Zack disappeared down the hall. Like most kids caught up in a divorce, he didn't know which side to be on and ended up just trying to stay out of sight. Fran was wearing stretch jeans and a polo shirt. She was one of those people who should avoid stretch pants. She had a round face and an usually pleasant demeanor. I'd known her briefly when I'd partnered with Zack in the West Valley, but that experience had colored her opinion of me. There was always a hint of disapproval. She gave me a cursory hug and then pulled back and fixed me with a hard amber-eyed stare.

"Get him out of here, Shane."

"I'll try."

"I can't do this. It was hard enough throwing him out the first time. What on earth was he thinking? In my bathtub? I come home with the boys and find him bleeding, with Sinatra singing on the CD."

"What's going on with him, Fran? It's like all of a sudden the bottom just dropped out."

She snorted out a bitter laugh. "You don't know the half of it."

"If I'm going to help him I gotta know what's eating him up."

"You can't help him. His problems go all the way back to his childhood. I didn't even know about most of it till his mother called a month ago. Since he got back from Florida, it's gone to a whole new place."

"Look, Fran, I need to—"

"I'm not getting into it, Shane. Can't and won't. Just make him go."

"Where is he?"

She led the way into the den at the back of the house.

Zack was in a big Archie Bunker chair parked in front of a dark big-screen TV. He was staring out the window at a small backyard with a lit kidney-shaped pool. His wrists were wrapped. The bandaging looked professional. I knew Zack wouldn't go to the emergency room. They'd be forced to report an attempted suicide and that would be career death for a cop. I remembered he'd told me that before they were married, Fran was an E.R. nurse.

We were standing in the threshold, but Zack was still staring out at the backyard. "Shane's here," Fran said. Her voice had the same detached, impersonal tone you'd use showing a plumber where the leak was.

Zack was wearing a maroon bathrobe and slippers. When he turned, I saw that he had removed the splint from his nose but still looked at me around a swollen purple mess. His eyes were expressionless, like holes punched in cardboard. Fran stepped back into the hall, closed the door, and disappeared.

"Intense," I said, as I crossed the room toward a wing chair by the window and sat on the arm. "Propped in the tub, wrists up, bleeding dangerously. Very operatic."

Zack didn't want to look at me, and turned his gaze back toward the window.

"What's the deal? Did that fancy Glock jam?" I said.

"Can it. I didn't call so you could come over and piss on me."

"Hey, Zack, what game are we playing? I'm not a psychiatrist and, obviously, I don't want to say anything that's gonna drive you over the edge, but my bullshit meter is redlined, man."

He still wasn't looking at me.

"How's this supposed to go now? You come over here and slash your wrists, but you don't quite get the job done and Fran and the boys come home and find you tits up in the tub with Sinatra singing, 'My Way.' "

"Get the fuck outta here," he said, his voice a whisper.

I stood and started toward the door, but then stopped and turned back. "Zack, I owe you a lot. You were there for me and I'm trying to be there for you, but you gotta admit, even at my worst I didn't pull a bunch a weak shit like this."

"I try and kill myself and you call it weak shit?"

"If you're gonna check off the ride, don't do it in a bathtub like some Valley transvestite. Screw that damn Glock into your ear and take care of business. You want my take?" He turned his eyes down so I continued: "You're hoping Fran will let you come back and this is some kinda guilt trip."

Then his eyes filled with tears.

"Get me outta here, Shane."

"Done."

I left him in the den and went to find Fran. She had washed his clothes. They were still warm from the dryer. In the harsher light of the laundry porch, I thought I saw the last remnants of an old bruise under her left eye. There was a darkening there, a faint smudge covered over with heavy pancake. I returned to the den, closed the door, and handed him the clothes.

He started rambling. "My boy looks at me like I'm . . ." He couldn't finish. "Like I'm some kinda monster."

If he'd been knocking Fran around that could be why. But I didn't know that for sure. I didn't have any proof. I was confused and conflicted. When he finished dressing, I said, "Let's go. You got everything?"

We walked to the car and I loaded him in. Then I went up to where Fran was standing on the front porch watching us. The strain of all this was adding years to her face.

"Where're you gonna take him?" she asked, concerned. "I don't know if he should be alone. He could try this again."

"Look, Fran, he's a cop. He's got access to weapons, or if he really wants to open a vein, there're sharp edges everywhere. We can put him in a psychiatric hospital, but unless he agrees to stay no civilian facility is gonna be able to hold him." She stood there with her arms crossed, her mouth growing smaller.

"Has he been hitting you?"

"I wish it was that easy," she answered. "I need for this to be over. I need to move on." There was finality and a brief shudder as she said it. This suicide attempt was an ending for her, a door closing.

"He's got a brother. Don or something? He never talks much about him. Lives in Torrance, right?" I asked.

"They don't get along much anymore."

"I'm taking him there anyway. Give me the address and while I'm on my way, call Don and give him a heads-up. Tell him I need Zack to stay put until I can figure something out."

She promised to call, wrote down Don Farrell's address, and handed it to me. I walked back to the car and got in. Zack was slumped against the door.

"I'm taking you to your brother's house," I said.

He didn't reply, so I put the car in gear and headed off to Torrance. As we pulled up onto the freeway, I turned to look at him. The overhead lights played over his face, strobing across a swollen landscape of depression and despair.

"Have you been hitting Fran?" My voice was so soft it was barely audible.

He sat quietly for a long time. I didn't think he had heard me. "When I was little, my father . . ." Then he stopped.

"What? What about your father?"

"What you are and what you become is written in the Big Book before you're even born. It's in your DNA. There's no way to alter destiny," he whispered softly.

14

As it turned out, John Doe Number Five from Canoga Park was really Patrick Collins from Seattle. Some off-duty officers from the day watch scored the ID by showing his picture to the homeless miscreants around the freeway on ramp. He was a regular fixture on that corner.

I learned all this when I got to Parker Center at nine the next morning. The detectives assigned to the new Fingertip task force had already taken over an empty cube farm that was to be our new, designated area on the third floor. The space was available in the overcrowded administration building because it was about to go under construction as a computer center. Deputy Chief Ramsey had run the contractors off and temporarily given the area to us. Two dozen detectives from five citywide homicide divisions were milling about, industriously moving ladders and fighting over the few window desks left behind by the contractors. Claiming prime office space was an important first day priority in task force geopolitics. The less desirable, center of the room locations were relegated to underachieving latecomers like me.

The detectives who were there had also commandeered the few available chairs and determined that Patrick Collins had no outstanding warrants by running him through our database, CID, and the National Crime Index computer. They had to use their cell phones because we still weren't hooked up to the main switchboard. Under all the bustle there was organized excitement here. Movie and book deals hovered on the horizon.

A swift, connect-the-dots series of phone checks quickly confirmed that Collins was an Army medic in 1970, assigned to the Big Red One, the First Combat Infantry Division in Vietnam. Thirty years before he took up residency under the overpass he had also been a resident of Seattle, Washington, where his seventy-five-year-old parents still lived.

As the task force milled and joked, a shrill whistle suddenly sliced through the confusion, bringing the volume down instantly. "Everybody, shut the fuck up!" an unfamiliar voice shouted from the back of the room.

I was still standing in the threshold, carrying my murder book and Rolodex, feeling out of it, like a kid on the first day of kindergarten, when the sea of humanity in front of me parted and I was looking at a pale, narrow-shouldered man with blond-red hair of a strange orange hue. He had it chopped short and his gray eyes glared through wire-rimmed glasses. A big, black gun rig hung upside down under his left arm like a sleeping bat and screamed asshole. My guess? The ranking fed.

"Okay," he said as soon as it settled down. "Everybody, we're meeting in the coffee room in thirty. Bring an open computer file, an open mind and a chair."

Already, I was hating this guy. I turned to a detective standing beside me and asked, "Who's he?"

"Dat be muthafuckin' Judd Underwood of da muthafuckin' FBI," the cop said in a theatrical whisper.

More furniture arrived ten minutes later on rolling dollies. Somehow I ended up with the worst desk. A dented, gray metal monster with a bottom drawer that was jammed and wouldn't shut all the way. A perfect place for our sacrosanct murder book. I lost a frantic game of musical chairs and ended up standing.

I knew a few of the other cops in the room. Mace Ward and Sally Quinn were from the Valley Bureau. Mace was a weightlifter with steroid cuts, who shot anabolics but had a furious hatred of junkies. His mild-mannered partner, Sally, resembled a kindly homeroom teacher until you noticed her kick-ass green-brown eyes that were hard and flat, and the color of bayou mud. I'd worked an Internet sting with both of them a few years ago when I was in Van Nuys.

Ruben Bola and Fernando Diaz were a Cheech-and-Chong homicide team from the old Newton Division, an area so rife with violent crime it was known citywide as Shootin' Newton. It had been reorganized into part of the Central Bureau but the old station house down there was still a hot spot. Wisecracking Ruben was smooth and cool, so he was Suave Bola. Fernando was round and loud, with a chunky diamond chip crucifix, making him Diamond Diaz. There were a few other familiar faces whose names I couldn't remember. Some were playing Who Do You Know; some were wondering aloud who was going to be in charge of solving the phone problem. The rest of us were still trying to find a chair and an open mind to bring to the coffee room.

The briefing started exactly on time. Judd Underwood had scrounged a blackboard from someplace and moved the vending machines out of the room. He had all five morgue photos of the Fingertip murder vics taped to it with dates and locations. While we settled in, he kept his back to the room, frantically scribbling on the blackboard like some harried criminology professor getting ready for class. Even after we moved inside pushing the few available rolling chairs, he didn't turn. For some unknown reason, under each photo, he was writing the lunar phase for the corresponding kill, which was puzzling because our unsub was on a fourteen-day calendar, not a lunar cycle.

For those who keep track of such nonsense, *Manhunter*, the 1986 motion picture adapted from the Thomas Harris novel *Red Dragon,* was about the FBI Behavioral Science Unit and featured a serial killer who killed on a lunar cycle. In one scene, the FBI hero actually stated that the moon had a powerful effect on most nut-job killers. Not exactly earth-shaking news since *Luna* is both Latin for *moon* and the root word for *lunatic.* I couldn't help but wonder if Underwood was about to reenact a scene from that film.

Finally he turned and faced us, the chalk still in his hand. "Good morning," he said, softly.

He was such an obvious asshole, nobody answered.

"My name is Judson Underwood."

And then, so help me, just like it was the first day of school, he turned and wrote it on the blackboard.

"D-E-R-W-O-O-D," he announced over the chalk strokes. "I'm a GS-Fourteen and the ASAC of the local FBI office here in L.A. I specialize in criminal behavioral science and serial crime profiling."

He finished by writing GS-14, ASAC, and BEHAVIORAL SCIENCE with a flourish in chalk, then he underlined it before turning again to face us.

"I run kick-ass units, so if you're a slacker, get ready for an ass kicking. Around here, brilliance will be expected, excellence will be tolerated, and standard work will get you transferred out with a bad performance review." He looked around the room. "Are we all square on that?" Nobody answered.

"Good. In case any of you humps have problems with an FBI agent running a city task force, you should know I've been asked to head this show by your Director of Field Operations, Deputy Chief Michael Ramsey. I'll handle the investigation; he's going to handle logistics and communications."

That fit my take on Great White Mike. If the case tanked, our media-savvy deputy chief would be perfectly positioned in front of the TV cameras to point an accusing finger at the entire task force, including our new, narrow-shouldered, kick-ass FBI commander.

"To begin with, we're gonna have some rules," Underwood said. "On this task force, nobody hoards information. Everything is written down and e-mailed to me daily. All facts, wit lists, and F.I. cards are in my computer at EOW."

For those unfamiliar with cop acronyms, F.I. stands for *Field Interview,* EOW for *end of watch.*

Underwood cleared his throat and continued. "We're going to have full disclosure. I don't ever want to find out that some piece of this case was not transmitted, no matter how seemingly insignificant. Woe be it to the detective who neglects to include everything in his daily report. Are we all completely square on this condition?"

Now everybody nodded. They all smiled and looked very pleased with this rule. A few even muttered, "Thank God for that."

But you can't fool me. It was just stagecraft. Both of the previous task forces I was assigned to had started with the full disclosure speech. From this second on, everyone in this room would be lying and hoarding like crack whores. It was a career case—the fast lane to the top of the department with big money stops at the William Morris Agency and CAA. It was a chance to become famous and add that new game room onto the den.

"Let's begin with the givens," Underwood pontificated. "Given: we have five DBs, all males, all mid-fifties to mid-sixties. Given: all have been disfigured with their fingertips amputated at the phystal phalanx of each digit. Given: all five vics have a symbol mutilation carved on their chests, an act of homicidal rage. We now know this symbol represents an approximation of the Combat Medics insignia. The first four bodies were on a two-week clock, then it dropped to seven days. That roughly corresponds to Lunar Phase Three of the calendar. I'll pass out a lunar chart to help you with lunar phases. From this point forward we will run all time frames on both a lunar, as well as a standard calendar. I know technically, these murders don't appear to be lunar phase killings, but it has been my experience that the moon exerts a powerful psychological pull on abnormal psyches and that most irrational acts have metaphysical constructs."

Right out of *Manhunter*. Sometimes I'm so good at reading assholes, I surprise myself.

"Using the moon as well as a conventional calendar could yield insights," he finished. "Are we all square on this?"

A few cops nodded but most were looking down, not engaging his eyes.

"Okay, moving on then," Underwood said. "This last killing, Patrick Collins, shortens the time frame between events to a four-day clock. That means he's only off lunar phase by a scant two days, well within a predictable margin of error depending on TOD estimates." TOD stood for time of death.

Underwood went blithely on. "The fourth John Doe, the one found at Forest Lawn Drive, appears to have been beaten first, then shot. What this means is, our unsub is closing to a lunar cycle as well as degenerating badly, becoming more violent and increasingly dangerous."

I needed some air, but I was stuck. As Underwood droned on, my mind started to wander. I had been instructed by Captain Callaway to keep Forrest in the serial case despite my growing suspicion that he might be a copycat. Cal also instructed me to keep this theory to myself. However, if we pulled Forrest out of the Fingertip case, it would shred all this lunar nonsense. But, for reasons of my own, I decided to hold on to my suspicion. . . . Was that hoarding? Should I start thinking about getting a book agent?

Judd Underwood raised his voice, bringing me back. "Most serial criminals are underdeveloped personalities who crave authority. Very often we find they have tried to become police officers or often impersonate police and will frequently attempt to insert themselves into the investigation. So look closely at anyone calling in with tips or questions and report them directly to me."

"I'd like to report Detective Diaz," Ruben Bola grinned. "He's an underdeveloped personality; he volunteered us for this case, and when it's a full moon, this Cuban asshole goes into Santeria mode and starts killing chickens in the backseat of our Crown Vic."

The room broke up, but Underwood wasn't smiling.

"Are these murders in some way amusing to you, Detective?"

"No, sir." Bola pulled his smile down as Underwood continued.

"Crack wise again in one of my briefings and I'll talk to your supervisor. This unit will not engage in comic nonsense. Is that absolutely clear?"

The room sobered quickly as Underwood gave us his best Murder One stare.

"So, ladies and gentlemen, if we're through making stupid jokes, I'd like to bring this into sharper focus. The murdered men are selected at random. Victims of opportunity. The beating of John Doe Number Four found at Forest Lawn Drive, along with the mutilations, in my opinion, indicates severe sadosexual rage and a disorganized killer."

I disagreed, but I didn't raise my hand or shoot my mouth off. I just wanted to get out of here.

Underwood continued. "Since females constitute less than five percent of the known serial murderers and because they are rarely known to mutilate, I'm predicting that our unsub is male."

Finally, I agreed with something this dink was saying.

"Further, since the mean age of all serial killers is twenty-five, and because disorganized killers tend to be younger, I'm going to subtract two years. This takes the profile on the unsub's age down to twenty-three. Are we all square on that?"

Nobody said anything, but a few in the room nodded. Again, I showed my maturity and held my silence.

"Generally there is an inverse relationship between the age of a serial killer and the age of the victim," Underwood pontificated. "The reason for this is serial murder is generally a desperate act by an unsub who has lost control over his everyday life. He's stressed out, so domination and control are big motives in the crime. Young unsubs are generally more worried about controlling their victims, and often target the old and infirm, people they feel they can dominate. Because of this, I'm lowering the perp's age again, this time to twenty."

He looked at us. "This is pretty damn important stuff. Aren't you people going to take notes?" All over the room keyboards started clicking.

"Regarding the matter of modus operandi where the unsub covers the victim's faces, I have a theory on that." The typing stopped until Underwood went on. "The unsub covers the eyes because I think our killer believes he is ugly. He might even be disfigured. He's embarrassed of his appearance and doesn't want his victims to stare at him, even in death."

Another beat right out of *Manhunter*, and just for the record, that wasn't part of the MO. It was part of the killer's signature—a completely different category.

"So pulling it all together, my preliminary profile says we're looking for a possibly disfigured twenty-year-old white male with sado-sexual rage against older males, probably father substitutes." Underwood looked around the room. "Questions or comments?" he asked, obviously not expecting any.

"Agent Underwood?" someone asked. I wondered what idiot would prolong this silly meeting by asking this asshole a useless question. Everybody turned around and looked in my direction. Naturally, the idiot was me.

15

YOU'RE DETECTIVE SCULLY, one of the original primaries on this. Am I right?" Underwood said, glaring.

"Yes, sir."

He looked down at a roster sheet. "Where's your partner, Detective Farrell? How come he's not here?"

"My partner's out running down a lead. He'll be along shortly," I lied.

Underwood looked thoughtful, then agitated, then like he was about to pass gas. "Well, what is it?" he finally asked impatiently. "What's your question?"

"I've been on this case for seven weeks and I've given it a lot of thought. I'm not sure I agree that the unsub is a disorganized killer."

"You're not?" Agent Underwood sneered. "And this insight, I

presume, is a result of your endless study in the field of criminal psychology." A snooty tone rose out of him like swamp gas fouling an already overheated, sweat filled environment.

"I don't think—"

"Because, Detective Scully, when an unsub kills an older person in a murderous rage, then mutilates and takes fingers off, we're looking at a sadist who is psychologically and pathologically immature, probably just a few years past puberty."

"I just don't think these are disorganized crime scenes," I persisted. "The unsub moves the bodies and dumps them at secondary sites. That indicates a high level of sophistication. The killer seems very knowledgeable about police techniques. This act of dumping is analogous to cleaning up after the murder. He's disguising evidence, even leaving the body in flowing water to eliminate trace evidence. That's pretty smart. I think that constitutes organized, post-offense behavior."

Underwood just stared. Since all the eyes in the room were on me, I lurched on. "Further, while there is certainly rage involved with these murders, in my opinion the mutilations are not rage based. He's removing the fingertips so we can't get prints and identify the victims. Since the chest mutilations are postmortem wounds, they don't necessarily indicate rage. I think he's labeling these victims with this. For that reason, I have him classified as organized and older, maybe even thirty or thirty-five. He knows what he's doing and he's been at this for a while. I don't think these homeless men are victims of opportunity as you suggested, but victims of choice. The different geographical locations all over town indicate he's searching for a victim that suits a certain profile. We need to look closely at the victimology. Something about these particular homeless men drew him to them. Maybe something as simple as the signs some were holding saying they were Vietnam vets. I think it's also possible he's a transient who has committed similar murders in other cities."

"You're aware that there are no similar murders listed in the VICAP computer," Underwood replied.

VICAP is the FBI's Violent Criminal Apprehension Program, a computer database. Police departments all over the country were encouraged to enter all ritual-type killings into VICAP so other departments could match up signature murders that occurred in their cities. Serial killers tended to move around, but their signatures rarely changed. The problem with VICAP was, not all police departments went to the trouble of listing their ritual crimes on that database.

"The missing fingertips, the chest symbol, would jump out on a VICAP scan," Underwood defended.

It was now dead quiet in the room. My remarks had dropped the temperature in here a few thousand degrees. I had only one more thing I wanted to say. Might as well go down swinging.

"I think you may be inaccurate about the reason he's pulling the coat up and covering their faces. By the way, that's not part of the modus operandi. MO is something a killer does to avoid being caught. The act of covering the eyes is part of his signature, something emotional that he can't help himself from doing. I see covering the face as avoidance and guilt. I agree he may be killing a father substitute. Patricide is a very heavy psychological burden for him to bear. After the killing, the unsub most likely is ashamed of his act and doesn't want to deal with a father substitute's disapproving gaze even in death, so he covers the face."

Underwood just stood in the center of the room with a strange, bewildered look on his narrow face. "One of us must be a complete idiot," he finally said. "And I'm sure it's not me."

"You asked for comments."

"After this briefing we'll have a chat." Jabbing the chalk at me. Dotting the I in *idiot.*

Underwood had printed up his profile and now he passed it out. So far, beyond what he'd already told us, his unsub was an unattractive twenty-year-old who lived at home with a female parent, wanted to be a cop, and had a childhood history of fire starting and violence against animals. It was all textbook stuff and not worth much to this roomful of potential authors.

In the end, Underwood couldn't escape the need to follow up on the one solid lead I'd supplied—the medical insignia and the fact that Patrick Collins turned out to be a combat medic in Nam.

We were instructed to designate four two-man teams to recheck each victim against VA records. Underwood selected a big, overweight detective named Bart Hoover to run this part of the investigation. Most all of us had heard stories about the aptly named Sergeant Hoover, who had major sixth-floor suck. He was a younger brother of a Glass House commander who headed the new Crime Support Section. Bart was a well-known fuckup who had actually once handcuffed a bank robber to his squad car steering wheel with the keys still in the ignition. The last he saw of that bust was his own taillights going around the corner. Despite bonehead mistakes, with the help of his brother, Bart had hoovered nicely up through the ranks.

Underwood closed by telling us we were having morning and evening briefings just like this one, right here in this coffee room at 0800 and 1700 hours. Attendance was mandatory unless we were in the field, and then we needed to get his permission to miss.

After the meeting broke, those with chairs pushed them back into the squad room. A few of my fellow detectives checked me out disdainfully. I had just marked myself as a troublemaker. I challenged Underwood, which could cause him to come down on everyone. Obviously I didn't understand task force group dynamics.

As I moved into the squad room, I was trying to keep from being put on one of the four background teams. I had other plans for the day. I ducked down and tried to hide while pretending to unjam my bottom desk drawer.

Underwood stopped beside my desk. "That was interesting

stuff in there. I want you to write it all down, every word so we'll have a record, then you and I will go over it," my FBI leader said pleasantly. Then he moved away, leaving me to that task. I smelled big trouble.

16

AN HOUR LATER I finished my profile on the unsub and flagged Judd Underwood over. He veered toward me.

"All done?" he asked pleasantly.

"Yes, sir." I handed four pages of profile material to him.

"Good. Follow me."

He headed out the door, into the lobby. I didn't know what the hell he was up to, but I tagged obediently after him. He was waiting for me outside the bathroom door.

"Come on, I want to show you something," he said.

I followed him into the men's room, wondering what the hell was going on. Then he dropped my four-page report into the urinal, unzipped his pants, took out his pencil dick, and started pissing on it. His yellow stream splattered loudly on the paper. When he was done he zipped up and turned to face me.

"That's what I think of your ideas," he said, his voice pinched and shrill. "On this task force there will be only one profile and one profiler. I'm it. Get the murder book and come into my office."

I wanted to deck him, but seventeen years in the department has taught me that the best way to survive assholes is to wait them out. So I choked down my anger and followed Agent Underwood out of the bathroom and across the squad room, stopping to retrieve the murder book on the way.

Underwood's office was very large, but had no walls. He had instructed someone from maintenance to chalk out the perimeters on the gray linoleum floor. I was surprised to see that he swerved to avoid walking through the nonexistent south wall and entered through the chalked out opening that served as his door.

I stopped at the line on the floor and looked in at him. Did he really expect me to walk around and not step over it? I paused for a moment to deal with this ridiculous dilemma. I was already in pretty deep with this guy, so I skirted the problem by finding my way into his office through the marked-out door.

Welcome to *The Twilight Zone*.

I waited while he sat behind a large, dark wood desk that he'd scrounged from somewhere. It was the only mahogany desk I'd ever seen at Parker Center and I had no idea where it had come from. He also had an expensive looking, oxblood-red executive swivel chair, and some maple filing cabinets. All that was missing was an American flag, the grip-and-grin pictures, and a wall to hang them on. His cell phone sat on a charging dock in front of him. Several folders decorated one corner of his blotter. The five Fingertip case reports were stacked front and center, the edges all compulsively aligned. Taking the invisible office and all this anal organization into account, it seemed Judd Underwood had a few psychological tics of his own. But who am I to judge? I only had two semesters of junior college psych where I didn't exactly bust the curve.

"Where did you get all that hopeless nonsense?" he sneered.

I smiled at him through dry teeth. "Since I got this case, I've been studying up on serial crime. I've read all of John Douglas's books on serial homicide, Robert Ressler's too, Ann Burgess and Robert Keppel—"

"Okay, okay, I get it. But it's one thing to read a book, it's another to actually go out and catch one of these sociopaths. Since you obviously like reading about it, I suggest you pick up my book *Motor City Monster*. It's on Amazon dot com. Been called the definitive work in the field. In fact, let's make that an order. You need to get some facts straight. Have it read by Monday morning."

"Yes, sir."

He tapped a spot on his desk. "Put the murder book there." I set it down while Agent Underwood settled into his executive swivel and picked up a folder. It was my two-week report. Every homicide detective routinely files a TWR with his or her supervisor. It details the workings of all active investigations. Underwood ran a freckled hand through his orange bristle, then opened the folder, licked his index finger, and slowly started to page through it, leaning forward occasionally to frown.

Once, about two years ago, I was working a fugitive warrant that took me to Yellowstone Park. It was rattlesnake season and I hate snakes. I was paired up with a park ranger who told me that when dealing with poisonous reptiles, the way to keep from getting bitten was to give them something more interesting than you to think about. It was time to put that strategy to use.

Underwood looked up from my TWR. "I hope you and your partner are getting in some nice days at the beach, because, if not, this whole last two weeks has been a total waste of time."

I launched into action. "Agent Underwood, I have a plan to draw your unsub out." Notice the clever possessive pronoun.

Disinterested gray eyes, magnified and skeptical, studied me behind those thick wire-rimmed lenses. Undisguised contempt.

"Really?" he finally said, stretching it way out so it sounded more like a wail than a word.

"Yes. I think we should throw a funeral for one of these John Does."

Underwood steepled his fingers under his chin and scowled at me. Then he heaved a giant sigh that seemed to say that dealing with morons was just one of the ugly realities of command.

When he next spoke, he enunciated his words very carefully so that even a fool like me wouldn't get confused.

"It probably hasn't occurred to you, but since the advent of DNA, we no longer hold unidentified bodies at the morgue. All of those previous John Does have been buried. Since you've been so busy misprofiling this unsub, it may have escaped your notice, but Mister Collins has requested that his son be immediately flown back to Seattle, leaving no corpses for your little scam." Then he tipped back in his swivel and regarded me smugly.

"John Doe Number Four is still available," I answered. "He's the one we found at Forest Lawn Drive seven days ago. I checked with the coroner and he's still on ice. We give him a phony name, publicize the hell out of the funeral, get some retired cops to be his mom and dad and see who stumbles in."

I could see he instantly liked it. It had flair. It was the kind of thing Jodie Foster might have come up with in *Silence of the Lambs*. But this only registered as a glint in his stone-gray eyes. His face never even twitched and you had to be trained at reading assholes to spot it.

"Our budget is limited," he equivocated.

"I can get Forest Lawn to work with us. I know a woman down there who's a funeral director. What if I could set it up for under three thousand? I'll get him embalmed on the cheap so we can have an open casket. We'll put on a full media blitz. I'm pretty sure I can rig it in a day or so."

He sat there running this over in his pea brain. It's a well-known fact that some killers have an overpowering urge to attend the funerals of their victims. Judd Underwood should have suggested it himself instead of filling our briefing with psychobabble and lunar charts. But that's a complaint better left to the book and movie guys milling in the squad room beyond the invisible walls of his office.

"You get it set up for under three grand and I'll get Deputy Chief Ramsey to approve it."

I didn't believe that Forrest was part of the Fingertip case, so why stage an elaborate funeral to see who shows up? Well, I had a devious plan building in the back of my head that might solve all of my problems with one brilliantly deceptive move.

I started to leave, stupidly moving to my right before I remembered and skidded to a halt. I had almost walked through the south wall again.

"Sorry," I muttered. "I keep forgetting that wall is there."

"I'm not a complete moron," Underwood said. "The reason that line is chalked out is so the contractors who are coming in this evening will know where to hang the partitions."

"Thank God for that," I muttered.

"I don't like your attitude, Detective."

"Don't feel bad. Nobody does. I'm not even sure I like it most of the time."

Then I stepped over the chalk line into the squad room where I used my cell phone to call my friend Bryna Spiros at Forest Lawn. Once I had her on the line, I explained what I needed. She cut me a great deal. Twenty-five hundred for everything, flowers, all park personnel and security services, even a priest to say a few words. I told her I'd have Rico From Pico get in touch to make arrangements for the body to be sent over for embalming. She said she'd loan me a casket at no charge because it was scheduled to be burned in a cremation later in the week.

With all this in the works, I decided to head up to Special Crimes to talk to Cal. On my way out two of my new task force brothers were shooting the bull by the elevators.

"Judd Underwood is legendary," one of them said.

I let the open elevator go and started stalling, fiddling with the buttons. I wanted to hear this.

"Over at the Eye, they call him Agent Orange because he defoliates careers. If something goes wrong, he'll pin it on the guys working with him."

A second elevator opened and Deputy Chief Michael Ramsey hurried out. He was tall, milk-white, and looked like a forties matinee idol, complete with the oiled black hair and pencil-thin moustache.

He turned and faced me. "You're Scully."

I reached out and stopped the elevator door from closing.

"Yes, sir."

"I'm looking for you to put this Fingertip deal down fast. Can you make that happen for me?"

"Gonna try."

"That's the ticket," he said with false enthusiasm. "We got a storm blowing in on this one. You wait 'til it's raining to pitch a tent, everybody gets wet." Sounding like a scout leader giving out instructions before a jamboree.

We stood there looking at each other. Me in the elevator, him in the hall. No connection. Nothing. We'd actually run out of small talk in less than ten seconds. So to end it, I slid my hand off the door and the elevator closed, cutting him from view.

17

I ARRIVED AT my digs in Homicide Special where the phones worked, and sat in my old cubicle without the murder book or my partner and rubbed my forehead. After talking with Fran Farrell yesterday, I had to admit I felt uneasy, unsure of what to do about Zack. All I knew was I was in a close race with Internal Affairs for his badge. But I couldn't dwell on it because now I was also stuck with this funeral. So I headed in to see Jeb Calloway, brought him up to date, and then begged for his help.

"Not my problem anymore," he said, after I finished. "Take it up with your task force commander."

"Deputy Chief Ramsey put some rat-bag ASAC from the FBI in charge of the task force. The guy's actually got us on a lunar calendar."

"Look, Scully, you're a good cop, but sometimes you complain too much."

"Captain, we're stuck in a Hannibal Lecter movie down there. His own people at the Eye call him Agent Orange."

"Whatta you want from me?" Cal said. "I didn't put this task force on the ground. Take it up with the head of the Detective Bureau." Some songs never change.

I switched tactics. "I need to get this funeral set up fast. I'd like to run it out of here."

"Jeez, Scully."

"I'll clear it with Agent Underwood," I pleaded. "We don't even have phones or furniture yet. There's hardly any place to sit."

After a long, reflective moment, Cal nodded. "Okay, you clear it with your task force commander and I'll let you work it from this floor temporarily." Then he frowned. "A funeral's a big expense for a copycat kill, or are you off that now?"

"I'm keeping every option open, Cap. Just like you taught us."

He gave me a tight smile. He knew blatant ass-kissing when he saw it.

"And I want Ed Hookstratten from Press Relations to handle the PR," I rushed on. "I need press about this funeral in all the papers and TV. I know you guys are tight and I was wondering if you could pin him down for me."

"You got a name for the DB yet? We can't put John Doe on the headstone."

"He's gonna be Forrest Davies."

"Okay. You get Underwood to sign off. I'll get in touch with Sergeant Hookstratten."

He fixed me with one of those hard-ass, Event Security stares of his and said, "Agent Orange?"

The rest of the afternoon I focused on the funeral. First I left a message for Underwood that I was working at my old desk until our task force phones were in. Then I did the casting for Forrest's immediate family, who I decided to name Rusty and Alison

Davies. I made a few calls and recruited two retired cops I'd worked with ten years ago. Detective Bob Stewart agreed to be Forrest's dad and Sergeant Grace Campbell would play his mom. Both were gray-haired sixty-eight-year-old vets who looked like they could be the parents of a fifty-year-old man. I asked them to send over personal portraits for a press packet I was making up to go with the artist's rendition of Forrest.

At three o'clock, Bryna Spiros called back. There was a chapel available at one-thirty tomorrow afternoon. I took it and thanked her.

By five o'clock almost everyone was back after an unsuccessful day at the V.A. I brought my team up to the Homicide Special break room for a pre-meeting. They were tired, and I was getting a decent amount of stink-eye. Big spender that I am, I bought everyone machine coffee. The funeral crew consisted of nine people including me.

Sergeant Ed Hookstratten was a six-foot-four, hollow-chested, Lurch-like piece of work with a long hooked nose to go with his name. The man always slouched, but he was, without question, the best media guy in the Glass House.

I'd picked the four cops that I already knew on the task force: Bola, Diaz, Ward, and Quinn. My long-lens photographers were Kyle Jute and Doreen McFadden, two patrol officers who were camera buffs. I'd used them both in the past. The last two players were the grieving parents, retired Sergeants Campbell and Stewart.

Everybody sipped watery coffee while I laid out the op. We would be on Handy-Talkies with earpieces and would stay well back, watch, and photograph everything, making sure to get close-ups of all the license plates in the parking lot for DMV checks later. We had no warrants, so we would make no arrests unless some overt crime happened right in front of us.

This was strictly a photo surveillance.

18

WHEN I GOT home that evening, Chooch and his best friend Darius Hall were huddled in the backyard with their heads together talking earnestly. Chooch had just been notified by the UCLA athletic department that head coach Karl Dorrell wanted to arrange a home visit. It was scheduled for the day after tomorrow at five-thirty in the evening. Delfina was in her room doing homework, so Alexa and I kicked off our shoes in the den and sipped cold beers.

"Good news about UCLA," she said.

"Very," I agreed.

"So how was your day?"

"Don't go there."

"Don't be an asshole," she smiled. "I want to hear about the task force. What's your take on the crowd Chief Ramsey picked?"

Instead of engaging in petty cheap shots, I told her about the funeral the following afternoon.

She was silent for a minute after I finished. "I thought you had John Doe Number Four down as a copycat kill."

"Might be. Might not be. Never can tell," I said, blithely sawing the air with an indifferent hand.

She looked at me critically. "Are you trying to get off this task force and be reassigned to this last John Doe murder?" picking off my brilliantly deceptive plan faster than a base runner stealing signs from second.

"Naw . . . get off the Fingertip task force?" I lied. "How can you say that? We got invisible offices and a neat FBI leader who will tolerate nothing but brilliance. No ma'am. This is a chance to get my name in the paper. Maybe I can even sell this case to the movies, and put a second story on this house so Chooch won't have to sleep in the garage."

"Don't hedge, Shane."

I looked at her and shrugged.

"Let me see if I'm reading this right. You absolutely hate task forces. You know Zack is in career trouble. With all the white light the Fingertip case is getting, he won't last two days on that unit, so you want me to split this last murder off and move you and Zack onto it, out of the spotlight, until you can figure out what to do to save him." Busting me like ripe fruit.

"Listen, I agree with you about the task force," she continued. "But we've been backed into this by the mayor. Tony didn't want to do it."

"Then why did you put an FBI agent in charge?"

"That was a deal we had to cut with the Eye so they wouldn't take the case away. You know how they love a high-profile media murder. And after seven weeks, if they just take it from us, it looks like we muffed the investigation. That's bad for Tony and for me."

"How do they just take it away? It's our case."

"Honey, with the new organization in law enforcement, Homeland and the FBI have gained major power. They can more or less have anything they want."

I sat there for a long moment studying my shoes. It looked like they were due for a shine. Actually, I was due for new shoes. I wondered if I should step up from Florshiems to designer moccasins, or maybe get a pair of those butt-ass ugly Bruno Maglis like O. J.'s.

"I need you on that case to be my eyes and ears," Alexa said, interrupting these weighty thoughts.

"I'm not a spy." My feelings were hurt that she would even suggest it.

"That didn't come out exactly the way I wanted," she said.

We sat together and finished our beers without speaking. Finally she got up and went into the kitchen to start dinner.

I wandered out and listened to Chooch and Darius in the backyard. They were talking about what they always talked about. Football. Darius was Harvard Westlake's star running back and was also being heavily recruited by UCLA. They had already offered him a scholarship.

"We should go as a package, dude," Darius suggested.

"Way cool," Chooch answered, excitement building in his voice. "I could tell Coach Carroll I won't go to USC unless they offer you a ride. You tell the same thing to Coach Dorrell."

"Keep the old backfield intact."

I stood in the doorway behind them and listened to few more minutes of this nonsense. I didn't think trying to blackmail a couple of blue-chip, Division-One college coaches was the best way to earn a full scholarship from either.

I went back into the den, switched on the TV, and caught the top of the seven o'clock news.

"Big advancements in the Fingertip murder case," the handsome blow-dry on Channel Nine declared triumphantly. "Today, Chief Filosiani announced the formation of a new task force.

The unit will be headed by famed FBI criminal profiler Judson Underwood. Underwood is perhaps best known for his capture of the Detroit Slasher and his subsequent best-selling book, *Motor City Monster*. The task force will be comprised of crack members from homicide bureaus all over the city."

Then my artist's rendition hit the screen. "Funeral services for the fourth victim, recently identified as Forrest Davies, will be held at the Old North Church at Forest Lawn cemetery at one-thirty tomorrow."

The shot switched back to the anchorman. "The funeral will mark the beginning of the second month on this horrific case where bodies have been mutilated and leads have been scarce. But tensions seemed to ease all around town today, as the details of this new, high-tech squad were revealed."

I wondered if our high-tech squad had any phones yet.

19

MY BRIEFING WENT off in the task force coffee room at 8 A.M. Ed Hookstratten had blanketed the media with stories of Forrest's funeral. Chief Ramsey and Agent Underwood stood in the back until I was finished.

"That's the skinny, then," Underwood said, as he walked to the front of the room. "I don't want to overload this funeral with suits, so I'm limiting attendance to ten people. One officer only from each Homicide Bureau. Work it out among yourselves and try not to show up looking like cops. No brown shoes and white socks." One of the few worthwhile things he'd told us.

After the briefing, Underwood paused in front of me as the others were pushing their chairs out of the coffee room.

"Where the fuck is your partner? I still haven't laid eyes on that guy."

"He needed to get gun qualified this morning or go on suspension. It's been scheduled for a month. He's over at the shooting range," I lied flawlessly.

Underwood stared at me for a moment, then turned and followed Deputy Chief Ramsey into his office, which had now been miraculously upgraded with walls and a door.

Once he was safely inside, the members of our elite squad circled me like a snarling pack of coyotes. I'd claimed the early lead with my bullshit funeral and was a looming literary problem.

Twenty minutes later, as I was getting ready to head out, one of the detectives from Central Bureau, a fireplug with a swarthy complexion, named either Brendan or Brian Villalobos wandered over. He stood across from my battered desk rocking on his heels.

"Pretty good," he said. But there wasn't much enthusiasm in it.

"Thanks."

"You really think this dickwad is gonna show up at your dumb-ass funeral?"

"Stranger things have happened, Brian."

"Brendan."

"Brendan."

Then we started staring each other down like twelve-year-olds before a schoolyard fight.

"Okay, look . . . you want, maybe we can come to terms on this," he ventured.

"Terms? What are we talking about, Brendan?" Giving him my dull stupid look, which unfortunately, I seem to affect very easily.

"This task force is just a crock a sixth-floor bullshit. But maybe you and I can get past that and turn it into something worthwhile if we work together."

"But we are working together, Brendan. That's what task forces do."

"Don't shine me up, pal." He motioned toward the room.

"This is a five-car accident. Still, there might be opportunity in all this chaos if we work it right." He leaned closer. "What if you and I trade everything we've got, but just with each other? These other humps can fend for themselves."

"You mean hoard shit?"

He smiled, "I know you're the original primary on these murders and you probably know stuff the rest of us don't. But if you team up with me, you're getting a skilled homicide guy with a seventy-percent clearance rate. If we end up with a book or a movie, we cut it right down the middle."

"Can I get back to you on that? My voice mail is loaded and I'm sort of obligated to evaluate all my offers before deciding."

His expression hardened. "I'm not going to let this opportunity get away. My partner is the buffalo in the checked coat over there." He pointed at Bart Hoover. "He's Captain Hoover's brother. They're filling his jacket with sexy stuff, hoping he catches this perp so he can make the lieutenant's list. But trust me, that jerk couldn't catch a cold in Alaska. It's also no secret your partner is a world-class alkie. Since we're both stuck working with lames, maybe we should unofficially team up. This funeral thing of yours has possibilities. I'm just saying, let's cut our losses and go in on it together."

"Interesting idea," I said. "But I'm not sure about the fifty-fifty book and movie split. I'll have to run that by my creative affairs advisor. I'll get back to you."

He wandered off looking dissed. Since I hadn't scored a chair yet, I sat on my broken desk and made a few calls.

At noon I drove out to Forest Lawn and met with Bryna Spiros, a short, dark-haired woman with a bright smile. She'd helped me on two similar occasions, knew what I needed, and led me to the small wood-framed North Chapel.

12:15 P.M.: My photographers, Doreen and Kyle, arrived in separate L-cars. They checked out suitable camera positions. I bought some leafy flower arrangements from the worship center florist to provide them with better photo blinds.

12:30 P.M.: The polished mahogany casket arrived on a rolling gurney and was placed in the front of the chapel. I really love the names they give these coffins. I actually saw one in the display room called the Sky Lounge. This one was a Heaven Sent. Since I have a less formal streak, when I die I want to get hammered into a That's All Folks!

I opened the half-lid and propped it up. Forrest was festively turned out in a black suit and gray tie, resting on white satin, all ready for his heaven-sent ride into the great beyond.

The embalmer did a reasonable job of cleaning him up. They taped over the gunshot wound and covered it with plastic skin, although his head still showed the lopsided trauma of the wound. He had that red-tinged robust complexion found only in wax museums and on the chalky faces of the dead. His eyes were closed and someone had decided to put heavy pancake over his eyelid tatts, covering the Russian Cyrillic symbols that said: "Don't wake up." This time he wouldn't.

"I'm gonna get this guy, Forrest," I whispered somewhat foolishly to the waxy corpse.

12:45 P.M.: Agent Underwood arrived and sat in the back, holding his ostrich briefcase, which undoubtedly had some kind of huge exotic, square-barreled automatic inside.

1:00 P.M.: Stewart and Campbell, dressed as grieving parents, walked into the church and were seated in the front row.

Members of the task force started to arrive, pulling into the parking lot in their personal vehicles. A few minutes later, they wandered into the church and spread out, everyone stylin' and profilin'. No polyester, white socks, or Kmart ties.

Some tactical ops like to use catchy radio code names, but I always feel like an asshole triggering my mike and saying, "This is Dogcatcher to Handy-Wipe," so I just assigned numbers. Underwood was One. I was Two. Bola was Three, and so forth.

There were a half a dozen people in attendance who I'd never seen before. The long-lens team was busy shooting close-ups of all of them. Kyle was inside the church, behind the viewing area. Doreen was in the trees, halfway between the chapel and the parking lot with a 350-mm lens. A CD of harp music played as a few more people ambled in and sat in the uncomfortable, wooden pews.

There was a very attractive, well-dressed, middle-aged, blonde woman in a stylish suit sitting in the back of the church looking as out of place as a debutante at a monster truck rally. Ice blue eyes, flawless skin, great shoes, and a single strand of pearls.

At one point, before the service started, a gray-haired, pear-shaped, three-hundred-and-fifty-pound man in a brown tweed coat entered the chapel, waddled up the aisle on swollen ankles, and looked into the casket. He reached down and rubbed the pancake off of Forrest's eyelids, then leaned close and checked the tattoos. Satisfied, he turned and limped back up the aisle and right on out the front door of the church. I triggered my mike.

"This is Two to Six," I whispered to Kyle using my Handy-Talkie. "You get that?"

"Roger, Two. Got him," Kyle's voice answered in my earpiece.

"Seven, this is Two. You got a huge bogie dressed in brown burlap coming out the front of the chapel."

"Roger, Two," Doreen McFadden said. "I'm photogratizing his sagging ass even as we speak."

I moved out the side door of the chapel and watched from the steps as she tracked him from a safe distance using the line of trees for cover, gunning off shots as he got into a black Lincoln Town Car, driven by another man. The car quickly exited the park.

"Two, this is Seven," Doreen's voice came back in my ear. "That town car has diplomatic plates."

"Get outta town . . . ," I murmured, wondering what the hell was going on.

A few minutes later, the attractive blonde got up, walked to the casket and looked at the body. Then she also left. Right after that, a medium-built bald man in a blue blazer did the same thing.

1:30 P.M.: The funeral started and the priest Bryna provided said some oft-used words. "God has seen fit to call his servant home."

The guy had a timid delivery and the short service droned unmercifully. By then the only people left in the congregation to hear it were all packing badges and creaking out yawns.

2:10 P.M.: Six members of the task force carried Forrest's Heaven Sent casket out of the church and loaded it into the hearse for the short drive to our gravesite two hundred yards up the hill. We had to keep up the charade until it was over. It was a good thing we did, because just as the priest was sprinkling holy water on the coffin, I saw a black guy in a Forest Lawn uniform taking pictures of the burial with a long lens from a grounds truck parked a hundred yards from the gravesite.

"Six, this is Two. African American in a park maintenance outfit behind the white truck."

"Roger. Already got him and his partner," Doreen answered.

I hadn't seen his partner.

2:50 P.M.: The funeral was over and everybody was gone. We retrieved Forrest from the elegant, silk-lined Heaven Sent and returned him to the harsher environs of the morgue refrigerator. Then we hurried to task force headquarters to look at the digital shots Doreen and Kyle had taken.

When I arrived, I had a surprise waiting.

20

ZACK WAS STANDING with his back to the window. He looked awful. Bloodshot eyes, purple nose, saffron cheeks. His swollen jowls were flush with the tropical colors of sunset. Making it worse, he was holding forth in front of six detectives on the worthlessness of task forces. "You bunch a ass-wipes couldn't find dog shit at the pound."

I walked over and grabbed him by the elbow. "Hey, Zack, come here. I need to show you something."

He pulled away. "Juss' splainin' what lame shit this is," he slurred.

Agent Orange was only a few minutes behind me. If he saw Zack in this condition it was over. But my partner was a big man who wasn't easy to corral under normal circumstances. Drunk, he was impossible. So I screwed my heels into the floor and let him have my best right cross. He wasn't expecting it and at the last second, turned into the punch. The sound bounced off the walls in the squad room, cracking like a leather bullwhip.

Zack fell forward, landing across somebody's new window desk, scattering pencils, pictures and a charging cell phone. He was stunned, but not out. I reached around behind my back, grabbed the cuffs off my belt, and slipped them on his bandaged wrists. Then, with a throbbing right hand, I straightened him up. A line of bloody drool was coming out of the corner of his mouth. These last few days had taken a heavy toll. I'd just added to the mess by splitting his lip.

I turned to the room full of startled cops wearing various expressions of jaw dropping disbelief.

"This guy is a vet with an outstanding record. I'm begging you people to forget what you just saw. He's going through a rough time. A divorce, a bankruptcy . . . cut him some slack."

I helped Zack to his feet.

"Why'd ya hit me, man?" he mumbled.

"To shut you up. Come on, we got people to see."

"Wha' people?"

I led him out of the temporary task force area into the bathroom across from the elevator, getting him inside just seconds before I heard Agent Orange in the lobby. I leaned Zack against the sink, his hands still cuffed behind him. Then I wet some paper towels and held them up to the fresh cut on his lip.

"You gotta get outta here, Zack. Don't come back till you're sober."

" 'S my new unit," he said dully. "Don't wanta get gigged on some bullshit nonperformance write-up."

"You're drunk. The fed running this detail's a total nutsack."

"Don't wanta stay at my place, can't stay at Fran's or my brother's. Hadda borrow his Harley. Fucker said he's gonna report it stolen."

"Zack, will you shut up and come with me?"

"Get these damn cuffs off," he finally said, softly.

I reached around and unhooked them with my key.

"Where we going?"

"To throw ourselves on the mercy of the sixth floor.

His big Irish face creased into a frown.

I found my wife in her office and left Zack sitting outside, breathing scotch on her assistant, Ellen.

"What is it?" Alexa said, looking up at me as I came through the door.

She was going over the monthly crime reports for the five detective bureaus. It was not an encouraging picture. Violent crime categories were up and clearance rates were down. That could largely be explained because there were not enough detectives to adequately cover the growing number of homicides. But commanders and deputy chiefs are notoriously deaf when it comes to down-trending job performance numbers. Alexa had to attend the bimonthly COMSTAT meeting and defend her clearance record. That meeting was scheduled for tomorrow. She looked impatient and worried.

"How'd the funeral go?" she said, her eyes still on the printouts, not giving me her full attention.

I pushed past that question, closed the door, and crossed to her desk.

"Honey, I haven't asked you for anything since you got this job but I'm about to break that rule."

"Please don't," she said looking at me with new, hard-edged determination.

I was her husband, and at home, there wasn't much we couldn't find a way to agree on. But we had carefully defined our two worlds. On the job she was my boss and we always found a way to keep it completely professional.

"Zack?" she asked, wearily.

I nodded.

She pushed the stack of crime stats aside and rubbed her eyes for a minute before looking up. The expression that formed when her hands came away was polite disinterest. This wasn't going to be easy.

"I've been giving this a lot of thought," I started by saying. "I owe this guy. We both owe him."

"How do I owe him? I never really knew him all that well until you two partnered up, and I'm just finding out he was already a big time lush by then. He needs a twelve step program."

"You owe him because he saved me. If he hadn't been there for me in the Valley, then there would be no us. I know he's behaving badly and something is going really wrong inside him, but I can't just walk away."

"Let's get something straight. Zack Farrell is only one of two hundred detectives under my command. If I give him a pass, or look the other way, how in the name of God, can I drop the hammer on the next drunk who stumbles through here? We have citizens to protect. This is a violent city." She pushed the crime stats across the desk toward me. "I'm supposed to be a firewall between all this and the law-abiding citizens we protect. How do I do that if I don't maintain guidelines and standards?"

"Honey, don't preach the police manual at me."

She just stared.

"Okay, look. It's complicated, but here's my problem. I'm not sure I really knew Zack back then. I was so out of it, I wasn't focused on much. Now that I am, I'm not sure I like what I see. But as a man, I can't accept what I accepted from him back then and not give something back. This is a debt and I've got to find some answer I can live with or it will change the way I view myself."

She considered this, then sighed loudly. "Where is he?"

"Right outside your door. He's drunk. Just got through cussing out half the task force. For all I know, one of them has already given him up to Underwood. The whole thing is out of control, but I've gotta try. He might be suicidal. I can't just stand around and watch him auger in."

She looked at me for a moment before picking up her phone and dialing a number.

"This is Lieutenant Scully in the Detective Bureau. Notify the Psychiatric section I want a two-man team to come to my office and pick up one of my detectives. I'm ordering a three-day hospital evaluation." She waited, then said, "He's undergoing extreme stress, both marital and financial, possibly suicidal. I want him held in the secure wing at Queen of Angels until you can make a determination. All reports on his condition are to be released only to my office." She waited again, then said, "Thanks."

She hung up and fixed me with one of her no-bullshit-all-business stares. "This puts him in the system, Shane. If he flunks the psych review, he's gonna get flagged. All this does is take him out of action for three days and keep him from doing something foolish. Maybe he comes back to us or maybe he gets marked unfit for duty. If that happens, he gets the gate."

"With a medical waiver he could go out on early retirement without affecting his pension."

"That would be up to Tony, the Commission, and the Bureau of Professional Standards," which was our new media-friendly name for Internal Affairs. I could see she was angry. "This isn't the way it's supposed to work," she added.

Thirty minutes later, two psychiatric paramedics arrived. Zack was led into the elevator. Just before the door closed, he turned and looked at me, a stunned, betrayed expression on his swollen face.

21

WHAT'S WITH ALL these embassy cars? Where's our intel on these people?"

Underwood was pissed, studying the digital photo blow-ups from the funeral. Brendan Villalobos, Mace Ward, Ruben Bola and I were crowded in his office.

The idea that foreign embassies might lodge a career-ending complaint in the federal hierarchy, definitely had Underwood worried. It was no fun being bait at the bottom of the political aquarium. While Underwood bitched about our inefficiency, I tried to get the image of Zack's swollen, disillusioned face to retreat to some dark place in the back of my mind.

"We gotta find out who these fucking people are," Underwood said.

"This big guy dressed in the tweed jacket left in a car from the Russian Embassy," Villalobos said, pointing at the pictures.

Ruben Bola followed his lead and picked up two photos. "This bald guy in the blue blazer left in an Israeli embassy car. The foxy blonde in the business suit was in a silver Jag. We ran her plates but they came back to a company called Allied Freight Forwarding. Answering machine, post office box address. Probably a phone drop."

Brendan Villalobos picked up photos of the guys wearing Forest Lawn jumpsuits. "Anybody been able to identify these two cream machines?" he asked.

The African American was implausibly handsome. The shot of his partner showed a thin, narrow-waisted white guy with tattoos. He had an uneven, sandy flattop that looked like he'd done it himself with hedge shears.

"Where's their car?" Brendan asked.

I rummaged around and found a shot of an old Dodge Charger pulling out of the lot. Darleen and Kyle had printed several blow-ups of the rear bumper giving us a readable view of the license plate. "California plate Ida-Mae-Victor three-seven-five," I said. "It came back to somebody named Leland Zant."

"And?" Agent Orange had lost patience with us.

"Extensive drug record," Ruben added quickly, keeping his eyes on his notes. "Guy changes addresses a lot. Sally's trying to dig through the clutter and get a current."

As if on cue, there was a knock on the door and Sally Quinn stuck her head in. "Zant is doing a third strike in Soledad. He's been up there since last August."

"So if he's in the cooler, who's driving this Charger?" Underwood barked. "Come on, don't make me pull it out in scraps."

Sally continued, "Zant went down for moving forty kilos of cut. With that much weight, we popped him for felony dealing and the car became an LAPD asset seizure. The registration just transferred."

"This Charger is an LAPD undercover?" Underwood frowned.

"Looks like it, sir," Sally answered.

"So keep going. . . . Who was driving it? Getting a full report outta you is worse than dental surgery."

Detective Quinn was turning red with anger, but to her credit, her expression didn't change. She took a breath and held his gaze. "It was checked out of our motor pool to CTB."

"I give up." Underwood was getting snotty now.

"Counter Terrorism Bureau," she clarified. "They're upstairs on four."

Underwood started rubbing his forehead with a freckled hand. "What the hell is going on here? Did we just accidentally stumble into some multinational anti-terrorism case?"

Nobody answered.

"Who in CTB checked the car out of your motor pool?" he asked Sally, holding up the two pictures of the Forest Lawn workers. "Was it these two? Did you get their names or did you even bother to ask?"

"Don't know who they are, sir. It was checked out on what they call a blind borrow." Detective Quinn's voice was strained. She'd had her fill.

"I wanta know who these two people are. If they're cops, I want their names." Underwood was apoplectic, waving the digital pictures at us.

After a long silence, I volunteered. "Homicide Special shares the floor with CTB. I've gotten to know a few people. You want, I could wander around up there and see if I can find out who these guys are."

"Hey . . . that sure sounds like a plan." Underwood rolled his eyes in undisguised frustration.

I glanced at my fellow task force members. They all wore deadpans that would have won poker tournaments in Vegas.

I went upstairs and wandered around with our digital prints stashed out of sight in a manila folder. CTB was divided into two sections. The operational side was a regular squad room with partitions, which housed your basic, high-testosterone, door-kicking commando types. Across the main aisle from them was the Intelligence Section. It was a cluttered cube farm full of nerdy boys and girls with fluorescent tans, plastic belts, and intense expressions.

The way it was explained to me, CTB Intelligence worked on background, accessing computer data banks, and looking for known associates of terrorist cell members. Once a new list of potential bomb throwers was compiled, Intelligence would turn it over to Operations. Operations would then make a determination on which targets looked promising and the lieutenant in charge would assign one of the surveillance squads for a twenty-four-hour look-see. Sometimes they'd spot the target buying drugs. Sometimes they were conspiring with other known terrorists or buying street guns. Sometimes they were just picking up prostitutes. Whatever the crime, Operations would arrest them and pull them in for questioning.

What CTB had learned since 9/11, was that once a terrorist was arrested, most hardcore operations like Al Qaeda would never deal with him again. One minor bust, even one that didn't stick, eliminated a cell member forever. As a result, the terrorist cells were so busy rebuilding, they didn't get around to running plays.

I walked slowly down the corridors looking for a friendly face, somebody that I could show my packet of photos to. Then I looked up. Coming right toward me was the handsome black detective from Forest Lawn. He was now wearing a snazzy designer suit with an open-collared blue silk shirt. Fruity cologne trailed him like expensive exhaust. After he passed, the guy flicked an F-stop glance back in my direction.

We have ignition.

I followed him into his small, cluttered cubicle. He was taking off his coat and settling behind his desk as I came through the doorway.

"Something I can do for you?" he asked.

Instead of answering, I dropped his picture on the desk in front of him.

22

I SETTLED INTO the chair on the opposite side of the partner's desk in his cubicle, and gave him my best blank stare.

There was a long moment while he tried to decide how he wanted to play it. I obviously wasn't going to go away, so he heaved a deep sigh and said, "I'll show you mine if you show me yours."

He was one of those guys who had scored big in the gene pool. Mocha skin, square jaw, white teeth, piercing black eyes. But there was also a healthy dose of arrogance.

I reached into my back pocket, fished out my worn leather badge case and dropped it onto the desktop between us. He did the same. Then we each slid them across the three-foot polished surface at each other.

He was Roger Broadway, Detective III. On the job since '87.

The picture looked like it came out of a modeling portfolio. We airmailed our creds back, both plucking badge cases out of the air simultaneously.

"You don't have a clue what you stumbled into, Scully. Your John Doe is in good hands. Cut your losses." I gave him more attitude so he continued. "This is a CTB special op. My best advice is, dial it way down, go back to that task force piñata party you got going, and forget this."

"That's kinda shitty advice, Roger. Especially since I'm working a front-page serial murder, and I got half the deputy chiefs in this building walking around in my asshole with flashlights." I tapped a picture of the coffin. "So in the spirit of interdivisional cooperation, why don't you start by putting a hat on this guy for me?"

"He ain't Mike Eisner," Broadway said, holding my gaze. "And he also ain't one of your Fingertip murders. He's an international intelligence asset. Beyond that, you don't have to know."

I reached into the envelope and pulled out the rest of the pictures and dropped them onto the desk. "This was a very eclectic turnout."

He picked up the pictures of the lumbering Russian in the brown tweed, and the bald man in the blue blazer from the Israeli embassy. He studied them for a second before he shrugged and handed them back to me.

"I want some answers," I said. "Why were you there, and why did all these embassy people show up?"

"Leave it be," he said softly.

Yeah, right . . . I thought. *Pushing on then . . .*

"I think my John Doe victim is a foreign national, possibly Russian. Maybe even Odessa Mafia. I agree, he's not one of the Fingertip murders, but my bosses want me to keep him in the mix. If I stumbled into a CTB covert op, I can walk softly, but this is still my one-eighty-seven, and the sixth floor wants it put down. So if you hardball me, I'll be forced to take it to Deputy

Chief Ramsey and we can do this hair-pulling thing in his office."

"Great White Mike can't cover you," he said, but there was worry flickering in his coal-black eyes.

"Help me and I'll help you. I have no desire to bitch up your investigation, but I'm not going away, especially after throwing this funeral and watching half the spooks in L.A. show up."

"I hope that ain't no racial epithet." A smile found the corner of his mouth. "Hate to have to one-eighty-one your Gumby white-slice ass." Talking about an Internal Affairs complaint.

"Your best bet of containing me is to trade with me, Roger."

"Right. And once that happens and you share our covert information with that buncha literary hopefuls downstairs, how long till it's on sale at Amazon?"

"I'll keep what you tell me strictly between us."

A bald-faced lie, because I knew I probably couldn't do that. I had to report this meeting to Underwood, and he could do anything he pleased with the information. My last line of defense was Alexa, but right now my beautiful wife wasn't all that happy with me. However, now wasn't the time to hesitate.

I pulled out the picture of the attractive blonde who had been sitting in the back of the church and showed it to him. "Teammate?" I asked.

He didn't take the picture out of my hand, but I saw another flicker of something in his black eyes.

Then a shadow fell over me. I looked up. Standing in the doorway was his partner—pencil-thin, bad haircut, hips like a wasp, chewing a soggy toothpick.

"You're in my chair, pard." His Southern accent was thick as pork gravy. All that was missing was the banjo solo from *Deliverance*.

I stood up and handed him the packet of pictures. He sorted through them quickly.

"That puts some hair in the biscuits, don't it, Rog?" He glanced over at Broadway.

"I'm Scully, Homicide Special."

"We know who you are, Joe Bob," he drawled around his toothpick. "You're the dummy running that mess down on three."

"Not running it anymore. We have a cool new FBI leader. Lunar calendars, party hats. Come on down and get a shit cupcake."

Broadway said, "This is my partner, Emdee Perry. Emdee is a name, not initials. This cracker's from the hills a South Carolina, so he ain't above burnin' a cross on your lawn. But the motherfucker sure knows how to kick up a shed."

"This cracker-bashin' Oreo finally got somethin' right," Emdee deadpanned.

I knew they were just stalling, putting up smoke, doing the dozens.

Broadway said, "Detective Scully's wondering who he was getting set to bury. That's how far off the pace the boy is."

Perry studied me, rolling the toothpick to the other side of his mouth. "We ain't actually getting set t'deal with this fool, are we, Snitch?"

Then I knew who they were. They had flashy nicknames—Rowdy and Snitch. Two colorful characters who were fast becoming LAPD legends.

"Don't make me take this to Deputy Chief Ramsey," I said. "He has big pressure coming down from the super chief. He won't like me being stonewalled."

"Great White Mike can shit in his hat," Broadway said. "We report to Deputy Chief Talmadge Burke in Support Services, and he doesn't like us to stand around and yap about secure cases with people who ain't been baptized."

"I can't believe you two humps want to start a turf war over a little deal like who my dead guy is. I'm gonna find out anyway."

Broadway and Perry exchanged some kind of subliminal look. The trick for them was to only give me info I would eventually discover on my own, and keep the rest hidden. My job was to run a good bluff and get things they shouldn't reveal.

Finally, Roger Broadway leaned back in his chair. "Your stiff is named Davide Andrazack. He's an Israeli black ops agent working for the Mossad. End of story."

"Except the guy had a contact lens for an eye condition called Keracotonus. According to our lab he was damn near blind. Are you two trying to tell me that a world-class black ops service like the Mossad is down to hiring blind guys?"

Emdee Perry cleared his throat, then threw the chewed toothpick into the wastebasket. "Since his eyes went bad, Andrazack don't work black ops no more," he said. "These days he's more of what you'd call an electronic plumber. Fixes computer leaks."

"Before he caught the big bus, he was their best guy for E-ops," Broadway said. "A master cracker." He glanced at Emdee. "A term of endearment." Emdee bowed his head magnanimously.

"Our file on him says he once penetrated Level Four Pentagon security. We think he was in the U.S. scoping the Israeli computers looking for a leak at their embassy."

"I'm still not buying this," I said. "A foreign intelligence agent with a record of hacking Pentagon data gets a visa from our State Department to come over and hack embassy computers? Not in the post nine-eleven world I live in."

"You're over cookin' the grits here, Joe Bob. Just accept what we're tellin' ya and move along," Emdee said.

"You guys haven't heard the last of me. See ya up on six."

I started to leave, but Emdee grabbed my arm.

"He was over here off the books. When they can't get a visa, the Israelis have been known to drop one a these hog callers in a rubber boat from a mother ship three or four miles offshore and run the man in. Not just the Mossad. Everybody does it. Any given day we got enough unidentified illegal spooks in this town to haunt a house. Idea is, they only stay here long enough to do one quick job, then it's back to the beach and *adios*."

"INS never knows they were here," Broadway said. "Only this time, looks like Davide didn't move quite fast enough and somebody skagged him. Whoever did that piece a work knew it was gonna stir up trouble, so they dressed Davide in homeless clothes and tried to ditch him in your Fingertip case."

"End of story," Emdee said firmly, and glanced at his partner. Neither of them wanted this to progress any further.

I didn't mention that we had held back the symbol carved on the chest and that there was no way the espionage community could have dumped Andrazack into our serial murder without knowing about that. Instead, I asked, "If Andrazack's dead, why are you guys still involved?"

They looked at each other, and I could see they were through with me.

"I guess you can just take it up with Great White Mike then," I said.

"Tell you what," Broadway replied. "Why don't you leave all these pictures with us? We'll run it past Lieutenant Cubio and if he signs off on you, we'll give you a call." Lt. Armando Cubio ran CTB.

"Make it happen, guys," I warned. " 'Cause there's big trouble hiding behind Door Number Two."

"Man, I think I just shit my drawers," Perry drawled.

23

ARE YOU WITH the family?" the county psychiatric evaluator asked, looking down at a clipboard with all of Zack's pertinent information. We were standing in the lobby just outside the secure psychiatric wing of the Queen of Angels Hospital. The doctor was tall and bald, peering at me through rose-colored lenses, which seemed to me like a bad visual metaphor in the sensitive field of mental health. His name tag identified him as Leonard M. Pepper, M.D., but he was pure vanilla.

"I'm Don Farrell. Zack's brother," I lied.

He found Zack's brother's name on the clipboard. "Okay." He had that kind of spacey, nonconfrontational manner usually found in westside head shops.

"I'm just wondering how he's doing."

"How he's doing is a subjective measure of what he's willing to accept minus what he's willing to admit to."

Oh, brother.

"Is he suicidal, for instance?"

"I'm not sure. He's very depressed."

I tried the direct approach. "Is it possible for me to see him?"

After a long moment, he nodded and punched a code into the electric door we were standing next to. Once it kicked open he motioned for me to follow him down a narrow corridor that had rooms every thirty feet or so on both sides. The doors were solid metal. Each had an eight-by-ten, green tinted, wire and glass window. As we walked, he droned on.

"Has your brother ever undergone psychiatric analysis before?" he asked.

"No, I don't think so."

"He said he went through it once in the army."

I didn't know Zack was ever in the army. He'd never mentioned it. I wondered why. But of course I couldn't say any of that. I was supposed to be his brother. "He never mentioned undergoing analysis in the service," I dodged.

Dr. Pepper turned to face me, taking a gold pen out of his pocket. "Was he truant a lot when he was in lower school?"

"Once or twice, maybe."

I was flying blind here. I didn't want to contribute to an incorrect diagnosis, but a brother couldn't be completely ignorant, either. I decided to just vague this guy out.

"Was he often engaged in fights as a child?"

"No more than anyone."

"What kind of answer is that?" The doctor peered over his rose lenses at me.

"It's *my* answer, Doctor." Now he was pissing me off.

"He indicated he had problems with bed-wetting into middle school," Pepper said. "Do you recall when it stopped happening?"

"What is this?"

"Just answer me."

"I don't remember . . . I don't think so . . . I don't know. I had my own problems. I wasn't paying attention." The asshole actually noted that down. "Why don't you just tell me what the hell you're getting at?" I demanded.

He clicked his pen closed. "This is still very preliminary. He's only been here six or seven hours, but your brother exhibits signs of cognitive disassociative disorder, along with what might be described as massive clinical depression. The depression is so strong I'm wondering if it might be a calendar reaction stemming from some event in his childhood. Often our subconscious stores dates and revisits them annually through bouts of depression, even though the event itself may be blocked in our memory. Do you remember something severe in his youth that might have caused that?"

"No," I said. "All I know is, right now he's under a lot of stress with his upcoming divorce. He's having money problems. He's also afraid he's losing his relationship with his sons."

"If my diagnosis is right, I would doubt any of that is responsible for the depression. Cognitive disassociates don't treasure emotional relationships. It's what that behavior is all about. But it's hard to tell, because right now, he's just trying to bullshit his way out of here."

"But you're not going to let go of him, are you?" I said, getting this guy's drift. He was bored with the endless drug overdoses and soccer moms who felt trapped by the monotony of carpools and Saturday sex. He wanted to hang some high-drama diagnosis on Zack, add some excitement to the revolving door litany of petty complaints he was forced to deal with daily.

"Your brother also may be a narcissistic personality," he added, really piling it on. "It's characterized by a predominate focus on self and a lack of remorse or empathy. This is only a preliminary diagnosis, and mind you, I could be wrong, but I want to keep him here for a while to sort it out."

He turned and led me further down the hall, stopping in front of a locked door. "Tell your brother he needs to cooperate with me if he wants to go home."

Then he took out a keycard and zapped the door open, letting me pass inside alone. I heard the door close and lock behind me.

Zack was slumped in a white plastic chair next to the window. The cell-like room was a concrete box painted dull white. In a salute to insanity, the bed and dresser were both bolted to the floor. Zack turned his swollen face to look at me. Without saying anything, he returned his gaze to the window and the distant traffic on the 101 freeway half a mile down the gentle slope from the hospital.

I motioned to the room. "This seems pleasant and clean," sounding like a friendly realtor instead of the traitorous bastard who put him here.

He wouldn't look at me.

"I just talked to your psychiatric evaluator," I continued. "He says you can work your way out of this, but he wants you to open up to him more."

Nothing from Zack.

"He also said you gotta come to grips with the divorce. Once that happens things are gonna get better, the depression will go away."

He hadn't mentioned any of that, but I was on a roll, here. I waited for Zack to say something like, 'Gee, that's swell, Shane,' or 'I don't blame you for ratting me out and ruining my life.' But he just sat there. Over three hundred pounds of Irish anger stuffed in a too-small hospital gown.

"It's hard," I monologued. "I know how much this is ripping you up . . . but the thing you gotta know, Zack, is I'm in your corner. A lot of people are."

He scooted his plastic chair further away from me, giving me almost his whole back now.

"Listen, Zack, I know you think I sold you out, but I was only trying to . . ." His shoulders slumped so I stopped.

I grabbed a chair and brought it closer. I sat next to him but I couldn't engage his eyes. I was talking to the side of his head. "Zack . . . listen to me, Zack. I'm really worried about you. I know it's hard for you to understand, but this is the best course. You can get help here."

He turned his chair even further away.

"I've got a plan, Zack. Will you listen to me?" I was starting to sweat, but I kept going. "This doesn't have to be as bad as it seems. We've got Alexa on our side and I'm about to split Forrest out of the Fingertip case. I think I can fix it so we can work on that murder and get off the task force. I'm pretty sure now that Forrest is a copycat. He was a Mossad agent named Andrazack, in this country illegally. I think he was killed by some foreign agent, not the Fingertip unsub. You're gonna be getting a clean bill in a few days, but in the meantime, I wanta come by and run some of this stuff by you, get your take on it. That sound like a plan?"

He just sat there.

"Zack, don't give up here, buddy. Zack? Hey, come on man, look at me."

Nothing.

I wondered if I was getting a look at cognitive disassociative disorder.

24

WHEN I GOT home my head ached and my eyes felt grainy. All I wanted was a glass of scotch to wash my treachery away. But getting wasted was my old solution. I'd moved past that now. In a gesture of determined sobriety, I settled for a Coke and a bag of chips and walked out into the backyard where I sat in one of my rusting patio chairs and looked out at the wind-ruffled water on Venice's narrow canals, thinking you really did need a sense of humor to appreciate its corny charm.

Every time I have problems I find myself sitting here, drawn to Abbot Kinney's faded dream, as if some part of my soul will be reborn in the stagnant water of these shallow canals. Sometimes, I feel as if he had designed this strange place with me in mind. I fit right in, a romantic in a fast-food world, lodged hopelessly in a moral cul-de-sac just like the McDonald's wrappers that collected under the fake Venetian bridges. But there was a sense of past and future here. The throwback architecture, the scaled-down plot plan from the 1400s, all managed to coexist in some kind of insane proximity to the strip malls two blocks away and the Led Zeppelin music that drifted across the narrow canals from my hippie neighbors windows. If only I could find such an easy truce with my disparate emotions.

Half an hour later I heard the back door open, and then Alexa dropped into the chair beside me and heaved a deep sign. She had a beer in her hand, and I listened while she pulled the tab, the chirp mixing neatly with the sounds of a hundred keening insects.

She grabbed a handful of chips and said, "I'm fucked with these crime stats. The chief is gonna redeploy at least twenty of my detectives. It's gonna foul up my whole grid plan."

Tony Filosiani was famous for his constant shuffling of manpower after COMSTAT meetings. He had installed a big, electronic map board of the city in the sixth-floor conference room. It was a complex son-of-a-bitch, which almost required a Cal Tech graduate to operate. Different colored lights represented different categories of crime that had occurred in the previous two weeks. One little light for every criminal incident. Murders and Crimes Against People were red; Burglaries—blue; Armed Robberies—green. While carjacking was technically a CAP, it was also such a growing category it had acquired its own color—yellow.

The division commanders would walk into the darkened COMSTAT meeting and see the board twinkling like a desert sky at midnight. Then Chief Filosiani would flip a switch and white lights would appear all over the map in clusters. The white lights indicated our deployed police presence. In one glance you could see if you had your troops in the right place. If a street gang like the Rolling Sixties went hot and started jacking cars and houses, you could see if there were enough cops at Sixtieth Street and

MLK Boulevard to handle it. If there were too many white lights where nothing was happening Tony would move people around. Just like that, cops got transferred to new divisions.

At the end of this light show, the chief would extinguish all of the cleared cases and embarrass any commander who still had too many colored lights burning in his area.

It was Alexa's job to move detectives and balance caseloads. The short-term problem for her was handing off old cases to new detectives and all of the confusion this produced.

"I need to cover some business," I finally said, setting my Coke on the table next to us. "I've got a couple of things to discuss."

"Look, baby, I'm sorry about this afternoon and Zack. I understand what you're feeling, I just don't agree, that's all. Can't we leave it at that?"

"I went by the hospital to see him after work."

"How'd you get in? He's supposed to be incommunicado."

"I told the psychiatrist I was his brother."

I waited while she sipped her beer. Finally, she responded. "I keep forgetting how stubborn and resourceful you are."

"I don't usually get slammed and complimented in the same sentence."

"You're also an asshole who's kinda cute," she said, doing it again.

"I give." I didn't have to look over to see that she was smiling.

"Okay," she said. "Gimme the second chorus."

"Zack's really screwed up. Wouldn't look at me. Wouldn't even talk. I was there ten, fifteen minutes, and he didn't say one word."

"Unless he's gone completely over the falls, he'll get over it."

"I don't think so. His psychiatric evaluator thinks he has a narcissistic personality with cognitive disassociative disorder, whatever the hell that is. I thought it was BS until I saw him. He's beaten, and he hates me."

"He doesn't hate you," she said.

"Yeah, well, you weren't there."

She thought for a moment before she turned to face me. "A while back, when I was in patrol, I caught a payback hit in Compton. This was two, three years before we met. The mother of one of the dead boys was this big, floppy soul with drooping eyes. I'm trying to take her statement, she's crying because she lost a son, and I say to her, 'These kids must really hate one another.' It was just nervous chatter. But she turns to me and says, 'Where you been, child? It takes powerful love to do a thing like this.' Then she said, 'Hate needs love to burn.' "

Alexa stopped and put her beer down. "At the time, I thought that was nuts, but you know something? Working murders all day long, I've come to realize that she was mostly right. Hate is just a few degrees past love on the dial. Hate and love feed on each other."

"And all of this tells me what?" I said, frustrated.

"That Zack loves you. He's stressed and feels abandoned, so yes, right now there's some hate, but it's built on love, Shane. Right now, you both have the volume up too high. Turn it down and see what happens."

I sat next to her and tried not to argue. I remembered what Zack said to me in the bar. "Everything I say, people hear too loud." But I also remembered the psychiatrist's words: "His personality type doesn't treasure relationships." I was too confused to sort it out, so I just said "Okay" and moved on.

"You said there were a couple of things," Alexa pressed. "What's the other?"

So I told her about Rowdy and Snitch, and the strange guest list at the funeral.

"Sounds interesting," she said, softly.

"Whatta I do?" I asked. "I've got Deputy Chief Mike Ramsey on one side and Deputy Chief Talmadge Burke on the other. Broadway and Perry are gonna try and get me conferenced in, but they have to clear it with their lieutenant."

"And since John Doe Four turned out to be an Israeli spy, the case falls into some kinda no-man's-land between CTB and the Fingertip task force," she said. "So what do you want?"

"I want off the Fingertip case. I want to work this homicide out of CTB with Broadway and Perry. I really can't stand that task force. I'm not doing any good. The boss doesn't like me. He's gonna backwater all my leads anyway."

"Shane . . . I can't take you off the Fingertip killings and I can't reassign you to the Andrazack case."

"Why not?"

"Armando Cubio runs a tight operation at CTB. He won't want you in the mix."

"I think you're wrong. He'll want to work it, but he'd also just as soon keep Andrazack in the Fingertip case. Strange as it seems, it's lower profile if it stays there, lost in the mix with five others. I had to tell Underwood what's going on and he's agreed not to make Andrazack's name public. CTB doesn't want a news story on how some black ops Mossad agent in the U.S. without permission got murdered."

Alexa looked beautiful, her black hair picking up fleeting specks of moonlight, her mouth soft and inviting. But she wasn't about to answer, she was mulling it over.

"Okay, then here's another plan," I said. "How 'bout we skip dinner and get naked. Maybe I can change your mind in the bedroom."

"You mean sexually entertain your division commander in an attempt to affect a duty assignment?"

"Something like that."

So we went into our bedroom, took off our clothes, and lay on the bed holding each other. She nuzzled my neck.

"This is beginning to make my Southwest crime problem seem irrelevant," she said, reaching for me.

I was already breathing hard when she stopped suddenly and looked into my eyes.

"Sometimes we're going to be on opposite sides of things."

"I understand," I said softly.

"But I want you to know I respect where you're coming from. What I treasure most are your complexities."

25

THE NEXT MORNING I drove down Abbot Kinney Boulevard heading toward IHOP for a stack of cakes and some coffee, before going into the office. As I pulled into a parking space in the adjoining lot, a tan Fairlane that looked like it had been painted with spray cans from the drugstore, screeched into the space next to me. The doors flew open and Rowdy and Snitch got out.

"This is nice down here," Broadway said. "Smell the ocean and everything."

"I'm assuming this ambush is because your lieutenant signed off on me," I replied.

"You buy the grits; we'll see how it goes," Emdee said and turned to lock the door of the car. It had to be force of habit, because there was nothing worth stealing on that wreck. It didn't even have hubcaps.

The IHOP was strangely quiet for 7 A.M. We found a booth in the back and settled in. Broadway and I ordered pancakes, bacon, and coffee. Emdee Perry had what he called a hillbilly breakfast. Pork sausage, oatmeal, and Red Bull.

"Alright," I said, taking out my spiral pad and pen.

"No notes," Broadway said.

"Why not?"

"In this game we don't put stuff on paper. Nobody wants t' face a bunch a subpoenaed notes we can't explain in federal court."

I put the pad away.

Emdee said, "We done some background checking and it seems you're okay, but we also found out Detective Farrell's bread ain't quite out of the oven. Frankly, you bein' hooked up with him makes us wonder how loose your shit is. The Loot says you been in some tight scrapes and didn't leak, but what we're gonna tell you's gotta stay with you. You can't go blabbin' none a this to the task force, or yer partner, or anybody else and that includes your wife."

Roger Broadway leaned forward. "Most a this shit won't stand up under a policy review. That's why we need your word."

"You got it."

The food came and everybody dug in.

"Okay," I said between bites. "Why don't you start by telling me why half the L.A. intelligence community was at Andrazack's funeral?"

"That wasn't half," Roger Broadway said. "That was just Russians, Jews, CIA, us, and two guys from the French embassy. You didn't get no pictures, so you musta clean missed the Frogs. They were up on the roof of the main building."

"I can't believe this dead Mossad agent was that popular."

"Classified information is getting out," Emdee Perry said. "Even our shop is leaking. The embassy players in town are freaking. All we got in this business is our secrets, and all of a sudden, it's like nobody's data is secure. We think Davide Andrazack was over here to help the Israelis find out who and how." He pushed his plate away. "We're getting fucked worse than sheep at an Appalachian barn dance."

"Andrazack must have found out something," Broadway added. "We think whoever is bugging these embassies caught Andrazack and whacked him to keep it quiet."

"So who's planting the bugs?" I asked. "Russians or Israelis?"

"Them two ain't the ones doin' it," Emdee said.

"You sound pretty sure."

"Behavior indicates result," Roger explained.

"I love when Joe Bob talks pretty like that," Emdee drawled. "But he's right. If they's the ones planting bugs, they wouldn't be running around like their hair's on fire."

"Andrazack had Cyrillic symbols tattooed on his eyelids," I said. "Translation: 'Don't wake up.' I got a call from a friend on the Russian gang squad this morning. He says that's a Ukranian hitman's curse. Sounds like Andrazack was more a Russian than a Jew."

"He was both," Broadway said. "Russian Jew. He repatriated from Moscow to Israel when he was nine. Joined the Israeli Army when he turned nineteen, then he joined the Mossad. He was fluent in Balkan dialects, so they sent the boy back to Moscow when he was twenty-five. His specialty was assassinations. Close kills behind the Iron Curtain. In the early eighties he botched a hit in Moscow and was sentenced to twenty years in Lefortovo Prison. Since Andrazack's criminal specialty was murder, he used his skills on the inside to stay alive. He was whackin' enemies of the Odessa mob for smokes. Ended up being the most feared killer in that prison. That's why he had the

Russian tatts on his eyelids. After the Soviet Union fell, somebody in the Mossad paid off a Russian commissar and he got released, went back to Israel. By then he was almost blind and became a computer geek."

"With a history like that, sounds to me like he would've had a lot of Russian enemies," I said.

"Bam-Bam Stan wouldn't have been at that funeral if his Black Ops guys did the hit," Broadway answered.

"Who the hell is Bam-Bam Stan?"

"The whale wearing the burlap tent. Stanislov Bambarak. Ex-KGB. 'Course nobody cops to being a KGB agent anymore. Stan says he works for the Russian ballet and symphony, but according to our intelligence file he wouldn't know an oboe from a skin flute. He went to the Russian language and culture schools in the Balkans in the early sixties. He came out and mostly worked infiltrating MI-5 until they moved him back to Moscow. Guy speaks English like a Saville Row faggot. Putting the cultural stuff aside, the fact is, he's still a frontline Kremlin operator. Back in the eighties, before his ankles started swelling, that bad boy was an fire-breathing sack of trouble. Still wouldn't want to go up against him."

"And the guy from the Israeli Embassy?" I asked.

"Jeez, you sure want a lot for a crummy stack of cakes," Broadway complained. "Maybe you got something to tell us about the Andrazack murder first."

I gave it a moment's thought. "Okay. The bullet we dug out of Andrazack's head was a five-forty-five caliber. We think it came from a PSM Automatic."

"The best damn piece ever for close kills," Emdee said. "You get a ballistics match?"

"Still waiting. I'll let you know if the slug ties up to any old cases."

They both nodded.

"This gun was issued to KGB agents, but you still say the Reds didn't pop him?"

"Theoretically, anything's possible," Roger conceded. "But Bambarak was at that funeral to make sure Andrazack was really on the Ark. He's too hands-on for one of his agents to have done it and him not know."

"So who's the Israeli with the bald head who left in their embassy car?"

"The guy ain't no Israeli," Emdee said. "He's a U.S. citizen of the Jewish persuasion—a retired LAPD sergeant named Eddie Ringerman. Worked Homicide before nine-eleven. He pulled the pin two years ago. Now he's a consultant for the Israelis. Helps them get favors and information out of the Glass House. Not a bad guy. He just forgot which flag he's supposed to salute."

"I think we need to talk to Ringerman and Bambarak," I said. "Can you get them to open up?"

"We're tricky bastards who have good relations all over town," Emdee said. "In the spy business, a guy does you a favor, you owe him. Reds, Ruskies, CIA, Frogs, Germans, us—everybody keeps track of old debts and pays off. The people who owe us will pay us back. We'll get something."

He looked at Roger. "Only people you gotta stay clear of is the FBI. The feebs will take everything you got and hand you a shit sandwich for your trouble. Nobody trades with those pricks."

"How about the CIA?"

"They're cool," Broadway said. "You can do business with them. The chilly fox in the designer threads who showed up at your funeral is CIA. Special Agent in Charge Bimini Wright.

"We should take a meeting with the gorgeous Ms. Wright," Emdee suggested. "Give us something to look forward to."

"Sounds like it's going to be a full day," I said, and paid the bill.

We walked out into the parking lot and then I followed their rusting Fairlane out of Venice. We had decided to start by talking with Eddie Ringerman at the Israeli Embassy in Beverly Hills, but we didn't quite make it.

Two blocks after we exited the freeway in West L.A., three gray sedans rushed us from behind, running both our cars to the curb. Half a dozen guys who looked like ads for genetic engineering piled out and waved badges in our faces. A few pulled guns.

"FBI!" one of them yelled. "Stay where you are."

"Hands on the hood of your car and nobody gets hurt," another screamed.

"We're LAPD," I shouted.

"Not anymore," Broadway growled. "I think we're now federal detainees."

26

THE OFFICES OF California Homeland Security were located on the top three floors of the old Tishman Building on Wilshire Boulevard. The Tishman was a monument to the concept of temporary architecture—a cheaply constructed twenty-story high-rise that was built in the '60s. The *L.A. Times* had recently reported it was already under discussion as a possible teardown.

The three gray sedans swept into the underground garage to the bottom parking level, and pulled up next to a single secure elevator with a red sign on a metal stand that read: U.S. GOVERNMENT USE ONLY. The car doors swung open as Rowdy and Snitch were pulled roughly out of separate sedans. I was yanked out of a third and pushed toward the elevator.

The agent in charge, a narrow dweeb named Kersey Nix, put his hand on a glass panel for a fingerprint scan. The doors yawned wide immediately and we were pushed into the elevator.

When the elevator opened on the top floor, a few more guys with identical haircuts were waiting. They led us down a corridor and put us in three separate lockdowns where the decor was half dungeon, half dental office; windowless, ten-foot square rooms with peach pastel walls, Berber carpet, and Barry Manilow wafting through a Muzak system. There was a thick metal door with an electronic lock. Before he left, my muscle-bound federal escort confiscated my wallet, cell phone, and watch. My gun had been confiscated back at the site of our arrest.

"You gonna tell me what this is about?" I asked.

"National security."

The door closed. The lock zapped. Barry Manilow crooned. There was no place to sit, no furniture, no shelves. Nothing. I was trapped in a musically bland, peach-colored environment.

I took off my jacket, sat on the carpeted floor, and tried to shake off my anger at these agents who felt they had such an overpowering mandate that they could treat three LAPD officers like criminals. I wanted to hit somebody. My rage flared so suddenly it surprised me.

When I was going through Marine Corps training, I remember once watching a videotape of an Army psychology program run at Fort Bliss using military police officers. The psychologists divided all the guards working one of our military prisons into two groups. One group of officers was assigned the role of temporary inmates; the others remained prison guards. The real reason for this test was not revealed.

What army psychiatrists were actually attempting to determine was how the act of granting complete power to one group over another might escalate both groups toward extreme violence. The MPs who were to remain guards were only told that the military was evaluating escape possibilities in Super-Max and to be especially vigilant. The guards pretending to be inmates were told to resist authority and look for any possible way to break out.

What transpired was amazing. The guards assigned to the role of prisoners didn't like being inmates. They had done nothing wrong. But their old friends were now hazing them, walking down the prison tiers ringing their batons across the bars, keeping them awake all night so they would be too tired to attempt anything. The men under lockdown became angrier, the captor guards more aggressive. After a week, sporadic incidents of violence broke out between men who had only a few days before, been close friends. In the second week, the army called off the test because a violent fight broke out between the two groups, which almost resulted in the death of a guard.

The lesson of this video was that absolute power without oversight can quickly morph into murderous rage. By the same token, complete loss of power, without appeal, can escalate behavior to exactly the same place.

If I was going to make the best of this, I would have to stay cool. I couldn't let indignation and self-righteousness turn to rage. Whatever was going on here, I was being tested. Anger would only result in failure.

So I waited. How long did I sit there? I have no idea. At first I tried to keep track of time by counting the Muzak songs. Figuring each at three to four minutes long, I sang along, counting on my fingers. By the time I'd heard "Mandy" four times, my brain stalled and I lost count.

Next, I tried to pass the time by concentrating on the Andrazack case, trying to come up with something fresh. Several things festered. I knew Broadway and Perry suspected somebody in the foreign intelligence community of bugging embassy computers. Broadway said he thought there might even be bugs or computer scans inside the LAPD's Counter-Terrorist Bureau. Forgetting for the moment how that could be accomplished, it raised an interesting possibility. If some foreign power was stealing information from inside CTB, had they also found a way to penetrate the LAPD mainframe?

The media was making a big deal of the Fingertip case and everybody in L.A. knew the basics of those crime scenes. But Zack and I had withheld the symbol carved on each victim's chest. If some foreign agent had hacked into our crime data bank or more to the point, the medical examiner's computer, it would explain how they knew to carve that symbol on Andrazack before dumping him in the river under the Barham Boulevard Bridge.

Further, if Davide Andrazack wasn't one of the serial killings, but a political assassination, all of the ritual evidence surrounding that hit was just staging. That meant most of the theories I had on it were no longer operative.

I started over and reevaluated. Maybe there wasn't just one killer. Maybe two guys threw Andrazack off the bridge into the water, which explained how they could shot-put a two-hundred-pound man thirty feet out into the wash. A bullet to the head doesn't always produce instant death. Maybe Rico was right and Andrazack's heart was still beating when he hit the concrete levee and that's why his right ribcage was bruised. The more I thought about it, the more it seemed to hang together.

Time clicked off a big, invisible game clock while Barry Manilow messed with my mind. Finally, I curled up and tried to sleep. As soon as I laid down, a voice came over a hidden speaker. "Don't do that," a man commanded.

I stood and looked up at the air-conditioning grate. The camera and speaker had to be in there, but it was too high up to get to. I was beginning to fume.

I needed to go to the bathroom, so I yelled that out. Nobody answered. In defiance, I unzipped and wrote my name on the tan Berber carpet in urine. Foolish, I know, but I have a childish streak.

"Don't do that either," the voice commanded again.

"Come on in here, asshole. We'll talk about it." Nobody answered, so I moved away from my yellow signature, sat down, closed my eyes, and waited.

It might have been four or five hours. It might have been ten. I completely lost track of time.

Finally the door opened. Kersey Nix was standing in the threshold.

"Is it recess?" I said, trying to sound faintly amused, even though underneath, I wanted to rip his throat out.

I noticed he was wearing a different suit. So while I'd been doing sing-alongs with Barry Manilow and writing my name on the carpet, this jerk-off had been at home resting up.

"I will give you some advice," Agent Nix said in a reasonable, but bland voice. "Tell us everything you know. Hold nothing back. You are at the beginning of a dangerous adventure. How it ends is going to be entirely up to you." Then he favored me with a sleepy-eyed half smile.

"I really need to go to the can," I said.

"Come on."

He turned and I had a weak moment where I was tempted to kick his skinny butt up between his ears. But I held off. It was a good thing I did, because two identically shaped androids were waiting in the hall just out of sight.

The four of us marched down the corridor toward the men's room. I saw a window. It was dark outside. We'd been picked up at 9 A.M. and sunset was four-thirty, so doing the math, I'd been here a minimum of eight hours.

After I used the facilities and washed up, I followed Agent Nix to a large set of double doors on the east end of the building. He led me inside a huge office, with an acre of snow-white, cut-pile carpet under expensive antique mahogany furniture. The U.S. and California State flags flanked each side of a Victorian desk big enough to play Ping-Pong on.

I'd seen the man standing in the center of the room waiting for me before, but only on television. He was in his late fifties, tall and handsome, with silver hair and a patrician bearing. He was flanked by two assistants—gray men with pinched faces. Everyone wore crisp white shirts, and a blue or a red tie. Patriotism.

"I'm Robert Allen Virtue, head of California Homeland Security," the tall, handsome man said. "I hope this hasn't inconvenienced you too much."

"Only if you don't like Barry Manilow," I replied.

27

I WAITED A few feet inside the plush office and tried to work out a good strategy to use on this guy.

Robert Allen Virtue was a political heavyweight who was chosen by the governor of the state of California and anointed by the U.S. Secretary of Homeland Security. He had a law degree from Princeton and dangerous connections in the political community.

I, on the other hand, was a Detective III in a city police department with a junior college education. My only dangerous connections were a sorry bunch of dirt bags I'd put in jail. Adding to my dilemma was a pile of anger I didn't quite know what to do with. Survival instincts told me Robert Virtue was not a profitable adversary for me. He could sink me with one torpedo.

"I'm sorry for the long wait," he said, equitably. "I was in Sacramento and couldn't get down here before now."

He pointed to a chair that had a black briefcase on it. "Just move that case and have a seat," he said.

"I'd prefer to stand."

"I'd like you to sit. Please," he said sternly, as if even this small challenge to his will was annoying to him.

I decided to save my shots and not get into it over trivial bullshit. I picked up the briefcase, which was surprisingly heavy, put it on the floor beside the chair and sat.

"Where are Detectives Broadway and Perry?" I asked.

"For now, let's stick to you."

"Alright. What do I have to do with Homeland Security? I'm a homicide detective working a serial murder."

"There are things going on in this world that would appall even you, and I'm sure you've seen your share of atrocities. A life-or-death espionage game is being played in the streets of most major U.S. cities every day. In Los Angeles we have one of the most vigorous contests. Unfortunately, you got mixed up in this because someone in the foreign intelligence community elected to hide a political killing in your grisly serial murder case."

He crossed to his desk and picked up a blue LAPD folder. I recognized it as a Professional Standards Bureau file with my name on the cover. Under Title 2 of the Police Bill of Rights, that folder, which contained all the complaints ever filed against me, was a confidential document and could only be accessed with my written permission. He set it down without mentioning it, just showing it to me to let me know he could cut right through my wall of rights anytime he chose.

"You are to turn the Andrazack killing over to me, and agree to no longer pursue it. He's not in your murder case. He was an alien intelligence officer in this country illegally, who also had a high threat assessment rating."

Virtue seemed to know all about my investigation. I only ID'd

Andrazack twelve hours ago, and the identification was supposed to be under a CTB Cone of Silence. I couldn't help but wonder how he came by his information.

"Mr. Virtue, excuse me, but despite the dead man's nationality or illegal immigration status, I don't think my bosses will want this investigation removed from the Fingertip case. It's certainly possible that he could have stumbled into the wrong place and was targeted by our unsub. Beyond that, the man was murdered in Los Angeles. Shot in the head, mutilated, then dumped into the L.A. River. That certainly makes it a city case. If it's not going to be worked by LAPD, who's going to handle it?"

"I will," he said, and gave me his warm political smile, acting as if he had just decided we were going to be buddies after all.

"You will," I repeated. "Personally?"

"Well, not personally, but I'll put someone from the local office of the FBI on it."

"Excuse me again, sir, but the Bureau doesn't have jurisdiction. Since this is an L.A. street crime, Homicide Central represents a better option."

Now he was getting frustrated. "Homeland Security and the FBI will take the case as a matter of national security," he said flatly.

"I see. Okay, well, then I'll need to hear that from my supervisor. I can't just walk away from an active case I've been assigned to. Somebody from my division has to give me the nod."

Virtue had again picked up the blue folder and was tapping that Bad Boy file on his fingertips letting me know what an asshole he thought I was being. "Let me make that call then. Excuse me."

He turned and walked into an alcove where there was a secure communications hookup. A big black box scrambler sat next to a digital phone. He dialed a number.

While he talked softly into the instrument, I made a little trip over to his I Love Me wall. A mahogany-framed plaque announced his graduation from Princeton. Another frame displayed his graduation diploma from the FBI Academy at Quantico. He'd been in the January class of '68. I remembered hearing that Virtue was once a Cold War warrior for the FBI. There were fifty or more pictures of R. A. Virtue shaking hands with world leaders, national sports celebrities, actors, and U.S. politicians. I saw shots of him standing with President Jacques Chirac in Paris and with former USSR President Brezshnev in Lenin Square. There was one of him with Jimmy Carter in an African village, surrounded by children with distended bellies. I moved further down the wall where a few big-game shots were displayed. Guys with two-day growths wearing fur-lined vests, smiled vacantly at the camera with large bore rifles broken open over Pendleton sleeves. All of them were grinning proudly while some freshly slain longhorn sheep or elk looked into camera with that same startled look you find on old people in wedding pictures. In one of these shots I saw a narrow-shouldered man with orange hair. I leaned closer.

Agent Underwood of da motherfucking FBI.

"Okay, your chief and the head of your Detective Bureau, whom I'm told is also your wife, are on the way over," Virtue said as he reentered the room. "Apparently they want to do this in person so they can get a case transfer form signed for legal reasons. You can wait in the outer office."

I exited into the waiting room and sat on a chintz sofa, fuming while picking imaginary lint off my jacket. The light blue-and-green furniture in this suite was cool and restful but did little to calm me. After seeing Underwood's picture this made a little more sense. When I told Agent Orange, my temporary supervisor, about Davide Andrazack, I broke my word to Broadway and Perry. Although he'd pledged to keep it confidential, that lying dickhead had obviously blabbed everything to Virtue or Nix.

A little while later Roger Broadway arrived looking tired and pissed, escorted by his own super-sized steroid case in a black suit. Roger sat in an expensive high-backed wing chair. I started to speak, but he caught my eye and shook his head. Then Emdee Perry joined us. Another huge fed had him in tow.

Perry didn't sit, choosing instead, to look out the window at the lights on Wilshire Boulevard. "These boys are startin' t'get my tail up," he muttered softly.

Finally, Chief Filosiani and Alexa arrived with someone in a brown suit who was introduced as George Bryant, from LAPD Legal Affairs. They stopped in the waiting room to make sure we were okay.

I nodded a greeting at Alexa who nodded back. She looked under control, but I knew she was pissed. She's my wife and I can read the storm warnings. A minute or two later, we were ushered into Virtue's plush office. Tony introduced Alexa and Bryant, and we all sat on the plush furniture.

"I'd like to know under what authority you detained these detectives working under my command," Alexa challenged, going right at Virtue the minute everyone was settled. Tony hung back and let her vent.

"I have a situation here," R. A. Virtue said.

"You're damn right you do," she snapped. "These men are not criminals. You can't kidnap police officers and hold them without cause."

"You might want to try and contain yourself, Lieutenant Scully," Virtue said coldly.

"I think she's right," Tony said. "You've held these men since eight-forty this morning. We didn't know what happened to them. A major situation alert went down."

"This involves national security," Virtue said.

"You can't just pick up our people and hold them without warrants," Alexa challenged.

"Our powers are sanctioned by the Homeland Security and Patriot Acts of two-thousand-one," Virtue countered. "These three men were involved in a sensitive case, and we simply held them as material witnesses until I could get down here and deal with it. Now, do you want to stand around and argue that, or can we get on with the business of this meeting?"

Tony was fuming, but Virtue didn't seem to mind. "You are to turn loose your fourth Fingertip John Doe murder."

"Why's that?" Tony demanded.

"The dead man was, in fact, an Israeli national involved in an act of deadly espionage. The case affects national security and falls directly under the Foreign Intelligence Surveillance Act. I'm not asking for your permission, Chief. I'm simply notifying you of what's going to happen."

"As far as I'm concerned, he's still a Fingertip murder," Tony argued. "What proof do you have that he's an Israeli national?"

"This." Virtue handed over a Homeland Security identity sheet with a picture of Davide Andrazack, his name, and dental records. "Run this dental scan against your dead body for verification, but I'm claiming the case under FISA, USPA, and the U.S. Immigration Act. All your evidence and crime scene materials are to be immediately sent to Agent Nix at the L.A. office of the FBI on Madison."

"I'm not sure those three acts grant you that authority," Tony challenged.

"Tell them, Mr. Bryant," Virtue said, turning to our attorney.

"I'll have to check the specifics, but if Andrazack was here illegally and involved in espionage, then it's probably their case," Bryant said.

"I'll sign the case transfer document now if you brought one," Virtue said. "The officers' cars were sent over to the LAPD motor pool on Flower Street." Indicating with this piece of housekeeping, that as far as he was concerned, the issue had been settled and the meeting was over.

Ten minutes later the case was transferred and we were standing in front of the Tishman Building. Filosiani waved to his LAPD driver who pulled the chief's maroon Crown Vic to the curb. Perry, Broadway, Alexa, and I all squeezed into the backseat. Alexa was almost in my lap, it was so crowded. The legal affairs guy, Bryant, was up front with Tony and the driver. It was a full, angry car.

"That was short and sweet," Alexa said once the car doors were closed.

"When I get fucked, I usually get kissed," Tony growled.

"What are we really supposed to do?" I asked.

"We give him the case," Tony said. "I don't like it any better than you do, but it ain't like we don't have enough murders to solve. It's just that arrogant asshole pisses me off, is all." Then he turned to the driver. "Get us the hell out of here."

In the spirit of the moment, the sergeant behind the wheel floored it and laid an unintentional strip of rubber up Wilshire Boulevard.

28

I RODE THE elevator to the sixth floor with Alexa. She was quiet, still angry. The door opened and we walked the green carpet to her small office. It was a few minutes past 9 P.M. and Ellen was gone. The streetlights below Alexa's window were rimmed with tiny halos of fog.

"That was certainly a thorough mauling," she said as she started dropping things into her briefcase, getting ready to go home. "God, Shane, when I couldn't reach you on your cell or on your MCT or police radio, I almost died. I couldn't imagine what happened. Ten hours of not knowing . . ."

I put my arms around her. "Who does that asshole think he is?" she continued. "I've got half a mind to file charges of illegal detention." She rested her head against my chest.

"It's borderline, babe. Virtue's got too much political juice.

It's best to wait till his own sense of self-importance lures him all the way over the line and then hit him."

"I've heard he has his eye on the governorship. That he's arm-twisting Hollywood celebrities and business people into investing in his campaign. He's already got a website. After he's governor, I've heard he even has plans for the presidency." She shuddered. "Just what this country needs, another self-serving power junkie in the White House. God help us."

I held her until she calmed down.

"Listen, Alexa, one thing did come out of all this that we need to pay some attention to."

"If it has to do with this case, forget it. We've been ordered to hand it over to the FBI." She pulled away from me and continued angrily slamming files into her briefcase.

"Someone in foreign intelligence popped Davide Andrazack and made it look like a Fingertip killing. Somehow, that shooter knew to carve the correct symbol on his chest. I find that very troubling."

She stopped packing up and turned to face me. "You're right. How did they know about that?"

I ran through what Broadway and Perry had told me about how there might be a bug, or a computer scan on CTB. I also shared my suspicion that maybe the leak went further than that.

When I finished, Alexa's brow was furrowed and her mouth pulled down into a scowl.

"I think we need to get someone from the Computer Support Division to sweep this place. Start with CTB and move to our main crime computers. Don't forget the ME's office."

She nodded. "Thanks," she said. "I'll get right on it."

"I'm gonna go down and check on my messages. I'll meet you at home in an hour."

The task force on three was still humming. It had progressed remarkably since this morning. Nobody seemed to miss me much. The detectives were all settled in. A chair with a broken back was pushed up to my desk. The phones were hooked up and I had been assigned extension 86. Someone's idea of a joke?

Word had already reached the cubes that John Doe Number Four was being yanked out of the serial case. It was officially logged as a copycat and was being worked by Justice. I got a few smug looks. I was back in the shallow end with the rest of the kiddies, my early lead eviscerated. Nobody wanted to be my secret partner anymore.

I sat at my desk, picked up the phone and tried the Queen of Angels Hospital. I was told that Dr. Pepper had gone home for the day and that Zack was resting and not receiving calls. I knew that after nine in the evening they had a phone cut-off but the woman on the switchboard made it sound like Zack had made a choice.

I listened to my voice mail. Some were callbacks on old cases, a few were people asking about Zack, and one was from a CSI criminalist in ballistics named Karen Wise who said that she had a report on the 5.45 slug we'd pulled out of Andrazack's head.

Since that wasn't my case anymore, I was tempted to e-mail her to contact Kersey Nix at the FBI, but curiosity got the better of me, and I dialed her number.

"CSI," someone answered at the Raymond Street complex.

"Detective Scully, Homicide," I said. "I'm looking for Karen Wise."

"She went home. If it's about an active case, I can connect you to her residence."

"Please."

I waited, and then a girl with a sexy voice came on the line. She had one of those low, fractured contraltos, that gets your fantasies boiling.

"Shane Scully," I said. "You called about my slug. Get anything?"

"We got a cold hit on an open homicide from the mid-nineties," she said, referring to a situation where a bullet or cartridge from one crime had striations or pin impressions that matched it to a bullet in what seemed like a totally unrelated crime.

My interest picked up at warp speed. "Wait a minute while I get a pencil."

I looked in my battered gray desk. Nothing in my pencil drawer but bent paper clips and dust, so I stole the supplies from a neighbor, then sat down again and snatched up the phone. "Okay, go."

"The striations on the slug from homicide victim HM-fifty-eight-oh-five, line up perfectly with the striations on a bullet that killed a man named Martin Kobb, in June of 'ninety-five. Kobb was shot in the parking lot behind a Russian specialty market on Fairfax in West Hollywood. The case was never solved. What makes this even more provocative is Marty Kobb was an off-duty LAPD patrol officer working a basic car in Rampart. He was in plainclothes on his way home when he entered the market and interrupted a burglary in progress. Looks like he just stumbled into it, pulled his off-duty piece, chased the robber into the parking lot, and got shot with the five-point-four-five slug."

"A burglary and not a robbery?" I asked.

"According to the case notes, the perp was rifling through the cash register while the owner was in the back. Since it wasn't a stickup, it was technically classified as a burglary that turned into a one-eighty-seven."

"Sounds like you have the case file there with you."

"I thought you'd want it, so I had Records send me a copy. I brought it home in case you called."

"Thanks, Karen. Now listen, because this is very important. Tell nobody about this cold hit. I don't care where the request comes from—how high up. If someone asks, just refer them to me."

"Why? What is this?

"Trouble," I said. I gave her the fax number for Homicide Special and asked her to fax the file to me immediately.

"I can e-mail it."

"No computers. Send me a fax."

I raced up the stairs instead of waiting for the elevator. When I got to the Xerox room the fax was already coming through. I plucked it out of the tray and carried it over to my old desk. The summary was just as Karen Wise reported. In June of '95, Martin Kobb, an off-duty patrol officer, walked into a Russian specialty market on the corner of Melrose and Fairfax and interrupted a burglary in progress. There were no witnesses to identify the shooter because the storeowner was in the back supervising a delivery of vegetables, and the robber had simply been emptying the register when Kobb came in. He chased the suspect out to the parking lot and the burglar dumped him with a 5.45 slug. Now, ten years later, the bullet in his death matched up perfectly to the striations on the one we dug out of Davide Andrazack's head five days ago.

29

THE FBI HAD called Red's Roadside Towing to haul our cars to the main police garage on Flower. I ran into Roger Broadway as we each forked over forty-five dollars to buy our cars back.

Broadway dug into his wallet and complained. "This rusting piece-a-shit Fairlane ain't worth forty-five bucks." He paid the civilian working the police garage who had fronted the money to the tow operator.

"It's a motor pool car. At least you can expense it. I'm probably stuck 'cause this is my personal vehicle," I said, as I handed over my cash.

He was about to get into the tan Ford, when I stopped him. "Hey, Rog, you don't think maybe there might be a tracking device or something on that old beater?"

He frowned.

"Because I keep wondering how those FBI guys knew where we were to run us off the road this morning."

"Damn good point," he said.

We went over the undercarriages of both vehicles with a mirror on a pole that the police garage used to check for bombs. We found a miniaturized transmitter attached by a magnet to the left rear fender wall of Broadway's Fairlane and pulled it off.

"Satellite tracking device," Broadway said, bouncing the tiny, aspirin tablet sized transmitter in the palm of his hand. "Never seen one this small before. That's probably our tax dollars at work."

"Who planted it?" I asked.

"My money's on the FBI." He put it in his pocket. "Gonna get Electronic Services to trace it."

"I get the feeling that Virtue's guys kinda slipped the leash somewhere," I said. "You need a warrant and a bunch of probable cause to plant one of these. Especially if it's on Los Angeles cops."

"Lemme lay some background on you, friend. Before the Twin Towers went down, them gray cats in Justice had a bunch of legislation sitting around that they didn't know how to get through Congress. After nine-eleven they loaded it all into the USA PATRIOT Act. Once USAPA was enacted, the FBI got handed tremendous new powers. They already had the Foreign Intelligence Surveillance Act. FISA was passed in 'seventy-eight, and as far as federal law enforcement is concerned, it's a kick-ass piece of legislation. Those two acts together give the Frisbees power we lowly city coppers can only dream about."

"How so?"

"Let's say the feds think a foreign agent is involved in anti-U.S. intelligence that might compromise national security and they want to bug him. They go before a secret FISA court. The way Lieutenant Cubio explained it to us, that court has nine federal judges. Maybe now it's up to thirteen. The FBI or Homeland makes their case to this panel of judges and asks permission to plant a bug. The spooky thing is there's no record of any of these requests. It's a completely secret proceeding."

"Like a star chamber?"

"Exactly. Once they get their request approved, they're good to go."

"But this court can say no, right? The FBI still needs the same level of probable cause."

"Technically, yes," he said. "But since 'seventy-eight, according to federal records, there have been over twenty thousand requests and not one denial. After nine-eleven the number shot up. One other nasty thing. The Attorney General of the United States can bypass the court anytime he wants. He has emergency powers that he can invoke at will. After nine-eleven, when John Ashcroft was in office, he used those emergency powers more than any other Attorney General since FISA passed."

"And now they're bugging you and Emdee?" I asked.

"Ain't no fucking AM radio we just pulled off this rust bucket." He kicked the fender of the old Fairlane, then held up the bug. "This little pastry means we've probably all been targeted for roving bugs."

"And just what the hell is a roving bug?" This was all news to me.

"Used to be, the feds wanted a phone tap, a computer scan, or to bug some guy's pen register, they had to write a warrant on a location just like us. They'd have to get permission to bug a building or a computer or a car phone, and then the warrant made them specify *which* computer, room, or phone you wanted bugged."

"Yeah, you can't get warrants to just bug some guy's whole life, and the courts only approve most bugs for short time frames. Then they have to be removed. That's the way it still is. You're telling me that's changed for the FBI?"

"The PATRIOT Act altered everything. Most citizens don't know this, but instead of getting warrants on locations, the feds can now bug a person. It's called a 'roving bug.' They listen to a suspect's cell phone and get his pen register—the numbers he's called. According to the act, they aren't supposed to listen to the conversations, but who's not going to listen in once they've got the tap? They find out where the suspect's heading and then, if they want, they can even do a black bag job on the structures he's going to visit. With a roving bug they can tap anything: buildings, restaurants, and in our case, even this old piece-of-shit Fairlane. I don't know how the feds knew we were working Davide Andrazack's murder, but somehow Virtue must've gotten wind of it. Once he found out, he got Homeland to attach a high threat assessment to us and got the FISA court to issue the warrant."

I felt like shit. I was the one who told Underwood about Andrazack. Virtue only knew about it because of me.

"If the FISA court gave them permission to rove with us," Broadway continued, "that means my house and our office phones, the computers—everything is probably compromised. It's a new world, Shane. Big Brother is definitely watching."

He shook my hand. "Nice working with you, even if we did get our water turned off in the end. Stay in touch. We'll go bowling some Saturday." Then he got into the Fairlane and pulled out of the garage.

I took my time driving home and thought about all these changes in the law. As a cop I wanted to catch dangerous criminals, and I certainly wanted terrorists behind bars, so any expansion of police powers seemed welcome. But as a citizen, I wasn't so sure. In the wrong hands was this unlimited power dangerous? Were the Fourth Amendment rights afforded me by the U.S. Constitution being abridged? This new roving bug, created by the PATRIOT Act, seemed to give the government too much leeway. If abused, would it be at the expense of important constitutional freedoms?

All the agency had to do was get permission from their secret court, which, according to Broadway, was not accountable to any higher power. That raised a lot of questions. For instance, what happens to these roving bugs after the suspect leaves a particular building? Were they deactivated or just left in place? What were the legal guidelines in a completely secret proceeding? What provisions, if any, were there for oversight of the FISA court? If the suspect under surveillance worked in the Glass House as the three of us did, could the feds actually bug the police administration building without getting a municipal warrant?

Worse still, for reasons I couldn't comprehend, the Justice Department and R. A. Virtue seemed to have convinced the FISA court to target the three of us. If Roger was right, we couldn't even petition the court to find out why.

Alexa was at her desk in our bedroom working on more case material when I got home. She'd had a bad COMSTAT meeting yesterday, and was transferring half-a-dozen homicide detectives. Orders to move these guys had to be cut and she needed to approve the protocol. It was a lot of paperwork.

"What took you so long?" she asked as I came into the room. "I was beginning to wonder if Justice had kidnapped you again."

"Had to get my car back from the motor pool. Forty-six bucks."

"Right. I forgot."

"You want to take a break?" I asked. "Get a beer?"

"Gimme fifteen minutes."

I went into our bathroom, stripped off my clothes, took a hot shower, and washed ten hours of confinement off my skin. I put on a pair of frayed jeans and a T-shirt, went into the kitchen for a beer, then headed barefoot out to the backyard and Abbot Kinney's five-block fantasy.

I sat down in time to watch a family of ducks paddle by. I felt just like those ducks, serene and composed on the surface, but underwater, paddling like crazy.

A few minutes later, Alexa joined me. "Picturesque," she said, looking at the moon on the canals, or maybe the ducks. I knew she wasn't talking about me.

"Yep."

"All and all, a pretty wild day."

I could tell from her tone that her anger had dissipated.

She looked over at me. "Not knowing where you were made me realize how much I need you. So I guess there's some good that comes from everything."

I had decided to push ahead regardless of my new jeopardy with the feds.

"I got a cold hit on the bullet we dug out of Andrazack's head," I said, positioning myself for an argument.

"Send it to Agent Nix."

"Right." I took a sip of my beer. "Problem is, it matches a slug that killed an LAPD officer named Martin Kobb, in 'ninety-five."

She peered at me in the dark. "Really."

"Yep. Unsolved case. Open homicide. This guy Kobb was off-duty and walked into a Russian market on Melrose, interrupted a burg in progress. He pulls his piece, badda-bing, badda-boom, he gets it in the head. Bullet is from the same gun that killed Andrazack."

"You're sure?"

I'd come prepared. I pulled out the fax pictures of the two bullets and the case write-up that Karen sent me.

Our ballistics lab has a comparison microscope, which is basically two microscopes mounted side by side, connected by an optical bridge. She had retrieved the Kobb bullet from the cold case evidence room and photographed it next to Andrazack's using 40X magnification. The photo lined both slugs up back to back. Bullets can have as few as three, or as many as thirty different land and groove impressions. This one had twelve, and they lined up perfectly.

I handed the photo to Alexa. She held it to the light and studied it for a full minute or more.

"So here's my question," I said. "How does the Los Angeles Police Department look the other way on this? This guy was a brother officer. With the addition of this new ballistic evidence, how can we refuse to reopen the Martin Kobb investigation?"

"Shit. You're a tricky bastard," she said softly.

"A lucky one, too. Just as one mount gets shot out from under me, along comes another horse to ride."

"And you want . . . ?"

"This cold case. Assign me, and Detectives Broadway and Perry to investigate."

"And when you run straight into Agent Nix and his flock of drooling jackals, what do you say?"

"We'll say, 'Nice to see you, Agent Nix. Hope all is going well on the Andrazack hit. We're just over here investigating this poor, dead LAPD officer from 'ninety-five.' "

"And you think they won't go right up the wall?"

"Let 'em. You tell me, how can they take Marty Kobb away from us? The fact that it may be the same shooter who killed Andrazack is just one of those things."

Alexa sat for a long time, thinking about it. She knew I was on solid ground technically. We had standing to work our own police officer's murder. But still, it put us in direct violation of an order from the head of California Homeland Security and the SAC of the local FBI.

This is the kind of wonderful stuff that, when it happens, makes me relish police work.

"I'll need to clear it with Tony. Write everything down so I'll have it for him to review."

"You don't need to clear it with him. You're the head of the Detective Bureau. All you have to do is reactivate this cold case and give it to me."

"I'm gonna talk to Tony."

"Chicken," I challenged.

"Maybe," she said softly. "But a lot is on the table, here. Not the least of which is the safety of a man I love."

"I like the sentiment, but you're still a wuss."

She put the ballistics report back into the envelope then smiled and said, "Nice save."

30

I ARRIVED AT Parker Center for the 8 A.M. Fingertip task force meeting. I decided there was little point in getting into it with Underwood over leaking Andrazack's identity. He'd just deny it anyway. Besides, if Tony approved my transfer, this would be my last day in Underland.

"I have good news to report," Underwood called out, bringing the morning coffee din under control. "I put the hat on John Doe Number One." Making it sound as if he had gone out and beat the pavement for the ID himself. Then he turned, and under a picture of John Doe Number One taped up on the rolling blackboard, he wrote in magic marker:

VAUGHN ROLAINE

Something about the name sounded familiar, but I couldn't pin it down. "This identification was a direct result of canvassing the VAs," Underwood said. "Vaughn Rolaine was not a medic, but was in Nam. He held a panhandling sign near the 101 freeway claiming to be a vet. This vic is a fixture in that neighborhood. He's been living for years in Sherman Oaks Park. Starting this morning, we're gonna be out there talking to everybody. Maybe someone saw the unsub target this man."

As Underwood droned on, my mind flashed back to the night Zack and I caught the first Fingertip murder, now identified as Vaughn Rolaine. We were next up on the call-out board at Homicide Special, so we went home early. It was a Friday night and we were pretty sure we'd get some action. Fridays, Saturdays, and Wednesdays were big homicide nights in L.A.

We got the squeal at midnight. Zack beat me to the address. The body was in the river at Woodman Avenue near Valleyheart Drive. The L.A. River and the 101 freeway ran next to each other in that part of town, but the body had been dumped about a half a mile beyond where the freeway and the riverbank separated, probably so the unsub wouldn't be seen from the 101. That meant that if Vaughn Rolaine lived in Sherman Oaks Park, he was moved almost two miles. We were called because the patrolmen who were first on the scene told dispatch that all the victim's fingertips were cut off. Any mutilation of that nature was deemed outside the norm, and caused the case to be kicked over to Homicide Special. That was seven and a half weeks ago, but it seemed more like a year.

I kept circling my memories of that night. Zack was sitting in a brown Crown Victoria from the Flower Street motor pool, having left his windowless white Econoline van at home. I stood on the curb waiting for the MEs to arrive. I remember looking into Zack's car and noticing that he was crying. Later that night, after we left the crime scene, he broke down and told me that

Fran had thrown him out the day before and was demanding a divorce. After that, Zack deteriorated rapidly. His drinking got worse. He seemed to stop caring.

The name Vaughn Rolaine again flickered like a faltering light bulb in my brain. I almost had it, but just as I came close, the thought went dark again. When I tried to coax the memory back, it was gone.

"Everybody break up into your teams," Underwood shrilled, jolting me into the present. "Scully, you're in my office."

Damn, I thought. *How do I get off this guy's shit list?*

I pushed my broken chair out of the coffee room, and after parking it at my dented desk and checking good old extension 86 for messages, I headed into his office.

As soon as I entered he said, "So far, my friend, you have been a colossal waste of time, money, and energy. We wasted a full fucking day and three grand on that dumb funeral idea of yours, and what does it come to? Nothing! I want you to call Forest Lawn back and knock down their expenses. Get it under a grand. I'm not approving these numbers." He held up the invoice. "The Andrazack murder isn't even part of this Fingertip case anymore. I'm not approving money spent on a crime I'm not even assigned to."

"It's too late," I said. "You already approved it. Besides, how can it not be part of the case? The body had the secret medic's symbol carved on his chest." Since I knew he was ratting us out to R. A. Virtue, I was just pushing him to see what would happen.

"I have been told by the special agent in charge of the FBI office downtown, that this murder is no longer any of our concern," he snapped.

"But how do you explain that carved symbol?" I persisted, and watched him fidget.

"You don't listen very well, do you?" he said.

"I listen fine. I just don't get this. Either this building is leaking info and we have a huge security problem, or Andrazack was killed by our Fingertip unsub and should still be part of this case."

"The case has been transferred. Get over it." He had raised the volume, so the good news was, at least I was getting to him.

"I know you want off this task force," he continued. "Worse than that, you're a vindictive son of a bitch who's looking to screw me up any way possible. But I have a way to fix that." He smiled coldly. "Who was it that said, 'Keep your friends close, and your enemies closer'?"

"Daffy Duck. No, wait, don't tell me Donald."

"You're a funny fucking guy. But the fact is, you're gonna be stuck right here, close to me. You're our new inside man. You sit at your desk where I can watch you right though that window." He pointed at the plate glass that faced the squad room. "You'll coordinate paperwork and answer calls."

"Evidence clerk and switchboard operator?"

"I'll have somebody brief you on exactly how I want it done. There's going to be protocol right down to the phrase we use to announce this task force when we answer phones."

"Right. A good phrase is always helpful." I turned and started for the door.

"And Scully . . ."

I turned back.

"I've read your Professional Standards Bureau folder. It's a train wreck."

That file was supposed to be secure, but everybody in law enforcement seemed to have a copy. When this case was over, instead of trying to write a best-selling Fingertip book, maybe I should just go with all this overwhelming interest and publish my 181 file.

He continued. "I don't like what I see in there. You seem to do things any old damn way you please. Reading between the lines, and judging from what you just said, it would be just like you to try and go around this direct order from California Homeland, and work on Davide Andrazack's murder without jurisdiction."

"Why would I do that?"

"Because you have authority issues."

"Right."

"You're down to your last straw with me, mister. Make one more mistake around here and you'll be hammered dog shit."

I turned and walked out of the office. *Jesus H. McGillicutty. How do I keep stepping into it with guys like this?*

I walked through the squad room and decided to get into the elevator, go down to the lobby and step outside for some air. But instead of pushing L, for some reason I pushed *4*.

A few minutes later I was in the small cubicle office of Roger Broadway and Emdee Perry. They both looked beat up and subdued. I figured Lieutenant Cubio had rained all over them like Underwood had just done with me.

"There's a life lesson here," Perry drawled. "It ain't never smart ta dig up more snakes than you can kill."

With that sentiment hanging in the air, I told them both about Martin Kobb.

31

AT THREE O'CLOCK that afternoon I was summoned to the chief's office. Alexa met me in the hallway as I came off the elevator.

"Tony came through," she said.

"Great."

She nodded, but looked worried. We walked down the hall to where Broadway and Perry were seated in the chief's outer office with Lieutenant Cubio.

Cubio always reminded me of a Latin street G—short and dangerous, with a dark complexion and spiked black hair. But he spoke four languages and had thrown himself in front of more than one pissed-off superior to protect his troops. He was a Glass House legend and Detective Division fave.

The three men stood as we arrived. Bea Tompson, the hawk-faced guardian of the chief's time and space had already announced us.

Tony came to the door with his jacket off and motioned us inside. The office was spacious, but sparsely decorated. His gray metal furniture was all from the Xerox catalog and was pushed up against the walls giving the room the look of a dance studio. A huge window that looked out over the city dominated the east wall.

"I read your briefing." Tony said, facing me. "You guys sure you wanta do this? Homeland plays rough. They can skirt my authority pretty easy. I might not be able to cover you if it gets nasty."

"Yes sir. We want to do this," I said, glancing at Broadway and Perry who both nodded in agreement.

"Okay. Armando, gimme your take," Tony said. "What's really going on with these humps over at Homeland?"

"Sir, I've told you about the embassy and consulate leaks, but bad as that is, in my opinion it's just a symptom, not the disease. There's more at stake here than just leaks or who killed this Israeli national. It's also more than some foreign embassy rogues going off the reservation. Something dangerous is shifting the ground, and we're completely in the dark. We gotta find a way to get in the game or risk being set up and embarrassed."

Tony looked at me then held up my case notes. "Your brief says you think there may be a roving bug planted on the three of you. Is that right?"

"That's what Roger and Emdee think." We told him about finding the transmitter on the Fairlane and our suspicions that it was planted by the feds.

"Man, I've got a big problem with that whole new roving bug idea," Tony said. "How do you supervise it?" He looked at Alexa. "You got an electronic sweep going on our shop? Computers, phones, everything?"

"Yes, sir. Sam Oxman in the Electronic Services Division is

handling it. Top priority. I had him sweep your office first thing this morning. So far he's found nothing."

Tony looked at us for a long moment, rocking back and forth on oxblood loafers that were shined to a diamond brilliance.

"Okay, good," he finally said. "I'm gonna authorize you guys to work on the Martin Kobb murder. I agree something ain't right here. I'll tell ya this much. If we find bugs in this building, I'm gonna go ballistic. If the FBI or anybody else in the Justice Department is planting bugs on a sister agency, then all bets are off. Whatever happens from this point on, only the six of us will be involved. I want everybody to keep your phone and e-mail communications to a minimum, and if you do use 'em keep it vague. Talk between the lines until our electronic sweep is complete. Also, we've got some new scrambled SAT phones in ESD. They're state-of-the-art and can't be breached. Lieutenant Scully will get one for each of us. We gotta assume we're wide open here. Only discuss the case outside this building or on those secure ESD phones."

"Sir?" I said, and Tony turned to face me.

"I need to be reassigned off the Fingertip task force. Agent Underwood has me on files and communications. I'm not supposed to leave the building."

"Pissed him off, didn't ya?" I didn't answer, so Tony said, "Okay. You're reassigned. Where's your partner? You probably want him on this with you."

I looked over at Alexa.

"He's on medical leave right now. I don't think he's currently available," she said.

"Alright. Shane, you're temporarily reassigned to CTB. You'll work out of their offices under Lieutenant Cubio's supervision. That's it," Tony said.

We waited in the hallway outside the chief's office while Alexa remained behind for a short operations meeting.

Cubio was frowning. "I don't like R. A. Virtue," the lieutenant said. "Never trust some asshole who uses initials instead of a name. Besides that, he's got a very unique take on the law." Not exactly news to three cops who just spent ten hours locked up in the Tishman Building.

The chief's door opened and Alexa came out. "Okay, it's done. I'll notify Underwood."

I headed down to CTB with Roger, Emdee, and Armando.

"You really think somebody has a wire inside this division?" the lieutenant asked, as we entered his office. He started scanning the walls as if some high-tech bug might actually be beeping there, ominously.

"Could be," Broadway said.

"Then let's get outta here until ESD finishes with this floor."

He led us down to the lobby and half a block away to an outdoor restaurant. We sat on hot metal stools in the late afternoon sun and ordered coffee.

"One thing I want you guys to know," Cubio said. "Whatever is happening with Homeland, there's still a dead patrolman in the mix. When a brother officer gets shot somebody's got to pay the price." His face hardened. "Kobb's murder might be ten years old, but somebody has to go down for it."

32

THE NEXT MORNING, while Broadway and Perry ran an extensive background on Davide Andrazack, using something they referred to as covert resources, I visited the Records Division on the third basement level of the Glass House and started digging out the case notes filed by the two sets of detectives who worked on Kobb's murder. In 1995 nobody filed old cases on computer disks so there was a ton of paper.

The two primaries who caught the original squeal were Steve Otto and Cindy Blackman from the Internal Affairs Division. Back then IAD handled all cop killings. Under the current scheme, police officer shootings were investigated by Homicide Special. Otto and Blackman were finally replaced after the '01 reorganization, and Al Nye and Salvador Paoluccia from Homicide Special got the case.

That was before I was transferred here, but I knew Sal from my time in the Valley. He had a good sense of humor, loved baseball, was a popular guy, but was sort of a screw around. He was no longer assigned to Homicide Special.

I found a desk and started plowing through the reams of case notes. Otto and Blackman were thorough and meticulous. Detective Blackman had neat handwriting with a slight, backward slant and she drew cute, feminine circles over her Is, something I'm sure heckling, fellow officers had broken her of by now. Otto printed in bold, angry, slashing strokes. You could tell a lot about detectives from their paperwork. It was apparent from the thorough nature of their notes that they had desperately wanted to clear this case and had worked it vigorously.

In 2001, Paoluccia and Nye took over. By then it was officially a cold case—a grounder that had rolled foul. Nobody wanted it because there wasn't much chance it would ever be solved. Sal and Al had done what is known commonly in police parlance, as a drive-by investigation. Their notes and case write-ups looked slap dash. What it amounted to was they had blown it a kiss and moved on. Kobb's wife had left L.A. after his death and gone back to Iowa. She died a year later of ovarian cancer.

Even though I knew Detective Paoluccia, I decided I'd skip getting in touch with Sal and Al and would contact the more thorough team of Otto and Blackman.

As I paged through Detective Blackman's background notes some interesting things caught my attention. First and foremost, Martin Kobb was a second-generation Russian-American. His original family name, before it was shortened, had been Kobronovitch.

First I find Andrazack, a dead Russian dumped in the river. Then ex-KGB agent Stanislov Bambarak comes limping into his funeral on swollen ankles to make sure Andrazack's actually dead. Now I find out Kobb was Kobronovitch, and was killed outside a Russian market ten years ago with the same gun that got Andrazack. Way too claustrophobic and way too many Russians. I made a note to follow up on that.

Next I read Blackman and Otto's initial piecing together of the incident. It was pretty much the same as the case summary, but with a few more details. Kobb had been shot off-duty in the parking lot of a specialty market in Russian Town at around 7:50 P.M. on June 12, 1995. A Monday night.

According to his family he liked to cook old-country style. He had gone grocery shopping and stumbled into a burglary in progress. Yuri Yakovitch, owner of the Russian market, who everybody called Jack, had apparently left the cash register where he normally worked, and gone to the loading dock to supervise a vegetable truck delivery. Yakovitch said he was in the market alone because his regular stock boy was ill. He thought he had a pretty good view of the front of the store and his cash register from the loading dock, but he somehow missed the burglar and Kobb when they entered the market.

The burglar had a gun, but apparently ran, leaving the money behind, when Kobb pulled his off-duty weapon. They ended up in the parking lot where Kobb was shot in the northeast corner. He died next to a fence that backed up to an adjoining Texaco station.

Yuri, a.k.a. Jack Yakovitch, stated he hadn't seen the burglar, but had heard a single shot and ran through the market into the parking lot, where he found Kobb dying. He never saw a getaway car.

The lack of any witnesses stymied the investigation. Because a cop died, the case remained active until '98 when it was officially marked cold.

Given the dearth of material, there was actually damn little here to work with. Since the case was unsolved, I really hadn't expected much. But I knew for the most part, we would be coming at this through the Andrazack killing anyway.

I made copies of the top sheets and the crime scene diagrams and handed all the rest of the material back to the clerk. I also put in a written request for the murder book, which had been sent back to Internal Affairs Division where the case originated.

Next I decided to take a run out to the corner of Melrose and Fairfax and get a look at the crime scene. Maybe Yuri Yakovitch still ran his market there.

Over the last two days, the temperature in L.A. had switched from cold and damp, to hot and dry. Sometimes in January, just to remind us that we shouldn't have built this town in a desert, God cranks up his Santa Ana winds. They come whistling out of the east and drive the mercury up into triple digits. Today was one of those days; bright, hot, and clear, but with air so full of pollen that antihistamine sales would quadruple.

I dialed the main LAPD switchboard from my car and asked the operator to find me department extensions for Steve Otto and Cindy Blackman. Otto wasn't listed, so he might have retired or left the job, but there was an extension on file for Cindy Blackman. I called and found out she was now stationed in the Central Bureau, Area 13, which by the way, was good old Shootin' Newton. She was new in Robbery Homicide, but wasn't at her desk, so I left a message for her to call me.

As I drove, I let my mind crawl back over the festering mound of guilt that I will loosely label My Zack Problem. I didn't want to leave him parked in the psych ward at Queen of Angels, yet he seemed far worse to me the last time I saw him. I was really worried and searching for some middle ground. I remembered that the LAPD had a psychiatric support unit located somewhere in the Valley. It existed to help suicidal cops or those with drinking problems. I made a mental note to call and see if I could get Zack some help there.

By the time I arrived at the corner of Melrose and Fairfax the air conditioner in my new gray Acura had cranked the interior temperature down to a brisk sixty-eight degrees. I sat in the car with the engine running and pulled out Otto and Blackman's crime scene sketches of the area. They detailed a layout of the market in 1995, including the spot where Martin Kobb's body was found near the Texaco station. Now as I looked at the actual terrain, nothing was the same. The corner had been completely redeveloped. A giant Pay-Less Drugstore took up the entire area. The Texaco station was also gone, folded into the huge drugstore complex.

I stepped out of the car into a blast furnace of hot, late morning wind and hurried into the air-conditioned drugstore. Nobody working there was older than twenty-five. Memories were short.

"Only been here since April, dude," one guy told me. "We get a lot of turnover."

"The boss here is a jerk," a young girl added. "Nobody puts up with that Barney for long,"

None of them remembered the old Russian market. Nobody remembered Yuri "Jack" Yakovitch, or a policeman named Kobb who had given it up in the parking lot ten years ago.

As I trudged back to the car and tossed my coat into the backseat, the name Vaughn Rolaine flashed in my memory again, along with a vague notion of where I'd heard it. My house? The backyard? I made a frantic grab for the recollection and missed, coming up with a handful of nothing. The memory slipped quickly back into the tar pit that sometimes serves as my mind.

33

CINDY BLACKMAN CALLED me right after lunch and we agreed to meet for coffee in an hour at a Denny's halfway between the Newton precinct house and Parker Center. She turned out to be a tall, slender redhead in a tan pantsuit. After introducing herself, she slipped into the window booth and dropped her purse on the seat next to her.

"I swear traffic is getting to be a bigger bitch every year," she said. "I don't know which is worse now, the four-oh-five or the seven-ten."

In L.A. this is good opening dialogue. We bond over our hatred of freeway traffic. Cindy was a Detective II and since she was in IAD back in '95, that meant she had at least fifteen years on the job. But she looked about eighteen. Her red hair was done in twin braids and freckles sprinkled the bridge of her nose. An impish smile hovered at the corners of her mouth like a child on the verge of a prank.

The waitress took our orders. Because it was so hot, we both asked for Cokes. After a few minutes of Who Do You Know, where we discovered we'd once had the same, humorless, iron-fisted captain in the Valley, I got into it.

"Looks like you and Detective Otto were all over this case," I said, setting her notebook on the table between us.

"Didn't help much." A frown darkened her bright demeanor; not accepting the compliment, or giving herself much credit.

"As I said, I'm on it now. Third time could be the charm." I smiled, trying not to sound like I was sweeping up after a bad job.

"I hope you do better than Steve and me, or Sal and Al."

The Cokes came and we tore the paper off our straws.

"I dropped by that crime scene address. The Russian market's not there anymore."

"Yeah, I know. They put up a monster drugstore." She frowned again. "I hope you can solve it. The Kobronovitch family were nice people. Came over here from Minsk. American dream and all that."

Cold cases usually don't get solved because somewhere along the way the investigators have accepted a particular construct of facts that turns out to be false. The trick is to look for tiny holes in logic, and once you clear them away, hope they're hiding bigger problems.

"If you think back through the case," I said, "what fact or idea did you come across that jarred your sensibilities before you finally accepted it?"

She sipped her Coke. "That's an interesting question. What jarred me? Anything? Doesn't have to be crime related?"

"Yeah, anything."

She thought for a minute, then smiled. "Well, this is stupid, but Kobb's wife said he liked to cook Russian dishes and that's why he went shopping. But it was a Monday and Yuri's market was all fresh food. Fish, vegetables, everything right from the boat or the garden. Marty Kobb was working patrol, and with a baby coming, he'd been putting in a lot of overtime. His wife said he was coming home after ten o'clock almost every weeknight, only taking Saturday and Sunday off. So I'm thinking, who goes to a market to buy fresh fish and veggies on a Monday night if they're working late all week and can't cook until Saturday? It just didn't hit me as quite right. I like to cook and I wouldn't shop five days ahead of time."

She paused, thinking about it. "But that doesn't necessarily mean he wouldn't do it. Maybe he was planning on freezing the food or surprising his wife by taking Monday night off from work to cook. I don't know. It just felt a little strange. Is that the kind of thing you mean?"

"Exactly." I wrote it down, but didn't have a clue how to use it.

She sat thinking some more, then remembered something else. "His aunt was so distraught when we interviewed her, she almost couldn't talk to us. She would start to say something and then she'd break down into tears. I know families can be close, but an aunt doesn't usually get that emotional. She was an immigrant who didn't speak very good English, but they lived a few blocks from the Bel Air Country Club on Bellagio Road. It was a very nice house—not a mansion exactly, but nice. I remember thinking these people were doing pretty well, coming over from Russia and all. My parents were born in L.A. and we didn't have anywhere near that nice a house."

"What was her last name?" I asked. I had skimmed some of the notes but didn't remember seeing anything about an aunt.

She hesitated. "Damn, what *was* her name?" She snapped her fingers. "I think it's in here."

She reached for her spiral notebook and started flipping pages. "Jesus, look at this. I was actually circling my I's back then. What a ditz." She finally found the page she wanted. "Yeah, here it is, under V.R. That's my shorthand for victim's relative." That's why I'd missed it. "Her name was Marianna Litvenko. Her husband was deceased." She looked up from the notebook. "Not very earth-shattering stuff, is it?"

I wondered if the Litvenkos had a big house because Mr. Litvenko had a Russian mob connection. I thought Minsk was somewhere up by the Black Sea. But I didn't know Russian geography very well and wondered if it was anywhere near Odessa. Back in '95, Little Japanese was just getting the Odessa Mob started in L.A., so Blackman and Otto wouldn't have thought to check Kobb's uncle to see if he was in Russian Organized Crime.

"What did the husband do?" I asked.

"Y'know, I don't even remember his first name. If it's not in our notes, maybe we didn't ask. He'd been dead almost a year by the time Kobb was murdered." She frowned. "Probably should have checked that out, huh?"

"Not necessarily. You weren't investigating the Litvenkos. It was the Kobb murder you were working."

I gathered up the rest of the case books. "Listen, Cindy, if I get these notes copied and send them over to you, would you mind going through them to freshen your memory, and then call me if anything else occurs to you?

"I won't be able to get on it until the weekend. I'm jammed. Our murder-robbery board in Newton is mostly red," she said, referring to the common practice of listing the month's open cases on the duty board in red magic marker and the closed ones in black.

"Tough beat," I told her, and it was.

We exchanged business cards. I left Denny's, then sat in my car in the parking lot as she drove off in a department slick-back, overworked and underpaid. I got the air going and once it cooled down, I tried to free up my mind. I wanted to come at all this from a different angle. Get a fresh take. I started by trying to put myself in Marty Kobb's head. I leaned back on the seat and gave it a go.

So now I'm Martin Kobb. I've got a baby coming and I'm taking on extra work to pay the bills. I'm in Patrol, but watch commanders won't book a patrol officer for double shifts, so how am I getting the OT? Maybe I'm loaning myself out on various department sting operations after hours. A lot of patrol guys will volunteer for undercover assignments if they're trying to make a move out of A-cars into detectives. I wondered if it was possible to get Kobb's timesheets from back then. Would the LAPD even save old payroll stuff from '95? Probably not, but I took out my spiral pad and made a note to check the patrolman's time cards and log books.

I went back to being Kobb. After my shift, what am I working on? I didn't think the LAPD was actively working the Russian mob back then, but the divisions that could always use a fresh face were Drug Enforcement and Vice. Maybe I was working as an undercover for one of those outfits and pissed off some street villain. Maybe I wasn't killed by a burglar. Maybe I pushed too hard or got made, and some angry suspect pulled my drapes behind that market. I sort of liked that, so I made a mental note to revisit it, then moved on.

Yuri Yakovitch reported he was out back on the loading dock. He said he kept an eye on the cash register, but missed seeing the burglar. I started to wonder about that. What shop owner, working alone, leaves the cash register unattended to go supervise the unloading of a vegetable truck? I let my mind go, surfing the ozone. Maybe Jack Yakovitch was the suspect Kobb was working. Maybe he was running drugs or Russian whores out of his market. Maybe there was never a burglar. Jack Yakovitch makes Kobb as a cop, pulls a gun, and dumps Marty in the back of the parking lot.

None of this felt quite as promising, but I picked up my cell phone and dialed an extension in the Records section. Rose Clark came on the line. She's a researcher in the Computer Division who for some unknown reason thinks I'm sorta cute. She had done some background searches for me in the past, and usually put me at the head of the line.

"Rosy? It's Shane."

"Parker Center's coolest boy toy," she teased. "What can I do for you, honey?"

I ran the Kobb case down for her, then told her what I wanted. "I'm looking for background from 'ninety-five on a guy, named Yuri 'Jack' Yakovitch, who ran a Russian market on Melrose. I don't know what happened to him. I need to find him. Run him through our Russian Organized Crime computer. Also, is it possible to get Martin Kobb's time cards and log books from that time?"

"I'm sure we don't save that kind of stuff from that far back," she said. "But I'll check."

"And can you also run a guy named Litvenko? Check him for an ROC connection. I don't have his first name, but he was Martin Kobb's uncle. He died in 'ninety-four or 'five. He lived in the Melrose area on Bellagio. The wife's name is Marianna."

"This is turning into a pretty big job."

I was losing boy toy points.

"This is important, Rose. A dead policeman. We can't let him fall between the cracks," I said, appealing to her sense of department loyalty. She agreed and I rang off.

As I put the car in gear, the name Vaughn Rolaine floated past my foggy view plate once again. This time I slapped it down, pinning it on the edge of my consciousness. Only something was wrong. It wasn't Vaughn. It was . . . Army . . . No, *Arden* Rolaine. That was it. Arden Rolaine. Who the hell was Arden Rolaine? Man or a woman? Where had I heard it?

Then slowly it all started to seep back, filling old ruts in my memory like seawater on a rising tide. My house. The backyard. Barbecuing. Last summer. I'd heard the name from Zack. He and Fran were over for dinner. This was right after we'd partnered up for the second time, or shortly after, only a few weeks into it. Alexa and Fran were inside setting the table and Zack and I were trying to decide what to do with our existing cases.

We wondered, now that we were partners, if we should throw all of our old unsolved homicides into the mix and work them together. I had three that were still active, he had four. That's when he mentioned Arden Rolaine. She was one of his unsolved cases.

Zack told me Arden was sixty or so and had been murdered in her house in Van Nuys. I couldn't remember what was unusual about her case or why it was being worked out of Homicide Special. We'd discussed it for only a minute or two before deciding to keep our prior cases separate, work them on the side. We wanted to start our partnership fresh with no unsolved cases to go against our clearance rate as a new homicide team. That's all I could remember.

I sat in the car with this strange fact still flopping around on the floor of my memory. I wasn't sure what the hell it meant, or how it fit in with the first Fingertip murder. Was Vaughn Rolaine a relative of Arden's? Vaughn and Arden were both unusual names. Some parents will do that. Give all their kids unique handles. You wouldn't expect somebody named Vaughn to have a sister named Sue.

34

I DIDN'T HAVE to talk to Doc Pepper because the floor nurse remembered me and let me in without an argument.

Zack was lying on top of the bedspread staring at the ceiling of his sterile, white box room at Queen of Angels Hospital. He was dressed in a polo shirt, tan slacks, and flip-flops. Fran, or one of his boys, must have brought him fresh clothes. His hands were laced behind his neck, and as I was buzzed through the security door, he looked over at me with heavy lidded eyes. His face had returned to its normal shape but the discoloration had darkened to an ugly bruise.

"Look who's come to visit," he said, slowly. "The career monster."

"You sound tranqed. You on something?"

"Hey, if you're gonna make a buncha bullshit judgments, then take it on down the road, Bubba."

He struggled into a sitting position and hugged his fat knees. "Fran had me committed. Now I can't get out. Can you believe that? The bitch is divorcing me, but since we're still technically married, she can do it. My joint custody of the boys will be dust after this bullshit."

"I'm sorry I suggested this, Zack. I thought you were about to commit suicide."

He waved it off and changed the subject. "So how's the book club? You humps got a line on our unsub yet?"

"I'm not down there anymore. Like I told you, I'm working this stand-alone murder now. Davide Andrazack."

His face showed nothing.

"So you ain't gonna be able to give me any updates?"

"Nope. That circus moved on without me."

His eyes suddenly seemed feral, his mouth set in a hard, straight line.

"Too bad," he said. "I was hoping to catch up with that."

"I can tell you this much. We finally made the first vic. John Doe Number One."

"Yeah?" He pulled his eyes into sharper focus.

"Turns out his name was Vaughn Rolaine. Vietnam vet."

I watched closely as he processed it.

"No kidding." He looked puzzled.

"You ever hear that name?" I asked.

He seemed to be searching his memory, then said, "Should I?"

"Didn't you have an open homicide before we teamed up? A woman? Arden Rolaine?"

"Jesus. You're right. Vaughn was the brother. Shit. These tranqs they're giving me really maim my brain. How'd I forget that?"

"Doesn't it strike you as a little cozy that Vaughn Rolaine, our first Fingertip kill, turns out to be the brother of one of your uncleared one-eighty-sevens from last summer?"

He sat for a long moment trying to pull it together. "It is a tad close," he finally said. "How do you suppose?"

"I was hoping you'd tell me."

He got up, lumbered over to the sink, and turned on the tap. Then he jammed his head under the faucet. Water blasted off the back of his head and splattered onto the concrete floor. After a minute, he stood up, turned off the spigot, and dried his face and hair with a towel.

"Hang on a minute. My brain's oatmeal."

Then he began doing jumping jacks. His huge belly flopped up and down as his rubber-soled flip-flops slapped the concrete floor. After doing about thirty, he dropped and did fifteen pushups, rolling into a sitting position out of breath when he finished.

"Better?" I asked.

"Not much."

"We need to talk about Arden Rolaine. Can you remember the details of that case, or should I go to the Glass House, pick up your murder book, and bring it back here?"

"I haven't really worked on it in five months, but I remember."

"Let's hear."

He got up off the floor and sat on the bed. Then he rubbed his eyes as if to clear his vision before starting.

"Okay. My old partner, Van Kelsey, and I caught the case last June. Arden Rolaine was this sixty-one-year-old widow. Husband died in Nam thirty-odd years ago. Never remarried. She lived alone in Van Nuys. Little cracker box nothing of a house. Spring of last year, a pizza delivery kid saw some street freak jimmying her window, trying to get into the place. The kid didn't call it in and didn't come forward till he saw the story about her murder on TV. The way me and Van figured it, she musta come home and surprised the perp goin' through her place. He turns and bludgeons her to death. Used a brass candlestick from her mantle. A real blitz kill. The ME stopped counting at a hundred blows."

"Why did Homicide Special get the case?"

"Arden Rolaine was part of an old singing group in the sixties. The Lamp Street Singers. Folk music and love songs, mostly. They had three or four albums. Had one chart-topping single."

"Yeah . . . 'Lemon Tree,' I think."

"That was the Limelighters. The Lamp Street Singers had that drippy ballad, 'Don't Look Away.' They were gone in about a nanosecond, but somebody in dispatch was a fan and it got kicked over to Homicide Special because it was a quote, Celebrity Case, unquote. Fact is, hardly nobody even remembered her or the folk group. But Arden had saved her money and had enough squirreled away to make it to the finish line until this asshole climbed through the window and clipped her."

"You said it was a blitz attack?"

"Classic overkill. Lotta anger. The doer pounded her until her face was mush. Van and I figured with that much rage, it had to be somebody close to her. Somebody who maybe once even loved her."

Hate needs love to burn.

"Because of the blitz attack we started looking at old boyfriends and relatives," he continued. "Finally turned up her brother, Vaughn. I never could find him though, 'cause he moved around. Homeless bum. According to her neighbors and the guy who did her hair, Vaughn was this wine-soaked mistake in a tattered raincoat. He was always trying to hit Arden up for cash. She finally got tired of fending him off and told him to never come over again. My theory was after she said that, he got pissed, came back, climbed through the window to steal her money and little sis caught him. They argued and Arden got put down with extreme prejudice."

"So you never brought him in for questioning?"

"Like I said, I couldn't find the son-of-a-bitch. Homeless. No address. I had his picture up all over the place—liquor stores, bus stations. Nothing. It's a big city. Thousands of homeless. I figured eventually, I'd run him down."

"So Vaughn Rolaine was your lead suspect in Arden Rolaine's murder and he ends up being our first Fingertip victim," I said. "Pretty big coincidence."

Zack frowned. "What's the first thing they tell you in the Academy?"

"Never trust a coincidence in police work."

"Exactly," Zack said. "So it can't be a coincidence. Gotta be some logic to it. We just gotta find it."

"So how does it fit?"

He sat for a long moment, thinking. "Okay. Remember when you said you thought that the Fingertip unsub was maybe another homeless guy with rage against his environment? Hating the other bums he had to live with, seeing himself in their misery and killing himself over and over again?"

"It was just a theory. I'm not even sure it's psychologically valid."

"Yeah, but I always kind of liked that."

Zack had snapped back to his old self. His mind seemed focused. For the first time in months he was sorting facts like the old days.

"What if Vaughn lets it slip to some other homeless bum that his sister has all this money?" Zack reasoned. "After Arden is murdered, this other bum thinks Vaughn's inherited his sister's scrilla and goes after it. Ends up killing Vaughn."

"With a single shot to the back of the head, execution style like the fucking mafia? That doesn't track. And what about the

Medic's symbol on the chest, the mutilations, all of that other post-offense behavior?"

"We don't really have that much listed under victimology," Zack continued. "Just Vietnam vets. Rage. Father substitutes. So let's build on this a little. This rage-filled, homeless guy hates his father. Maybe he was sexually abused as a kid and he's a ticking bomb but hasn't gone postal yet. Vaughn told him about his sister's money and the unsub is hassling Vaughn, trying to get the dough. But Vaughn doesn't have it, because he was my number-one suspect in his sister's murder and couldn't exactly go to the probate hearing. But let's say the unsub doesn't believe him, starts working Vaughn over, maybe cutting fingers off, trying to get him to talk. It gets out of control and he eventually kills Vaughn."

"I guess it could have happened that way," I said.

"Damn right. And then comes all the other postmortem behavioral stuff we profiled—the latent rage against his father—everything is unleashed. Vaughn is dead, but this other bum, the unsub, carves the symbol on his chest anyway. A postmortem mutilation. Maybe the unsub's dad was a medic in Nam, or he hates all vets, sees his father in them. He cuts off the rest of Vaughn's fingers to frustrate identification, then dumps him in the river. After this first kill, our serial killer is born. He realizes he's got a taste for it. A blood lust. He keeps on killing. One bum after another."

I sat in the room thinking about it. A few things worked, but too much didn't.

"How's some homeless guy transport the body?"

"Okay. Maybe the unsub's not all the way homeless yet. Maybe he's living in his car."

"Maybe." At least Zack was trying.

"I'm just coming up with some options here," he said.

"Yeah, I know, I know." I didn't want to discourage the first spark or interest he'd shown in months.

"Listen, maybe you should pick up my murder book after all," he said. "Maybe there's old case stuff in there that would jog my memory. Van Kelsey retired four months ago to grow grapes in Napa. I'll call him and see if he remembers anything."

"Okay. I gotta tell the task force about this, so I'll swing by Parker Center on my way home. After I bring Underwood up to date, I'll pick up the murder book. Is it in your desk?"

"Yep."

I stood to go and Zack rose with me.

"I made a decision today," he said.

"What is it?"

"I don't want to be a drunk. I don't want my life to be fucked up like this anymore. I want to get better."

"That's great news, Zack," I said. For the first time in two months I was feeling hope.

35

IT WAS ALMOST four-thirty in the afternoon and the sun was just going down when I got back to Parker Center. This day had flown by. I stopped at our cubicle in Homicide Special and pulled the Arden Rolaine murder book out of Zack's bottom desk drawer. It was pushed to the back. As soon as I opened it I saw that Zack hadn't even mounted the crime scene photographs. They were still in an envelope, just thrown in along with the coroner's report, autopsy photos, and the rest of his case notes. The book was little more than a catch-all. Nothing was in order. No time line or wit lists. His interview notes were a mess.

I shook my head as I sorted through the grisly crime scene pictures showing the living room of a small cluttered house. It looked old and musty. The dark red velvet furniture had lace doilies on the arms. Sprawled on an Oriental carpet, on her back, wearing a blue terry bathrobe and rolled down stockings, was Arden Rolaine. Whoever killed her had done a damn thorough job. There was nothing left of her face. Her gray hair was matted and thick with dried blood.

I replaced the pictures in the folder. Then I noticed a Federal Express package on my desk. It was the book I'd ordered from Amazon.com. My reading assignment from Agent Underwood. I picked it up and headed down the hall to CTB. I wanted to check in with Broadway and Perry. Their cubicle was empty, but Lieutenant Cubio found me and handed me one of the secure satellite phones. They were only a little smaller than an old Army field telephone.

"These came in from ESD and hour ago. Pretty easy to operate. You've gotta access the satellite. To do that, you use these six numbers first." He handed me a slip of paper. "Then dial the regular ten-digit phone number you want. There's an extra two-second delay because of the satellite scramblers."

He handed me another piece of paper with the SAT numbers for Tony, Emdee, Roger, Alexa, and himself. "You're good to go," he said.

"Where are Rowdy and Snitch?"

"Off minding the wool."

I raised my eyebrows.

"Women," he explained. "Broadway's wife Barbara is a Ph.D., teaches African studies at Mount Sac college. Emdee dates strippers. I think the current lamb is a lap dancer named Cinnamon or Ginger . . . one of those spices. She works at the Runway Strip club out by LAX."

"If they call in, tell Roger and Emdee after I check in downstairs, I'm going home. I have a coach's meeting at five-thirty."

"A what?"

"My son is being recruited for football at UCLA. Karl Dorrell is coming over. I gotta bust ass or I'm gonna miss it."

"No shit? Karl Dorrell? Really?" I'd finally said something that impressed this hard-eyed, boot-tough Cuban.

I rode the Otis to three and found that the task force had slowed down since this morning. Half the troops were gone; the rest were talking softly into their phones.

Agent Underwood was in his office getting ready to go home. His ostrich briefcase was open, and I couldn't help but notice the oversized Glock with a big Freeze Motherfucker barrel.

"Well, look who's here. I thought you were too good for us. On a special assignment for the chief. Didn't have time for our cheesy little serial murder case."

"When you urinated on my criminal profile, I figured we weren't gonna make much of a team."

"What do you want?" he snapped, as he turned his back and continued to load things into the briefcase.

"There's an old murder case that's touching this Vaughn Rolaine Fingertip kill," I said. "Happened early last June. Vaughn's sister, Arden, was beaten to death. Completely different MO from the Fingertip murders so it's probably not the same doer. The victim was pounded into oblivion with a brass candlestick."

"Is that MO? I thought a rage-based act made it a signature. Of course, I keep getting this stuff all confused." Really getting pissy now.

"You're right. It's a signature."

I dropped the packet of crime scene pictures on his desk. He picked them up and thumbed through them.

"My partner had the case. He put it together when he heard Vaughn Rolaine's name."

"Your partner, the invisible Zack Farrell." Underwood smiled. "How is that guy? Since he works for me, I keep meaning to meet him."

"He's sick, Judd. He's in the Queen of Angels's psychiatric ward. He had a complete emotional breakdown yesterday."

Underwood stared at me for a long time. Then he nodded. "Sorry to hear it."

"Thanks." We stood in awkward silence. "Anyway, by the middle of June, Detective Farrell had Vaughn Rolaine down as the key suspect, but wasn't able to find him because he was homeless and moving around. I don't know how this all fits, but it needs to be looked at."

"That the murder book?" He pointed to the blue binder in my hand.

"Yeah, but it needs work. I'm taking it home to organize it. I'll drop it off here in the morning."

"Okay."

I held up the FedEx from Amazon and he frowned.

"*Motor City Monster,*" I told him.

"Since you're not on the task force anymore, you can forget reading it."

"I know we didn't hit it off, Judd, but you caught this Detroit killer. I never even got close to our Fingertip unsub. I'll have it read by Monday, because it's never too late to learn something. Good luck catching this guy." I turned and walked out of his office.

Driving home, I thought about Zack. He'd really perked up while sorting facts on Arden Rolaine's murder. Even though most of his ideas seemed farfetched, there were one or two that tracked. I liked the idea that the unsub might also be a homeless guy who got started by killing Vaughn Rolaine because he wanted the sister's money. That one murder could have kicked him off.

I got to our house in Venice at five-twenty-five. When I opened the door and walked in I saw Alexa, Chooch, and Delfina all sitting in chairs out in the backyard. I joined them on the patio and they turned to face me. Chooch looked angry.

"I made it before five-thirty," I defended. "Dorrell isn't even here yet."

"The coach isn't coming," Chooch said.

"Whatta you mean? Why not?"

"The Athletic Department called," Alexa said. "Apparently, he's in a tug of war with Penn State over some blue-chip quarterback from Ohio. He's fighting Joe Paterno for him so he moved that meeting up and cancelled us."

I could see the devastation on Chooch's face. Delfina was holding his hand, trying to console him.

"Okay," I said. "Stuff happens. Don't let it sink your boat, bud."

"But Dad, he said he wanted me. If Joe Paterno also wants this guy from Ohio, that probably means Penn State's not going to want me. What if neither USC or UCLA offers a scholarship? Then I've got nothing." His voice was shaking.

"We should talk about this," I said. "Just you and me, okay?"

He nodded.

"Come on. Let's take a walk."

We went out the back gate onto the sidewalk that fronted the Grand Canal. Millions of spider-cracks crisscrossed the pavement under our feet; fissures in another man's dream. My son followed me in silence.

We made our way up onto the main arched bridge, climbing its subtle slope until we were at the top, looking down the long canal. Chooch stood next to me, his face awash in anger and frustration.

"When I was sixteen, I didn't believe in myself." My voice was thin, blowing away from us in the weakening Santa Ana winds. "I wasn't a true believer. Didn't think I counted. I was an orphan who nobody wanted, and that fact was proven to me over and over because five different sets of foster parents all gave me back. So instead of working to improve myself, or understand why it was happening, I tried to tear down everybody around me. I had a code back then. 'Do what I say or pay the price.' But even when people did what I wanted, I didn't enjoy it, because I knew they did it out of fear and not respect."

"Dad—"

"No. Listen to me, son, because I don't talk about this stuff often. Showing weakness to people I love is hard for me."

He fell quiet, so I continued. "Growing up, I knew if people thought I was weak, they'd take advantage of me. Underneath my bully's bluster was a frightened kid who didn't believe. I kept trying to impress people with threats. But I could see in their eyes that they weren't impressed. They were simply tolerating me, and that just made me angrier."

I turned to face him. "Chooch, if there's one thing I can try to give you, it's this: You don't have to impress anyone to be important. Around us you can be yourself. You can have big dreams, and all of us will help you live them."

"I do," he said, softly. "Playing football is a dream."

"I'm worried that football isn't as much of a dream as it is a device—a way for you to elevate yourself or prove yourself to others. For some reason, it looks like Coach Dorrell may choose this other guy over you. Coach Carroll likes you, but hasn't offered you a scholarship yet, and he might not. Same with Penn State. So right now you don't feel so important anymore. But try and think of it this way. You're the sum of all your experience and your experiences have helped forge who you are. If you were valuable yesterday, then regardless of what anybody else thinks, you're valuable today. It doesn't matter what Coach Dorrell or Coach Carroll do. It doesn't change who and what you are, unless you let it. Everybody suffers defeats, son. You'll come to realize some day, that it's your defeats that define your victories. The way to true happiness in life is to love what you're doing, not how well other people say you're doing it. It's an important distinction."

Chooch stood looking down stoically at the wind ruffled water on the Grand Canal.

"Even if you don't get an athletic scholarship to any university, and you go to one of these schools as a walk on, if you really love the game, love the process; you will succeed. Maybe not in exactly the way you once thought, but success will come."

My son was looking at me now, his face a strange mixture of emotions.

"But you won't ever be happy if you let other people grade your paper, Chooch. It has to come from inside you. You've got to be a believer before anyone else can believe.

"And you think that I play ball just so other people will think I'm a big deal?"

"Nothing in life is all one thing or all the other. In failure, there can also be accomplishment. In jealousy, there is usually envy and respect. The trick is to get the balance right. I think some things got out of balance for you this year."

He stood beside me, his eyes again fixed on the water, pondering my words.

"In whatever you choose to do, I want you to compete, and hopefully you will succeed. But most of all, I want you to love the process, because that's where happiness lies."

"So it's not important that Coach Dorrell cancelled his visit?"

"Not in the long run."

"What if he doesn't reschedule? And what if I don't hear back from USC either?"

"We can only play our game. We can't play anybody else's. You are a lot of things, Chooch. You are a combination of cultures and emotions. Your genes come from me, and your mother, Sandy. Alexa and I try to be good role models and show you how to behave through actions, not just words. But you get to choose what, and who, you want to be. You get to decide how you want to behave."

"I should calm down?" he said softly.

"Yep. And you gotta believe." I put my arm around him. "If it's meant to be, it's gonna happen."

36

AT SEVEN THAT evening I was at my desk in the den working on the Arden Rolaine homicide book. As I went through the old case notes, trying to put them in chronological order, I noticed a margin note that read, "Re-interview VR about Jan. 3rd time line."

I wondered if VR was shorthand for Victim's Relative like in Cindy Blackman's notes, or if it stood for Vaughn Rolaine, the victim's brother. Since Zack said he was never able to locate Arden's brother, I started looking around through all this disorganization for interviews he'd done with other family members.

As I was doing this, the doorbell rang. I got up from the desk, walked to the front door and peered through the peephole. The distorted images of Emdee Perry and Roger Broadway were stretched comically in the fish-eye lens. I opened the door and saw they were both decked out in snazzy Lakers gear—purple and gold jackets and hats. Roger handed me a ticket.

"What's this?"

"Lakers game," Broadway said. "Staples Center. Ninth row. We scored the seats from the Mexican Embassy. For some Third World reason, the *se hablas* are Clippers' fans. Never use their Lakers' seats."

I looked at the ticket. It was for the Spurs game, eight o'clock tonight.

"I'm in the middle of something."

Emdee drawled, "We like you okay, Scully, but we sure as shit wouldn't waste great Lakers tickets on you 'less we had to. Tip-off's in fifty minutes. Giddy-up, Joe Bob."

"Something's going down?"

They looked at each other in disbelief.

I told Alexa what was up, grabbed a jacket, and headed out. Roger and Emdee were waiting in a motor pool Navigator with smoked windows. I climbed in the backseat and Roger steered the black SUV up Ocean Avenue to the 10 freeway. Once we were heading east, Perry turned and handed me the transmitter Roger and I had taken off the Fairlane.

"ESD found out who made that little pastry," he said. "Designed by a private firm here in L.A. name of Americypher Technologies."

"Never heard of them."

"It was founded in 'ninety-three by a Jewish cat named Calvin Lerner," Roger said. "Man's got an interesting history. In 'ninety-five Lerner gave up his Israeli passport and became a naturalized U.S. citizen. This was very good news because Americypher specializes in state-of-the-art listening devices and transmitters. It turns out Uncle Sam is one of their biggest customers."

"We don't make our own surveillance equipment?" I was a little surprised that we would subcontract out work like that.

"It all comes down to horseshit and gun smoke in field operations," Emdee drawled.

Roger picked up the story again. "About two years ago Calvin Lerner, who still owned controlling interest in Americypher, went missing on the Stanislaus River in Central California during a trout fishing trip. Wandered off up the river alone, and did a *Beam me up, Scottie.* Never found any trace of him. No tracks, no blood, no body. His widow took over running the company. Americypher is still going strong."

"Americypher *sounds* like it should be a good American outfit," I said.

Emdee smiled. "One a the things ya learn working this beat is the more American a company sounds, the less Americans are probably involved with it.

"The bugs Americypher makes are years ahead of the curve. That's one of them," Broadway said, pointing to the tiny transmitter in Emdee's hand. "They're designed to use miniature low-volt batteries with twenty-year lives, but apparently because of the low voltage they're a bitch to install. The way we hear it, the engineers from Americypher go out on black-bag installations to help their customers plant these things."

Now I saw where this was going. "And you think since Americypher knows where the bugs are located, they could sell that information."

Broadway said, "Counter-intelligence plays a big part in world politics."

"But would Americypher double-cross big federal clients like Homeland Security and the FBI?"

"The old team put together by Calvin Lerner probably wouldn't," Roger said. "But nobody knows much about his widow. She's still an Israeli. Never took the pledge of allegiance. We just cranked up a new investigation on Americypher. The dicks in Financial Crimes are gonna hit that piñata and see if it spits out any candy."

We pulled into VIP parking at the Staples Center and ten minutes later I was sitting in the best seat I'd ever had at that arena. Nine rows up, center court. The tip-off was at eight o'clock sharp.

While I watched the game, Broadway and Perry took turns getting up and going to the bathroom, or out to buy beers. Something was definitely up, but when I asked them what, they waved it off. I decided to just wait them out. Whatever we were doing here, it had nothing to do with the Lakers.

At the half the home team was only up by three points. Fans were stretching and going out to the concession stands. Broadway said he wanted another hotdog and headed toward the exit.

Ten minutes later, Perry grabbed my arm. "We're leaving," he announced.

"We need to wait for Roger," I said. "He's getting food."

"Roger's in the car. Come on."

We hurried up the steps through the midlevel tunnel. As we joined the crowd milling toward the food courts I caught a glimpse of the same bald-headed man in the blue blazer who had come to my phony funeral. He was now wearing a Lakers jacket and was about twenty people ahead of us, moving toward the exit.

"Isn't that Eddie Ringerman?" I asked.

"Small fucking world," Emdee said as he pulled me along.

"Why don't you spit it out? What's going on?"

He hesitated, then said, "We got direct orders from the chief not to confide in the competition, but he didn't say we couldn't follow 'em. Ringerman's a rabid Lakers fan, but if our boy gets up to leave with the game in doubt, something's goin' down. So we follow Ringerman, see if we can catch him in *politicus flagrante*. Then we'll jerk a knot in his tail and make the boy give up something."

Ringerman headed out the main entrance onto the street, then crossed with the light to the east parking lot and got into a gray Lincoln.

Perry still had my arm, pulling me along. "Hustle up," he said. "Game's on."

37

BROADWAY DROVE THE Navigator out of Staples VIP parking and onto the city streets. I couldn't see the gray Lincoln Town Car that Ringerman was driving. We'd only been following it for three minutes and already we'd lost sight of him.

"I like a nice, loose tail," I said, "but isn't it usually a good idea to keep the target in sight?"

Broadway opened the glove compartment revealing an LD screen. He turned it on and a city map came up displaying a two-mile moving grid. I could see a red light flashing down Fourth Street towards the freeway.

"Satellite tracking," Broadway explained. "The feds aren't the only ones with goodies. While you and Perry were watching the game, I hung a pill on Eddie's ride. We're following him from outer space."

We followed the embassy car from a mile back as it turned off the Hollywood Freeway at Highland, then shot across Fountain and down the hill on Fairfax. We turned on Melrose and were right back where Yuri's market had once stood. The center of Russian Town.

This three-block area was the L.A. version of New York's Brighton Beach. Russian liquor stores featuring signs advertising expensive brands of Yuri Dolgoruki and Charodei vodka. Restaurants with names like Sergi's and Shura's dotted the landscape. Posters were plastered everywhere advertising an upcoming Svetlana Vetrova concert.

Roger finally pulled up across the street from a restaurant called the Russian Roulette. It was on Melrose at the west end of Russian Town, nestled close to the boundary of Beverly Hills. The building was stucco, but had a slanted roof with fancy trim. I spotted Ringerman's gray Lincoln in a jammed-to-overflowing parking lot.

"Unfortunately, as it turns out, this ain't the best place for me and Afro-Boy t'attempt a covert surveillance," Emdee said once we were parked.

"Shane, you're gonna have to go in there and check it out for us," Broadway added.

"Me?"

"We're unwelcome personages in there," Broadway said. "A month ago, donkey brain over there, attempted to end the criminal career of one Boris Zikofsky, a known L.A. hitter and Odessa shit ball."

"The man deserved the bust," Emdee protested.

"Instead of following this hat basher into the parking lot and cuffing him out there like he's supposed to, the Hillbilly Prince badges the motherfucker right in the restaurant without backup, and starts World War Three. My man ended up by dancing Boris through a pricey pastry cart from fifteen hundred Czarist Russia. Cost the department seven grand. The Loot shit a blintz."

"Not my best polka," Emdee admitted.

"So if we go in there, we're gonna get made, turned around, and run right back out, then reported to the lieutenant." Broadway handed me an old, taped together digital camera. "Take lots of pictures."

"I don't even know who the players are. Who do I take pictures of?"

"Everybody." Broadway reached into the glove box and retrieved a big, clunky tape recorder with a directional mike that was about the size of a Kleenex box.

"What happened to all our miniaturized, state-of-the-art goodies?" I said.

Broadway handed the recorder to me and said, "If you can find the complaint box up on five, slip it in as the saying goes."

Then he pointed at the camera. "No flash. It's digital, but just barely," he smiled. "Directional mike on this tape recorder has a short, so watch the transmission light to make sure it's recording."

"What are you two gonna be doing?"

Emdee switched on the radio. The Lakers game was in the third quarter. He gave me a lazy smile.

"Right," I said, and headed across the street.

I decided not to go in through the front. I didn't want to be seen, so I went to the rear of the restaurant.

The back of the Russian Roulette was littered with empty produce boxes and used-up liquor bottles. I looked in the trash and found some soft lettuce heads that didn't look too bad. I put my clunky camera and recorder in one of the boxes, then arranged five heads of wilted lettuce on top. I took off my jacket, tied it around my waist, and rolled up my shirt sleeves.

With this brilliant on-the-fly disguise in place, I carried the rotting produce right back into the restaurant.

The kitchen was noisy and full of cooks turning out that vinegary smelling food that Balkan people seem to love. Without warning, a burly guy in a white tunic who looked like a cross between Boris Spassky and Wolfgang Puck, grabbed me and started rattling away in some language with way too many consonants.

"Sorry, pal, I'm just the relief driver," I said into his guttural windstorm. "No speaky da Rooskie," trying to do it like some zooted out delivery guy from Saugus.

He ranted some more Russian at me then grabbed a head of rotting lettuce out of the box and shook it under my nose.

"No can this . . . this . . ." He was sputtering. "Thing no to eat!" Then in frustration he turned to find somebody who could speak my language.

As soon as he was gone, I set the box down, retrieved my camera and tape and went lickity-splitting down the hall connecting the kitchen and restaurant, moving past two doors marked (женщины) and (люди), which I figured were either Egyptian crypts or Russian toilets.

I moved into the back of the dining room. The place was packed and noisy. The predominant language sounded Eastern European—Armenian or Russian. I scanned the room looking for Ringerman.

Halfway down, seated in a wall booth, there he was. Next to him sat Bimini Wright, the Ice Goddess with the silver Jag from the funeral.

I crowded behind a flower arrangement and took pictures of everybody in the restaurant. Then some patrons in the booth next to Ringerman's got up to look at the pastry table. Apparently the priceless rolling cart hadn't made it back from antique repair. I slipped down the aisle between tables and slid into the recently vacated spot next to my targets. Then I turned on the tape and laid it under my jacket close to the next table.

They were speaking softly in Russian. It surprised me that Ringerman and Wright, two Americans, would choose to converse in a foreign language. I couldn't understand a word. They acted like people who were plotting something. I taped them for about ten minutes until the people from my borrowed booth headed back, carrying dessert plates. Then I bailed.

Minutes later, I was back in the Navigator, where Broadway and Perry were still listening to the Lakers game.

"You see him?" Broadway asked.

I scrolled through some digital shots of the two of them.

"Bimini Wright?" Broadway said as soon as he saw her picture. "Maybe the Israelis are using Eddie to build a bridge to the CIA." He looked up at Perry. "Something is sure as shit in the wind." Then he turned to me. "What were they talking about in there?"

"Beats the hell outta me." I punched Play on the tape recorder and we listened while their whispered voices, speaking Russian, filled the car.

38

We pulled out of Russian Town while Emdee hunched over the tape recorder in the front seat with an open notebook on his lap, translating the conversation. It surprised me that this transplant from South Carolina actually spoke Russian. These two were full of surprises. Listening to my bad recording, I could barely distinguish Eddie Ringerman's whispered baritone or Bimini Wright's elegant soprano. They spoke softly, their voices all but drowned out by the loud background chatter in the restaurant.

"Since they're both American, why are they talking in Russian?" I asked.

"They're both fluent. Both went to spy school. It's the kinda stuff these spooks live for," Broadway said. "Besides, it puts a crick in our dicks when we try to eavesdrop. Now this ignorant cracker gets to practice his night-school Russian."

I glanced out the rear window of the Navigator at traffic piling up at a stoplight half a block behind us. Suddenly, the headlights on a blue Ford Escort swung wide and the car roared around waiting traffic into the oncoming lane. It ran the light and rushed up the street after us.

"She's bitching about something called the Eighty-five Problem," Emdee was saying, playing a section of the tape over. "It happened when she was stationed in Moscow. She's pissed. Eddie is trying to calm her down."

"Bimini Wright was at the U.S. embassy in Moscow for ten years in the mid-eighties and nineties," Broadway said as the tape ran out.

"This all you got?" Emdee complained.

"Yeah. I had to leave the booth I was in."

I was still looking out the rear window. The blue Escort now ducked in behind a Jeep Cherokee, trying to hide.

"Hey, Roger, make a right."

"I don't want to make a right," Broadway said. "I'd like to go back to Parker Center."

"How'd you like to go back to the Tishman Building?"

Broadway grabbed the rearview mirror and repositioned it.

"Which one?"

"Behind the Jeep Cherokee. The blue Escort."

"Get serious," he growled. "Nobody runs a tail in an Escort. They got less horsepower than a Japanese leaf blower."

"Turn right and see what happens."

Roger hung a hard right and started down Pico. A few seconds later we saw the Escort make the same right and follow.

"Go right again," I said.

Roger swung onto a residential street. Only this time, after he rounded the corner, he didn't stick around to watch. He just floored it. We flew down the narrow street over speed bumps that launched the Navigator into the air each time we hit. I wasn't buckled in and shot up into the headliner with the first landing, slamming my head into the roof.

"Ooo-ee!" Rowdy shrieked, loving it.

When Roger got to the end of the street he hung a U and headed straight back toward the pursuing Escort. The two guys in the front seat suddenly started rubbernecking houses, pretending to be looking for an address.

"Look at these two dickwads," Broadway said. "Comedy theater."

We passed them and turned back onto Pico the way we came.

"We need to get outta here, Roger. One of those guys was the steroid case who walked us through the Tishman yesterday."

"Danny Zant, the FBI area commander," Roger said, and floored it again, heading for the freeway.

Just as he did, two more unmarked Toyotas skidded onto Pico, leaning sideways, burning rubber from all four tires with the turn. "Two more bogies," I said. "Blue Toyotas."

Roger had his foot all the way to the floor and the engine in the black Navigator was in a full-throated roar. He found an on ramp for the San Pedro Freeway and flew up onto the eight lanes of concrete, heading east. The next few minutes were a white-knuckle experience. We merged with unusually heavy 11 P.M. traffic. Roger was smoking around slower cars, tailgating, honking his horn, and passing in the service lane. Despite all his frantic driving, every time I looked back, the three federal sedans were still right back there.

"Can't you shake these assholes?" I said. "They're not in Ferraris, it's a fucking Escort and two Toyotas."

"Gotta have more than just stock blocks under the hood," Broadway said.

He put more foot into it, careening between slower vehicles, finally hitting the off ramp at Fifth Street and roaring down the hill toward Parker Center.

"Let's see if these humps want to have it out in the police garage," he said.

He broke a red light at Sixth, and another at Wilshire, then hung another right and headed straight toward the Glass House. The huge, boxy building loomed in front of us.

"Going under," Broadway shouted, sounding like a crazed subcommander as he drove into the garage.

He grabbed his badge, and as we roared up to the guard shack, held his tin out to the rookie probationer guarding the parking structure and frantically signaled the young cop to raise the electronic gate arm. The wooden bar went up and we went down.

I turned just in time to see the Escort flying into the garage after us. The driver didn't wait for the closing arm. He broke right through, snapping it off. Splintered wood went flying. The two Toyotas followed.

The startled police rookie pulled his gun and ran down the ramp. A siren went off somewhere.

Roger held the SUV in a hard right, our tires squealing loudly on the concrete as we descended level after level. Emdee pulled his gun out of his shoulder holster and laid it on his lap.

"You aren't really planning on shooting FBI agents are you?" I asked.

"Depends," Rowdy answered, his mouth set in a hard line.

We finally reached the bottom level, four floors below the street and were flying toward a cement wall.

"Bottom floor," Broadway announced. "Perfume and body bags." The Navigator spun right, and skidded to a stop, inches from the concrete. We bailed out just as the federal sedans squealed to a stop behind us. Doors flew open and six guys with thick necks and hard faces jumped out. Everybody had a badge in one hand and a gun in the other. Then came the shout-off.

"You're under arrest! FBI!"

"Stick it up your ass, Joe Bob!"

"Federal agents! Throw the guns down! Assume the position!"

"Eat me!"

The sound of police sirens now filled the garage, growing louder, echoing in our ears. Seconds later four squad cars, called in by the garage probationer, roared down the ramp and careened to a stop. Eight uniforms from the mid-watch jumped out with guns drawn. I heard more running footsteps pounding on the pavement.

"LAPD! Drop your weapons," a burly uniformed sergeant from an L-car boomed. It was chaos. Everybody was pointing guns, waving badges and screaming.

Then the elevator on the far side of the garage opened and Tony Filosiani charged out, gun in hand. The garage security alarm sounded in his office and had brought him running.

"What the fuck is this?" the Day-Glo Dago bellowed.

"These men are under arrest for failure to heed a direct order from the head of California Homeland Security," Agent Zant shouted hotly. "We're FBI! They're coming with us!"

"No they're not," Tony said.

"This is a federal issue," Zant brayed. "It involves national security."

"No it ain't," Tony yelled back. "It's the LAPD garage, and it involves your fuckin' imminent arrest and custody."

Zant looked startled.

"You guys may not have noticed, but you're way the fuck outnumbered here," Tony growled.

The FBI agents slowly turned. By now thirty cops had them surrounded with their guns drawn. Some were in uniforms, some in plainclothes. The feds turned back to Tony.

"And just who the hell are you, fat boy?" Zant asked angrily.

"I'm the Chief of the Los Angeles Police Department and you

six cherries got thirty seconds to get off LAPD property. Failure to comply gets you a bunk downtown."

"We're federal agents," the big, pockmarked ASAC said. "You can't jail us. Are you nuts?"

"You obviously ain't been reading my press releases," Tony sneered.

After a minute of indecision, Zant knew he was beaten. He motioned to the others and they got into their cars.

What followed was low comedy. Everyone was so jammed in down there that turning their vehicles around was next to impossible. Finally they got it done and a trail of red taillights retreated up the ramp.

Tony's chest was still heaving, out of breath from all the adrenaline. "This parking lot ain't secure," he finally said. "We gotta get a metal arm on that entrance." Then he turned and pointed at me. "This was supposed to be a covert op. Where's the fucking marching band?"

"I think this Navigator may still have a few bugs on it," Broadway said.

"All three of you. My office! Five minutes!" Then Tony turned and strode back to the elevator and left us there.

"We're in deep doo," Broadway said.

"Yeah, but at least we won't have to listen to Barry Manilow," I answered.

39

YOU GUYS WERE supposed to be running a low-profile no-see-um ground op, but less than ten hours after you leave this office, half a dozen feds chase ya into the police garage." Tony was a red-faced, five-and-a-half-foot blood pressure problem, standing in the center of his office with his feet spread, glaring at Rowdy and Snitch, Cubio and me.

"Don't you get it?" Tony continued. "If the humps down at Homeland decide to make all of you disappear, I can't do shit. It's worse than just them catching you out there disobeying Virtue's direct orders, they also probably know exactly how you're doing it."

"How?" I asked. "All we did was go to a Lakers game and to a Russian restaurant."

He crossed to his desk, retrieved a small box, and emptied it onto his blotter. Ten or twelve miniaturized bugs, none of them any bigger than the transmitter we pulled off the Fairlane spilled out onto his desktop.

"So far this is what Sam Oxman in Computer Services found in our phones and ceiling fixtures. We also turned up scans on half a dozen computers, including Alexa's and the main databank at CTB. So far, thank God, we haven't found anything in the ME's office."

"Keep looking," I said. "There has to be something down there."

"We're still on it, but after finding this stuff, I also notified the DA and the Superior Court. If somebody wants info on our activities this bad, it could also extend to other branches of municipal law enforcement, like prosecutors and judges."

I glanced around the office with concern and Tony waved my look off.

"This room is clean now," he said. "We went through it twice. Found four transmitters on this floor alone. Somebody in our own house must be planting these things, 'cause security's too tight for anybody else to get in here and do it. I'm gonna give everybody in ESD a close look and a lie-detector test." He grabbed up a couple of the bugs from the blotter and held them up. "Some of this stuff is so new we've never seen anything like it before. We had to use a microwave zap to shut the damn things off. They've got batteries the size of a pinhead, and they're sound activated. They run on such low power that our ESD analyst said they could have up to a twenty-year life."

"If ya let hornets nest in yer outhouse, it's hard t'get pissed when they buzz down and sting yer ass," Emdee contributed wisely. Tony groaned at the analogy.

"Do you think these came from Americypher Technologies?" I said, looking at Emdee and Roger. Each picked up a bug and studied it. It was hard to tell because none of them had brand markings. Finally, Broadway shrugged.

"Okay, we're running completely without cover now," Tony said. "I expect to hear from Robert Virtue any minute. He's bound t' sic his bunch of crewcuts on us. He's also probably gonna demand I hand the three of you over for obstructing justice—failing to obey a direct order from Homeland. Depending on what's going on, they might even be able to gin that up into a threat against national security."

Tony picked up the transmitters and put them back in the box. "The FISA court doesn't have to divulge its reasons for approving wire taps or arrest warrants. They can bust you and hold you without ever saying why. We can't beat these guys. Once you go into the system, you could be reclassified as enemy combatants or people of interest—whatever they need to put you on ice till this is over."

The room got very quiet.

Cubio said, "I think, under the circumstances, we need to put these men into a deep-cover assignment. Get them the hell out of here, find a secure location, and have them report in on SAT phones."

"I agree," Tony nodded.

"Chief, this morning you mentioned we needed to be totally covert and not confide in anyone," Roger said. "But if we're going to be effective, we need to confide in a few people."

"Such as?" Tony asked.

"Something strange is happening between the CIA and the Israelis," Broadway continued. "Eddie Ringerman and Bimini Wright were meeting tonight at the Russian Roulette. Ringerman used to be an LAPD detective. Now he does security for the Israelis. Bimini's head of the CIA's Western section station. We may need to start by getting them to brief us. Eddie used to wear blue and Wright's a straight shooter. She also owes us on the Lincoln Boulevard shooting last year. We put the case down without questioning any of her people. We could've blown a lot of covers and we didn't."

Tony stood thinking about it, and then looked over to Cubio for his opinion.

"Might as well. We ain't foolin' anybody anyway," Armando said.

"Okay, but not Ringerman," Tony said. "I don't trust a guy who changes sides like that. Start with Agent Wright, but don't talk to anybody else unless you clear it with Lieutenants Scully and Cubio or directly with me."

"Yes, sir," Broadway said.

"And we need to code name this," Tony added. "I don't want the feds to subpoena any internal memos using your names."

"How about Unusual Occurrence?" Cubio suggested. "It's the section in the CTB Operations Guide pertaining to tactical and covert operations. It's vague and it's already in our literature. Shouldn't attract much interest."

"Unusual Occurrence it is," Tony agreed. "All communications will be under that heading. No names. Broadway, you're One. Perry, you're Two. Scully, Three. Cubio, Lieutenant Scully, and I will be Four, Five, and Six."

We left the chief's office and moved into the hall. Alexa was just coming out of the elevator. She'd made it back to headquarters from home in less than twenty minutes. A new record.

"We'll meet you across the street in the park," Cubio said, nodding a greeting at Alexa.

Once the doors closed, Alexa took my hand and led me across the hall toward her office.

"Tony called and told me what happened in the garage," she said.

"I must be kicking over some of the right rocks," I smiled.

"I'm worried. It's one thing fighting criminals; it's something else when it's our whole federal government."

"This is not the U.S. government," I responded. "And it's not Big Brother either. It's just five or six assholes on a power trip. Tony wants us to work this undercover from a secure location."

"I think that's a good idea." Then she looked furtively around and planted a quick, secret kiss on my lips. "Once you get settled I want a call every five hours. If I don't get that call on schedule, I'm going to crank up this department and come looking."

It was almost midnight when I walked into the park across from the Glass House. Lieutenant Cubio was pacing in the mist-wet grass, talking on his cell. Emdee Perry was on his SAT phone, speaking low, gesturing, trying to explain to some lap dancer in Inglewood why he was going to be out of pocket for a few days. Broadway sat on a concrete bench a few yards away under a streetlight, doing the same thing with his wife. When they rang off, their faces were tight.

The lights from the windows in Parker Center shown through the trees and made strange patterns on the grass where we stood. Bums drinking wine out of Evian bottles eyed us suspiciously from the benches near the sidewalks. We were standing out here because we didn't think ESD had found all the bugs inside Parker Center.

"You guys know that asset-seizure house off Coldwater?" Cubio asked.

"Yeah," Broadway said. "The stilt house on Rainwood where we busted the gun drop last spring."

"It's still in our property inventory and it's furnished. That's where you'll set up." Cubio handed us a set of keys. "Except for the chief, Lieutenant Scully, and the four of us, nobody else will know that's where you are. We're gonna run outta clock fast. If you don't get the shit in a bag by Monday, we're gonna be facing a flock of subpoenas and federal court demands."

"We're full throttle," I said.

He nodded. Then he shook each of our hands, wished us luck, and walked briskly back across the street.

"I guess church is over," Emdee drawled.

40

THE MECHANICS AT the Flower Street garage pulled two bugs off my Acura. The Navigator also had two. Broadway selected a blue Chevy Caprice from the motor pool. Perry took a gray Dodge Dart. I arranged to meet them at the safe house in an hour because I had something I needed to take care of.

It was after midnight on Saturday, so the psych ward at Queen of Angels was crowded. Doctor Pepper was still on duty, but he looked like an assembly line worker whose conveyor belt had overrun him. He clearly wasn't happy to see me.

"Who are we going to be tonight? How about Detective Farrell's Uncle Harry?"

I showed Pepper my badge. "We're working an important case. I didn't think you'd let me in."

He glanced at one of his clipboards then handed it to a passing nurse. "I couldn't seem to help your partner, so I'm not his doctor anymore. I'm having him transferred to an abnormal psych unit that's better equipped to deal with his kind of problem."

I didn't like the sound of that. "I need to see him," I demanded.

"This time I guess I should find out if you're armed. It's considered terrible form to allow firearms inside a psych ward."

"Locked in my car." I opened my sport coat and showed him.

I waited while he called a male nurse to escort me to Zack's room. I was lugging the LAPD murder book on Arden Rolaine in one hand, and my briefcase in the other. The nurse pushed some buttons, cleverly hiding the combination with his body. The door swung open, I entered and heard the disconcerting sound of the electric lock buzzing the door shut behind me.

Zack was at the window, still dressed in the same clothes. He looked up as I entered, then leaned against the wall and studied me. There was something different about his demeanor, something distant and slightly lost.

"Hi," I said.

He nodded but said nothing.

"Brought the Arden Rolaine binder like you wanted."

He just stood there, so I handed it to him.

"You got a minute? I asked.

"Do I have a minute?" he finally repeated, and shook his head in disbelief.

"Hey look, Zack . . ."

But he waved me off, his big hand polishing the air between us.

"I have a few questions on Arden Rolaine's murder," I said, and pulled up one of the plastic chairs. After a moment, he took the other.

"Questions," he said flatly.

"Stuff we discussed that doesn't quite track. I want to get it all straight before I give Underwood this murder book."

"Pretty anal compulsive. Maybe you're the one ought to be in here."

"I'm just trying to find some answers."

"So what is it? What's the big head scratch?"

We looked into each other's eyes. His were empty as train tunnels. Mine probably showed confusion. There was something eerie in Zack's relentless stare.

"Turn to page twenty in the book."

Zack smiled. "Ain't no page twenty. I never filed any of this."

"I know. I did it for you."

He finally opened the book and started flipping pages, shaking his head in wonder. "Boy, Shane has been a busy, busy boy."

"Page twenty," I said. "Your case notes from the fifteenth. The margin note, middle of the page."

He scanned the page then looked up. "So?"

"Says there you were planning to re-interview VR for the June third timeline. Who, or what is VR?"

"VR?" he looked puzzled. "Re-interview VR . . . shit, I don't remember writing that."

I didn't like where this was going.

"Can't stand for Vaughn Rolaine," he went on. "Cause I never met the guy. Couldn't ever find him." He started looking through the book. "If I wrote re-interview, it was probably just a fuck-up. A mistake." He hesitated. "I don't know," he said, finally looking up.

"Could VR be shorthand for victim's relatives?" I asked.

He thought about it. "To be honest, I'm not sure. I was getting pretty hammered most nights last June." He thought some more. "Y'know, though, now that I think back on it, you may be right. VR for victim's relatives. Makes sense." He closed the book. "Mystery solved."

He sat opposite me, looking down again at the binder in his lap, shaking his head in wonder.

"Lotta unanswered questions on this case," he finally said softly.

"Yep. I need to get everything nailed down before I give it over to Underwood. We need to start at the top and run through everything again."

Zack sat quietly for almost a minute, looking at the painted concrete floor between us. It was almost as if he was trying to come to some sort of decision. Then, without warning, he exploded out of his chair. I'd never seen him move so fast.

I lurched up, trying to stand as he smashed me in the face with the murder book, driving me back. I hit the concrete wall hard. The air rushed out of my lungs. Before I could stop him, he had his hands around my throat and was lifting me off the floor, right out of my Florsheims.

I felt my stocking feet kicking, hitting his legs. I wanted to scream out, but my throat was constricted in his powerful grip. We were eye to eye; his face, a mask of rage.

First, my vision blurred.

Then everything went black.

41

I WAS IN *Yuri's market.*

Everyone around me was speaking Russian, and just like the Russian Roulette, I couldn't understand what anyone was saying. I was wearing Lakers' gear and Martin Kobb had the shopping list. He moved along beside me, young and handsome in his off-duty clothes. We were buying ingredients for a dinner he was going to cook.

"We'll need to baste with a heavier motor oil," Marty said, reaching for a can of Texaco 40-weight. "And we'll chop up some of these for the salad." He pulled several boxes of windshield-wiper blades off the shelf.

"What's in this recipe?" I asked.

"Wait'll you taste it," Kobb said, checking his list. "You get the transmission fluid. I'll find the antifreeze."

Then I was back at the Staples Center. The Lakers game was still in progress, but I was walking around in the cheering crowd, unable to find my seat.

"You're in the way!" someone shouted, angrily. "Sit down!"

"If you can't find your place, go home!" Another fan yelled. I looked down at a lady wearing hoop earrings and a UCLA sweatshirt.

"It's in the ninth row. Seat twenty," I said, hoping she could direct me.

"How come you're here?" Her voice and expression hateful. "Nobody wants you anymore. They should just give you back to Child Services like before."

And then I was wandering in a desert. I had my shirt off and was looking for Chooch and Alexa. The sun burned my face and shoulders. I finally saw my wife and son, far away, standing in the shade of a huge Texaco sign. They were waving for me to join them. I started running, but the desert sand was deep and my legs were sluggish. The faster I ran, the further away they seemed.

I heard somebody behind me. I looked back and saw Zack. He was moving much faster, and was about to catch me.

"I saved your ass," he shouted angrily. He was almost on top of me now. "I saved your ass, and this is how you pay me back."

He lunged and caught my shoulder, pulling me down.

When I opened my eyes, I was looking at Alexa. She had a cool hand on my forehead. Chooch was standing behind her, worry on his face.

"Dad, we love you. Please be okay," he said softly.

I had a tube down my throat and was breathing through an oxygen mask. My jaw ached where Zack hit me. I tried to say something but Alexa put her finger on my lips.

"Don't talk. You were strangled and hit on the head. You have a severe concussion."

"Zack . . . ," I managed to say around the throat tube.

"Don't talk," she said.

"How?" I struggled to sit up.

She pushed me gently back on the pillows. "He choked you unconscious. Then he either knocked you in the head with your briefcase, or kicked you. He called in an orderly who didn't know him. You were lying on his bed under the covers, the orderly thought he was you and you were him. Zack just used your badge and walked right out.

"The trauma physician wants to keep you very quiet for at least a day. If your brain swells, or fills with fluid, they'll have to operate to relieve pressure. The next six hours are critical. You've got to lie still."

So I closed my eyes.

For the next ten hours I slept. When I woke again, the sun was up and my room was empty. Someone had removed the tube and the oxygen mask.

My head throbbed, my spirits buried in emotional mud. I pulled myself upright and experienced a wave of dizziness.

My briefcase sat open on the table next to the bed with Agent Orange's book still inside. I had so many questions I didn't know where to start. After a minute I pulled out the book, set it on the covers beside me, and tried to collect my thoughts.

Like a buzzard circling a rotting carcass, I scavenged my bleak history with Zack, looking for something to hang on to. The more I thought about it, the worse it got.

I rang the nurse's bell, and a minute later a pleasant African-American woman with a wide, happy face appeared in my doorway.

"I need to talk to my wife," I said.

"She was here all night. Once you were out of danger this morning, she and your son went home. She said she wanted to take a shower, then go to the office and finish up some things." The nurse looked at her watch. "She'll be back later."

"Thanks," I said, and watched as she left. Then I hefted Agent Orange's *Motor City Monster* up onto my lap and thumbed it open to the contents page.

Chapter one was entitled: "Growing Up to Kill—Social Environments and Formative Years."

I turned the page and began to read.

42

ALEXA ARRIVED AT a little past five that afternoon. The sun was already down as she walked into my hospital room and kissed me on the lips, letting the moment linger before pulling me close and gingerly hugging me. Then she looked over and saw Judd Underwood's book on the nightstand.

"You're reading this?" She seemed surprised as she picked it up.

"Just finished it," I said.

She thumbed through a few pages before setting it back down. "I thought you said he was a jerk."

"Actually, there's a lot of good stuff in there."

She settled in the chair beside the bed and took my hand. "Okay, let's hear it. Something's on your mind."

I took a moment to gather my thoughts. "I need to know what's going on with Zack," I said.

"Nothing. He's in the wind. Of course, after what he did to you he's probably dust on the LAPD. We could file on him for assault with attempt to commit and battery against a police officer, but for that to stick, you'd have to be willing to press charges and testify. Knowing you, I'm guessing you won't."

I nodded my head.

"So that train probably doesn't get out of the station," she said. "It'll still have to go to the Bureau of Professional Standards. But so far, all we've got is a psychologically distressed cop who went momentarily nuts, knocked you in the head, and split. Since he was legally committed here by his wife, there's some monetary and civil complaint issues, but that's it."

I nodded. I was reluctant to get started because once I did there was probably no turning back. She sensed my hesitancy and pressed me gently.

"Where Zack went isn't what's bothering you. I can't help if you won't tell me."

"Some of this is theory, some just guesswork. So if you go proactive on me before I get this completely straight in my mind, then there's a good chance it's going to ruin what's left of Zack's life, 'cause I could be completely wrong."

"Shane, stop dodging. What is it?"

"Okay, but you won't like it."

She let go of my hand to pull an LAPD detective's notebook out of her purse.

"It starts with an old open homicide that Zack was working before we partnered," I began. "We agreed to handle all of our prior cases separately, but he told me about this open murder case the first week we teamed up."

Alexa started making notes.

"The victim was a woman named Arden Rolaine. She was

clubbed to death with a brass candlestick in her house in Van Nuys back on June third of this year. Zack and Van Kelsey caught the squeal. The one-eighty-seven was sent to our division because she used to be in a singing group called The Lamp Street Singers, and it got classified as a celebrity homicide."

"Let me jump ahead," Alexa said. "You're about to tell me Arden and Vaughn Rolaine were related." Writing it down as she said it.

"Brother and sister." I took another deep breath. "Arden had some substantial money saved up from her music career, but Zack and Van never found any of it after she died."

"And you think it was under her mattress or buried in a fruit jar in the backyard. The doer beat it out of her, dug it up, and took it."

"Yes. Zack's prime suspect in that murder was Arden's brother Vaughn. He was homeless, but was always coming around and mooching money from his sister. Finally, she got tired of it and told him to buzz off. Zack's theory was Vaughn got pissed and came back in early June to burgle her place. She surprised him. He smacked her around, got her to give up the dough, and then put her down with the candlestick."

"Pretty straightforward," Alexa said.

"What's troubling me is how Vaughn Rolaine could be the prime suspect in one of Zack's murders last June, and then turn up as the first dead body on the Fingertip case this December."

"A little coincidental, isn't it?"

"Yeah, but not impossible, I guess."

She nodded and finished writing that down.

"The Arden Rolaine murder book is a mess," I continued. "Zack didn't organize anything. Maybe because by then the spark was out and he'd stopped trying, or maybe it was all unfiled because he never planned on solving it. I was going through the binder, getting it in shape before giving it to Underwood and

I came across this margin notation: 'Re-interview VR, on timeline for June third.' Zack told me he never spoke to Vaughn Rolaine. Couldn't find him. They never met."

"Then how could he be re-interviewed?"

"He couldn't. Just before he jumped me, I asked Zack if it was his casebook shorthand for something else, like Victim's Relative. He couldn't remember at first, then changed his mind and told me that, on second thought, that's what it stood for." I waited for her to finish writing and look up. "How long you been a cop?" I asked.

"Seventeen years."

"If you use shorthand in case notes, you think you'd ever forget what your abbreviations stood for?"

She shook her head.

"Me neither. So if VR doesn't stand for victim's relative, then it probably stands for Vaughn Rolaine, and that means Zack talked to him once before and was lying to me. Zack said he couldn't find Vaughn because he moved around a lot. But the homeless people we talked to in Sherman Oaks Park two days ago, said he was a fixture down there. So which is it?"

"Where's this going?" She stopped writing.

"I don't have a shred of evidence for this. It's all total speculation, but I keep wondering if it's possible that Zack was the one who killed Vaughn Rolaine. It's the only construct I can come up with where all of these coincidences line up and make sense."

"What's his motive?"

"The missing money. Arden's recording industry dough. His case notes say he and Van couldn't find it in any bank accounts of hers, no safety deposit boxes. According to Zack's theory, Vaughn forced his sister to tell him where it was before he killed her. So if her little brother found it and took off with it, then maybe Vaughn buried it in the park somewhere."

"And you think Zack waited four or five months until Arden Rolaine's case cooled down and then went after it."

"His divorce probably helped determine the timetable, but yeah, that's what I'm wondering. Zack goes to the park, drags Vaughn up into the foothills, stuffs a rag in his mouth and clips off the guy's fingers to get him to talk, ends up killing him. Zack's a cop. He'd know clipping off the fingertips and moving the body to the L.A. River would bitch up our investigation. With no fingerprints, there'd be nothing connecting him to the case, 'cause we'd never ID the body. And we almost didn't."

Alexa blew out a long breath. "If your theory has him catching the Vaughn Rolaine murder himself so he could control the spin on the investigation, then the big question is how did he set it up so you two would get the case?"

"The night we found the body in the L.A. River was a Friday. That previous afternoon, Zack and I moved to the top of the murder board. We knew we'd get the next one-eighty-seven. We even went home early to get some sleep. Zack would have known those mutilations would get the case sent to Homicide Special where we were on deck. He left Parker Center at four o'clock Friday afternoon. That gave him plenty of time to find Vaughn, torture him, get the money, and do the murder. That first body was easy to see from the river bank, so he knew it would be found quickly. He also knew we'd probably catch the squeal because, as the killer, he had control of the timetable.

Alexa was still frowning as she made a few more notes.

I picked up Agent Orange's book and handed it to her. "According to Underwood, stress is the big precipitator for serial murder. The big stressors are marital, financial, and work related. Zack hits bars and stars on all three.

"When we got to Vaughn Rolaine's body it was midnight, and while we were waiting for the MEs, I remember looking into Zack's car, and seeing that he was crying. Later he told me that Fran had thrown him out on Thursday and asked for a divorce."

"And you think that's what snapped him," Alexa said. "He's lost his marriage; he knows the divorce will bankrupt him, so he goes to see Vaughn Rolaine to get the stolen money. Starts chopping off fingers, and kills him in a rage."

I nodded.

"What else?"

"Well, lots of stuff. None of it alone is very earthshaking, until you add it all up."

I retrieved *Motor City Monster* from her, opened it to a chapter entitled "Antecedent Behaviors in Criminal Profiling," and then gave it back.

"According to this book, the first murder done by most serial killers is close to home. Underwood calls it killing in the comfort zone. Zack and I worked for two years in the West Valley. That area was definitely in his comfort zone."

She was writing again.

"After the unsub kills Vaughn, he goes postal. All the latent rage from his childhood comes out, the signature elements of the murder. He carves the Medic symbol on the chest—all the other postoffense behaviors. If these victims are father substitutes, he covers up the vic's eyes so his dead father won't stare at him. That chapter you're looking at is about parental abuse and the early psychological factors that help form serial criminals. Parents play a big role. If his father sodomized him or abused him physically, that could be a huge factor. If his dad was a medic in Nam, that explains the symbol on the chest.

"Zack told me a few days ago, when I was driving him to his brother's, that he wished his father hadn't done something. I asked him what, and he wouldn't say, but said something about not being in control of his destiny. That his actions were written in his DNA long before he was born."

"And you think that's why he's killing father substitutes?"

I nodded. "According to Underwood, most serial killers vacillate between extreme egotism and feelings of inferiority and self-contempt. They're not in control of their lives or emotions, so they crave control in the commission of their murders and often look for jobs that give them a sense of authority."

"Like a cop," Alexa said.

"Exactly. There's a thing Underwood calls the sociopathic or homicidal triad. It includes bed-wetting, violence against animals or small children, and fire starting. This book says if two of those three conditions are present, you're heading for big trouble. They're often precursors to serial crime. His psych evaluator hinted that Zack used to be a bed-wetter and I found out that he ran over the family dog the week after Fran threw him out."

She was just looking at me now, her notepad forgotten on her lap.

"Stress plus rage equals blitz kills," I said. "The doctor psychoanalyzed Zack for two days and said he appeared to be a cognitive disassociative personality, incapable of having relationships. He also said Zack might be a narcissist. According to Underwood's book, that's a pretty classic mindset for a homicidal sociopath."

"You want my opinion, Shane?"

"Of course. It's why I'm telling you all this."

"Okay, let's take your points one at a time."

She looked down at her notes. "'Re-interview VR' could stand for re-interview victim's relatives as you suggested, and Zack was so drunk, he simply forgot. But it could also stand for half a dozen other things. To name a few, it could mean 'Re-interview victim's Realtor,' or 'victim's rapist' if she had a prior sexual assault. You've still got some back-checking to do on that."

She kept her eyes on her notes. "Forgetting for a moment that huge leap you just made that Zack's dad was a corpsman in Nam, let's just deal with natural probabilities." She paused, then asked, "How many of the homeless men in the West Valley would be Vietnam vets?"

"I don't know."

"Ten percent?"

"Maybe."

"That makes the odds of our unsub killing a vet about ten to one. So far, we've only identified three. It's not impossible that it's a coincidence they're all vets."

"I guess you're right," I said. "But I don't think it's a coincidence. How could that be?"

"I don't know. I'm just playing defense here. Putting in the exculpatory evidence." She consulted her notes again. "If Zack was planning on stealing Arden Rolaine's money, why would he include the fact that it was missing in his case notes? Wouldn't it be smarter to just leave out that fact all together?"

"Van Kelsey was his partner. How could he leave it out?"

"Yeah, but Van Kelsey retired well before Vaughn Rolaine was murdered. Zack could have easily gone back and removed that material from the Arden Rolaine case files. But he didn't. Why?"

She had a point.

"Then there's the whole question of Davide Andrazack," she continued. "You don't really believe Zack killed Andrazack, right?"

"That's right. It was a political assassination."

"We've completed our computer sweep of the Glass House and none of the bugs we found in the police department was on computers that included Fingertip case information or a description of the chest mutilation. That means it's still possible that Andrazack *was* killed by the Fingertip unsub and that it *wasn't* a political assassination. So, which is it?"

I didn't know. "What about the polygraphs the chief was doing on the ESD techs?" I said. "If we could find out who planted those bugs, maybe we could roll him."

"Nothing yet," she said.

"What about the medical examiner's computers?"

"Still checking, but so far they're clean."

Alexa was slowly shooting down my entire framework.

"So you think I'm nuts."

"No, I'm just showing you some holes in your theory. So far, you have nothing that directly ties Zack to any of these murders. It's just intriguing speculation. You better find some evidence if you want a municipal judge to write an arrest warrant."

"Alexa, believe me, I don't want this to be true. It might just be a lot of coincidences, but don't we need to find out?"

"What do you want me to do?" she asked.

"Zack lived in Tampa as a kid. Contact the police department there and find out if they have a record on him. You might have to get somebody to unseal a juvenile record if he had one. Next, we need to find out, was he a loner? Did he beat up younger kids? Did he kill or torture pets? Was his father a medic in Vietnam? You know the questions to ask, but we have to keep this strictly to ourselves. If we're wrong and it gets out, it could destroy what's left of him."

Alexa closed her book and frowned. "Of course, you know, either way this turns out, we're gonna end up being wrong."

43

AFTER ALEXA LEFT I began to feel cooped up. It was impossible for me to be officially released until ten o'clock the next morning, so I pulled a Zack, got my clothes out of the closet, and just split.

The Acura was still in the visitor's lot where I'd left it. Now that I was moving around, I could see how much damage Zack had done. I hurt like hell. My body ached and when I bent down to check under the car for new bugs, I almost passed out. I got behind the wheel, waited for my head to clear, and then dialed Emdee on the SAT phone. After three rings, he picked up.

"Howdy." His voice coming from outer space, and sounding like it.

"It's me. Number two or three. Whatever I am."

"You're three."

There was a long delay after I spoke and before he answered. The scramblers were doing their work.

"I'm outta the hospital."

"Good goin', Joe Bob. Next time ya pick a partner, get one who won't kick the caddie-wampuss outta ya when he gets spiky."

"Good advice. Where are you guys?"

"Market. House ain't got no protein, 'less you eat roaches."

"I'm on my way over. Where's the key?"

"Under the pot."

"Under the pot? Why not over the doorjamb?"

"Before y'start complaining, wait'll y'hear which pot."

The pot was on the front porch of a vacant house across the street. *Okay. Not bad.*

I put the car in gear and headed toward the safe house. The dull pressure behind my eyes was spreading, morphing into a throbbing headache. I stopped at a 7-Eleven for a bottle of water and some Excedrin. As I walked down the aisle, the unexpected shadow of last night's crazy dream flew over me. I remembered walking down the aisle of Yuri's market with Marty Kobb at my side, buying forty-weight oil and windshield wiper blades for a salad. Nuts.

I paid at the counter, got back into my car, and swallowed three pills. Then I drove onto the freeway, still thinking about Zack. After Alexa shredded my murder theories, I was no longer happy with the dumb-ass criminal profile I'd done. As I drove, I came up with even more exculpatory information.

According to another chapter in Underwood's book, serial killers were fractured personalities who were marginalized by their early upbringing and subsequent life experiences. For this reason, they often had difficulty holding jobs. Yet Zack was a veteran on the LAPD. Was it possible that he could have existed in a stress-filled environment like police work and moved up the ranks to Detective II while still being a dissociative personality? I doubted it.

I rode with him for two years in the Valley. Wouldn't I have known if he was some kind of monster in training? Instead of a disassociative personality I had seen a savior. He'd protected me from that bunch of tail gunners at Internal Affairs for the better part of a year. I believed I had a true friend in Zack Farrell. How could I feel that way about a disassociative, narcissistic personality?

I reached for my satellite phone to call Alexa and tell her to forget that background search in Tampa, when a random thought hit me. If you were a cognitive disassociative narcissist; if you were prone to fits of rage and excessive violence; who would you want as a partner? How about good old, drunk-as-a-skunk, throw-up-in-the-backseat, Shane Scully? Passed out most of the time, unable to observe anything except my own belt buckle, so self involved and depressed that I wasn't focused on anything. The perfect partner for a murderous sociopath. I put the phone back on the seat beside me and took the Coldwater off-ramp.

The asset-seizure house on Rainwood looked small and unimpressive from the street. The LAPD wasn't wasting any money on maintenance and the yard was overgrown. I pulled past and parked half a block away, then got out of the car and walked slowly toward the vacant house opposite the one we were using. There was a big, potted rhododendron on the front porch. I leaned down, my vision going gray for a moment as I bent to retrieve the key. I had to pause to let my head clear before walking across the street.

I opened the front door of the safe house and entered a one-story, cheaply constructed California A-frame. Broadway and Perry had left a few lights on and I walked through the exposed beam, lightly furnished living room and out the back door onto a large wooden deck, which was cantilevered on long metal poles hanging precariously over the canyon.

The view was the money with this place. To my right, a million twinkling lights spread across the San Fernando Valley. A soft wind blew through the canyon carrying with it the sweet, peppery smell of lilac, eucalyptus, and sage. I sat in one of the canvas deck chairs and looked down at the valley.

I needed to get my mind off of Zack Farrell and Vaughn Rolaine, and back on Davide Andrazack and Martin Kobb. Right now there was nothing I could do for Zack. I tried to tell myself it was out of my hands.

I smiled as my Kafkaesque dream resurfaced. Forty-weight motor oil for God's sake, trani-fluid, and antifreeze? Some gagger of a salad that would have been. What the hell was that all about?

And then, just like that, I knew. A series of memories tumbled over each other. I took a minute to calm down then tried to put them in some kind of order.

I started with Cindy Blackman's notes and our brief discussion at Denny's. Cindy didn't think an experienced cook would buy fresh groceries five days in advance. Yuri Yakovitch said he was on the back loading dock of the market, supervising the vegetable delivery. He had a good view of the cash register but in his statement, said he somehow missed seeing the burglar, as well as Kobb, when they entered the store. Marty Kobb was supposed to have pulled his gun, and chased the robber out into the parking lot, where he was shot to death. But the money was, for some unknown reason, left behind in the cash register, Nobody saw a getaway car.

I ran it over in my mind and marveled at the simplicity of it. How had we all been so stupid?

An hour later, Emdee Perry and Roger Broadway returned, carrying groceries. They must have been in full Bubba mode when they shopped because their market bags were full of beer and chips. They left everything in the kitchen and we walked back out onto the deck. I returned my aching ass to the sagging canvas-backed chair.

"'Bout time for us to all snap on our garters and get this case movin'," Perry drawled.

"You come up with anything new since we seen you last?" Broadway asked. I took a moment and then nodded.

"What if Marty Kobb wasn't buying food at the Russian market?" I said, giving voice to my new idea. "What if he was buying gas at the Texaco station?"

44

WE SAT ON the back deck of the Coldwater house drinking beer and talking it over. If Martin Kobb had been at the Texaco station when he was shot, it was a major shift in case dynamics that could change everything. But it still didn't mean we could solve his murder. On the other hand, if the killer was doing a gas station holdup instead of ripping the market, there could be witnesses we'd completely missed.

One looming question doused some of my enthusiasm. If the shooting happened at the station, why hadn't the manager or a customer come forward to clear up the misunderstanding? Still, it was a promising new direction.

"If this turns out to be right, then the department just spent ten years paintin' the wrong house," Emdee observed.

"First thing in the morning I'm gonna call Texaco's executive offices," I said. "See who used to own that station, see if I can get the employee list, and if there's a record of credit card sales receipts from back then so we can start making up a new wit list."

"Good thinking," Roger said, as his cell phone rang. He dug it out of his pocket and put it on the table in front of him without opening it.

"What do I do now?" he said. "If I answer it and they have a satellite track on there, will the feds know where we are?"

"Ya ask me, there's a big difference between being careful and just bein' a pussy," Emdee drawled.

Roger frowned, snapped up the phone and answered it. "Yeah?" He listened for a moment, and then gave us a thumbs up. "Good. No, that's okay. No problem. Now's as good a time as any. See ya in twenty minutes." He disconnected and smiled.

"Good thing we bought you some deodorant," he said to Emdee. "Bimini Wright returned my call. We're invited to midnight tea with the CIA."

Ten minutes later we were in Broadway's blue Caprice heading down Coldwater Canyon on our way to the CIA offices on Miracle Mile, a favored location for U.S. intelligence agencies.

"She ain't gonna be easy," Broadway said as he drove.

"Long as you don't plow too close to the cotton we'll do fine," Emdee answered.

"She doesn't like you, so let me do the talking," Broadway cautioned.

"Lay some Ebonics on the woman. That oughta light her fire."

The CIA building was actually called the Americas Plaza. I wondered if that meant it was owned by some foreign government. We parked in the basement. Zack had my badge, so Broadway and Perry vouched for me and signed me in. We took a secure elevator up to the twenty-fifth floor and exited into another beautifully decorated hallway. Our tax dollars were certainly getting a good workout in the Los Angeles counterintelligence community. Lion claw feet held up polished Queen Anne tables with tapered legs.

But the best tapered legs in the joint belonged to Agent Wright, who was standing on the ivory cut-pile carpet wearing three-inch heels and a short, tan skirt. Her Icelandic blonde hair was done in a graceful cut that curled in just under her chin. Blue eyes the color of reefwater gunned out of an ivory complexion, clocking us. If I worked on this floor, I'd never get anything done.

"Let's go," she said, without even waiting to be introduced to me. Of course, after the funeral she'd probably run a full profile.

Agent Wright led us through a door marked Fire Exit, up a flight of stairs, and out onto the roof, which had a flat, tarred surface. We followed her to a spot between two huge, boxy air-conditioning units, which were roaring even though it was midnight. The hot Santa Ana weather had the cooling system working overtime.

Bimini Wright stopped between the A/C units and spoke, just over the roar. "This is far enough." Her voice mixed with the loud, growling exhaust. It was the rough equivalent of turning on faucets in a bathroom before a covert meeting.

Broadway introduced me. "This is Detective Scully."

We shook hands. She had a surprisingly strong grip, as if she'd been taught by some butch station chief that, if you want to make it in a man's world, you better shake hands like a trucker.

"Okay, guys. Your call. What's the deal?"

"It's the Davide Andrazack murder," Broadway said, not giving her much. She shrugged, so he dribbled out a little more. "It was in Shane's serial murder case, but now it's been stripped away from us by Homeland. The Andrazack hit is involved with another investigation we're still working. We were hoping you could give us some background."

"Davide Andrazack was never one of your serial murders," she said, looking over at me. "He wasn't a homeless bum. He was killed by Red Shirts."

"Company speak for enemy spooks," Emdee explained.

"You three need a Come to Jesus meeting," Bimini said. "So here it is. If you don't back off, you're gonna get spun and hung. You need to do exactly as Mr. Virtue instructs and leave the Andrazack thing alone. Robert Virtue lacks humor, and there's lots of heat coming down on that situation. You work it without portfolio against his wishes, and you're gonna be swept so far out into the bush we'll never find the hole you're buried in. That's the best advice I have."

"What about my murder case?" I asked.

"Believe me, they're all over it," Bimini said. "R. A. Virtue and the FBI come off a little headstrong, but they've got huge national security concerns to deal with so I try to cut them a little slack. Take it on down the road and leave this to us."

"'Cept, somebody's planting bugs all over town," Emdee said. "We pulled a basketful outta the police administration building yesterday. It's not hard to guess that Davide Andrazack was over here trying to find out who was bugging the Israelis. I'm also guess'n we're not all standing up here on this roof, 'cause you like the smell of L.A. smog. You ain't all that sure about your shop either."

Just then, the air filtration system switched off, banging loudly as the spinning fans stopped. It was suddenly very quiet.

"We know you met with Eddie Ringerman at the Russian Roulette last night. We were in the next booth and got it on tape," Broadway said.

She smiled. "You're really gonna try and bluff me with no face cards showing? You've gotta do better than that, Roger."

"Are we just completely forgetting about the Lincoln Avenue shooting?" Broadway countered. "I thought you were good for your old debts."

"That's five levels below this on the threat assessment board."

"Then why don't you tell us about the 'Eighty-five Problem?" I ventured, and saw immediately that I'd hit a nerve.

She looked at me sharply. "I guess you *were* in the restaurant listening," she said, coloring slightly, not enjoying being busted. After a moment she added, "Okay, since it's only history, I guess I can tell you a little about that."

"We're waiting," Broadway said, frustration showing in his strained voice.

"Back in the eighties, I was stationed at our embassy in Moscow," she began. "It was the Cold War, and we were mixing it up pretty good with the Reds." She looked over at me. "I know you're probably interested in Stanislov Bambarak since he also came to your funeral. Back in the Cold War days, Bam-Bam Stan was a KGB legend. Our paths crossed a lot when I was in Moscow. We never hit it off, because I managed to recruit quite a few of his frontline officers as double agents. It really pissed him off. He got so jacked he ran me in four times and questioned me at the Moscow Motel, which was an interrogation center the KGB had under the Kremlin. Stan couldn't understand how I kept infiltrating his Apparat. But I was young, pretty, and flirtatious, and his station officers were lonely, horny, and alcoholic. A perfect recipe for defection. The trick was to cook up their emotions, get them half in the bag and see how scared they were that Soviet Union was about to collapse. The Cold War was winding down and it looked to everybody like we were winning. A good many of these KGB officers were willing to give me covert information in return for a promise that I would arrange for them to come to the States after the Cold War was over. Once the Berlin Wall came down, everyone knew it was only a matter of time before the Soviet Block fell apart."

"We can get all of this on the History Channel," Roger said, still pissed that his Lincoln Avenue trade hadn't worked.

"I was really on a roll in those days," Bimini continued.

"More and more agents were taking my deal. Then, one night in August of 'eighty-five, there was a roundup. Stanislov picked up all of my Russian double agents in the middle of the night and took them to Lubianka Prison in Moscow. Lubianka was a shooting prison. People would go in there and never be heard from again. All of my doubles were interrogated, and then summarily executed. That fat bastard gave the order. They were all shot in the back of the head."

"With a five point four-five millimeter automatic," Broadway said.

"That was how they did it back then," she concurred. "I was devastated. I couldn't conceive of how Stanislov could have learned about every single one of my assets. I had spread out the case info, distributed their encrypted files to a lot of different service computers. NSA, FBI, CIA . . . It shouldn't have *all* leaked. It became pretty damn obvious that somebody far up in our own system had sold us out. Some embassy official with high security clearance was giving up these Russian double agents. We investigated diligently but couldn't find out who it was. It came to be known on station as the 'Eighty-five Problem."

"And you never caught the guy?" I asked.

"A few years later, R. A. Virtue got a phone tip at the FBI in Washington, giving him the name of one of our ex-CIA Moscow agents. After a lengthy investigation, Virtue and some other D.C. counterintelligence types finally turned up man named Edward Lee Howard. He'd been passed over for promotion and had gone into business with Stanislov to help beef up his CIA retirement fund. We searched his records, and found out that he had probably given up some of my double agents. But the more we studied him, the more it became obvious that he didn't know anywhere near all of it. And then before we could bust him, he shook his tail and got out of the U.S. and back to Russia. But I know there was still another traitor out there."

"You were in charge of the investigation?" Roger asked.

"It was my op. But it was Virtue who really made his bones on the 'Eighty-five Problem." Bimini took a deep breath. "In February of 'ninety-four, Virtue caught another anonymous tip. A CIA officer named Aldrich Ames was eventually arrested for treason. He too, had been selling the identities of Russian double agents back to the KGB. But again, when we checked his exposure to the names, there was no way he could have known about all of them either. By then Virtue was a rising star in the FBI, and was put in charge of large aspects of the case. We all knew there was still another traitor involved. With the arrest of FBI agent Robert Philip Hanssen in two thousand one in Virginia, it finally seemed that we had uncovered the last of them. But as we debriefed Hanssen, we realized that we still couldn't account for all of the lost KGB doubles. That's when we knew there had to be a fourth man. Somebody with connections high up in our operation, who also had damn good contacts inside the KGB. In effect, a double-double. Covert intel I'm not willing to give you, leads me to believe the fourth man is hiding in L.A. It's why I'm stationed here today."

The air-conditioning unit switched on again, and this time Bimini's nerves must have been getting to her, because she flinched.

"Stanislov was probably the one who recruited Howard, Ames, and Hanssen, just like you recruited his double agents," I said.

"That's right," Bimini replied. "When you boil it down, he had the exact same problem as I did. The fourth man was selling assets to both sides. Stanislov Bambarak's trying to find him, same as Virtue and me. Bambarak would do anything to get even. Both sides were losing their doubles. We arrested our traitors. Stanislov, asshole that he is, executed his." She took a breath. "I'm still looking for my last traitor. Hopefully, I'll beat him to it this time. That's all I can tell you. The rest is classified."

45

IT WAS ALMOST 2 A.M. when I finally flopped down on my bed in the sparsely furnished safe house. I closed my eyes, but my mind wouldn't shut down, so I lay on top of the covers, picking at an array of troubling self-doubts. When I'm in these self-analytical moods, attempting to dissect my confusing life journey, I often start with my police academy graduation, the most fulfilling day of my life to that point. I stood at attention in Elysian Park and received my badge, full of pride and a sense of accomplishment. But as the years passed, my pride dissolved in a brutal mixture of street violence and bad rationalizations. As my pride left, the sense of accomplishment I'd won disappeared with it. Then came the drinking.

But in the beginning, right after graduation, I felt very righteous in my new uniform, armored by its ironed blue fabric and the LAPD badge. It gave me a stature I'd never had before, and I was comforted by the ballsy sound of my own gun leather creaking. I rode the front seat of a department A-car, secure in the belief that my turbulent upbringing had taught me how to survive. I also knew that loners rarely got double-crossed, so I affected a carefully orchestrated isolation. If I didn't depend on anyone, even my partner, I reasoned, then I was in complete control of my environment. But the obvious flaw in this thinking was since I didn't depend on anybody, nobody depended on me. I told myself that I treasured that. I was a lone gunman.

What I had really become was an afterthought on the job. Underneath my strutting arrogance were hidden doubts and a lurking suspicion that I had chosen to isolate myself because I never really mattered to anyone and couldn't figure out how to change that. I thought if I just didn't look inward, I wouldn't have to deal with the insecurities and could believe in that uniformed power image that looked back at me from my mirror each morning. But I was wrong.

As I stared up at the exposed beams in my borrowed bedroom, I realized that in the last four years I had made a complete transformation. Now I depended almost too much on others.

I had Alexa and Chooch to share my feelings with. Broadway and Perry were becoming more than just case-mates. I could bask in their banter. It felt good, but I had sacrificed control. This all happened because I opened myself up; made myself vulnerable to others. But just when I finally reached the point where I was maturing into someone I could actually respect, I found myself miles from my wife and son. I was back where I'd started. It surprised me that my new, hard-won sense of self lay behind such a transparent veil of doubts.

At that moment, my cell phone buzzed. I looked over at the bedside table, watching it pulsate every two seconds doing a little vibration dance. I didn't give this number out, and Alexa would use the SAT phone, not my cell, so I knew who it was. The phone just kept taunting me, moving stupidly to its right, every time it buzzed.

There's a difference between being cautious and just being a pussy, I thought. So I rolled over, opened it, and put the cell up to my ear.

"Shane," I said, and waited for Zack to reply.

"We need to talk, Bubba."

His voice sounded tight.

"Turn yourself in, Zack. Then we'll talk."

"You need to meet with me, just us, face to face."

"I'm not meeting with you."

"I know what you think. That's why I jumped you. I had to get outta there." Then there was a long pause before he said, "I didn't kill Vaughn Rolaine. You owe it to me to listen. You've got to hear my side. I know how it looks. You're my last chance."

I took a deep breath and decided to press him hard and see what happened. "I've been wondering about something, Zack. You were getting into a lot of shootouts back when we were in the Valley. How many perps did you light up? Three or four in twelve months? Wyatt Earp didn't drop that many guys in Dodge City."

"We had big problems in that division. IAD investigated. You know they wouldn't rate them clean kills 'less they were."

"Were you covering my ass because you were trying to help me, or because you wanted to keep me on the street 'cause you needed a partner who was too out of it to hurt you at any of those shooting review boards?"

His pause seemed a fraction too long.

"Come on," he finally said. "Whatta you talking about? That's nuts." Then he lowered his voice. "You gotta help me. I can't explain how Vaughn Rolaine ended up in both my cases. It makes me look bad. You gotta help me come up with something."

"I'll meet you in Jeb Calloway's office anytime you pick," I said.

"Get serious. I ain't goin' nowhere near Mighty Mouse till I got some answers. I'm not some drooling monster. How can you think that?"

"It's there, or nowhere." Another long silence stretched between us. "Turn yourself in, Zack. If you're straight on this, then it's gonna all come out fine. Nobody is out to sink you, not Alexa, not Jeb, and especially not me."

"Yeah, right. Fuck you very much, asshole."

Then he was gone and I was listening to a dial tone. I closed the phone and turned it off.

I got up, went out onto the deck, and sat on one of the canvas chairs under a three-quarter moon. When I looked out at the beautiful canyon, I noticed a pair of feral yellow eyes turned up at me from the sagebrush. They glinted gold in the moonlight for a flash, before disappearing.

Probably a mountain lion or a coyote. But I'd been on the street long enough to recognize a killer's eyes. There was predatory hunger in that crafty yellow stare.

Then a strange thought hit me. When that beast looked up at me, what did he see in my eyes? Was there nobility and honor, or did he see another killer?

46

THE NEXT MORNING I called Texaco. After sitting on hold for almost five minutes, a stern woman came on the line and identified herself as franchise manager. She sighed loudly after I explained my time-wasting errand.

"We don't generally give out the names of our franchisees," she snipped. "Wait one moment."

More recorded music followed as I dealt with the corporate ego of Chevron Texaco.

"Okay," she said. "I guess we can supply that."

"Thank you."

"Where was our station located again?"

"The corner of Melrose and Fairfax in Los Angeles."

"One moment."

This time she didn't put me on hold, but came right back on the line.

"You're mistaken. We have no franchise located there."

"This was back in 'ninety-five. It's not there anymore. I told that to the first woman I spoke to."

"But you didn't tell me, did you?" Frigid. Finally, I heard computer keys clicking.

"Okay, 'ninety-five. That station was actually not on a corner, but one up from the intersection with a Melrose Avenue address."

"Thank you, ma'am, I'll make a note of that. Could you tell me who owned the franchise?"

"Yes."

More silence.

"Would you mind telling me now?"

"I'm trying to pull it up, if you'll please give me a second."

We definitely weren't hitting it off.

"From 'eighty-three to 'ninety-five, that station was owned by Boris Litvenko. Then it was sold to Patriot Petroleum."

"Excuse me. Litvenko? Did you say Litvenko?"

"L-I-T-V-E-N-K-O." She spelled it.

My heart was beating faster now. Boris must have been Marianna's husband and Martin Kobb's uncle.

"Do you happen to have the ownership names for Patriot Petroleum?"

"No, we wouldn't have that."

"Thank you, ma'am. If I have any more questions, I might need to talk to you again."

"I'll be right here," she chirped, not sounding too happy about it, either.

I found Emdee and Roger eating prefab waffles at the kitchen table. They put two in the microwave, zapped them up for me, and handed me the butter and syrup.

"Anything?" Broadway asked.

"We're in business. Marianna Litvenko sold the station in 'ninety-five to an outfit named Patriot Petroleum. No surnames on the paperwork."

"Whatta ya wanta bet there's no patriots employed at Patriot Petroleum?" Perry said.

"So, like you said, Marty Kobb wasn't at the market. He was over visiting his Uncle Boris's gas station when he was killed," Broadway said.

"Why didn't Marianna Litvenko or anyone else mention that they owned a gas station right next to the market, and that Marty was there right before getting shot? When Blackman and Otto talked to her in 'ninety-five she never mentioned it."

"That ought to be our first question once we find her," Emdee said.

We spent the rest of the morning looking for Boris's widow. She wasn't listed in the phone book. Maybe she was listed under another name or had remarried. I thumbed through my shorthand of Blackman's and Otto's notes looking for the Bellagio address. I found it, picked up the phone, and ran it through the LAPD reverse phone directory. No Marianna Litvenko. The directory listed the people who owned the house at that address as Steve and Linda Goodstein. I called the number and Mrs. Goodstein said the house had sold twice since '95. She had never heard of the Litvenkos.

Emdee Perry finally found Marianna in the LAPD traffic computer. She had three unpaid tickets for driving with an expired license from three years earlier.

We agreed that since I'd turned this angle, I would run the interview on Mrs. Litvenko. Roger and Emdee would be there for backup. The address was way out in the Valley, in Thousand Oaks.

"Wonder why she sold the nice place on Bellagio?" I said as I unlocked my sun-hot car and we piled in.

Roger shrugged and took shotgun. Perry stretched out sideways in the back. We headed down Coldwater, onto the 101. Just after two o'clock we pulled up to a slightly weathered, not-too-well-landscaped, low-roofed complex of cottages in the far West Valley.

When we parked in the lot, my question was answered. There was a large sign out front:

WEST OAKS RETIREMENT CENTER
AN ASSISTED LIVING COMMUNITY

47

AS WE WALKED up the stone path to the lobby building, I glanced over at Emdee. "Don't you think since you speak Russian, you'd be better equipped to handle this?"

"You get in a crack, I'll help ya out. But I don't put out a good Granny vibe. I look like I skin goats for a living, so old ladies mostly hate me on sight."

"Listen to the man. He knows his shortcomings," Broadway said.

We entered a linoleum-floored waiting room furnished with several green Naugahyde couches, bad art, and a long vinyl-topped reception desk. An old man with a turkey neck and two-inch thick glasses peered at us over the counter as we approached.

"Ain't seen you folks before," he announced, loudly. "Means

you're either guests, undertakers, or family of our next resident victim." Then he smiled. He had most of his lowers, but not much going the other way.

"We're here to see Marianna Litvenko," I said.

"Ever met her before?"

"No, sir," I said.

"Then get ready to be disappointed. Whistler's mother with more wrinkles than a Tijuana laundry. And ta make it worse, the woman is a communist."

He picked up the phone and started stabbing at numbers, made a mistake, and started over.

"Can't see shit anymore," he growled.

"Are you employed here?" I asked, a little surprised at his demeanor.

"Hell, no. Volunteer. I'm Alex Caloka of the Fresno Calokas. Not to be confused with the San Francisco Calokas who were all fakers and whores."

He finally got the phone to work. "Folks to see Russian Mary," he bellowed into the receiver. Then he waited while somebody spoke. "I ain't shouting!" he said, and listened for a minute before hanging up.

"Unit B-twelve, like the vitamin. Off to the right there. She's getting massage therapy. If they got her clothes off and ya don't wanta puke, cover your eyes."

We walked out onto the brown lawn that fronted the paint-peeled cottages and turned right. The single-story, shake roof bungalows were arranged in a horseshoe. A few frail-looking, old people with blankets on their laps, sat in wheelchairs taking the sun.

"Be sure and sign me up for this place after I retire," Emdee told Roger.

B12 was identical to the other units. The only difference was the color of the dying carnations in the flowerbed out front. We went to the door and knocked.

"Just a minute, not quite finished," a young-sounding woman's voice called out.

We waited for about three minutes, listening to occasional hacking coughs, which floated across the lawn from the row of parked wheelchairs. Finally, the door opened and a thirty-year-old blonde goddess in gym shorts and a sports bra came down the steps carrying a canvas therapy bag.

"You're her guests?" she asked.

"Yes, ma'am," Broadway and Perry answered in unison, both of them almost swallowing their tongues.

"You're lucky. She's having one of her good days."

Then the goddess swung off down the walk using more hip action than a West Hollywood chorus line, and headed toward another cottage.

"As long as we're here, maybe I oughta see if I can get that painful crick worked outta my dick," Perry said, admiring her long, athletic stride.

We stepped inside the darkened room and stood in the small, musty space for a moment waiting for our eyes to adjust. Then I saw her sitting in a club chair parked under an oil portrait of a stern-looking baldheaded man.

Suddenly, she leaned forward and pointed a bony finger at Emdee Perry. "Dis is man who stole my dog," she shouted, loudly.

"I'm sorry?" Emdee said, taking a step back.

"Took *Chernozhopyi*. Right out of yard."

"Chernoz . . . ?" Broadway said, furrowing his brow, unable to finish the word.

"Means black-ass," Emdee said.

"Beg your pardon?" Broadway sputtered.

"You ain't bein' insulted. Probably was a black dog. So don't go sending no letter to them pussies at the N-Double-A-C-P."

"I want dog back!" She yelled.

Perry looked chagrined and took another step back, glancing at me.

"Your witness, Joe Bob."

I moved forward. "Mrs. Litvenko, we're police officers."

I turned to Broadway and Perry. "One of you guys show her your badge."

They both pulled out their leather cases, and as soon as she saw them, Marianna Litvenko shrank back into her chair like a vampire confronted by a crucifix.

"Ma'am, this is about your nephew's murder in nineteen ninety-five," I said.

"I no talk. You go!" she said, her voice shaking.

"Ma'am, Martin Kobronovitch was an L.A. police officer," I pressed. "This is never going to be over until we catch his killer."

"No." Her lower lip started to quiver. "Not again. Please."

I moved over to her and kneeled down looking into dark eyes.

"Mrs. Litvenko, we're not here to hurt you," I said gently.

"Please, I have nothing left. They have taken everything."

"Why didn't you tell the detectives who talked to you before, that your husband owned the gas station on Melrose next to the parking lot where your nephew was shot?"

"No good will come of this," she whispered.

"I know you cared about Martin. The other detective told me how upset you were."

"Martin is dead. We cannot help him now. We can only save those who still live."

"Your family was threatened? That's why you kept quiet?"

She put her wrinkled hands up to her face. "These men, they are *gangsteri*."

"Russian Mob," Emdee clarified. He had retreated to a spot behind the screen door on the porch, where he now stood with Broadway, looking in.

"Mrs. Litvenko, this is America. It's not the old Soviet Union. We're not KGB. The police are not your enemy. We're here to protect you."

"Did you protect Baba?" she challenged.

"Your husband?"

"Killed. Murdered! Did the police stop that?"

"Ask how he was killed," Broadway coached through the screen.

Marianna looked up, angrily. "They must leave. I will talk only to this one." She pointed at me.

I walked to the door and looked out through the screen. "Why don't you guys go get that physical therapy?"

I closed the door on them and turned back.

"Mrs. Litvenko, I want to find out who shot Martin. I know now, he was at the gas station, not the market, when it happened. I understand you're frightened, but whoever is threatening you, I will protect you. This is America. You'll be safe. You have my word."

She shrank further into the upholstered chair and then, the dam broke. Tears rolled down her face. It was as if a decade of anguish was flowing down those wrinkled cheeks. Finally after several minutes, her crying slowed. I found a Kleenex box and gave her a tissue.

"How did Boris die?" I asked.

"He owned six Texacos," she said, haltingly. "Very smart. He work hard, my Baba. Then one day, the *mafiozi* come. Boris say one of these men is huge and ugly. They want to buy stations. Boris say, 'This is Land of Free. We can dream here.' These men laugh. They tell him he has one week to sell. Boris is very frightened. He tells Martin, who is policeman. But Martin say he can do nothing without proof. Then Baba goes to be checking his two stations in Bakersfield. He is coming home; a big truck swerves and there is accident. Boris only one to be dead."

"And you don't think it was an accident."

She snorted out a bitter laugh. "Martin, he start to investigate after work. He find out man who drove truck is named Oliver Serenko from Odessa. Odessa. This is a place of many evil men. Serenko was never arrested. He just disappeared. Martin, he goes to Boris's gas station on Melrose. He talk to people, try to find someone who saw the *gangsteri.* That night, they come again. The manager of our station, Akim Russaloff, he tells me Martin is angry, threatens the men and then the ugly one with the broken face, shoots him."

"Where is this manager?"

"Disappeared. A week later. Dead."

She sat quietly now, looking away and remembering.

"There was nothing we could do. I could not help Martin then, and I cannot help him now."

"They forced you to sell all six stations?"

She nodded. "They threatened my sister's babies. These are men who keep their promises. I had no choice."

I looked at the guilt in her eyes. That's why she cried when Cindy questioned her. Martin had been at the gas station because of her. She felt guilty about his death, but could do nothing without risking the lives of her sister's children.

"Who were they, Mrs. Litvenko? Who killed your husband and your nephew?"

"No. They will kill my grandnieces."

"You give me their names and I will see that they all get protection."

I held her hand again. "This has gone on long enough. Only you can make it stop."

The tears started flowing again. I stayed beside her until she was finished crying. After a few more minutes, she had no more tears.

"Please, Mrs. Livenko," I pleaded. "It's time to finish this."

"*Nyet,*" she whispered.

48

I CALLED TAMPA and talked to the chief of police there," Alexa said. "You were right. Zack had some problems."

We were standing out on the deck of the safe house. The evening sun was just setting behind a dense wall of brush in the overgrown canyon; sliding below the hills, shining gold on the limbs of a nearby stand of white eucalyptus. Broadway and Perry were in the kitchen opening beers and preparing a plate of crackers and dip.

"What kinds of problems?" I asked, fearing the worst.

"The chief wouldn't unseal his juvie record, but he remembered the worst of it. A lot of fights, half a dozen D and Ds."

D and Ds were drunk and disorderly arrests. My own juvie record was three times worse.

"Anything else?"

"Nothing the chief could remember. If he was killing dogs or beating up classmates, it didn't make it to the booking cage." She reached into her purse and retrieved some temporary credentials with my name attached. "Here. I figured you'd need these until Personnel gets your new ones made."

I put them in my pocket without looking at them. No cop likes to lose his badge. It was embarrassing.

Perry brought out the hors d'oeuvre plate and set it on the table with a flourish. It contained a three-by-two-inch block of something covered in brown goo with crackers arranged around the edges.

"I hope that didn't come out of the toilet," I said skeptically.

"This here ain't some possum I scraped up off the highway, Joe Bob. What we got here is a quarter pound a cream cheese with A-1 Sauce. Prime hillbilly cooking."

"I think I'll pass," I said.

Broadway came out on the deck, balancing a tray with beers and four glasses he'd found in the kitchen. All this party formality was because it had finally occurred to these two dingbats that Alexa could actually enhance their careers. As if cold beer and cream cheese would zip them right up onto the Lieutenant's List.

After the Heinekens were poured, Alexa opened her briefcase and pulled out some folders.

"This is everything from the Russian organized crime databank on the Odessa mob," she said. "The guys who seem to be currently in charge are the Petrovitch brothers. Samoyla and Igor. They're both foreign nationals here on long-term visas. Neither of these guys has a wife or family, but that's pretty standard. Members of the Russian mafia are prohibited by their criminal code from getting married, seeing or talking to relatives, or even working for a living."

"They're celibate?" I asked, surprised.

"They can have girlfriends, but no children," she responded. "They brought a strict thieves' code over from Odessa. It's all pretty desperate stuff. Never work, never marry. Never, under pain of death, give truthful information to police. And my own personal favorite; sit in on trials and convocations and be willing to personally carry out all death sentences."

"Nice," I muttered.

"The file on the Petrovitches is mostly a lot of surveillance reports and broken search warrants that never came to anything," she said, handing it over. "Every time OCB thinks they have Iggy or Sammy set up for something, and convince a judge to write the paper, the search always turns up zilch."

I looked at the file. There was no picture of Iggy Petrovitch, but there was a booking picture of his younger brother, Sammy, clipped on the front of his yellow sheet. If this was the guy who threatened Marianna, no wonder she wouldn't talk.

He looked massive and his face was a hideous mask of scar tissue, the result of some horrific disaster. Height and weight were listed in metrics courtesy of some European police agency. For the record, he weighed 127.01 kilograms and was 2.032 meters tall. Somebody else would have to do the math, because I don't get the metric system.

"This guy is right out of a forties horror flick," I said, showing the shot to Broadway and Perry who nodded, but didn't take the photo. They knew him from the street.

Alexa continued. "According to the background check from Interpol, Sammy was rumored to have been doing covert incursions and death squad assassinations for some secret branch of the KGB during the Russian war in Afghanistan. Setting bombs in mosques and blowing up buildings. He was driving away from one of his booby traps in Kabul when a Sunni militia man hit his vehicle with an American-made shoulder-fired Stinger. We had some green berets over there advising Afghan warlords. They found him and one of our corpsman patched him up. The world would've been a lot better off if we'd just let him die. Now he's in L.A. and according to our gang squad, Sammy is the

Odessa mob's designated hitter here. He's dropped ten or fifteen people since he showed up, only we've never been able to prove it. Down in Russian Town, this guy's like the Black Death. They call him *Ebalo*. It means The Face."

"Two questions," I said. "If he was a KGB agent with such a dark past, how does U.S. Immigration and Naturalization let him in here? And since the Petrovitches aren't citizens and we suspect them of being Odessa mobsters, why don't we just deport them?"

"Can't deport them if we can't prove they're guilty of anything," Alexa answered. "The one time we actually tried, it was squashed by INS in Washington with instructions not to pursue our case."

She leaned forward, picked up a cracker, and spread some cream cheese on it. Then she put it tentatively, in her mouth and chewed. Everybody watched.

"That's excellent," she exclaimed.

"Our street intel puts Iggy and Sammy in L.A. since 'ninety-five," Broadway said, picking up the story. "The Petrovitches started out as finger breakers, but were so good at it that within three years, they were promoted to authorities, or brigadiers."

I must have looked confused so he clarified.

"That's like an enforcer. In 'ninety-eight, these two guys staged a bloody coup and took control of the entire L.A. branch of ROC. When I say, bloody, I mean like in, 'the streets ran red.' Rumor has it that Iggy is the boss. He was also some kind of covert assassin for the KGB during the Soviet Union. He does the thinking, and Sammy, with his ghoul's face, does the wet work. During their coup a few years back, we were pulling dead Reds outta every drainage basin in L.A. But like their code instructs, nobody talked or stepped up. We couldn't prove the Petrovitches were behind the slaughter."

"Then how can you be certain they did it?" I asked.

"Negative physics," Broadway said. "Somebody creates a vacuum and you wait to see who rises. The Petrovitches rose like the cream in a root beer float. After they became *pakhans*, or supreme bosses of the Odessa mob here, everything quieted down again. They started branching out and taking over legitimate businesses, usually by some kind of threat or extortion."

We all sat and thought about this while a hoot owl, way up the canyon chanted his mournful cry.

"Okay, I'm gonna jump to a not very tough conclusion," I finally said.

"Get froggy," Emdee smiled.

"I've read some gang briefings, and I understand the Russian mob is very big on gas tax scams. But to run them you need to pump gas, and that means you need to own service stations. The Petrovitches couldn't strong-arm Boris Litvenko, so they killed him and forced Marianna to sell the six Texacos. Then Sammy shot Martin Kobb when he started looking into his uncle's death and got too close. A week ago, he gets Andrazack with the same gun. That means Sammy still has that five-forty-five stashed somewhere."

"Yeah, but how do we find it?" Broadway asked.

I looked over at Alexa. "You could have Financial Crimes open up a gas tax investigation on Patriot Petroleum, I'll bet a year's pay it's a Petrovitch company. Make the warrant for financial records, but tell the judge to write it as loose as he can. It needs to be served on Sammy's home office as well as his business. Once I get in, I'll push the edges and see if I can find that pistol."

"I'll do my best," she said. "But there's no probable cause. I may not be able to find a judge who will write the paper."

"In the meantime, give the three of us permission to talk to Stanislov Bambarak," I said. "Sammy's an unguided missile, but I bet Bambarak's got big problems with the Petrovitches. The Russians are supposed to be our allies now. Maybe it's time to put that theory to the test."

49

STANISLOV BAMBARAK AGREED to meet us at his house in the Valley at nine the following morning. We arrived in Broadway's blue Chevy Caprice and pulled into the driveway of a beautiful California Craftsman house on Moorpark Avenue bordered by beds of colorful red and white impatients brimming behind well-trimmed hedges.

We rang the doorbell, and a few minutes later heard heavy footsteps coming down the hallway, followed by the sound of latches being thrown. The massive wood door swung open and Stanislov Bambarak greeted us in the threshold, holding a long-necked watering can. A wrinkled Hawaiian shirt and stained khaki shorts draped his mammoth body like a badly pitched tent. Watery brown eyes inventoried us carefully.

"Ah," he finally said, letting out a gust of breath ripe with the tart smell of breakfast sausage. *"Da vafli zopas."*

"Flying assholes," Perry translated, and smiled. "You gonna let us in, Stan, or you just gonna stand there and insult us?"

Stanislov stepped aside. Then he held up the watering can and said, "Been feeding my pretties." This mystifying remark was delivered in perfect tally-ho English, courtesy of some Black Sea KGB spy school where he'd trained so he could infiltrate MI-5 in Great Britain.

Without further discussion, he turned and limped down the hall toward the back of the house. The screen door to the porch was open and he led us across a manicured lawn, past a brand new Weber barbeque with the sale tags still attached. We followed him into a greenhouse that took up most of his backyard.

Glass walls coated with sweet smelling condensation drove the temperature up over ninety. The hothouse shelves were stacked four high, and held hundreds of orchids in every size, shape, and color. A worktable at one end of the shed served as a splicing area where Stanislov was grafting exotic hybrids.

He pointed with pride at a particular plant. "Grew that Pirate King Crimson Glory for the orchid festival in Bombay. Bloody first place."

I tried to appear interested and impressed, but so far I had absolutely no feel for this guy. So I looked to Roger for help.

"What can you tell us about the death of Davide Andrazack?" Broadway said, sledgehammering the question with absolutely no preamble.

"I'm a cultural attaché working to get the Leningrad ballet and symphony booked into the Dorothy Chandler Pavilion for the season. That's all I'm focused on right now."

You're a cultural attaché like I'm a proctologist," Emdee said, showing him a set of brown teeth, but no humor. "You went to his funeral. We got the pictures. So fuck you and your cover story. Keep it up and you'll be picking pieces of my boot outta your ass."

I thought they were misplaying this guy, coming on way too strong. Stanislov had diplomatic immunity and wasn't going to crumble because of threats or fear of an arrest. But maybe that was the reason for Emdee's performance. Either way, we were already off on this game of bad cop, so I just shut up and listened.

Broadway continued. "For the last month Eddie Ringerman and Bimini Wright have been pulling bugs out of secure computers. They think you and your embassy guys are planting them."

Stan picked up an orchid. "The only bugs I worry about are mealy bugs and spider mites." He showed us some outer leaves with holes in them. "Bloody hard to kill what you can't see."

"But you *could* see Davide Andrazack. How hard would it be to kill him?" Broadway challenged.

"Such an unsophisticated question belittles you, Detective."

"There's an old rule in murder cases," Broadway pressed. "A lot of killers seem drawn to the funerals of their victims."

"I used to have some espionage connections," Stanislov allowed. "I don't deny I had a few run-ins with Davide, but it was a long time back. I went because I don't like crossing people out of my Rolodex unless I'm absolutely certain they've actually passed on."

"Sounds like horseshit," Broadway said.

Stanislov set the orchid down. "Mr. Broadway, you and I have had minimal contact over the three years I've been here. I know you believe that I'm some sort of deadly agent, doing bloody what all. But I'm just a boring cultural attaché who grows orchids, while trying to foster our Russian culture in America. If sometime, you were to have actual information and not just idle threats, I might make a transaction and trade with you. However, I'm not going to risk my residency in your country because you come over here blathering a bunch of nonsense and accusing me of a clumsy murder that we all know I'm way to smart to commit."

"Bimini Wright thinks all this has something to do with her 'Eighty-five Problem," Emdee said.

"Ms. Wright is a lying, round-heeled twat who shagged half my Moscow bureau."

Sweat was beginning to trickle down my back as I stood in the hot greenhouse. Roger and Emdee weren't getting anywhere with their bulldog approach, so I decided to try another angle.

"What about Samoyla and Igor Petrovitch?" I asked. "Our department has a very thick file on them. Some people in our counterintelligence unit actually believe that they work for you."

"I don't believe I've heard of them. Are they involved in the arts?" His expression didn't change, but there was a smile in his wet, brown eyes.

"Blood artists," I said. "And if we ran them through a CIA check, your name would start popping up everywhere. But it's all ancient Kremlin stuff. I don't think they quite fit this new calling of yours. They probably make too much trouble for a man of your obvious refinement. I think you might hate the trouble they cause for your own people over here."

His eyes gave away nothing, so I went on.

"Maybe there's a way we could take care of some of that for you. Arrest the Petrovitchs and ship them off to some slam dance academy, where they'll remain permanently incarcerated."

He stood very still. "Finally, in all this hot air comes a useful idea," he said. "I have wondered many times, why your country let these two mobsters stay. Of course, when you examine it, there can only be one answer. Somebody important is profiting from their activities. If I were you, I might look into that."

"You haven't answered my question," I said.

"Your question is a political conundrum with many permutations. If you care to be more specific about how we might cooperate on such a project, then yes, maybe I'm interested. It's got to make sense, however."

Broadway looked at me and shook his head slightly. Stanislov saw it.

"No?" he said, then set down his watering can. "Okay, if that's everything, I have a dance audition at ten-forty."

He turned and led us out of the greenhouse to the front door. I stopped him before he showed us out.

"Sammy and Iggy both live in expensive houses in Bel Air. There must be lots of money coming in to afford those ten-million-dollar spreads. What businesses are they in?"

"They take what isn't theirs."

I thought it was all he was going to say, but then he added: "By the way, they don't just have those two houses in Bel Air. The Petrovitches also own a villa up at New Melones Lake in central California. I've often thought that if that lake were dredged, it would give up the bones of many disillusioned people."

50

THAT PRETTY MUCH sucked," Broadway complained.

"Maybe if you hadn't taken out your street baton and started raising knots on his head, we would a done a little better," I countered.

"Don't let the fey Brit accent fool you," Roger cautioned. "Bam-Bam killed his share of cowboys. He's deadly as an E-Street gangster. You gotta go at him head-on. Besides, it's almost impossible to role-play spooks with political immunity. He probably wasn't going to give us squat anyway."

Perry nodded, chewing on a toothpick. The three of us were sitting at a concrete picnic table on the long wooden pier that stretched out from the beach into the ocean at Santa Monica. The structure included an amusement park and restaurants, which were almost empty at this hour of the morning. A ten-foot hurricane break from a storm in Mexico was rolling in, pounding the sand, slamming against the concrete pilings. Not that we were overly paranoid, but we chose this location because even with a powerful directional mike, it would be next to impossible for the feds, or anyone else, to record our conversation over the crashing surf.

"I'm open to suggestions," Roger said. He had bought a hotdog from a vendor and was peeling back the paper.

"You know what this feels like?" I said. "Feels like everybody is holding a piece of the same puzzle, but we're all so locked into security concerns, the bunch of us will never put the damn thing together.

"We need to bring these people together. The Russians, Israelis, and the CIA. Get them all talking to each other and to us."

"You ain't gonna get Bam-Bam Stan and Bimini Wright in the same room together 'less you turn off the lights, and give 'em both switchblades," Emdee drawled.

Roger took a big bite of the hotdog and added, "Their rivalry is personal. Goes all the way back to the eighties in Moscow."

"What if we start the bidding by throwing something useful on the table? Give them a couple of good pieces of our intel."

"You're loadin' the wrong wagon, Joe Bob. We ain't got nothing they want," Perry said.

"We got the ballistics match on the five-forty-five automatic that could end up putting Sammy behind two murders. If Stanislov wants to get rid of the Petrovitches like he said, that gun could do it."

"You nuts? We can't give these people that part of our case." Broadway stopped chewing and his mouth fell open in astonishment.

"Close your fuckin' mouth," Perry said. "Bad enough I gotta look at ya without watchin' that mess a chaw get goobered."

Broadway swallowed and shook his head. "If we give that information to Stanislov, and it turns out he was lying and the

Petrovitches really are working for him off the books, then that murder weapon gets dumped in the ocean and we'll never make our case."

"I didn't say it was perfect, but we need to find a way to unstick this."

Broadway threw the half-eaten hotdog in the trash. Apparently, I'd destroyed his appetite.

"They won't come to a meeting, no matter what we give 'em," he finally said.

"We don't know that," I persisted. "Look, we're out of moves, and with Homeland circling us, we gotta set up something fast."

Suddenly, Perry snapped his fingers and we both turned.

"How 'bout we call in your Uncle Remus," he said to Roger.

"We don't have a warrant to plant a bug, and he won't wire one up without court paper. I ain't ready to put my badge in Lucite," Roger said, referring to the department's practice of encasing a cop's badge in a block of plastic as a souvenir to take home after he left the force.

"Not plant a bug, dickhead. I'm thinking Remus should just turn one of his old ones back on."

"Who the hell is Uncle Remus?" I asked.

"Ain't named Remus," Broadway said. "That's just what this gap-toothed cracker calls him. He's talkin' about my Uncle Kenny. He's an electronic plumber for the National Security Agency in L.A. When NSA gets a warrant to plant a bug, Kenny and his technical engineers do the black bag job; go into the location at midnight and plant the pastries. These boys are real craftsmen. Dig up floors and run fiber-optic cable all through the walls. Got electronics so small, the lenses and mikes are no bigger than computer chips. They plaster everything up, paint it over, and leave the space just like before. In less than eight hours, they got the place wired up better'n a Christmas window and you'd never know they were ever there."

"So how does that help us?" I asked.

"After the cases go to court, most of this shit is never pulled out," Broadway explained. "It's usually too dangerous to go back and remove the hardware, so they just turn it off and leave it. Uncle Kenny's got deactivated bugs in buildings all over town. The beauty of Perry's idea is, maybe since the bugs are already in place, we don't need a warrant to turn one back on." He looked at Emdee.

"It's a unique concept, untested by law," Perry answered. "Who knows? I'm saying we don't."

"I still don't get it," I said, wondering how random bugs in buildings around town helped us.

"Since the bugs ain't where the Petrovitches are," Perry said, grinning. "All we gotta do is get the Petrovitches to the *bugs*."

Then he told us what he had in mind. It was smart but also risky. There was no way our bosses in the department would ever sanction it. That meant we'd have to run a dangerous operation off the books without LAPD backup.

We sat on the pier feeling the warm sun and the thundering surf.

Finally, I stood and said, "Okay, but if we're gonna do this, we need to find somebody to watch our six."

"Except, we can't go to Alexa, Cubio, or Tony," Broadway said. That means we've gotta get these intelligence agencies to help us."

"We can't have dickwads and liars holding our back," Emdee argued.

"We've got no choice," I said. "Sooner or later, we're all gonna be dead anyway."

51

I'D BEEN AWAY from home way too long, and tomorrow was going to be a busy, dangerous day, so I decided to sleep in my own bed tonight and make love to my wife. I also wanted to sit down and have a long talk with Chooch.

I exited the freeway on Abbot Kinney Boulevard, then glanced in my rearview mirror. Coming down the off-ramp several cars back, was a familiar vehicle. A white Econoline van.

Zack?

I doubled back, made two quick rights, and came around behind it. But the van took off, accelerating up the street. It shot through a light just as it was changing, and I got totally blocked. I never got close enough to read the plate. All I could do was watch in frustration as the taillights headed back onto the freeway and disappeared.

Almost immediately, my mind started to deconstruct the incident. I hadn't actually seen the driver or plate number, so how did I really know it was Zack? How many white Econoline vans were there in Los Angeles anyway? And here's a big one. How could Zack know I'd be on that freeway at that exact time? Wasn't it more probable that it was just some random white van that sped up to beat the light?

I was trying to smooth it over, to make it go away so I wouldn't have to deal with it. But somewhere deep down, I already knew the answer.

It was Zack and he was coming after me.

I approached my house from the Grand Canal sidewalk, pausing to look around before opening the white picket gate and heading across my backyard. If Zack or the feds were following me, coming home could be a major mistake, but I needed to be near the people I loved and who loved me. I moved to the sliding glass porch door and found it locked. Just as I getting ready to go around to the front and use my key, Delfina appeared in the living room holding Franco in her arms. She spotted me through the glass, ran across the carpet, and opened the slider.

"Shane," she said, leaning forward and kissing my cheek. "I'm so glad you're out of the hospital! But Alexa said you wouldn't be coming home."

"Changed my mind."

Franco was stretching out a welcoming paw, so Delfina handed the marmalade cat over. As soon as I took him, he started purring and nuzzling my chest. It's nice to be wanted.

"Guess what?" Delfina said. "This afternoon we got a call from Pete Carroll. He wants Chooch to come to the school next week and meet all the coaches. It's an official visit. Chooch thinks it means they're going to offer him a full scholarship. If he wants to go there, he needs to sign a letter of intent by February fourth.

"That's great!" I said, happy that it was finally working out.

"He's in his room calling the world," she laughed.

I walked into the makeshift garage bedroom. Chooch hung up the phone and turned as I entered.

"Dad, it's so cool you came home tonight," he beamed. "Mom said you were undercover for a few days. You gotta hear what just happened!" One sentence fell on top of the next.

"Del just told me."

"Is this sweet?" A grin spread, lighting his handsome face.

"You bet it is."

I put Franco down and sat on the foot of Chooch's bed as he spun his chair around to face me.

"Y'know, Dad, I've been going over what you said, and you getting hurt and going in the hospital sorta put a lot of this in perspective. I think you were right about most of what you said."

"I was?"

"Yeah, about using football so people would think I was special. But that's only part of it."

He paused and furrowed his brow. I knew he was coming to an important realization so I sat back and waited.

"When I was a kid growing up with Sandy, it wasn't like she was even my mother," he finally said. "She was always off doing whatever, and she had me stashed at one boarding school or another, always safely out of the way, so I wouldn't judge her. But I was so young I didn't understand it was about her. I thought it was about me. I thought I wasn't important enough to her."

I understood what he was saying. When I first met Sandy Sandoval in the late eighties, she was a high-priced L.A. call girl who I had eventually recruited as a civilian undercover to work high-profile criminals. She was Hispanic, and so beautiful that people often turned to stare whenever she entered a room. Because of her looks, she had no trouble getting my criminal targets to confide in her once she had them in bed. In return for any information that led to a bust, she would collect an amount from LAPD equal to half of the money we had spent trying to catch that particular criminal in the proceeding year. It often came to several hundred thousand dollars. She was making ten times more as a UC than she ever had as a call girl. Sandy and I only made love one time, but without my knowing it, that union had produced Chooch. For the first fifteen years of his life, before I knew he was mine, Sandy had more or less ditched him, putting him in expensive boarding schools so he wouldn't be exposed to her line of work. The day she died three years ago, she told me that I was his father. Chooch grew up feeling angry and rejected, much as I had. This history had produced insecurities in him, and that's what he was talking about.

"So I guess in some ways you're right," he continued. "Having everybody saying I'm good at football, well it just felt real good to me, y'know?"

"Son, I know. I've been there."

"But I've been acting like a total jerk. And you're absolutely right about my Montebello game. It was lousy. Who do I think I'm kidding, saying Terrell Bell has rotten footwork and a bad arm? The guy is great, and I'm scared he'll beat me out if he goes to USC. With two Heisman-winning quarterbacks in five years, they're really loaded at that position. Terrell's not my problem. *I'm* my problem. If I want to succeed, all I have to do is make myself better. I've got a lot to learn from these other guys, and if I get the scholarship, I'm gonna go in with the right attitude. I'm gonna be a team player, 'cause I really love this game, Dad, and it does come from the inside."

"That's the right way to look at it, son." I was incredibly proud of him.

"You and Alexa are invited on Sunday of my weekend visit. They're gonna take us around the athletic department to meet the staff and show us the facilities."

"I'll be there." I only hoped I'd be alive to keep the promise.

Alexa came home at eight o'clock and was surprised to find me sitting in the backyard. She walked outside shaking her head slightly.

"Is this smart?"

"I don't know. Probably not."

"Honey, I think you need to leave," she said.

"Not exactly the response I was hoping for."

I stood up and kissed her. Her arms went around me, and for a moment we clung to each other.

"Since I don't trust the phones, I figured I'd tell you this in person," I said.

She held my hand and waited.

"I need you to get a search team up to New Melones Lake in Central California and drag the bottom for Calvin Lerner's body. I think he may be down there, wired to an anchor. If he is, and if he was shot in the head like Davide Andrazack, then maybe we can tie the bullet to Sammy's five-point-four-five automatic."

"Drag the whole lake. That's gonna cost a fortune. There's over a hundred miles of waterfront."

"The Petrovitches have a house up there. Get somebody to check with the real estate tax board and find out where it is. Then start somewhere near the house. These guys are so arrogant, I wouldn't be surprised if they just threw Lerner's body off the end of their dock."

She nodded, then said, "I'm trying to get you the warrant, but I'm afraid it's not going to be what you want. It'll be pretty narrow. The judge wrote it for tax records only, and limited it to Patriot Petroleum, which is one of their companies like you thought."

"Sammy won't have an old KGB assassination pistol hidden in his office. If it's anywhere, it's in his house."

"I know, but I set this up using your gas tax idea. The judge wouldn't write a warrant on their houses. This isn't like a FISA court where we can get whatever we want. I had to twist Judge Bennett's arm to even get it at all. I hardly had any PC." Alexa pulled her hand away. "So far the only address we have for the damn company is a post office box in Reseda. Maybe the fucking gun is locked up there." She was getting frustrated.

"Okay, okay. Don't get hot. I'll get an address for the warrant."

"I'm not hot, I'm worried because I think I know what you're up to."

"No, you don't."

"You don't really give a shit about these tax records. It's a nothing financial crime, and at worst the Petrovitches will only get a lousy eighteen months. You're not going through all this just to drop a pound and a half on them. Since finding the gun is now pretty much of a long shot, I think you're gonna try and piss this goon off."

"How can you say that?" I said, trying to look innocent.

"You're gonna roll over there, insult this lunatic, then lure him into an ambush and try to take him down for assault on a police officer. Once he's in custody, you're hoping to roll him on his brother. That's the dumb-ass plan, right?"

I decided if I wanted to get laid tonight, I better change the subject. So I brought up Zack.

"I don't want to talk about him right now," Alexa said.

"I think he's been following me."

"Great. It's not enough you're flipping off a leaking stick of nitro like Sammy P, but now your number one suspect for a multiple homicide is also after you. By the way, what are you doing for laughs?" She was frustrated with me, but I wasn't finished.

"Look, Alexa, to be safe, I think we need to move everybody out of here. Take a hotel room down by the beach."

"We can't afford to do that."

"We can't afford not to." I took her hand again and held it.

"Sometimes I get so weary of this." Her voice was softer now, almost pleading. "When I'm not battling with Tony and my crime stats, I'm worrying about you. I know you're doing what you feel you have to, but I wish you'd just take a job on the sixth floor so I could stop looking at my watch and wondering why you haven't called. I can't change how I feel."

I sang Billy Joel's song to her, warbling the tune comically off-key: "I want you just the way you are."

"Great." She smiled. "I wish you weren't such an impossible hard head." Then she put her head on my shoulder.

So I led her into the house.

We closed the bedroom door and slowly started to undress. Looking at Alexa, I couldn't help but think how my wife seemed more beautiful and incredible to me with each passing day. If Zack or someone else took advantage of my family, would I be able to go on? Would I have the courage to keep fighting if either she or Chooch were in serious jeopardy? I suddenly understood the wisdom of the Russian mafia rule to never marry or have children. My wife and son gave me strength and emotional stability, but they also made me extremely vulnerable.

I needed to get my family relocated tonight.

Alexa and I lay on the bed and caressed each other for a long time. I felt her breath on my neck, her hands on my back.

She turned her face up to mine and kissed me.

"Darling," she said. "I'm so afraid. Sometimes I think if I lost you, I couldn't go on." Voicing my exact fears.

I knew how vulnerable we both were to misadventure and my heart suddenly raced. I vowed to protect us, even at the expense of my own life.

We began to make love, slowly taking each other higher and further than we had ever been before. As we coupled, the intense pleasure of desire, primal and pure, washed over us. I wanted to be closer than our bodies would allow. It was almost as if I needed to be her, to wear her skin as my own. In this act of love, the longing and closeness we shared made me crave even more.

Afterwards, we lay on the bed listening to the innocent sounds of our home. The kids were laughing about something in the living room. The TV was blaring. The normalcy of all this was a bitter contrast to my lingering fears.

"I think you're right. We need to get out of this house," Alexa said, sitting up and looking at me. "I don't trust it here right now."

We dressed and went out to tell the kids to pack; that we were spending the night somewhere else.

The phone rang. I caught it on the fifth one. It was Roger Broadway. He told me that the Financial Crimes Division had just called him back with troubling news on their reactivated investigation into Americypher. Ten months ago, Calvin Lerner's widow had sold controlling interest in the company to an offshore Bahamian corporation called Washington Industries. I wondered what that meant, but told Roger I'd call him back once I was resettled.

As I was locking the house five minutes later, Alexa slid into her department slick-back with Franco purring on the seat beside her. Chooch and Del piled into his Jeep. They pulled both vehicles out, headed for The Shutters Hotel on the beach in Santa Monica.

I followed half a block behind them in my Acura, on the lookout for gray sedans with government plates, while also scanning the road for any glimpse of a white Econoline van.

52

KENNETH BROADWAY WAS a broad-shouldered, fifty-year-old man with ebony skin, and the deepest-set eyes I'd ever seen. He had a megawatt smile that could instantly light his semi-serious face. He was standing next to his nephew, Roger Broadway. Emdee Perry was facing them, his back to a two-story building located across from the Coast Highway in Long Beach. I pulled in, got out, and was introduced.

It was ten o'clock the next morning.

We were a block from the ocean, a mile northwest of the old Long Beach Naval Yard. The empty, warehouse-sized building we were parked in front of was dominated by a giant, two-story high, rooftop cutout of a slightly cartoonish blonde of extraordinary proportions. She was a luscious creature with overdone curves, wearing platform heels and a painted-on black miniskirt.

Large corny lettering proclaimed our location as the West Coast factory for Lilli's Desert-Style Dresses.

"Lilli is Butch Lilli. Human dirt," Roger Broadway said. "He's currently doing a nickel in Soledad. This was his front. We took it down in two thousand three when I was still in Narcotics. The guy moved a shit-load a flake outta here. The upstairs is nothing but a big room full of long sewing tables. He made the *brasseros* who bagged his dope in cellophane twists work in their undies, so he'd be sure they couldn't steal any powder."

Kenny boasted, "I put more cameras and mikes in this joint than they've got over at NBC Burbank."

Emdee Perry had the key from the real estate agent and he opened up. We walked into a dim, musty, downstairs corridor decorated with cheap wood paneling and years of petrified rat shit.

"If you guys wanta use this place, we'll need to turn the electricity back on so you'll have enough light to get a video image," Kenny said, as he led us up the stairs. "I kept meaning to come over here and pull the electronics out, but I did this job off the books for Rog, so I had to be cool about it. It's all outdated anyway. We don't use fiber-optic cable anymore. It's voice-activated radio transmitters now. This stuff still works, but it's three generations past prime."

We entered a large open area on the second floor. Sewing tables stretched the entire length of the room—perfect for making dresses or bagging cocaine.

"Uncle Ken put five cameras in here," Broadway said. "It was great, because Butch Lilli loved to bring his dirtbag dealers up and show them the operation. Ran the sting for six months before we took the joint down. Forty coka-mokes hit the lockup."

"See if you can find a camera," Kenny said, with a tinge of professional pride. "I'll give ya a hint. It's right there." He pointed at a place on the wall.

I walked over and studied the spot where he was pointing, but couldn't find it. Then he came over and showed me where a piece of plaster had been chipped four feet up from the baseboard.

"That little dot there," he said, proudly.

"That's a camera?" I could barely see the pinhole.

Kenneth nodded. "Fiber-optic line on this bug runs down a channel we cut in this concrete column here, then behind that baseboard, down the air shaft, out into the lot. When we did this sting, Roger parked one of the ESD minivans in the culvert forty yards to the east, loaded brush all over the thing, and then plugged everything into monitors we put in the van. Television City."

We walked the room. "This is gonna work good," Perry said, studying the layout. "It sits out here all alone. The Odessa *bandas* will like it. If I was gonna stomp your gonads, Shane, this is where I'd do it."

"I'm beginning to have second thoughts," I said, a cold chill descending. "I'm not doing this unless we get some decent backup."

"No problemo, Joe Bob." Then Emdee shot me a yellow-toothed smile. "Once we set that up, all ya gotta do is get Sammy out here and get him talkin' before he kills ya."

"What makes you so sure he's gonna chase me down here?" I asked.

"Sammy's got no impulse control," Emdee explained. "He's a gag reflex with balls. We got ten pages of withdrawn complaints to prove it. Piss him off and he'll come after ya. No insult goes unpunished. It's his thing."

I looked around. "This place is pretty deserted. If he's gonna fall for this, it's gotta look like I'm here to meet someone. I can't just come to an abandoned building way out in butt-fuck-nowhere, and wait around to get captured. He'll know it's a setup. One of you guys is gonna have to be up here waiting so it looks like we're having a meet."

"I'd do it, but my back's been acting up," Broadway grinned.

"You ain't gonna skip out that easy," Perry said.

"Okay, what then?" Broadway said. "Draw straws? Eenie-meenie-miny-mo? If we measure dicks you know you lose."

"Ahhh, yes," Perry grinned. "The old African dick myth." He pulled a coin out of his pocket. "Call it," he said, and flipped.

"Tails," Broadway said as the coin hit the floor, and spun for a moment before lying down.

Tails.

"Okay, Emdee's in here waiting for me." I looked at Broadway. "You're in the van outside with whatever backup we can score this afternoon. If Rowdy and I look like we're about to get harp lessons, you gotta make some big-ass trouble, man."

"I got your six," Roger assured me.

I looked over at Perry. "Let's stash some guns up here, just in case."

We both pulled our nines and started looking for a place to hide them. I found a spot under one of the sewing tables near the cameras, and taped up my Beretta using a roll of silver duct tape I'd brought in my briefcase. Perry had a big .357 Desert Eagle that he taped behind a heater six feet away.

We all went downstairs and watched as Kenneth Broadway reactivated the bugs. He turned on each camera and checked it on a portable monitor for picture and sound, then ran some fresh cable from the building outlet through the brush to the spot in a gully where one of his NSA surveillance vans was parked. Inside the vehicle was a bank of monitors.

After two hours, we were ready to go.

I unfolded the warrant that Alexa had procured, and showed it around. "Open warrant for the tax records on Patriot Petroleum once we find where the damn company is located. They're not listed, so we're checking with the IRS. We can forget looking for the gun 'cause he won't have it at his office. I'll just raise as much hell as I can and blow outta there."

"Whatever you do, make sure you get all the way down here," Broadway cautioned me. "I wish this place was closer, but tactically this is the best location that was prewired and fit all the other parameters. If they pick you up before you make it here, you're pretty much up on The Wall."

The Wall was the marble monument to dead police officers located in the main lobby at Parker Center. Hundreds of brass nameplates were mounted under a plaque that read: "E.O.W." End of Watch. Every name on display had died in the line of duty. One of my main career goals had always been to stay off that damn wall.

I was praying Stanislov Bambarak, Eddie Ringerman, and Bimini Wright were going to help me keep that goal alive.

53

I'M BLOODY TIRED of waiting," Stan said, glaring at his watch. "Give us a bell if you ever decide to get serious about this."

We were standing on the end of the Santa Monica Pier in the blazing noontime sun waiting for the others to arrive. Both of us had our coats off. A quarter mile up the beach I could see the Shutters Hotel where I stayed with my family last night. Just as Stan turned to go, Broadway's car pulled up and parked. Roger got out, and then the passenger door opened, and Bimini Wright, looking very hot in a sundress and heels, joined him. They started walking toward us.

"What's she doing here?" Stanislov glowered at the beautiful CIA station chief who was now only twenty or thirty yards away.

"Calm down, Stan."

He threw his coat over his shoulder and started to walk away.

I grabbed his arm. "I told you I had something that would interest you. You don't get to hear it unless you stick around."

"Not interested."

This was in danger of unraveling before it got started, so I said, "What if I can put Sammy Petrovitch in Pelican Bay for murder? I also have a decent shot at getting his brother Iggy on conspiracy to commit."

Stanislov stopped walking and looked at me. "If you could really do that, we bloody well wouldn't be standing out here gassing about it, would we?"

"Don't be so sure."

But I had him interested, so I went ahead and told him about the ballistics match on the bullet that killed Martin Kobronovitch. "If Sammy was the triggerman on both hits, and if we match the bullets to a gun in his possession, he's gone."

"Those are big ifs," Stan said. He shifted his weight and looked at Bimini Wright, who slowed as she approached. You could feel the negativity jolting back and forth between them like deadly arcs of electricity.

"Roger," she said, looking at the handsome African-American detective, as they came to a stop where we were standing. "You didn't say anything about this son-of-a-bitch being here. If he's involved, I'm gone."

"Strange remark from a woman who flat-backed half my Moscow Bureau," Stanislov growled nastily.

"Hey, Stan, it's not my fault all you recruited was a bunch of alcoholic hard-ons."

Just then, out of the corner of my eye, I saw Emdee Perry approaching with Eddie Ringerman. It distracted Bimini and Stan, and they both turned as the two men approached.

"Now we got the whole, bloomin' free world," Stan groused.

"I already filled Eddie in on what we're up to," Emdee said as they joined us.

"Anybody want a Coke or something?" Broadway offered, ever the perfect host.

"Let's just get this over with," Bimini snapped.

"To start with, I want to compare notes on one fact," I said quickly before our guests sprinted to their cars. "All of us have computer leaks. Our ESD technicians think the bugs were manufactured by a company here in L.A. called Americypher Technologies. I'm assuming your people have made similar discoveries."

"Not exactly news," Eddie Ringerman countered, removing his coat in the heat, revealing bulging biceps under his short-sleeved shirt.

"The original owner of that company, Calvin Lerner, was an Israeli national who disappeared ten years ago," I continued. "Our financial crimes investigators told us yesterday that Lerner's widow is now listed as the CEO, but she isn't really running the company. It looks like she's just some kind of management front. We also found out that Americypher is really owned by a private Bahamian holding company called Washington Industries. Our analysts haven't been able to penetrate the stockholders list yet, but since Americypher sells surveillance equipment to everyone in the intelligence community, if they're owned by the wrong people, it could be a problem."

Ringerman rocked back on his heels and glanced at Bimini Wright before responding. "You should be able to penetrate a Bahamian corporation with the IRS."

"Our Financial Crimes division thinks Washington Industries is a burn company that has all their assets and stockholder tax records in numbered accounts," I said. "They think if we lean on them too hard, they'll transfer the assets and corporate paperwork to Europe and all we'll get is a shell."

"The Petrovitches own it," Stanislov interrupted, his gravely voice almost lost on the warm breeze.

"You're sure?" I said.

"We also traced those surveillance devices," he continued. "Washington Industries funnels cash back to the Petrovitches' holding company, Patriot Industries, through a Swiss bank. You need better financial analysts."

I looked at Eddie Ringerman. Something was going on with him. He looked stricken, so I said, "Are you just an interested spectator or do you want to add to this?"

Eddie hesitated for a moment, then spoke. "Davide Andrazack found seven Americypher bugs inside our embassy and several in the ambassador's car. If the Petrovitches are secret partners in that Bahamian company, then it's a major problem because Davide found out that those bugs were reverse engineered. They operate on two frequencies. One broadcasts to the office of Homeland Security, who I guess had them installed, but the other frequency transmits to a site somewhere in Century City. Davide was murdered before he could trace it. Since then, that second receiver went dark. We tried to triangulate on it, but whoever owns it took it down. Now that it's shut off, we'll never find it." He paused, then added, "As an interesting point of fact, the Petrovitches have new offices in Century City," giving me a location for Alexa's warrant.

"Without busting that receiver, you don't have much of anything," Bimini observed.

Everybody pondered that for a moment before Stanislov said, "This is all frightfully interesting, but I don't see what any of it has to do with catching the Petrovitches."

So I told them what Roger, Emdee, and I had planned, and how we needed everybody's help to back us up if things went wrong.

When I was finished, Stanislov just stood there frowning. "Rather dicey, that," he growled. "I certainly can't involve my embassy on that kind of risky project, but I wish you blokes all the best."

Then he turned and, without another word, just lumbered off the pier. The rest of us watched him go.

"I'm afraid I'm with him," Eddie Ringerman said. "My embassy won't sign up for anything like that either. Hope you pull it off."

He followed Bambarak into the parking lot.

I felt my spirits sinking. We couldn't go it alone. That left only Bimini Wright.

"What's your excuse?" Broadway asked her.

"Shit, fellas, this is a domestic espionage situation. CIA is tasked to international cases only. I'd like to pitch in, but if I took a swing at something like this, the FBI and Homeland would shit a brick and I'd bitch up a twenty-year ride. Sorry."

She turned and followed the other two off the pier.

Once the three of us were standing there alone, I turned to Broadway and Perry. "Whose dumb-ass idea was this anyway?" Since it was mine, nobody answered. "We could use a new plan, guys," I said. "Whatta you think?"

"I think, besides learning those bugs were set by Virtue and reverse engineered by someone, the filly looks the best going away," Emdee drawled, watching Bimini's long, sexy stride.

"We could try and recruit a CTB surveillance team," Broadway suggested. "Most of our Special Ops cowboys have more testosterone than sense. We'd have to do it without sanction and that could cause them trouble. But if we make it a challenge, maybe we could recruit a few and get them to keep it on the DL so the Loot doesn't fall on us."

The CTB surveillance teams were mostly reassigned hard-ons from SIS or SWAT who loved a good dust-up. But still, it did involve some career jeopardy.

"Okay," I told them, "but I'm not throwing down on this guy unless we have backup."

"Say no more, Joe Bob. Rowdy and Snitch always deliver."

54

TAKE THE ENTIRE top floor of a Century City high-rise; buy every bad Russian painting you can find; stick them in overdone gilt frames, then hire Donald Trump's decorator, and you have a reasonable idea of what the offices of Petrovitch Industries looked like. There was enough nude statuary and crystal swag to decorate every whorehouse in New Orleans.

The receptionist was a beautiful Russian girl with flawless skin, piercing eyes, and a sculpted jaw. She also had a bitchy attitude and a graceful swan neck acceptable for wringing.

I was standing with Danny Dark and Sid Cooper, two detectives from the Financial Crimes Division. They were both carrying thick briefcases with notebook computers inside.

"And this is regarding?" my Russian goddess asked. Only the

slightest sound of the Ukraine still remained in her clipped, chilly presentation.

"I will only discuss it with Samoyla himself," I said.

"And he won't agree to see you unless you first state the nature of your business," she replied coldly. Ice started to form on the mirror behind her.

I laid my temporary creds down on the marble desk. "See if you can get Mr. Petrovitch to change his mind so he won't have to take an uncomfortable ride chained to the inside of a big gray bus."

"Really?" she said, arching plucked eyebrows as if she would really like to see me try that.

I held my ground under the weight of her disapproving stare, but after a second she folded, and deserted her post like an Afghan army regular. On her way past, she reached for my ID and started to leave with it. I grabbed her wrist.

"Where are you going with that?"

"I have to show Mr. Petrovitch."

"You don't get to take it. You tell him you saw it and then he gets to come and see it for himself. That's the way it works." I was playing it very ballsy and tough for a guy in a Kmart suit, standing in a lobby surrounded by two million dollars worth of crystal and art. But what the hey. You gotta believe in yourself, as I'm so fond of telling everyone.

After a minute, the receptionist departed and the three of us were left alone to study a huge lobby painting of thousands of Cossacks on horseback charging across a wooded field. Glorious carnage and romantic death.

We waited for almost five silent minutes before the Russian princess returned. "If you're the one in charge, he'll see only you," she intoned coldly.

I turned to the financial dicks. "You guys wait here while I get this guy set up."

She led me away from Cooper and Dark, down a hallway full of art depicting the Greats. Peter, Ivan, and Alexander. The Russians have produced a lot of Greats. Most of them in braided jackets with warlike personas.

I was ushered through a Russian Barbie section where half a dozen beautiful blonde secretaries, all perfectly groomed with arched backs and jutting breasts typed diligently at computers. I followed my princess into an executive suite that faced the Avenue of the Stars. A Louis XV desk and a high-backed swivel chair covered with expensive gold brocade sat- in front of a glass wall overlooking the street twenty stories below.

"He'll be here shortly," she clipped. Almost no accent this time. I had to really strain to hear it now. She left me standing there and closed the door. After a minute alone, the side door opened and the most frighteningly ugly man I have ever seen walked into the office. His booking picture didn't begin to capture the essence of him. In person, he radiated evil.

Where to begin?

He was a dermatological mess—much more so than I had realized from the photograph. Scar tissue everywhere. I've seen a lot of scars, even have my share, just not ones where the crude stitching so horribly altered what had been there before. All that was left was a hideous mask. He had at the same time, both a ghoulish smile and a frightening scowl. This amazing expression was accomplished because his restitched mouth curved up on one side with a scar that ended in the middle of his left cheek. On the other side, the scowl side, the scar collapsed down from the corner of his mouth to his chin, ending at his destroyed uneven jaw line. It was as if the Riddler had gone into a psychopathic rage, ripped his own mouth wide open, then stitched the mess back together using a staple gun.

He was huge, so those metric measurements now translated to about six-foot-eight and almost three hundred fifty pounds. He had shoulders like a water buffalo and hands the size of anvils. All that was missing were the neck bolts.

"Shto tibe nado?" he said, in Russian. His voice was a strange whispery squeak from vocal cords wasted in all that carnage.

"Sammy Petrovitch?" I asked, knowing there couldn't be two like this.

"Da?"

"You speak English?" I said, wondering if it was possible that this guy could have been in the U.S. since 'ninety-five and still not speak the language.

"Ya, I speak. Vat is?" he said. It was not that his voice was high, as much as it was a whistling, muted wheeze. I'd never heard anything quite like it.

"I have a subpoena to gather up all of the records for Patriot Petroleum," I said, holding out the paperwork. He didn't look at it, didn't care about it. But that's okay. Neither did I.

"I also have two financial crimes detectives in the lobby who need access to your computers and all the electronic records and transactions for that same company."

"We have done nothing," he squeaked. "We have rights."

Time to throw sand in the giant's eyes. "The only right you have is the right to suck my dick, yakoff."

His huge, flat brow furrowed. Rage began to climb up his neck and redden his destroyed face.

"Did you hear me, dummy? You're under investigation for running a federal gas tax scam. This subpoena orders you to give my detectives full access to your computers. Then we'll see about getting you and your limp-dick brother, Igor, downtown to answer some more important felony charges."

The first part of our plan was to insult him. Get him operating on impulse so he'd make a mistake and follow me after I left. It never occurred to me that this guy might decide to just flat out whack me right under the crystal chandelier in his overdecorated antique office. But apparently that's what he planned, because without warning, he started a murderous shuffling advance across the room. That ruptured face became a distorted mask of rage. His scarred lips pulled back in a snarl, exposing teeth, big and square as tombstones.

I don't like giving up ground under any circumstance, but in that instant Sammy Petrovitch had me spooked. I was now close enough to read unchecked insanity in his stone gray eyes. He had at least a hundred fifty pounds and five inches on me, so I started backpedaling until I slammed into a paneled wall and rocked an oil painting. One of the female greats—Catherine, was hanging from a hook in a thousand-dollar gilt frame, looking down her aristocratic nose at me.

Sammy took another shuffle step, then paused, bringing both hands up into some kind of combat strike position, methodically sizing me up, deciding how he was going to annihilate me.

"Back up, asshole," I commanded. "You touch me, I'm taking you in for aggravated assault on a police officer."

It didn't begin to dampen his enthusiasm. He shuffled in closer. His eyes glinted with pre-combat intensity.

This wasn't going at all as I planned.

Just then the side door burst open and out of the corner of my eye, I saw another man moving into the office. "Samoyla! *Stoi! Shto ti delaesh? Nyet!*" he shouted, as he grabbed Sammy and pulled him back.

I was propped up against the brown paneling next to a disapproving Catherine the Great, who was still swinging wildly from her hook.

"Who are you?" the man demanded. Judging from the expensive suit and the size of his diamonds, it was Iggy. He was one third smaller than his brother with a strong face and greased-back hair that was the texture and color of poured concrete. He looked nothing like Sammy. But then a Stinger missile in Afghanistan had forever ended the notion of any sibling resemblance.

"What do you want?" he said, his English far better than his brother's.

"I have a subpoena for records on Patriot Petroleum," I said, holding it out. "You and your company are being audited by the LAPD for financial crimes."

Iggy snatched the paperwork out of my hands and glanced at it. "Our attorneys will deal with this. You go."

"Not that easy," I answered. "This ape was threatening to attack me. A threat of violence constitutes felonious assault." Sammy was rocking from side to side, his eyes had now gone slightly blank, someone not in complete possession of his faculties.

I certainly hadn't been ready for the mammoth insanity of Samoyla Petrovitch.

"He did not touch you. You have served your papers. It is done and you go. This is America. We know our rights," Iggy said.

"I love it when you noncitizen mob assholes throw your American rights around," I growled. "That's a real crack-up. From now on, I'm gonna make you a full-time project," I said, glaring at Sammy. "You're both Priority One on my shit list. I'll stay on it until I get both of you either jailed or deported back to Odessa. There are two officers from the financial division in your lobby. They need a place to work. You give them everything this warrant calls for or I'll be back here with another fucking warrant for obstruction of justice and failure to comply with a legally obtained court order. You don't want to test me on this."

I moved toward the door, paused on the threshold for a moment and looked at them, trying to judge my jeopardy and how much damage I'd done.

Sammy and Iggy were both glowering, standing side by side in a nice little homicidal tableau.

"This is the beginning of the end for you two pukes. When I'm through, you're both gonna be chained to a wall."

Samoyla lurched forward, but Iggy pulled him back. I turned and exited the office, heading down the gilded hallway past the Greats, into the lobby. Behind me, I could hear voices yelling angrily in Russian. A door slammed somewhere in the hall.

"What the fuck is that all about?" Detective Cooper said, looking a little alarmed.

"This isn't going to be exactly like running an audit on Enron," I told them. "These guys are a little looser than I thought. I'm going to radio for some Blues to come in here to watch your back. Stay frosty till they arrive, then make as much trouble as you can."

More Russian shouting leaked out into the lobby.

"I'm outta here," I said, and stepped into the elevator and pushed the button. As the doors closed I heard more shouting and doors slamming.

The Acura was parked in a red zone in front of the building with my handcuffs draped over the steering wheel so I wouldn't get towed. It's the universal signal to traffic cops identifying a detective's car. Once I was inside with the engine running, I called dispatch and ordered immediate backup for Cooper and Dark. Then I waited to see if Sammy was as nuts as Emdee said.

He was.

Three minutes later a black Cadillac exploded out of the underground parking garage and turned in my direction. There were four burly guys, including Sammy, packed cheek to jowl inside. All were wearing strained blank expressions. They spotted me as they sailed past. Brake lights flashed. The Cadillac skidded to a stop and began a Y-turn, coming back after me.

55

THE BLACK CADDY was only four cars back, tracking me on the 405. It was the worst tail since Hef designed the bunny costume. At any given moment, I could see them in two of my three rearview mirrors.

Somewhere near San Pedro I caught sight of a white, windowless Econoline van.

Please don't let that be Zack, I thought. *I've got enough trouble right now without adding him to the mix.*

I lost sight of the van when I exited the freeway and turned left onto the Coast Highway heading toward the recently decommissioned and razed Long Beach Naval Yard.

The massive property slid by outside my left window—hundreds of acres of freshly paved parking lots loaded with multicolored marine shipping containers.

I looked back. The black Cadillac was now caught at a light; so, without making it look too obvious, I slowed down and timed it so I missed the next signal. Then I spotted the Cad coming up on me again. Sammy must have somehow reined in all that homicidal rage because they were being more careful now, staying further back.

Up ahead loomed the two-story-high, curvaceous blonde cutout in her black miniskirt. I pulled into the abandoned dress company parking lot and stopped next to the entrance of the main office. Then I stepped out of my car and headed toward the building.

I took the stairs two at a time, quickly reaching the second floor. When I got to the sewing room, Emdee was waiting.

"They follow you?" he said, looking out the window.

"Yeah. You were sure right about Sammy. He almost unpacked me right there in his own office. If his brother hadn't walked in, I wouldn't have made it out of there."

"If they followed you, then we're in business, Joe Bob."

So we waited.

I walked over to one of the camera positions and spoke into the pinhole to Roger who was in the ESD van out back with four CTB surveillance guys he'd recruited. I brought Roger up to date, told him the Russians were about to make their move.

But nothing happened.

Emdee and I sat around until well after sunset. Then we walked downstairs and checked the parking lot and the road out front.

No sign of the black Caddy anywhere.

Finally we climbed down to the ESD van hidden in the culvert. I knocked on the back door. Roger opened up. The four CTB surveillance team members inside were all wearing black Kevlar with heavy ordnance strapped to their sides.

"He didn't take the bait," I said.

"What the fuck is wrong with that boy?" Roger said.

We turned the surveillance team loose and watched them drive out of the parking lot in their black Suburban.

"So what do we do now?" Emdee asked after they were gone.

"We regroup," I said, softly.

56

I HEADED BACK to the Shutters Hotel in Santa Monica. All the way there I kept my eyes on the rearview mirror. No white vans. No black Cadillacs.

Before transitioning onto the Santa Monica Freeway I pulled a lane change maneuver that an old motorcycle officer in the traffic division taught me. He swore it would shake any tail. You stay in the fast lane going about sixty and look for a pattern in traffic that allows you to abruptly cross all four lanes in one move, and shoot down an off-ramp. No car following will be able to find a similar hole and will overshoot the exit.

I executed the maneuver twice and then drove on surface streets to Shutters, which sits right on Santa Monica Beach and, in my opinion, is one of the most delightful little hotels in Southern California.

I handed over my car to the valet and went upstairs to our ocean-view suite on the second floor. Delfina and Chooch were both inside doing their homework.

"Hi. Where's Mom?" I asked, as I came through the door.

"Gonna be late," Chooch said. "She called and said she wants us to get dinner without her."

Franco was out on the balcony leering at seagulls swooping in over his head, turning back and forth, watching them with hungry eyes. I got a beer from the minibar and joined him. The beautiful white sand beach stretched out beyond the bike path where the surf thundered in, making turquoise and white foam. Off to the right was the Santa Monica Pier where we had our disastrous noontime meeting.

I sat on the balcony taking in the view as the afternoon sun set; thinking about the events of the afternoon.

A wasted day.

Worse still, we'd exposed ourselves without any result and put the Russian mob on alert, giving them the opportunity to destroy key evidence.

So far, nobody at Parker Center had been told how badly we'd screwed up, but I knew I was going to have to fill Alexa in when she arrived.

The phone rang, so I walked inside to answer.

"Good, you're there," Alexa said. "How'd it go?"

"Terrific," I lied, chickening out, telling myself I'd rather give her the bad news in person. "I left Cooper and Dark down there to scan the computers and dig out anything they can find on the forged gas tax records."

"Yeah. I know. I got a call from the Petrovitches' attorney. Some Eastern Euro shyster named Sebastian Sebura. He's been all over us with temporary restraining orders and show cause writs. Guy's a real meat grinder. I called Detective Cooper. He says, so far, it looks like a grunion hunt. If they're running a gas tax fraud, they have it pretty well papered over. I told Tony I wouldn't pull them out without your okay, but everybody down here thinks it's a wasted play."

"Take 'em out," I sighed. "I'm gonna work on coming up with something else."

"I think that's a good idea," she said, then hesitated, adding, "Listen, we found out who planted all those bugs in the Glass House. A tech in ESD named Ivan Roson—short for Rosonovitch. He hanged himself two hours before he was scheduled to take his polygraph. It's a circus down here. We're working on a statement for the press. Take the kids down to the Pier and get them something to eat. That fancy restaurant downstairs is nice, but it's a little pricey for our budget."

I told her I loved her, and we hung up.

At a little past eight, the kids and I left the hotel and walked along the beachfront bike path to the pier. It was a warm night and now there were hundreds of people milling around on the rebuilt wooden structure. I bought Delfina and Chooch hotdogs and ice cream, and we sat on a bench, not a hundred yards from where I'd sat that morning. Funny how savvy our plan seemed, just eight hours ago. Now it felt like total nonsense.

"Hey, Dad, wanta go on the Ferris wheel with us?" Chooch asked, after finishing his food.

"Yes, Shane. Come with us," Delfina pleaded.

"You guys go. I've had a bad day. Got a lot on my mind."

"You've been really quiet," Del said. "Maybe if you tell us, we can help."

"You guys help by just being here. Go ride the wheel. I'll buy a camera and get some pictures."

I handed them twenty dollars and they went off to get in line. I walked down the pier to a vendor's stand and bought a Kodak throwaway. As I headed back toward the big, colorful wheel, someone suddenly pressed hard against me on the right. Then a big body leaned in on the left.

"Hey," I said. "Watch where you're—"

I heard a loud *Zap*. Intense pain shot into the small of my back. When the department gave us Taser training at the academy, we were forced to take a jolt to see what it felt like. Once you've taken a Taser shot, you don't forget it. I tried to lurch away as my muscles twitched and jumped with electrical overload. I staggered forward and fell.

"My friend is having a heart attack!" somebody with an Eastern European accent shouted out in dismay.

Then three or four faces belonging to overfed men in their mid-thirties, were peering down at me.

"This way! He needs a hospital!" one with a Euro accent shouted.

They grabbed me. My muscles were still convulsing with the charge.

"No!" I tried to say as they lifted me. But my voice wouldn't work. I was helpless.

"My car's this way," another shouted. Then I was being hustled off the Pier.

They ran with me down the steps into the parking lot. We stopped in a dark area of the lot. Somebody stood me upright and held me. My muscles were chattering and my hands jerked uncontrollably. One of the men took a syringe out of his pocket, removed the plastic tip, and shoved it into my thigh, depressing the plunger, and emptying the cylinder.

In seconds my vision started to dim.

I vaguely heard a trunk open and I was dropped onto a hard, rough surface. The lid slammed shut. Everything went black.

57

I OPENED MY eyes.

I was sitting in a wooden chair.

"This is un-fucking-acceptable!" someone was yelling in American English. It was coming from another room.

I recognized that voice. Agent Kersey Nix. The mild-mannered FBI agent from the Tishman Building.

My body ached and my head buzzed like a broken radio. I tried to move, but discovered that all four of my appendages were securely taped to the chair with black electrical tape. The chair seemed to be bolted to the floor because it wouldn't budge. I looked down and saw what appeared to be dried blood on the concrete underneath me. Then I took a careful inventory of the room. I was in a garage. A single, exposed lightbulb hung from a cord in the center of the space and a black Cadillac Brougham was parked under it. Somewhere I heard the distant sound of thundering surf.

". . . He come . . . he say, 'Suck my dick, yakoff.' " It was Sammy Petrovitch complaining. "Fucking asshole—fucking piece-of-shit asshole."

"You shut up!" Nix shouted. "Talk to him, Igor. This isn't working anymore. He's gonna put our whole thing in the shredder."

"Sammy has . . . he has problems. He will get this worked out," Igor said.

"He didn't used to be like this," Nix responded.

"He say, 'suck my dick, yakoff!' I no listen to this shit—motherfucker!"

I'd really stirred up some trouble with my trip to Century City. I realized dully that I'd actually accomplished what I set out to do this morning. I'd frightened the Petrovitches enough to get them to grab me. But I'd underestimated them. They were smart enough to do it on their timetable, not mine. I wondered how they found me. While we were inside the dress company, did one of them sneak over the fence and plant another bug on my car? However it happened, they'd waited until I was separated from my backup and made their move. Now I was alone and in big trouble.

The side door into the house suddenly opened and Kersey Nix stood backlit, in the threshold. Behind him I could see a modern kitchen. He moved toward me followed by Iggy Petrovitch. Sammy loomed in the doorway, watching.

I kept thinking, *What the hell is Kersey Nix doing here?*

"You were told by Mr. Virtue to go away," he said. "Apparently, you don't hear so good."

"I'm kind of tone deaf. But I'm getting over it. I get the message now."

"Too late."

"Too bad." I took a deep breath. "Where are we?"

"A long way from L.A.," he said.

"What the hell do you and R. A. Virtue have to do with these Odessa thugs?"

"This is not a deal where you get to ask questions, asshole. You tell me what you know, then I decide what to do about it."

"I don't know anything. I'm a fuck-up. I never score."

Nix's cell phone rang. He answered. "Nix." A pause. "Yeah, they got him, sir. Zapped him on the Santa Monica Pier. Lately these guys are fuckin' outta control. I have two agents down there now, laying down some counterintelligence. Finding witnesses who saw it and telling them the guy just had an epileptic seizure. So far so good. But we've got a problem with the big guy. You or Iggy are gonna have to deal with this now. Sammy needs to go home. We need to put him on a plane tomorrow." Nix paused, then added, "Okay . . . fine . . ." Then he disconnected.

"How's Mr. Virtue?" I said, trying to sound self-assured and in control while a little puddle of flop sweat was forming under my ass.

"Okay, Scully. Here's the deal. I want to know what you know, what Broadway knows, what Perry knows, what your wife and Lieutenant Cubio know. You're gonna debrief me completely."

"None of us knows anything. We're just local cops. We're slow and stupid."

"Right now, even though you're sitting up and breathing, you're just a corpse that hasn't been buried yet. The question here, as far as you're concerned, is how you die, not *if* you die."

"I don't know anything."

"I think you're going to change your mind and come up with something. You can buy your way out of a very painful ending with a little useful information. Stonewall, and I'm gonna let Sammy fuck with your psyche."

I looked over and saw the silhouette of Samoyla Petrovitch standing in the doorway, leering with that horrible face.

"Igor, get the box," Nix said.

A moment later, Iggy Petrovitch returned carrying a black metal suitcase. He set it down and opened it. There was a strange looking device inside that had all kinds of wires and clips attached.

"What the hell is that?" I asked in panic.

"It's a polygraph," Nix said. "We're going to debrief you on the box. That way we know everything you say is righteous."

"Doesn't look like any polygraph I ever saw." There was no graph, or stylus, but it had an LD screen on the back.

"State of the art," he said softly. "You don't need to give yes or no answers on this. It reads the truth in sentences." He looked at Igor. "Hook him up."

Iggy Petrovitch grabbed my shirt and ripped it open. Buttons flew off and danced across the concrete floor. He spoke to me softly as he hooked up the skin sensors and finger clips. "You make big mistake coming to our office. There is nothing there. So you will find nothing. You say you make a project of us, now we make a project of you."

"You can't just kill a cop," I said.

"Yes we can," Iggy said softly. "We do it all the time."

Once the box was connected, he stepped back.

Nix took his place in front of me. "We're going to start with your partners, Broadway and Perry. How much of this do they know?"

I sat strapped to the chair feeling like a death row inmate.

I'd once taken a weeklong capture and survival course at Fort Bragg where we spent a day working on anti-interrogation techniques and polygraph deception. I knew if I was going to get through this, I had to lock my mind on something other than my imminent demise because fear of death would cause me to produce excessive amounts of adrenaline. Polygraph machines operate on body chemistry. A lie produces a physical response that speeds the heart and sends an impulse down your nervous system causing sweat and increased skin electricity.

If I could get my mind and emotions to quiet down, I had a better chance of focusing on a deceptive thought that would allow my responses to register as inconclusive on the machine. But everything in me wanted out of here, wanted to survive this, so I wasn't having much luck. I tried a slow breathing technique to bring my heart rate down.

"You are going to be debriefed," Nix said. "You should also be advised, I'm not beyond using extreme techniques."

With Sammy standing in the doorway, I didn't even want to speculate as to what 'extreme techniques' might include.

"Answer me. How much information do Detectives Broadway and Perry have?"

If I talked, I would be signing Roger and Emdee's death sentences. If I didn't talk, I was going to go through a very bad session here. Not a great choice, but since I was probably a lost cause anyway, I knew I'd feel a lot better about going down if I didn't give these guys anything. I set my jaw and said nothing.

"Sammy," Nix said. The big man moved out of the doorway and over to the black Cadillac. He opened the trunk. A moment later he slammed it shut and walked toward me carrying a short-handled tree limb cutter.

"What the hell is that for?" I asked.

Nix stepped aside and without warning, Petrovitch placed the limb cutter over the index finger of my taped down left hand at the first joint near the fingertip.

"You can't be serious," I managed to say as the horror of what they were about to do dawned on me.

There was no further discussion.

Sammy simply bore down with the gardening tool and cut off my fingertip. It flew off the end of my hand liked a discarded cigarette butt and hit the floor. A second later, the pain hit.

I howled. My mouth was open and somebody stuffed a rag into it, choking off my screams. I watched in horror as my mutilated finger spurted blood. As my blood mixed with the dried blood under the chair, I wondered how many people before me had sat here and gone through this.

My senses were on overload. When Nix leaned in to speak, I could smell his breath. "I ask you again," he said. "What do Detectives Broadway and Perry know?"

He nodded to Iggy, who pulled the rag out of my mouth.

"Go fuck yourself," I wheezed through gritted teeth.

Nix stepped forward with a roll of surgical tape and a gauze pad. He carefully wrapped and taped my finger stemming the flow of blood so I wouldn't pass out.

"We can get Samoyla to clip you apart one piece at a time," Nix said. "How 'bout a toe, or the last two inches of your dick? I can make this last all night."

I tried to hold on, but I could feel my resolve weakening. Then suddenly, my eyes filled with water, and though I made no sound, I knew I was crying.

"Sammy," Nix said, and the giant stepped forward, this time, placing the clippers on my right index finger.

"No . . . no, don't," I said. The panic and desperation in my voice surprised me.

"Talk," Nix said.

"We . . . I . . . I think Davide Andrazack was an Odessa mob hit. Martin Kobb, too."

Then the dam broke and I was spilling my guts, telling about the cold hit and how we wanted to use the 5.45 slugs from the PSM automatic to tie both murders to Sammy. I said that Broadway and Perry knew about all this, but that we couldn't prove it without the gun. Basically I puked up our whole case.

When I finished, Nix checked the LD screen on the polygraph, then sat down on the bumper of the car and regarded me carefully. "You see, you could have saved yourself a lot of pain if you just told me that earlier."

He speed dialed a number on his cell. After a minute he said, "Okay, I think we can contain it. Sammy has to ditch his little assassination pistol and he definitely needs to go visit his family in Russia tomorrow. These guys have the gist of a case, but they can't make it without Sammy's gun or a witness. I think we can make this go away."

There was a long pause as I sat with my head on my chest, feeling lower than I ever had in my life. You like to hold the idea that you can withstand anything—that you can take torture, or the worst man has to offer and not break. But I hadn't been able to do it. I had a much lower threshold than I had imagined. I'd fallen short, and now, even though I was probably not long for this world, I had to live with that uncomfortable knowledge until they killed me.

Nix said into the cell phone, "Fine. I'll go with them and make sure it's done right."

He disconnected and said, "Put him under."

One of the brigadiers stepped forward with a needle and jammed it into my leg again. Whatever was in that syringe was powerful stuff. I was out before they untaped me from the chair.

58

When I regained consciousness I was back in the trunk and we were moving.

I wasn't sure how long I'd been out, but my whole body ached, and my left index finger was throbbing like a bitch.

Memory started to return, and as it did, I knew I was going for a ride I wouldn't come back from.

I now had some of the "hows," but the "whys" still eluded me. To keep my mind from disintegrating in fear, I tried to reason them out.

Nix was Virtue's right hand, so that meant Virtue was, for some reason, allied with the Petrovitches. Why?

Virtue and the Petrovitches were all in Moscow in the mid-eighties. Stan Bambarak and Bimini Wright had also been stationed there. Was this part of Bimini's '85 problem? Alexa told us that Sammy had been an assassin for the KGB. Was he the shooter who did Bimini's Russian doubles in that Moscow prison? How did all of that tie to R.A. Virtue? Why would Virtue take such a risk? I wasn't sure, but it felt as if it started back then.

Then came a wave of frustration and anger, most of it directed at me. For the past three years, I had gotten into the habit of playing just outside the boundaries. I was usually able to pull it off, but little by little, I had become overconfident. Past successes had blinded me to current weaknesses. I had allowed myself to be taken and then hadn't held up. I'd given our case away. It would now come to nothing. That memory shamed me.

I started to review the events that lead me here. There was now little doubt that Samoyla Petrovitch had degenerated from whatever he'd been in Moscow into a much more dangerous, murderous psychopath. He had pulled that tree-limb cutter from the trunk of his car. Then he'd snipped off my fingertip. Did it without a hint of hesitation or a flicker of emotion.

A question began to bump up against that gruesome memory. *What the hell was Samoyla doing with a tree limb cutter anyway?* Maybe he bought it to cut off Davide Andrazack's fingertips so the Mossad agent could be dumped in our serial murder case. Then a new idea struck me.

Alexa told me about the Stinger attack in Kabul. How Sammy had been stitched up by a U.S. corpsman who saved him, but also disfigured him for life. I'd seen firsthand that Sammy was an impulse killer. He almost murdered me in his Century City office.

As I lay stuffed in the trunk of the moving Cadillac, I tried hard not to curse my stupidity. I had been so locked on the idea that Zack was the Fingertip Killer, that I had completely overlooked Sammy.

The hub of my case against Zack hinged on the fact that

Vaughn Rolaine was involved in both of his murder cases. But Alexa had pared that coincidence down. As she had said, it was statistically possible that Zack and I just happened to catch the Vaughn Rolaine murder on that Friday night two months ago.

I suddenly wondered if all of the logic I'd used to tie Zack to these murders might just as easily apply to Sammy. Maybe Vaughn Rolaine was the precipitating murder that got Sammy started killing homeless men. He'd been ordered by Virtue or Nix to kill Davide Andrazack because Davide was finding those reverse-engineered Americypher bugs and tracking them to a receiver station on the roof of their Century City office building. But maybe Sammy was so ritualized by then that he just continued the same rage-based techniques he'd been employing during all the other homeless murders.

We didn't find any bugs or scans on the ME's computer, so maybe that chest carving hadn't leaked after all. Maybe Sammy had been using it all along, carving a Medical Corps insignia on Davide Andrazack as well as all the other homeless vets he killed. All of it because of psychopathic anger over that botched field triage in Afghanistan. Maybe Davide Andrazack wasn't a copycat kill, but part of the same series of murders, and the only thing that was different was the motive.

I had to admit that Sammy fit the unsub's profile at least as well as Zack. I remembered Underwood's suggestion that the unsub was covering the eyes of the vics because he thought he was ugly and didn't want them looking at him even in death. I had scoffed at that, but now with Sammy as a suspect, I wondered if I was wrong, just like I was wrong about the unsub being an organized, methodical killer. Sammy was an impulse killer with a questionable IQ who didn't plan his murders. But he was also a KGB-trained assassin. He knew how to cover up his crimes, and those acts made the crime scenes appear organized when in reality they weren't. He was a classic example of a mixed unsub, and cutting to the bottom of it, Judd Underwood's profile was a lot closer than mine.

Clever detective that I was, I had actually managed to get myself caught by the very serial killer I was investigating. It doesn't get much worse than that.

The car slowed slightly, and I felt the tires humming on asphalt. We had left the highway and were now on a winding road.

Suddenly, the car passed over something, and intense vibrations rattled the chassis. A cattle grate? It seemed we were outside of L.A., far out in the country.

Half an hour or so later, I felt the car tilting and tipping as the driver negotiated what felt like deep rain crevices.

After what I estimated was about a half mile, we made a long sloping turn and came to a stop.

Car doors slammed.

A minute later, the trunk opened and I was looking up into the sunlight. Looming over me, looking like something a mad scientist concocted in his basement, was Samoyla Petrovitch. He reached down and scooped me out of the trunk, using so little effort, it shocked me. Then he turned and threw me on the ground nearby.

I thumped in the damp grass. When I looked around, I realized I was about a hundred yards from a beautiful, blue lake. Wherever we were, it appeared deserted. No neighbors or houses in sight, no docks or boats. I saw Kersey Nix getting out of a gray government sedan, which was parked behind the black Cadillac Brougham I had ridden in. I took a head count. Including Nix, Sammy, Iggy, and their five brigadiers, there were eight all together.

I started to lose it.

To begin with, no full-grown male likes to be lifted off his feet and thrown around like a sack of laundry. Secondly, eight against one is lousy odds unless you're the star of a kung fu movie. I couldn't see any way to change that. I was in terrible shape—beat to hell with one fingertip gone, taped up, and weak from loss of blood, miles from civilization. I wasn't going to get out of this.

I craned my neck and saw that we were on a rolling lawn in front of a sprawling mountain lodge in a garden framed by low brick walls. The house was designed to look like a Swiss chalet with wood carved eves and Disney-esque pastel colors. The Petrovitches' summer place on New Melones Lake. I was going to disappear up here just like Calvin Lerner.

I glanced at Sammy. He had a blank expression on his ruptured face and was again rocking side to side. Two brigadiers were standing behind, watching him sway, frozen by his murderous intensity.

"Sammy . . . ," I said.

He didn't answer.

"Listen, man, you don't want to kill me. This is a very bad plan. I'm a cop. You kill a cop, it doesn't go away." Thinking even as I said it, that it hadn't slowed him down, or hurt him much when he shot Martin Kobb ten years ago.

59

THE PETROVITCHES AND Kersey Nix went into the house, leaving me on the lawn with a few brigadiers assigned to guard me. Ten minutes later Sammy came back out carrying a fifty-pound Danforth anchor in his left hand. Then he grabbed my bound feet in his right, and began dragging me down toward the lake. My head kept hitting rocks on the path as he yanked me savagely along, rounding a point to a small cove, just out of sight of the main house.

There, tied to the end of a private dock, covered by a canvas tarp, was a classic, varnished wood Chris-Craft.

Sammy dragged me to the end of the pier and dumped me next to the boat, then pulled out his 5.45 PSM automatic. It disappeared quickly into his enormous hand. He jabbed the barrel behind my left ear, its cold muzzle pressing hard against my skull.

I gathered myself together, trying to prepare for death, but all I kept thinking was, *I'm not ready yet.*

Then Sammy wheezed, "Suck my dick, yakoff."

I steeled myself, waiting for the bullet. Instead, he just laughed. It was a high-pitched squeak that shot over ruptured vocal chords, hee-heeing across the silent mountain terrain in a breathy, whistle. He pulled the gun away, leaned down, and fastened the heavy anchor to my legs with a rope.

The idea of getting shot in the head was bad, but going swimming with a fifty-pound anchor didn't exactly cut it either.

Sammy lumbered back toward the house as one of the brigadiers unzipped the canvas cover on the speedboat, peeled it off, and then jumped down into the cockpit. He slid behind the wheel and turned on the blower, waiting for the gas fumes in the bilge to clear. Then he pushed the starter.

A rolling ball of fire blew straight up into the air, sending wood splinters flying into my face as the classic speedboat exploded. The blast rolled me across the dock and almost knocked me into the water. From where I lay, I saw the brigadier who had been behind the wheel catapult through the air engulfed in flames. He fell toward the water, finally splashing into the lake, extinguishing himself and sinking without a trace thirty yards out.

Sammy Petrovitch screamed something in Russian. I craned my neck and saw him running across the lawn, heading back toward the dock.

He was so intent on the burning speedboat, he didn't see the white Econoline van speeding out of a dirt road in the woods, coming directly at him from behind. Just as it was a few feet away, Sammy heard the engine and spun. The front bumper clipped him and the impact knocked him sideways. Then the speeding van roared right on past, heading toward the dock where I lay. It hurtled out onto the pier, its tires clattering on the wooden planks, and finally slewed to a stop just inches from the water.

The side door flew open. "Some fucking mess you got here, Bubba," Zack said, as he jumped down onto the dock, a big square-muzzled Glock in one hand, a fishing knife in the other. He put the knife between his teeth, then pulled out his handcuff key, leaned down, and quickly unlocked the metal bracelets.

"Gimme a gun!" I yelled.

He threw the automatic to me. I tried to catch it, but with my wrapped and painful left index fingertip missing, the Glock went right through my grasp, hit the dock, and splashed into the water.

"Nice catch, asshole," Zack cursed. "My last backup piece."

Gunfire erupted, coming from the direction of the house. I turned and saw Sammy, Iggy, and their remaining brigadiers all shooting at us from the lawn with Kalashnikov submachine guns. Kersey Nix ran out of the chalet firing a handgun. The barrage of bullets zapped and sparked against the dock while pieces of the burning Chris-Craft still rained down around us.

The wood pier was disintegrating under a steady stream of 7.62-mm machine gun bullets.

"Get in the van!" Zack yelled.

I managed to pull most of the tape off my ankles and untie the anchor. Then I half-hopped, half-threw myself through the open side door as gunfire riddled the vehicle. Rounds punched through the metal sides, ricocheting and sparking around me.

Zack jumped into the front seat and threw the van into reverse. "The metal case in the back!" he shouted. "Get the SAR out and get busy," referring to a semi-automatic rifle.

I scrambled to the back where there was a metal case with LAPD SWAT stenciled on the top. I could barely raise the heavy lid on the box because the missing fingertip made my left hand all but useless. I finally heaved it open and wrestled a semi-automatic .223 AR-15 out, slammed in a clip, tromboned the slide and jammed the muzzle through the back window, breaking the glass.

We squealed backward off the dock, once swerving very close to the edge, almost going into the water.

I let loose with the semi-automatic rifle.

The AR-15 had been modified to fire four shot bursts and the 55-grain JSP rounds scattered the mobsters and FBI agent on the lawn.

Zack powered backward onto the grass and made a sharp turn, taking my scrambling targets from view. I rolled to the front of the van and, kneeling in the open side door, began firing again, squeezing off short bursts like an aircraft waist gunner. I saw Kersey Nix break for cover, and fired in his direction. I took his legs out and he screamed as he went down. Then I swung the barrel and took out a brigadier who was just running off the porch, gun blazing.

Then we were back in the woods on the same dirt road Zack had come out of earlier. The van's engine must have taken hits from those monster 7.62-mm slugs, because it was now running rough, coughing and sputtering.

"This thing is trashed! Gotta find some cover," Zack shouted as he pulled the van into the brush and parked. We both bailed out.

I saw the black Caddy rounding a distant turn, heading toward us, throwing a dust cloud out behind as it came. I waited until it got close enough so I could see Sammy and Iggy and maybe three other men crowded inside. Then I let loose with two bursts from the assault rifle, breaking the windshield first, then taking out the front grill of the speeding cad. The men all ducked down and the cad lurched right and skidded to a stop. Then I saw their heads pop up and they all jumped out of the car. The long gun was empty so I turned and ran into the woods, following Zack.

We scrambled up a hill, finally coming to a small clearing.

"How many?" Zack asked.

"Four, maybe five. I didn't hit anyone, but I took out the block."

Zack saw the slide on the AR-15 was locked open and took the rifle out of my hands and pulled the last magazine out of his back pocket and began changing clips, dropping the empty, slamming the fresh one home.

"The fuck happened to that boat?" I asked.

"Snuck over there, opened the gas line. Drained half the tank into the hull. My idea was to hit it with a hot round, blow it up and use it for a distraction. I almost shit when they took you out there and that asshole hit the starter."

"How did you find me?"

"Been tailing you for two days. Got pretty worried when they had you in that garage near Pismo Beach. Had to wait it out, hopin' they didn't kill you. I been watchin' your six, Bubba, just like the old Wild West days in the Valley. Nothing changes, huh?"

Then he reached into his pocket and pulled out my badge case and handed it back to me.

"Here. If we get lucky enough to arrest these hair bags you might need this."

I felt like shit as I took my shield. I'd just spent two days trying to drop a serial murder case on this guy while he'd been following me around trying to keep me from getting killed. "I had it all wrong," I said. "I'm sorry, Zack. I should've believed in you."

He looked up, his face hard to read. "I know I'm a strange flavor, man. It's why I don't have many friends." He didn't speak for almost ten seconds, then said, "I gotta look after the few buds I've got."

I was too choked up to say anything, so I just nodded.

He finished reloading the SAR and tromboned a fresh round into the chamber. "Glock's in the lake, one thirty-shot clip left for the long gun. One knife. And it's five against two."

Then my partner smiled. "I don't know, Bubba, seems like a pretty fair fight to me." He handed over the hunting knife. "Whatta ya say we go kick some commie ass?"

60

ZACK AND I made our way slowly back down the hill toward the road, our footsteps deadened by a heavy bed of pine needles. I heard Zack wheezing in front of me, breathing through his mouth. After about ten minutes we stopped and kneeled in the dense brush beside the road.

"We need to set up an ambush," he whispered.

"We should sneak back up the road to their car," I responded.

"Right." But he stayed where he was, hunkered down in the brush. "You didn't really think it was me murdering those homeless guys, did you?"

I didn't want to talk about this now. We needed to keep moving.

"I gotta know," Zack said. "You really thought I was the unsub?"

"I'm sorry, Zack. But you looked pretty good for it. I couldn't get past the Vaughn Rolaine coincidence and how fucked up the murder book was. It was almost like you were trying to tank the case. And then after you damn near killed me . . . I'm sorry, but for a while, that's the way I saw it."

He shook his head, looking down at his shoes. "Guess loyalty just ain't one a your strong suits," he said, softly.

"What's important is, I was wrong."

He was still kneeling there, shaking his head while cradling the automatic weapon in those huge, fleshy forearms. "You know how completely fucked that is?" His voice was loud, carrying in the still forest.

Suddenly, I felt very strange about all this. I hadn't exactly proved that Sammy was the unsub. Boiled down to its essence, that was just a promising theory. I gripped the hunting knife tighter, wondering whether I'd just made another terrible mistake.

When Zack looked up at me, he had tears in his eyes. "I'm afraid to let the people I love get close," he said.

"Zack—"

"My dad committed suicide when I was eight. It hurt so much I swore I'd never let anybody hurt me like that again. The day he did it, he told me he was gonna go help pour out the rain. Thought he was talkin' about our rain cisterns out back. But that wasn't what he was talking about at all."

"Zack, we gotta keep our mind on business here. These guys aren't pushovers. We gotta keep moving."

I looked up the hill behind me. I couldn't see or hear anybody up there, but my combat training told me we'd stayed in one spot too long.

"Zack—"

"Shut up, okay?" he interrupted. "I gotta tell you this. It may be our only time." He took a deep breath. "I found him down in the basement. His brains were on the ground, maggots crawling in his head. I puked. Couldn't touch him—my dad, and I couldn't touch him." He shook his head. "After that, Mom stayed drunk for two years. Her liver was so stewed they had t'put her in a hospital to dry her out. Kept my brother but dumped me in foster care, same as you. Only I was this fat kid nobody wanted and my foster folks kept throwing me back."

Then he looked directly at me. "You asked me why I hung on to you when you were so wasted. That's the reason, man. That's why I did it. I knew I couldn't let you go, 'cause you were just like me. It wasn't that you were too drunk to testify at my shooting reviews. It was because I understood you, Shane. I understood because your demons were the same as mine."

We were quiet for a minute, both thinking about that shared emptiness.

Then we heard voices in the distance. Zack rose out of his crouch. "Let's go."

We took off, moving just off the road, hiding in the brush. It took us almost twenty minutes to travel three hundred yards. When we finally got close enough, Zack held up his hand, signaling me to stop.

We could just make out the black Cadillac through the brush, parked on the road about twenty yards away. One of the Russians was leaning against the car. Then, almost as if inviting an attack, he set his pistol down on the trunk to pull out a cigarette.

Zack pointed at me, then at his eyes, indicating he wanted me to keep an eye on him while he moved up closer. I was only armed with a knife, so I wasn't going to be much backup unless I got in close. I held up my knife and pointed at myself, then to the car. He shook his head violently, and before I could argue, moved off in a low crouch, staying by the side of the road.

He was almost halfway there when he stepped on a piece of wood.

There was a dry snap and all hell broke loose.

The Russian grabbed his gun off the trunk as simultaneously Zack fired the .223, blowing him out of his loafers and halfway across the road, taking out most of his chest with one four-shot burst. The man flopped on his back, dead before he landed. Zack moved out onto the road toward him.

At that moment a Kalashnikov RPK opened up from somewhere further up the road. Zack was spun around by a stream of bullets as the barrage turned him. Blood sprayed out of his chest. He went down hard. I spotted the Russian with the machine gun crouched behind a rock twenty yards further up the road.

We were the ones who'd been lured into the ambush. Sammy Petrovitch, also a combat veteran had left two rear guards and split them.

I ran toward Zack's fallen body, keeping the Cad between me and the second guard. The Kalashnikov started chattering again. Bullets thunked into the car, breaking windows. I ducked down, then rushed out, grabbed Zack by the heels, and dragged him off the road. The machine gun suddenly went quiet. The brigadier had emptied the weapon and was changing clips. A few seconds later, the machine gun started up again, but by then I had my partner behind the car. I rolled Zack over and checked his wounds. He'd been hit by more than half a dozen rounds. Blood was seeping out of both sides of him, but his eyes were still open.

"That didn't quite work," he whispered weakly.

I knew the gunfire would bring the Petrovitches and henchman down on our position. There wasn't much time. I sprinted out into the road where Zack had dropped our .223. As soon as I showed myself, machine-gun fire erupted. I scooped up the long rifle and took off into the woods on the opposite side of the road. The Russian tracked my run with a stream of lead, hitting trees and boulders as I disappeared into the heavy foliage. I took cover in the deep forest, then started moving back toward him. I needed to clear the guy out before going back for Zack, and I knew Sammy and the others were headed this way.

Suddenly there was motion on the road. The brigadier had changed positions and was now standing below me with the

Kalashnikov on his hip pointed up in my direction. He spotted me and started spraying bullets.

The cover was thin now and I was pretty much his for the taking. At that moment, I lost my sense of self, as rage over Zack and everything else that had gone wrong flooded over me. Without judging the danger or fearing for my safety, I ran straight down the hill at the Russian, firing the AR-15—charging right into his chattering Kalashnikov, squeezing off short bursts one after another, guided by some insane force.

"Motherfucker!" I yelled as I charged.

When we were only twenty feet apart, the Russian mobster swung his gun barrel toward me and pulled the trigger. But the Kalashnikov fired just one round and jammed. The slug went a foot wide and flew past my head, whining into the forest. The brigadier crouched, struggling frantically with the slide, trying to clear the breech.

I squeezed the trigger. A four shot burst caught him in the neck. He flew backwards into the road, landing on his back.

I hurried toward the man and checked his pulse.

Dead.

Then I grabbed the Kalashnikov and ran back to Zack.

He had pulled himself into a sitting position, leaning against the Cadillac, but his eyelids were sagging. He was pale and losing blood fast.

"Let's go," I said, reaching down for him.

He whispered. "Time ta go pour out some rain, Bubba."

"You're not done, Zack. We're gonna make it."

I threw the jammed Kalashnikov far into the woods, then pulled Zack onto his feet. He weighed over three hundred pounds, but I got him over my shoulder in an awkward fireman's carry and started lumbering down the road toward the chalet and my potential getaway car—the remaining FBI sedan. I couldn't carry him far without stopping. I was still weak from lost blood, but adrenaline was fueling my effort.

When we finally reached the clearing by the chalet, the gray sedan was gone. I spotted a woodshed off to the side of the property and ran toward it, stumbling as I went, finally going down, sprawling on the grass with Zack on my back ten yards from the shed's door. I was so weak, I dragged Zack the rest of the way across the grass, into the shack.

Once we were inside I closed the door, then leaned down and checked him closer. He was still gushing blood from seven or eight holes. I knew if I didn't stem the flow immediately, he'd be dead in minutes. I sat next to him with his head in my lap and started ripping my already torn shirt, stuffing the fabric deep into the bullet wounds, pushing it down as far as I could using both hands, ignoring the pain from my clipped off fingertip.

"No—" Zack said. "Stop." His eyes were open again, but he was dangerously pale.

"Lemme go, Shane."

"No."

"Leave me. Save yourself."

"Zack, I can't leave you. I'm getting you outta here."

"I got nothing left to live for," he whispered.

"Don't do this."

Then a thin smile split his lips. "I saved your ass here, Bubba. When you get back, put me in for that medal. Do that and we're square. When they have the ceremony, I'll be watching. I'll know."

He was talking about the dumb-ass Medal of Valor. "You want that fucking medal, I'll get it for you," I said. "But you gotta stay alive to receive it."

Then he started coughing and blood flowed out of his mouth. After a minute, he got the spasm under control. "Shane . . . listen." His voice was so weak I could barely hear it. "The department—with what happened at the hospital—they'll try to freeze my line-of-duty death benefits. I need that cash for Zack

Junior's college. Promise me you'll make sure Fran and the boys—make sure they—"

And then, in mid-sentence, his eyes lost their shine. I watched him shrink back inside his own body as his spirit left.

I sat there, overwhelmed with an intense feeling of loss. How had this happened? How had it all managed to go so wrong?

Suddenly, one of the light machine guns opened up outside.

Then two more.

Bullets started punching holes in the thin, cedar walls of the shed. I threw myself down on top of Zack, protecting his dead body.

Good instinct, I thought, bitterly. *But I should have protected him when he needed it.*

I heard Sammy's high-pitched, breathy shriek yelling in Russian, "*Ti—mertvyetz, svoloch!*"

More bullets rained into the shack.

How did they know I was in here? Then my eyes fell on the trail of blood that Zack had left as I dragged him inside. A gory path pointed right at us.

Another barrage of bullets hit the shed. I dove for cover behind a pile of cut firewood and cowered while Zack's body was rocked with occasional hits.

Splinters of flying pine flew as more lead rained in on me.

I was pinned down and out of options.

61

Every time I raised my head to fire the .223 through the walls, more death rained in on me from all sides. I ended up just hunkered down with my head tucked between my knees, making myself as small a target as possible.

Then I heard the faint sound of an incoming helicopter. As the sound grew louder, the machine guns stopped firing at the shed and began cranking off rounds into the sky.

The shed hadn't taken any hits for a minute or more, so I crawled out from behind the woodpile and wormed my way across the dirt floor. Using the barrel of the gun, I pushed the door ajar.

Hovering out by the lake, was an LAPD red and gray Bell Jet Ranger. A skinny man with a bad haircut was crouched in the open side door. Even from this distance, it was easy to recognize

Emdee Perry. He was holding a large weapon in both hands, and while I watched, he opened fire.

Tracer rounds streaked out the door of the helicopter, across the lawn, toward Sammy and his men. The stream of lead was followed by a loud, ripping noise. I knew that sound well. Perry had commandeered one of the M-60s from the LAPD SWAT house in the Valley. The big machine gun scattered the Petrovitches and their brigadier. They ran across the grass toward the chalet, firing at the helicopter as they went.

I could now see that there were two other passengers in the hovering bird. Their faces became clearer as it neared. Alexa was seated next to the pilot. In the backseat, peeking out from behind Perry, was Roger Broadway.

The chopper landed on the lawn close to the lake and the three dove out finding cover behind one of the brick walls that framed the driveway. I got to my feet and stepped out of the shed onto the lawn, waving my hands so they would see me.

"Stay down!" Alexa screamed over the roar of the chopper, just as the Kalashnikovs opened up from the second floor of the house, chasing me back.

Then I heard the first, deadly KA-WUNK.

The sound of an RPG grenade launcher. The ground in front of the Bell Jet Ranger suddenly exploded. Pieces of dirt and turf flew into the air, and landed on the shiny red and gray nose of the chopper. The pilot immediately powered up, pulled back the collective and took off, banking quickly away.

The grenade launcher fired two more pineapples at the brick wall where my rescue party hid. Pieces of grass and brick flew high in the air. Roger, Alexa, and Emdee all rose out of their positions behind the low garden wall. Roger had a SWAT team Benelli M1014 combat shotgun in his hands. He let loose with two blasts while Emdee ran to the right, firing the M-60. Alexa and Roger went left.

Suddenly, Alexa spun away from Roger and made a suicidal

run across the open lawn toward the shed where I stood. The Kalashnikov opened up. Bullets tore at her heels as she ran. I stepped away from the shed, faced the chalet, and fired three bursts from the .223 at the upstairs windows, driving the shooter away from the opening. Alexa was almost to me so I ran toward her, grabbed her hand and slung her toward the riddled cedar woodshed. She fell through the door and I dove in after her.

KA-WUNK! KA-WUNK! KA-WUNK!

Three explosions followed and the walls of the structure were ripped apart, shredded by exploding hand grenades. I stood to get out of there, but Alexa was transfixed, looking down at Zack's dead body.

"What's he doing here?" she asked, shocked.

"Looking after his partner."

I grabbed Alexa, pulled her up and led her through the smoke and debris. We ran through a large gap in the back wall out into the bright sunlight. The loud, sharp burp of Emdee's M-60 tore a hole in the wall of noise.

Alexa and I made it to the cover of the woods and knelt down. She carried a 9 mm pistol in her right hand. From this position we could cover the back of the chalet through the dense foliage.

"Nice save," I said. "How'd you find me?"

"The kids saw it happen from the top of the Ferris wheel. They called me, hysterical. I figured it had to be the Petrovitches. We had the address on their lake house, so I got Rowdy and Snitch, commandeered Air One, and here we are."

Then she saw my bloody left hand, crudely wrapped and taped.

"What happened to your finger?" she asked, concerned.

"What finger?" I said, ruefully.

Just then we heard the grenade launcher fire, followed a few seconds later by three more explosions. I moved a few yards back to my right, and saw that Emdee was pinned down behind another garden wall. Sod and brick fragments were raining down on him. I couldn't see Roger, but Emdee suddenly stood up from behind the ruined wall, exposing himself to the deadly Kalashnikovs while letting loose with the M-60. His slugs tore through open windows on the second floor and ripped holes in the front wall of the chalet. Then he ducked down again, as two more grenades exploded ten feet from his position.

"That RPG is murder," Alexa shouted over the racket. "Once they get the range dialed in, we're done."

I had an idea. "I'm gonna sneak up to the house from the back and see if I can set fire to the place. Smoke 'em out."

I started to go, but Alexa grabbed me. She unbuttoned her jacket and pulled a long, fat pistol out of her belt.

"Flare gun. It was in the chopper. If we can get a shell through an upstairs window, it oughta do the job."

I took the gun and fumbled it open using my right hand. There was one fat phosphorous round in the breech. I closed the gun and took off the safety.

"I'm gonna get closer."

I turned for the house. Again, she stopped me.

"Give that back," she ordered.

"You're not doing this."

"What was your last range score?"

I didn't answer because we both knew I barely qualified.

"A lousy seventy-eight as I recall. I shot marksman."

She snatched the gun out of my hand and took off in a crouch, using the tree line at the back of the house for cover. I followed, staying close on her heels. When we were about fifty yards away, directly behind the back door, she kneeled down and aimed the flare gun at the second floor. After sighting carefully, she pulled the trigger.

There was a loud bang. The flare streaked across the lawn and went right through a second story window.

"Great shot!" I said. She'd hit it dead center.

Then the M-60 cut loose out front. Twenty yards to our right in the trees, a second gun barked. I turned and spotted Roger

Broadway in a crouch, firing the riot gun at the house. He had retreated deeper in the woods and established a position just east of us, cutting off an escape from that side. The four of us had the chalet more or less surrounded.

The upstairs took about ten minutes to catch fire. After that, the flames spread rapidly. Smoke started pouring out of all of the upstairs windows, igniting the roof. Then the intense heat lit drapes and furniture on the ground floor. Alexa dialed a number on her cell phone.

"How's it look out there?" she asked.

Emdee's voice came back through the earpiece, loud enough for me to hear. "We're turnin' Joe Bobs into shiska-babs."

"We'll hold the back," Alexa said. "If they come toward you, give 'em one chance to throw down their guns, then blow them away."

"Done," Emdee replied.

Suddenly, the back door opened and Sammy appeared in the threshold carrying his machine gun. Alexa and I let loose with a barrage, driving him back inside. I caught sight of Roger working his way toward us, hugging the tree line. Then a single shot sounded from a back window. He yelled out and went down.

"How bad?" I shouted. I couldn't see him where he'd fallen in the foliage.

"Through and through," he screamed back. "Fucked the bone up!"

"Stay down. We'll do this."

The Kalashnikovs started firing from the front of the house. Alexa's phone was still open in her hand and I heard Perry shouting over the earpiece. "They're in the door, gonna make a run at me!"

"Right," Alexa said and started toward the front. I grabbed her arm.

"You stay here," I told her. "Hold down this position."

Without waiting for an argument, I took off, heading around

to the front of the house. I got there just in time to see Sammy and Iggy Petrovitch, along with the last remaining brigadier, run out of the chalet into the yard. All of them were on fire. Their clothes burned brighter as they ran.

I unloaded the AR-15 at them until the clip was dry. Iggy went down first, then the brigadier behind him. Sammy was the last one standing. He was taking hits from the Perry's M-60. But even as several rounds spun him, the giant stayed upright, lurching forward like the monster in a Japanese horror flick.

Then he veered to his right and started toward me. The back of his shirt was still blazing, blood covered the front of him. The Kalashnikov in his hand kept firing, but he was spastically jerking the shots off. The bullets went wide. I tried to return fire, but I'd forgotten that my weapon was empty. Petrovitch continued toward me, bringing his gun up as he advanced.

He was now only five yards away, too close to miss. His ruptured face and giant teeth were pulled wide in an ugly grimace.

Then, as I watched him start to pull the trigger, two loud reports sounded from behind me. I spun in time to see Alexa in a Weaver stance, her 9 mm extended in a two handed grip. Her first shot was a little wide, but hit Sammy in the shoulder, knocking him sideways. The second was perfect—right between the running lights. His huge block head flew back, then forward. He teetered for a moment before he fell forward, landing with a thud, facedown on the ground directly in front of me.

Is this woman great? I thought, as relief swept over me.

Then everything was quiet.

I looked around and saw bodies sprawled all over the front lawn. Kersey Nix, Iggy, Sammy, and their brigadier.

When we finally got around to checking the Russians, they were all dead. When I reached Kersey Nix I got a surprise.

The traitorous son of a bitch was still breathing.

62

MY FRIENDS WHO work in forensic entomology tell me that green bottle flies have many amazing characteristics. They can home in on a dead body from miles away, sometimes arriving in less than ten minutes. They feast on the remains and lay thousands of eggs in the cadaver's moist cavities and crevices. Those larva soon hatch and become maggots. Thirty-six hours later, these maggots grow into a new generation of ugly green flies that lay more eggs. The process continues, cycle after cycle. By counting generations of fly larva, and measuring outside temperature, which affects the breeding cycle, it's possible for an entomologist to establish an approximate, long-term time of death estimate.

I don't want to be overly harsh, but in my opinion, the press shares many of these same characteristics. They arrive without warning from miles away and feast hungrily on the dead. The greater the carnage, the more reporters and stories they breed, reproducing their ugly offspring news cycle, after news cycle. With the media, the outside temperature doesn't seem to affect the process.

The first TV chopper landed less than ten minutes after the last shot was fired. Whether they picked up a broadcast from our chopper, or whether some neighbor on the lake called it in, it didn't really matter. The blue and white Hughes 500 settled down on the grass like a big hungry bottle fly and discharged two maggots carrying video equipment at port arms. One had an HD-24 camera, the other, a digital sound unit and sun gun. They had a variety of spectacular targets to chose from. The house was engulfed in flame; bodies were strewn everywhere.

A few minutes later, two more choppers landed, followed by another after that. All had their call letters and station logos emblazoned proudly on the sides, and of course, there were plenty of catchy slogans:

Channel One Is the One in the Inland Empire.

Stay Up to Date with Channel Eight.

Channel Six Gets It Right on Time.

I was trying to set up a police line and hold them back but we were outnumbered, and worse still, out of our jurisdiction, so I was getting a lot of arguments. The press knew this was big.

The NBC affiliate KSBW landed a chopper. The story was about to go national.

While I struggled to keep the news crews at bay, Alexa was on her cell phone to Chief Filosiani in Los Angeles. The LAPD pilot had already radioed the local sheriff and requested a fire team, backup troops and EMTs. Roger was in considerable pain, but Emdee had stemmed the bleeding with his belt. Kersey Nix was unconscious and going into shock.

The fire department arrived with three pumper units and immediately started knocking down flames using water from the lake. The chalet was a loss, so they concentrated on protecting the trees to prevent a wild fire. Once the perimeter was contained they worked to extinguish the burning house.

There were two EMTs with the fire crew and I led them over to Broadway and Nix.

Roger was sluggish from loss of blood, so the paramedics went right to work tying off bleeders and applying pressure compresses. Nix was critical and needed an immediate dust off. Alexa commandeered the chopper from Channel Six. Amid a chorus of complaints, we loaded Nix inside, along with a paramedic, and the news chopper took off for the nearest hospital. After the second EMT finished the field dressing on Roger he took a look at my hand.

"What caused this?" he asked, as he peeled back the temporary bandage Nix had applied in Pismo Beach.

"I got in the way of a homicidal tree trimmer."

The EMT shot me a puzzled look, but when I didn't elaborate, told me it had to be treated at a hospital, then he splinted and wrapped it up tight with fresh gauze and tape.

The local sheriffs finally arrived at 4 P.M. and ten deputies in Smokey the Bear hats took control of the crime scene.

Alexa closed her phone and came over and stood with me. "The chief is worried that once the news story breaks, Virtue will rabbit."

"Yeah." I pointed to the NBC chopper, which had a satellite dish affixed to the door. "Probably Brian Williams's lead story already."

She nodded. "Tony went to the FBI. With Nix off the flowchart, Agent Underwood becomes the temporary SAC in L.A."

"Good luck," I said.

"Tony said the guy is actually kicking some big-time ass for us in the Bureau."

"Jerk had to be good for something eventually," I grumbled.

"I need to get back to L.A., she said. "The Sonora sheriff is choppering in a local ME right now, to handle the crime scene."

Just then, a paramedic chopper landed on the lawn to pick up Roger. I found him lying on a blanket Emdee had scrounged from somewhere. Blood was already seeping through the new bandage the medic had put on his leg.

I shook Emdee's and Roger's hands. "Thanks for the rescue. See you guys back in L.A."

Alexa and I got into the LAPD chopper and left the scene. As we circled the lake on our way back to the city, I turned around and looked down at the smoking house. The fire was now out and there were twenty or thirty dots moving around on the lawn. From this far away, it was impossible to tell which ones were the maggots.

63

WE STOPPED AT the Queen of Angels emergency room where the docs did thirty minutes' worth of needlework on the end of my left index finger. When they were finished, my finger was half an inch shorter and my hand was wrapped in a pound of gauze, suitable for ringing a Chinese gong.

It was around 8 P.M. before Alexa and I got back to Parker Center and rode the elevator to six, where we went directly into the chief's office. Great White Mike occupied the only chair. Armando Cubio and Agent Orange were there, along with half the LAPD command staff and deputy chiefs. Tony Filosiani was pacing the room, fully in charge. As soon as we walked in, the chief told us that R. A. Virtue had disappeared from his home at 6 P.M. His wife didn't know where he'd gone and neither did his people at Homeland Security.

"Musta seen the early news and figured to get outta sight till he could assess the damage," he said.

"If Nix survives his wound and talks, Virtue's in a big jackpot," I said. "As it is, I think we have enough to get a warrant to arrest him as a material witness."

"I'm already working on that," Cubio said.

"Agent Underwood's got us dialed into the regional Homeland Security office," Tony continued. "They're in full stammer. They can't believe Virtue and Nix went off the res like that."

Underwood's narrow shoulders were pinched together. His bright orange hair bristled angrily under the fluorescent ceiling lights in Tony's office. He held up two sheets of paper and said, "We've got all the airports and border crossings covered. This is a list of asset-seizure planes in the FBI inventory. There's a twin-engine Challenger corporate jet—tail number Sierra Mike eight-six-eight. It went missing from the federal hanger yesterday."

"It's gotta be pretty damn hard to steal a federal jet without stirring up a flock of questions. Where'd it go?" Tony asked.

"Don't know," Underwood said. "Virtue has his own pilots. He probably has enough juice to commandeer one of these federal planes without paperwork. But if he tries to fly it anywhere without filing a flight plan, the FAA will have an unauthorized blip going through their airspace. Since nine-eleven, if we don't know who you are, you land or get shot down."

"So if he can't take off, how does he plan to escape?" I asked.

"If it was me, I'd park that Challenger in a secure hangar and change tail numbers," Underwood suggested, running a freckled hand through his orange bristle. "Then when he's ready, he files a flight plan under somebody else's ownership numbers."

"Okay. From now on, any Challenger jet that requests a flight plan has to be checked, regardless of who owns it," Tony said.

Underwood nodded. "Big job, but we can do it."

After the meeting broke up, I found myself in the elevator with Judd Underwood.

"Got pretty tough up there in Central California," he said. "Heard one of your guys got it."

"My partner."

"Farrell?" His brow creased in thought. "You know, I never got to meet him."

"Too late now."

Thankfully, the door opened. I didn't even know what floor we were on, but I didn't know what to say, and needed to get away from him, so I stepped out.

"Hey, Scully," he said, stopping me. "What you did? It was good."

"Thanks."

"Lord Acton's Law. 'Power corrupts, and the love of power corrupts absolutely.' " He seemed to want to bury the problem between us. "With guys like you around, maybe we can keep the corruption at bay."

I nodded, shook his hand, and watched the elevator close. After I turned around, I realized I was on the second floor.

Accounting. It seemed like a good time to stop in and get the paperwork moving on Zack's survivor death benefits.

When Alexa and I got home, Chooch and Delfina made a big deal over my being safe. Once the excitement was over, they went out to a movie to celebrate. We went out to the backyard with Franco, who gazed sadly at the shallow canals. I think he preferred the ocean view from the balcony at Shutters.

I told Alexa, for about the tenth time, how happy I was to see her choppering in with Rowdy and Snitch to save me.

"Enough," she finally said, "I can't take another thank you."

So I told her I didn't ever again want to hear a criticism from her about my taking chances. Not after that suicidal run across the lawn toward the woodshed.

"Gotta look after my honey," she grinned.

I was transfixed by the graceful curve of her neck, the slant of her high cheekbones, all of this exotic beauty lit by soft moonlight.

Then I took her hand, and finally worked into a discussion about Zack's survivor benefits. The family of a police officer who dies in action is entitled to 75 percent of his final average salary plus a death in service benefit.

Alexa shifted in her chair. "All this stuff with Zack—I'm afraid it's not quite over yet," she said softly.

"Whatta you mean, it's not over? The guy's dead. He died saving my ass. End of story."

"After you went missing, everything you told me, your suspicions about Zack being the unsub—I took it all to Tony."

"But, I told you Zack was not the killer, Sammy was. Before he died, Zack told me the department would try to use this stuff to screw him out of his line-of-duty death benefits, and now that's exactly what's going on. I'm not gonna stand by and watch the number crunchers on two steal money that's rightfully his."

"We're not stealing anything," she said, coming to the defense of the department. "But now that it's in the system, things have to take their course. I can issue a favorable opinion, which I will do, but it's not something I can control anymore."

Sitting in the dark, I realized she was right. With both Sammy and Zack dead, there was no way I could ever really prove which of them was the Fingertip Killer.

At one o'clock in the morning, Alexa and I were lying in bed, but were still both awake, tossing and tangling our sheets, too keyed up to sleep.

The phone rang.

Alexa snatched up the receiver. "Yes?" She paused. "Where?"

She hung up, rolled out of bed, and started putting her clothes on.

"Gotta go."

"Somebody filed a flight plan?" I said, swinging my feet to the floor.

"Stay in bed."

I got up and started dressing.

"You're not going, Shane. It's an order."

"An order's not gonna be enough. You're gonna have to shoot me."

Ten minutes later we were speeding down the 405 toward the Van Nuys Airport. Alexa was driving. I was slouched in the passenger seat watching the lights from the freeway streaking across her face.

At 1:35 A.M., we pulled into the parking lot of Peterson Executive Jet Terminal in Van Nuys. Tony Filosiani, Lieutenant Cubio, and Judd Underwood were already there, along with a dozen cops and FBI agents. A heated procedural argument was in progress.

"It doesn't matter to me if it belongs to John Travolta or John the Baptist," Tony was saying. "It ain't takin' off. We gotta make a move." Then he turned to face us. "An hour ago, Travolta's Gulfstream filed a flight plan for Berlin."

"I thought we were looking for an asset-seizure Challenger with altered tail numbers," Alexa said.

"We are. Were," Underwood said. "This was filed as an emergency flight plan. According to the paperwork, Travolta's supposed to be aboard heading back to Germany where he's shooting a movie. When the printout came in it seemed fishy to me because I remembered reading somewhere that he has a big new seven-thirty-seven that he uses for long-distance flights. According to his production office in Berlin, Travolta's still in Germany. He doesn't know anything about his Gulfstream leaving from here. The flight plan has the plane taking off in five minutes. It's taxiing now."

"That's enough talk! We're gonna shut this down," Tony said angrily.

The tower was alerted that we wanted to halt the takeoff and board the Gulfstream. The message was relayed to the pilot, but the plane kept rolling.

"He's not responding," the FBI agent who was on the phone to the tower reported.

In less than a minute we were in our cars and out on the tarmac. Four cars streaked down the taxiway. Tony took the lead, driving his Crown Vic at high speed, his Kojack light flashing red. Judd Underwood was in the front seat with him.

I was in Alexa's slick-back while she drove. We were doing close to seventy, following Tony's Crown Vic so closely, our headlights only lit the car's trunk. I could barely make out the shiny white shape of the jet turning at the end of the runway, positioning itself for takeoff.

Then the Gulfstream began to accelerate.

"Cut across the grass," I yelled. "We'll never block him if we stay on the taxiway!"

Alexa swung the wheel and we shot across the infield. Tony and the other vehicles must have had the same idea because suddenly we were all on the main runway.

The Gulfstream thundered toward us, engines at full throttle, while four police cars closed the distance, speeding straight at it on a deadly collision course. When we were halfway down the tarmac, Tony spun the wheel, skidding sideways. The other cars followed suit, blocking the runway four across. There didn't appear to be enough space for the big jet to get airborne, but it kept coming, powering toward us.

"Get out!" I screamed.

Alexa and I dove out of the car and ran for our lives. The other cops and feds all did the same.

At the last minute, the Gulfstream swerved to miss the blockade of cars and left the runway heading out onto the grass. It tore up the turf as it tried to brake to a stop. With both engines now screaming in retrograde, the big jet finally began to lose speed. As it did, the undercarriage started to sink into the grass, followed a minute later by a loud, tortured bang, as the wheels set themselves in soft turf and the landing gear snapped. The heavy jet nosed down and shuddered to a stop.

Everyone surrounded the plane with guns drawn. A few tense moments passed before the hatch attempted to open. Because of the nose down attitude, the hydraulic door stuck halfway open. After a moment, Robert Allen Virtue appeared in the threshold and peered through the jammed hatch.

"Somebody will have to help us out," his patrician bearing still in place.

"You're under arrest," Chief Filosiani said.

Agent Underwood stepped forward. "FBI," he bellowed.

"I know who you are, asshole," Virtue snapped. "You work for me."

"Not anymore," Underwood replied, his pale complexion coloring.

Minutes later Virtue was helped out of the crippled jet. He didn't expect to see me alive, and stopped to face me as he passed. A strange look shadowed his face as if, for the first time, he realized he might actually be in some trouble.

"You'll never assess the damage you've done to your country," he said.

"You're the one who's been damaging it," I answered.

Virtue seemed stunned by this. Then came self-righteous anger. "People like you are great moralizers, but have damn few solutions when it comes to getting this country where she needs to go."

"You're certainly not getting us there by trashing the Rule of Law and the Constitution."

"The Constitution?" he snorted. "What's any of this got to do with the Constitution? I'm talking about global terrorism. This country has fought its last war of nations. We're now engaged in a war of ideologies. The rules have to change when your enemy has no conscience or borders. But you'll never understand that."

"I understand that the Patriot Act and FISA are rolling back the search and seizure rights provided by the Fourth Amendment. The FISA court trashes the Eleventh Amendment limiting judicial powers and the Sixth Amendment right to a speedy trial. We're supposed to beat terrorists by becoming despots?"

"Traitors always accuse patriots of despotism," he shot back.

"No," I said softly. "Despots always accuse patriots of treason."

64

SOMETIMES THINGS JUST have to get a lot worse before they can get better. A wise, if somewhat painful concept.

I just wanted my current string of downers to come to an end. But it wasn't to be. Zack's funeral and my son's USC visit were on a collision course for the same day.

I pulled Chooch aside and tried to explain it to him. "This guy was my partner and he died saving my life."

We were in Chooch's bedroom two days before the funeral and the scheduled USC visit, which were both set for Sunday. "There's not much that would keep me from doing this with you, son, but I can't miss the funeral. I owe Zack too much."

"It's okay, Dad. I understand," Chooch said, but his face was long and there was real disappointment in his dark eyes.

Saturday night I decided to take the family out to dinner to make up for it.

The dinner didn't work out either.

On the way to the restaurant, Alexa happened to mention that accounting had just notified her they were holding up Zack's Line of Duty death benefits because of questions pertaining to his possible involvement in the Fingertip murder case.

"How many times do I have to tell you, Sammy killed those homeless guys?" I said, hotly.

"Shane, I feel terrible about this, but it's out of my hands. As soon as Homicide Special closes the serial murder case, and as long as Zack's not involved, then the paperwork can proceed. We can't give Zack Line of Duty benefits or the two extra years on his pension as long as he's in any way a suspect. The same goes for you putting him up for the Medal of Valor. The press would skin us alive."

So to keep the bottle flies happy, we were going to deny Zack the only two things he'd ask me to do when he died.

I started brooding like a ten-year-old and ruined my own dinner party. But I knew how the game was played. There would be no more murders, so the task force would disband and the case would eventually go cold. Zack would remain a suspect and his survivor benefits would be frozen forever.

At the restaurant, Alexa and I fell into a chilly silence. Dell and Chooch made small talk and tried not to get us going again.

Later, sitting in the backyard, Alexa and I attempted to clean up the trouble between us. I admitted that I knew it wasn't technically her fault this had happened to Zack.

"Technically?" she said, seizing on this one, carefully parsed word.

"You were worried about me," I added. "You went to the wrong window. Shit happens."

"I was trying to save your life."

"Yeah, but Zack was the one who actually did."

As I said it, I remembered that in the end it was Alexa who smoked Sammy Petrovitch. She and Zack had both saved my life. It seemed my life took a lot of saving. I needed to calm myself down. Yelling at Alexa wouldn't solve anything. After about five minutes of silence, I tried to change the subject.

"How do you come out on Virtue, and what he did?"

"He's just bad material. He's going away. The system is good. You can't blame the system for one bad apple. Fortunately, Nix survived, or we wouldn't be able to file against the son of a bitch. As it is, once Nix turns state's evidence, Virtue is toast. If he wants to stay in politics, he'll have to run for the convict council in Soledad."

I thought about what she said, and then asked, "Is this new, redefined system really good, or are we little by little, losing what this country once stood for?"

"We're cops, Shane. We need all the powers we can get to put dirtbags away."

"Virtue was using USPA and FISA to take away due process. Do we really want these emergency powers and lack of due process in the system?"

"Cops are getting overrun by crime," she argued. "If you don't believe me, just take a look at my monthly stats."

"Yeah, maybe." I fell silent.

"Go ahead and say it." She knew I didn't agree.

"I just don't think it's smart to give up our freedoms in an attempt to protect them."

She sat quietly for a long moment, then without saying anything else, got up and went into the house.

On Sunday, Alexa and I went to Zack's funeral. It was a very small turnout. He told me once that he didn't have many cop buddies, and this sparse event surely proved it. Fran was there with their two boys. I was glad to see Broadway and Perry. Roger was on crutches with his leg wrapped to the hip. My bandaged left hand wasn't quite so huge now, but I still couldn't open a can of beer. Between the two of us there was enough gauze to wrap a mummy.

Emdee and I helped Roger hobble across the lawn to the gravesite. Alexa and I spoke to Fran and both of Zack's sons. They looked confused and rigid. This isn't the way anybody planned for it to end. Too much had been left unsaid. We took our places in a small group of mourners.

Just before the service began, I was surprised to see Stanislov Bambarak pull up in his embassy car, followed a few minutes later by Bimini Wright in her silver Jag. They made their way over to us. Bimini looked gorgeous in a simple black dress. Stanislov, as usual, was as big and wrinkled as a walrus.

The service was mercifully short. After it was over, we walked toward the parking lot. The Russian and the CIA agent shook hands with Roger, Emdee, Alexa, and me.

"Bit of hard cheese, this," Stanislov said, indicating the coffin. "Sorry I couldn't help out."

"Lotta people had to die to keep me alive," I said.

"Come on, Shane. Stop it," Alexa said sharply. She was determined to get me past this.

Bimini agreed with Alexa. She looked at me and said, "Sometimes freedom comes with a high price tag, Shane."

I had asked others to pay so much that I really didn't know how to respond.

Then she smiled brightly. "Guess what? After you got us all together, Stan and I decided to compare some more notes. We finally solved the 'Eighty-five Problem. Kersey Nix filled in the blanks and confirmed our theory two days ago. Guess who the fourth man turned out to be?"

"Virtue."

I'd had three weeks to ponder it since the frustrating hours spent locked in the trunk of Sammy's car. Virtue was an FBI agent stationed in Moscow in 1985. Virtue was heartless and ambitious. He paid the Petrovitches to be his moles inside the KGB, then brought them to L.A. to work for him off the books. I figured back in '85, he sold information to both sides to gain power. It was a brilliant political move. By giving up some of Bimini's Russian double agents, he gained influence with the bureaucrats inside the KGB, and that allowed him to learn the identity of the American traitors. By catching Aldrich Ames and Robert Hanssen, he subsequently became a star in Washington. He was a traitor who thought he was a patriot.

"I guess there is some good that comes from everything," Broadway said. "If Sammy Petrovitch hadn't snapped and started killing homeless men, who knows, it might have ended with R. A. Virtue in the White House."

"Now that we've put the hat on that piece of business, I guess my people will be sending me home," Stanislov said.

"What people are those?" I deadpanned. "Are we talking about the directors of the Moscow Ballet?"

He chuckled. "Rather silly, I know, but you take the post they give you." He smiled at Bimini. "I've sort of grown used to it here—the warm weather, the sunshine in winter. Agent Wright said if I retire and promise not to dabble in espionage, she'll look into getting me permanent resident status."

"You know what they say?" I said smiling, "Once you buy your first barbecue you'll never leave L.A."

They asked all of us to join them for lunch, but I needed to talk to Fran. Alexa was going in to the office, and Roger and Emdee had plans, so we begged off and watched them go. As they headed toward their cars, Stanislov accidentally bumped up against the beautiful CIA agent. Or was it an accident?

After everybody left, I waited for Fran to leave the gravesite and took her aside. We stood under the shade of a beautiful elm.

"I put Zack up for the Medal of Valor," I said. "He's always wanted it. I think what he did, saving my life, certainly qualifies him."

Even as I said it, I realized that my chances of getting him that medal while he was still on the Fingertip suspect list were somewhere near infinitesimal.

"I don't care about that damn medal. That was Zack's fantasy. My needs are more basic. Zack Junior goes to college next year. I can't afford to send him without Zack's line-of-duty benefits."

"I'll find a way to get it for you," I took her hand and squeezed it. "Now both of you have my word."

65

CHOOCH SIGNED HIS letter of intent in mid-February. He was going to USC on a full athletic scholarship.

A few weeks later, to celebrate, I planned a weekend boat outing to Central California, and the whole family, including Franco, was loaded into the car with our luggage and scuba gear. All the way over the Grapevine Chooch talked about college. You could hear how happy he was.

"You gotta go with me during spring ball, and meet the rest of the coaches, Dad."

"I'm looking forward to it," I told him—and I was. Chooch had sorted out his priorities and I was proud of him.

We arrived up at New Melones Lake at 10 P.M. and checked into the Pine Tree Inn. The next morning, we got in the car and drove up to the lake. On the east shore was a rental dock where you could lease houseboats. We picked a bright blue one named *Lazy Daze*. After a short instruction course on how to run it, we loaded the scuba equipment aboard and headed out onto the lake.

I could see the Petrovitch's burned-down Swiss chalet across the water. We maneuvered up close to their dock and put the anchor down.

As I was putting on my wetsuit and air tank, Alexa said, "I'm sorry I couldn't get the department to foot the bill for this." She smiled sheepishly. "With the current budget crunch and the Fingertip case inactive, I couldn't scare up much enthusiasm."

"Right."

It was a beautiful morning. The unusually warm weather continued and the temperature was already in the mid-seventies. She was wearing a tiny string bikini, sitting in the back of the houseboat. I was tempted to jump her right there, but Franco and the kids were watching.

On that Saturday, Chooch and I made ten dives, filled our air tanks four times and found nothing. Sunday was more of the same. I dove, Chooch dove. The mountain stream that fed the lake was ice cold, and even with our wetsuits we could only stay down for twenty minutes. We were working a grid pattern I had drawn up, trying hard not to miss a patch of lake bottom. We started close to the Petrovitches' dock and moved out, circle grid by circle grid. It was tough, demanding work. The wind blew the houseboat at anchor and I had to keep sighting against points onshore to keep from missing sections.

On the last dive Sunday evening just before sunset, I found an oil drum secured to the bottom with two Danforth anchors. Chooch and I hooked a line to the drum and floated a buoy. Then I called the sheriff's office.

Monday morning a police dive boat with an electric winch was trailered up from Sonora. We finally hauled the big drum topside and set it on the rear deck of the houseboat. We had to cut the welded top off with a torch.

Inside we found Calvin Lerner.

His body was well preserved due to the icy water at the bottom of that mountain lake.

My luck had finally changed. I found what I'd been searching for.

All of Lerner's fingertips had been cut off and the Medical Corps symbol was carved on his chest, proving once and for all, that Sammy Petrovitch was the unsub.

Later that day the ME retrieved a 5.45-mm slug from Calvin's head. Ballistics matched it to the gun we found on Sammy's body—the same gun that had killed Martin Kobb and Davide Andrazack. With that, the Fingertip murders were finally down.

The Police Commission met the following month to decide on the annual Medal of Valor recipients awarded in May.

Roger Broadway, Emdee Perry, and I were recognized, but Zack Farrell was not awarded a medal.

The commission never explained why. I think, given everything that had happened, it was easier for them if Zack just faded away. "I'm not a hundred dollar bill," he'd once told me. "Not everybody's gonna like me." It was certainly proving to be true.

The LAPD Accounting Office released Zack's survivor benefits and Fran called to tell me that with the money, Zack Junior would be able to go to USC. He would be a freshman in the same class as Chooch. We made arrangements to get our sons together before school started.

That was pretty much it, except for one last thing.

On a cold day in late May, Alexa and I drove back to Forest Lawn. Rain clouds were threatening on the horizon. We stood by Zack's grave as the air grew heavy with moisture and lightning bolts shot shimmering streaks of electricity toward the San Gabriel Mountains.

Some promises are hard to keep. Where Zack was concerned, I had made too many, and kept too few.

"You're sure you want to do this?" Alexa asked. "Somebody will just steal it."

"I don't care."

I reached in my pocket and took my own Medal of Valor out of its velvet box. The gold medallion hung on a red, white, and blue ribbon. Awards and medals had never mattered much to me. They were only symbols, usually given by people who hadn't been there and didn't know what had really happened. Like love and respect, some things only gain value when you give them away.

I laid the glittering medal pendant on Zack's headstone, then said a prayer and told my partner how sorry I was. How terrible I felt about the way it ended.

"I love you, but you're a strange man," Alexa whispered, holding my hand. "How does giving your medal away help? Zach's dead. He doesn't even know."

Thunder shook the hills. "Don't worry," I told her as the first heavy drops of rain fell. "He knows."

ACKNOWLEDGMENTS

Researching is one of the great joys of novel writing because of all the wonderful people I get to meet. This time a very special thanks goes to John Miller, Chief of the Counter-Terrorism and Criminal Intel Bureau at the LAPD, where I met Captain Gary Williams, Lt. Adam Bercovici, and Sgt. Nick Titirita. These men are the real heroes in the war against terror. Thanks for letting me hang for a while and see how it's done.

Helping me understand the inner workings of Homeland Security were Bill Gately and Dick Weart, both retired U.S. Customs agents. Also Joe Dougherty at ATF.

Norman Abrams, professor of constitutional law at UCLA Law School, explained the USA PATRIOT Act along with the Foreign Intelligence Services Act. Dr. Abrams untangled the confusing legalese of these two pieces of legislation and helped me to understand what their real strengths and dangers are.

Even with the dedicated help of these technical advisors, I admit that I still sometimes don't get it exactly right and any mistakes in fact are mine alone.

In my publishing and business world are the same great cast of people. My agent, Robert Gottlieb, adds vision and strength to my efforts. At St. Martin's Press, Charles Spicer edits and advises with a firm but gentle hand. Matt Baldacci and Matthew Shear keep the presses and the book tours rolling, and overseeing it all is my publisher, Sally Richardson, who has been my friend and supporter from the beginning.

Closer to home in Los Angeles is my great support team. First and foremost is my assistant, Kathy Ezso, who fields my first draft pages and works as my right hand all the way through to publication, adding suggestions and editorial comment. Next to her is Jane Endorf, who imports and does revisions. Kathy's husband, Dan Ezso, stepped in on this book and gave me a push in the right direction when I had one wheel stuck in the mud. Jo Swerling, as always, reads my first draft, comments, and cheers me on.

Of course, at home I am blessed. Our beautiful daughter, Tawnia, has navigated the difficult career rapids in Hollywood to become a sought-after television director, without losing any of her gentle humanity. She and our wonderful son-in-law, Tim, have blessed us with three amazing grandchildren. Our equally beautiful daughter, Chelsea, has graduated cum laude from SMU and is now beginning her career in TV journalism. She is a joy to her mother and me. Our son, Cody, earned the dedication on this novel with his hard work as he enters his senior year of college. Thanks for making your dad proud. And, of course, there is Marcia, who after forty years of marriage is still my best friend. Without her, none of this could happen. I love you guys.

W9-BUZ-831

PRAISE FOR *FALSE LIGHT*

"Eric Dezenhall is a genius writer, and *False Light* is a masterwork—smart, funny, unpredictable, freewheeling, and start-to-finish entertaining. The plotting is brilliant, the dialogue always sharp. Better yet, perhaps, this novel is a good-news reminder that we can always find measures of virtue and fairness and hard truth in justice's difficult alchemy."

—MARTIN CLARK, author of *The Substitution Order*

"*False Light* is *The Big Chill* of the #metoo era—I want the soundtrack of this terrific, timely book! I also want a buddy like the hilarious, loyal Sandy 'Fuse' Petty. On probation either because he's too old or too good, Fuse has the press chops to help his friend's daughter when her internship with a celebrity goes south. All he wants is justice, and for his teenage daughter to laugh at his jokes."

—MARY KAY ZURAVLEFF, author of *Man Alive!*

"In *False Light*, Eric Dezenhall combines a wickedly funny take on the demise of journalism and the fragility of reputation in the Internet era, with a clear-eyed view of the complex costs of sexual predation, despite the best efforts of the #metoo movement. A grown-up fantasy for our troubled times."

—DAVID O. STEWART, author of *The Lincoln Deception*

"For any parent who spends sleepless nights worrying about what could happen when the universe gets ahold of their child, *False Light* is an acerbic tale of revenge in the form of reputation obliteration, the only currency a certain type of climber understands. Eric Dezenhall mixes the serious topics of our times with a riotous look at middle-aged crushes, long marriages, insane relatives, and fears of professional obsolescence."

—LEE WOODRUFF, author of *Those We Love Most*

"No one knows the world of damage control better than Eric Dezenhall. His portrait of what a savvy operator can do in a crisis is as real as this vehicle for talking about the battles between good and evil. You'll feel like you're reading or watching an exposé on national television—or getting to see the whole truth of what our real world doesn't tell you. Highly entertaining and informative."

—JAMES GRADY, author of *Six Days of the Condor*

FALSE LIGHT

a novel

FALSE LIGHT

Eric Dezenhall

GREENLEAF
BOOK GROUP PRESS

This book is a work of fiction. Names, characters, businesses, organizations, places, events, and incidents are either a product of the author's imagination or are used fictitiously. Any resemblance to actual persons, living or dead, events, or locales is entirely coincidental.

Published by Greenleaf Book Group Press
Austin, Texas
www.gbgpress.com

Distributed by Greenleaf Book Group

For ordering information or special discounts for bulk purchases, please contact Greenleaf Book Group at PO Box 91869, Austin, TX 78709, 512.891.6100.

Design and composition by Greenleaf Book Group and Brian Phillips
Cover design by Greenleaf Book Group and Brian Phillips
Cover images used under license from ©Shutterstock.com/Lukasz Pawel Szczepanski

Publisher's Cataloging-in-Publication data is available.

Print ISBN: 978-1-62634-749-6

eBook ISBN: 978-1-62634-750-2

Part of the Tree Neutral® program, which offsets the number of trees consumed in the production and printing of this book by taking proactive steps, such as planting trees in direct proportion to the number of trees used: www.treeneutral.com

Printed in the United States of America on acid-free paper

20 21 22 23 24 25 10 9 8 7 6 5 4 3 2 1

First Edition

To Lincoln,

Love you, Bud

"You can escape from prison, but how
do you escape from a convincing story?"

ERROL MORRIS

• • •

"The modern world will not be punished.
It is the punishment."

NICOLAS GOMEZ DAVILA

Contents

Part I

FORGOTTEN MAN

"They were both cool—handsome, charming, ambitious, ironic, self-deprecating in the slightly underhanded way that the people with the best cards can afford to be."

JEFF HIMMELMAN, ***YOURS IN TRUTH,*** **ON BEN BRADLEE AND JOHN F. KENNEDY**

1

WHATEVER THE HELL I had been doing at work the past few years no longer mattered. I thought for sure my investigative series on the presidential candidate's proven mob ties would have caused a ripple with readers, but he'd been elected anyway. Nobody gave a damn.

It wasn't easy, tipping into the latter half of my fifties, to reach the conclusion that a decades-long career at the *Capitol Incursion* as one of the good guys added up to nothing more than a grease smear on a windshield. On my way out the door, after the newspaper had suspended me pending a disciplinary investigation, an inspirational quotation by the bug-eyed comic Marty Feldman had caught my eye. The scrap of paper was tacked to a cubicle and read *The pen is mightier than the sword, and considerably easier to write with.* What I'm getting at, I guess, is not just that my work didn't matter anymore, but that *I* didn't matter.

If you're sensing that I was in a funk, you'd be right. I know it's not an attractive quality, and I admit I'd become prone to tedious rants on certain subjects. But you can't control how you feel—you can only control what you do about those feelings. Maybe. It was about more than the impending loss of my career. Even before journalism had wilted toward extinction, my mind had become a panorama of catastrophe, and I had this sense that the modern world was saying to me, *Look, we don't want you here.*

Case in point: I hate technology and technology hates me. I use a flip phone. I don't know how to text. My wife, Joey, forbids me to use the television in the house because whenever I operate the remote control, I take down the whole system. Joey is responsible for getting the cash from the bank because the last time I tried to use an ATM, the cash jammed and when I tried to pull the bills out of the slit, the cops came and commanded me to put my hands flat against the wall. If it weren't for Joey, I could not function in the modern age. As I once told her, my theme song should be Tom Petty's "Forgotten Man." That I share a surname with the artist only made it seem more profound.

When I worked at the *Incursion,* I always took the stairs because the elevators wouldn't move when I pressed my floor. I couldn't tell people this, so I said that I used the stairs for exercise, which eventually became true. I have never once in my life successfully opened a hotel room door with a digital key card. Automatic doors rarely detect my presence and usually remain closed when I approach.

I call all these gadgets "TICU" (pronounced *TEEK*-yoo) for "Things I Can't Use." I know you must be thinking, *C'mon,* but I'm absolutely serious. Plus, if people really want to talk to me, I tell them to call the landline at the house, because nearly all my mobile phone calls drop—which is where this adventure begins.

My friend since middle school, Kurt Rossiter, left me a voice message one evening a few weeks after my *Incursion* leave began. It just said, "Fuse, call me. It's pretty urgent."

My nickname deserves a little explanation. I was Sanford "Sandy" Petty until ninth grade. My father had changed our last name from some Eastern European abomination because he hated his brother, "the-son-of-a-bitch-who's-always-shovin'-it-up-my-ass-and-who-I-always-helped-out-and-never-said-a-goddam-word-of-thanks." In other words, my father didn't want to share his name with Uncle Barry, whom I'd always liked and whose son, my cousin Mitchell, I had been close to growing up.

That first year of high school, there was an incident where my reputation changed overnight from class clown to Mr. Unpredictable, at least when certain variables converged. A group of us were in the woods behind the school on the Saturday after it happened: The Thing. At least that's what it eventually became known as. The others were passing a bong around when Kurt said, "I'll tell you, Sandy, you've got the world's longest fuse, but man . . . whatever set you off last weekend brought down the *riot cops*!"

The stoners all started chanting, "Fuse! Fuse! Fuse! Fuse!" The Elton John song "Rocket Man" was getting a lot of play at the time, and it contained the lyric about rocket man burning his fuse out. Given that I had once been a target of bullies because I was so skinny, The Thing was the best thing that had ever happened to me.

After Joey, that is.

She'd already gone up to bed before Kurt left his message. I was still downstairs putting the finishing touches on the first draft of a freelance story I was writing—by hand, on a legal pad—for some online rag. They were paying me $1,500 for a story on homemade bombs—it was the only income I was getting beyond my *Incursion* paycheck, which could end very soon, depending on the outcome of the investigation.

While I didn't want to finish my career in scandal, I couldn't imagine going back to work at the paper. Compared with most Americans, I suppose I had a cushion, but we were only one year away from sending our daughter, Finn, to college, and the idea of taking a penalty for borrowing from my retirement fund was terrifying. My earning years were effectively over. Thankfully, Joey made some money from her graphic design work. But my father's resources were dwindling too, with his round-the-clock dementia care, which meant I had to take up the slack.

I put my financial worrying on hold and called my friend back. "Kurt. Fuse."

"Yeah, man . . . I have a situation," he said. "A real situation." He sounded shaken. The only other time I'd ever heard him like that was one day in high school when he thought Angie might've been pregnant. But of course, she wasn't.

"Okay . . .?"

"You mind if I come over?" Kurt asked.

This was not a typical request. Among other things, Kurt knew Joey and I rarely stayed up past ten. Correction: we preferred not to stay up past ten, but ever since our teenage daughter had cultivated a taste for dangerous teenage boys, I had been staying up until . . . Actually, I didn't really sleep anymore.

Joey and I had tried to enforce a curfew, but Finn had been sneaking out of the house to hang with her increasingly punchable boyfriend, so we'd decided to loosen the strings or risk losing her completely. Last summer, she had thrown beer bottles onto passing cars on the Beltway from an overpass near our house on Bradley Boulevard. Had she not known a cut-through into our neighborhood, the Montgomery County cops would have nailed her—as they should have. A few kids from another school were arrested and charged with vandalism and reckless endangerment. Finn claimed that she didn't know them, but I didn't believe her—she'd become a skilled liar when it came to self-preservation. She eventually admitted to the bottle-throwing, but still denied being linked to the kids who got nicked. No matter how many times Joey and I told her she could have killed somebody, her adolescent brain lacked the capacity to fathom consequences. Truth be told, I pulled some stupid shit when I was her age, but it was different, because I had been invincible. My baby was not, according to parental logic.

"Um . . . okay, sure," I told Kurt. "Come on over."

"Be there in ten."

2

AS I WAITED for Kurt on my front porch, I took in the warm early October air. The lingering scent of burning leaves reminded me of how the autumn smelled during my college years on Philadelphia's Main Line. These days, Kurt and I both lived in Bethesda, Maryland, where we'd grown up—Kurt in his parents' old house on Arrowood, with me a mile away in a colonial built during World War II. Our place was the last on our street not to be torn down and replaced by a suburban Versailles. That's what was going on outside Washington: old houses were being vaporized and supplanted by structures so big that they left very little yard. I liked our cozy house. Setting aside our limited resources, I never understood why anyone would want to build a house so large that they would never encounter anyone they loved while wandering through its hallways and rooms.

Kurt had eventually married Angie, which made sense because of their commensurate perfection, although I'd always assumed he would have found another Angie-type when he was at Stanford. But among our childhood gang, only Haddon Seagull (legally Segal) had flown away because, well, that's what she did, like a desperado leaving a trail of heartsick mopes who wondered why she hadn't married them, because they had thought for sure she was their destiny.

I wondered what the hell was making Kurt so anxious. Everyone had seemed all right at brunch last week. Kurt's son was at Stanford, and his daughter was doing well at the University of Virginia. Angie still looked like she was thirty. And Kurt—as president of the Wheelock Foundation, a progressive policy think tank in Washington—was always seated beside some world leader opining about climate change—the very social issue, by the way, that was most likely to get him laid. The only thing that ever seemed to worry Kurt was environmental Armageddon, his foundation's focus, as opposed to absolutely everything else, which was what worried me.

An ungenerous part of me kindled the impulse to be glad Kurt had hit a pothole. Maybe it was his marriage. Perhaps he'd gone one extramarital *shtup* over the line. Joey and I had our own civil wars, and it occurred to me that nothing could unite a middle-aged couple more than the notion that somebody else's marriage was more flawed than theirs.

Kurt swung his Tesla into my driveway.

As he approached, even in the darkness, he appeared haggard. There were lines around his eyes, which prompted a wave of concern from me as he emerged fully under my floodlight, his diabolical thicket of graying blond hair coming into focus. My hair had largely vanished with the Clinton administration, and I buzzed it myself once a week. I hung on to a sense of achievement that I would never again have to spend money on a barber. The rationalizations we make to accommodate loss.

Kurt came under the porch light, and I sighed. He really was the sandy-haired, sailing-tanned, square-jawed anti-Christ. "Can we talk outside?" he asked. "Really don't want Joey to hear this."

"She's asleep."

"Still."

"Fine."

We walked across the grass and onto the street. Kurt appeared hunched. He was usually about six feet tall but tonight seemed closer to my height of five-eight. "What's going on?" I asked. "You look like ten pounds of shit in a five-pound bag."

"It's Samantha."

His daughter. My goddaughter.

"What happened?" I asked.

"Her internship last summer . . ."

"With MyStream?"

"Yeah."

MyStream was a virtual news network of self-styled citizen journalists who did their own investigative reporting, mostly in the form of bursts of short "gotcha" videos that were long on embarrassment and short on substance. MyStream positioned itself as a more thoughtful version of YouTube, but I detested it to the point of psychosis. At least YouTube didn't deny that it welcomed videos of drunk college kids who lit their farts on fire, which was at least something I could respect.

"Samantha went back to visit the MyStream people on an exam-prep break," Kurt continued. "She called us yesterday from school and asked us to come and get her. She told us in the car"—Kurt made an unnatural gagging sound—"that Pacho Craig . . . that he . . ."

"What?" I asked.

"Attacked her."

"Attacked her? Like *sexually*?"

Kurt nodded.

Pacho Craig was MyStream's star "reporter." In his late thirties, with a long, thick mane of chestnut hair and a perpetual shadow of beard stubble, Craig had become the Digital Age's dashing Prince of Confrontation. With a huge millennial fan base, Craig would use social media to blast out a one-sentence allegation, often featuring an unfortunate faux pas or video clip of some poor Joe who happened to be in the wrong place at the wrong time. He would stumble upon his hapless prey at some point during the week, and by Friday he would release a video of himself confronting his victim-of-the-week in a brief segment called "This Is Your Chance." When the target balked at speaking with him,

Pacho would flip back a fugitive strand of hair, point to his watch, and say, "Time is running out, friend. This is your chance. Only a coward wouldn't take it."

"Did Sammy go to the police?" I asked.

"No. We're trying to figure out what to do. Still getting just bits and pieces out of her. I'm not sure why she went all the way back to school before telling us—we were right here. I guess her mind is a jumble."

"I hate to ask this, but . . . uh, do you know any details yet? I mean, did he just get handsy or was it, you know . . . rape?" There was something about that last word I had trouble getting out.

"I don't know yet, Fuse. She's been really upset, so we're giving her time to get everything out. We're still reeling, but with the way she's acting, I think it was . . . the second thing."

"Jesus, Kurt. I don't know what to say. How can I help?"

"I'm not sure. But we have to do *something*. We just don't know what. Angie and I thought because you've covered stories like this and, you know . . . talked to vulnerable people—plus Samantha has known you her whole life—you might talk to her. You're good at getting people in tough situations to talk. Samantha trusts you. Besides, she and Angie aren't so high on me these days about matters of sex."

I tried not to roll my eyes. Kurt had gotten involved with a young woman, one of his interns—Bonita Weller. He had broken off the affair, but that hadn't gone over well. I'd advised him on how best to reverse-engineer what could have been an explosive scandal. The solution involved Kurt paying off the woman from private family funds and me speaking with both Kurt's attorney and opposing counsel to ensure there would be no end-arounds where the story would get out via other means. These days, nondisclosure agreements or "gag orders" were rapidly becoming obsolete, as aggrieved parties would take your money *and* go to the press, thinking they could have both their cash and their richly deserved publicity. Part of my job had been to help convey that if an unsigned letter, a flash drive, a call from a burner phone, an anonymous email, or a voice-disguised witness were to find its way to the press, the Wellers would cease to enjoy their windfall and the new life they had established for themselves on the other side of the country. So far, so good.

Despite our success in tamping down the scandal, Kurt clearly remained on shaky ground with the women in his family.

"What's the end goal here for Sammy?" I asked. "The tactics vary, depending on your decision."

"What do you mean?"

"Do you want justice? Peace? Money? Revenge?" I said.

"Justice."

"That's what everybody says at first."

"What's so bad about justice?"

"Samantha will be on trial. They'll rip into every aspect of her life. Your lives. Your situation." I took a step closer to him, but not too close. "Bonita Weller could resurface."

"That wasn't a rape."

"But it could become one, under the wrong set of circumstances. We're in the vortex now with the #MeToo movement."

"Like I said, mine wasn't rape." Kurt kicked something imaginary. "It was barely an affair."

I wasn't surprised at his take on the Bonita Weller situation. Everybody, without exception, wants to think of themselves as a good person. To maintain that self-image, people twist their account into a pretzel, trying to convince themselves that they're someone other than who they are.

"You're right," I said. "It was about an immature girl who thought that after one tumble in a Gaithersburg motel, she was going to be Mrs. Rossiter, heading off to Davos and having dinner with George and Amal Clooney in Lake Como."

“I want what’s best for Samantha,” Kurt sighed.

“I’m not angling for a particular outcome here. Just let me know what you want to do, and I’ll walk you through your options. I’m happy to—scratch that—I’m *willing* to speak with her.”

Kurt smiled for the first time since he’d arrived. “Thanks, bud. How’s the *Incursion* situation?”

“The investigation? Sign of the times. They want an old fart out, so they whip up an ethical violation. I’m meeting with my lawyer the day after tomorrow, and we’ll see where things stand. Helping you guys out would be a nice distraction.”

Kurt narrowed his eyes.

“Well, not nice, but you know . . . still a diversion.”

“I knew you’d know what to do,” Kurt said.

“I’m not sure that I do,” I replied. “But I know I’ll do something if you need me to.”

3

FOR THE BETTER part of six decades, God had adored Kurt Rossiter—but God, it turns out, can be a moody chap. I pondered this as I climbed the steps to our bedroom. Joey was facing the outside of the bed, toward the mattress ledge. I knew she was awake, though, because in the reflection of the lamp base, I saw her open eyes as I crawled under the covers.

With full lounge-lizard smarm, I put my arm around her midsection and murmured, "Hey, what's goin' on?"

She sniffed out a chuckle.

"You know," I said, "there's a fifty-fifty chance if we can get things going here, something marginally pleasurable might come of it."

"Those are feeble odds," she said. "Pretty lousy seduction you got there, fella."

"I only peddle what I've got in stock. I'm getting old."

"I dunno. I've heard 'dad bod' is becoming a big online search category—"

"*Dad bod?*"

"The kind of bodies aging dads have. Some women like that. I got a pop-up ad on my phone."

"Pop-up, huh?"

"Were you talking to somebody outside?" Joey asked.

"Yeah. Kurt came by."

"Why?"

Time to lie. I wasn't ready to tell Joey what was really going on with Samantha, because she would likely tell Angie that she knew, either directly or by some other cue. Joey didn't have much of a poker face. I needed Kurt to know he could trust me.

"He wanted to see if I'd be on a panel at Wheelock."

"He came by for that?" Joey said.

"He had some other stuff on his mind." Okay, I'd eke out a technical truth to paper over the lie.

"Like what?"

"Boring midlife guy stuff."

"Affair?" Joey asked, suddenly alert.

"Yes, I'm having an affair with Kurt," I said.

"Seriously."

"Political nonsense at his foundation. Getting too old to fight the bullshit. Things like that."

My statement was sufficiently boring to cause Joey to roll back away from me. A familiar theme. When I was younger, adversity had been a bold challenge. Not anymore. I thought you were supposed to get tougher as you got older, but that's not how it works. When the *Incursion* said I had to take some time off, I just grabbed my backpack and faked a lighthearted stride to the stairs so it wouldn't appear anything was amiss. In fact, right now I couldn't think of anything I felt strongly about anymore, besides Joey and Finn and a lingering conviction that America was tapping its watch, wondering when I'd climb aboard one of Jeff Bezos's space shuttles and go to Neptune already.

"By the way," Joey said, her voice sounding muffled as she rolled over, "your father left seven hundred and ninety-six messages."

"How many were suicide threats?"

"All of them."

4

AT SEVENTEEN, AND wearing an oversized hoodie, Finn looked like a kindergartner dressed up as a teenager for Halloween. Of course, I probably treated her like one. This drove her nuts. Slim and athletic like Joey, only smaller, Finn had my darker coloring. When she was younger, I used to joke that the smallest unit of measurement known to man was Finn's nose.

"Have everything ready for school, Cheeks?" I asked as she sat eating cereal at the kitchen counter. I had called her Cheeks since she was a baby.

"No. It's stupid. I mean, tell me one time you've ever had to know geometry," she said.

"Easy. When you were born, I needed to confirm you had a round head and a little triangle nose. I wouldn't have known if I hadn't taken geometry."

"Stop being queer."

"Queer? Like homosexual or part of a sexually fluid community? Is geometry gay?"

"Dad! No, queer like strange—"

"I guess a rhombus *is* attracted to another rhombus—"

"Ugghh." She suppressed a smile.

"Wanna do something with me after school?" I asked.

"Like what?"

"Maybe rob an elderly person in a retirement community?"

"That's not funny," Finn said, again betraying evidence of a smile.

"I'll hold the knife and you can tie her up."

"Her? We're robbing an old lady?"

"Yeah, they're smaller and easier to carry. You know who Mother Teresa was?"

"The saint?"

"Yeah, Cheeks," I said. "I interviewed her once. I'm pretty sure I could take her too."

"You're horrible."

"We have to pay for college somehow."

"I'm not going to college."

"That's okay. You can just hang out with me. We can rob the elderly together."

Finn clomped away as I convinced myself that someday she would like me.

• • •

Like a moron, I answered the house phone despite seeing that it was Aunt Judith calling. She was one of my father's dwindling number of ambassadors, the people he was able to mobilize to tell his children they were neglecting him. She wasn't a real aunt, just a family friend. Had Joey been near the phone, she would have picked it up and told Aunt Judith never to call again. Joey had grown to despise the ambassadors as much as I did, but she didn't feel the compulsion to hear them out. I *did,* because of the guilt.

"Hello," I said.

"Hi, Sandy. It's Judith."

"Yes, I saw the number."

"How are you?"

"I'm fine, Aunt Judith. Look, I'm running out the door." I had no intention of running out the door at any point in the next several hours.

"Oh, I won't take long." She'd take long.

"What do you need?"

"I was talking with your father, Sandy. He called me. You know, he loves you. I'm very worried about him. He's such a gentle soul. I'm worried he will take his life."

"He's fine."

"He loves you, Sandy, and he needs his son. He's all alone."

"Did it ever occur to you that there's a reason for that, Aunt Judith? You should be ashamed of yourself."

"*I* should be ashamed of myself? What kind of person leaves an old man to suffer alone—"

"Please don't call here anymore. He's not going to kill himself."

"I can't call anymore?" Judith said, her voice in retreat.

"No. Never. Don't even let the thought cross your mind."

I hung up.

It would be different if I'd been just dealing with an aging parent with dementia, but my father, Nat, had been this way my whole life. One of the reasons for my exhaustion was that I had never experienced one day in my decades on this planet without Nat threatening to kill himself. He usually called to do this at dinnertime, but he especially liked disrupting holidays when I was with my family. He had not, to my knowledge, ever been formally diagnosed by a psychiatrist, because he didn't think there was anything wrong with him. But I had done research on my own with contacts at the National Institute of Mental Health in Bethesda. I figured he had some combination of schizophrenia, bipolar disorder, and borderline personality. At some point, you don't care what the diagnosis is—you just want the abuse to stop.

At least when I was a kid, I was subjected to his rants only a few times a day and on a somewhat irregular basis. My mother would refer to him as a human landmine. When I became an adult, it turned into robocalling: I heard his speeches all day long, every day. And he never got exhausted or heard a word we said. He was always broadcasting, never receiving. It never wore him out. You hear these stories about rage giving people cancer, but with Nat, his blood had long ago morphed into bile, and the bile sustained him and gave him strength. His explosions released the energy, and the radiation deformed everybody else's nuclei and eroded our immune systems.

When I was in college, my mother and I went to a doctor and asked how long my father could sustain behaving like this—implying, of course, the question of how long *we* could sustain his behavior. The doctor informed us that a human being's nervous system could take a lot of stress. That was nearly forty years ago, and Nat was still going—still getting thrown out of pharmacies and restaurants for pestering young women and, in front of me (but no one else, of course), clutching his chest and falling to the ground with fake heart attacks.

My mother had the most efficient strategy for coping with Nat: she got cancer and exited the planet a year after her diagnosis. I was in my last year of college.

I recognized long ago that no one besides me could possibly understand what we had endured and why I acted toward Nat the way I did. I spoke to him as if we were in an absurd stage production where all dialogue was meaningless. My goal was to simply get through any and each encounter with him without having my immune system impaled.

The question you have to answer when dealing with an insane family member is both an existential and a practical one: just because a blood relative is crazy, precisely how much of your life are they allowed to destroy? My current rule was that I would visit him once per every fifty suicide threats.

I put on my favorite black felt fedora, along with my regular warm-weather uniform that consisted of a black pocket T-shirt, khaki pants, and low-rise boots, and drove the two minutes over to Nat's. He still lived in the modest split-level I grew up in near the National Institutes of Health, in a neighborhood called Huntington. For both financial reasons and convenience, I had tried to get him to move, but—ever committed to making everyone's life a long stay in Guantanamo, Nat opted to dig his heels in even more firmly, and proceeded to pretend to fall down the stairs several times a week. I'm fairly convinced this was because he read someplace that old people fall.

I felt the usual palpitating in my throat—the sensation of choking I always had before seeing him. Twice, my mother had taken me to the hospital to see why I was having difficulty swallowing and breathing. The doctor had said there was nothing wrong with me, which only reinforced Nat's stance that I was a spoiled brat who didn't know how good I had it.

I inserted my key in Nat's door and opened it, and an intangible sense of strangulation reached for me, which is how my anxiety usually manifested itself.

"Hey, I'm here," I said.

"Son of a bitch," Nat said from the den, down the steps.

Nat sat in his favorite chair. He looked smaller every time I saw him. His face was square and harmless. The chair enveloped him. He looked about as dangerous as the old tailor who had been shuffling around Valley Cleaners on Old Georgetown Road with a tape measure around his neck since the Truman administration.

"Who's a son of a bitch?" I asked.

"They're all shovin' it up my ass," Nat said.

"Really? How far? All the way up?"

"I fell down today. I broke my knee and my hip. They have to operate on me. I may die. I'm broke." Every data point in this series of statements was a lie, but Nat betrayed none of the hesitancy one usually associates with lying.

"I'll do the operation myself then," I said. "Save you some money.

I have a hip in the car. They had a two-for-one at Safeway in Potomac Village."

"Potomac. All the rich people. That's who you're with now while I'm here dying of malaria?"

"They don't have malaria in Montgomery County."

"You think I've never been to Potomac before? I've been to Potomac plenty. That's where Roger Friedman lives. Now there's money. He knows me, Roger Friedman."

"Maybe he has a spare hip we can use, seeing as how you broke yours."

"It's not easy living with sickle cell anemia," Nat said.

"Sickle cell, huh? You see that on a TV ad?"

"I'm dying of it, the doctor said. They have to operate on me to take out the mesothelioma."

"They do that outpatient now. I can take you over to Suburban Hospital. They've got a deal going. They take out two sickle cells and one mesothelioma if you trade in an old laptop."

"I don't use that nonsense."

"Good for you," I said.

"Your bastard Uncle Barry has one, that son of a bitch who's always shovin' it up my ass and who I always helped out and who never said a goddam word of thanks. Without my help, he wouldn't have a laptick."

"Laptop."

"Your Uncle Zeke . . . now he's got the best kids. Supportive. They would let him live with them."

Uncle Zeke was a childhood friend of his. A sweetheart and profoundly generous.

"I have no family around," Nat continued. "No support. I'm gonna blow my brains out."

A few years ago, when Nat was over at my house for a barbecue, I'd actually handed him my gun and suggested he get it over with while we were all together. He was so terrified of the firearm that he tossed it underhand back at me as if it were ablaze. I realized for the first time in my life—at age fifty—that Nat would never kill himself. It was a half-century too late.

Omar, Nat's caretaker, came in from the kitchen. A gentle soul from Somalia, he had developed diabetes and high blood pressure since coming to work for Nat two years ago. All of Nat's vitals were those of an eighteen-year-old triathlete.

"Hi there, Sandy," Omar said. "Nat is glad you're visiting."

"It seems like it."

Omar always enjoyed listening to my banter with Nat, even though I could tell he thought we were out of our minds. To the extent anyone understood what we had been managing with Nat all our lives, it was Omar, but he only understood about ten percent of it. Nat was not *his* father, after all, and he wasn't affected on a molecular level like I was.

"You know how dementia is," Omar would say earnestly after Nat said something particularly vicious. No matter how many times I told him that Nat had been doing these things since Pearl Harbor, Omar would repeat, "You know how dementia is." Every trade has its anthem.

"They're all shovin' it up my ass," Nat was saying now. "You have your own life. Go lead it. Be selfish. I'm alone. You have no frame of reference."

"What exactly have people been shoving up your ass all these years? Just curious."

"We should go to that deli."

This was a no-go. Nat had begun to follow attractive young mothers around Attman's Deli over in Potomac, pretending to be a sweet paternal figure, thereby earning their temporary affection—sometimes even a gentle pat on the hand. It made me furious that he clearly had total control over his behavior, but he rarely managed to turn on this charm at home. One day, after watching him pull his Cuddly Grandfather act, I vowed never to take him out again. And I stuck to that.

"You never take me out to the deli anymore," he complained. "The apple don't fall far from the tree." He always used this phrase as generic filler.

"You know who likes trees?" I said. "Farm animals. I'm very attracted to them. You know what I'm talking about."

"You know who's good-looking? Those Victorian models."

"Victoria's Secret?"

"They want money," Nat said. "They steal from me."

"They steal from me, too. They wrestle me to the ground, strip me naked, and take everything."

"They're unsupportive."

"That's why they have those bras, I guess," I told him, forming cups with my hands and giving my invisible breasts a boost. "To help with the support."

"You were always talking about yourself," Nat said. "It was always about you."

"I know. I'm unsupportive."

"Exactly! You understand now."

"Of course I do. I'm going to hell."

"Don't fucking curse about hell! You're not going to hell. You're just selfish. I always took care of everybody," Nat said. "All I ever did was help people." He sighed and settled back in his chair. "I'm going to end my life."

"What do you want for your last meal? How about a big steak?"

"Too much cholesterol."

"I could be wrong, but I don't think cholesterol is the top concern before suicide."

"My vessels are clogged."

"Right. You'll survive with the cockroaches after the nuclear war with North Korea. You and Kurt."

"Now there's a winner. Kurt Rossiter. He's on TV with President O'Bonner."

"Obama. He's not Irish. And he's not president anymore," I said.

"I was all right with him, in spite of . . . you know."

"Yes, I know."

"That Kurt. There's a winner. Very supportive of his parents. His parents probably live with him."

"No, in fact, they don't."

It occurred to me that one thing Kurt didn't need right now was quality time with his parents.

5

INDEED, KURT HAD been on TV with Obama. When I got back home after my spiritual colonoscopy with Nat, I took a rare foray onto the internet and was able to find some videos of my all-grown-up childhood buddy: Kurt at Davos. Kurt with Obama, talking about climate change. Kurt meeting with lecture attendees at the Wheelock Foundation, wearing his best *I'm listening* face and scooping his thick hair off his forehead. The more I watched Kurt and his invocations of all the Davos buzzwords—*sustainability, tolerance, inclusiveness, transparency, authenticity, social justice, engagement*—the more I wondered what those words actually meant. They struck me as hollow incantations, obsessive-compulsive gestures.

Then I found my way onto Google to check out Pacho Craig. Given his nickname, I assumed he had some kind of Hispanic bloodline, but he looked like he could be Kurt's younger brother. I clicked on Pacho zinging a Food and Drug Administration official, then making the talk-show rounds to amplify his takedown. From my search, I discovered he had a particular dislike of evangelical preachers, corporate exploiters, Republican cabinet members, and polluters. He liked taking on the same causes as Hollywood stars—tried-and-true topics like climate change, gun control, abortion clinic bombers, and family values–obsessed public servants. His segments would trigger a round of breast-beating by legacy news organizations about the dubious triumph of digital media.

I noticed that in more than one video, when an interview subject would come back at Pacho in a tense exchange, he would tilt his head to the side in mock submissiveness and chuckle nervously before counterattacking. It was probably an unfair comparison, but it reminded me of the interviews I had seen with Ted Bundy, the serial killer. It wasn't an expression of true shyness, but a maneuver designed to convey a puppy-dog vulnerability to female viewers: *He can't be that bad. Look at his dimple!*

I wrote the word "shtick" on my notepad. Pacho was always telling targets that their time was running out, and his constant uniform was a long Australian Outback coat that had the whiff of a superhero cape. He wore Western boots with ornate designs, and had taken to collecting priceless watches that he displayed during tours of his eclectic townhouse in Georgetown, which had been featured in *Architectural Digest*.

Pacho's stock had risen two years prior, when he took down the chief of the Federal Emergency Management Agency for not responding properly to Hurricane Todd, which had engulfed Camden, New Jersey. It had not been an easy hit job. First, Pacho had attempted to portray the head of the agency, Henry Lockridge, as a racist, claiming that Lockridge's use of the phrase "chink in the armor" to describe a weakness in Camden's rapid-response plan was a swipe at the city's half-Korean mayor. Lockridge had objected, and attempted to explain that it was a common expression, to which Pacho asserted that Lockridge was "widely known to be racially intolerant." When a CNN host pointed out that Lockridge was, in fact, half black, a gobsmacked Pacho slip-slid his way to a new catch all rhetorical prison, insisting that Lockridge's leadership constituted a "failure of imagination." And that was the precise term the president used when dismissing Lockridge for supposedly mismanaging the hurricane. Poor Lockridge then dissipated into a bottomless depression, developed stomach cancer, and died within the year.

I had briefly interviewed Lockridge's daughter, Abigail Case, for a potential *Incursion* story about his downfall, but I didn't end up quoting her. I will never forget her waiflike appearance and her dark, haunted fawn eyes.

As I thought about what Pacho had done to Samantha, it occurred to me that the man would be a hell of a moose head on a reporter's wall. In the past, the press had avoided cannibalizing ideological soulmates like Pacho or Bill Clinton, but the margins of the culture had shifted. He was a rich white man who had been sailing through life on a following sea. No wonder women in America were furious.

I called Kurt, who was still at home, to check in on him.

"I was just going to call you," he said. "Any chance you could swing by to talk to Samantha?"

"Of course. When do you want me?"

"You can come over now."

I was in my car in thirty seconds and at the Rossiters' nine-thousand-square-foot house at the Burning Tree Country Club sixty seconds after that. Kurt and Angie lived over on Arrowood Road, widely considered to be the poshest street in Bethesda. After a neighborhood barbecue at Kurt's house a few years ago, I remember muttering to Joey that Arrowood was a street of millionaires who aspired to be billionaires. Even the turn onto Arrowood from Burdette Road was elevated, in the event motorists didn't get the message that they were entering higher ground. Rising to the main drag, I remember experiencing a burst of anticipation, as if a golden unicorn might be spotted chewing grass under a tree raining squash racquets.

Mr. Rossiter had worked for the State Department during the Nixon and Ford administrations, but the Rossiter lifestyle was financed primarily by something called a "family trust," which was a vastly mysterious and alluring concept to me as a kid. I envisioned secret ceremonies, blood oaths, and elaborate handshakes that only trick-jointed WASPs were capable of executing, like Vulcans. I always wondered what they talked about at family trust meetings, and imagined it had something to do with the burdens of being better than everybody else.

During the course of our forty-plus-year relationship, I'd often asked myself whether I really liked Kurt or only remained close to him out of sheer fascination that God could love one man so much that He gave him everything.

I let myself in through the garage as usual, and found Angie standing by the kitchen counter. Kurt and Samantha were sitting at the table.

I hugged Angie, and we both sighed at each other at the same time. What else could be articulated? As always, Angie was beautiful in her cool, blonde *Town & Country* manner, but the sun streaming into the house through a skylight revealed the crow's feet around her eyes. Maybe such features can appear overnight. Until this moment, I had seen both of the Rossiters as being remarkably ageless.

Given her recent ordeal, I chose not to embrace Samantha, who was wearing loose-fitting sweatpants and a red sweatshirt with the hood up around her pale face. She had the appearance of someone seeking cover. Kurt was standing beside her like a sentry, with his palms on her shoulders.

"Hey, kiddo," I said. I tapped her button nose the way I had done since she was little, and she offered a nodding grin.

"Hey, Uncle Fuse."

I took a seat beside her. She tilted her head to one side so that her ear almost touched her father's hand. Kurt had always adored her and was more affectionate with her than he was with his son, Steven. Samantha held her knees up against her chest, making herself into a dense cannonball, which at this moment gave her the appearance of a cute kid more than the twenty-year-old that she was. She had Angie's light coloring, was attractive and voluptuous, but landed a few degrees shy of her mother's acute beauty, which made her more approachable. The last few times I'd seen her, I couldn't help but project back to my own college years and think about what I would have felt had I seen her on campus: heartbreak.

"Sit down, Kurt," Angie said.

He reluctantly moved away from Samantha.

An excruciating silence permeated the room. There was an odd juxtaposition between the pain being felt here and the hypnotic sway of upper-class ecology playing outside the picture window overlooking Burning Tree, arguably the most exclusive golf club in America.

I would not directly confront Samantha about her version of what had happened with Pacho Craig. As a reporter, I found that I was better able to build a narrative by nibbling at the edges. When you demand that people describe an event, they tend to perform, but when you let them ramble, you get their humanity and, therefore, the truth.

"Well, kiddo, I'm really sorry you're dealing with all of this," I began.

"Thanks. Me too." Her lower lip appeared heavy, her eyes unfocused. I wondered if she had taken a tranquilizer. Her eyes betrayed a resigned fear, despite the slackening of her face.

"What can I do to help?"

Samantha said, "Mom and Dad thought that, because you've worked with some bad people . . . I mean, you've been around people who've done bad things . . . so maybe you might help me figure out some stuff."

"If I were God, Sammy, what would you want me to do? Ask for anything. Let's start there."

"Cut it off," Samantha said. Her face lost its slack, and her eyes flashed anger.

Kurt winced. It wasn't the kind of cringe men associated with the act of castration. It was more of a psychic pain. This was his baby.

Angie opened her mouth and began to form an objection but then said nothing.

"Okay," I said and chuckled a little.

"Sorry. That's how I feel," she said, slouching again, her confidence receding.

"I get it. Let's file that away for a second. Did you think about going to the police?"

"Yeah."

"But you didn't like that idea?"

"No," she murmured, looking down.

"Why not?"

"Because," Samantha said, "he'd get away with it."

"Why do you think that?"

"He's good-looking, rich . . . and people like him." She gazed in her father's direction.

"That concerns me too," Kurt said. "The cops."

"And why don't you want to involve the cops, Sam?" I asked.

"They'd make me into something I'm not. Like someone dirty—how I see myself now." She glanced at her parents, who stared back blankly. "They'd say I was looking for attention. That I made it up because I liked him and he didn't like me back."

"And is that true?" I asked.

"No!" Her mouth curled into a snarl as if she had been anticipating such an accusation. I was comforted to see some fight in her, even if it was momentary.

"I know this is hard, but I need to ask you: what *is* true?"

"I just stopped by MyStream to say hi to everyone. And then in his office, we were alone . . . on the sofa." Samantha looked at her parents and then back at me. "He put his arm around me and kissed me. But then he started getting . . . rough." There was reverberation in the word "rough," as if she were reliving it.

"Okay. So what did you do?"

"I let him." She glanced mournfully out the window. She shook her head. "God, I'm such an idiot. Why did I even go back there?"

Angie shut her eyes and held her face in her hands.

"Sorry, Mom," Samantha said.

"No, no, it's—" Angie began.

"We can stop," I said.

"No," Angie said. "It's just hard."

"It's very hard," I said, swallowing a lump in my throat. I couldn't imagine the horror of Finn ever finding herself in this situation. "Sammy, did you know when you went into Pacho's office that he might want to . . . get personal?"

She exhaled. "When he closed his door, part of me thought something might happen. But not what *did* happen." Sammy was now staring at a houseplant, her mind bobbing in another hemisphere. Her rage had dissipated, and she was reduced to being a barely functioning organism without agency of its own.

"Not that it would go so far."

"Right."

"And it went as far as it could go?" I asked. "Intercourse?"

"Yes."

"And you said no?"

"Of course I did." I saw a flicker of fury in her eyes again. Her hands balled into fists, and the veins bulged on the backs of her hands.

"And what did Pacho do?"

"He said that it would be all right. I mean, I said no, but he just kept going."

"Okay, kiddo. That's all I need to know."

"Um, there was protection," Samantha added.

"That's good. That's good," I said, turning my head toward the picture window that overlooked the pool out back and the golf course beyond.

"What do you think, Fuse?" Kurt asked. He'd been struck silent by his daughter's account, and I'd almost forgotten he was in the room.

"So," I said, "Kurt mentioned justice to me. And Sammy wants revenge. At least castration sounds like revenge." I grinned, and Sammy did too. "But there are a few other options . . . just so we're clear."

"Like what?" Samantha asked.

"Well, like money. You could always sue him. I know you guys don't need money, but it would make a point."

"We don't want his goddamned dirty money," Angie said.

Kurt and Samantha nodded.

"Maybe you don't sue him for money," I suggested. "But maybe you could get an admission that he attacked Sammy. He could give money to some charity, maybe one that helps women who've been abused. A lawsuit would shield you from any accusations by Pacho of defamation."

"How's that?" Kurt asked.

"If Samantha makes a claim in a civil filing, it has certain legal protections. And it also allows the media to report on a legal filing versus just the allegations, which could be seen as libelous. If, say, the *Incursion* prints allegations of rape based on the lawsuit, they're simply reporting news based on a civil complaint." I explained that the publication itself wouldn't be alleging anything, and that the revelation would allow the rest of the media to start scratching around, asking questions, and contacting the cops. "The cops, especially nowadays, would have no choice but to investigate. And some prosecutor—given your profile, Kurt—will surely want to take it on."

"Do you think the media will go after one of their own?" Kurt asked.

"Yes. Look how many of these media types have gone down for sex-related offenses along the spectrum: Matt Lauer. Charlie Rose. Mark Halperin. Les Moonves. Hell, they're even going after Tom Brokaw and Chris Matthews, and I think those allegations are pretty thin."

I had seen the way some of these boys in Congress carried on in the eighties and nineties, but plenty of them were liberals, so nobody covered it. It wasn't worth stirring up because plenty of these scumbags were good on certain issues. Of course, the right-wingers didn't want to hold investigations, because they were doing the same thing. Hell, a lot of the guys in the media were also grabbing interns. And when we eventually did cover it during the Lewinsky deal, it was the feminists who were hammering us for digging around on Clinton.

I explained all this to the Rossiters. "But now we've got a revolution brewing, and revolutions don't discriminate. Blood needs to flow. Outrage demands severed heads. It's preferable to get guys of the wrong political persuasion, but it's not required."

I stopped my rant and looked over at Kurt. He'd been nodding along with my diatribe, but Sammy's forehead was wrinkled, and I realized this wasn't the time or place to air my jaded laundry.

Angie cleared her throat. "I don't see an easy way out of a lawsuit."

"Neither do I," I said. "Now, what about quietly going back to your life? Maybe seeing a therapist? Trying to find some peace with this . . . wound? It's not like you can just forget it, but you may learn to live with it."

Samantha breathed in quickly. "And let him get away with it?"

"That's right."

"But he could do this to someone else!" Sammy's lips remained parted in a rictus, and her eyeteeth appeared pronounced like fangs. "No fucking way is he—"

"Sammy!" Angie said, and then paused for a moment. "I'm sorry. You can say whatever you want."

"All right, then let's come back to justice," I said. "We go to the police. You tell your story. They prosecute him. I encourage some friends in the media to cover it. He gets exposed, embarrassed, maybe fired. Maybe he even goes to jail."

Angie asked, "Can we report it anonymously?"

"No. There's no way to keep a secret in this day and age. Samantha will have to testify. You'll have cameras outside your house all the time. And there's something else. Pacho will probably argue that it was consensual. He'll claim that Sammy was into it and when it didn't turn into a full-blown romance, she decided it was a sexual attack. Pacho will admit to using bad judgment, his rep will get tarnished, no doubt, but it could very well end there."

Sammy balled her fists. "And for the rest of my life, I'll be the star-struck girl who asked for it."

I nodded. "Sad but true."

"Do you remember, Sammy, how upset you were when those girls put that nonsense on Facebook a few years ago?" Angie added. "About *Sweet Charity*? How supposedly you only got the part in that school play because we pressured the principal? If this went public, the attention would be a million times worse than that."

I hadn't heard this story, but I was glad Angie mentioned it. If Samantha had been unable to handle online teenage gossip, then the exposure of a sex crime case would destroy her.

"Look, you don't have to decide right now, but you can't wait forever," I said. "A lot of women coming forward these days are making allegations about things that happened years ago. Decades, even. Many of them have legitimate reasons for waiting, but to the public, those reasons sometimes don't look so legitimate."

"How come?" Samantha asked.

"It can come off as opportunistic. It looks like the woman woke up one morning, decided she wanted attention or money, and made her move."

The air escaped from Samantha's lungs as her fighting stance deflated to surrender once again. "That's so unfair."

"Yes, Sammy, it is. But I want you to understand what your options look like."

Samantha pulled back her red hood and shook down her hair,

which added about five years to her age. She leaned forward and told me, "I want my life to go back to the way it was before. And I want him to look in the mirror at himself and see what I see. What I think everybody else will see when they look at me."

"What's that?"

"Nothing."

My heart broke a little more.

"And Uncle Fuse, I just want to know why he did it."

6

I SAID MY goodbyes, and Kurt walked me out to my car. When we got outside, I said, "I can't tell Sammy why he did it."

"I know," Kurt said. "I think the cops are out of the question."

"You've made that clear," I said.

"Seems like vengeance is high on the list."

"Is that what Sammy wants, or is it what *you* want?" I asked.

"I think it's what we all want."

"I'm not so sure, Kurt. I think what she wants is her old life back, which of course I can't get for her. But I can follow her lead." It was clear to me that Sammy didn't want to get jammed up in anything that made her an active, front-and-center participant in what we decided to do. "Going to the police or suing this bastard would be brutal on her."

"I agree," Kurt said. "So that leaves vengeance. Maybe it *is* just because *I* want to do something. *Anything*. I can't do nothing."

"It's not like a vending machine, Kurt. You don't just feed a buck into the slot, push the button, and watch vengeance drop."

"You're not taking Samantha literally, are you? About chopping his dick off?"

"Genital mutilation isn't in my bag of tricks," I said, tapping the roof of my car. "There are other ways to screw with this guy."

"Where would you begin?"

"Takedowns are part of what journalists do. We look at a bad guy's weakness—a high-profile person's, that is. What makes them tick."

"For example?"

"Okay . . . The press corps always knew about Senator Gary Hart and women. That he couldn't help himself. He was so lost in his JFK fantasy that he didn't know a few generations had come and gone—that the rules had changed. You couldn't just cheat on your wife and get away with it anymore."

I paused, and Kurt had the decency to lower his head.

"With reporters," I continued, "there's a harsh reality. We have to please our employer. And they want to go after people they don't like, which plays into it. I covered Iran-Contra, which my bosses loved. They were so pissed when we couldn't prove Reagan knew about it. They wanted tape recordings like Nixon had, and there just weren't any. Reagan acted befuddled, and that worked for the most part."

Kurt grinned. "Sure did."

I nodded. "I had this source. Once of Reagan's top guys. He told me this great story. Nixon had called him one day during Iran-Contra, said to him, 'Let me tell you how to advise Ronnie. He should hold a press conference and say, *Look, I'm just stupid*. And the whole thing will go away.' Then Nixon hesitates for a beat and goes, 'Now of course, I could never have gotten away with that.'"

Kurt laughed. "So Reagan the dunce survives, and Nixon the genius goes down."

"Who was the genius in the end?"

"So what human weaknesses does my Fusey-boy exploit?"

"Remember years ago, when you asked why I wasn't afraid of those gangbangers I'd write about when I was covering crime?"

"Sure."

"It was because I never ambushed them," I said. "I always went in as a passive listener and never as an investigative badass. There was that drug lord, Big Noodle Jackson, back in the late nineties—"

"I remember him," Kurt said. "From Anacostia."

"Right. I just walked into the 'hood and said I was with the *Incursion,* and within days Big Noodle reached out to me." I ended up spending almost a month with the guy. He didn't tell me about specific crimes, but he shared his outlook on the world. How he was just providing a product that the marketplace wanted. That Al Capone *I'm-just-a-businessman* line. "I finally wrote that magazine section cover story on him, photos and all. He looked like a gangland genius. He framed the magazine cover, so I'm told."

"The cops took him down after," Kurt said.

"They surely did. But he never linked it to the media profile. He knew they'd get him at some point, but I guess he loved the fame almost as much as his freedom. That was his weakness. His successor, Eddie Fontaine, apparently loves the Big Noodle stories. Low-key guy. I tracked him down, and he thanked me for doing the feature on Big Noodle. It put Noodle away and made Eddie the boss. Now Eddie's talked to me from time to time, off the record—I just had to promise never to do a profile on him. That was the deal. He thinks I'm his friend."

"What's your point?"

"There's always something that moves a person from Point A to Point B. For Big Noodle, it was fame. For Eddie Fontaine, it seems like he wants to quietly build his fortune and send his kids to good schools. He wants to live a quiet, affluent life. He just happens to deal drugs to get there."

"Hoods have always liked you, Fuse. Why is that?"

I shrugged. "Maybe because I never try to act badass around them. They let their guard down, and we talk politics, families—"

"That's not it, my friend. I think they see a kindred spirit," Kurt said with a wink.

"I'm the squarest guy in the world, Kurt."

"Yeah, but there's a thread in that mosaic that they must see. As your friend, I've only heard about it. But I know there's that narrow thread, black as coal."

"Sounds mysterious," I said.

"So where does all this talk leave us?"

"Reporters these days can't pass up an opportunity to take somebody down and see their face on TV. This generation thinks journalism is just big-game hunting, a vehicle for fame—"

"I've never heard you talk that way."

"Something's changed. I'm not a part of this wave."

"Do you think getting fired has something to do with your change in attitude?"

"Maybe," I said. "But I'm just 'on leave.'" I rolled my eyes. "Anyway, I haven't thought the whole thing through. I need to look into Pacho a bit. See if there's something that's feasible here. I'd sure like to nail the bastard."

"Why?" Kurt asked with a sly grin. "Because of what he did to Sammy, or what he did to journalism?"

"Sammy, asshole," I said.

"Do you think we can get him for the way he treats women?"

"People aren't often punished how we want them to be—or when. We need to find out what he values and find a way to take it from him."

Kurt sighed. "This whole thing is brutal, Fuse. I can't compartmentalize. I can't not think about what happened to my baby."

I put my hand on Kurt's shoulder. "Compartmentalizing is just another American horseshit myth. Like 'closure.' And 'soulmates.' Where do we come up with this stuff?"

"Of all the things that I thought might destroy me," Kurt said, "I never thought it would be something like this. My mother's brother died pretty young. The one I look like. His heart just stopped one day when he was on the tennis court. I thought that might be the thing that got me. Every time I exercise, I wonder if the heartbeat I feel will be my last."

"I've watched hundreds of people go down during my career," I said. "Played a role in some of them. The one thing they all had in common? They thought they were special. Sorrow and defeat were for other people. Inferior people." I looked into Kurt's eyes. "They looked at people with problems as jackasses who brought misfortune on themselves. These were people, men mostly, who loved to say, 'You make your own luck.' Which is the kind of thing only lucky people say."

"You sure have given a lot more thought to trouble than I have," Kurt said.

"That's because you didn't know trouble until now. Trouble is all I know. And one of the biggest things I know about it is that trouble talks. And trouble had better keep its fucking mouth shut to make sure there's no blowback."

"I understand."

"No, you don't. But if we end up doing anything here, you had better understand it. That's why you can't tell Samantha any details. I can't even tell you details."

"You don't trust me?"

"I don't trust human nature. Every conspiracy begins to break apart when somebody leans across a table in a coffee shop and says the words 'You have to swear not to tell anybody.' People can't help themselves. Especially people who have never personally paid a terrible price for yapping. So tell me, Kurt, have you ever paid that price?"

"I don't think so."

I nodded. "Let's just say a lot of things have to break the right way for something like this to work."

As I drove the mile back to my house, my thoughts returned to Pacho. We all have dark impulses, but most of us don't act on them. Plenty of married guys—women, too—want to screw around, but we don't. Some of what stops us is morality. Or love for the person we're with, despite everything. Other times it's the fear of consequences—the understanding that a crushing tax will have to be paid. When a yellow dashboard light goes off in your mind, you stop and check it out. But if you're Pacho, and you have no feeling for anything besides your own animal impulses, you say to yourself, *I'm covered*. And you take what you want, no matter who gets harmed.

7

I DIDN'T WANT to imagine the scene taking place on Arrowood Drive right now, when the Rossiters reconvened. Would the Rossiter women rehash Kurt's adventures with Bonita Weller, and any other Bonita Wellers I didn't know about? Who knew what went on in a family—what kind of unspoken deals were cut, what quiet sobs were released, what complaints were registered to friends and therapists?

I shut the door of my study and called a district police lieutenant I knew, Mike Adams. He was a twenty-five-year veteran of the force and an expert marksman I sometimes went shooting with. I could bounce something off him without fear of it going further. I gave him the key points of the Samantha crisis without using her name.

"College student, huh?" Adams barked.

"Yeah."

"Finals?"

"Huh?"

"Was she in the middle of final exams?" he asked.

"Actually, her parents brought her home before the finals began."

"Be careful, buddy."

"I'm not following," I said.

"Finals season is when the sexual assault calls start coming in from George Washington, American, Catholic, Georgetown, and all the rest."

"Why finals? What am I missing?"

"Simple, Petty. You're feeling the stress. How do you get out of exams? Fastest way out these days is to be a victim of a sex crime."

"You can't be serious," I said.

"It's these bullshit claims that fuck it all up for the real victims. We go and hunt these cases down, and we get these mushy allegations. When we press, half the time we get some lousy, awkward regretted sex. Not assault. Not rape. Just unpleasant sex. And if you tell anybody I said this, I'll fuckin' deny it."

"Believe me, that'll never come out of my mouth. I don't even like thinking it's possible."

"Welcome to my miserable fuckin' world, man."

I hung up and stared at a window shade for twenty minutes.

• • •

I told Joey I wanted to take her to dinner. I pretended it was a spontaneous thought, when in reality it was part of my plan to inform her about what was going on with Sammy. I chose a Greek place downtown that was near my old *Incursion* office, because she liked it and the chef worked wonders with fresh vegetables. I asked Finn to join—I'd have to tell her about Samantha at some point—but predictably, she had no interest in coming with us. She wanted to be with that boyfriend of hers, who had recently read a few things online about Woodstock and decided he was a sixties radical. I heard Finn say something about making placards for an upcoming march.

Joey and I ordered our food, and I took her slim hands in mine and pinched a millimeter of skin on one of her knuckles. "Very obese knuckle," I said.

"Women like hearing about their obesity. So what's going on with Kurt?"

I flashed surprise.

"What?" Joey said. "You didn't think I noticed the furtive phone calls and disappearances?"

"I guess I thought I was more clever than I am."

"I've been married to an investigative reporter since I was a fetus."

I nodded. "I guess I never thought you were that bright. I was only into your looks."

"If you were all about looks, you would have gone for Angie."

"Not my type," I said.

"I know, you married me for that nose freckle."

"The heart wants what it wants."

"Isn't that what Woody Allen said about his relationship with his stepdaughter?"

"Yes, I base all of my relationships with women on what Woody Allen does."

"Encouraging. Ever think you made a mistake with me?" Joey asked.

"Oh, definitely. I think I would have been happier with Haddon, at home while she was out, flitting from man to man, collecting broken hearts and tacking them to the corkboard of her soul."

"Yes, you would have done well with Haddon, my Prince of Routine." Joey couldn't suppress a smirk.

"And Kurt?" I asked. "What about you and him?"

"Oh yeah, he would have been very happy with a tomboy who's in her pajamas by dinnertime."

"But wouldn't you be happy with him and all his hair?"

"Yes, Fuse, that's what I was looking for. Hair."

"How about ease? Wouldn't you have liked living in a Ralph Lauren ad?"

"That's not what I wanted."

"C'mon on, Joe. Isn't Kurt what all women want, the way people want a mountain or a sunset? You see beauty and everything you ever wanted, and your brain goes, *BAM! Yes! That!* Certain people are fantasies in human form. A woman looks at Kurt and sees the sunset, not the heartbreak."

"Thanks for acknowledging my depth. Let's not get into anything stupid here."

I nodded that I wouldn't.

"Is Kurt is behaving these days?" Joey asked.

"I figured you saw him as being perfect," I said.

"I see the Rossiters as *looking* perfect. You're the one who thinks they *are* perfect."

Joey was right. But I wasn't sure I could sit on the Samantha bomb any longer now that Joey was probing. "Okay, here goes. Sammy was, um . . . assaulted."

Joey's glass slipped in her hand, but she managed to catch it. "Oh my god." She lowered her voice. "As in, raped?"

"Yes."

"Shit. Did you talk to her?"

"Yes."

"Who did it?"

"That swashbuckling Pacho Craig character."

"The guy she was interning with?"

"Yes."

"With the long hair, the cape thingy he wears—"

"Right."

"Did she go to the police?"

"Not yet. We're trying to figure out options. That's what they wanted my help with."

"Options? There's only one option. Go to the cops."

"It's not that simple." I explained all the ways reporting Pacho could boomerang on Samantha.

"How's Kurt holding up?" Joey asked. "Sammy's like a little doll to him. I always thought he was cold to Steven. And what about Angie?"

"She looks hollowed out."

The waiter brought our salads. Joey stabbed a tomato. "And Sammy?"

"She was sitting there in a hoodie, hugging her knees to her chest like a little kid. I can't get it out of my mind."

Joey conjured a brief flicker of puzzlement.

"What?" I asked.

"The way you described Sammy as a kid. I haven't seen her in that way for a few years."

"What do you mean?"

"Oh, come on, Fuse. It's hard to deny that she's grown up into a very sexy woman."

The thought of burning in hell flashed through my brain. "What? I don't know. Sure, she's very pretty. A pretty . . . you know . . . *girl*."

"What are you, a moron? Of course she's sexy. There's nothing wrong with noticing that. And I'm sorry I brought up Kurt and his women," Joey said. "Angie always wonders about him, you know? She hoped he'd get it out of his system."

"That's a myth," I said. "Getting it out of your system. People who tend toward monogamy keep tending toward monogamy. People who tend toward variety tend—"

"I follow."

"Think Angie will always stick by him?"

"She loves him. Loves their life," Joey said. "He says he's knocked it off. Besides, where would she go?"

I glanced at a man a few tables over who was holding up his coffee cup and waving over the young waitress.

"Stick your finger in it!" the man demanded of the waitress. "Cold!"

His wife sat cowering as the waitress's lower lip quivered.

"Do it," he insisted.

"I'm sorry, sir. I'll get you another cup," the waitress said.

"No way. There's no excuse for this. Put your finger in it," the man said again.

I sized him up: fifties, medium height and build, with a mean look embossed on his face conveying that he reigned supreme in his home but nowhere else.

His wife shot the waitress a pleading expression.

The waitress tried again. "I'll . . . I'll, uh, get you—"

"Stick your finger in it!"

"I can't, sir. It would be unhygienic." The waitress turned away.

"Don't bother bringing another one," the man shouted after her. "You're not getting a tip!"

The other patrons in the restaurant sat gaping at the scene.

I felt heat behind my eyes. It was a peculiar but familiar sensation—the feeling of my blood percolating in my skull. Joey was watching the proceedings, knowing how this kind of thing affected me and why. *Nat.* Still, my default reaction was usually to seethe quietly. This time, I saw Joey's eyes narrow, and she shifted in a way that made me think of her tomboy days, when she hadn't hesitated to kick a kid named Randy Gerson in the balls after he said something about seeing her bra in gym class. She'd really hurt him, too.

The waitress passed me and caught my eye. I held up my hand, and she came over.

"You all right?" I asked.

She shrugged and said, "This happens sometimes. It's part of the job." But the tightness in her expression betrayed the pain that came with customer confrontations like this one.

"Dissatisfied customers are part of the job. Abuse is not. You look shaken."

"I'm fine."

"What's your name?" I asked.

"Tracy."

"Do me a favor, Tracy," I said. "Bring him one of those bread puddings with the vanilla ice cream on top. Add it to my bill."

"Fuse, what are you doing?" Joey asked. I could tell from the familiar twitch on her upper lip that she sensed some aggression coming on.

"I'm just trying to express my admiration for a man who gets what he wants." I made a muscle.

Joey shook her head, but I could see she approved.

The waitress shot us a quizzical look.

"What if he sends the cake back?" Tracy asked.

"Just say it's compliments of me. Oh, and do you happen to know his name?"

"He comes in here from time to time. Roy Nickerson." She walked away, leaving Joey and me to finish eating.

"Are you going to pull something?" Joey asked. She knew I had a dastardly streak, although she still wasn't aware of some of the adolescent actions I had taken over the years.

"You may want to finish your wine."

Joey's expression fell on the spectrum between mischief and resignation, not outright anger. I knew when Joey was angry—and had she angrily ordered me to retreat, I would have obeyed.

"I'm going to the restroom," I said.

When I got back, Tracy set down the bill in front of me. I left cash, both for expediency and because I didn't want to give Nickerson a chance to find out who I was. A few tables over, Tracy placed the bread pudding and vanilla ice cream before Nickerson.

"I didn't order this!" he said.

"It's courtesy of the gentleman over there," Tracy said, nodding my way.

He glanced at me, wearing a facial expression like he'd just stepped in dog shit.

I held up my water glass as if in a toast. Joey held up her wine, wearing a huge, insincere grin.

Nickerson scowled and pushed the bread pudding away from him.

"Ready, Joe?" I asked.

"Oh, God."

We stood and proceeded in the direction of Nickerson and his wilting wife.

"Hey," Nickerson said as we approached his table.

I picked up the dessert plate with my left hand and pressed the pudding into his face. With my right hand, I grabbed his impressive head of hair and said, "Stick your finger in it!"

When I sensed some resistance, I dropped the plate against his shirt, grabbed his throat with my left hand, and forced his head down toward the table with my right.

His wife recoiled.

I spoke to him through gritted teeth. "Now listen to me, Roy Nickerson. You just sit here for a few minutes and think about your dessert. I'm gonna look into you, and I may wake up one morning four months from now, track you down with a bunch of Albanians, cut out your organs, and sell them on the black market. If you scream at your wife after I leave, that'll be reason enough. And I'll *know*."

When I was certain that he'd be too busy gasping for air for the next few minutes and in no frame of mind to challenge me, I nodded at the nearby patrons. "I hate rude behavior, and I'm not gonna tolerate it."

It was a line I paraphrased from Larry McMurtry's *Lonesome Dove*.

"C'mon, darlin'," I said to Joey.

Joey glanced at poor Nickerson's wife and said, "You oughta dump this asshole."

On the way out of the restaurant, Joey said, "Unemployment has made you intrepid as fuckall."

As we were walking to our car, which was parked on a side street, a dirtbag wearing a gray hoodie jumped out of an alley and growled, "Your wallet! Gimme it!"

Joey jumped back and held her hand to her chest.

But I recognized the thug. I gave him a hard look and said, "Knock it off, Freddie!"

Freddie hung his head. "Sorry, Petty," he said. "I didn't know it was you." When I took out a five-dollar bill and gave it to him, he vanished back into the shadows.

Joey just looked at me. "Who *are* you?"

8

THE FOLLOWING MORNING, I awoke to Joey facing me on her pillow and arching her eyebrows.

"What did I do? Snore again?" I asked.

"Well, spouse-o-mine, that was quite an adventure we had last night. What was that performance at the restaurant?"

I rubbed my eyes. "I just couldn't take what that asshat was doing to that girl."

"Does this have something to do with Samantha?"

"I don't know. Probably."

"Or memories of your mother, as your father was spewing?"

"Maybe. I just did it."

"That's my point. You usually think things through. Have you done this before when I'm not on the scene?"

"I don't think so."

Joey studied my face, assessing whether I was telling the truth. It wasn't as if she thought I was a serial liar, but I had been known to evade complete answers when I didn't want to get into something.

I said, "I was in the car a few days ago. I had the seventies station on satellite. I caught the beginning of 'Suite: Judy Blue Eyes.' That opening line . . . when he talks about how it's getting to be where he's no fun anymore."

"Yes?" Joey said.

"I heard it a million times but never really paid attention. All of a sudden, I felt like I was about to give a speech and that was my walk-on song."

"You're plenty of fun still."

"Thanks. I'm trying not to be a leaky vessel like my father," I said.

"A leaky vessel that never runs out of poison. You're not him, Fuse."

"Thanks."

"Do you regret what you did last night?"

"Is this where I lie and tell you that I have reflected upon my actions and now regret them? Truth is, I don't. Actually, I wish I could do it more."

"Be careful. You're not Dexter."

"Dexter?"

"The vigilante serial killer on TV and from those books."

"I'm squeamish about blood." I kissed her and got out of bed.

I hadn't been entirely truthful with Joey. I had, in fact, done other things over the years that were perhaps equally as . . . *assertive* as what I had done in the Greek restaurant. A few years ago, there was a girl at school bullying Finn. It was mostly verbal stuff accompanied by the occasional locker shove. I did some research on the bully's family and learned that her father was a lobbyist for a big pharmaceutical company.

Sweet.

I called the lobbyist during lunchtime, when I knew he wouldn't be in, and left a message from "Sanford Petty with the *Capitol Incursion.*" When his assistant asked me what the inquiry was regarding, I said simply, "Malfeasance."

I assumed that he crapped a cinderblock when he returned from lunch and got his messages, because he called me back in the midafternoon. I didn't return the call until the next day because I wanted him to have a very unpleasant evening after he checked me out and saw my pedigree.

When we finally spoke, I told him about his daughter bullying Finn. He vowed to look into it, and I believed him. Before we hung up, I asked him what kind of lobbying work he did, and he gave me an anodyne answer. Not a threat had been uttered, but one had been delivered. The last thing a guy like him who operates in the shadows needed was sunlight, courtesy of the *Incursion*. He didn't want to be on my grid, and he knew that Washington runs on payback. And what was politics anymore but the implementation of spite?

The bullying stopped.

• • •

Later that morning, as I drove to my latest meeting with a media attorney named Frankie Waterman, I honed my purpose of getting a read on what the *Incursion* had been telling her about its investigation into yours truly. I had retained Frankie after I was put on leave. She had experience in taking on big media organizations on behalf of both defamed clients and inconvenient journalists.

Last spring, I had begun an investigation of my own: into the suicide of a character named Guido Reni, the head of a free-enterprise think tank known as Running Dogs—so named because of how communist revolutionaries had referred to the "running dogs of capitalism" or "running dog imperialists." Reni was a bohemian provocateur who liked challenging organizations—from environmental groups and radical gender outfits to plaintiffs' lawyers, labor unions, and short sellers—that he believed embodied the encroaching forces of socialism, in the form of the hegemony of certain lefty causes over the news media.

Despite his free-market bias, Reni was not rich, and his appearance ran toward homeless couture. I never agreed with him on much, but I admired his subversive attitude. During the Obama years, he'd had a point about how we in the press had become the handmaidens of the White House. And it wasn't just about favorable reporting on story ideas submitted to us by those we agreed with. What a lot of people didn't understand about media bias was that the things we chose *not* to cover often said more about who we were than the things we did cover.

I started digging into Reni's suicide—he shot himself while hiking on the high rocks of the Billy Goat Trail, and his body fell into the gnashing Potomac River, leaving blood and brains spewed all over the boulders. A source of mine from back in the Clinton years informed me that Reni had been murdered by Hillary Clinton along with the financing of left-wing billionaire George Soros. I found nothing to confirm this tedious blather.

However, I did find something more nuanced: Reni had been the target of a "cancellation campaign" to destroy his livelihood, orchestrated by a loose affiliation of organizations that were all clients of a progressive PR firm called the Sunshine Collective. He was getting fired from teaching gigs, having speaking engagements and consulting work nixed, and seeing his book contracts voided. Although the firm took its Sunshine name from a supposed commitment to transparency, my experience was that whenever anyone used that word, the next thing they said would surely be a lie. "Transparency" simply translated into *I want dirt on people I don't like*.

As I began to trace the organizations that had moved against Guido Reni and Running Dogs, an interesting thing happened. My editors started getting calls from the Sunshine Collective's charismatic founder, Mario Candell, and my bosses started riding me on why I had been chasing down Reni's suicide. It wasn't unusual to receive complaints from media targets, but usually such complaints made us dig in even harder. In this case, I found Candell's ability to impede my story through calls to my editor a little clubby. I also didn't like the looks I began getting in the newsroom. I really had no great affection for somebody who shilled for big business, but all Reni had been trying to do was throw punches back at those of us in the press who hadn't returned his phone calls.

So I did what any pain-in-the-ass reporter does. I dug deeper.

The Sunshine Collective eventually prevailed upon the *Incursion* to kill my pursuit of the story on the grounds of "tortious interference," a potential legal claim that I was disrupting their business. The truth was, we messed with people's careers and personal lives every day of the week with impunity, so why did the *Incursion* care so much about Sunshine? I asked the paper's brass how they would feel if a left-wing activist had blown his brains out after making claims of harassment by big business or right-wing dirty tricksters.

Then others at the *Incursion* started complaining about my "abrasive presence"—in particular, a thirty-something, Pulitzer Prize–wanting reporter named Gretchen Kramer, who wouldn't be happy until every aging white guy's carcass was roasting on a spit. And in the wake of billionaire Peter Thiel's financing of pro-wrestler Hulk Hogan's fatal defamation lawsuit against Gawker, the *Incursion* editors said they had to investigate any journalistic endeavor that could potentially bring down the newspaper. They demanded my investigative notes, put me on paid leave, and informed me of the possibility that if journalistic malfeasance were discovered, I could lose my pension and perhaps any severance pay.

Me. A man of destiny. Hell, didn't these things happen to other people—to life's losers? When my mother once illustrated my Great Future in prolific and hyperbolic terms, the prospect of being downsized hadn't been part of her sketch. She may have envisioned such a crummy future for my booger-laden neighbor Allan Borowitz, with his finger perpetually up his nose and his little green rabbit teeth. But not for me.

Frankie's office was in the Bender Building on Connecticut Avenue near the intersection with L Street. That spoke well of her. The building was one of the older ones in the high-rent district, and its tenants were serious but not ostentatious. If somebody had told me ten years ago that the great legal and lobbying powerhouses like Howrey & Simon and Patton Boggs would have collapsed, I would have thought that person was insane. Outfits like that were more solid than the Adirondacks, but when collapse came, it came overnight, leaving hundreds of thousands of marbled square feet empty.

A pundit once said that in Washington there are two worlds: "talk-show world" and "shadow world." There are denizens of the capital who appear on talk shows—occasionally powerful men and women whose main qualification is picking up their phone when a producer needs somebody to jump in front of a camera and say something that will fire up Twitter. Then there are people like Frankie Waterman, who quietly toil day after day, decade after decade, in offices that no one photographs for the *Washingtonian*. Shadow world.

Operating the boutique legal practice of Pollard Waterman & Cooper for two decades, Frankie was a litigator's litigator from somewhere in the South who had come north for her education at Wharton and Yale Law. Just shy of sixty, she had reddish hair, a sun-kissed complexion, and a soft, almost mesmerizing voice. I was relieved when she agreed to take me on as a client.

I pushed Frankie's floor in the elevator, but the button wouldn't light up. Typical. I went out to the front desk in the lobby and told the attendant my problem. She waddled over to the elevator, pushed the floor, and it lit right up.

Frankie's office overlooked the Mayflower Hotel, where the Bender Building's inhabitants had watched Monica Lewinsky take her walk of shame to where her attorney was based, a few floors above Frankie. There was nothing special about Frankie's office save the equestrian paraphernalia and an over/under shotgun resting on a wall mount.

I sat on Frankie's sofa while she leaned back in a comfortable chair. She wore an Oxford shirt with a vest and khaki pants over her slim frame, and on her lap was balanced a legal pad on a clipboard.

"What do you have so far, Frankie?" I asked.

"Well, Petty, they don't tell you much about internal investigations."

"It's only my life."

"I know. The gist is that the very act of you calling around qualified as push-polling."

Interesting term. "Push-polling" is a device used by political campaigns to spread false rumors about an opponent under the guise of polling, such as *Does Barack Obama being a Muslim extremist suicide bomber make you more or less likely to vote for him?*

"That's what Guido Reni was saying the media were doing to *him*—different media outlets calling around, asking questions to defame him," I said.

"Accusing your enemies of the very thing they're doing to you," Frankie said. "A common trick."

"I know. It was one of Goebbels's favorites. All I did is what reporters do: ask informed questions." I thought about all those years I had phoned my targets and said, *This is Sandy Petty from the* Capitol Incursion. There were times I felt like offering up a Dracula-style *Mooohooooohaahahah!* Reporters love scaring people, but in the Reni case, I really hadn't done anything over the line.

"They have put some of their reporters onto the investigation into your conduct—not for publication purposes but for investigative ones," Frankie explained.

"Do we know who?"

"The *Incursion* wouldn't tell me, but I have a source there who said one of them is Gretchen Kramer."

"Shocking. She hates me."

"Why?"

"I red-inked the hell out of one of her story drafts. I told her she wanted to be Joan Didion but didn't want to immerse herself into the worlds that made Didion great. She didn't like constructive criticism about needing to spend more time digging than writing Pulitzer-posing essays. Very millennial. Pretty sure I said something else that offended her, too."

"More than that?" Frankie smiled.

"We were talking about Bill Clinton and the whole Monica Lewinsky drama. Gretchen didn't dispute that Clinton had an affair with Lewinsky, but was dismissing the rape and harassment charges from the others—Juanita Broaddrick, Kathleen Willey, Paula Jones. I had gotten sick of women blindly rallying behind Clinton, so I might have said something along the lines of 'You'll need to decide whether you're against men who prey on women or you're against men you don't find attractive who prey on women.'"

"You said that?" Frankie asked.

"I say shit sometimes. I don't edit until something gets into type."

"No wonder the *Incursion* doesn't like you. You're a stegosaurus. Which brings me to another point. See, Petty, there are problems with old white guys in the media. For one thing, you're expensive to employ. For another, you don't write stuff that readers these days care about. They want coverage of Kim Kardashian's ass and whatever hits their algorithms. They want stories about transgender this and that, and aerial views of billionaires' houses. But employers don't want age-discrimination lawsuits, so they have to bounce guys like you with buyouts and malfeasance allegations."

"I'd take a buyout."

"That would be nice, but we have to get through this investigation first."

"Look, Frankie, all I did on Reni was what I've been doing for thirty-plus years. Investigate. Make calls. Do interviews. I'm not harassing young interns—"

"But you were pursuing an inconvenient story."

"Look, a prominent Washington gadfly blew his brains out," I said. "That's a story."

"It's a story, Petty, that the paper didn't want to do."

"Fine, but why does that warrant an investigation?"

"Because they think you crossed a line." Frankie stood, presumably for emphasis, and crossed her arms.

"But I didn't."

"But they think you did."

"Bullshit. They *want* to believe that I did."

"Let's cut the Oliver Stone lunacy and get down to it. Why, realistically, do you believe they didn't want you pursuing the Reni story?" Frankie asked.

"For one thing, like you said, they want to bounce the old farts out."

"Fine, but they could have told you it's time and given you a buyout."

"They don't have the money they once did, when the Baldessari family owned the paper. And when that unctuous Jacobin Mario Candell called my editor, the paper told me to back off."

"All right, so the *Capitol Incursion* ordered the murder of Guido Reni," Frankie said, setting down her clipboard.

"Of course not. But they have some reason they don't want that story written."

"Editors kill stories all the time, I bet."

"Not because some PR flack asks them to." I threw my arms up. "So, what I've learned today is that you don't know anything new other than that a reporter who hates me has been assigned to dig into me. And I guess you're telling me that I have to let the process play out?"

"What else do you have in mind?" Frankie asked. She winced a little, waiting for my response.

"I'd like to scratch around a little," I said.

"Investigate their investigation?"

"Yeah."

She dropped her pen on the floor. "Are you nuts? They already want you out."

"I know, but I'm not one to just sit around waiting for the stampede to roll over me. They're obviously worried about something," I said. "It may not be super-sinister, but it may be embarrassing. I'd like to do a little more research on what Guido Reni had been working on and what might have pushed him over the edge."

"Did you ever think that maybe he was just depressed?"

"Sure he was depressed. But he was also a pretty tough guy. He was used to controversy. Yet all of a sudden what he's been doing for thirty years makes him do a ballistic backflip into the Potomac?"

"Petty, I don't take on lost causes," Frankie said, picking up her pen. "I can't control you, but I can tell you that if you get nicked investigating further, it will inflame the *Incursion.*"

"They're already inflamed."

"Then they'll be so inflamed that they'll say you've lost your mind, that you're trying to cover up whatever you did wrong, and then we'll have no chance of a buyout. Plus, they may even retaliate in some way. The media are no different from any other corporate enterprise I've represented. They deny, they lie, they stonewall, they smear their own whistleblowers—"

"I'll be careful," I reiterated. "They're hiding something, Frankie. And if we find out what it is, it may call them off and get me a better deal."

Frankie blew out her cheeks. "Fuse? Isn't that your nickname? Where does it come from?"

"That's another story," I told her. "When I got that name, I could very well have needed you. Almost did. I was a kid."

"Sounds ominous."

"Yeah, it kind of is. Someday I'll tell you the story. In the meantime, I have something else to discuss with you."

"You haven't done something crazy, have you?"

"Always. No, not this time. This is something else. I have a friend who has a problem."

"A friend?" She bit the side of her cheek and cocked an eyebrow.

"Honestly, a friend. His daughter worked for a well-known media guy. She claimed he attacked her—"

"Rape?"

"Yeah. I'm pretty sure I know what I'm going to do. But I want to know if you have thoughts about cases like this."

"Do you believe her?"

"I've known her since she was born. I do believe her."

"What are the chances it was a little romp gone bad? The guy 'hit it and quit it,' as they say, and she's pissed? I've seen it happen."

"Always possible, but this guy strikes me as a real shit."

"Everybody strikes you as a real shit. You're a reporter. Is it possible she thought the encounter was one thing and he thought it was another, and now she wants to punish him for this disparity in expectations? Because if I was repping the guy, that's how I'd play it. Did you say the girl worked for him?"

"Yeah, but as an unpaid intern."

"Let me tell you what's happening all over this country right now. At this very moment, there is an employment attorney calling up his male client and asking to go for a walk together around the block to discuss the current state of affairs. Literally." Frankie wagged a finger to underscore her point. "On that walk—away from prying eyes and ears—the attorney tells his client that this is a privileged conversation, that it never happened. He's telling that man not to meet with women in his office privately. He's telling him not to travel with women or mentor them or take them out to lunch. He's telling him that if there's a job applicant you find attractive, don't hire her, because temptation is trouble."

"Would you ever give that advice? As a female lawyer?"

"No comment."

"What about going to the police?" I asked.

"I would argue that if it really was a rape, then of course you go to the police. I'd tear somebody apart who made an accusation like that and didn't go to the cops. The risk is that you can't control where it goes, where the ball bounces—trials, investigations into her behavior, anonymous posts on the internet about what a big whore she is. She'll be the crazy girl who just wants attention. Meaning, her name will get out. It always does."

"Her family is a big deal—"

"Well, there you go. She could always hire a victims' lawyer and try this in the press, but those lawyers are rarely honest about the downside or the risks. Like losing and being tagged as a rape victim for life."

"But she *is* a victim."

"But that isn't her identity to the outside world," Frankie said patiently. "If this goes public, as you know, that's what she'll be. The victim. Forever. In some circles, there's an outside shot she'll be the tough woman who stood up to a bastard, but I wouldn't oversell that. It's more likely she'd be the crazy victim or the victim who asked for it. When you say her family is big, do you mean rich?"

"Rich . . . connected."

"Then she doesn't need cash."

"No."

"How badly does she want to burn him down? You said the bad guy's famous?"

"Yeah."

"Everybody wants to burn down a big shot. Even his friends in the media will want to eat him alive. You guys love lighting up high-profile newsmakers. My sense is you already know what you're going to do to him."

I felt the heat shoot up my spine and then turn frigid. Maybe this was because I had begun to suspect that of myself, and I sensed she had tweaked me on purpose. It was one thing when *I* trashed the press—it was like complaining about your kids to a friend—but another thing when somebody else trashed the institution.

I drove home contemplating whether there was a way to "light up" Pacho Craig in a manner that wouldn't boomerang on a woman I had carried around as a baby. If there was, I hadn't thought of it yet. But I did know that if Samantha did decide to come forward, she should not be alone.

9

WHILE AT THE *Incursion,* I had gotten to know a consultant to the National Security Agency who did a pretty good job at translating for me what intelligence agencies did and did not do when they spied. We had never spoken on any of my regular phones—I always contacted him through a burner—and we would meet at Attman's Deli, where he would answer my questions about the mischief going on in the American electoral process. I usually met with sources at places that held no appeal for Washington insiders, because at prestige restaurants it wasn't unusual to overhear someone at the next table saying something they shouldn't to somebody just like me. I did not want to be overheard. I usually chose delis or diners, where we might look like insurance estimators grabbing a sandwich before getting back to a body shop in Rockville or Herndon. As a result, I'd become a diner and deli regular around town.

I'd never asked my NSA friend for his name, or precisely how he made his living, or who else employed him. And this was a good thing. I'd told him my name was Boz Scaggs, but given his line of work he surely found out long ago who I was. I took to calling him "Goblin" because he taught me new forms of mischief, and because his ears were just a tad pointy.

Goblin was seated across from me now, at a table in an isolated alcove at the deli. He looked to me to be about thirty, though it was hard to tell exactly, and I made it a point not to press him for personal details. Cajun and African American, with a jolly, round face and a body to match, Goblin once joked that his employers favored him in part because few people would ever suspect him of being a cyber spy. Whenever he had to enter a location under less-than-honest circumstances, he made a convincing Washington-area utility worker who was all too happy to tell you about the new valve he'd just installed in an HVAC system.

He hadn't been surprised when I'd once told him that in the course of my reporting, I'd been known to leverage the inherent racism in our culture by mobilizing people of color to pose as maintenance or service workers for reconnaissance, such as eavesdropping on restaurant conversations. He would have been insulted if I had given him some politically correct speech about how I would never stoop to such a thing. Like me, he lived in the real world.

"You want lunch?" I asked.

"Sure, Boz, yeah, yeah."

I got a kick out of the way he repeated words at the end of his sentences, which had taken some getting used to. "I like the club sandwich."

He said to the whip-thin young waitress, "I'll have a lox and bagel, *cher.*" The Rossiter Family Trust was paying.

"Any thoughts about the latest Russian stuff?" I asked. "You know, screwing around in our politics?"

"I think if a federal prosecutor wants to find something, he'll find something," Goblin said. "Sure, the Russians put the gris-gris on us. And we screw around with them. It's what we do."

"Gris-gris?" I asked, pronouncing the unfamiliar word *gree-gree* as Goblin had.

"Voodoo."

"Ah. Yes, that we do. Years ago, I interviewed an old KGB guy. Long retired, living in America. He asked me if I'd ever heard the theory that the CIA killed President Kennedy. I told him everybody knew that theory. He asked me if I knew where that got started. I said no. He said, 'What do you think I was doing in the sixties and seventies?' He'd been running around paying college professors who already believed the CIA killed Kennedy to write books and articles saying they did it."

Goblin grinned. He knew a lot about the current state of intelligence, but I knew more history. "Who did your Russian friend think shot JFK?" Goblin asked.

"Oswald! He said they knew it was Oswald as soon as our people arrested him."

"The Russians had their eyes on that *couillon*," Goblin said.

"They knew him, but not how people think. They were aware of him because he had settled in the Soviet Union for a while, married a Russian woman. But they thought he was a nut. When they heard the news about Kennedy's murder, the KGB guys said, 'That idiot actually fucking did it?'"

"What about the cover-up theories?"

"It was really the kind of bureaucratic cover-up we see all the time in Washington—worker bees covering their asses, afraid they're going to get dinged for not preventing a product flaw by reporting it up the chain. J. Edgar Hoover was worried that his guys had interviewed Oswald and didn't stop him. All it takes is one couillon, as you say—just one wackadoo—to get lucky, and he can turn the world upside down."

"Or somebody with an agenda. Like Eddie Snowden, no?" Goblin replied, mentioning the NSA consultant who gave up much of the Americans' spy game to the media.

"Right," I said. "Were you surprised when Snowden went public?"

"Look, I met the guy when he worked with a consulting firm. I'd love to tell you I was smart enough to know he was special, but he was just another kid like me. It's scary, scary. People are obsessed with cyber war, cyber intelligence, like it's all about technology. Meanwhile, some asshole had to get the thumb drive out of the building."

Lunch came, and we started eating. "I guess you wanted to see me for a reason, *bon ami*," Goblin said. "What are you working on? I know you're not at the paper."

"Yeah, how'd you know that?" I asked, rearranging the jelly packets on the table.

"Your cell phone is pinging from Bethesda, not DC." Goblin pointed to the sky.

"You guys spy on reporters?"

"Never," Goblin answered, feigning offense. "But when you called, I thought I'd find out where you'd been, to see if I could guess what was up."

"Let's just say I'm on a *special mission*." I emphasized the last words like a secret agent would.

"All right, right."

"You know Pacho Craig?" I asked.

"Yeah, the news guy on MyStream, yeah."

"You know anything else about him?"

"Chicks dig him. He seems to dig himself. What kind of things do you want to know?" Goblin asked quietly, holding his hand to his mouth as a patron walked by.

"I want to get to what makes him tick, what moves him from Point A to Point B. But let's start with the basics. Has he been sued? Does he have debt? Also, his MyStream videos. There's one where he shows off his expensive watches. I'm wondering how much those are worth and where he gets the money to buy them. I know he has a corporate sponsor: Blue Ridge Summit, the outdoors co-op. But I don't get the economics of sponsorships these days. Do they pay hundreds of thousands? Millions?"

"Okay." Goblin shrugged. "But not sure if any of this will tell you what makes him tick."

"That's why I want to go back to where he grew up. I may do that personally. Get a feel for it. Maybe talk to some of his old teachers."

"Why?"

"That's where people's fantasies about who they are begin to form. And maybe you can poke around on his social media, which I can't do that well myself. What does it say about him?"

"You're not on Facebook or Twitter, I take it?" Goblin asked, smirking.

"No. When I have a story, the *Incursion* tweets it out."

"What do you say in meetings when social media comes up, Boz?" He raised his eyebrows.

"One of my great geniuses is pretending that I understand stuff. I did it all the way through school. I hardly paid attention, but when the teacher asked me if I understood, I'd pull a knowing face—the way I do now when my accountant tries to explain my tax returns to me."

"Must help being a reporter, too, yeah? So let me make sure I'm hearing you. You're not asking, um, anybody to look at Pacho's computer or phone?"

"That would be tricky business," I said.

"That's also where things can fuck up. As Mr. History, I'm sure you remember that old 'third-rate burglary,' yeah?"

"Watergate was before my professional time, but yes."

"I'd love to tell you that somebody who might do something like that is a ghost in the night, but the reality is, it doesn't matter whether you're talking about FBI, CIA, or NSA. People are people. Fuck-ups happen, yeah."

"I thought you guys were monitoring everybody."

"See, that's what people don't get," Goblin said. "We *can* monitor everybody if we have sufficient provocation—and ideally a warrant—but we're not monitoring everybody's calls, texts, emails, and online activity."

"But you *can*."

"Of course we can, yeah," he said in an incredulous whisper.

"Well, my friend, I may need that kind of deep dive at some point."

Goblin's eyes bored into mine. "Somebody may be able to help, if it comes to that." He always said *somebody* or *it,* never *I* or *me.*

"What would somebody need to take a whack at this?" I asked.

"Fifteen to twenty-five thousand. Cash."

I nodded. "I'll have it next time. What's your gut on our chances here?"

"Bad news and good news," Goblin said. "Bad news is, I have no idea whether your guy is dirty."

"The good news?"

"Egotists like him memorialize everything, *bon ami.* Absolutely everything. God forbid the world should miss one of their fingernail clippings."

"There's something else I need help with. Have you read about that free-market activist, Guido Reni?"

"Yeah, suicide on the canal."

"Billy Goat Trail. I was starting to dig around on what happened there when my editors got spooked. I want to get back into it but need to do it off the books. I know he had financial problems, but I didn't get around to doing a whole litigation search on him. Can you check into that? Maybe social media, too?"

"You think Reni and Pacho are connected?"

I didn't, but divulging my true agenda wasn't necessary at the moment. "Not sure yet."

Goblin shook his gleeful round head. "Never a dull moment with you, is there?"

"No."

"Laissez les bons temps rouler."

Let the good times roll.

10

WHEN I GOT home from meeting with Goblin, Finn—praise be to Allah—was doing her homework at the kitchen counter. No sign of Frigging Alex, Finn's boyfriend, hanging around, so fortunately Joey and I wouldn't have to dismember him that night. He played guitar in a band (of course he did) and had convinced Finn she should be their female lead (of course he did). She was pretty good, with a sweet voice, so Joey and I were torn between wanting to encourage her and the reality that it was only a matter of time before we buried Frigging Alex's body in Rock Creek Park and covered it with lime.

Our red Labrador retriever, Wagatha Christie—or Wags—was at Finn's feet, dusting the kitchen floor with her happy tail. I envied the dog's lack of worry.

"Hey, shortcake," I said to Finn.

"Hey," she said without looking my way.

"I was wondering if you could help me out with something I'm working on."

"What?" she said, somewhat less civilly.

"What kind of social media do people in high school and college go on these days?"

"Why, so you can spy on me?"

"No, I already have a transmitter implanted in your butt that communicates with the drone I have following you."

"No, really."

Concocting another lie in the course of Operation Pacho, I told

Finn that I was considering doing a story on how young people get their news from social media. She seemed to buy this, and I wondered whether I had ever lied to her before with such ease.

"My friends are on TikTok, Instagram. Some guys are still on Facebook. Geeks put stuff on Twitter because it has news and stuff. There's Tinder for hookups."

I didn't like the sound of hookups, but didn't want to trigger a nuclear war by delving into more detail. I asked if just anyone could access these apps, and she looked at me as if I had broccoli hanging out of my nose.

"Duh."

"Duh, yes? Or duh, no?"

"Yeah," Finn explained with an eye roll. "You just go on the page and type somebody's name and see what they're posting. Well, unless they have it private. Then they have to invite you in." Picking up her phone, she pulled up some of her friends' social media profiles but made me swear not to stalk or "friend" them. That was a promise I could keep. I could bring about Middle East peace before I could friend anybody.

"Hey, can you help me use that U2 thing?"

"What U2 thing?"

"The website with all the videos."

"YouTube."

"Right. Tube."

"U2 is a band. God, Dad."

"I know U2. Sonny Bono," I said, just to piss her off.

"Bah-no, Dad." She shook her head in disgust. "It's Bono. Not Sonny *Bone*-oh."

"Oh. Is that how it's pronounced, then?"

"How do you function in the world?"

"I don't. Function in the world, that is. I want to see MyStream, too." I hovered beside Finn as she typed *MyStream* into the internet browser window. The website came up. "Okay, so is this the best way to look somebody up and see their videos?" I asked, typing a name in the browser window.

"Pacho Craig?" Finn said. "He's hot."

"Yeah, that's why I want to see him."

"Gross. Why do you really want to see him?"

"Everybody's been talking about his reports. I want to see what it's all about." A list of thumbnails came up—an index of all the latest Pacho Craig videos.

"Yeah, that's all you have to do," Finn said. She went upstairs, and I started watching Pacho in action.

In the first clip, he was interviewing a Catholic priest. "There's a lot of disrespect for religion these days," Pacho said.

"I can understand why," the priest replied. "We've let down a lot of people with these abuse scandals."

Pacho cocked his head, allowing a strand of long hair to fall over his eyes. "I don't think people understand what somebody in your position goes through . . ." And from then on, he owned his victim.

The priest continued. "When the bishop in our region got the report about my predecessor, he did everything according to the rules."

"But your predecessor remained in his job."

"You can't just remove someone every time someone makes a claim," the priest said. "You have to investigate."

"You can't remove someone," Pacho repeated, leaving off the end of the priest's sentence. The video then cut to an altar boy who had claimed abuse—a teenager with a vacuous expression, the kind you see on people who have been violated.

The next video was Pacho confronting a child molester on how he stalked elementary schools. Then there was Pacho ambushing an oil company chief. Pacho grandstanding at a presidential news conference.

Ambushing an evangelical Christian pedophile. Few of his segments lasted more than three minutes. There was a minute of background about a topic, followed by a minute of Pacho stalking his prey.

The final minute showed Pacho confronting the Satan of the moment by pointing to his watch and launching his catchphrase: "Time is running out, friend. This is your chance. Only a coward wouldn't take it." One thing was for dead certain—Pacho must have accumulated a fair amount of enemies during his run.

There were a few interviews with late night comedians. Pacho had even brought a long-haired wig and an Australian bush coat for Stephen Colbert to wear during that interview. Then there was a stand-alone segment from when he gave a talk-show host a tour of his Georgetown townhouse and displayed his collection of watches. There must have been fifty of them, and I wondered exactly how much money his short little terrorist broadcasts actually made. I knew Blue Ridge Summit was a sponsor, but still. Maybe he had family money. He had that whiff about him. I couldn't help but think that if I had a fortune in watches lying around, I wouldn't be inviting cameras in to film my collection. Alas, I was from another era. Today, discretion is a cultural sin that ranks up there with child abuse.

I hopped on Google and discovered that Paul Charles "Pacho" Craig had been raised in a well-to-do family in Baltimore and spent his summers on Gibson Island, an exclusive enclave on the Chesapeake Bay. Real money. His dad was a spine surgeon with Johns Hopkins and was known as "Almighty Craig" around the hospital. Early in Dr. Craig's career, the *Baltimore Sun* said he had the "hands of God" because he was able to help so many accident victims walk again.

Pacho's fancy background, in my view, conflicted with his desire to be seen as a badass, with his beard stubble and the weathered Outback coat he wore in his interviews. He had played lacrosse at prep school and at the University of North Carolina at Chapel Hill. None of this meant much, other than that my biases pointed me in the direction of entitled douchebaggery.

I was at the beginning of the beginning.

Pleased with my limited cyber skills, I stayed online for a while. Apparently, one of the internet's great offerings was photos of dead celebrities, thus the huge reward paid to a despicable relative of a rapper I had never heard of, for a snapshot of the rapper in his casket after he was gunned down in a Los Angeles strip mall. Technology never ceased to validate my theories about the voyeurism that really drove it.

I looked at Samantha Rossiter's Facebook page. Nothing was particularly provocative other than perhaps some party scenes, but it became clear when I looked up some of Finn's friends that most kids her age had similar photos.

Next I found a few more videos of Pacho, and an article about him in a celebrity magazine that began the way all puff pieces do:

> At first, I thought he might be a Spanish mercenary in search of a long-hunted Basque separatist, but only as he drew closer to me in District Commons did the rugged man betray the quirky charm of a man with two different-colored eyes. This man in his worn Australian bush coat appeared younger than he did while populating the globe's iPhone screens, closer to thirty than the thirty-eight he really was. His shy, off-center smile and tentative handshake lent the impression of a talented undergraduate who nonetheless would have to be persuaded to study indigenous tribes in barely discovered lands.

Holy jumpin' Jesus. If ever prose had made me feel that I could set a record for projectile vomiting, this was it. Why do some writers always feel the impulse to characterize obvious media whores as being camera shy—the Reluctant Celebrity who is nevertheless always diving in front of cameras?

I took a deep breath. As an editor once told me, I'm a "human-frailty guy" and not a "data guy." I have good instincts about targets versus being the kind of reporter who just wades through documents. I would be spending a lot of mental time with Pacho Craig in the weeks ahead. And my human-frailty meter had detected a self-absorbed prick with a suppressed rage problem who had plagiarized Indiana Jones's persona without any compunction.

11

HADDON SEAGULL SENT an email to Joey and me.

> Spoke to Kurt and Angie. Worried about them—what the hell is going on with Samantha? Holy shit! Coming up from Key West to Rehoboth. You guys in?

Kurt and Angie still had his family's house in Rehoboth Beach, Delaware, which overlooked a vast pond that, in turn, nuzzled the Atlantic Ocean. Most Washington-area families like mine who went to the beach in the summer rented gamy motel rooms in Ocean City, where every square inch was an invisible monument to the former location of a condom wrapper. But our gang had been visiting Kurt's sweet digs in Rehoboth for decades. Our group had congealed in seventh grade, in 1975—the quintet consisting of me, free-spirit Haddon Seagull, remote beauty Angela Pfeiffer, my Joey Morris, and (insert sigh here) Kurt Rossiter.

The minute I saw Haddon's email pop up, my heart skipped. What was wrong with me?

Haddon Seagull. Who had a name like Haddon? It was a cross between Britain and Heaven. Or maybe it wasn't, but who cared? When we were kids, I always thought "Segal" was "Seagull," which was fitting. Haddon was perpetually on the verge of elsewhere, flying away, which always made me wonder where she was going that I wasn't. She saw me spell her name S-E-A-G-U-L-L in homeroom once and thought it was cute.

Now she was an artist of some kind in Key West and actually went by Seagull. None of us knew how she made a living or what her art was, which added to the free-love mystery that had always surrounded her. Last I heard, she had been going through a contemplative, ascetic stage and working at a monastery on the Amalfi Coast of Italy, an enterprise that went unfulfilled after she fell in love with a ceramics restorer named Enzo, who was a marvel with his hands and other appendages.

Apparently she had been conceived at Haddon Hall in Atlantic City, or at least that's what she told us at Steven Waldman's bar mitzvah. *Conceived*. I've never heard that word without thinking ribald thoughts. Her parents were a few years younger than the rest of ours and had a hippie-dippie thing going on. They were rumored to smoke pot, which was cool to seventh-graders in the way that hearing Johnny Cash had been in jail was cool. I vaguely remembered Haddon saying she had been a seven-year-old at Woodstock, a legend that—in the minds of our crew—was the height of counterculture groove. Kids our age always felt a twinge of bitterness about being too young to be part of the Woodstock generation. The best we could do was let our hair grow a little long, fire up a hookah, and wear a Jimi Hendrix T-shirt to show that we knew the music, that we "got it."

One of my most vivid memories of becoming aware of sex as something that could potentially involve people we knew was of Haddon at a campfire on the beach during a bicentennial party, her eyes closed, singing the lyrics to Bad Company's "Feel Like Makin' Love," her hair swaying with her head movements. None of us had the nerve to sing those lyrics aloud. We were out of our sexual depth just hearing the damned song. But not Haddon.

Since the administration of Gerald Ford, I've had Haddon floating around my brain like Tinkerbell. One drive-by kiss near the Liberty Bell in college had taken on the neural significance of the moon landing, even though to Haddon it was just one of a million grazed affections.

My lingering thoughts were not something I'd ever told anybody about. Well, I had told Kurt once, years ago, with a little misdirection. I saw these notions about Haddon as something like obsessive-compulsive disorder, this need I had to touch the corner of my night table four times before going to bed. I'd always felt such notions were a betrayal of Joey.

I'd gone to college at Haverford, outside of Philadelphia. Haddon was at Rutgers. There was some kind of festival going on, and I'd invited Haddon down with considerable trepidation. Joey and I had agreed to a be-free period, something I had consented to solely out of fear that things would have been worse had I balked. Haddon was about five-four, with brown wavy hair that took on golden highlights in the sun. She had high cheekbones, a straight nose, and big brown doe eyes. She had what my mother called a "va-va-voom figure" (it had concerned me that my mother noticed such things). The first time our group saw Haddon in a black bikini, we all wept. The boys shed tears from the sexual ache, and the girls—even Angie with her Grace Kelly bearing—felt their eyes moisten because some foreign part of them fell in love with her too. You just had no damned choice.

When Haddon visited me at Haverford, I momentarily achieved rock-star status among the guys and among the women of Bryn Mawr, our sister school, too. I remember seesawing between the pride of a newly discovered stud and the desperate insecurity when some of the men—with the Main Line or Fifth Avenue pedigree that I lacked—had the swagger to distract her from me. Yet I took Haddon's hand on our way out of one party, and she didn't hesitate to intertwine her fingers between mine. Ecstasy. If I couldn't have Joey, this could work just fine. That weekend, I had arranged for Haddon to sleep in the dorm room of a Bryn Mawr friend. It never would have occurred to me to assume she would stay in my room, and I didn't ask.

The following day, we went into Center City, Philadelphia, so

Haddon could catch a bus back to Rutgers. We stopped by the Liberty Bell, and for an interminable eleven seconds, I contemplated moving in to kiss her. I finally made my move, just before she got on the bus, momentarily thinking I was Steve McQueen—a sentiment that remained for days afterward, because there really was lightning inside this woman. The off-center kiss, which landed somewhere between her nose and her eye, lasted for a nanosecond. Yet I decided I would survive without Joey after all.

Once Haddon left, the best I could do for correspondence was to call Haddon's dorm hallway phone or write letters. This was the stone age, before cell phones. I didn't see Haddon again until our five-year high school reunion.

We were nice to each other, but whenever I saw her thereafter (which wasn't often), I felt the way one of those Looney Tunes characters did after he transformed into an actual horse's ass in a thought bubble on the TV screen. Joey once casually observed that Haddon brought out the worst in me. I never discussed with her why that might be so.

• • •

Finn had lobbied to stay with a girlfriend while we went to Rehoboth, which we approved only because it was the best of our terrible options. What the hell did you do when your baby just didn't want to be with you? I carried the sensation of an impending hailstorm, one of those where the sky turns blackish-green and you think, *I've never seen that color before,* and then, boom, the roof of your carport is gone. We knew Frigging Alex would be on the scene in some way, but until we dissolved him in acid, there was nothing we could do about it.

We met on Friday evening at the Rossiter place in Rehoboth, which hadn't been modernized much since we were in high school. There's a reason why certain families keep their money—they buy good stuff at the front end and never replace it. Kurt and Angie had asked Samantha if she wanted to join us, but she'd declined. They were worried about leaving her alone in Bethesda, but they also didn't want to send the wrong message: that they thought she might be so fragile, she needed constant supervision.

Haddon, as always, arrived last, the subtext being that she had just flitted in from someplace exotic. This time, she had managed to find an airport that none of us knew existed. We had already started eating dinner on the Rossiters' indoor-outdoor porch. The sun was retreating, and the lake that separated the Rossiter place from the beach had a soft orange glow.

Haddon came on the scene wearing a beige number that offered exposure of her toned brown arms. Her hair was lighter than I remembered—I hadn't seen her for about five years—and the only aging I could detect from our last visit together was deeper smile lines around her mouth. She hadn't lost any of her carbonation. In comparison, I guess I looked all right. My hair was mostly gone except for my action-hero buzz, but I was in better shape than most men my age.

Conversation was stilted during dinner, which consisted of a stir-fry whipped up by a young woman who served as the Rossiters' Rehoboth caretaker and cook. With Samantha's tragedy, there wasn't just an elephant in the room—it was more like a glowing purple woolly mammoth. After the plates were cleared, with the October air tiptoeing through the screens, we all sat around the porch like ghosts of the 1970s.

"When did we all become a thing?" Haddon asked. "Fall of '74? Seventh grade?"

"No," I said. "Spring of '75. Later on in seventh."

"Listen to Mr. Investigative Reporter." Haddon flicked me on the shoulder.

"I remember by the songs that were playing," I said. "It was the year with all the bar mitzvahs. We were all here in Rehoboth. It was summer but a little cool outside. Nice. One night we were on the boardwalk. Elton John had released 'Philadelphia Freedom' a few months before—"

"I thought we were listening to that song 'Jackie Blue,'" Haddon said.

"No, 'Philadelphia Freedom.' Remember?"

Haddon shook her head, and the others stared at me blankly.

"Yes, you must. There was a group of kids our age on the boardwalk who had come down from Philly, and they were singing really loud, pumping their fists. They were all cocky because Springsteen had just come out with 'Born to Run' and Philly was close to Jersey, so somehow Springsteen was their achievement. And 'Philadelphia Freedom' was their triumph, too. Philly fans. Nobody knew the lyrics. I don't think there was an album out yet, so no lyrics on the jacket. One Philly kid was singing with a lot of confidence, *'Philadelphia freedom, sha na, to the ass of the one on the right.'*"

Everybody laughed, remembering now. "What were the actual lyrics?" Joey asked.

"Something about freedom and shining the light through the eyes of the ones left behind," I said.

Joey asked, "What does that even mean?"

"I don't know, Joe, but I remember you had started running track and your hair had gotten really blonde and your freckles were coming out. Angie and Kurt's hair was feathered. Haddon was sunburnt and wearing those puka beads around her neck."

"Was I?" Haddon said. "Oh my God, what an embarrassment."

"That whole era was an embarrassment," I said. "I actually had a leather peace band around my wrist."

"That was the sixties for you," Haddon said, making a peace sign.

"A lot of the sixties happened in the seventies," I said. "We think things are crazy *now*? Remember the couple thousands of bombings by radicals every year? Serial killers like Son of Sam? And Manson's lunatics were still running around shooting presidents. The Moonies. Gasoline lines. And yet we were all pretty happy, weren't we? And I looked so cool with that peace band on my wrist." I smiled. "If only I'd been able to feather my hair like Keith Partridge—and Kurt. Instead, I ended up looking like a poodle just curled up on my head and died."

"And where is all that hair now, Fuse?" Kurt asked. "I thought Angie was more likely to go bald, with all that blow-drying she did to get the Farrah Fawcett look."

"Genes, baby!" Angie said. It was the first time I had seen her smile since the Samantha drama began.

"But you're all forgetting the big thing we did that weekend," I said. "We went to see the movie *Tommy.*"

"Roger Daltrey rock opera!" Joey said.

Angie grinned. "'Ballroom Blitz.' 'Fox on the Run,' by Sweet—"

"'The Night Chicago Died,'" Joey threw out. "Paper Lace." Simultaneously, we all sang the opening lyrics.

And then Haddon blurted out, "How can we help Samantha?"

Everyone grew quiet.

Angie, after an interminable silence, said, "She wanted to be with friends this weekend. We needed to show her we had enough confidence in her to leave her alone."

There was something defensive in Angie's voice, as if she were justifying leaving Samantha behind. I understood it completely. When your child is suffering, it is a biological impulse to believe it's somehow all your fault.

"Fuse is helping us," Kurt volunteered feebly.

"Really?" Haddon said, turning to me. "Fuse, what are you doing?" She leaned forward and grabbed an apple slice, exposing a touch of cleavage.

I wasn't thrilled to be getting into this. Even though I hadn't done anything yet, telling anyone anything at all was really indiscreet.

"Just consulting on options," I said. "There are press implications if this were to go public. And of course, Pacho is a media figure."

Haddon squinted. "Really? And what can *you* do? They're going to write what they're going to write."

"Probably best that I keep my thoughts for the lawyers," I said. I figured that invoking legal counsel might shift the focus from me.

Haddon leaned back and stroked her jawline. Her mouth fell open in a hint of revelation. "You should rip into that bastard, Fuse."

"How?" I asked.

"The *Incursion,"* she said.

"We're not going public with this," Kurt said. "Not yet anyway."

"So you're going to let this creep get away with what he did?" Haddon asked.

"We didn't say that," Angie said.

I turned to face Haddon. "You and I both know how the press goes after women who accuse men of sex crimes. The victims are put on trial, and a defense team or reporters rip into them. We have to consider these things."

"Believe me, I know what they do," Haddon said. "But Sammy's pretty scrappy. Don't you think she can handle it? There's a bigger cause at work here, and she can be a part of it."

Angie and Kurt squirmed. Angie said, "She doesn't deal well with negative attention. Somebody put some nasty remarks about her on Facebook a couple years ago, and she went into a tailspin for weeks."

"You know better," Haddon said with a shrug. "I was just asking."

"Things are nuts out there," Angie continued. "It's open season on boys too. I think about Steven at college. There's a backlash brewing. That's one of the things we're worrying about if we go after Pacho. Do you know how college campuses are defining sexual assault? If a guy makes a move and the girl says no, even if he takes his hand away, he's still committed an assault. Now he has to ask and get what they're calling 'affirmative consent.'"

"Maybe he should," Haddon said.

"But that's not my point," Angie said. "Even the antidotes to assaults are now considered overkill, which could swing in Pacho's favor."

I turned to Joey. "When I put my hand up your shirt when we were watching *The Rockford Files,* I don't remember asking you to sign a waiver."

Everybody chuckled, then seemed to wonder whether we should have.

"No," Joey said. "Because I was okay with it."

"I didn't know you were okay with it until I did it. These days, we'd each have to bring an attorney. 'Ms. Morris, I'm Mr. Schoenstein from Schoenstein & Wilkins. My client, Mr. Petty, would like to move his hand from your side to just slightly above your belly button.' Then your lawyer would hop up and go, 'Objection!'"

Haddon was shaking her head.

"What?" I said. "What's with the face?"

"I have a face?" Haddon said.

"Yes. You have a face."

"You can be so tone deaf, Fuse."

"Ah, the great sin of the age."

"You're just so judgmental."

"That's what qualifies as being an asshole now? Judging? Suggesting there should be some standard? What are you afraid I'm going to say?"

"Easy, Fuse," Joey said.

"I'm just trying to understand the rules, Joe," I replied. "Did I commit some violation on your parents' sofa forty years ago every time *The Rockford Files* came on? That theme song was like a Pavlovian experiment. The minute I heard those drums and that synthesizer, I got going. That's totally different from what happened with Sammy."

"By today's standards, maybe you did commit a violation," Haddon said.

"And what do you require today of your gentlemen callers?" I asked.

"Enough," Joey said.

"You're slut-shaming me now?" Haddon asked me. "Like when women wear low-cut tops and men's eyes start popping out and they drool like a St. Bernard?"

"Well, maybe if you didn't want men looking, you wouldn't be firing your gazongas out the top of your shirt like Tomahawk missiles," Kurt said.

Angie shouted, "Kurt!"

Kurt laughed nervously, while Haddon made oinking noises.

"I remember you defending Bill Clinton, Had," I continued unwisely.

"Nobody defends Clinton anymore," Haddon said.

"Okay, fine. I'm just trying to figure out what changed—when the whole school of fish suddenly turned left—and how the guys that women went for in college are now cultural villains."

Haddon said, "Nobody's saying that."

"C'mon, you two," Joey said.

"I want to understand what the violation is," I pressed. "As a reporter. What makes a bad guy? Is it a man making a sexual move? A man making a sexual move without clearly articulated permission? Is it having the wrong politics? Passing judgment? Or is it just anything a man says? Or being a man? Anybody who waves the grievance flag has the power. If everybody has a grievance, nobody has a grievance."

"Well, you're an ass," Haddon said.

"You love me and you know it," I said.

"I know I do." Haddon smiled and put her hand on my knee, and I felt a few butterflies. "But you're still an ass."

Me, an ass? I felt like Butch and Sundance, with a new age bearing down like that angry, huffing train full of assassins—all the boys really could do was jump off that cliff and hope they hit the water, not the rocks. I remembered what the sheriff said to Butch and Sundance about their time being over and them dying bloody, and the only choice left being where they died.

Thank God, we spent the rest of the night discussing songs from junior high, followed by a little update on my father. "Lady Marmalade" brought up memories for Joey of Julie Thornton's barbecue and Debbie Dawes throwing up her whiskey sour in a bush. Neil Sedaka's "Bad Blood" made me think of my father in the basement screaming, "They're all shovin' it up my ass!"—which drew a laugh.

"Nat did a good job regulating his behavior when we were around, didn't he, Fuse?" Haddon said. "All those stories you tell . . . We never saw him do any of it."

"Yes, he was a genius at knowing precisely when to misbehave," I confirmed, grateful that she'd acknowledged some of my humanity.

"Do you think when he dies, they'll finally find what everybody's been shoving up his ass?" Kurt asked.

"No," I said. "For one thing, nobody was ever shoving anything up his ass. For another, he's never going to die."

Joey nodded. "After the nuclear war, there will only be the cockroaches and Nat Petty."

And on that note, we all agreed it was bedtime.

12

WHEN I WOKE up the next morning, Joey wasn't beside me. I went downstairs. Angie and Haddon were having coffee at the kitchen counter, with a mist of dust particles swirling around them like tiny admirers. They were both wearing sundresses, and I was conscious of the long odds that our little group was so densely packed with lovely women. I very much included Joey in that calculation, even though hers was a beauty that tiptoed up next to you rather than hit you over the head.

"Where's Joey?" I asked.

Angie said, "She and Kurt took a walk on the beach."

"Huh," I said, trying to conceal the high-school level of threat that I felt. "I'll probably take a morning walk down there too. Either of you want to go?"

Both women held up their coffees to convey they had just gotten started. They didn't ask if I wanted any, because I don't drink coffee. Still, I felt a twinge of rejection.

I flipped on my Orioles baseball cap and headed down to the beach. Which way would Kurt and Joey be walking? I saw a flag blowing on one beach house, indicating the wind was coming from the south. Joey and I always liked to walk into the wind first so that the walk back would be easier. I figured that they had probably gone south toward Dewey and Bethany beaches, so that's how I went. I walked down about a mile but saw no human shapes that appeared to be Kurt and Joey.

I'd loved Joey from the second I saw her up in the big tree behind Western Junior High School in Bethesda, Maryland, just outside Washington, DC. When so many of the kids in the spring of 1974 were test-driving coolness by smoking after school, Joey—skinny, and dirty blonde—crouched observantly among the leaves just watching the "cool" kids, like a shy, freckle-nosed monkey. She had one particular freckle just right of center on her turned-up nose that I found especially adorable, and I regretted that it had faded over the years. On more than one occasion when she was sleeping, I've taken a fine-tip Sharpie and dotted her nose where the freckle once was. She thinks I'm insane.

When we were kids, I didn't like the whole smoking scene myself—I was afraid of getting cancer from cigarettes and afraid of going insane with pot—so, like Joey, I hung back when it was time to light up. At that age (or at any age, really), I would have never had enough nerve to approach a girl, but there was something about the emotional cover provided by that vast, sprawling tree that allowed me to inch closer to Joey. Could I help it if I started out on one limb and happened to find myself via some circuitous route on Joey's branch? I've met plenty of great women over the years but only one I thought I could have a life with, and it all started on that tree while a novelty song called "Life Is a Rock" played on a nearby transistor radio.

As I turned around now and looked down the beach, I felt sweat forming along my spine. My heart started skipping. Kurt *had* Joey! I stood on the hot sand feeling like a five-year-old kid who couldn't find his parents. Of course, I knew where mine were: Mom long gone, and Nat at home shrieking at somebody and giving them an illness.

What were Joey and Kurt doing? What were they talking about? Joey had always exhibited a weakness for the poignantly damaged. And that was part of Kurt's genius, his shtick—faking vulnerabilities when the joke was that he had none.

A small group of women was gathered near the water's edge. One was pointing to something. Curious, I made my way over to them. One of them volunteered that a deer had run onto the beach from God knows where and then into the ocean. "Look there!" she said.

Indeed, a deer's head was bobbing among the waves, the rest of its body submerged and whatever damage it had sustained invisible. The head was darting around, and the deer was clearly terrified.

"Should we call someone?" I asked.

"Who do you call?" the woman responded.

"I don't know. Maybe the Rehoboth police?"

"By the time they got here, the deer would be gone."

"Maybe they could call the Coast Guard and get her," I said.

"Hmm. You think it's a girl?" the woman asked me.

"Yeah, I guess I do."

"I figured it was a male. Straying from the herd and all."

By this point, I no longer could see her. The deer. She had either gone under or been swept too far out. Maybe a shark would get her soon—the way Pacho got Sammy, or the way Nat exhausted my mom until she gave up.

Turning despondently to the north, I saw Joey and Kurt approaching—him tall and lean in a floppy bucket hat that somehow looked stylish on him, and Joey in a comfortable baggy sweater emblazoned with a faded *HAVERFORD* that made her perfectly huggable.

"Are you waiting for permission to go in the water, Fuse?" Kurt asked. The group of women had dispersed.

"My mother always told me to wait an hour to properly digest before going in," I replied. "But sometimes I go in after forty-five minutes. That kind of dangerous behavior is why the chicks dig me."

"He's a real bad boy," said Joey.

I told them about the deer. They glanced toward the horizon and didn't see anything.

"How far did you guys go?" I asked, instantly regretting my wording.

"Just a little bit. Toward Henlopen," Kurt said.

I checked out Joey's nose and, for a moment, thought my favorite freckle had reemerged.

"What are you looking at?" she asked.

"Oh, nothing. I thought I saw something. It was just a funny angle."

She smirked. "The freckle?"

"Yeah."

After Joey turned to walk back to Kurt's place, he lingered for a minute, his gaze moving over the horizon. "Fuse, you've had dark moments. Have you ever wondered if you'd actually survive?"

"I've had more of those periods than I would care to admit."

"Like what?"

"Not being able to get out of bed. Being afraid of being homeless. Being on a plane and not caring if it went down. I've been feeling a lot of that lately, to be honest."

"About the job?"

"The only thing I know how to do is write. Report. What am I going to do now? Be one of those asshat middle-aged guys at the Apple store in Montgomery Mall, selling iPhones to kids with trust funds?"

"You? You still use a flip phone."

"Point being that outside of Joey and Finn, I see no role for myself on this planet, and if I can't make enough money to live, I could lose them. So, in answer to your question—yeah, I have dark periods. Now, do you want me to gerbil this guy Pacho or what?" I asked with a smirk.

"Gerbil him?" Kurt asked.

"You know the rumor about Richard Gere going to the emergency room with a gerbil up his ass?"

"I heard that thirty years ago."

"It's bullshit. Like J. Edgar Hoover in a dress. But somebody lit that match. I figured we could spread some gerbil-esque rumor about Pacho," I said through an impish chuckle.

"It never occurred to me that a rumor like that had a ground zero."

"And that was before everybody walked around with a computer glued to their hand."

"Wait . . . you don't think Hoover was gay?"

"He sure as hell wasn't wearing a sequined gold evening dress to parties with senators."

Kurt laughed. "Is something like that even possible? Spreading a totally false rumor? I mean, things can be vetted online nowadays."

"The internet is about velocity and venom. Those things overpower fact. If the garbage moves fast enough, you can't hunt it down and kill it. But whatever the smear is, it has to be plausible. I read a line from Virgil years ago: 'Consider what each soil will bear, and what each refuses.' The soil has to be right for a particular plant to grow. We just have to figure out what will grow in this soil we're living in."

Kurt's knees buckled suddenly, and he dropped to the sand. "Do it to *me*!" he cried. "Do it to *me*!"

What the hell?

I bent down and put my arm around him. "What's wrong? Do what, Kurt?"

He put his head between his knees, his floppy cap making him look like a boy. "What happened to Sammy . . . Why her? Why didn't God punish me? I'm the one He wants. He should've just done it to me."

"What did you do? You mean the affair?"

"He should have just punished me. Just me."

I was short on advice because I tended to see events move with similar logic. I'd always assumed my misfortunes were punishment. But right now, I would say what I had to say to make a friend who was suffering feel better. "I'm not sure that's how the world works. Punishment, that is."

"It's punishment—believe me," Kurt mumbled. This made me think that even more had gone on with Kurt and women than I knew, but now wasn't the time to probe. I had never seen such jagged humanity in him. I had never witnessed him pushed to this kind of rage and desperation. I realized that before me was a man who had spent his life getting away with things but was suddenly caught up in the slipstream of another man who had spent his life getting away with things—and the turbulence and disorientation were fierce.

"Fuse, help me get this son of a bitch. Obliterate this Pacho fucker. Rip him apart." Kurt's face suddenly appeared to be deeply creased, and the way his skin pulled along his jawline made him look skeletal. "I want him to blow his brains out. I want to look him in the eyes, and I want to see his brains fly out of his head. I want to record it and watch it over and over again on a continuous loop. I've got money. I don't care what it costs."

"I don't want to profit personally, Kurt. I'd have to pay others for their help, though."

He nodded. "Whatever it takes. Make him suffer. I can't help my baby, but I can't do nothing. I don't want him to do this to someone else's child. I don't want another father or mother to know what it's like to watch the universe devour their kid. I know how you worry about Finn . . . You understand. And I don't want to hear that this can't undo what's been done. I know that. At the beginning, you asked what I wanted. Justice, peace, all that. I want all of it, but the only thing I think I can get is vengeance. You have to help me."

"I'll help you. Sam won't ever know it was us."

"But I'll know. And that will have to be a tiny little victory in this shitty world. And if we bring him down, she'll get to see him lose something, pay something. Even if not directly for his sins."

"We'll be the hyenas."

"Hyenas?" Kurt asked.

"I was watching a nature documentary on the treadmill. Last week. The cheetah killed an antelope and was taking its sweet-ass time eating. Then a pack of hyenas came over the rise with these sly looks on their faces and oozed their way toward the feast. They chased the cheetah off because they had sheer numbers. It's nice to be the cheetah that kills the antelope. It's not so nice when the hyenas show up to eat what you killed."

I put my arm on Kurt's shoulder to emphasize my final point.

"Just understand one thing: perfect vengeance is when the target has no idea who did it to him. That way, if we succeed, he'll be wondering his whole life, checking under his bed, agonizing over if or when it will happen again. I know the satisfaction it would be to stare Pacho in the face and tell him you're the one punishing him for what he did, but that can't happen here. There can't be any winking or nodding or 'you have to promise not to tell anybody, but this is what I did.'"

Kurt nodded. "I promise."

"Haddon already knows I'm helping you. Don't say any more."

"I won't."

"Okay, brother, then let's light him up. When we get back, make arrangements to take a wad of cash out of your bank."

He nodded, and I helped him up from the sand. Then Kurt and I traded a glance that had an instant sensation of déjà vu. When we were kids, while everybody dawdled before getting in the ocean, we would submit ourselves to "banzai baptisms" by nodding at each other and then running into the surf, shrieking, "Banzai!"

I pointed to the ocean now. We both charged in fully clothed.

"Banzai!"

It was peculiar, looking at the world with just one's head above water. Kurt and I must've looked like morons—two middle-aged guys, our clothes floating around us like prom dresses collecting seawater. We were the only people in the cold sea.

"Well, there go my balls," Kurt said with a shiver.

"Something tells me if I were naked in front of a woman, I wouldn't show well right now," I said.

"How are we still thinking that?"

"Guess we're not ready to give up," I said. "Hey, remember the days when pissing in the ocean was the most wicked, stealthy thing you could do?"

"Oh yeah," Kurt said.

"Let's go up, dry off, and plan something a hell of a lot worse than that."

"Pacho?"

I nodded.

• • •

The gang was digging into bagels that Angie had brought from a local shop. She didn't touch the carbs, but everybody else did. After last night's intense discussion, nobody had the energy for a sequel.

"How long are you staying up north, Haddon?" I asked.

"Not sure. I'd like to see some friends in DC and Annapolis," Haddon said.

I couldn't help but imagine who these fascinating friends were.

We all dragged some chairs back to the beach and sat around in the autumnal cool. I preferred the beach in the off-season. There was no pressure to get tan, no expectation of having to go to a party and Meet People—my least favorite activity. Our chair arrangement was divided along gender lines: Kurt and I facing south, and the women about ten feet away and angled slightly to the north. Kurt and I watched Haddon put sunscreen on her calves.

"When did you and Haddon have your session?" I quietly asked Kurt.

"How do you know we did?"

"Because I know the laws of physics."

"When Angie went to Florida with her family one Christmas break," Kurt conceded.

"Tenth grade?"

"Think so," Kurt said.

"All the way?"

"Yup."

"Fucker."

"I wasn't her first," Kurt volunteered.

"Well, there's a surprise. I figured you were everybody's first."

"That's your mental bullshit starting."

"Probably. Do you still think about her?" I asked.

"Of course I do. A long marriage . . . You know how it is. Even if you love the person and think she's beautiful. One person is one person. There's something about new territory. Besides, a man is only as loyal as his options allow." Kurt laughed.

"Some men don't seriously consider their options."

It was clear to me that Kurt just didn't think as much about this stuff as I did. Despite being an academic and obsessing about climate change, something which he had no control over, he simply did not reflect on the behaviors he *could* control. He'd clearly been shaken by the Bonita Weller crisis, but the devastation came more from the affair's potential to strike at his reputation. Angie must have been suffering deeply inside, but here we all were, together, at the beach. Kurt knew Angie would always stand by him, and this certainty informed the choices he made.

"You're not at all uncomfortable around Haddon now? After being with her?" I asked.

"No, Fuse, I'm not. You can be such a fucking girl. That was a lifetime ago."

I glanced at the women. As Angie and Joey let the sun beam onto their faces, Haddon went down to the water and swept her toes along the foam.

I lost control of my filter. "You know, Kurt, I covered guys like you for years—like Teddy Kennedy and his crowd. There's a reason guys drive women off bridges. It comes from never having to deal with guardrails."

"I didn't kill anybody. That's not fair," Kurt barked.

"No, it's not. But the metaphor works. It would never occur to me to bang a subordinate and then try to get away with it."

"You're so pure of thought?"

"Of course not. I'm a reptile at heart, like all of us. But there are thoughts and there are actions. I can't imagine that the rewards of a quick romp would outweigh the lifelong hell of hurting Joey. I could go a thousand lifetimes without finding anyone like her."

"Yep, you didn't do so bad, Fuse."

"True . . . Kurt, now stay with me here. This is going to be a long fight with Pacho and getting Sammy through this. Some nasty action is going to go down before it's over, and I'm sorry about it. But stay with me. We'll punch out of it."

Haddon turned from the surf and headed back in our direction.

"Watch her walk," I said.

"Yup," Kurt said. We both started laughing like seventh-graders.

13

JOEY AND I didn't talk much on the car ride back from Rehoboth. It was that walking-on-eggshells sensation that made you feel that if you exhaled the slightest bit, it would be the equivalent of running naked into the Vatican and blasting a fart as the College of Cardinals solemnly voted on a new pope. I didn't know how much of the drama in my head was just a slow-motion panic attack, but ever since I couldn't find Joey when she was walking on the beach with Kurt, I had this feeling of doom. I couldn't assign it to anything in particular except the Petty curse—a hardwired sense of dread.

The one thing I learned you can always do when you feel tension in a marriage is bring up a common enemy.

"How should we do it?"

"What?" Joey said neutrally.

"Kill Frigging Alex."

"Oh. Do you really think he'll end up getting Finn in some kind of trouble?"

"Trouble? Like pregnant?" I said.

"Oh God. Stop it!" She looked over at me, frowning and biting her lip. I imagined her freckle. "I guess so, yeah."

"That's what I worry about. That and her going all Patty Hearst. Remember when Patty became Tania with the Symbionese Liberation Army and robbed that bank?"

"Of course I do. I think it was sixth grade."

"Right. 'Seasons in the Sun' had just come out."

"It's sick that you remember that, Fuse."

"Depressing song," I said.

"You're depressing me."

"I'm depressing myself."

"When did they arrest her?" Joey asked.

"Patty? September '75. Around when we all became friends."

"You link the two? Patty Hearst's arrest and when we became friends?"

"Definitely."

"What's the connection?" Joey asked.

"I'm thinking 'Rhinestone Cowboy'?"

"The Glen Campbell song?"

"No, the Shakespeare play. Of course the Glen Campbell song," I said. "For some reason, I associate it with Patty Hearst getting arrested."

"So you think Finn is going to become a radical terrorist?"

"Yes."

"All Finn did was throw some bottles off a bridge. And we're not rich like the Hearsts," Joey said.

"I think you're taking this Patty Hearst metaphor too literally, Joe. I'm just saying I'm worried about Finn."

"How would you do it? Kill Frigging Alex?"

"Remember that terrorist Patty Hearst hung with—"

"Again with Patty Hearst?"

"Stay with me. There was this radical criminal, Donald DeFreeze. He kidnapped Patty. He went down in this gunfight in Los Angeles. He shot it out with the cops, and the house blew up and caught fire. Maybe we can call the Montgomery County cops and tell them Frigging Alex is in his house with all kinds of explosives."

"This seems like a very sound and rational plan. What could ever go wrong? What if Finn's there, nitwit, when we light this shock-and-awe bonfire? Just trying to stay with your ingenious strategic plan."

"We'll make sure she isn't there, moron. We'd do it when we see Finn's sleeping in her bed. This way, we don't have to do anything directly violent."

"Your plan blows, Fuse. And it concerns me that you seem to give these things such intricate thought."

"Do you remember the cartoon I started developing?"

"Remind me," Joey said.

"There was that girl who was torturing Finn in third grade—"

"Loretta Marcus."

"Right. I came up with this idea for a cartoon character, a kid who went into schools undercover and humiliated bullies. Poured paint on them, tripped them up, smacked them around," I said.

"Fuse Petty, Patron Saint of Bullied Children."

"Joey, you know if Patty Hearst married me, she'd be Patty Petty."

Joey slapped her forehead. "You're a very deep thinker, Fuse. It's what I admire most about you."

• • •

Sure enough, Frigging Alex was at our house, and he and Finn were watching *Lady and the Tramp,* which momentarily gave me a sense of warmth. When Finn was little, she'd held on to me like a koala bear while we watched Disney films. And now Frigging Alex, with his stringy, late-Beatles haircut and his three chin hairs, had my place on the couch.

Finn hopped up and hugged us, right in front of Frigging Alex. A burst of color flushed Joey's cheeks, and I wished I could tell Finn—and every other child in the universe—that she could not begin to fathom what such a gesture means in the life of a parent. Screw reversing climate change. If you want to help the world, just hug your parents.

Finn darted upstairs to retrieve something from her bedroom while I opened the mail that she had kindly placed on the desk in my office. This was about the only chore we could expect from her these days. I overheard Frigging Alex talking to Joey. Encouraged, I sidled closer to the door of my office and heard him ask, "Mrs. Petty, why do they call Mr. Petty 'Fuse'?"

This would be interesting.

Joey didn't answer immediately. Then I heard her say, "Oh, it was some stupid thing from when we were kids."

"Is it because he has a short fuse?"

I hoped she would answer, *Yes, yes, it is. In fact, he is a psychopath of the worst kind, and if you lay one hand on our child, he will flay your skin with a red-hot carrot scraper and take you apart piece by piece.*

"No, Alex, he actually has a very long fuse. Did Finn ever say he has a bad temper?"

"No, um, she said he never gets mad. Like ever. She said you get madder than he does."

"She said that?"

"Oh, it's not like she said you get real mad," Frigging Alex backpedaled.

When I heard Finn's footsteps come down the stairs, I decided this was my moment to return.

Frigging Alex appeared nervous, pulling at his upper lip where a moustache was supposed to be.

"We were just talking about you," Joey said to me.

"I wasn't actually *convicted* of the thing with the chainsaw and the Girl Scout troop," I said.

Frigging Alex's jaw fell open for a moment. When he saw me smirk, he returned the expression to show he got the joke. He asked, "So, Mr. Petty, do you really interview spies and gangsters and terrorists?"

"Yes."

"Where do you find them?"

"Sometimes they find me. Other times I find them."

"How do you find them?"

"When you've been a reporter as long as I have, you build a big list of contacts."

"When you did those stories, you know, on the big guy when he was running for president, did you actually talk to the gangsters he did business with?"

"I did."

"Were you, like, scared?"

"Not really. They don't have a history of hurting reporters in this country. Sometimes they even like guys like me, because they think they might need us someday."

"For what?"

"To give us information. About their enemies, or a dirty cop or politician."

"So, like, if you wanted to call up a terrorist or a gangster, um . . . you could?" he asked.

"If I had good reason, I guess I could."

"Even though you're not with the *Incursion* right now?"

"I don't have a reason right now to talk to anybody like that. Why, do *you* need to talk to one of these reprobates?" I asked.

"Me?" His eyes, which tended toward sleepiness, popped wide open. "No, not me."

"Well," I said very slowly, holding his gaze, "if you ever want to meet a psychopath like that, I'd be happy to make the connection. So, are you taking care of my baby girl?"

"Yeah. Yeah, I am," he almost yelled. Probably to make sure his girlfriend's psycho dad heard him loud and clear.

14

"ONE OF THOSE watches alone, the Corum, is worth about a quarter million, yeah," Goblin told me, after downing a pickle at Attman's. He'd arrived with a bunch of papers stuffed into an envelope that appeared to have barely survived Hiroshima.

"A quarter million for a watch? Who wants to know the time that badly?" I said.

"My guy tells me that if the Patek that Pacho was showing was the one he thought it was, it could be worth more than four hundred grand. *Beaucoup,* yeah?"

"How many watches would you say were on that display case in the MyStream video?" I asked.

"I don't know, maybe fifty. But keep in mind, Boz, they're not all in that league. My guy was focusing on the big ones."

"Jesus. Our Pacho has got a couple of bucks."

"I would say so. His townhouse is worth five million, and his mortgage is about three and a half. Both of his parents are still alive, yeah. They've got a nice place on Gibson Island and a condo in Naples. Not gaudy, but each residence is worth a few million and they don't have mortgages. They're not Warren Buffett rich, but they're certainly one-percenters."

"He could be living on a trust. At least in part."

"A guy like that must have a trust, but his sponsorship from Blue Ridge Summit is worth *at least* several million a year," Goblin said. "And his expenses don't seem to be that high."

"In other words, it's conceivable he could be paying for the townhouse and those watches through legitimate, self-generated income."

"There's no reason to believe the guy's a crook, no," Goblin said. "A few other things. He's got something called heterochromia, meaning he has two different-colored eyes. One green, one blue."

"Yeah, I heard that. Exotic."

"As I'm sure you know, he's had some legal spats with the people he's targeted, but they've never gotten to court."

"Of course not."

"Why? Why don't people ever sue him full-on?" Goblin asked.

"Sue him for what?"

"Libel. Defamation."

"Very hard to prove. You have to show malice and reckless disregard for the truth. For malice, it basically means you have to show his state of mind and intent to cause harm. For reckless disregard, it means showing that he didn't care enough about the facts or the consequences of his story—but should have," I explained.

"Pshaw, that's bullshit."

"Tell that to the Supreme Court."

"You media guys can get away with anything," Goblin said. There was a question mark in his voice, and he rubbed his temples. It wasn't an unusual reaction when even sophisticated people found out that the US has no real laws that prohibiting biased and inaccurate reporting.

"The only real constraint we've had over the years has been reputation. Standards. Integrity, really."

"Doesn't have a lot of teeth in it."

"Not anymore."

"You want to talk about your boy, Guido Reni?"

"Very much."

"I can see why the man blew his brains out, *bon ami*. He had more litigation against him than a tobacco company," Goblin said.

"Personal stuff or . . . ?"

"A little bit of everything. He had six active lawsuits against him when he checked out."

"Six?"

"One from the Planet Society. Redleaf. American Knitting Union. Creative Protection League. Implant Victims Network. And his kids."

I tried to process this. "Okay, let me get this straight. All these crunchy groups and labor types, plus his *kids* were suing him? What were all these suits about?"

"Different things, yeah," Goblin said, studying his notes. "Tortious interference. Fraud. Conversion, whatever that is—"

"Basically stealing proprietary stuff."

"Uh-huh. And RICO. Yeah, they say Reni engaged in a criminal conspiracy to hurt some of these groups. I thought RICO was for the Mafia, Boz, no?"

"It started that way," I said. "Now they're using it in civil suits to suggest they were conspired against in an illegal way. It's designed, of course, to tar the target with the underworld brush. Do we know the status of these suits when he died?"

"A few dismissed. A few in discovery."

"Were they dropped when he died or transferred to another target?"

"Dropped. Running Dogs, his organization, folded right before he died. Financial collapse, *pauvre bête*."

"His enemies got what they wanted. They stopped him in the ultimate way. What about his kids? What did they want?"

"They wanted a divorce from their father."

"Were Reni and his wife still married?"

"As far as I can tell, yeah," Goblin said.

"Crazy."

Goblin slid the messy envelope over, and we talked for a little while about what was happening in the spy world. Goblin said something about the media worrying too much about the Russians and not enough about the Saudis, and then he left.

I hated reading legal filings. Among other things, it reminded me how misguided I had been in ever considering becoming a lawyer. So many lawsuits could have been summarized in one sentence, but they never were. The suits against Guido Reni could have simply read: *We don't like you, and some people told us you did bad stuff to us, and we want to make your life hell.* And that would have been the truth.

After a half hour of skimming the documents, three things struck me. One was that the complaints were worded with purple prose, suggesting that they were written more for the media than for a court. Second, the suits were all filed by law firms associated with progressive causes. Third, they were short on proof, which betrayed either that they were hopeful they would find the truth in discovery or that they didn't care. It all added up to one thing: ruining Reni, either with legal fees or in the media, had been the end goal.

I called a young *Incursion* reporter I had been mentoring: Eva Liora—one of the few kids of her generation who actually thought she might learn something from an elder.

"Eva, Sandy Petty here."

"Ooh, my favorite bad boy! Wazzup?"

"I am calling to exploit our relationship."

"I don't know much about the protocols. Is this kind of thing against the rules of suspensions?"

"They haven't revoked my credentials or pay and haven't said I couldn't talk to people. Talking to me may not be wise, but it's not a clear violation. Are you wise?"

"No, I get by on my looks," Eva said.

"Me too! So you'll help?"

"I like forbidden fruit. What do you got?"

I told Eva about the suits against Guido Reni. "I need a LexisNexis search on all the media these suits got when they were filed and during the life of the suits, including *Incursion* coverage. I also need you to cross-reference the law firms that filed these suits with their known clients."

"What's your thesis?"

"I want to understand Reni's enemies. I'm also trying to understand the legal merits of these cases—"

"As opposed to what?"

"The aim of just ruining Guido Reni's life."

Part II

ASYMPTOTE

—

"As in all great affairs, Mark Sanford fell in love simultaneously with a woman and himself—with the dashing new version of himself he saw in her molten eyes."

—MAUREEN DOWD

15

I TOOK A call from Kurt in my study. When I came out, Finn was sitting on one of the living room chairs, playing with her iPhone.

"What are all these calls with Uncle Kurt and you? Something about Samantha?"

She and Samantha had never been especially close. Samantha was a few years older, and she was more of a mainstream kid than Finn, who was a little offbeat. These differences were a big deal at her age, but beyond the occasional eye roll, I didn't sense that the two girls actively disliked each other.

"Well, kiddo, this is family stuff, so not a word about it to anyone. Not even the boyfriend. You got it?"

"Got it."

"Samantha was, ah, she was assaulted . . . sexually. By a man at work."

Finn appeared stricken. Her eyes changed shape and her lips trembled.

"Raped?" she said.

"Yes, that's what she said."

"What do you mean, 'that's what she said'?"

"After it happened, Kurt and Angie asked me to come over to talk to all of them about it."

"Why you?"

"For a few reasons, I think. Samantha likes me and may find it easier to talk to me than Uncle Kurt—"

"Why, because Uncle Kurt had an affair?"

I didn't know Finn knew about that, but I saw no use in litigating the point. "I'm not sure, but I think they were trying to figure out what to do."

"What do you mean, 'what to do'?" Finn wrinkled her brow. "Call the police."

"That's what we're trying to figure out. See, there are consequences to calling the police. Sammy's name could go public, and the guy could start trying to discredit her."

"But she said he did it?"

"Yes, she says he did it."

"Then tell the police that!"

One thing that is so hard to learn about dealing with children—even adults—is that you cannot tell them about the terrible things you have learned in your particular trade. It wasn't that Finn's opinion was wrong, but she couldn't factor in what the world had taught me on my unique and narrow path. I wanted to give her an experience transfusion, but I couldn't simply hook her up to a device and transfer knowledge via a tube into her soul. This was the crux of the problem I'd had with Nat my whole life. When people saw a sad little man threatening to kill himself, they took it at face value. They didn't understand the sophistication of the scheme, and the more I tried to explain it to somebody, the worse I looked. There are limits to what communication can accomplish, due to restraints in the life experience—and sometimes the intelligence—of the other party.

I would do my best.

"It's not that simple, Finn," I said. "I had to explain to Sammy and her parents what happens when these cases hit the courts. Everybody looks into the victim's life, not just the bad guy's. They find everybody who ever disliked you—even if they have to go back to fourth grade—and they quote them in news stories that say you were the kind of person who lies."

Her eyes were wide. "That makes no sense. The guy should be in jail."

"Yes, he should, but we have to look at what Sammy wants."

"She doesn't want him to be in jail?" Finn asked.

"Of course she does, but a number of hurdles would have to be crossed or jumped or whatever to get to that point. The police don't just grab someone and put them in jail."

"They do it all the time."

"Yes, they do. But somebody like this guy has resources—"

"So if you're rich, they can't get you?"

"They can get you, but it's harder. Sammy might get death threats, or rocks through her dorm window. Her professors might avoid her, saying she's trouble. Guys might not want to date her, for fear of getting accused of something or just because of the stigma. She could get sued for defaming her accuser. The internet would be filled with guys calling her a whore. Sure, they'd be complete lies, but she would log on to some website and see what people were saying about her. Some of them would go on TV and lie, which they're allowed to do under the First Amendment. Sure, she could sue them for lying, but she'd have to spend a fortune, and once it got to court, all the lies—and maybe even some true things, like her medical records—would be out there all over again."

"Medical records?" Finn asked.

"They could ask whether she's taken medicine for anxiety or depression. If she had, they would say she's crazy or unreliable. They could ask if she was ever on birth control, and she'd have to answer under oath. If she was, she'd be a slut. In our system, the bad guy has every right to defend himself, to poke holes in her story."

"That's ridiculous!" Finn threw her arms in the air.

"How would you feel if somebody accused you? You'd want to find the best lawyer to make it hard for the police to get you."

"Well, I wouldn't do anything that bad in the first place," Finn said.

"Well, there was the little incident with throwing beer bottles from the Beltway overpass that could have gotten people killed had the wind blown the wrong way. That could have gotten you charged with manslaughter or murder—"

"Dad, that's not what happened!"

"That's not what *ended up* happening. Anyway, then there's the issue of Sammy's career. She wants to do something in media. If she goes into that field, nobody will want to touch her. They'll be afraid of getting sued. Even if she breaks through, she may get tagged as a loose cannon or a victim. Only bad options . . ."

I could see the mechanisms of Finn's brain whirring, and I knew the conclusion she would reach: that the human adventure is painful and unfair. That bad people win and good people lose. That "the system" doesn't work, and may never work, because of the soupiness of allegations that are subject to interpretation—unlike science, where a molecule is a molecule.

And perhaps there was another conclusion she would reach as well: that her dad couldn't protect her from any of it.

16

FRANKIE WATERMAN AND I met in the lobby of the *Incursion* and were escorted up to the boardroom by a male student intern in a boxy suit, trying to look grown up but failing spectacularly. Fortunately, our escort pushed the elevator button, sparing me the embarrassment of another failed encounter with modernity. We used the boardroom when we wanted to convey to a source or target that we were taking them seriously. It was an imposing room decorated with the *Incursion*'s big headlines from across the decades. The JFK assassination. Vietnam. The moon landing. The Pentagon Papers. Watergate. 9/11.

As we waited for whomever they were bringing in for my career X-ray, Frankie reminded me to answer their questions slowly and to be mindful that the *Incursion* needed to perceive enterprise risk—that *they* were also being questioned.

"Sandy, I'm not going to be as aggressive as I would be in a courtroom, because I want to try to resolve this peacefully first and not send signals that you're legally vulnerable. We want them to get the impression that this could be painful for them—"

"Even though we don't know what they're so afraid of—"

"If anything at all," Frankie said. "They may legitimately believe you did something wrong."

"I got it."

I didn't get it.

I was dressed business casual in a blue blazer, as was, it turned out, the general counsel—Joel Mayer, a man of about my age who had once been a prosecutor in New Jersey. Following him through the board-room entrance was the paper's editor, Stuart Gilmore, a longstanding supporter of my work. Entering from a side door was none other than reporter Gretchen Kramer.

What the fuck? This is an ambush.

Frankie had warned me against appearing too afraid. I had to let it go.

Gretchen had the weak-chinned look of a just-hot-enough high-school teacher who was banging a sixteen-year-old male student. She nodded at me and removed her cell phone from the back pocket of her pants, setting it down on the table.

A camera had already been set up and was pointed straight at where I was sitting. A tech kid named Ryan came in and sat behind the camera. He wore a sorrowful expression and avoided eye contact. I'd always sensed he liked me, and wondered what he'd been told about the inquisition.

Mayer went through a list of the milestones in my case, in clinical fashion. After several minutes of pretending this farce was something other than what it was, he said, "I'll remind you that even though Sandy has the right to have an attorney present, this is not a legal proceeding—"

"Which is why the *Incursion*'s general counsel is presiding over the interview and a camera is filming us," I said with a smirk.

"That's just policy," Mayer said.

Gilmore, a tall, athletic man with a shaved head and a full beard, took over. "All right, Sandy. As you know, we're conducting a due diligence review of the reporting you were doing on Guido Reni. This isn't an inquisition."

"Aside from it being an inquisition," I said, "this reminds me of when we tell targets we're not after them—we just want to confirm a few facts."

Gilmore and Mayer grinned tightly. Gretchen Kramer did not. She wore an expression as if she had just discovered she had stepped in doggie diarrhea. I wanted to blow her a kiss but thought better of it.

"Before we get started, do you have any questions?" Gilmore asked.

"A general one," I said. "Why is there an inquiry? Usually these things happen when there's a suspicion of malfeasance. Plagiarism. Fabricating sources. I haven't heard a word about what's driving this, especially since I never actually published anything. My investigation was killed right off the bat."

Mayer and Gilmore were quiet—they knew I had a point. Kramer narrowed her eyes. Mayer nodded and said, "Sandy, there's no suspicion of a giant crime against journalism."

"Then what brings us here?"

"Frankly," Gilmore said, "there was a feeling among some who originally covered Reni's career that you were undermining their work."

"You mean Gretchen," I said, meeting her icy glare.

"We're not getting into names," Mayer said.

"It sounds like this is an inquiry into hurt feelings. Tell me, how was I undermining anybody?"

"We're not sure you were. We're just trying to find out," Gilmore said.

"Let's consider the worst-case scenario," I said. "Just for fun."

"Hypothetical, of course," Frankie interjected.

"Of course," I echoed. "Let's say that some of my reporting did create some heartburn among my younger colleagues." I wanted to throw in an age reference to tweak discrimination anxiety. "What would they have been so afraid I was going to find out?"

"I don't think it's that, Sandy," Gilmore said. "It was more like a feeling you were looking to counter what they had discovered about Guido Reni."

"And let's say, hypothetically, I believed our coverage was inaccurate or incomplete and would have embarrassed the reporters who covered Reni. If my reporting was correct, so what? Aren't we about transparency?" I hissed the last word.

"Were you trying to embarrass your colleagues?" Gilmore asked.

"Of course not. You seem to be forgetting that I didn't do this behind your back. I openly approached you to look into this, and my pursuit was killed."

Mayer and Gilmore visibly squirmed. I saw the corner of Frankie's upper lip rise. Gretchen, still wearing her dog-shit expression, wrote something on her pad and underlined it furiously.

"What were you trying to accomplish?" Mayer asked.

"Look, there were all these articles that resulted in the death of a high-profile subject, and I thought there may be more to the story. Stuart, you didn't even wave me off initially."

Nobody spoke for a moment.

"So what's the sin?" I added.

"The *concern,"* Mayer said, "was that you were deliberately fomenting dissent in the newsroom."

"Really, Stuart?" I asked. "What are you even basing this on?"

Mayer held up a palm, presumably signaling Gilmore not to answer the question. "We're asking you, Sandy," Mayer said.

"Asked and answered," Frankie said.

"When you were asking for support internally, did you ever raise with other reporters that you thought some of our folks had gotten their coverage wrong?" Gilmore asked.

"I don't think so," I said.

"Do you remember how you asked for assistance from junior reporters?"

"I don't really remember asking for assistance per se, but I'm sure I said 'please.' I was looking to cover the coda of the Reni affair. We'd done so much reporting before his demise, I figured why not cover the epilogue."

"Or write it," Gretchen Kramer said with a forced smile and hard eyes.

Mayer and Gilmore swiveled their heads toward Kramer.

"Which brings up another question," I said, boring in on her. "What are you doing here?"

Mayer took this one. "She did a lot of the coverage. We wanted her expert input solely from a content perspective."

"And to send her a message that she is part of this inquisition, lest she sue you for discrimination for not inviting a woman to join Murderer's Row here."

"That wasn't necessary," Mayer said.

For the next forty-five minutes, my three interrogators grilled me about who I had interviewed for my Guido Reni story, the kind of research I had done, and whether I had begun to write a story, which I had not.

Gretchen Kramer's final question was telling. "What made you think of doing this story?" she asked. As if this was any of her business. As if she believed she had the right to know what was in my mind.

"I've covered this already. To finish a story we'd already begun. A man we had been hounding for months blew his brains out the top of his head and made certain that his body tumbled down a cliff into the rapids of the Potomac. Compelling, don't you think?"

Kramer didn't answer.

"What I wondered was why no one else was covering the story! Gretchen here spent so much time on it when Reni was alive, why not follow up on his newsworthy demise? Seems logical, right?"

Kramer shook her head in a generic registration of protest.

"What didn't you want people to know, Gretch? Aren't you the transparency queen?" I continued.

"Did you have a thesis? A conclusion?" Gilmore asked.

"As to Reni's suicide? Not really. But there is a part of me that wondered why we targeted him as opposed to a progressive think-tank guy." I stared down Kramer when I said it. I knew she didn't like right-of-center operatives, but I suspected something else was at play. "The only thing that's nagging at me now is, why did my nascent interest in this subject matter get me suspended?"

I studied the body language in the room. Gilmore and Mayer remained poker-faced, but I thought I saw a twitch around Mayer's right eye. Gretchen underlined something on her notepad with alacrity and drew something that appeared to be a three-dimensional cube.

"Let's go, Frankie," I said. "No new information here."

Frankie and I left the meeting with nothing answered and nothing resolved. Nevertheless, I was happy for purely psychic reasons. I had gotten some shots in and had seen my employer's discomfort when I'd barked the word "transparency" at Kramer. That word, which the free press clings to in the way some Americans invoke "freedom"—to mean absolutely anything—is the very one that kills them when it's probed. And that's exactly what I intended to keep doing. Everybody has secrets.

17

MY JEEP WAS in for an oil change, so I took the Metro to Union Station and then hopped a train up to Baltimore to pay a visit to Marsh Academy, where Pacho Craig's Wikipedia biography indicated he had gone to high school.

On the train ride up, my misanthropic impulses were raging. People were speaking too loudly on their cell phones, engaging in intimate and unnecessary conversation. I could understand making urgent calls from the train, but these people were just jabbering about routine issues. One guy—he was sitting across the aisle from me—began to FaceTime with his family without using a headset, so that his two-way discussion was broadcast to all of his fellow passengers. In what world was this not antisocial behavior? Even the other passengers began eyeing each other, appalled by this asshole's obliviousness.

I took out my flip phone and pretended to dial a number. Then I held the phone up to my ear and began speaking loudly. Really loudly.

"Yeah, Bruce," I said, "I'm producing a lot of mucus. I mean *a lot* of mucus. Red, inflamed. What do they call it when there's blood in there? Sputum. Right, sputum. The thing is that the mucus is a deep green when I hock it up. It's the kind that really sticks to the sidewalk when you loogie it out, know what I mean? I guess I shouldn't be hocking all that phlegm right out there on the sidewalk where people can step on it and get that yellow-green goo all over their shoes, but when it's coming out of your lungs like Old Faithful, what are you gonna do? You gotta share that phlegm with the world. Cut the people in, baby!"

Mr. FaceTime glanced over at me with a sneer. "Excuse me," he said, visibly annoyed. "Would you mind keeping your voice down?"

"Me? Why?" I asked.

By this point, a young guy diagonally across from me was trying to restrain himself from laughing.

"What you're talking about is not very pleasant," FaceTime said.

"You know what else is not very pleasant?" I said. "Listening to you yammer and cluck with your family so loudly that the Taliban in their caves ten thousand miles away are covering their ears. I'll make you a deal. You get off your damned phone and I'll get off mine."

"There's a big difference—"

I held my phone back up to my ear and shouted, "And the hemorrhoids! Like bloody little sacks. You slide your ass one way a bit too far and . . . BOOM!"

"That's enough!" FaceTime said.

"You know the deal. You hang up. I hang up. If I had a smartphone and could record you, I'd broadcast you all over the internet so maybe you'd get some feedback from civilization."

We both hung up and glared at each other. A couple of people on the train clapped. It was a small victory against the TICU culture of oblivious self-absorption.

• • •

Marsh Academy was in a pleasant section of town near Johns Hopkins University's Homewood campus, which combines urban neighborhoods with bucolic private schools. The scrubbed-looking kids milling about appeared to have been raised like veal, protected from every element in nature. In a year or two, they would be transported to Duke, Bucknell, and Yale. After that, of course, things would get interesting.

The rapids of prosperity that had carried them to a certain point wouldn't always flow as swiftly once these kids were washed into the delta of adulthood.

I wore a tweed sport jacket and khakis, purposely affecting a non-threatening, cool social-studies teacher vibe. I wandered around, appearing pleasantly confused. I made a point of talking to some of the students, who probably thought I was wearing my fedora ironically as opposed to wanting to protect my scalp from sun and breeze. They were all very bright and enthusiastic about the school when I told them I was looking at Marsh for my daughter.

I entered the main administration building—a converted mansion. While wandering around with a moronic grin and reading plaques and other items of historical significance to the school, I made eye contact with most of the grown-ups who passed by. I was waiting for the right person to intercept, someone who appeared senior without being too stern. Posing as a parent of a prospective student, I tried to appear appropriately awestruck, as if every soul I encountered was a major decision maker with the power to either nod my child into Xanadu or cast her into the fire pit of rejection. After forty minutes, my curious examination of the school newspaper, *The Martian,* intersected with a hip-looking man with a graying ponytail and a hiking vest who was emerging from an office.

I tapped the glass case holding the latest edition of *The Martian* and said to Ponytail, "Whoever said millennials can't write never read this newspaper."

"Yes," Ponytail said, "some of our students are pretty good."

"Most kids write too flowery, and you have to whittle the excess off the page."

"We take writing seriously. These kids are competing with serious characters in the college race, and as much as we push the liberal arts, it can't all be squishy."

"I get it. I'm a writer, and I'm watching my trade vanish into oblivion. Just happy to see a ray of hope."

"What kind of writing do you do?" Ponytail asked.

"Oh, boring old obsolete journalism, but I didn't mean to get into that. I'm Sandy Petty." I extended my hand.

"Josh Culling," Ponytail said.

"Are you a teacher here?"

"Vice principal. But I teach a history class."

"Great. I was just in Baltimore interviewing a guy at Hopkins and wanted to swing by to check out Marsh for my daughter. I didn't mean to take you away from anything."

"You should bring your daughter to look around the campus."

"Honestly, I think it's too late for her to make a switch, but I'm a worrier—and a reporter—so I'm obsessive."

"How old is she?"

"Starting junior year in high school in Bethesda." I brightened.

"Well, it's late in the game, but you never know . . . What kind of journalism do you do?" When his forehead wrinkled, it shifted his hairline.

"Politics, corruption, crime, things like that."

"Freelance?"

"No. *Capitol Incursion*."

"Wow. No kidding?" Culling said, his eyes widening.

"Don't be too impressed. With newspapers collapsing every day, you might want to check in with me tomorrow. I might be applying for a maintenance job here. Run out of business by Facebook, Twitter, and MyStream."

"That's where it all seems to be going. And one of our alums is leading the way."

"Who?" I asked. "Mark Zuckerberg?"

"Nobody that big."

"Jack Dorsey? Twitter?"

"No. Pacho Craig," Culling said.

"Who?" I asked.

"Pacho Craig. He's on MyStream and some other online sites. He does these short—"

"Oh! The guy with the cape!"

Culling laughed. "It's not a cape. It's an Australian bush coat."

"Excuse me," I said in mock apology.

"I was a class ahead of him. I graduated in 1999," Culling said.

"No kidding? I can't imagine a guy like that in high school."

"We have the yearbook to prove it."

"Man, I gotta see that."

"C'mon." He waved for me to join him, and I kept the eager smile plastered to my face.

I followed Culling down the hall to a miniature library. As we entered the room, I asked Culling what Pacho was like in high school.

"Popular. The girls liked him. He didn't have that long hair then. Real preppy."

"Handsome Spanish guy getting all the girls, huh?"

Culling looked at me like I was daft. "Aw, that Pacho stuff is bullshit. He was just Paul when he was here. His blood is bluer than George Washington's." Culling shrugged. "I guess Pacho's just some stage name."

At the beginning of my career, journalists tended to be kids from modest backgrounds who pounded the pavement covering local news, as I did. As my career progressed, mainstream journalists began coming from affluent backgrounds instead. They went to top-flight universities and moved pretty quickly to covering big social issues. Now at the top of the food chain, they were multimillionaire Manhattanites who commanded six figures for a speech. In the eyes of this new generation, Democrats were correct-thinking progressives fighting the good fight, and Republicans were racists and brutal capitalists who occupied themselves by mowing down protestors like that lunatic at that Charlottesville white power rally. But if the Pacho Craigs of the world actually knew the people they were covering, they would see things differently or at least with greater nuance. The recent backlash against all of this was the bloody shriek from the far right on the internet, talk radio, and cable TV—which only made things worse.

"Really? Not Spanish? I could have sworn I saw an interview where Pacho said he was named for a relative. Pablo, Carlos, or something."

Culling rolled his eyes. "That's showbiz, I guess." Culling wasn't nasty about it—after all, Pacho was a famous alumnus he didn't want to trash—but there was a subtext here. In our modern culture, there was special resentment toward someone who was capable of just manufacturing an image. In the eighties and nineties, Madonna was often praised for her metamorphoses, but these days, when she was accidentally-on-purpose photographed wearing a burka, it screamed of desperation.

Culling went to a shelf and pulled out a yearbook from the Class of 2000. He opened up the senior photos and thumbed to the *C*s. I was surprised to see that the senior portraits were in color. On the top right corner of the page was a color photo of a grinning, baby-faced Paul Charles Craig, with short hair and a side part. He seemed to be genuinely laughing at something. A child of affluence, he sported a wrinkled, button-down Oxford cloth shirt with one of the collar flaps askew, as if to say, *My collar can be a tad off if I want it to be, because I just don't care.*

"Heh, there he is," I said, and then looked closer. "Hmm. What color are his eyes?"

Culling studied the photo. "Blue," he said. "Why?"

"Huh, a strange glare," I said. "So was Pacho a good student? Just curious."

"More of a shrewd student," Culling said.

"What do you mean?"

"He knew how to work the teachers. Knew how to get the brainiacs to help out with papers."

I flipped through to another page that had a photo of Pacho. In one, he was posing with several other guys. The caption read *El Banditos*.

"Who were El Banditos?" I asked Culling.

"Oh, just an ad hoc group of chuckleheads."

"What did they do?"

"Various and sundry mischief."

"Who were the other El Banditos?"

Culling studied the photo. "Well, that's Paul there—Pacho. This guy here is David Burns. He was a lacrosse player. I don't remember the other two guys so well."

"Do you remember anything about them? I always wondered about who big stars hung out with when they were younger."

"This guy here, I'm pretty sure he was in theater. He played Pippin in the school play. Joe or Josie somebody. I think this other guy was a stoner, always showing up late for class."

"Were any of them Hispanic?" I asked.

"Hispanic? No, I don't think so. Because of Banditos?"

"Yeah. I mean, why not call themselves the Bandits?" I suspected Pacho had a fetish for Spanish culture to protest his white-bread roots.

"I don't know." Culling squinted and shook his head.

I shrugged, thanked Culling for his time, and made my way out of the building. I pulled my small Moleskine notebook from my breast pocket and wrote "shrewd student/worked the teachers." Then I jotted the word "heterochromia." Did one just develop two differently colored eyes over time? Of course not. I also wrote down the names of the other Banditos Culling had mentioned.

Now, I knew there was nothing wrong or unusual about being

mischievous in high school—Lord knows, I pulled some crap—but there was something about the head fake toward ethnicity that smacked of self-invention. Banditos. Pacho. A lot of big shots had a good line of bullshit, but they also had something else. Bob Dylan was a shtick artist, but look at what he wrote. Steve Jobs had his monk routine, but look at what he made. Ronald Reagan had a lot of charm, but he had a portfolio of thought, whether you liked it or not. And what did Pacho have?

All I could think was that this guy was a real piece of work.

18

EVA, MY YOUNG mentee from the *Incursion,* had left a message on my cell when I was in the shower. It was four days after we had initially spoken. She had an update. I called her back from the hard line in my home office.

"Hey, Eva, have you secured the Pentagon Papers?" I asked.

"What are the Pentagon Papers?"

"Jesus, I—"

"I'm screwing with you, Petty."

"Thank God."

"You got a pen?"

"Yeah."

"All right. I can't tell whether I've got anything of value," she said, "but here's what I know. The law firms that sued Guido Reni all use the same PR firm, the Sunshine Collective. The organizations that sued are also all clients of Sunshine. They're this liberal PR firm—"

"I know."

"Here's the thing," she said. "All of these suits against Reni were dismissed with prejudice by the DC courts, so the plaintiffs filed them again in federal court. Is that unusual?"

"It's not that unusual to refile a suit in another court, but it is kind of strange that *all* these cases were dismissed with prejudice."

"What does that tell you?" she asked.

"It tells me that they were bullshit suits. Vexatious litigants."

"Okay," Eva said slowly, which I interpreted to mean that she didn't know where I was heading.

"These are suits you file for purposes other than winning in court."

"Like what?"

"Like fucking with somebody. Maybe bankrupting them," I said. "What about press coverage?"

"I did a search on the lawsuits. There was extensive coverage when the suits were filed."

"What about the dismissals?"

"No coverage of dismissals at all," Eva said.

"None?"

"None. And I looked at Sunshine's client list and went into our database."

"Whose?"

"The *Incursion*'s. We did seventy-three stories on various Sunshine clients. Exposés of corporate dirtballs and polluters. Puff pieces on women with defective breast implants suing manufacturers, heroic plaintiffs' lawyers, Republican sexual harassers, whistleblowers who were silenced by their employers . . ."

"How would you characterize our coverage? Favorable? Unfavorable?"

"Very sympathetic to Sunshine clients."

"Surprise, surprise," I said.

"Petty, what are you mucking around in?"

I dodged the question. "Who wrote our stories?"

"Different reporters, but Gretchen Kramer did the bulk of them," Eva said.

"How many?"

"About half."

"Hmm. That's a healthy percentage. How many stories did we do hostile to Guido Reni?" I asked.

"I'd say ten. You don't want to tell me what you're into here? Maybe mounting a defense for your suspension?"

"There's some overlap," I said, mostly honestly. I thought about asking Eva to do something else for me, but I didn't want to get the kid in trouble. "Look, let me think about this a bit and get back to you."

I hadn't found a smoking gun on my fair Gretchen, but I had enough to tell me to keep going.

19

MY SCHEME FOR a reckoning with Pacho was taking shape in my mind. Nevertheless, a good idea can seem like a brilliant strategy inside your head until it collapses under the weight of practical tactics. From the beginning, I kept asking myself the same question: Who hates Pacho? One name kept floating back to me.

I called Abigail Case, the daughter of disgraced FEMA chief Henry Lockridge, whose life had been destroyed when Pacho Craig ambushed him after the Camden hurricane. She had changed her surname, switching to her mother's maiden name after her father's downfall and death from cancer. I'd met Abigail when I was "collecting string" on a potential story about Lockridge. At the time, she'd still been figuring out her life path. Now, after Goblin's help in doing some superficial digging, I thought she might be game for what I now had in mind.

I met Abigail for lunch in Chevy Chase, at Clyde's. A pretty, multiracial young woman in her early twenties, she bore a passing resemblance to Meghan Markle. I usually came here with Joey and Finn, so the waiter was probably wondering who this attractive young woman was, at least until we got down to business.

"The thing is, Sandy," Abigail said, "I'm not a hateful person, but I just can't find a place for this. I mean, my dad is dead. My mother had to become a secretary again after twenty years of hosting Washington parties. She lives in this little rental in Gaithersburg. My brother is a busboy at a California Pizza Kitchen. I'm forever between jobs. And then I think of *him*—it's hard for me to even say his name. Pacho Craig. I think of him as a murderer. No, he didn't shoot my dad, but the cancer came on right after he destroyed us in the press. My rage hasn't subsided at all."

"He's a son of a bitch, Abigail. I mean, beyond what he did to your dad."

Abigail sighed. "My dad was just an academic who made good. A poor, black kid from Baltimore who worked hard and got lucky. Until he got unlucky. I gather you have a reason to hate Pacho's guts?" she asked with wide eyes. I had a vision of what she must have looked like as a little girl. "Hate his guts" may have been a grade-school term, but it only reaffirmed that the destruction of her father had rendered her helpless.

"I do. I just can't tell you everything now . . ." I had to see how my plan would unfold first, piece by piece.

"Sometimes I watch his little show just to hate him more," she went on. "I read the comments under his videos. All these stupid girls in love with him, talking about how interesting he is with his 'oh-so-cool' blue and brown eyes."

I grinned like a James Bond villain.

"What?" Abigail said.

"They're fake."

"What's fake?"

"His eyes. At least I'm pretty sure they are. I've found old photos of him. Both eyes are blue. He must use a contact lens to alter one eye."

"Why would he do that?"

"Have you ever read Joan Didion?"

"No."

"She said that people tell themselves stories to live. That's what Pacho is doing. Marketing. Like everybody these days, he needs shtick.

A hook. A trademark. He uses props that he thinks make him sexier—the intrepid journalist. I'd say it's working pretty well."

"Geez," she said, scrunching her nose.

"Abigail, I'm looking into something, and I want to run a little game."

"Ooh, sounds cool." She leaned in closer and rubbed her hands together.

"Yes, but very sensitive," I said.

"I understand."

"No, you don't, but you'll need to. Can you keep a secret?"

"Yes," she said, crossing her heart with a finger.

"Few people can. They always say they won't tell, until they get together with someone and say, 'You have to swear not to tell anybody.' And then they tell."

"I swear I won't."

"Okay, I trust you."

I didn't. But I didn't trust anybody lately. After trust, the next best thing was deniability. Layers. I'd have to be sure I left no trail. Besides, what were my options?

"Have you heard of a man named Oliver Shackley?" I asked.

"Nope," she said.

"That's how he likes it."

"Who is he?"

"He's a guy worth six billion. He makes things nobody thinks about unless they have to. Dental implants, chemicals that make plastics more bendable, and the little tips at the ends of shoelaces that let you slip them into holes. His company is privately held. General Commodities. I presume he picked the name because it's boring and could mean anything. And nothing. Shackley also bought a confectioner that makes gummy bear–like treats. They fly off the shelves."

"I love gummy bears!"

"I do too. Even though I shouldn't. The whole gummy bear bonanza led to a story the *Incursion* did years ago, called 'Candy From Strangers.' It was a play on Shackley's reclusiveness. The dude lives in a modest colonial in one of the older neighborhoods in Rockville. He mows his own lawn with a .357 Smith & Wesson revolver strapped to his hip."

Abigail laughed.

"Shackley hired the most aggressive defamation lawyers and tried every legal trick in the book to try to kill the story. He failed, but he forced the *Incursion* to ensure that its reporters verified every single data point. I was on the fact-checking team and remember being disappointed in how bloodless the story ended up being because of how heavily edited the piece was. That was Shackley's second best outcome."

"Wait, I thought this was about Pacho. Shackley's mixed up with *him?*"

"Hold on. Patience. You millennials, I swear," I said with a smile.

Abigail twisted her face and then grinned.

"Anyway," I continued. "Sometime after 9/11, the *Incursion* was on to General Commodities again, because of his partnership with a Saudi Arabian petrochemical company. The bin Laden family was also an investor. Could've been a great story, right? Well, Shackley's legal counteroffensive was so savage that not even the *Incursion* felt it was worth the risk to include his name in the story. So we didn't. The bin Laden family was vast, and there was no reason to believe that they were all involved with terror."

"You guys think before you ruin people's lives," Abigail said, chewing on the side of her lip. "Unlike some."

"Right. I clearly got the impression that Shackley was one of the few men in the Age of Media Whoredom that truly did not want to see his name in the press for any reason. He seems to understand that the American dream of prosperity has been overwhelmed by the American dream of publicity, and he is happy to stick with the original one, thank you very much."

Abigail nodded. "There's a lot to be said for that."

"I later learned from a reporter friend who worked at *Forbes* magazine that Shackley sent a team of attorneys and accountants into the CEO's office to argue that he *wasn't* rich enough to be on their annual top billionaires list. He failed. They put him at $6 billion."

"So we know the guy is rich. Now what does this all have to do with Pacho?" Abigail asked.

"Okay, here's the deal. I need you to approach Pacho Craig. He obviously can't know who you really are. If you sense he might, we'll abort. Because your name isn't Lockridge, he has no reason to tie you immediately to your dad. Tell Pacho you work for Shackley's company, General Commodities—"

"Can't he check on that?"

"The company is privately held. They don't give out their address, and they don't even acknowledge they exist. Also, Pacho isn't known for his journalistic rigor. I'll help you get enough information to make you credible. You're playing the part of whistleblower. Do you know the name Adnan Sabbag?"

"The reporter who was killed."

"Right. He was a Saudi reporter doing investigative work for American media outlets. He was killed while investigating human rights abuses in Saudi Arabia. He called bullshit on their supposed reforms."

"Terrible," Abigail said.

"Awful. The pitch to Pacho is that Oliver Shackley was involved in Sabbag's murder. That Shackley has business with Saudi Arabia, and that Sabbag was investigating this relationship. Tell Pacho that Shackley sent up a panic signal and the Saudis lured Sabbag to Turkey and killed him."

A strand of hair fell in front of Abigail's eyes. It's strange how the slightly altered placement of a woman's hair can make a man's heart skip. Abigail blew the lock back to the side of her face. Yep, Pacho would like her.

"Wait, is any of this true?" Abigail asked.

"It's true that the Saudis killed Sabbag. It's true that General Commodities has business with the Saudis. It's absolutely false—at least to my knowledge—that Shackley had anything to do with Sabbag's murder. Shackley is a tough customer but I doubt he's a killer. If this plays out, he'll only get grazed. I'm using him as a whale for Pacho to hunt."

Abigail leaned back in her chair. I could see the component parts in her brain whirring. "What do you think Pacho will do?"

"I hope he'll pursue the story."

"But it's not a story," Abigail said, twisting her face.

"Leave that to me."

"But I want to understand what you think Pacho will do—what you want him to do."

"We'll get to that," I said.

"From what you've told me about Shackley . . ." Abigail stopped and covered her mouth as if captured by a religious awakening. "If Pacho comes after him, Shackley will tear him apart."

I nodded.

"Won't Pacho know that?" Abigail asked.

"How would he? He wasn't inside the *Incursion* newsroom when all this stuff went down with Shackley's legal team. He can search, but all he'll discover is that Shackley is a very rich, very secretive guy. Media outlets get threats all the time that go nowhere. This will make him a more appealing target."

"And this is for a potential *Incursion* story?"

"This is for a potential everything story," I said. "I want to show Pacho being reckless with people's reputations and expose what he does to people. Shackley is a big boy. He can take care of himself, and he can take care of Pacho."

"Can you do this?"

"Set up a pretext? Absolutely!"

"Is it ethical?" she asked.

"No, it's not ethical, but it's not illegal either." Probably. "Think about the end goal here."

"How will I approach him?"

"He goes to a coffee shop near his house in Georgetown. I think we take him there. My hope is that he'll want to meet with you to get more info. We'll figure out those details later. Now, I apologize in advance for this . . ."

"Okay . . ." Abigail said, narrowing her eyes at me.

"Uh, it's not lost on me that you're a very attractive woman—"

She gave a shy smile. "Um . . . thank you?"

"No, no. I'm not making a pass at you."

"I didn't think—"

"I'm just telling you explicitly that I am using your good looks"—I almost laughed as she gave a simple shrug, as if this sort of flattery happened all the time—"and I'm using your motivation. I'm using what Pacho did to your family to make this move on him. And of course, you're smart. That's key to pulling this off. But there's something else you need to know. I have reason to believe Pacho is . . . well . . . *aggressive* with women. That's what's motivating me to do all of this, which is all I can tell you now. I don't like putting you in this position, and I'll be listening and close by the whole time. I'll also give you pepper spray and a taser just in case. I'm serious about this."

"You're sweet, but I can take care of myself. I'm a millennial woman, remember?" She winked at me.

"I'm serious," I said. "I have a daughter who isn't that much younger than you are. I think—"

"I understand. I'm not futzing around here with this creep. I want my go at him."

There was a hardness in her eyes that assured me she was up for the job.

"Let me do a little more research. I'll get you some background materials, and we'll prep you to meet up with him." I reached into my pocket and pulled out a small bank envelope. "There's two thousand dollars in there, but I want to assure you that you'll keep getting paid."

"Wow, thanks. I appreciate it."

"One final thing. Do you ever wear glasses?"

"I'm wearing contacts now."

"Perfect. When you get the chance, get me your prescription."

I left the meeting knowing full well that putting Abigail in any position with Pacho was risky. But the look I'd seen in Abigail's eyes could only come from tamped-down fury. I realized then that I knew the sensation, and that she was probably tougher than I was.

20

I GOT TO Eddie Fontaine, the gangster, through his cousin Tiger. I called Tiger's cell phone, and he gave me the number of one of his burners. Once on a secure line, I reminded him who I was and said that I had an idea I wanted to bounce off Eddie. He said Eddie would meet me at a recreation center in Anacostia.

I wasn't thrilled about meeting in Anacostia. It was one of DC's roughest neighborhoods and considered one of the nastiest in the country. I hadn't wanted to ask Tiger for a guarantee of protection, because I didn't want to insult him or come off as being weak. I figured that if I drove directly there and carried some pepper spray, I'd have a decent chance of getting out unscathed.

Arriving at the rec center early, I got out and watched a group of young black men playing basketball on an outside court. A few kids nodded at me, and I figured if I stayed close to the sporting area, I'd be all right. There was one guy, about twenty, who might have been giving me a hard look, but that could've been me being paranoid. Or maybe not. A Stevie Wonder song from long ago, called "You Haven't Done Nothin'," was pulsing from a speaker in the distance.

Right on time, I spotted Eddie in the passenger seat of a black Buick Enclave SUV. It was smart, understated—no giant, sparkling white Cadillac Escalade, the king of vehicles within the drug rackets in the nation's capital. Eddie lived like an upwardly mobile African American businessman rather than a bling-laden rapper.

I waved, and he approached me with a firm handshake and a clap on the shoulder. "I was happy when Tiger told me you called," he said.

Eddie was exactly my height: five-eight. His all-gray goatee matched well with his tightly cropped, silver-flecked hair. In his mid-forties, he was in good shape, but perhaps five pounds heavier than when I saw him last. Dressed in khaki pants and a blue polo shirt with no discernable label, he wore a pair of Clic reading glasses around his neck. I knew he was a bibliophile and had a special fondness for Latin quotations. His only surrender to flash was a Rolex Submariner.

Once seated, Eddie said, "Sandy Petty, the man himself." He chuckled.

"It must be a big moment for you to see me in person after so long. You'll probably tell all your friends."

Eddie grinned broadly, showing perfect white teeth. "I'll take back an autograph. Just please tell me that you're not looking into me."

"No, Eddie, it's nothing like that. Completely unrelated. So unrelated, you may think I'm crazy."

"Now I'm intrigued," Eddie said. "You reporting on anything big these days?" He motioned for me to follow him and proceeded along the back edge of the basketball court, toward a picnic table. Everyone took a step back as we walked. The fellow who had given me a tough-guy look made it a point to nod at me, as if to convey we were cool.

Eddie and I sat across from each other at the table, which was shaded by a gazebo. A few big men that I assumed were bodyguards stood back a good twenty feet, well out of earshot. The basketball players occasionally glanced in our direction. No one approached.

"I'm taking a break from the *Incursion,* actually," I told him. "I have some side projects going."

"What, you're not into reporting anymore? That's crazy, my friend. It's your gig."

"Honestly, Eddie, my trade is dying. The Kardashians and MyStream have taken over the world, and I'm not much for that."

"Yeah, man, me neither. My kids are all over that shit, but I don't even like to touch a smartphone. Especially in my business."

I nodded. "Even the more legitimate media outlets are going in a direction I don't like."

"More and more, you people are putting over a point of view," Eddie said.

"That's one of my top grievances. We still say we're only reporting the news, but the fact is, we're just hunting big game now."

"When there's money in the pot, anybody can justify anything. I usually stick to CNN and CNBC," Eddie said.

"CNBC, huh?"

"Oh yeah. I like to follow the markets. Long time ago, late nineties, I asked Tiger to get me a book down at the Borders store. They didn't have it. So my daughter—she was pretty young at the time—says we don't need to go to no store. Any store. She jumps on her computer and types in the name of the book, and two days later, I get it at my front door. I ask my broker about the company. Amazon. He said, 'Don't buy it.' Some kind of tax dodge. I said, 'Dodge, my ass. Those guys brought a book to my front door.' So I bought the stock. Spent maybe twenty thousand. Now it's worth almost a million."

"Geez, Eddie. You should be a professional investor."

"I *am* a professional investor. Key is knowing when to get in and when to get out."

"Do you still like what *you* do?" I asked.

"Trying to make that turn, you know, man? Trying to figure out what I'll need to get out."

"How much of staying in is about money, and how much is ego?" I asked.

Eddie pointed at me and nodded. "That's what I ask myself. Am I staying in because of the cash, or do I need to be the king?"

"What's the answer?"

"I still need to work to live my preferred lifestyle. Investments alone—legit ones—don't pay diddly. There's more to the ego thing than I probably want to admit." Eddie knocked on his head and laughed. "You know, word on the street is that the big man's outta the game and such. That I'm retiring. It's just trash talk, but I gotta pay it some mind. Every year there's more risk, more chance of getting clipped. The need to be king gets less and less powerful each year. All the pressure. These kids looking at you, and you know what they're thinking: 'What's so great about him? Why's he up there and not me?' *Forna bonum fragile est*. All good things end."

"So where does that leave you?" I asked.

"I gotta start thinking like them Buddhists. That it all passes. That it's dumb to think anybody will care, in a few short years, whether you controlled this or ran that. My instinct, you know, is to plot, to scheme, to think a dozen steps ahead and outmaneuver them, but—" Eddie closed his eyes.

"But you're tired," I said.

Eddie nodded. "Man, you're like a psychic. Like Hannibal Lecter, knowing what people's thinking."

"Nah, Eddie, it's just that I'm tired too. That's all."

He nodded again. "When I smell these kids close on my heels, I'm gonna do something they didn't never imagine."

"Should I be hearing this?"

"It's no mind. I'm gonna give it to 'em. Step aside. Hand over the business. Not to my own blood, mind you. But that's why I need the money. Be rich enough to walk away and fund places like this. Not fight. It's not one of them businesses you can sell stock in."

"You built this rec center?" I asked.

"I converted the building. We got an indoor basketball court. Volleyball. Ping-pong. Weights and stuff. Makes me feel good. I dunno." He paused. "What do you got for me?"

I laid out my proposal to get Pacho.

Eddie knew who Pacho was. *"Vasa vana pluribum sonant,"* he said.

"What does that mean?"

"'Empty pots make the most noise.' Looks like to me, Sandy, you're in a different business than journalism on your so-called break."

"You're right, Eddie. I am trying to make news, but I'm not cooking up something that benefits me. The man I mentioned did a very bad thing to the child of a friend of mine."

Eddie squinted at the word "child." "What kind of bad thing?"

"To a young woman."

"I see," Eddie said, stroking his goatee. He glanced toward the basketball court and gave one kid a thumbs-up. Then he looked behind him and to the sides. I couldn't tell if he was searching for cops or surveillance equipment, or if he was just thinking. "You looking for a favor, Sandy?" he finally said.

"No," I said, deliberately waiting to offer up the prize. "A business deal. Pacho has a watch collection. Some pieces are worth well into the six figures. One alone is worth a quarter million or more. I'm just informing you of their existence and letting you know I'm aware that there may be a specific occasion when someone may have access to his residence. If all goes right, that is."

"One watch worth a quarter? How many watches he got?"

"Two, three dozen at least. They're not all worth that much, but I can't imagine a scenario where the collection is worth less than a million. It's probably double that at least."

"And you don't want a cut?"

"I demand to *not* get a cut."

Eddie's eyes were illuminated by the chip in his brain. He was doing the calculations. Worst-case scenario, he gets a million for the watches, launders it through his businesses, and it lands in stocks, bonds, or real estate. He gets closer to retirement. And Pacho gets fleeced, not to mention embarrassed by some of the other services I had in mind for Eddie to perform.

"Normally I wouldn't ask about all the ins and outs of a deal," he said, "but you got me curious about not wanting anything."

"Oh, I want something. And I'm getting something very much of value, Eddie."

"Yeah?"

"What I get out of this is his image. I mean, I take it from him."

Eddie rubbed his palms together. "Man, I thought I'd done been in on every kind of scheme. You got others helping you with this?"

"Oh yeah. But I don't want anybody in our crew to have any contact with each other, unless I say so. I like having firewalls—if somebody starts getting treacherous thoughts, there's only so much damage that person can do."

"You shoulda been in my racket," Eddie said with a playful grin. "Now, Sandy, if we're gonna have a little gang, my man, we need a name."

"The Callous Sophisticates," I blurted out.

Eddie almost spit out his drink. "Say what?"

"There was a cartoonist when I was growing up, named Kliban. He drew these crazy drawings with nonsensical captions. One of them showed a group of snobs snickering at this one woman at the party who had a freakishly little head. The caption read 'The callous sophisticates laughed at Judy's tiny head.' Something about it got to me, and I've been laughing about it for forty years."

"The Callous Sophisticates. If you say so," Eddie said. "You're one strange motherfucker. Well, *ex nihilo nihil fit.*"

I shrugged because I didn't know what that meant.

"Nothing comes from nothing," Eddie said.

"No, sir, it does not."

21

I ASKED FREDDIE—THE street urchin who had lived in the alley behind the *Incursion* for years and who tried to mug Joey and me after dinner last week—if he knew any good pickpockets. His answer was "The best." So I showed him a photo of Gretchen and told him where she always stopped for her morning coffee by the *Incursion*'s office.

Freddie reported back to me the next morning, after he had waited for Gretchen to come out of Starbucks with her grande latte and faked a bad fall at her feet. While she was distracted helping poor Freddie, his buddy Skinny the Pickpocket had simply slipped her iPhone from her back pocket. After meeting Freddie, I went to a dead drop near a small playground on River Road and left the phone in a paper bag for Goblin.

On my way home, I felt the impulse to drive by Joey's old house. I was experiencing a freakish surge of nostalgic girl-craziness. The Morris family had lived in a Cape Cod in the Hillmead section of Bethesda, where the houses were small but tidy. As a teenager, I would ride my bike over in the evening after dinner to "do homework." I could never wait to leave my house. Dinner was always the roughest part of my day, but it must have been sheer torture for my mother because she couldn't leave—at least not by the values of the day, which were very much her values.

After Mom was diagnosed with cancer, she became delirious from the medication and kept muttering something that sounded like "crow nose." Years later, I took an art history course in college and came upon a painting by Goya of the Titan Cronus eating his son. Then it clicked. Not "crow nose," but *Cronus*. The painting was terrifying—Cronus had these maniacal eyes, and the son was headless—and it shook me to the core. It was less that I identified with the son being consumed than that my mother apparently thought I should recognize the danger I was in. What else had she seen that I never knew about?

I found Joey's old house in Hillmead and felt so grateful for her. I'd always loved that she loved simple things, like trees and the moon. After biking to her house in the evening, I would look at her baby pictures and ask her parents about when she started paying attention to the moon and when her freckles came out. As miserable as I felt living in the Petty insane asylum, I knew that after dinner, from eighth grade through high school, Joey's house was only a bike ride away.

The first time I knew I liked a girl was in kindergarten, when this adorable little Italian doll sat in front of me and her presence there made me dizzy. But nothing ever actually happened between a girl and me until Joey and I started going down to her basement. We did some homework, but not much. I don't know how I did so well in school, because most of what I remember about those days was watching Joey read, which she sometimes did with her lips moving. She would tuck her long hair behind her ears, and as her head tilted toward the bottom of the page, her hair would flip forward and she would push the strands back behind her ears again.

But the best part of the week was Friday night, when we would hang out in Joey's basement and then . . . and then . . . *The Rockford Files* would come on. That was always when I made my move. It really was Pavlovian: the synthesizer of the theme song started, and either I would jump on Joey or she would jump on me. I'm not sure I ever actually watched an episode until reruns aired when I was in college. Turns out, it was a pretty good show.

It was a freezing-cold night in February—Joey was wearing an

Olivia Newton-John T-shirt, and I put my hand up the back of it. Joey shook her head, and I pulled my hand away. Of course I did. But I hadn't requested permission, and a couple of weeks later, I tried again. And Joey didn't say no.

After a while, I began to think I was some kind of criminal for leaving my mother home with Nat, his pants undone after dinner, ranting in the corner of the sofa about all the sons-of-bitches, while I was in the midst of a sinister bliss that I thought was unique to me in the history of civilization.

I always dreaded the bike ride home. Not because it was dark. Not because those were the days before flashing bike lights and helmets. Not because on narrow Bradley Boulevard there was no sidewalk to ride an arm's length away from traffic. Not because those were the days before backpacks, so I carried my books under my arm and steered one-handed. No, it was because I was leaving Joey to go home to the cuckoo's nest, all the while harboring a sense of having done something monstrous for having fled my parents' home in the first place.

I shook the memories free and drove home. I was in my office, looking over my notes about my next moves on Pacho, when an email pinged. It was a note from a family friend known as "Uncle Murray." A decent-enough fellow, Uncle Murray was a retired pharmacist who could always be counted upon to traffic in Nat's velvet-encased poison. I had no doubt that Nat had put Murray up to the email. If I had had any brains at all, I wouldn't have opened it, but instead I made the fatal click.

Dear Sandy,

This is your Uncle Murray long time no talk ha ha. I just wanted to mention that I saw your father who loves you very much and is always so proud of you and your success. You know Sandy that you only have one family and blood is thicker than water and you only have one set of parents and you should cherish every moment you have with them. Nat says how much he misses you and he is an old man and only has so much time left. Sure he can be a bit crotchety but that's what happens when you get older believe me. You don't want to avoid your parents because believe me you will regret it later when you don't have them. Regards to Joey.

Murray

I felt my blood vessels constrict and thought I sensed a shooting pain in my left arm, but that was probably because I read somewhere that one sign of a heart attack was shooting pains in your left arm. I began typing back:

Dear Uncle Murray,

You are a fucking idiot and if you had any idea what went on in that household you would keep your Mother Goose theories about families to yourself and ram them up your ass broadside ha ha.

Sandy

After reading my words on the screen, I sighed and deleted my response as well as Uncle Murray's email, an action that had taken me five and a half decades to achieve. I was not put on earth to explain things to people. It was vanity to think otherwise, but I was guilty of vanity and had, in fact, made a career out of explaining things to people—something one can do only if they think they have an exceptional gift for explaining.

Still, the emotional blackmail worked: I stopped at Nat's place before dinner. Given that I had been feeling pretty good, I figured God wanted me to have a little punishment to balance things out.

When Nat saw me, he started sobbing, so Omar gave him a pill. When Omar turned his back, my father slipped it into the pocket of his robe. He didn't like taking medicine, because he didn't think anything was wrong with him.

"Calm down," I said. "I'm here."

After a few minutes, the sobs stopped, and the only residue was the moisture on his face and the sensation I had a football lodged in my throat. "There he is, the Portugal son," Nat said from his favorite chair.

"You mean prodigal."

"What did I say?"

"Portugal."

"What's the difference?"

"One means wasteful. The other is a country near Spain."

"Maybe the son was from Portugal," Nat said. *And maybe a chartreuse gorilla was going to fly out of my left nostril.* I wasn't up for an argument. This was strictly a guilt-alleviation visit.

"He probably was from Portugal. You're no dummy," I said.

"You don't need to go to a fancy college and spend all that money to know a thing or two," he said.

"I agree," I said. "There's nothing like street smarts."

"The school of hard knocks, we used to call it. And believe me, I've had plenty."

"Is the school of hard knocks anywhere near Fort Knox?" I asked.

"Pretty sure it's nearby, yes," Nat said without a trace of irony. "That was some picture of your friend."

"What picture?"

"This morning in the *Incursion*."

My heart accelerated. I grabbed the newspaper on the table beside

Nat. Indeed, there was a photo of Kurt moderating a panel of leading members of Congress on climate change.

"So," Nat said, "is he still shtupping around?"

"No, Dad, I don't think so."

"He's been shtupping around on his wife for some time though, am I right?"

"I'm sure he has in the past. Not so sure about now," I said.

"What's to stop him with those looks and all that money?"

"Maybe he cares about what it would do to his family."

"Aw, they'll be fine," Nat swatted. "How's that boy of yours?"

"Finn's a girl," I said.

"Don't be smart."

"I'm not smart at all. Just very attractive."

"You were a good-looking kid. All the girls thought so—I could tell. But you were too stupid that way to know it."

"Like I said, I was never very bright."

"You could have pulled in a lot more ass if you'd wanted to. Still can."

"Hard to pull a lot of ass when you're married," I said.

"There are ways. What do you like about that girl?"

"Huge bazooms."

"Your wife? No, she's like an athlete."

"Right, I was confusing her with Jayne Mansfield."

"Now there was a rack of lamb on her. I think her head fell off or something."

"She was killed in a car accident, Dad."

"Yeah, but her head fell off when Oswald shot her."

"No, Oswald shot Kennedy. Maybe her head fell off in the car accident."

"I liked Kennedy. Very attractive man, like your friend Ross who shtups all those girls."

"Rossiter," I said.

"Kennedy was very supportive of his father."

"His father was very supportive of him. Gave him the presidency, which was nice."

"His father was just paying him back for all the support. There's something you could learn from the Kennedys about being supportive."

"I don't think the Kennedys are great examples of being good to their loved ones," I said.

"I'm just saying they were very kind to their parents. They all live in that house together. High Anus."

"Hyannis. I'll make you a deal. If you give me eight hundred million dollars, I'll be more supportive."

"I was no lightweight in my day when it came to money, I'll tell you that, Mr. Smart-ass. I once had about a million seven," Nat said.

"That's a lot of money. You worked hard for it."

"This one steals from me," he said, nodding toward Omar.

"Omar doesn't steal."

"He's very supportive. I'll say that much," Nat said.

"That's because you pay him."

"I don't care for this president. I get the feeling he's a thief."

"Of course he's a thief."

"I don't like his mouth. It's like an asshole."

"Yes, it is."

"His kids are very supportive. That's nice to see. They all live with him."

"Why do you think he has that kind of support, Dad?"

"He raised them right," Nat said. "You were raised mostly right, but you were spoiled."

"Do you think the fact that the president's kids have been given everything they've ever wanted since birth, and would be working at a frozen yogurt booth in a strip mall otherwise, plays a role in why they're so supportive?"

"I should have a wife like he has. I just haven't been lucky."

"See, to get a lingerie model, there has to be a reason for her to want to be with you."

"What's wrong with *me*?"

"Nothing. I think a woman like the president's wife would find life with you very appealing," I said. "Think about it. A model, sitting in a little split-level off Old Georgetown Road in Bethesda, getting screamed at all day. I can't imagine why she'd balk."

"It's all about money. Don't kid yourself."

"I'm not." I started backing toward the door.

"Where are you going so fast?" Nat asked.

"I need to check in with Kurt about something."

"Those Rosses have had money for years."

"Rossiters. Hey, I've had four thousand in a money market since 1987. Old money, baby," I said.

"No, old money would have to be before 1987."

"Really?" I asked. "When exactly would old money begin?"

"Rockefellers."

"Right. They've had it a while," I said. "You know, I read that when John D. Rockefeller Jr. built a big townhouse in New York City, he invited his father to visit. John D. Sr. was appalled. He said, 'How can you spend so much money on a house? Who do you think we are, Vanderbilts?'"

"Vanderbilts. That's funny. You could have been rich, but you didn't go to Wall Street with all your education. You wanted to write poems or whatever the hell you did."

"Not poems. News stories," I said.

"One thing I'll say about this president. He always has a picture of his father on his desk."

Ah, the bad son. I got the message.

22

IN A SUBCOMMITTEE meeting of the Callous Sophisticates at the Hunter's Bar and Grill, Goblin told me how he'd gotten into Gretchen's phone. I begged him to spare me the tech details.

Goblin had correctly guessed her password as the day and month of her birthday and printed out any seemingly relevant emails and texts. Then he'd destroyed the phone.

"She had *beaucoup* data, yeah," Goblin said. "I didn't have time to go through everything, Boz, because I figured she'd know the phone was gone pretty fast and begin trying to track it down or check if somebody was accessing it."

"I get it."

"The only thing I found that mentioned you was a text to somebody named Anne Marie Bowles—"

"Another reporter."

"Yeah, well, Gretchen texted, 'Petty is defensive as hell. I think we've got him.'"

This made me want to kill her, but I pretended it didn't bother me. I wanted Goblin to think I was a cool customer. If he saw weakness in me, it might panic him.

"Did Bowles write anything back?" I asked.

Goblin slid a printout of the text to me. Bowles had written back:

Keep at him.

"Boz, what do you think that means?"

"Malice. It means they want reporters like me out of the newsroom. Old white guys."

"You're not that old, no," he said.

"I'm old enough. Anything else of interest?"

"Her emails from the past few days."

He handed me a large manila envelope with pages of printouts. I quickly sifted through the ones that were of potential interest.

Gretchen Kramer had forwarded my emails with different sources to Bowles, Stuart Gilmore, and Joel Mayer. These emails included ones I had sent to Guido Reni's former colleagues at Running Dogs. There was nothing sinister about the emails, just questions about Reni's life leading up to his suicide—things he might have said to others that would have exposed his state of mind. Clearly, Kramer saw these exchanges as efforts to undermine her reporting. Fortunately, I rarely put anything of value in emails. In fact, I read Mayer's email to Kramer indicating that he and Gilmore hadn't seen anything in my correspondence that pointed to journalistic malfeasance.

But Kramer wasn't content. She responded to Mayer and Gilmore:

> Petty is undermining our reporting by treading over old ground. And who knows what he's saying to these sources.

Gilmore—an old white male like me, God bless him—wrote back:

> Gretchen, how is contacting the people you contacted for your stories undermining? We use the same sources in our stories over and over again. If we report on, say, the Red Cross repeatedly, we repeatedly call the Red Cross. What are you so concerned about?

I pumped a fist in the air.

"What is it?" Goblin asked.

"They know they don't have me on anything, and the brass is starting to chafe."

Gilmore had hit on the big question that I couldn't get past: *What are you so concerned about?*

In a follow-up email, Kramer groused:

> I think Petty is trying to do a story saying we essentially murdered Guido Reni.

This time Mayer responded with:

> Gretchen, you seem to be suggesting that Petty's fundamental sins comprised things we don't even know he did. Per your earlier email, we do not know what Petty is saying to others. Besides, what he says to others does not rise to the level of an ethical violation. You don't know that he was working on a story saying we "murdered" Guido Reni, and he's too seasoned a hand to be that histrionic. So far what we have here is a savvy reporter who has a long history of being a pain in the ass who is guilty of being a pain in the ass. You need to do better than that.

The minute I saw the word "histrionic," I knew Mayer was in trouble. Kramer wrote back:

> I bitterly resent your use of the word "histrionic" to describe my concerns about Petty's reporting. It is endemic to the problems the *Incursion* has with women who raise any issues of concern about the management of this institution. You seem to have made your mind up about Petty already.

Mayer didn't respond until several hours later, which told me that he likely had consulted with the newspaper's external counsel, Lily Gibbs. Gibbs was not a paper-shuffling risk-avoider. She fought fire with nuclear weapons, which presumably led to this response from Mayer:

> Gretchen, allow me to double down. "Histrionic" means theatrical and has nothing to do with gender. Your desire to drag gender into this argument undermines your case. Nor did I use the word to describe you; I used it to describe the kind of story Sandy Petty would not do.
>
> Further, you are leaving the *Incursion* vulnerable to a suit by a respected journalist. We agreed to suspend Petty because by having a few of your colleagues support your position, you made a case that his behavior had been disruptive to the newsroom—not that he had committed a demonstrable ethical or legal violation. In an abundance of caution, we agreed to suspend him. I've known him for many years, and he will hit back hard if this inquiry continues. And he will be well within his rights to do so.
>
> We brought you into this investigation because you reported concerns initially and seemed to have the greatest knowledge of the situation. At the moment, you appear to have conflated your dislike for Sandy and his pursuit of a storyline that you dislike with his having committed some violation.
>
> Please do not attempt to leverage the current climate to prosecute an unrelated agenda.

Kramer shot back an allegation that I had threatened a source at Running Dogs, demanding dirt on Kramer's reporting, to which Mayer shot back:

> Bring me proof or back off.

"What do you think, *bon ami*?" Goblin asked.

"It's interesting how she focuses on what she doesn't know about me."

"How so?"

"You see, proof of a conspiracy often comes from a lack of evidence," I explained.

"That makes no sense," Goblin said.

"It's how the best conspiracies sustain themselves. The fact that you can't prove anything allows your imagination to go wild. Your target becomes the symbol of all evil, so clever that they're able to cover their tracks perfectly."

"Will that work on you?"

"It probably won't be good enough to bounce me from the *Incursion,* but it says something about the sustainability of her passion. When people believe there are shadows on the grassy knoll, after a while they start actually seeing men in ski masks."

What I didn't tell Goblin was that, knowing what I now knew about the *Incursion*'s internal correspondence, they would be very nervous about me suing them. The paper's legal counsel would know they'd have to produce emails in discovery admitting their skepticism about the case against me.

I pored through more of the texts and emails, few of which were especially interesting. Kramer's reporting priorities appeared to be what they always had been: lawsuits against powerful companies, environmental issues, and women's issues.

There was one thing that gnawed at me: the sheer amount of time devoted to Kramer's media appearances and speeches. It seemed as if a person named Ariel Lindy coordinated them. When I was on the job, speeches and panels were a rare annoyance. As for TV appearances, I almost never did them, because they were about the theater of journalism, not journalism itself. Still, self-promotion had become our national religion and certainly was not unique to Gretchen Kramer.

I thanked Goblin and pushed the documents back toward him.

"Burn 'em," I said. "The *Incursion* knows what's on their system and what would come out in discovery."

"Pshaw, you think you have to tell me that, Boz?"

"Sorry."

"You know where to go from here?" Goblin asked.

"I think so. Something about all of her speeches. Let me scratch around on my end."

The petite waitress arrived, and Goblin picked up the menu. "I think I'll have the pastrami."

I ordered the same. "While we're waiting for the food, I need one more thing: start sending blind emails to Pacho."

"Saying what?"

"'I won't forget what you did to me.'"

"That's what you want me to write?"

"Yeah. Just a few times, maybe a couple of days apart."

"That's it, yeah?"

"No. Then I want you to see who Pacho searches for online. I'm looking for women he's googling. Even though he's a prick, he's a prick with a self-preservation instinct, and he'll think about the universe of people who could be coming after him. I want him looking at everybody suspiciously."

"Got it. So, Boz, given what we know so far, what do you think makes him tick? Forgive the watch pun."

"I've always flown on a combination of data and instinct with these things. Let me ask you, do you know any big-time surgeons?"

"Can't say that I do, no."

"They think they're God. As you know, Pacho's father is a big gun at Johns Hopkins. Almighty Craig. That's his nickname. Surgeons hold life and death in their hands, and the more success they have, the more certain they are that they're God. These guys tend to be cold bastards. I found a picture of Craig online. Looks like an icier version of James

Brolin. Handsome. Square jaw. Wears a sneer. Taller than the people standing beside him. Pacho's mother looks pretty but fragile. Goes to social things, but I get a cowering vibe from her. Pacho's a rich kid, a pretty boy. I can just imagine a guy like Almighty Craig looking at little Paul as though he's a total fuckup, even if he isn't."

I concluded that Pacho needed an identity of his own. So what did he do? He invented a guy who's basically a suit of armor—some badass in a bush jacket and Western boots. Indiana Jones or something, even though Pacho's from fucking Baltimore. It was his shtick: the two-colored eyes, the watches, the Tom Cruise–style catchphrases. Paul Charles Craig became Pacho Escobar, El Bandito.

"He wanted to be a real man, to show everybody, like his mama—"

"No, his father. He doesn't respect his mother, the way the Kennedy boys didn't respect Rose, despite the smiling family pictures. Pacho is attracted to women, but he doesn't like them."

"So he likes to ask the ladies, 'Who's yer daddy?'" Goblin said.

"You're in the right neighborhood. He likes playing God. Having power over who lives and who dies, just like Daddy does. And Goblin, even if I'm wrong about some of this, I know I'm not wrong about all of it. This isn't a standardized test. I just have to be right enough to get Pacho to do what I need him to do."

Then it would be payback time for all the people he'd screwed over the years—literally and figuratively. And I was just the guy to make it happen.

23

THE NEXT DAY, the stock market crashed, and the president called the prime minister of Malaysia a "gigantic douche nozzle," then observed on a hot microphone that the leader's wife was a "four" on a scale of one to ten—"at best, at best." This was what was on the television news in the neighborhood coffee shop where Pacho Craig liked to snag his latte before going to work and where I was sitting wearing workman's clothing, including a utility belt and sunglasses. I'd parked myself at the table nearest the counter, hoping to keep a close eye on our target.

I had a perfect view of Abigail Case, who had walked through the front door minutes before, looking achingly beautiful in a sleeveless red dress that displayed her toned arms, and was waiting in line right behind Pacho. She wore light makeup, enough to make her lips pout and cheeks blush, but not enough to look like a painted chief-of-staff/cynical mistress/hopeful first lady/eventual bitter lobbyist. She glanced at me and winked.

Pacho apparently sensed the lovely presence behind him and looked back to better assess Abigail. He gave her the sort of smile that conveyed the intangible confidence endemic to Washingtonians—the understanding that those all around him knew precisely who he was. This sentiment had the added convenience of being accurate.

Abigail smiled back and glanced at her shoes. I followed suit and glanced at mine, trying to blend into the background, as the two weren't but a few feet away. Abigail said quietly, "I know who you are."

"Who am I?" Pacho asked with a grin.

"Lady Gaga," Abigail sassed.

"I get that a lot."

I saw Abigail bat her eyelashes. *She's good*. "Full confession," she said to Pacho. "I know you come here sometimes."

"How did you know?"

"I have a friend who's seen you here some mornings."

"Do I know this friend?"

"I don't think so. She's just a girl I know."

Pacho allowed Abigail to go before him in line. She accepted the offer and ordered. Pacho told the young, dreadlocked barista to put Abigail's drink on his tab and ordered his own.

"You don't have to do that," Abigail said. "Especially since you're the one already doing me the favor."

Pacho squinted. "Favor? I'm sorry, but I—" He brushed a fugitive lock of hair from his forehead.

"I had to get up enough nerve to speak to you about something," Abigail said.

"About what?" Pacho asked. His upper lip had an anticipatory Elvis-like curl to it.

Abigail scratched at her collarbone, and Pacho stole a glance at her cleavage. Whereas most men would then glance away quickly, his line of sight held fast. "I work for a company that may have had something to do with the murder of that Saudi Arabian reporter," she said, holding her open hand against her chest.

"Sabbag?"

Abigail nodded.

Pacho frowned. He'd probably thought this not-so-chance encounter was a pickup, as if he'd expected Abigail to say, *I came here to gaze upon the very emblem of male sexuality*. "Oh, I see," he said.

"Can I talk to you in absolute confidence?"

"Of course. Let's get our drinks and sit down."

"This is a good spot," Abigail said, pointing at the table next to mine. *Perfect.* She sat down across from Pacho and only about a foot away from me. I sat at the ready, eager to take him down if he tried anything untoward. "I'm sorry for the cloak and dagger," she continued, "but I'm really nervous."

"I deal with that all the time with my sources. What do you want to tell me?"

"I work for a billionaire. He has a lot of business with the Saudis. I think Sabbag was investigating him. The next thing I know is, the man's dead and there are high-fives in the office."

"Actual high-fives?" Pacho asked.

"No. More like smirks and winks. Look, I can't really tell you any more now. I have to get to work. I'd rather meet someplace—not now—where people can't overhear."

"I live down the block. I have plenty of meetings in my home office."

"Not now. I just wanted to know if you're interested. Somebody has to expose this, but I don't want to get myself killed in the process."

"Of course not. When can you meet?"

"Maybe tonight. After work?" Abigail said.

"Can you tell me who you work for?"

"A company in Rockville. General Commodities."

"And the billionaire's name?"

"Oliver Shackley. Google the name."

"I've never heard of him."

"That's just how he wants it."

"Look, I know we've both gotta run, but I'd like to talk more," Pacho said, standing. "When can you come by?"

"Let's try for eight," Abigail said, gathering her things and following him to the front door.

Pacho scribbled something on a piece of paper, gave it to Abigail, and then walked out the door heading east. Once he was out of sight, Abigail looked back at me and smiled. I flexed my arm in an exaggerated fashion to mark her strong performance.

She flexed back.

24

I COULDN'T ASK Eva to dig deeper at the *Incursion,* but I had already formulated a working theory: the *Incursion* and other media outlets had become overly dependent on a steady drumbeat of prepackaged news stories supplied by the Sunshine Collective PR company. These marketed stories were products of the predictable formula that reliably drew eyeballs and journalism awards—they comprised evil villains, vulnerable victims, and alas, the free press, which galloped to the rescue and untied the fair maiden from the train tracks as the locomotive bore down. These articles were the lifeblood of newspapers like the *Incursion*. The narratives were packaged, and the paper didn't have to expend time, energy, and money on endless research and sourcing. Moreover, the *Incursion*'s stories had disproportionately ripped into Guido Reni, which may have contributed to his suicide. On that account, if my theory was correct, Kramer had been right to suggest that I was inclined to hold the newspaper partly responsible.

Having grown somewhat more confident in my online skills, I googled the name Ariel Lindy, Kramer's speaking agent, and discovered that she was affiliated with a group called the Charisma Bureau. Of course, this begged the question: if one were charismatic enough, would one need to retain the Charisma Bureau? It was like all the companies with "quality" in their motto that made me want to establish *Petty Plumbing: Mediocre. Amateurish. Unresponsive.*

I paused for a moment to wonder how, given the state of my career, I would go about becoming a plumber if I had to.

Returning to the task at hand, I navigated to Gretchen Kramer's personal website. It featured a glamour photo and a turgid bio that described her as a "sought-after speaker." The website referred all inquiries to Ariel Lindy. I typed *Gretchen Kramer* and *speaker* into Google and came up with several hits. She had spoken to the US Trial Attorneys Council, the Redleaf environmental group, a labor union, and a few granola-type outfits.

I picked up my burner phone and called Ms. Lindy at Charisma.

"Yes, Ms. Lindy, this is Donald DeFreeze from the Southern New Jersey Litigation Council."

"Yes, Mr. DeFreeze." Her thousand-watt smile and saleswoman's self-assurance radiated through the phone lines.

"I'm a conference coordinator for my group, and we're looking to have a speaker at a meeting we're doing this spring in Atlantic City."

"Yes, excellent."

"A lot of our litigators are interested in how the media covers high-profile lawsuits against corporations, you see, and we thought it might be good to have a tough reporter speak to us."

"Sure. May I ask how you heard of Charisma?"

"My co-worker used one of his internets and found your name. Said you were listed on one of the web styles or whatever it's called."

"I see," she said, clearly stifling a laugh. "Well, there are two journalists we represent who might be a good fit for something like this."

"Great."

"There's Ben Schwartz of the *Boston Globe,* who covered those pharmaceutical trials a few years ago with the talc suits, as well as one of the church scandals."

"I read about those. He's big-time."

"Yes," Lindy said. "He's in demand right now because he's on TV a lot."

On TV? Well, then, he must be a genius.

"What kind of fee does he charge?" I asked.

"Ben's rate is twenty-five thousand, not including travel."

I whistled. "Any others? He may be out of our price range."

"Yes, well, there's Gretchen Kramer from the *Capitol Incursion*."

"Uh-huh. What does she do?"

"She also covers big controversies. Lawsuits. Oil spills. Things like that."

"That could work. What's her rate?"

"Ms. Kramer charges fifteen thousand, not including travel."

"Does your fee come out of that?"

"Yes."

"This may sound like a stupid question, but do your speakers always charge a fee for every speech they give?"

There was a moment of silence. Ms. Lindy was sensing a deadbeat on the line. "If the speaker goes through us, they charge."

"Are there specific groups you know of where Ms. Claymore has spoken?"

"*Kramer.* We don't give out complete lists, but we do have references we can point you to."

"Oh, that would be great."

"I can email them to you."

"Gee, I don't use email. Still living in the eighties."

Lindy laughed. She gave me three names. An attorney, a union PR flack, and a representative of something called the Ozone Conference. They would hear soon enough from Don DeFreeze.

25

I DROPPED BY Frankie Waterman's office to give her a sense of what I was hearing about the *Incursion* investigation. I knew she'd give me a lot of crap, despite the fact that I would not officially tell her I had been spying on my erstwhile employer.

Frankie was in casual mode, wearing jeans with leather boots and a denim shirt along with silver and turquoise jewelry. We got into my case right away.

"All I can tell you, Frankie, is that the boys at the top are skeptical. Kramer is pushing hard, but she doesn't know the difference between things she doesn't like and things that are actionable."

"I'm not going to ask how you know this, Sandy."

"Good. Kramer also claimed that I threatened somebody at Running Dogs. You know, 'Give me dirt on how the *Incursion* pursued its coverage, or else.'"

"Did you?"

"No. I know my weaknesses," I said. "That wouldn't be in my bag of tricks."

"Do you think she's got an off-the-record source saying that?"

"I wouldn't put it past her to make it up, but Mayer and Gilmore told her to prove it. You shouldn't hesitate to suggest—at the right moment—that you intend to follow through with a suit that will result in discovery. They will *not* want discovery, Frankie."

She closed her eyes as if this would help her unhear what I had just said. "I don't want a suit, Sandy. I want you either on the job again or getting a nice severance package. Where are you leaning these days?"

I gazed somewhere above Frankie's head. "I don't see myself going back there, Frankie. I just don't. In any other period in history, this suspension never would have happened. I'm on the wrong side of the historical locomotive. I should have never marked up her damned story and told her to pound the pavement."

"You wouldn't miss the game?"

"I'm not sure there is a game anymore. At least not the one I once played."

"So you want the money."

"I think I want the money," I said.

"That's good to know. And whatever the hell you're up to, make sure you don't get caught, or you won't have a job *or* money. Remember, what doesn't kill you makes you weaker, but it also makes you smarter. It's science. A body your age can't do what a twenty-five-year-old body can. All you can hope for is added wisdom."

"I agree. I can't stand how we're living in an age that requires us to preach what won't get us into trouble instead of what we believe. I want the damned money. Screw the greater good for now." I noticed a paperweight on Frankie's desk that I hadn't seen before. I stood and picked it up. "Brass knuckles?"

"Indeed," Frankie said.

"Spectacular." I paced with the knuckles. "Where did you get these?"

"An uncle of mine was a cop. I carried those before I started up with guns."

"I love it," I said, caressing the smooth metal.

"Just don't leave with them. They're illegal to carry."

"I won't."

"You know, Sandy, I've seen a lot of people who think they're a big deal fall or otherwise be fatally disappointed. Nobody who blows up thinks that was their destiny. They believe catastrophe is for those who aren't chosen by God."

"You're telling *me* this? I practically invented that theory," I said.

"I gotta say something. Given how you conduct your life, you never struck me as a big risk-taker. But I'm getting a cowboy vibe from you."

"You're the one dressed like the cowgirl. As you see, I'm in my usual mourning black." I tugged at my shirt. "I guess I'm feeling like time's running out. It's almost a physical sensation. Like I'm in an hourglass on the upper container of sand and I'm falling down into the lower glass. It's hard to describe."

"Are you . . . depressed?"

"I have a gift for catastrophe."

• • •

I turned right outside of Frankie's building, and Gretchen Kramer was leaning against a newspaper vending machine. She was wearing jeans but had on a formal-looking sport coat, and her hair was styled. The television appearance look.

"Sandy," she said.

"Gretchen. My little petunia in her greenroom uniform," I responded in my most palpably insincere voice. "I was going to ask what you were doing here, but then I remembered you still work down the street."

"And I remembered that you don't."

"I see you're providing support to that poor vending machine."

"What are you doing downtown?" Kramer asked. Her tone was that of a cop rousting a vagrant.

"Interviewing proctologists," I said. "I like to be thoroughly examined by as many of them as possible before I make my selection."

"Still with the dark humor."

"Proctology is dark, yes. Colons and all."

Kramer looked up and down the Bender Building. "Are there a lot of proctologists in there?"

"Well, it is the Bender Building. What do you think?"

"Charming. Seriously, what are you up to?"

"Seriously, interviewing proctologists."

"Visiting Frankie Waterman, I guess," Kramer said.

"Are you following me, Gretchen?"

"You're paranoid."

"No, I'm suspicious. Paranoia is an irrational fantasy that somebody is out to get you. You really are." She said nothing, so I kept going. "That's the kind of thing reporters like to expose. Spying on other people. I guess when *you* spy, it's ethical, but when people you don't like spy, it's sleazy."

"I could look up proctologists on my phone, but it seems to have gone missing," she said bitingly.

"Damned Putin. He doesn't know when to stop."

"What do you think Putin wanted with my phone?"

Always resist the opportunity to show your enemy how smart you are. Showing all your cards is a powerful impulse but a stupid one. It betrays too much information and affords them the weaponry for a counterattack.

"Porn," I replied. "I understand Putin hacks women's phones to see what porn they're looking at."

"My phone is missing, Sandy."

"Then go to the fucking Verizon store, Gretchen."

"You don't know anything about it?" She was studying my facial expression, which was obscured by my sunglasses. Or so I hoped.

"I'll call Putin," I said.

"Are you still reporting on Running Dogs? Freelance?"

"No, Gretch. My lawyer told me not to touch it, pending your investigation."

"It's the *Incursion*'s investigation."

"No, it's *your* investigation. You won, kiddo. You don't know that yet, but it's your world now."

"'Kiddo'? Really?"

"What year were you born?" I asked.

"1984."

"I was covering a presidential race when you were in Pampers."

"Are you speaking for old white guys everywhere?"

"No, I only speak for NAMBLA."

"Who?"

"The North American Man/Boy Love Association," I said. "I decided I want to get involved with a cause I believe in."

Kramer actually laughed. "You are one ice-cold bastard, Petty. Ruthless like a shark. A machine."

"It's sad that you need to make your monsters a hundred feet tall in order to justify slaying them, Gretchen. Read Janet Malcolm's *The Journalist and the Murderer.*"

"What's that?"

I snorted. "It figures you don't know."

"Let me know if you find that proctologist."

"When I do, you're welcome to join me. Maybe he'll find your phone."

So, I was now operating with a Pulitzer hound on my trail. This was what is known in the trade as Not Fucking Good. It left me with two options: One, stop everything I was doing, dead in the tracks. Well, that wasn't going to happen. Two, dig in deeper on everything—and not get caught.

Number two was the only real option, of course, but I would have to take precautions. After all, while Gretchen Kramer's agenda and conclusions might be questionable, her suspicion that I was up to something was quite on point.

26

I HAD INSTRUCTED Abigail to meet Pacho at his coffee shop again that evening so they could walk back to his house together. I wanted her to watch how he got inside. Did he use a key? Where did he put the key? Did he have an alarm system? If so, she should try to discover the code he punched in.

Goblin had given me a laptop that would carry a video and audio feed from Abigail's vantage point. This would allow me to observe her interaction with Pacho. I was worried about her being alone with him, given his penchant for attacking young women. But Abigail was determined to go forward. I trusted her instincts but not Pacho's. I also didn't trust the damned laptop to work. At least I'd convinced her to take the pepper spray.

Abigail's transmission device was in a pair of glasses Goblin had rigged for her. Audio *and* video. I had seen this work once with a source who had infiltrated a nuclear laboratory in Pakistan and had filmed a meeting with a lens in his glasses. I wanted not only to see and hear what Pacho was saying to Abigail, but also to get a sense of his house: the layout, the style, the artwork. I also wanted to see Pacho's watches up close to check for authenticity. The video capacity of such a small camera wouldn't be ideal, but it was better than having no visual sense at all.

Pacho and Abigail crossed the leafy Georgetown intersection in front of my parked Jeep. Pacho was taller than Abigail but not by much. *Good,* I thought. Less chance that he could overpower her easily—although my assumption was that Pacho's modus operandi was not straight-up, ferocious rape. No, that would conflict with his self-image as a smooth operator. If Samantha's story was any indication, he would wait until some clothes were off and there was some relative sense of the consensual—and then he'd get mean. If I heard something I didn't like, I would start banging on the door and calling the cops, our scheme be damned.

Pacho's place was a four-story brick townhouse attached to a similar structure on the right. There was an alley on the left side of his house, which separated it from smaller, less imposing homes. His entryway, where he stood with Abigail for a moment before disappearing inside, was recessed by about four feet. There was a thick oak door with a metallic keypad to the right.

I opened the laptop, which Goblin assured me would immediately broadcast what Abigail was seeing. It did not. Although I did hear the audio feed, all I saw was a black square where there should have been a picture. I called Goblin on my cell and cursed. He said he would "remote on" to get me the video feed. Within thirty seconds, I could see the cursor moving on the screen.

"Now don't go too far from your cell," I demanded, "because the minute I'm left alone with it, this piece of shit will crash!"

"Let's have a seat in the living room," Pacho was saying. "Do you want something to drink?"

"No, thanks." I had told Abigail not to accept anything from him.

"I like your glasses," Pacho said.

"Thanks. I wear them when I have a lot of reading at work or when my allergies are kicking up."

"Do you mind if I sit down here?" I could see, through Abigail's camera, Pacho's gesture to the seat beside her on the couch.

"Sure, it's a big couch," Abigail said. Nevertheless, she scooted back a few inches. Then she began to establish the ground rules we had discussed. "Mr. Craig—"

"Pacho."

"Pacho. Okay, I wanted to say a few things before we started."

"Sure."

"I'm very nervous about all this. Very. I assume you know a little more about Oliver Shackley than you did this morning?"

"I do. Quite a character," he said.

"What was your impression?"

"In this day and age, most billionaire types are diving in front of cameras. Not this guy. I can only find one photo of him, and that's from 1980 or something."

"What does that tell you?"

"It tells me that he has something to hide."

Perfect. Of course a man like Pacho would equate discretion with corruption. It never occurs to born publicists like Pacho that some people genuinely don't want to show their bathrooms to *Architectural Digest,* visit Bono in Ireland, or have their children kidnapped. If someone has the temerity to be discreet, the twenty-first century demands they be destroyed.

"Well, Pacho, he certainly has that. Something to hide. But listen, I do *not* want to be on camera. I do *not* want to be quoted. I want only to be a source who is tipping you off, and you will have to do whatever you do to verify that there is a story here."

"I know you're worried, Abigail, so I'm not going to record this." He handed her his iPhone to show her that the microphone was not on. "I'll take notes. We can communicate by WhatsApp on our cells. It's virtually impossible to hack."

"If you can't verify what I'm telling you, you won't run anything, right?"

"As a journalist, I can't run what I can't prove. For now, the best I can do is dig around and see what I can find."

Yes, he can dig around, I thought. But what he couldn't discover, he could compensate for through ambush interviews, innuendo, and crafty camera work. A long-distance camera shot of an executive wearing sunglasses and walking into a restaurant could be used to paint him as a mafioso going into a sit-down to carve up garbage truck routes.

"Okay," she said. "Okay."

"The floor is yours, Abigail. Tell me what you know." Pacho leaned into her when he said this. I could see his face expand through the lens in Abigail's glasses. He leaned his chin on his fist, presumably thinking himself adorable.

Abigail took a deep breath. "General Commodities had a lot of business in Saudi Arabia. Plastics and chemicals that go into making other stuff. Shackley figures if the American military orders a bajillion lacquered shoelace tips with General Commodities plasticizers, nobody will notice or give a damn. He doesn't make nuclear warheads—he produces the red dye that goes into the glass screens that makes the timing counters easier to read. Boring shit. But profitable."

Pacho nodded. "Keep going."

"Then along came Adnan Sabbag. Sabbag figures that Shackley is making products—using Saudi resources—that the United States will buy. Shackley is worried that Sabbag will report that the US is relying for defense materials on a country that may have been complicit in the 9/11 attacks. Saudi Arabia."

"I *know* Saudis were involved in the 9/11 attacks, Abigail," Pacho said, as if speaking to a junior high school cheerleader.

"Okay, sorry," Abigail said, her voice cracking a little. "Anyway, when Sabbag's investigation began to cut too close to the bone, the Saudis invited him to a meeting about his passport and killed him."

"I know," Pacho said. "They never found his body. Wow." He was scribbling furiously.

"I know," Abigail said.

"I have a few questions, obviously."

"Of course."

"Everybody assumes the Saudis killed Sabbag. Why do you believe Shackley had anything to do with it?"

"People around the office were very nervous about these deals falling through. Shackley and his people took a lot of trips to Saudi Arabia, and some of their people came here."

"To the offices in Rockville?"

"Yes. And other meeting places. I know from one of the guys I work with—kind of a friend—that they hired lawyers and PR firms to try to figure out what to do with Sabbag. One day, Mr. Shackley came out of his office after this other guy—an intermediary, I guess. The guy left, and Shackley seemed super pleased. Later, I heard from my friend that somebody in the meeting said Sabbag wasn't going to do the story after all. A week later, Sabbag was dead."

"Interesting. So . . . while we don't know who gave the order, what you're saying is that there was a lot of relief around General Commodities that this big news story wasn't going to happen."

"Right. Is this something you can work with?"

"It's a hell of a start. I mean, we're obviously not going to get an email or any definitive confirmation that Shackley gave the order, but the timing here is very interesting. I'm wondering, Abigail, if you have access to any documents. The thing is, as a young, pretty girl, they probably don't take you seriously enough to think you're a threat. Your eyes are such an unusual brown—"

"Like what kind of documents?" Abigail said curtly.

"Maybe emails. Orders for supplies. Anything that shows business transactions between Shackley and the Saudis."

"Boy, I don't know."

"Think about it. Think about what you may have access to—"

Abigail drew in a deep breath. "It couldn't come back to me?"

"Of course not. Of course not. So maybe you can look . . . ?"

"Maybe Elijah would know." Abigail let the name fall out of her mouth like a wet toothpick.

Pacho put down his notepad. He slid closer to Abigail. "Who's Elijah?"

Abigail froze as if she might have said something that she shouldn't have. "Um, he's like . . . ah, this . . . I work with him sometimes. He's one of the guys on the Saudi account. They like him because he's Muslim. But he seems skittish about all that's been going on. We talk about it sometimes."

The visual glitched, and I saw that she'd inched back away from him. Then the video crashed again.

I called Goblin again on my cell. "What the fuck, man?" I said. "I don't have audio or video of our girl!"

"Hold on, *bon ami*," he said. "I just went to the bathroom."

"What did I tell you? The minute you step away, my feed crashes. I'm serious about this curse! Don't leave me!"

Goblin did his remote thing, and I saw the cursor dance on the screen again before the video feed returned.

"Abigail, do you think there is any way Elijah would speak with—"

"I don't know. He has no idea I'm doing this."

"Maybe there's a way to make it seem like I approached you? Like we met somewhere, and you realized I was pursuing a story?"

"I don't think so."

"He wouldn't be surprised by a man approaching you. Look, you're gorgeous. Your skin is like cappuccino—"

"I . . . I don't know about any of this."

"Do you think he knows more than you do?" Pacho asked.

"Way more."

"All right then. Here's what I want you to do. Think about whether you can get Elijah to meet with me. Anywhere he wants. You can either be there or not. You can play as dumb as you want."

"Be a dumb chick, huh?"

"Hey, I don't mean it like that. I'm not saying you *are* dumb—I'm saying Elijah doesn't need to know you originally approached me. You can say I approached you and you're scared. This is how these things work. One thing leads to another, and the original source fades into the background and even disappears."

"I have to think about this," Abigail said.

"That's all I'm asking."

"Okay."

"This is important, Abigail. A man was killed. You can make history."

"I don't want to make history," she said. "I just want to do what's right. And live my life."

"I get it. This can be our secret. But this is your chance to do something very good. Very important."

"I know. I just have to process this. I feel like I'm in a movie."

"I'm sure it does feel that way, yes."

"If they make a movie—if this becomes big—will you tell them how you got the story?"

Pacho oozed back on his couch, clearly enjoying this sudden prospect. I had asked Abigail to find a way to raise the issue of a movie. "The way Hollywood works is, they get the basic story right, but they fill in all the details and characters with made-up stuff. For example—and I'm just being hypothetical here—they could get, say, someone like Bradley Cooper to play me. I would never tell them about you, but I could give them a composite. In other words, your role might be played by a couple of people. Maybe Seth Rogen—"

"We don't exactly look alike," Abigail said with a chuckle.

"That's what I'm saying. They could get somebody totally different so nobody would put it together with you."

"And if they wanted somebody closer to me, who do you think they might get?"

"Maybe somebody like Zoe Kravitz. Or maybe a little bit older, like Kerry Washington. Or even mix things up with a Blake Lively type."

"And maybe Will Smith or Denzel could play Elijah," Abigail said.

"Right. But we're getting way ahead of ourselves."

"I was joking."

But Pacho wasn't.

Abigail had done a pretty good job of looking around the room and letting the small lens in her glasses record Pacho, his bookshelves, the artwork, and the view through an archway into his kitchen.

"What kind of watch are you wearing?" Abigail asked.

"This is a Santos de Cartier." Pacho took the watch off and handed it to Abigail, who put it on her wrist.

"I like how you can see through it and watch all the gears move," she said.

"Yeah. All these shapes doing their own thing, you mean?"

"No. More like you can't tell which widget is pushing what gizmo. Hard to figure out what's making the whole system go."

"Uh-huh," Pacho said. He awkwardly removed the watch from Abigail's wrist and repeated *uh-huh* slowly, as if he were still trying to make sense of what he had just heard.

27

A FEW NIGHTS later, Joey and I went into Finn's room as she was getting ready for bed. Joey hugged her and said, "I love you, baby girl."

"I know, Mom," Finn said.

I grabbed Finn's face and said, "I don't like you all that much, Cheeks."

This had been a running joke between us, ever since she once complained about how I told her I loved her way too often. She had stomped her feet and said, "All you ever do is tell me how much you love me. All you ever do is ask me about my day. All you ever do is want to do things with me." Despite being in grade school at the time, even Finn appreciated how unsympathetic her complaint had been, and we'd both started laughing.

"Should I just tell you how much I don't like you from now on?" I had asked her.

"Yes!" she'd said, cracking a smile. So that became our standard line.

Joey headed to our room and slipped into bed first. I stood at the end of the bed and began flexing as if I were in a bodybuilding competition. Joey rolled her eyes.

"You like?" I said, turning around and attempting to make my back ripple.

Joey rolled in the other direction and said into her pillow, "Very alluring."

I gestured toward my torso while holding out my arms as if I were too muscular to let them fall by my sides. Then I climbed into bed and shut the light off.

"This is the first time I've seen you jazzed about something in months," Joey said.

"Jazzed?"

"You seem excited.

"Probably more like anxiety."

"About what?"

"I can't stop thinking about Samantha and that there's no way to erase what was done," I said.

"And you think it's your job to erase it?" Joey asked, wrinkling her brow.

"I think it's my job to do *something*. At least help Kurt get through this."

"I know how you feel about Kurt down deep."

"And how's that?"

"You think he glides through life while you've had to slug it out at every step."

"Am I wrong? Every impulse he's ever had has been indulged." I stopped there. Contrary to what the shrinks of the 1970s lectured, there was something to be said for long-married couples *not* communicating about everything.

"We both love Sammy, but I don't think she's your sole motive here," Joey said.

"Kurt is my friend. I feel for him, as a father. And Samantha's our goddaughter. I keep seeing her face looking at me, wondering why I'm not doing more."

"There's something more. I think you hate that Pacho Craig. Aside from Sammy. That Gretchen Kramer woman too. I think you want to kill them both."

In the absence of an articulate answer, I stuck my tongue out at her.

Joey's analysis was incomplete. To be fair, however, I hadn't even figured the whole thing out in my own head. And she wasn't exactly wrong.

• • •

The next morning, I left our house and went for a bike ride to think. Or perhaps I wasn't really thinking—just ruminating on the same themes. Sammy's vulnerability. Smug Pacho, marching on and ruining lives with his ambush journalism, and not a single consequence on the horizon for him. How lucky Kurt had been to make it to our age without ever having his ass handed to him. Was it easier or harder to deal with misery for the first time in your life in one's fifties? I didn't know.

Despite my initial instinct not to accept money to go after Pacho, I had to admit that mine hadn't been the most violent of refusals. Who knew? I might yet decide to take some serious money to work on the case—to allow my desire to pay for Finn's college to trump my pride. Besides, it wasn't like I had been posing for forty-some years as Kurt's financial equal, so he knew my resources were limited. It wouldn't surprise me if he reiterated his offer to compensate me.

As I waited to cross River Road at Bradley Boulevard, a Lexus pulled up next to me with its windows down. The driver was blasting that Tom Petty song—"Forgotten Man." It had never hit big, but I liked it. The lyrics about being "forever damned" made me ruminate about the demise of journalism and what it had become during my tenure in the trade. Maybe Joey was right: although Pacho's violation of Samantha may have catalyzed my hatred for him, his violation of my life's work had been brewing long before that, and even before my suspension from the *Incursion* at the hands of Gretchen Kramer—someone cut from the same tinsel.

Journalism had gone from being an instrument of chronicling to an instrument of vengeance. Pacho Craig and Gretchen Kramer were angry about some perceived assault on their concepts of themselves and what they deserved, and were using journalism to strike back. Reporting was now big-game hunting—smart-asses like Pacho taking shots at people who were, as Teddy Roosevelt once said, "in the arena," trying to get something done.

And here were people like Kramer—and me, I had to admit—sitting on the sidelines, digging up dirt on people in public life. Sure, we exposed bad actors. But with every passing year, I thought more and more that I was just shooting at living things because of a dark shadow in my character, a hidden closet that housed glass jars preserving resentments. Resentments about having a father like Nat who just wouldn't die, a mother who died way too soon, a world dominated by TICU, and the demise of a career I had once been proud of.

So no, it wasn't just that I adored Samantha and loathed what had happened to her. It was also that I hated the world that seemed to be drawing a bead on me.

When I got back home, I said to Joey, "Whatever else this thing with Sammy is, it's a story. I'm in the middle of a story again. And I'm on the right side."

• • •

That night, Joey was fiddling around with the TV as we were trying to find a movie to watch on Netflix. *The Price Is Right* was on. A towering and comically blonde woman in a slinky outfit was gesturing grandly toward a NEW CAR. The announcer repeated, "NEW CAR!" loudly when informing the audience of the potential prize.

"When do you think pointing toward products became a thing?" I asked Joey. "Do they think the viewer doesn't know the car is there?"

"You really ask the big questions, don't you, Fuse?"

"Think about it. You've got a shiny new Honda Accord smack-dab in the middle of the screen. Then this fashion model comes on and points to the car in a dramatic way. What's the value-add there?"

"If people see the model pointing to the car, it adds to the excitement," Joey explained.

"Possibly. But then she walks to the other side of the car and extends her arms out toward the vehicle so you get the gesture from another angle. Do they think we missed it the first time?"

"I'm sure they don't, love. You may be overthinking this," Joey said.

"Maybe. I'm just trying to think economically. Now that I've been downsized."

"You were suspended, not downsized."

"They want me out. That's the takeaway. Why am I losing my job for doing something of value, while this model gets to keep coming on TV to point to stuff that we already know is there?"

"You're missing the point," Joey said. "Her value is not that she's telling us the car is there. It's the cheese factor. It adds to the excitement. Especially when she walks from one side of the car to the other and you get to see her legs and ass."

"I'd be excited about the prospect of getting a new car even without the cheese. I think the contestant from Terre Haute, Indiana, would be excited about it too," I said.

"Oh, I'm sure he is. But his friends at the local Arby's are saying to themselves, 'Not only is Vern about to win a new car, but he gets to meet Brittany too.' Then Vern's friends start thinking, 'Maybe I'll go on *The Price Is Right* and maybe win a new car and get to meet Brittany.' They're going for sensory overload."

"And wasn't I, as a journalist?" I raised an eyebrow.

"Nope. You were just reporting what was happening in Washington. Were there young boobies involved in your reporting?"

"Rarely," I conceded.

"Well, there you go. Speaking of which, do you think you're making progress with whatever you're doing for the Rossiters?"

"I do."

"But you still can't say what it is."

"I'm protecting you, believe me."

"You really believe that if Sammy came forward, she'd get shredded?"

"Absolutely. There's no good mechanism for dealing with this stuff within the system. This is why women don't come forward. The press loves crazy-slut stories. And, look, the kid wants to have a career in media. It would kill any serious chances she has."

"You're going to blow up this Pacho jerk, aren't you?"

"No comment."

"Does he remind you of anybody?" Joey asked.

"Who, Pacho?"

"Yes."

"You mean Kurt? Of course. Presumably without the rape," I said.

"Yes, he has a lot of qualities like Kurt's," she said. "Did you ever think that Kurt wanting to get this guy is like him wanting to kill himself?"

"That's a little overly psychological, Joe. I think he wants to get the guy who hurt his daughter. Kurt is in the middle of a Greek tragedy—you know, how the Greeks punished their heroes. All that fatal flaw gibberish. Kurt was just cruising along, doing whatever pleased him in life—with total impunity—and suddenly he finds himself eating the filthy exhaust of someone who lives his life the same way."

"And you wonder if you'd be so lucky?" Joey asked.

"That's in there somewhere, sure."

"Has Kurt ever expressed remorse to you about his cheating?"

"Not really. He's referred to 'when I screwed up.' That kind of thing. He crosses lines because he lives with the confidence that he'll always have women who support him, regardless of what he does. It's a question of degree with people. I know a drug lord who no doubt has killed people. I think he'd prefer not to kill people, but he's not tortured by it. I think in Kurt's heart, he doesn't think his cheating is a big deal. He knows it's hurt his family, and he doesn't get any pleasure out of that. But I don't think he's racked with guilt."

"How do you think he'd react if Angie cheated on him?"

"Has she?"

"No," Joey said. I studied her face to see if I could detect any deeper knowledge of the situation, but I couldn't glean anything. "Why, do you think it would bother him?"

"I think his world would cease to make sense. I mean, he loves Angie, but there's also the ego thrown in there."

A concerned look descended across Joey's face like a curtain. "Did you ever wonder whether Samantha may have embellished her situation as a way to strike back at Kurt? Hurt him?"

"I can't say I know anything for sure, but I believe Sammy."

"You've always loved that little girl. I have, too, but you were always so demonstrative. You're more like that, I guess, with your goofiness. Kids like that."

"I love kids."

"You want to protect them all," Joey said.

"Let's not get into that."

"Didn't you say that Kurt didn't seem keen on going to the police?"

"I did."

"Doesn't that strike you as odd?"

"Maybe a little. But there are plenty of reasons not to want to go down that road. What are you getting at?" I asked.

"I'm not sure. I'm just surprised that as an investigative reporter, you aren't more suspicious."

I held back my pleasure that Joey didn't think Kurt was such a golden boy after all. "I may have been more suspicious when I was twenty-five, but not anymore."

"Why is that?"

"Do you know why Nixon wanted the Pentagon Papers kept quiet?"

"No."

"He wasn't implicated in any of what was in there. It was all before his time. But if the press could blow up the Pentagon Papers, what else could they unearth? There may be other stuff Kurt doesn't want shaken loose, namely his own history with women. It doesn't mean he's a monster." I looked at Joey and waited for that to sink in. "As much as I want to go to the cops and bust this guy, I know the law doesn't work the way we want it to work."

"Why, because Sammy dug the guy?"

"How'd you know that?" I asked.

"Angie said something. It doesn't give him the right to rape her."

"You're talking morally, not realistically, in terms of how these things play out. Wicked people are supposed to be punished by God, and good people are supposed to enjoy the rapture. You and I both know better."

"I guess you're being a journalist in your own way with all this. Wanting the world to balance out. 'Comfort the afflicted, afflict the comfortable.'"

"I do want the world to balance out, Joe, but the comfort-the-afflicted business is pure Marxism. I never went in for that."

"I don't know about that, bud," Joey said. "I think that's why you detest Gretchen Kramer. She uses her power to ruin people, and hides behind the badge of journalism. You suspect, down deep, that you did some of that yourself."

"I went after bad guys, Joe."

"Kramer thinks she's doing the same thing."

"She's just an assassin. There's a primal hunting instinct in all humans, whether we act on it or not—some cosmic validation we get, even when we're just squishing a fly. People can't acknowledge that they have this irrational villain void that must be filled. It has to be sublimated and redirected. Journalists like Kramer can kill from behind a shield of sainthood and convince themselves they're exterminating vermin. If Mark David Chapman had social media, he wouldn't have shot John Lennon—he would have tweeted about him."

"You took down high-profile targets."

"Yes, I did."

"So you don't think the decisions you made during your career represented any personal agenda, but with her it does?"

"Things are always personal, Joe—we've talked about this. And I've argued with my friends in the business about it. They all identified as nonpartisan or as moderates, but all of us had the same politics. We were the Deltas in *Animal House,* wanting to screw with the country club Omegas. At least I admitted it. Gretchen Kramer wants to be Katie Couric or Megyn Kelly, and down deep she wants to be married to a guy like Kurt or Pacho. Best she can do is knock off people she detests."

"What's caused this soul-searching?"

"Same thing that always does. Misery. Being on the receiving end of unfairness."

Joey puffed out her cheeks. She looked like a chipmunk. I popped them.

"I don't think we're going to resolve these issues today," she said. "If you want to help Kurt, then do your best for him."

"I plan to."

"Just don't enjoy it too much."

"Me? Enjoy something?"

28

I WAS IN my home office in the late morning, right after Finn had gone to school and Joey had left for her parents' house, when an unexpected rap fell against our front door. It was Samantha. She was wearing University of Virginia sweats and an Orioles baseball cap, all orange.

"Hey, Sam," I said. "You look very citrus."

"Trick or treat," she said mechanically. Her voice was a monotone.

"You're a few weeks late. Come on in."

"I was just over at the co-op and thought I'd say hi." Her shoulders slouched lower.

Not good. "Get inside."

I guided her toward the back of our house, to the sitting area with a round glass table, an easy chair with a floral pattern, and a dark Crate & Barrel sofa I sometimes crashed on. We'd had it forever. Samantha sat on the sofa, and I consciously sat across from her on the easy chair rather than next to her.

"Does that co-op have anything interesting?" I asked. "I'm not sure I've ever gone in there."

"It's pretty crunchy. I get vitamins and natural shit there."

Okay, then. "What kind of shit?"

"Something to help me sleep. I grabbed some more melatonin."

"Does it work?" I asked.

"I don't know yet." She smiled and then put her head in her hands. "Not after all this. I need something way stronger to knock me out."

"Must be hard to stop thinking about everything, huh?"

"Uncle Fuse, I just can't shut off my goddam brain."

Samantha was looking slightly above my head, unfocused.

I was quiet. Waiting.

After a few moments, she stared at me. "How can he be two different people? Everyone sees just the guy on MyStream. They all think he's so great." In an instant, her eyes went from intense to sleepy.

"Is that what you wanted to talk about when you came here?" I asked.

"Not really," she said. "This really was on my way home. Besides, you always make me feel better."

"I'm glad," I said, even though I didn't feel I had been much comfort to her.

Sammy gazed off into the distance toward a clay pencil holder Finn had made me when she was in kindergarten. She smiled wistfully. Then she turned back to me and said, "This is why I can't sleep, Uncle Fuse. These are the things I think about—why people do what they do. Or don't. I stare at the ceiling for hours trying to find an answer. And I just can't sleep."

"You seem tired now, Sammy." I said softly. "I mean, right now."

"I *am* tired right now."

"Why don't you take a nap here on the sofa? I have some work to do in my office right over there."

Light from a window momentarily made Samantha's eyes look as if they were on fire. When a cloud slid past the sun and the room darkened, her eyes began to close, even though she was sitting up.

"Lie down, kiddo. I'll cover you up."

She did as I said, and I gave her a knit blanket that was draped over a chair in my office. Once she was asleep, I called Kurt and Angie to let them know that Samantha was here and okay. As okay as she could be.

Samantha slept for about an hour and a half. On the way out of our house, she smiled weakly. "Thanks for caring about me," she said.

"I've always cared about you. I always will."

When she hugged me, I felt her shoulder blades, which made me think of the skeletons I used to see in science classrooms. I never knew whether they were plastic or had been from a real person. I'd always felt too stupid to ask. Sammy's shoulder blades, however, were real, and it occurred to me that perhaps she didn't see herself as being real anymore—just a collection of parts held together by something intangible.

• • •

I had a rendezvous with Abigail scheduled for later that day, to go over her recent encounter with the author of Samantha's crucible.

"You were great with Pacho, Abigail," I said as we walked along the C&O Canal.

"Thanks."

"I laughed out loud when you mentioned the movie."

"Pacho liked it too. He leaned back on the couch and all but grabbed a cigar and said, 'Lemme tell you about showbiz, kid.'" She held out her hand as if she had a cigar in it.

"I know. I heard. Do you have your glasses?"

She handed them to me. I told her I'd give them back after I had the recordings downloaded.

"Now what?" she said.

"One step at a time. Did you see how he accessed his house?"

"He punched in a code that opened up the front door. It's an alarm-door lock combo. I only caught some of the numbers." She removed her iPhone and opened the notes section.

"0-3-2-6 were the first ones. But there were two other numbers. Sorry, but his hand was in the way, and I couldn't see them. Then he bent down to pick up a few boxes from Amazon, and when he stood up, he almost bonked me in the head, so I was kind of flustered. I hope I got those four numbers right."

"0-3-2-6. Let me see what I can do with that. Tell me about his house—things I may not have seen on the video feed."

Abigail started describing the art—from all over the world, including lots of African and safari-type things.

"How swashbuckling of him," I said.

"He's got a lot of books, too."

"Any pattern?"

"Celebrity biographies," Abigail said. "He has a whole shelf of Bob Woodward and Carl Bernstein books."

"The alpha and omega of investigative journalism."

"I guess. And on his refrigerator, there are all kinds of pictures with him and celebrities looking real casual, like he hangs with them all the time."

I had the impulse to make a jerk-off hand gesture but thought better of it. "The way you slid Elijah in was perfect," I said instead.

"You mean the way I slid in a person you made up."

I shook my head. "I have an Elijah."

Abigail frowned. "Where do you find an Elijah?"

"He's part of what I've been working on. For your protection. You don't need all the details. It's part of the ground rules of the Callous Sophisticates—"

"Who?"

"Oh, I keep forgetting . . . It's the crew. We're called the Callous Sophisticates."

She looked at me like I had just escaped from St. Elizabeths—the mental hospital. "There's a crew? With a name?"

"Look, I need to get with Elijah and brief him up. Drag your feet with Pacho. Don't contact him. I want him to get anxious that he may lose the scoop. If he calls, sound nervous. Tell him somebody from ABC News is calling General Commodities. Let him cajole you. Tell him you're still thinking about it. Then once I get Elijah prepped, you'll call Pacho and set up a meeting."

"Will I go to that?"

"Yes, if you want. But you'll be doe-eyed."

"What will be the purpose of the meeting?" Abigail asked.

"To give Pacho further confidence that there's somebody who knows a bit more about this than you do. We want to embolden him."

"But he asked for emails and memos and stuff."

"Then that's what we'll get him."

"I don't have anything like that."

"You're not paying attention, Abigail." I held her gaze. "I'm saying, *We. Will. Get. Them. For. Him.*"

"Ah. But wouldn't that be illegal? Manufacturing documents?"

"What law is being broken? You're not defrauding investors. You'll be feeding documents to a half-a-journalist who is going to use them to go after a rich guy on camera. Shackley will only get nicked a little. The thing that happens afterward is what we're really looking for."

"What if somebody brought documents to you at the *Incursion* for a story?"

"Between my editors and me, we would vet them harder than the Shroud of Turin. But that's the *Incursion*. We're talking about MyStream here." I backed away for a moment and looked Abigail up and down.

"What are you looking at?" she asked.

"Are you about five-four?" I asked, observing she was a few inches shorter than my five-eight. We were both wearing short hiking boots.

"A little taller. Why?"

"I was just thinking about why Pacho only wears swanky cowboy boots."

"Fits his style," Abigail said.

"I wear a lower-cut Western boot a lot. Not the all-out cowboy style."

"So?"

"Cowboy boots don't just make you fancier. They make you taller."

29

ELIJAH JONES WAS an accountant who did work for Eddie Fontaine. He focused on the legitimate side of Fontaine's enterprises, with an emphasis on slowly making Eddie's dirty money clean. He had a successful practice focusing on African American businesses in the Washington area. As a practicing Muslim who was active in the DC Islamic community, he also helped finance mosques and other charitable initiatives. Eddie said even though Elijah disapproved of narcotics like all devout Muslims, he justified his work because it put money into the Muslim and black communities.

For my purposes, Elijah's appeal had several features: his business credentials, his Muslim pedigree, his willingness to do whatever Eddie Fontaine asked him to do, and his penchant—unbeknownst to most others on Eddie's payroll—for community theater. If Pacho looked into Elijah, he would surely be able to confirm the first two characteristics, and I felt certain he would never uncover the third. I just hoped Pacho wouldn't be able to decipher Elijah's acting skills.

I met Elijah in his modest offices in Southeast Washington. A wiry man in his mid-forties, Elijah Jones was dark-skinned, soft-spoken, and buttoned-up. I shook his hand, and we sat down at a small table in his office. After a few pleasantries and a quick briefing on Pacho and his slimy character, I asked about Elijah's acting skills. He'd have to prepare well for this whistleblower part. I wasn't sure he was up for the job.

"As I told Eddie, Mr. Petty, I'll do anything for him," Elijah said.

"But honestly, I was also excited about taking on this little acting gig. I'm always looking for ways to branch out and explore creative spaces that I can bring back to the theater."

I grinned at him and slid him the stack of papers I'd printed with all the information on Shackley he'd need to memorize. "Now, the main thing to remember is that you're a key interface between General Commodities, this Shackley guy's company, and the Saudis who've grown disgruntled with the company after the murder of journalist Adnan Sabbag."

"What a shame, what happened to him. A real stain on the Muslim community," Elijah said, shaking his head.

"More than a shame," I said.

"So what's my motivation? My character arc?" Elijah asked.

I laughed. "Okay, you're really not happy at General Commodities—there's a new flavor-of-the-month consultant who's recently won Oliver Shackley's favor, and you're feeling threatened. Let Pacho know this. He might be smarmy, but he's not stupid. Most investigative reporters, even ones like Pacho, recognize that leakers and whistleblowers are usually motivated by personal indignities even if they cloak them in righteous indignation."

At the end of our meeting, Elijah was satisfied with his character sketch and seemed to be relishing the thought of his upcoming role.

When Abigail and Elijah arrived at a spare meeting room at the rec center Eddie Fontaine had built in Anacostia a few days later, I was sitting in my car a block away, praying to the laptop gods that all would go smoothly with my video feed. Once inside, they sat beside each other at a round Formica table with cheap matching chairs.

Pacho Craig arrived about five minutes later, wearing a baseball cap and sunglasses, presumably to send the message that he was incognito. Abigail, Elijah, and Pacho were the only ones in the room. After introductions, Elijah began looking around, mimicking perfectly the nervous little guy on the totem pole, trying to assess whether he was free to speak without being compromised by eavesdroppers or their equipment. When someone opened the door to the room, Elijah jumped—but the man simply shut the door when he saw it was occupied.

Man, he is good.

"So, Abigail told me a little about the situation with the company you work for," Pacho began.

"I'm a contractor, not an employee," Elijah said softly, his eyes narrowing.

"I'm sorry," Pacho said.

Abigail looked from one man to the other.

"No big deal," Elijah said. "Look, Mr. Craig, I know of your work, and I need to understand something. I need certain reassurances. I do not wish to be a visible part of this story. It could ruin my career. My business is anchored in confidentiality. If people believe I'm talking, I'm done. I'm not a pop singer who claims he just wants to be left alone but also wants a billion views on MyStream. Forgive me, I don't mean you."

Pacho said, "I completely understand."

I'd told Elijah that, to an investigative reporter, a source is a means to an end. The end is an award-winning story—promotions, accolades, prizes, media appearances, book deals, what have you. Sources are a necessary hurdle to getting there. Most reporters, especially one like Pacho, don't really stress about the well-being of their sources. If a source gets exposed, few reporters care about it in any emotional way. They simply have to evaluate what is in their self-interest: Should they burn the source in order to make themselves appear more credible? Or should they leave the source anonymous and expose themselves to criticism of their work due to weak sourcing? Nevertheless, *all* reporters care about what burning a source might do to their future prospects. If you became known for this, you won't get many more sources.

So it was critical for Elijah to be clear that he was worried about being outed.

"Let me give you some assurances," Pacho continued. "Do you know the story of Watergate and Deep Throat?"

"Of course," Elijah said.

"Then you know that Deep Throat was Bob Woodward's source, a powerful person who didn't want to be identified because it would ruin his life. Most of my sources make the same request you do. They have the same fears. You said something a few minutes ago about having seen my work. You know, then, that I have very limited screen time. That's on purpose. I interview very few sources and witnesses on camera. I build my case, and I confront the target. Then I air my report. Afterward, I blog a bit and do other interviews. I've never burned a source. It's in my self-interest not to, because if I do, I'm out of business."

God, this guy is predictable. Lucky for me.

"I appreciate that," Elijah said. "Will my name be in any emails or texts or computer files that can be hacked or subpoenaed?"

Pacho shook his head.

Liar.

Reporters often say they don't keep records on sensitive matters, but they do. The few—very few—of us who have actually been through litigation or endured surveillance know that with the proper motivation and resources, all information can be gotten.

"I keep no correspondence of any kind," Pacho said.

"People always say that, Mr. Craig," Elijah said.

"Please . . . just Pacho is fine."

"I prefer keeping this more formal. I don't want to be lulled into a false sense of brotherhood here."

Abigail chimed in. "We're dealing with a billionaire *and* the Saudis." She pointed to Pacho's cell phone. "They can get onto that phone, believe me. They can get to anything they want."

Elijah said, "And please don't say they wouldn't dare do that to you. They already murdered a journalist."

"Yeah . . . I get it," Pacho said.

"Good," Elijah said, "because this is very serious business."

"Agreed. Tell me, Mr. Jones, how did you come to work with Shackley?"

"I'd been doing some work for a company that General Commodities had acquired. GC is the whitest group of white guys you'd ever meet," Elijah said. "They wanted to show their diversity credentials to the House of Saud. And here I was, this Muslim CPA. They hired me to do some accounting work and included me when some of the Saudis came to town. In time, I became part of the team. I knew it was more for my religious and ethnic pedigree than my facility with numbers and tax law—even though I am very good."

"He did my taxes for me," Abigail said.

"When did you begin to sour on the company?" Pacho asked.

"Shackley and his team started getting antsy when Sabbag began digging around on Shackley's ties to Saudi royals. GC had contracts in the works with the US government—like military contracts. Sabbag was turning into more of a human rights activist than a reporter. He was just an agitator trying to make it hard for the American government to do business with a repressive regime. It didn't work. It was business as usual at GC."

Abigail seemed to collect her thoughts for a moment before continuing.

"Sabbag kept publishing investigative pieces for high-end magazines, but the US showed no sign of backing away from the Saudis. Shackley knows he owns the White House. He's a huge contributor to the campaigns. But Sabbag kept coming. There were a bunch of trips and meetings. To and from Riyadh and Jeddah. Then one day everything got better. People at GC were happy. I asked Shackley's top man—"

"Who?" Pacho asked.

"The chief operating officer. I asked him why things were looking better, and he said something about a high-level team being brought in to manage the Sabbag investigation. There were some rumblings of congressional investigations."

"What did you think that meant?" Pacho asked.

"I figured he was talking about lawyers, lobbyists, and PR types," Elijah said. "By the end of the week, Sabbag was dead."

"Do you believe Shackley and his people were involved with the murder?" Pacho asked.

"I have no evidence of that. You know the old story about the king in medieval times who said, 'Who'll rid me of this turbulent priest?' and then the priest was dead?"

I sighed from my perch down the street, wondering whether Elijah was going overboard with such a profound quotation.

But Pacho bought it. "I vaguely remember something like that."

"Well," Elijah said, "I only know that the stakes were huge. I know Shackley was feeling the pressure. There was a sense of euphoria in the days leading up to Sabbag's killing—"

"Before? Not after?" Pacho asked.

"Yes, before."

"Why weren't they happy after the murder?"

"These are not imbeciles, Mr. Craig. They wouldn't go jumping for joy if an adversary was literally dismembered. Bad form."

Pacho rubbed his temples. "This is really something. But we need to harden this. I need something to prove—"

"Hold on there," Abigail said. "Not by identifying sources . . ."

"No, no, no," Pacho said. "But do you think you can get your hands on some documents?"

"You're not going to find a memo ordering a murder, Mr. Craig," Elijah said.

"No, but I may be able to get some confirmation that Shackley had a lot to lose."

"Would that be enough for a story?" Elijah asked.

"It certainly wouldn't hurt."

When the meeting was over, Abigail and Elijah stayed inside the rec center. I backed up my Jeep to be closer to the main entrance and slowly lowered my passenger window to get a better view. Two young African American men were standing on either side of the door. One of the men pointed at Pacho, and I heard him say, "Yeah, you're that guy from MyStream. Pancho!"

"Pacho," Craig corrected with a broad grin.

"Yeah," the man said. "Pacho. I seen you. Where's your big coat at?"

"A little warm today for that."

"Warm, yeah," the young man said, extending his hand. Pacho accepted the gesture and they shook.

The quieter of the two went for a high-five, and Pacho met it in kind. "Pacho!" The quiet man finally spoke. "Like that name. Like macho."

"I guess," Pacho said. "Good meeting you guys."

"Pacho," the duo said at the same while the celebrity made his way to his Range Rover.

A perverse part of me was pleased to see Pacho enjoying his celebrity. If my calculations were correct, it wasn't going to last much longer.

30

"KURT CALLED WHILE you were on the other line," Joey said, standing in the archway of my home office. "He said Sammy wants to talk to you."

"Me?"

Joey shrugged. I called Kurt.

"She's pretty upset," he said. "I can't get much out of her. She says she wants Uncle Fuse."

I drove over to the Rossiters' house, which seemed to get bigger every time I was there. Or perhaps my house was getting smaller. Either way, something strange was happening—not just with the relative size of things, but with the fact that this poor, tormented young woman wanted to be with me, while my own daughter alternated between loving me and looking at me as if I were mucus.

Kurt and Angie were both in the foyer waiting.

"How's she been?" I asked.

"Pretty good, actually," Angie said. The light was hitting her face in such a way that all I saw were the lines created by the Venetian blinds, the shadows dividing her beauty into segments. "But today went south for some reason."

"Okay. I'm happy to do whatever I can," I said.

I walked upstairs and tapped on Samantha's door.

"Uncle Fuse?"

"It's me."

"Come in."

Samantha was rocking in her bed, with her arms around her knees.

It was obvious from her bloodshot eyes that she had been crying. She was wearing a yellow sweatshirt and matching sweatpants. She looked like she was closer to eleven than twenty.

I sat on the edge of the bed. "You look like a banana," I said.

Samantha laughed, and I heard the congestion in her nose.

"What's going on, kiddo?" I asked.

"I don't know. I think I'm going crazy." Her tears started up again.

"Why do you think that?"

"It's like I'm starting to doubt myself."

"What are you doubting?"

"If I'm even sitting here! I'm even doubting my name! I mean, what I told you was the truth, but in my head sometimes it's something else."

"You mean . . . with Pacho?"

"Yeah."

"What else could it have been?" I asked.

"It's so hard to talk about."

"Do you want me to be a reporter right now? Suggest things and talk you through it?" In my job, I often operated with a thesis about something that had happened, and when my subject found it too difficult to discuss things directly, I planted seeds around them—potential facts and scenarios. The more fertile ones would blossom.

Samantha nodded.

"Okay. I know that you and Pacho Craig had sex and that you didn't want it to happen."

"Right."

"Did you tell him that?"

"Yes. I mean, I told him no."

"But you didn't tell him no at the beginning, when you were first together?"

"No."

"But you did tell him no later, before you started having sex?"

"I did. I mean, I told him before and after, but things were happening by then. This is what's making me crazy. I remember it so many ways that I don't know what's true anymore. I was totally sure right after. I felt like a scum. Like a rag thrown on the side of the road. But now I'm starting to think there is something wrong with me. Like it was my fault. Look, Uncle Fuse, I know I can be flirty—"

"That's not a crime, Sammy. A lot of people flirt."

"I know. What I'm saying is that . . . I don't know how to say it right. What I'm saying is that I'm not exactly what I seem sometimes. Even with the flirting."

"You're not what you seem . . . how?"

Samantha covered her face and spoke through her fingers. "Nothing had . . . um . . . ever gone this far with anybody. God, I'm so embarrassed. Do you understand?"

"I completely understand. You were a virgin. And you don't need to cover your face. I have not heard one thing—*not one*—that you have done wrong here. If anything—" Here my voice cracked. "I am doing such a lousy job. I'm sorry."

This discussion was not making me feel better about the prospects of ever taking Pacho to court. They would absolutely kill Sammy.

I tried to get back on track. "Sammy, why *me?*"

"There's just some things I can't say straight to my parents."

My eyes scanned the room. Samantha still had posters on her wall from high school. I didn't even know who these pop stars were, but I did remember the ones from when I was her age: Farrah Fawcett for boys and Steve McQueen for girls. Shaun Cassidy for younger girls. A surge of cool air pushed its way through the open windows. A leaf blower was revving in the distance. There was an autumnal aroma to the atmosphere, and the sensory narrative transported me to specific moments a few miles from here in a much smaller bedroom.

Paul McCartney's "Silly Love Songs" and "Let 'Em In" settled in my ears with the breeze. I remembered the intensity of my heart racing along with adventuring hands, and the pangs of shame that I was doing something punishable.

Between Samantha's ordeal and the broader war in the nation's culture, I couldn't help but revisit my own past with women. Was it possible that, by today's standards, I had been some kind of creep but didn't know it? Was it possible that there was a girl somewhere out there—a woman now—whose memory of me had been dormant but would soon awaken in a panicked revelation of something terrible I had done? And would it destroy my life?

When it came to women, I didn't have much of a sample size, but I honestly didn't ever remember specifically, verbally asking any girl for consent. Things were just improvisational. They either moved along or they didn't. I assumed that what I was doing was probably all right, but I didn't know for sure until I did it. And even then, I wasn't sure. I remember agonizing over whether I had shown the proper regard for the other person after my mother said something about sex being an expression of love between two people. Is that what I was doing? Expressing love? Or was I just a libidinous slob?

I vaguely remember a time during college when Joey and I were on the outs, and I was in an unfamiliar dorm room getting into it with a girl and hearing her say, *Hmm,* as if raising a question about what was going on. I had stopped. We then sat awkwardly watching the end of a campy Aaron Spelling television drama. I never got together with her again. I didn't know whether I had committed a foul. Or had she been the felon for initially waving me in like a NASCAR pit board, and then sending up a wispy smoke signal that I couldn't read but, in an abundance of caution, responded to by retreating?

Here's my point: I've never had the ability to properly read girls' signals, and it made me feel like I was on a completely different side of the street from savvier beings. It was as if everybody except me got the formula in a secret sex briefing. Even so, I always knew that *No!* was pretty clear.

"Sammy, let me ask you this," I said, "and please tell me the truth, no matter how hard it is. Did you find yourself attracted to Pacho?"

She nodded.

"Do you feel like because you wanted some kind of . . . I don't know . . . contact with him, maybe you asked for what happened?"

She nodded. "He seemed so nice."

"That's the challenge. It's why clowns are scary. You look at them and see goofiness, but you don't know what's really lurking behind the outfit and makeup."

"I thought this great guy liked me." Samantha wept.

I moved up and hugged her while she shook in my arms.

When she caught her breath, she said, "He just seemed so angry."

I left Samantha alone after extracting permission from her to tell Kurt and Angie about our discussion. I sat with them in their family room, surrounded by photos of their kids in various stages of adorability, toothless awkwardness, and beauty.

"Is she okay?" Angie asked.

"Yeah, she'll be fine," I said.

Angie and Kurt exhaled.

"Here's the thing. She was attracted to him, so she's feeling guilty about the whole situation. I think she was fine with some initial . . . affection. But then Pacho got aggressive. Now I'm not a psychologist—"

"If you aren't, nobody is, Fuse," Angie said, which made me laugh.

"Anyhow," I continued, "she blames herself. She thinks she's culpable because she felt something for him and didn't wave him off in a definitive way early on. These things are messy, but my own opinion is that if you don't bargain for something rough, and you say no, that should be the end of it."

“Exactly,” Angie said.

“I mean, even if she didn’t state it in a definitive . . . I dunno . . . documented form, she didn’t want what happened to have happened.”

Kurt walked me out to the driveway. “Full speed ahead, Fuse.”

As I was leaving the Rossiters, Haddon pulled into the driveway in her rented car and asked if anybody wanted to go for a hike.

I volunteered. Every synapse in my brain was firing, my skull was hot, and I hoped being in the woods on the banks of Cabin John Creek would cool me off.

31

HADDON FOLLOWED ME home in her car after none of the Rossiters expressed interest in joining the hike. I ducked into the house to change into my hiking boots while Haddon waited. Finn was sitting at the kitchen counter with her laptop in front of her.

"Why does Samantha keep wanting to talk to you?" she asked.

"Because she trusts me," I said, with no small amount of self-pity, before turning and exiting the room. With Finn, I found that when I left abruptly after making a statement rather than lingering in the hope of further engagement, she was nicer to me during our next encounter.

"Are you up for eight miles on the Cabin John Trail?" I asked Haddon when I got back outside, displaying my hiking pole.

"Hell, yeah!" Haddon said. "Lead the way."

As we walked down Bradley Boulevard toward the trailhead, I felt a twinge of guilt. But I figured that if Joey could do a beach walk with Kurt, I could hike in the woods with Haddon. I thought about inviting Joey along, but I knew she was busy with a new graphics project. She had never come right out and said she had found Kurt attractive, but I had always operated with the suspicion that there might be a twinge of something there, largely because that appeared to be women's universal reaction to him.

Haddon wore jeans and a puffy down vest. She wore her hair in a ponytail beneath a baseball cap, all of which accentuated her features in a way that made me think of a young Julie Christie. Haddon could have worn a burka and been fetching.

"Love the hiking pole," she observed.

"Thanks. It helps when I go down a hill. My knees aren't what they were."

"Old fart."

"I keep getting membership invitations to join AARP."

"That's sexy, Fuse."

"I know, Hadd. That's why I said it. I've been thinking of starring in middle-aged porn. It's the hottest genre now."

"That's a great idea!"

"I'll be the lead in *Disappointment in the Dunes* and *Letdown in Las Vegas.*"

"Why so pessimistic? Why not make it hot?" Maybe her youthful perspective was why she had never adjusted to adulthood. That and the fact that she was still screwing like a college kid.

"Because the whole idea is to dampen expectations. Make middle-aged people feel better about the whole endeavor."

When we got to the entrance of Cabin John Trail, I asked Haddon whom she'd visited in Annapolis.

"I stayed with an old boyfriend and his wife and kids. Great people. He was a Navy SEAL I dated about twenty years ago."

Of course she did.

"How did his wife feel about your visit?" I asked.

"Penny's cool."

Sure, Penny was cool. Everyone in Haddon's world was cool. Except me. I nodded, pretending to be hip.

"Yeah, all the nice guys are taken, Fusey."

This made me want to push her down the hill into the ravine that snaked along the trail. "There is nothing more obnoxious than a beautiful woman whining about how she can't meet a nice guy. You don't *want* to meet a nice guy."

The finger gesture she shot me had the desired effect of defusing the judgmentalism. "Then who do I want to meet?" she asked.

"I assume you want a player, somebody exciting. There are certain traits that come along with being a player, and one of them is not niceness."

"I'm not sure I agree with you. All I know is that guys like you are long off the market."

"C'mon, you don't want a guy like me. See, there are sailboats and there are houseboats. Some of us are sailboats, built for adventure, for the variety of life, which is fine. I believe in freedom for all people, even so-called open relationships—which are all well and good until you're the one who gets opened. Now, a sailboat may look at a houseboat and think, 'You know, that would be nice to float beside and watch the sunset with every night.' But sailboats are drawn toward other ports when gloomy weather hits. That's how they're made. But a guy like me? I'm a houseboat. Sure, I think about other ports. I'm human. I'd like to see the world. But I'm built like a houseboat. I'm not made for the high seas."

"So I'm a sailboat?" Haddon asked.

"Yes, you're a sailboat. And good for you. You're one of the most interesting people I know. Sailboats attract other sailboats. Or suicidal houseboats."

"What do you mean, 'suicidal'?"

"If a houseboat is into you, he's gonna get torpedoed. You'll kill him, leave him sobbing in his cornflakes."

"I've dated nice guys. I thought this one guy, a Miami councilman, would finally leave his wife. But at the last minute, he didn't."

"Maybe he wasn't as nice as you thought. Why do you think he stayed with his wife?" I asked.

"He had kids."

"That was probably part of it. The rest is that he's a houseboat. He probably figured it was only a matter of time before you got bored and sailed off," I said. Then I added, "What's wrong with us, Haddy? Why do we argue?"

"Because we disagree on stuff."

Screw it. I was going to say it. "I think I've always been a bit bewitched by you. Do you think that plays into it? Why we spar?"

"Bewitched?" she said. Her nose was scrunched like a bunny rabbit's.

"I guess so."

"So that's what it is," Haddon said with a laugh. "I just thought that at some level you didn't like me. You were always so smart, and I figured it had something to do with that . . . So, are you still bewitched?"

"That was from when we were young," I said, looking straight into her eyes. *She doesn't have to know everything.*

"Maybe this whole thing is why I have such trouble meeting a nice guy."

I didn't want to lay into her about the fact that she was looking for a man she didn't really want, not for more than a few minutes anyway. How could a free spirit like her be tied down to a houseboat?

"You love your freedom," I said. "I just think that love isn't freedom."

"Then what is it?"

"It's being chained to someone you want to be chained to most of the time," I said.

Haddon stopped walking. "You know, a guy I dated who was a cowboy at a rodeo called me 'witchy woman.'"

"Of course you dated a rodeo cowboy," I said with a laugh. "Yippee-ki-yay."

"So where does Joey fit into these theories on women?" she asked, continuing along the dirt trail.

"I know something very few people know: that I'm with the right girl. Joey and I pretty much want to be where we are. I'm just trying to understand why I still think about college when you visited me at Haverford." It was true. For the life of me I couldn't figure out why I still cared about this stuff.

"You do? Why?"

"I kissed you before you got on the bus to go back to Rutgers."

"You did?"

I rolled my eyes. "Yes. And then I sent you that panda?"

Haddon stopped again. "Really?" she said, tilting her head.

"Just a little stuffed animal," I said.

"Oh, right." She didn't remember, which told me everything.

When Haddon had left me that afternoon after her visit to Haverford, I'd found a toy store and spotted this little stuffed panda bear. I had it wrapped and sent it to Haddon at Rutgers. I didn't hear back, so I rang and left her a message saying I would be near Rutgers the following weekend and would try to stop by. *Try*, my ass. Haddon was the only reason I'd driven to New Brunswick.

When I went by her dorm, she hugged me, but she seemed preoccupied. The little panda was on a shelf, facing the wall. About every two seconds, another guy would come to her door, and she answered every knock. I felt like deadweight, and after a few minutes of conversation that was like walking alone through a wilderness of molasses, I left. In the years since, I'd realized Haddon hadn't really wanted the panda, and then I'd come to realize something even more painful: Haddon hadn't wanted *me*.

"I was never able to make plans with you after that," I said. "I figured I did something wrong."

"Really? Oh, Fuse, it was just a silly weekend."

"Yeah, I guess so." I said it like I didn't care. Because I did care. Haddon had spent her life being given little pandas and had ceased to distinguish between all the stuffed animals. The gifts had all blended together: the pandas, the flowers, the cards, the kisses. But for me, the intrepid investigative reporter who faced down terrorists, criminals, and spies, that one stupid panda had meant so much.

I remembered having read a book a few years earlier about Ginevra King, the woman on whom F. Scott Fitzgerald based *The Great Gatsby*'s

Daisy Buchanan and other female antagonists. The upshot of Ginevra's assessment of Fitzgerald was: *C'mon, already. I had a crush on you when I was sixteen. Get over it!* An imbalance in expectations between two people. Haddon and me. Perhaps Kurt and his intern, Bonita. Somebody ends up on the downside of that seesaw, squatting in a puddle and pounding their fists.

"Did you ever wonder what it would have been like if we had gotten together?" Haddon asked, presumably to be polite.

"Honestly, no," I said. This was true.

"Why not?" she asked.

"Because I know exactly what would have happened."

"Which is . . . ?"

"Oh, Haddon, I wouldn't be enough for you. And you would be too much for me. I'd be perpetually waiting for you to say, 'We need to talk.' Always crawfishing."

"Crawfishing?"

"Crawfish walk backward when they want out. Reporters use that term when we cover politicians who don't want to answer our questions. Crawfish don't even bother to turn around. They just back away to their next gig." I smiled at her. "Besides, I wouldn't have my life with Joey. And that would just about kill me."

Haddon stopped and faced a curious direction. It was neither toward nor away from the sun. "Maybe I'm your asymptote."

"Excuse me?"

"Asymptote," she repeated. "It's from math. It means a line or curve on a graph that keeps getting closer and closer to another line, but it never intersects, never touches. I'm your asymptote."

"Hmm. Do you think it's possible that maybe I just *am* an asymptote?"

"No. Definitely not. You've intersected with Joey since you were twelve years old. Come to think of it, maybe *I'm* an asymptote—every guy's asymptote. They all think they love me. But I can't close the deal."

We came to a clearing that took us through a field with power lines, and after another quarter mile we entered another thicket that brought us closer to Tuckerman Lane.

"What do you make of this whole mess with Samantha?" Haddon asked.

"Tragedy."

"Do you believe her?"

"Oh, Jesus. Yes, I believe her," I said. "You don't?"

"Of course I do. But just a part of me wonders whether she's getting back at Kurt."

"For what, screwing around? Nobody ever said Kurt was a rapist—just a cheater."

"I know. But this Pacho guy could represent something."

"If she wanted to get back at Kurt, why not just be mean to him? Or bring home a douchebag? Daughters are good at that," I said.

"I don't know. Just grasping for explanations, I guess. Maybe there isn't one. So why do you think Kurt wants you involved?" Haddon asked.

"Because I'm a friend who knows the world."

"Any other reason?"

"Somebody to trust."

"Guys like Kurt are used to having their big-shot buddies cover for them," Haddon said. "He's a manipulator."

"Regardless, who do you go to if not your friends—whether you did something wrong or not? Anyhow, these fancy families don't want people looking too closely at what goes on inside," I said.

"That's what I was getting at. Something dark. Really dark."

"People don't necessarily have to be doing anything sinister. They may be doing things that *they* are ashamed of in their own heads, but that aren't necessarily diabolical. Image means a lot to Kurt and Angie. All the more reason to want a confidant who has an investment in them and won't blow them up."

"The Rossiters haven't kept their standing in Darwin's cruel world with any lack of skills. Kurt's dad was at State during the biggest foreign policy crises ever."

"So?"

"The Rossiters know how to find nice ways to get people to do things."

"In other words, I'm being manipulated."

"Maybe."

"They would have to be pretty good actors. And why would they have me talk to Samantha, who is so fragile? Is this *The Usual Suspects,* and Samantha is Keyser Soze, the unassuming mastermind?"

"She's not Keyser Soze. Maybe I shouldn't be throwing out horrible theories," Haddon said.

"We've all been throwing out theories. If it had been an attack in an alleyway and Pacho had been wearing a ski mask, we wouldn't be having this discussion."

"But you think he did it? Raped her."

"Yes, I do. But it wasn't in an alley, he wasn't wearing a ski mask, and the lead-up was probably romantic. Just like a huge number of rapes."

"I had to ask, Fuse."

I was quiet for a minute, looking up into the orange leaves surrounding us. The more I talked about Samantha, the more I missed Finn. I hoped someday she would want to walk in the woods with me again like she did when she was little.

"Are you okay?" Haddon asked.

"Yeah, why?"

"It looks like you're upset."

"Probably allergies," I said, wiping a tear from my eye.

"What are you thinking?"

I don't know why I did it, but I hugged Haddon. My voice broke, and I said, "I just wish Finn would like me again."

"She likes you now. She just doesn't know what to do with you. With Joey. With herself."

"It's hard to see your baby go into the world. I've been out there a long time, and I can't say I like it very much."

Haddon took my hand and held it in a way that made me think of my mother and something she said to me when she blinked awake during her last days. "You can have a life or you can have Nat Petty," Mom had said, "but you can't have both. You've been told." Then she'd gone back to sleep. Forever.

Part III

ACTUAL MALICE

"In his experience, people were seldom happier for having learned what they were missing, and all Europe had done for his wife was encourage her natural inclination toward bitter and invidious comparison."

—RICHARD RUSSO, *EMPIRE FALLS*

32

"**DID YOU FIND** anything about the door code to Pacho's house?" I asked Goblin as soon as he was seated at Attman's.

After my walk along the canal with Abigail, I had phoned Goblin on his burner with the four numbers and told him it wasn't the complete code. "Damn. Longer ones are more complex to break, *bon ami,*" Goblin had said.

I'd figured that. "Can you run one of those, I don't know, whiz-bang programs that you intel guys do?" I'd asked him. "See if those numbers mean anything to Pacho and his history?"

Goblin had agreed to run the numbers in addition to performing the other tasks I'd requested: reviewing the video feed from the glasses and taking a look at Pacho's Amazon account. I had a little theory about his ordering patterns and how we might be able to get them to blow up in his face.

"The numbers don't appear to be his birthday or anybody else's in his family," Goblin said now.

"Does March twenty-sixth mean anything in history?"

"I found a few things, yeah. The Camp David accords were signed on that day in 1979. Beethoven died. Mike Tyson got sentenced to prison for rape. Those Heaven's Gate *couillons* were found after the mass suicide." Goblin read a few others that didn't resonate, then added, "One that stood out was Bob Woodward's birthday. March twenty-sixth."

I brightened. "My girl said he had a whole Bob Woodward shelf at home."

"I know. I saw it on the video from the glasses, yeah."

"That's right. What year was Woodward born?" I asked.

Goblin looked at his notes. "1942. Pshaw! Maybe that's it, then. 03-26-42."

"Why don't you check it out when Pacho's gone? I'd try the Mike Tyson one too."

"You think he'd commemorate a rape, *bon ami*?"

"Who knows? Maybe it's a cautionary note to himself. Don't forget what can happen and all."

"Oh, I checked Pacho's Amazon orders, yeah. Nothing really unique." He shrugged. "But he orders everything delivered overnight."

"Yet he leaves everything stacked up without opening any boxes right away."

"So?"

"So it deepens my belief that he attacked my friend's daughter," I said.

Goblin laughed. "What does one have to do with the other?"

"It's a bunch of things. I believe the girl." I thought of Abigail too, and of the ponytailed Josh Culling. "Another woman I know reported a similar reaction—that Pacho was angry when he couldn't make his move. A high school acquaintance of his told me how he wasn't patient enough to wait in a cafeteria line. All this plus the Amazon Prime addiction, and it adds up to one thing: he's wired for instant gratification."

"Aw, a lot of people are these days," Goblin said.

"No doubt. I'm a monster in traffic, but this guy can't even hide it when he should." *And he definitely should.*

• • •

One of the things Goblin did with all the cash I had given him—about $30,000 so far—was buy an iPad onto which he uploaded all the data he had on Pacho Craig and Gretchen Kramer. He also taught me a valuable thing: how to use it. As we sat at the table playing with the device, he was visibly horrified when I initially pressed the icons on the screen and the iPad responded to my touch by immediately crashing.

"Oh, yeah, you're one of *those*," he said, and commented that he had heard about "us."

I wasn't sure what he meant.

He explained that there were certain people whose "ions are reversed" and who were simply loathed by modern technology on a basic, structural level. "I see it now!" he said. "It's like the new millennium is kicking you out, *pauvre bête*."

I had never heard of this theory and had always been quite pleased with my ions. But I was relieved that perhaps there was a scientific explanation for my problem with TICU other than my deep and abiding idiocy.

He showed me the recording Abigail had taken of Pacho's watch. "This Santos Cartier watch, or whatever you call it, it's real, yeah," Goblin said. "I showed it to a guy I knew who studied the way the thingamajigs move behind the glass. He said he hadn't ever heard of people counterfeiting this particular model, because you can see through it. With fakes, people don't want you to look at the mechanisms. Anyway, he said the movements are real."

"What's it worth?"

"My guy said this one is about sixty grand."

"A cheapie, eh?"

Before we departed my iPad lesson, Goblin shot me a curious look. One eye was closed and the other eye was wandering toward the pickle bar.

"What's on your mind?" I asked.

"You know I don't like to stick my nose in any more than necessary, *bon ami*," Goblin said.

"I know."

"But I think it might help me to know the endgame for the Callous Sophisticates."

"Sure," I said. "Are you going somewhere with this, Goblin?"

"Yeah, yeah. Is this a one-time caper or ongoing?"

"I don't know. I figured it was one time. Why?"

"For a pretty square guy, you're taking a lot of risks. I take risks every day, but you're Mr. Suburbia."

"I've spent my career talking to people who could hurt me if they wanted."

"Hurting reporters is rare."

"Tell that to Adnan Sabbag," I said.

"A Saudi. The Saudis kill troublemakers the way I grab a yogurt out of the fridge, yeah. I'm just wondering if somebody got in your ear about what a monster Pacho is. Gretchen Kramer too."

"Kramer really is out to get me. It's not a delusion."

"But this hard-on for Pacho . . . It seems like somebody whipped you up to take him out."

"I do feel an investment, yes," I said.

"Let me ask you again: if this gig works out, do you want to stay in this game?"

"What game is that?"

"This vengeance business. Or evening the score with bad people." Goblin shrugged. "Whatever you would like to call it."

A surge of frigid water shot through me. One of my mental characteristics is a tendency to have a guilty conscience—occasionally being prone to suggestion about my more negative traits. Working toward Pacho's peril was a Nat-like attribute—wanting others to get a dose of his misery. What did it mean if I possessed such a notion?

"Is there a reason you think that?" I asked.

"There is, yeah," Goblin said. "You know that old phrase about the spy world? 'Wilderness of mirrors'?"

"I've only used it a million times," I said.

"I've been in plenty of situations where somebody wants me to think I'm doing something for one purpose when I'm really doing it for another."

"If you're asking whether I'm keeping all the parts separate—I'm trying to. I don't want any one of us to know enough to hurt ourselves or each other."

"Except you," Goblin said.

"Right. And I don't plan on hurting myself. Am I answering your question at all?"

"I'm not sure if you even know the answer."

"I'm not sure if I totally understand your question. Are you asking if maybe I'm secretly working on a story for the *Incursion* and I'm drawing you in to set you up?"

"I'd find that hard to believe, yeah."

"Good, because I don't know how to assure you that this is as above board as a below-board operation can be. I have some vulnerability here, as you know."

"I know. I guess what I'm asking is whether you intend to keep taking off-the-books projects like this now that journalism is in the shitter. It occurs to me that your skills could be useful beyond this one situation."

"I haven't accomplished anything yet," I said.

"Okay," Goblin said. "But we may have something here. There's a market for taking down people who get through the system. A business, yeah?"

"We may have something indeed. In the meantime, let me know about Pacho's door code."

"I will. By the way, are you familiar with something called 'deepfake'?"

"No," I said.

"Let me tell you about it. I have an idea."

33

WHEN PACHO CRAIG opened the door to his townhouse, Abigail Case stood in the entryway, coyly holding a large manila envelope with several stray papers sticking out at the top as if they had been stuffed inside urgently. I could see on my iPad, via the camera in Abigail's glasses, that Pacho was wearing only a towel around his waist. I had to admit that the iPad worked better than the laptop. Maybe there was a reason people liked these gadgets after all. Nevertheless, I didn't like what I was seeing.

My stomach knotted. Pacho had known about their meeting well enough in advance to have gotten dressed. It brought me some relief that I was just down the street.

"Oh, I can come back," Abigail said, with no small amount of hesitation in her voice. I could imagine her feeling for the reassuring bulge of pepper spray in her front jeans pocket.

"No, that's okay," Pacho said. "I had to take an overseas call, so I was running behind after my workout. Come on in."

Abigail sat down in the living room, and Pacho offered her something to drink. He lingered in a doorway, with each of his palms flat against the frame. This had the effect of flexing his pectorals. Abigail pointedly looked away. I knew her revulsion of the man must be intensifying. Did he actually think she was so stupid as to believe his display was anything other than a calculated ploy? Of course, it wasn't lost on me that this must have worked on other women.

She sat on his sofa with her hands on her knees, looking straight into a bookshelf. As Pacho lingered, waiting for the response he'd been expecting, he just looked like an ass. He couldn't have liked it.

I felt my heart rumble against my chest, grabbed my own pepper spray, and felt for the crowbar under my seat. With my left hand, I took hold of the Jeep's door handle and prepared to yank it open. Pacho eventually huffed—with a surprising lack of subtlety—and slipped into a room just beyond his kitchen.

When Pacho returned to the living room, he was dressed. Abigail deliberately set the papers down beside her on the sofa so that Pacho wouldn't sit there. He took a seat on the plush chair across from her.

"So what do you have for me?" he asked. He seemed curt.

"I did the best that I could," Abigail said softly.

Pacho took the papers from Abigail and set them down on the coffee table that separated them.

"This," Abigail said, "is a list of products purchased by Saudi companies from General Commodities."

Pacho looked it over. I knew he would barely understand the items listed, any more than I did. Polystyrene clamshells. Polyethylene terephthalate fibers. Various insulation materials for military apparel.

"Basically, GC fabricates a lot of products from Saudi petrochemicals," Abigail explained. "And the Saudis buy the completed products."

Pacho grinned. "This is good."

The pages of purchase orders from Saudi companies to General Commodities were mind-numbingly boring, but they appeared to establish that Shackley had a lot of business with the Saudis through different firms. Pacho took a few minutes to read through them, including emails to and from Elijah Jones and other executives.

"Hmm," Pacho said. "Well, it's all very incestuous. The Saudis take the chemicals out of the ground and clean them up a little. They send them in some form over here. Shackley's outfit processes them into other stuff for consumer and military use, and then sells some of it back to the Saudis for their own uses, as well as to the US marketplace and Department of Defense."

"That's what I was saying, and it's not a crime," Abigail said.

"No, not at all. But if Sabbag was investigating the relationship, I can see where it caused heartburn for both parties."

"I was able to get a few emails between Sabbag and the PR woman for GC."

"Really? How did you get them?"

"Somebody forwarded an email to Elijah, and he printed it out."

"Let me see," Pacho said eagerly. When he was done reading the emails, he said, "Okay, so Sabbag is asking a bunch of questions. The PR woman gets back to him and threatens him with defamation action. I've gotten plenty of letters like that in my career."

"What does it mean?" Abigail asked.

"It means they have a lot to hide and don't want a meddling reporter scratching around in their business."

"But it doesn't prove they killed Sabbag?"

"Of course it doesn't. That's not ever going to be in an email. But it certainly shows a motive for why they—"

"Who's *they*?"

"Shackley and the Saudis. Why they may have wanted Sabbag out of the way."

The instant Abigail picked up the papers beside her and put them on her lap, Pacho stood up and moved around to sit down next to her on the couch. He put his hand on her knee and said, "This is really great. *Really* great."

Abigail jumped up and the papers fell into the ground. "Oh, good. I'm glad, ah, that helped. Oh gosh, sorry, let me get those." She bent over and gathered up the errant papers, gave them to Pacho, and hurried toward the door. "So, yeah, I'll be in touch. Or you will . . . Gotta go."

When Abigail made it outside and climbed into my Jeep, she was out of breath. "He tried to . . . He touched my knee," she said in a broken voice.

"I had the car door open and was on my way, but you were already up and out. Good job."

"You should have seen the look on his face."

"I did. Remember? I was about to pound on the door but decided against it when he went to put on some clothes. I'm sure he was disappointed," I said with nervous guilt.

"No, Sandy. He wasn't disappointed. He was angry. It was like his eyes turned red."

What? "Red?"

"I don't want to talk about it anymore. That viper took my dad from me," she said, looking down at her hands in her lap. "Look, I don't know how much longer I can do this."

"You can quit anytime, Abigail."

"No, no. We have to see this through. I'm just venting. I'm starting to feel badly about Shackley. He doesn't seem that evil. Like my dad wasn't evil."

"I don't think he is evil. I know it seems like Shackley is the target, but trust me, once everything falls into place, Shackley will be having the time of his life."

"I'll have to trust you on that, Sandy," Abigail said, her sigh conveying skepticism. "What happens now?"

"You should vanish a while. I don't want to pressure him, because he might get suspicious. I think he's going to move fast."

"Really? Why?"

"His thing is confrontation. The theater of confrontation. Now we wait. And I'm sorry you had to get that close to him."

"That's okay."

"No, it's not. I put you in harm's way."

"Listen, you warned me at the very beginning of all this. I'm a grown woman, and I knew what I was getting into. Besides, you were nearby if I needed backup."

"Still . . ."

"If we get him, it will have been worth it."

I thought of Samantha. A scheme well executed didn't mean a woman un-assaulted. I retreated into my own smallness and wondered how any sane person could ever conclude humans are in control of anything.

34

"THE CALLOUS SOPHISTICATES," I said in a singsong voice, picking up the phone. I'd seen it was Goblin. He'd tried to teach me to text on my burner before calling, but I couldn't get the hang of it. Besides, I was convinced that encryption was a myth to get you to confess your sins. Best not to text at all.

"Heh, *bon ami*," Goblin said. "I just wanted to take this opportunity to wish Bob Woodward a happy birthday."

"Oh, really? Good to know."

We had our entrance code to Pacho's house.

• • •

Kurt called me and said that Angie couldn't stop crying. He was at a loss and seemed to be under the impression that I was the Female Whisperer, given my talks with Samantha. If only he knew how useless Joey thought I was when it came to being a good listener and providing constructive advice. There had been so many times over the decades when Joey was upset and I thought I had been providing valuable insight. Then Joey would say, "You think this is all about fixing a broken doorknob or something."

As the saying goes, an expert is just a guy from out of town.

I went over anyway. Kurt let me in and made me pretend I had just popped in unannounced. Angie was sitting in the kitchen, wearing workout gear and no makeup. She appeared more bony than fit. And exhausted, like she had aged a decade in the past few weeks. But I knew this was temporary—her beauty was in there somewhere, reaching for an escape.

"Oh, hey, Fuse," she said, her eyes brightening.

I maintained the lie. "I was just cutting through Arrowood and wanted to see if you had any interest in making me a gourmet meal. I was thinking maybe a little surf and turf?"

"You can always make me feel better," Angie said.

"Put in a good word for me with Joey, would you? Soften her up for next time she's mad at me."

"Do you want something to drink?"

"Why, do you want me to stay?"

Angie glanced at Kurt as if asking him if it was all right. He had been leaning awkwardly against the refrigerator, unsure of what to do with himself. He shrugged.

I said, "I know it's awful to say this, but you look really tired."

She burst into tears and hugged me. "I just can't shake it, Fuse. It's all I think about. What happened to Sammy. My doctor tells me to compartmentalize—"

"Oh, screw him," I said. "Who the hell can compartmentalize?"

Angie emitted a hint of a laugh, and Kurt slipped out of our vision. I had dual reactions to her pain: one empathetic and one ungenerous. My empathy was because this was a woman who had been suddenly plucked out of the comfortable hearth where she had dwelled for well over a half-century and dropped headfirst into a snake pit. But even though it had nothing to do with the topic at hand, I couldn't quash my anger that she had been so tolerant of Kurt's dalliances for so long.

Had I behaved the way Kurt behaved with women, Joey never would have stood by me so steadfastly. So maybe I was just jealous. How did these guys—whom women claimed to despise—not only do well with women, but get them to tolerate the most outrageous things? Hell, when I left my biking shorts on the shower curtain rod, I was in the doghouse for a month.

"Let's sit down," I suggested.

Angie guided me into the kitchen, and we sat kitty-corner to each other at the table. From one angle, she looked like a portrait of actress Diane Lane—cool, blue-blooded, and perfect. But when the light hit her from another direction, she took on the appearance of needing a good nap, the kind where you sleep forever and when you eventually wake up, the pillow is moist and shaped like your whole head.

Were Angie and Kurt just another couple for whom the panacea of communication had simply fallen short, as it does with most of us who have stood the test of time? I rejected the theory that men cheat for the reason the "other woman" often cites—that there must have been something wrong with the marriage to begin with. Of course there's something wrong. It's a marriage! The notion that the enterprise is supposed to be completely fulfilling causes more divorces than the "miscommunication."

Of everyone in our group of friends, I was the least emotionally attached to Angie. We liked each other well enough, but we'd never had much to talk about. Finn had made me aware of the concept of "mansplaining" when I had helped her with a school paper on the Civil War, and I surely didn't want to commit that sin here. I got Angie a tissue from the counter and then sat at the table again with my hand on her shoulder. I almost brushed her hair back from her face but thought it too intimate a gesture.

"I appreciate all you're doing for us," Angie said.

"It's a labor of love," I said. "Painful, but our history means something to me."

"What does it mean? Our history?"

I took the tissue from her hand and dabbed her tear-stained face. "This is a weird age for our kids," I said. "But it's hard for us too. We have a solid block of time left, at least in theory, but it feels like the gate is closing. There's a German term for it: *Torschlusspanik*. It basically means that you're seeing the window of your life closing and you're terrified. You start thinking about your life, rewinding it. Thinking about what you want to keep, what you want to throw away, and what you may have missed."

"What have you missed, Fuse?"

"Oh, I didn't sow my wild oats, as they say. I never had the kind of fun young people are 'supposed to' have. Maybe I was wrong to have expected it. Here's my point, though. I've become more protective of what I do have, not what I didn't get. I think that when you get right down to it, love is just your history—"

"Love is your history?"

"It is. You and Kurt are my history. How could I not do my best to help you out?"

"I'm sorry—"

"No, no, that's not what I meant. I just meant to say that as alone as you feel, and as alone as you're allowed to feel, you're not completely alone," I said.

"I know. What are you actually doing for Samantha?"

"You're not old enough to know the answer to that. And you never will be."

"Why did he do it, Fuse?"

"Pacho? Because he's a rapist."

"I know, I know. I was talking about Kurt."

"Cheat?" I asked.

"Do you think that's all he did?"

"Yes, I do."

"Not anything worse?"

"No. Do you?" I asked.

"My mind is a jumble," she said. "I just can't differentiate between men right now."

This made me wonder if there was something I wasn't being told.

"So why did he cheat?" Angie pressed.

"Don't you dare fish for a defect in yourself," I said. "I don't think that's the way to go here. Not because you don't *have* a defect. We all do. But there are things operating at a level we don't even understand. I think men and women panic when the gate is closing, and they do things to keep their genes and their spirits alive—"

"Women too? I think that's a guy thing."

"Bullshit. You read about all these thirty-something women school-teachers screwing their students. They're bored with their husbands and their kids, so they start up with the younger guys. When we were growing up, the big cliché was middle-aged men banging their secretaries. Now the statistics show that men and women are evening out with that stuff. I'm just saying that you're right to feel awful about all this, but it doesn't mean you're deficient. Plus, you married Kurt Rossiter."

"But look at you, Fuse. You don't have all that . . . *Torschlusspanik."*

"How do you know? Who am I to say I'd never look at the way a woman's quadricep connects to her knee just right, or catch a glimpse of cleavage that topples my defenses? Under the wrong set of circumstances, I could think, 'Yeah, I'll ruin my life over that.'"

"My husband nearly blew up our lives over a knee?" Angie asked, exasperated.

"Maybe, Ange. Honestly, maybe. And I don't know what 'inner pig' Joey has going on—and no, I don't ask. Anyway, you must have thought about your options at some point."

"Well, yeah. And I don't think Joey has much of an inner pig going on."

I threw up my hands. "I don't wanna know what I shouldn't know."

"You know she loves you."

"I know I drive her crazy," I said, folding my arms.

"Well, not horribly crazy. But do you know what she said to me once, before all this started? 'Fuse drives me nuts, but he is always kind.

He has the biggest heart in the world. But never mistake kindness for weakness.'"

"She said that?"

"Yes," Angie said.

I put my hand back on Angie's shoulder, and she covered mine with hers. From this angle, with the indirect sunlight less piercing now, she sure was a masterpiece to look at.

She sighed. "Can we survive this? What we're going through with Sammy? With each other?"

I nodded. "Yes, Angie, you can survive this, and you will. It's just that it won't be the same. The future you imagined, with some kind of glowing destination at its end, may be—*will* be—different. Not every arc curves upward. I'm not going to give you any Ancient Mariner bullshit about the value of adversity and wisdom. And in case you're wondering, I've kicked your husband's ass over what he did—well, verbally. Because it was disgraceful."

Angie wiped her eyes again. "Do you know the origins of the word 'disgrace'?" she asked.

"I've never thought about it," I said.

"In Latin, *dis* meant 'away from' and *grace* meant 'being with God.' So 'disgrace' meant 'being away from God.'" She smiled at me sadly.

Thinking of nothing else to add to that, I kissed Angie on the cheek and left.

35

WHEN I GOT home, Finn was stomping out of the house. She wore that teenage expression that conveyed *I can't believe the singular stupidity of everybody in the world besides me*.

"What's going on?" I asked.

"Nothing, *Dad*. I'm going to Alison's house." Alison had been Finn's friend since grade school. A nice kid, but who knew anymore?

"Can I take you?"

"No!"

"Okay, okay!" I held up my hands in surrender. "Just offering."

At least she wasn't going to Frigging Alex's. But given her trouble with the truth these days, maybe she was.

It hit me that if Finn was engaging in theatrics outside of the house, then Joey might be upset inside the house. And while Finn had a history of snapping at me when she was in a rage, with Joey she tended to recite a litany of alleged flaws, which her mother took very personally as opposed to dismissing them as the rants of a teenager.

Sanford Petty, Manly Man, to the rescue! Or rather, off to make things worse.

I entered the house and commenced my bold search for the damsel in distress. First floor, clear. Onto the second. My intrepid search yielded quick results as I observed Joey curled in a ball on our bed.

"Hold on," I said and went into the bathroom. I reached behind me and stuffed the top of a towel down the neck of my sweater so it looked like a cape. Then I knelt down by Joey, arched an eyebrow, and said, "I'm Batman. What happened?"

"Finn says I suck."

"You suck?"

"Yes, I suck."

I took Joey's face in my hands. "Of course you suck," I said gently. "Nobody sucks more than you. When I first saw you on the playground, I said to myself, 'Whoa, look at that beautiful sucky girl over there in that tree. I can't imagine anybody ever sucking more than her.'"

Joey snorted a feeble semi-laugh through her nose.

"But," I continued, "the thing is . . . I fell for you because you sucked so much, and nobody sucked more than me, and I needed somebody who sucked as much as I did. And I was so lucky to find you when we were so young, so we could suck together. You think I'm kidding you whenever I say you saved my sucky life, but you really did—by sucking just the perfect amount."

Joey now had a snotty byproduct peeking out her nose.

"Look, you've got a little boog going on there." I put my forefinger in her nose.

Joey swatted my hand. "Get away from me, mutant!"

"C'mon. For better or worse, boogs or no boogs—"

"Stop it!" Joey put her head on my collarbone.

I whispered to her, "But you know who really sucks? Finn."

"Really?" Joey said.

"Yes. We have to consider the possibility that Finn sucks."

"Yeah, maybe it's *her* that sucks."

"At least she sucks now. Like Patty Hearst sucked as a teenager. But maybe Finn won't suck someday," I said. "Now, what caused the suckage?"

"I said we needed to start talking about colleges and we'd have to visit a bunch this summer. She told me she doesn't want to go to college and we're forcing her, and all she wants to do is be a singer with Frigging Alex's band and experience harmony."

"Harmony, huh? I hate harmony."

"I used to like harmony, but now I hate it," Joey agreed.

"We have to accelerate this murder. Frigging Alex."

"We do. I'm just . . . I'm just worried all the time. Why is that?" She took a sip out of a nearby water bottle.

"Well, sweetheart, when you are married to someone considerably more attractive than you are, it creates a lot of anxiety."

Joey gagged, then spit several ounces of water on my neck.

36

I WATCHED THE confrontation unfold on the iPad. Goblin had been on-site, recording the event on his iPhone, and had sent it to me. I was so impressed with myself for opening the video that I almost forgot to actually watch it.

Oliver Shackley was a pleasant-looking, round-faced man approaching seventy. Despite having a net worth in the multiple billions, he lived in an unimposing colonial in Rockville and stuck to middle-class routines.

One of those routines was having lunch on Sundays with his family at Clyde's Tower Oaks Lodge, a large restaurant set in the midst of a suburban forest and decorated with the trappings of a hunting lodge—a very different setup from the Clyde's in Chevy Chase, which had a global travel theme.

Shackley had gathered his family—wife, children, and grandchildren—around a table in a large bar area, and afterward he showed his youngest grandchildren the exotic fish in the koi pond that runs along a stone entranceway outside of the restaurant.

Shackley held his grandson over the railing to get a closer look at the giant fish. The moment Shackley put down the little boy, Pacho appeared on-screen in his unmistakable Outback coat and fedora, followed by a cameraman and another assistant carrying a boom microphone. He approached Shackley, who was wearing a bright red Washington Nationals baseball cap and aviator sunglasses.

Goblin had been too far away to pick up many actual words, but I saw Pacho say something to Shackley, whose mouth twisted into the shape of rage. He pointed a finger at Pacho's chest, flung some angry words in his direction, and then turned to his gobsmacked family and gestured them toward the parking lot.

Among the words that came across clearly were the ones at the end of the ambush, when Goblin was able to get closer. "Do you deny doing business with the Saudis?" Pacho asked. "Time is running out, Mr. Shackley! This is your chance. Only a coward wouldn't take it!"

Mrs. Shackley, a slim but unpretentious woman with short black hair and a hard-set jaw, and the couple's three grown children—a son and two daughters in their thirties—scowled at Pacho and his crew as Pacho shouted questions at a besieged Shackley, who hustled his family into two SUVs. The Shackley grandchildren, about a half dozen of them under age fourteen, were visibly terrified, but footage of their wide eyes and open mouths surely would not make MyStream's final cut. Viewers would see only the growling billionaire in sunglasses, dodging questions and fleeing. The crew filmed the dark Shackley vehicles pulling onto Preserve Parkway, presumably aiming to make it look like a Mafia motorcade.

Pacho turned to his cameraman, who gave him a nod and a thumb's up. He'd gotten it all on film.

So had Goblin.

• • •

Pacho Craig's story was promoted on multiple media outlets on Monday morning, beginning at ten o'clock. It included quick clips of his confrontation with Oliver Shackley. The full MyStream report aired the following Friday and featured Pacho baiting Shackley and browbeating him with questions about the Saudis, and Shackley looking alternatively like a deranged Air Force colonel or a two-bit pornographer carrying around small children. Shackley looked scared, weak, and most of all, guilty.

Then the venue shifted into the MyStream studio. In his report, Pacho referred to the emails he'd been provided by Abigail Case and Elijah Jones. He displayed a few of them in redacted form. These convincingly demonstrated that Shackley and General Commodities indeed had extensive business dealings with the Kingdom of Saudi Arabia. He also indicated that he had obtained email exchanges between Adnan Sabbag and GC executives.

Then Pacho said the legalistic weasel words: "None of this proves, of course, that Oliver Shackley ordered the murder of Adnan Sabbag, but the threat that Sabbag's investigation posed to General Commodities and Saudi Arabia certainly leaves many questions unanswered."

Pacho went on to explain that the threat of Sabbag's inquiries related to the problems associated with the US Department of Defense relying on manufacturing materials from a country—Saudi Arabia—that under reasonable standards could be considered an enemy. "Should American businesses be so cozy with the country of origin of fifteen out of the nineteen 9/11 hijackers? Should Americans be doing unfettered and unsupervised business with a country that so savagely oppresses its people? And finally, who gained from the elimination of Adnan Sabbag?"

After the report, social media immediately lit up with demands for congressional investigations of Oliver Shackley's potential violations of the Foreign Corrupt Practices Act, and with indignant shouts about the conflicts created by a US company supplying our military with items sourced from a foreign country that was likely a party to hostilities against Americans. Suddenly, Congress wanted to talk about the Sabbag murder. Within hours, a senator issued a press release demanding hearings.

That whole weekend, I sat at home and periodically watched

television as Pacho made the rounds on the cable news shows, repeating his insipid mantra of "unanswered questions"—the get-out-of-jail-free card of investigative journalism, which allows reporters to make devastating allegations with the justification *we were just asking*.

37

KATE STARK HAD begun her career as an intern at the *Capital Incursion* about ten years earlier. I had given her a handful of assignments, which she'd executed professionally. My sense of her was that she was a solid journalist, but that the print world wasn't enough for her. Her face was very pretty in a computer-generated, symmetrical way, and there was a certain amount of star quality, which could mean only one thing in terms of her ultimate destiny: TV. I didn't begrudge her this ambition. That was where the world was going.

I didn't want to meet Kate at her offices at the AGN Network because I knew too many people there, so I met her at Morton's on Connecticut Avenue, where the food was decent, we'd have a better-than-average chance of being neglected by the servers, and it was one of the last places in the city where you could actually hear people talk.

Kate spotted me at a booth within eyeshot of the entrance and waved effusively. She was wearing a button-down shirt with a linen sport jacket and khakis. Her hair was shorter than it had been when we worked together and was more styled, as one would expect from a TV news star. I got up and hugged her.

She set down her two mobile phones, pointed at my chin, and said, "Look at all the gray coming in!"

"Thanks for the reminder," I said.

Kate shared with me some AGN gossip and lamented that viewers were increasingly interested in the activities of non-entities like the

Kardashians and less concerned about public affairs, unless it involved congressmen tweeting dick pics. Her show, *Kate Stark's USA,* was doing well enough that she was considered someone who might go supernova someday. At some point, she'd have to do something huge, take a big journalistic risk, or marry Keanu Reeves to boost her career to the next level. Contrary to what life's lottery winners say about how you make your own luck, you don't.

"What are you doing with yourself now, Sandy?" Kate asked.

"I'm doing some freelance writing, exercising a lot—biking, hiking, treadmill—helping my daughter prepare for college—"

"Geez, I still think of Finn as a baby."

"She still looks like one when she sleeps, but she doesn't act like one. A few nights ago, I asked her what time she was going to be home, and she told me I was no different from Pol Pot."

"Hah. Sounds like teenage logic."

"I do have about three million Cambodian skulls piled up in my backyard."

"How do you think you'll handle the empty nest?"

"I intend to disembowel myself with a grapefruit spoon," I said.

"Vivid. I miss your warped humor. You were always a sap when it came to your girls."

"Still am."

"What made you reach out to me?"

"I'm helping a friend with something. I want to discuss it with you, with a paranoid level of confidentiality. If you don't like it, promise me you'll drop it and not make the story the fact that I came to you."

This was a serious point. The news today is largely arithmetic, and the number you need to keep in mind is infinity—which, as we were all reminded in high school, isn't even a number at all. Because the news goes on 24/7 and the old "legacy media" is rapidly fading, reporters are increasingly turning toward a new type of coverage to fill the endless void: the behind-the-scenes conspiracy of spin. For most of my career, if I didn't like a story pitch, I just wouldn't do the story. Beginning in the 2000s, however, we'd come under increasing pressure to run stories about the people pitching us on doing stories, as if this, in and of itself, was a shocking conspiracy. My favorite *Incursion* headline of this era was "CIA Has Pattern of Secrecy and Deception." Well, yeah. This story was the byproduct of a CIA person pitching us on something we didn't like, so the reporter simply decided to burn the poor flack who'd called us.

"I would never do that," she said. With a reporter of her generation, of course, this was not a guarantee.

"I appreciate it, Kate. I assume you're well versed in all aspects of the #MeToo movement."

I already knew the answer to this. She had been surprisingly balanced during the Supreme Court nomination battle over Judge Brett Kavanaugh.

"Of course. I'm covering it," Kate said. "You saw I got dinged for basically asking a question during Kavanaugh." She'd gotten some pushback on social media for saying, *Some of the women making sexual claims against him are more credible than others.* That was a no-no in this climate, where *all* claims against a powerful white man are equally credible.

"What are your thoughts these days?"

"I think it's long overdue. So many media men are pigs. You never were, by the way. You were always one of the good guys, Sandy."

"Why? Because I wasn't mauling women at their desks? Do I deserve a parade for that?"

"Good point. Just giving credit where it's due."

"You made a remark during the Kavanaugh thing that I thought was interesting. You said something about women needing to find creative ways to handle harassment and assault. What did you mean?"

"I meant that the legal system isn't really working. On one hand, men are protected because it's a 'her word against his' scenario. On the other hand, I do think there are women making false claims. I don't have a specific answer. Women need to be more subversive. I guess that's what I'm saying."

"Are you in the mood to be subversive?"

"Oh my. What do you got?

"Do you know Pacho Craig?"

She rolled her eyes. "I've met him."

"Why the eye roll?" I asked.

"Look at what he's doing to journalism. He's the human embodiment of Twitter."

"He raped a friend's daughter."

For a split second, her shoulders slumped. Then she hardened again. "I'm not surprised."

"Really? Why not?"

"Guys like him that have a sudden surge of fame . . . they want everything they didn't have before, and they want it now."

I couldn't believe how casual she was about it. "You're one tough cookie," I said.

"Not really. But my adventures with being suddenly high-profile have taught me things about human nature that I'd rather not know. When did this happen?"

"A few months ago. She was an intern. This is a child—a young woman now—I used to carry around in a Snuggly on the beach. To make a long story short, we made the decision not to go to the authorities, for reasons I'm sure you understand."

"She'll be the one on trial," Kate said with a smirk.

"Right. She's a sensitive kid and just couldn't take the pummeling she'd get. So I've been looking into Pacho. I think he's into some naughty stuff. The sexual stuff I can't prove, but I've got a line on other things. He's a massive fraud."

"Since when is that a crime in the media?"

"It isn't. But I've got my eye on something you can use. He's been tangling with the wrong guy."

"Is that guy you, Sandy?"

"Somebody way bigger. Oliver Shackley."

"Pacho just did a report on the man. Hadn't heard of him before. I haven't seen it."

"You should. It's bullshit. Shackley will be fine. He's been looking for an excuse to show that the media have been wrongly out to get him, and now he has his trophy example. I'd like to see Pacho go down for what he's done to this girl I care so much about. And you can help if you'd like."

"It depends on what you've got. Will it make good television?"

"The best. And yours exclusively," I said.

"Who would I interview?"

"Pacho himself. He'd be thinking it's a valentine, but it'll be something very different."

"You have my attention. And my cell number."

38

IT WAS A slow news day, which propelled the media's coverage of the shooting at Pacho Craig's Georgetown house to the top of most newscasts. While the *Incursion* avoided coverage of digital celebrities, the paper couldn't avoid doing a hard news story on this, because it had happened in the district. Waking up early, I had held my breath and logged on to the *Incursion*'s website.

Shooters Attempt to Kill MyStream Reporter in Georgetown Home

By Claudia De Botton

Washington, DC — Gunshots rang out shortly after 11 p.m. yesterday at the home of MyStream news personality Paul Charles "Pacho" Craig.

According to Lt. Jack Walsh of the Metropolitan Police Department, gunmen wearing ski masks forced their way into Craig's O Street townhouse and fired multiple rounds at Craig, who says he chased out his assailants by rushing them and throwing kitchen knives at them.

"He put up one heck of a fight given the odds he was facing," said Walsh, who observed that Craig's living room and kitchen were "shot to bits."

Walsh would not get into specifics about a possible motive other than to say the authorities are looking into the subjects of recent MyStream stories Craig has done. Craig is known for doing short segments that feature ambushes of those against whom he is alleging malfeasance. In his most recent report, Craig confronted billionaire Oliver Shackley about ties between his company, General Commodities, and Saudi Arabia. It is widely believed that top Saudi leaders were complicit in the murder of journalist Adnan Sabbag.

A source close to Craig said the online star suspects that the motive for the Georgetown shooting may be tied to this recent report. The police would neither confirm nor deny that this is one of their leads.

Abigail called and told me about her meeting with Pacho after the shooting. Everything had been so hurried, we didn't have time to set up the video feed. They had met at a horse barn in Rock Creek Park, where Abigail had expressed her concern about what happened in Pacho's townhouse the night before. Pacho had explained that the man at the door said he was from Amazon.

"He asked me to keep my ear to the ground at General Commodities' offices," Abigail said. "And—get this—when I asked him how he hadn't been hit, he said his training had kicked in. What training?"

"Probably Green Beret Delta Force Navy SEAL Army Ranger Mossad MI6 Squadron," I said.

Abigail snickered. "Pacho said I'd be safest going to work as usual. Then he said whoever did it was very afraid they botched it."

"Seriously? That's a line from the second *Godfather* movie. Good Lord. This guy, with the drama."

"Well, Sandy, somebody did try to shoot him," Abigail said.

"I know. And there's about to be some more drama headed his way."

• • •

"Holy shit!" Kate Stark said, when I answered my mobile phone.

"How about that Pacho?"

"What do you know about this, Sandy?"

"I know it's your blockbuster. You get him for an exclusive interview, and I'll give you everything you need to blow him up. I don't want to say more on the phone."

39

THE NEXT DAY, I walked through the woods near my house, dictating some thoughts into an old mini-cassette player that I hadn't wanted Joey to overhear. As I rounded a large, sharp boulder, there she was, standing by a stream: Gretchen Kramer, the chinless wonder.

"Why, Gretchen Kramer! Of all the hiking trails in the Washington area, I happen to find you hissing in my own Eden," I said with a smile.

"I thought we might talk, Sandy."

"Stalking ex-colleagues, huh? That's a little CIA, isn't it? Are you carrying a Beretta with a muzzle suppressor? I thought we were supposed to be against the police state."

"I'm a reporter, not a spook," Kramer said.

"I forgot. When *we* stalk people, we're doing it for God."

"*We?* You're not a reporter anymore."

"Hey, I'm still writing," I said.

"That's not all you're doing."

I half covered my mouth as if to convey a conspiratorial revelation. "Would you mind helping me with the bag of lime in my car? It's best I don't say any more now."

"Come on, what are you up to?"

"First of all, I think you're under the impression that you have rights here. You don't."

"There have been database searches at the *Incursion* of some of the stories I've worked on," she said.

"People can't google without your permission?"

"I'm talking about our internal database, Sandy."

"People can't search for public domain articles anymore?"

"That kid Eva signed in to the database—"

"Are you spying on her?" I asked.

"You've always worked closely with her."

"Sorry, I'll start just working with young male reporters going forward. Better?"

"And you've been asking people at the paper about Adnan Sabbag's murder like you have a lead. What are you into?"

My heart skipped. How could she know?

"Every journalist in the world is asking about Sabbag."

"And I've been hearing things about a pretty girl."

Abigail Case. Gretchen was tailing me. Or somebody had seen me talking to Abigail and said something to Gretchen. Small town, Washington.

I didn't think I covered my surprise very well, so I embraced it. "Ah, my sultry affair."

"I never knew you to be a player, Sandy."

"Huge player. Everything that moves. You got me." I decided there was a diversionary benefit to her thinking I was screwing around. If she had really known what I was doing with Abigail, she would have said more.

"Look, I don't think you're being very transparent with me," Kramer said.

"Really? Who are your sources telling you things about me?"

"Come on, you know I can't tell you that."

"Gretchen, I don't think you're being very transparent with me."

"Dammit—"

"Gretchen, our trade wants to destroy people and things that much of the country loves. Then they want to call it transparency. Please! This is why our business is dead."

"Nice sermon, Father Petty. And that's a little simplistic, don't you think? Since when did you start caring about what *Duck Dynasty* cretins think?"

"And there you have it. You're no different from when Fox News calls people 'libtards.' Think about what has transpired here in the last sixty seconds. You, a journalist who is presumably opposed to the surveillance of private citizens, stalk and confront me in the woods near my home. You've clearly been monitoring my activities, including my association with a certain young woman, because you think I'm questioning power. In this case, that power would be you. So what you're really saying is that you support thuggery, provided it's aimed at people you don't like. Maybe we can go over to Bed Bath & Beyond and buy you a mirror."

"You're talking in circles because you know I'm on to something."

"You're an assassin, a troll. What is this fascination with me?"

"Oh please."

"Did you ever think that maybe some journalistic rigor would get you that Pulitzer? Instead of this skeet shooting?"

"My, you're so virginal. You've knocked off plenty."

"Yeah, but I had doubts that always restrained me. You're just trophy-hunting."

"So we're trolls with Ivy League degrees, I suppose."

"I went to Haverford. Not Ivy League," I said.

"Just as competitive, if not more so."

"Do you think you're the only one who can dig?" I asked.

"Conclusion, please."

"Here it is: whatever you're into, Gretchen, there's likely to be somebody out there who doesn't think it's as noble as you do."

"That goes both ways, Petty."

"Oh, Gretchen, does it ever."

"You know I'm going to get to the bottom of this."

"That's what my proctologist told me. Heh."

Kramer hissed. She whirled around and peeled off toward the trail-head on Bradley. When she went over a hill, she appeared to twist her ankle, and I heard her yell, "Fuck!"

It would be my only pleasure that day.

40

KURT CALLED ME later that afternoon, said hello, and then said nothing. I suggested we meet for a walk. He readily agreed.

I leashed Wagatha Christie, picked Kurt up, and drove to the Capital Crescent Trail. We parked and made our way along the asphalt portion. When we came to a tunnel, Kurt surprised me by lighting a joint.

He began to hand it to me, though he knew that I'd never partaken, even when all of us were teenagers. I waved him off. I was not cut out for the mellow experience. After a few more hits, Kurt crushed out the joint, and we exited the other side of the tunnel and marched on.

"You know what I've always wondered?" he said. "How you get people to tell their secrets."

"Why, you got one?"

"No. More wondering about you."

"I'm an open book," I said.

"You're a mystery. I figure that's how you get people talking. You understand where to poke."

"The thing is, Kurt, most people find their lives fascinating and assume that their sins are significant because, well, their sins *are* significant. That's where my leverage as a reporter comes in—exploiting that innate sense of guilt, of worrying the authorities have something on them. Any reporter who tells you he hasn't gotten a secret thrill out of scaring somebody is lying."

"That's what you're betting on with Pacho, isn't it?"

"Partially."

At MacArthur Boulevard, Kurt suddenly said, "Tell me about The Thing. Ninth grade. Did you really deliberately push your father down the stairs?"

I didn't answer.

"The stories that went around had you sticking your foot out and shoving him, like it was all planned."

I stared at him. So that was my legend? The truth had been far worse.

"Nat started in on one of his rants," I told Kurt after a moment of hesitation. "His voice would get low, like he was possessed. And all the venom about everybody shovin' it up his ass started flowing. My mom froze. I suddenly lost sight in one of my eyes. It had happened once before, after a Nat-attack. My mom took me to a doctor, who told me it was called 'hysterical blindness,' something that happened when people were paralyzed with fear. Anyway, Nat started growling about all the people plotting against him and how he got no support and how we're all spoiled little bastards. Without thinking, almost catatonic, I stepped toward Nat, put my left hand around his throat and my right hand under his crotch, and picked him up. Then I held him over the railing and dropped him down to the floor below, onto a glass table. There were pieces everywhere. Of the table," I added.

"Holy shit—"

"I was really businesslike about it. I didn't even rush him. I was like a zombie. He felt like a sack of flour I was heaving onto a pickup truck from a loading dock."

"Why didn't you ever tell people that? You would have been even more of a badass."

"Because afterward my mother was so upset that she took me to a doctor to see if I was a sociopath. And because I didn't feel badly that I did it. And to be honest, I don't feel badly even now."

And I didn't. I feel so much about so many things, but to this day I feel as if dropping Nat off the second floor of our fucking split-level onto that table was a totally proportional response. I guess my brain just couldn't take it anymore. I short-circuited.

I'd been waiting for him to die ever since, but as much as he hated being alive, it seemed like he was put on earth to give everybody cancer, so there was reason enough for him to live.

"I don't know, Kurt," I said. "I just don't feel anything about him anymore. He makes me feel . . . not human. Maybe my mother was right about the whole sociopath thing."

"Maybe you're more like your mother," Kurt said.

"Yeah. She felt too much. She just felt so much, she died of it. Her system had reached its limit, and she wasn't capable of leaving him. I navigated Nat. My mom just crashed into the rocks. Or eroded from the inside."

"That makes sense," Kurt said, squinting and rubbing his temples. "But even if there were twenty Fuses who devoted their lives to absorbing his rages and his constant care, they never could have cured him. He needed to exploit your conscience just to get the amount of attention you did give him. Your career was fueled by getting the bastards who get away with such awful stuff. Even your beef with me is a channeling of your beef with Nat—"

"You think so?"

"Come on, Fuse, you're not that complex. Don't flatter yourself."

Kurt was right. My vanity was that I was hard to read. "When you heard what I did to Nat back then, did you understand why?"

"Nobody did. It took us all more than a half-century to even scratch the surface. We all thought that you went nuts. That you overreacted. We saw Nat as a harmless guy, maybe a little moody."

"That was his genius, his theater of harmlessness," I said. "Each time I've seen him over the past forty years or so, The Thing is always in the air. I know he has no idea why I did it. And I know how much he hates me."

"I remember when we started hearing the stories about him getting thrown out of stores, chasing perfume girls. When we were grown up, I mean." Kurt shook his head rapidly, as if trying to sober himself up. "You used to talk about how your mom would one day get cancer from him, and then she did. We thought it was a coincidence. That you were nuts. You know, the Fuse with his exaggerations."

"Joey saw it," I said.

"Joey's a quiet genius. Nobody sees good and evil like Joey. She saved your life."

"I tell her that all the time."

"And you saved hers."

"No, I didn't. She was fine."

"Joey was a tomboy, always in that damned tree. Then you guys started up and . . . she blossomed. She got involved with more stuff, talked more, had more guys noticing. The girls who are always worshipped, like Angie, come to hate men for their slobbering admiration. The girls who suddenly get it aren't quite sure what to do with their power."

"Tell me, did anything ever happen between you and Joey in college? You know, when her family came down to Rehoboth in the summers, and you guys were also there?"

"What makes you ask that?" Kurt said.

"I have a genius for catastrophe."

"We made out at the boardwalk . . . once," Kurt admitted after a beat. "Going into junior year in college."

"Motherfucker!"

I turned to head back, yanking Wags's leash to hurry her along. Was I ever wrong about Kurt? Seriously. When it came to anything awful happening to me or anything good happening to this anti-Christ, was I ever wrong?

Kurt opened his mouth to speak.

I cut him off. "Don't tell me it was nothing. Don't tell me that. These things are everything to me. And yeah, I'm judgmental and unforgiving."

"She didn't want me, Fuse. She was using me," Kurt said.

"Using you for what?"

"She was feeling good about herself, I guess. Enjoying college. More than you were. She used me just for . . . I don't know, for something stupid to do. After a little bit, we stopped."

"You probably kidnapped her. Like Patty Hearst."

"What the hell is with you and Patty Hearst?" Kurt asked.

The guy made out with my wife, and now he was asking me about *my* issues? I wanted to grab a serrated knife, cut Kurt's lips off, and leave him with a big skull smile. Let's see how he made out with chicks with only those choppers beaming out at the world.

"Neither of you ever said anything to me," I said.

"I'm sure it was because we both knew that you're a purist. Sensitive about that stuff. And in love with Joey. You'd only been apart for a year or so, and you've never been one of those let-it-go types. Even though nobody really knew what happened with Nat, we knew something that people on the outside didn't know."

"And what was that?"

"That you didn't kick your father's ass because you were tough. You did it because you were vulnerable. Uniquely so. Even the badass shit you pulled in your job was a reaction against vulnerability, not sociopathy. God knows what else you've done in the name of punishing bullies."

"And you swear that's all that happened with Joey?" I asked.

"Yeah. The only chick who ever used me. She wanted *you,* though. Most women want the guy who glides through life. Joey wanted the guy who hacked through it with a machete."

"If you say so."

"I don't say so. Look at the facts. Look at where she's been for forty-three years, minus a little gap in college."

At the moment, I could only see the two of them on the boardwalk at Rehoboth.

"Come on, what did you do in college when you and Joey were on the outs?" Kurt asked.

"Not much worth talking about."

"But there were other girls."

"Yeah."

"And you . . . you know?" Kurt made a gesture with his fist suggesting pounding.

"I'm not getting into that." I mimicked his gesture.

Then Kurt stared at me in an intense and curious way. "You didn't really make an effort to get serious with anybody else besides Joey, did you? Like you always thought you'd be back together any minute."

"I don't want to get into it," I repeated. I was intensely uncomfortable.

"You are from another planet, I swear. Now don't go telling Joey we talked about any of this," Kurt said.

"Why not?

"You'll look like a ween, Fuse."

"I *am* a ween, Kurt."

"Well, just don't."

"I guess you're not going to ask me about, you know, me and Angie?" I asked suggestively.

Kurt laughed. "No, I'm not. You're such a sap that, if you actually did it, you would have confessed in three seconds."

"So I guess I'm not a sociopath?"

"No, Fuse."

"What about you and Bonita Weller and the other girls? The whole truth."

Kurt looked me dead in the eye. "I've told you the whole truth."

"Not from the beginning."

"We screwed around," Kurt said. "Any suggestion she made during the extortion negotiations about it being unwanted is horse shit. Maybe the last time we did it, it was a bit of a hate-screw."

"So you got anybody waiting in the wings now?" I asked.

"That's not how it works, Fuse."

"How does it work, Kurt?"

"Propinquity."

"I'll have to google that."

"It means somebody nearby," Kurt said.

"Something tells me you're a tad more selective than that."

"Of course I am. You should have seen her though. Haven't you ever seen anybody who made you walk into walls?"

"The entire female gender makes me walk into walls. It's not exactly an aphrodisiac. Hard to pick somebody up after your head just bounced off a door."

"Look, I was an asshole. Not a criminal."

I felt badly about roughing him up, so I brought things back to guy talk. "I kissed Haddon once."

"You kissed Haddon?"

"Yeah, I did."

"Wait a minute. She's not the one you gave the panda?"

Now it was my turn for shame. "Yeah, she was."

Kurt slapped his forehead and laughed. "Oh, good Lord! The Fuse got her a fucking panda! Oh, dude, she didn't want the panda!"

"I know she didn't, and yet here I am, some old guy still wondering what happened on that stupid college weekend. She didn't want the panda—I mean, she just ignored it—and she didn't want me. Rejection. There is no other word for it. I'm telling you that Bonita Weller *did* want the panda. And what did you do? You screwed her brains out on the sofa in your office and dropped her like Introductory Macroeconomics!"

"Guess it's too late to get her a panda," Kurt said in a very, very sober tone.

"You've never been dumped, have you?"

Kurt twisted his mouth to the side. "A girl I was seeing at Stanford left to study abroad. Japan."

We had arrived back at my Jeep. "Get the fuck in the car."

When Kurt got in and closed the door, I took Wagatha Christie's head before I opened the rear hatch. "Wags, up until now that man has gone through life on a pass."

She stuck her tongue out and jumped up on me. No matter what I told this creature, she always seemed to understand.

41

I WENT HOME and showered. When I got out, Joey was getting back from a yoga class and ready for her own shower. I was numb from my conversation with Kurt. I knew I couldn't keep quiet about the Rehoboth make-out forever, but I decided against bringing it up right now. For one thing, Joey would have reamed out Kurt, and this would have caused him to distrust me at a time when I needed peace between us. For another, I had made a graceless attempt to kiss Haddon way back when, and I was afraid of looking like a sniveling dork. I needed some time to process this.

The funny thing was that, as long as Joey and I had been together, we had never discussed our dating activities during the times we were apart. I think it was because we both knew nothing good could come from it. We weren't very modern in that way.

"How was your walk?" Joey asked, turning the faucet.

"Good," I said. It was not good.

"What did you guys talk about?"

"Haddon," I said. We had not talked about Haddon that much.

"Really? What about her?"

"The massive affairs we've both had with her."

"Oh, great. I knew she and Kurt did it at one point."

"Sure, neither of them would want to skip over anybody."

"God forbid. When did you and Haddon get it on?" Joey asked, knowing damned well nothing had ever happened between us.

"When we hiked in the woods. You were out."

"Great. How was it?"

"She said I was fantastic. I did some cool stuff with twigs."

"You're such a loser."

"Chicks like losers," I said.

"I clearly must."

"Think I should use moisturizer after I shave?" I asked.

"It's a big decision," Joey said.

"Did you ever notice how when a dude shaves on TV commercials, he always looks at his face in the mirror and gives himself a confident nod, like he's really thrilled with his freshly shaved face?"

Joey turned off the shower. "I have noticed that, yes."

"The dude also usually has a hot chick standing next to him, stroking his face and conveying ecstasy at being in the presence of his epidermis. We should do that more. You and me."

"Oh, yes, that would be a nice activity," Joey said, making a towel turban on her head.

I shaved a strip of my face and winked like a game show host in the mirror. Joey stroked the shaved portion and covered her lips with her fingers in mock awe of the sexiness she had just beheld. I lifted the can of Edge, looked dead in the mirror, and in a pitchman's baritone, said, "Edge Shave Gel. For the man who likes to grin at his face after he shaves it."

Joey gazed into the nonexistent camera and said, "And for a woman who's equally a cretin."

We both gave the mirror a thumbs-up, and I added, "Smooth skin. Huge penis. Try Edge today."

"Gross," Joey said.

I was feeling good that I hadn't brought up Law of the Universe #1: Kurt-Gets-Everything-He-Wants, the Rehoboth edition.

"What is it about Haddon that all the men love?" Joey asked. "Do *you* want her?"

Good question. And I wasn't sure the answer made much sense to me. "She has a quality of bringing me back to when we were young and how my whole life was ahead of me. I met her before you. I'm just not sure if it has much to do with *her.* Honestly, I don't like very much about her as a person. With you, I like almost everything."

"Do you remember when you decided that?"

"Yes."

"When? Did it involve the tree behind Western?" Joey asked.

"No. We were at that roller skating rink."

"I couldn't skate very well. I remember that."

"'Lady Marmalade' was on the speaker system, and everybody was circling around on their skates. Haddon was zooming all over the place. It was her world. Everybody was showing how in-the-know they were because they knew the translation of the *Voulez-vous* lyrics—"

"What do they mean again?"

"Something like 'Do you want to sleep with me,'" I said.

"Right. Of course Haddon knew them. Yeah, we thought we were quite continental."

"Well, Joe, I knew *I* wasn't. Anyhow, everybody was zooming around. Kurt, Angie, Haddon. You were slinking around the edge of the rink, and I was just trying to stay upright by holding on to the wall. Then the song ended and another one came on. A slow one. 'I'm Not Lisa' by Jessi Colter."

"That's right. Everybody got off the floor and went to the soda fountain."

"Right. And I figured that would be my time to learn how to skate, when everybody was gone and nobody could see what a tool I was," I said.

"Didn't I come to get you?"

"You did. I managed to stand up. And we went around a few times. You held me by the elbow until the song was over and everybody came back."

"I wasn't Lisa. I wasn't Haddon," Joey said.

"No. If you were Haddon, I'd still be on my ass writhing around a bench."

"What if Haddon told you she wanted a go of it now with you, and I said okay?"

"No way. I have you. There's no earthly way to do better than you. Besides, I wouldn't want to be another chapter in her long book."

"I'm not a chapter in your book?" Joey asked.

"No. You *are* the book."

42

"WHO'S THERE?" NAT asked when he heard me opening the door. I'd dropped by to deliver some mail that was addressed to him, but at my home address. He had probably directed it to my house so I'd have to bring it over to him.

"It's me."

"Who?"

"Scarlett Johansson."

"No, it's not. She sounds different."

"It's Sandy."

Nat glanced up at me from his chair. "Nobody knows what I go through."

"No, no, they don't."

"That nurse they sent from the agency to check my blood pressure. Not exactly a turn-on."

"Not supposed to be," I said.

"Suppository?" Nat said.

"Supposed to be."

"You don't talk clear."

"I'm not very articulate."

"That's why you don't have the money like your friend. Kurt Rossiter."

Kurt, he remembers perfectly now.

"Kurt's father's family has had money since the Coolidge administration," I said.

"He's probably very supportive of his parents."

"He gets three-quarters of a million a year from his trust, on top of what he makes from the think tank. I'd be supportive too."

"I'm gonna kill myself," Nat said.

"You'll live forever. You're invincible."

"You can't see me?"

"I said *invincible*. It means you can't be destroyed. Not invisible."

"No, it's over for me."

"You spew it all out, and then you're fine."

"What about that number on that program *Friends*?" Nat said.

"What number?"

"The brown-haired one. Rachel. She's a callback. You never had any confidence with girls. With the way you looked? What's wrong with you?"

"How much time do you have?"

"Your kid doesn't visit me."

"Joey won't let her."

"Why not?"

"Last time she visited, you asked if she had any girlfriends for you."

"I did? That was just kibitzing."

"She's still a kid, Dad! She came home crying, asking if it was normal for a grandfather to ask his granddaughter to fix him up with a friend."

"Another one who doesn't know what I go through. No frame of reference. I don't have insurance."

"Sure you do. How else would we get the money after we smother you?"

"Uncle Zeke's kids are always around him. They're some kids, I'll tell you. I always took care of everybody."

"I took care of somebody earlier today. If you hear something going on out back tonight, it's just me, burying the body."

"You have to look out for yourself."

"That's what I'm thinking."

"You know, you were always a winner," Nat said. Then he started to cry.

Nat did this sometimes—said something nice out of nowhere after a torrent of lunacy. I took a few steps toward him and kissed him on his forehead. In that moment, I loved him.

• • •

On the drive home, my cell phone rang. I plugged in my earphones.

"Sandy," the voice said. "This is Steven Schlein. From Senate Judiciary." Of course, the sound emanated only from my left earpiece. God forbid they both should work.

"Of course, Steven. What's up?" Schlein was a prominent staffer at the Senate Judiciary Committee and a source I had used both on and off the record.

"I got a very strange call. I wanted to give you a heads-up about it."

My fingers and toes went cold. Just a sick feeling. "Okay."

"If I tell you this, it won't get back to your paper?" he asked.

"No. You're a confidential source, as always."

"I got a call from one of your colleagues. Gretchen Kramer."

My instinctive anxiety had served me well. "Yes," I said.

"She asked me . . . well . . . she asked if you had threatened me when you were working on that story about the election hearings a few months ago. You had been somewhat critical of our probe."

"If I'd threatened you?"

"Yeah."

"Well, did I threaten you?"

"No, of course not," Schlein said.

"Did you tell her that?"

"Yes. But she kept pressing. It was really weird."

"Don't worry about it, Steve. She's push-polling you," I said as if I wasn't worried. I was worried.

"Why would she do that?"

"It's a long and stupid story, and I don't want to drag you into something sticky. It has nothing to do with you. Someday we'll have lunch and talk about it."

"Okay. Sure was strange."

"I'm sure it was. And Steve?"

"Yeah?"

"I would never threaten you, but if you tell anybody about this call, I'll have you killed."

Schlein snickered, and we hung up.

Ah, Gretchen, Queen of the Trolls! She was pushing her crusade against me plausibly into the zone of *actual malice*—the standard for defamation. It was one thing to ask a source unpleasant questions; it was quite another to recklessly plant false notions to the point where that source felt the need to alert the targeted party. For the first time, I began to think the window on the Kramer's career might be closing. A few more things needed to fall into place and then, as they say in England, "Good night, Vienna."

Part IV
DEEPFAKE

"Only thing that matters in a murder case is did the fellow who's dead need to be killed, and did the right sonofabitch do the job."

—MARTIN CLARK, *THE LEGAL LIMIT*

43

MY MOBILE PHONE rang. *Nat.*

I would rather be dragged over hot gravel by a pickup truck than answer his call. I'd have to endure the ceaseless wave of rants and then days of emotional recovery until the next call. Maybe today he wouldn't be having a heart attack, but would just be cutting me out of his will—a threat I had been hearing since the Vietnam era. Omar would detect my pent-up rage and offer up some candied walnut about forgiveness. How many times did I have to tell him that I didn't believe in forgiveness—I believed in avoidance.

"Well, hello," I said, Mr. Cheerful.

"Sandy, this is Omar." Concerned voice.

"Yes, sir," I said.

"I'm sorry to tell you . . . but Nat did not wake up this morning."

"He's still sleeping?" *Good,* I thought. He couldn't hurt anybody in his sleep.

"No. He passed, Sandy."

"Who passed? Passed what?"

"Nat did. Nat passed."

This call had been on its way since the Kennedy presidency, but I never thought it would come. I figured Nat would be with me forever, like polio.

"How?" I asked.

"He just didn't wake up."

"Did you hear anything?"

"No. I put him to bed like normal, God rest his soul."

"We'll see about that."

"What?"

"Nothing. Where is he, Omar?"

"He's home."

"Are you sure, you know, he's . . . you know?" I asked.

"Yes."

"How do you know?"

Omar sighed. "He has no pulse."

"Maybe it's just low blood pressure."

"No."

"What do we do now? Do I call a funeral home? Does there need to be an autopsy?" I asked.

"Not unless you want one or something fishy is suspected. Do you want to come over?"

"No, I don't."

"You must forgive, Sandy."

"How's your diabetes, Omar?"

"The medicine seems to help, the doctor says. But it's strange—there's no history of diabetes or high blood pressure in my family."

Of course there's not, nimrod. Nobody has a history of anything until they come into contact with Nat.

"There's a funeral home in Rockville. I'll call them." I hung up and called the funeral home. The woman who answered asked me a few questions and said they'd go get Nat. I asked how they could tell if somebody's dead.

"You mean you're not sure?" she asked.

"Well, his aide said he was dead."

"Did the aide take his pulse?"

"Yeah."

"And?" the poor woman asked.

"Dead."

"That's what we usually go with," she said.

"Is there another test?"

"Test?"

"Yeah. What if there's a way to weasel your way out of the whole pulse thing?" I asked. "Like a loophole."

"There's no loophole, Mr. Petty."

"Okay, then. You sound like you know."

"I'll tell you what," she said sweetly. "We'll check, and if you don't hear from us, then just assume your father has passed."

"Good strategy."

I let Omar know the funeral home was coming.

I thought about the whole sociopath debate I'd had with my mother after I dropped Nat over our railing. I'd never been able to shake the terrible notion that it might be true, that I was a soulless golem roaming the earth. In my heart, on a cellular level, I had come to believe I was an unsupportive child, deserving of my suffering. No amount of rational argument or therapy would ever convince me otherwise. I was the child Nat Petty constructed, and the only way to deal with Nat was to develop a pocket of soullessness.

I didn't call Joey right away. I remembered her saying something about coming home after a doctor's appointment. I did about twenty minutes' worth of weights downstairs and then got on the ground and started my abdominal crunches.

I heard footsteps on the stairs, and Joey stuck her head over the railing. "Wanna go somewhere for lunch when you're done?"

"Sure," I said.

"Café Deluxe?"

"Great."

"How was your appointment?" I asked, mid-crunch.

"Fine. They just gave me eye drops for my allergies."

"Good."

"What did you do?" she asked.

"Not much. Nat's dead."

"No, he's not." Joey turned her head to the side, studying my expression. Of all the loony things I had said about Nat over the years, this was the most implausible. I had never joked that he was dead, largely because I didn't think nature would ever allow it.

"Omar called and said he was."

Joey sat down on the steps looking serious, recognition flickering on her face. I did another crunch. "He did?"

"Yes."

"What did he say?"

"Nat's dead," I said.

"No, he's not. How does he know, Fuse?"

"He said he had no pulse."

"Is that the only way to know he's dead? It couldn't be," Joey asked.

"That's what I said. I called the funeral home and told them to go get him. They'll probably know how to figure it out."

"Are you okay?"

"Why wouldn't I be okay?"

"Because, Fuse, your dad died."

"No, he didn't."

"Why would Omar say it?"

"Nat probably paid him to see what we'd do. He'll hop out of the hearse and tell us how the Kennedys were very supportive of their parents."

"What's with him and the Kennedys?"

"He's always compared us to the Kennedys," I said.

"What's the comparison?"

"I don't know. Maybe we're a dynasty and never realized it. Wanna start a dynasty?"

"We're not the Kennedys."

"Don't tell Nat that. He thinks he's a great patriarch."

"Maybe he can hang out with Joe Kennedy in hell." Joey covered her mouth. "I'm sorry. That was unkind. I shouldn't have said it."

"Wanna do it?" I said, smarmy grin and all.

"No, we're going to lunch."

"I just lifted weights. I'm huge."

"I see that. And it's very tempting," Joey said.

"We could do it, then go to lunch."

"I think there's something wrong with you."

"It took forty-some years for you to figure that out?" I said.

"I suspected."

"Let me know if Nat calls."

44

JOEY INVITED A group of my friends and a few of Nat's relatives over to our house after a very small graveside memorial service. Omar was there too, talking to people about forgiveness, even though I had explicitly told Omar that if he ever raised the issue of forgiveness with me again, I'd cut off his final paycheck.

Nat's brother, my Uncle Barry—the son of a bitch who was always shovin' it up my father's ass—showed up and, God bless him, told me, "You've had a rough ride." It was the nicest thing anyone had ever said to us about Nat.

Uncle Barry looked like Alan Arkin's younger brother and had a habit of talking out of the side of his mouth as if he were giving you a tip on a horse. He had always liked me, and I'd always liked him. A streetwise fellow who really did like to play the horses, he'd given me what was probably the best piece of advice I ever got. I was sixteen at the time, and it had shaped my worldview.

We'd gone to a diner to talk about colleges, and he'd asked, "Did your mother ever say you could be anything you wanted to be?"

I said yes.

He said, "That's bullshit—you can't."

I was stunned. This was the 1970s, when everything was flowery promises about empowerment and the sky being the limit. I said, "I can't?"

"No," Uncle Barry said. "All you can do is make the most of the abilities you have and see if the universe cooperates. In this life, it's about doing the best that's doable. If you're a genius with a lot of luck, you'll rule the world. If you're a genius with no luck, you're screwed. If you're a moron with a lot of luck, you can do pretty well. And if you're a moron with no luck, well, we know what happens there. All we know now is that you're a pretty smart kid. We don't know the rest."

The words "the best that's doable" have never left me.

I watched from across the living room as Uncle Barry's wife, Aunt Arlene, flitted about. Tiny, and still sporting the bob haircut that figure skater Dorothy Hamill wore in 1976, Arlene was a sweet and harmless little bird. Whenever the subject of Nat came up, she would hold up her palms and them push them down in a gesture that said, *Enough already.*

Uncle Barry stood beside me, slicing himself a piece of cheese. He slipped it onto a cracker, started chewing like it was going out of style, and then turned to me and grinned.

My uncle also liked me because of how accepting I was of his son, my cousin Mitchell, who was gay, and because of a related and unspoken incident in our family. Mitchell and I had been close growing up, and while there were many differences between us, we shared an introversion that made us content to stay home, interpret Beatles lyrics, or just read. Nobody in our world really knew straight from gay in the 1970s, and I remember my mom describing him as *you know, artistic.*

The summer before I went to college, Mitchell was beaten up in DC by three suburban yahoos who thought beating up gay people was fun. Mitchell, who was a year older than me, was hospitalized at George Washington University. His jaw was wired shut. It was terrible, and the cruelty of that particular act struck me deeply. I was all for killing terrorists and understood the complexity of violence in international conflicts, but harming a person who had done nothing to provoke anyone else? I couldn't find a place for it.

In addition to my tight crowd of Kurt, Angie, Haddon, and Joey, I also had a shadow group of friends who were the rough boys of Montgomery County, which simply meant they lived closer to Rockville and were not necessarily college bound. The guys who hurt Mitchell were from the Silver Spring area, and I was able to track them down by asking some questions of Mitchell's friends. Then, wearing ski masks bought from Sunny's Surplus, the rough boys and I systematically hunted down the three thugs, knocked them around pretty hard with baseball bats, and made the one who had a car hand over his keys. We promptly sold the car to some city lads in Adams Morgan who happened to be in the stolen auto trade. We'd used the money to help Mitchell with his medical bills.

"Question for you, Sandy," Uncle Barry said, still chewing his cheese. "Did you ever figure out what the fuck was actually wrong with him? You know, your father. You're an investigative reporter, for Christ's sake."

Kurt and Angie overheard the question, began laughing, and sidled up closer to hear my response. It was nice to see them laugh.

Uncle Barry gave the Rossiters a look of reverence, as they were the biggest celebrities here. I vaguely recalled Uncle Barry once referring to Kurt as "a bit of a roué," a term for a womanizer that I had to look up.

"Believe me, Uncle Barry, I looked into it," I said.

I remember my mom once persuading Nat to go to a psychiatrist. A few days later, the shrink was in our house, telling us we were all selfish and uncaring narcissists. That really broke her down. She was desperate to be seen as a good person.

"I talked to countless psychiatrists over the years," I continued. "I even wrote a story on the National Institute of Mental Health as a way to find more out about Nat. The best I could figure out is that it was some version of bipolar disorder and borderline personality disorder. Highly functioning, of course."

"Borderline? What's that?" Uncle Barry asked. "Like they're from Mexico?"

"No, on the borderline between psychotic and neurotic," I explained. "Someone who is pretty close to being insane, but they can also function, so you can't commit them. They're considered impossible to treat. Some shrinks won't take them on. Borderlines don't believe they have a problem. Same with many paranoid schizophrenics. They believe the problem is the people in their lives. People plotting against them. It has something to do with a fear of abandonment."

"Devastating!" Aunt Arlene said, breezing by.

"Abandonment?" Uncle Barry said. "All Nat ever did was chase people away who wanted to help."

"All he ever did!" Aunt Arlene echoed.

"But it took decades," I said. "His real genius was getting sympathy by playing into people's instincts to be, well . . . decent. Decent people want to help people who are crying, who fall down, who have heart attacks. That was Nat's power. It's strange—even though they say it's an illness, he had enough control to regulate it when he had to. He had brief relationships with a few women after Mom. They were, without exception, nurses or social workers—women who needed to take care of people and who maybe thought they deserved abuse."

Uncle Barry shook his head. "What the hell causes it? I don't have it. Our parents were nice people. None of us knew where he came from."

"None of them knew where he came from!" Aunt Arlene said.

"Nobody knows," I said. "They don't know if it's something to do with parenting. They don't know if it's a chemical or if the person was dropped on their head."

My uncle threw up his hands. "So what do you do?"

"You stay the hell away from them," I said.

"Not easy," Uncle Barry said.

Aunt Arlene said, "Impossible!"

"That's the key point." I threw up my own hands. "Everybody has an answer except the people who have to deal with it. Nat's and my mom's old friends, you'll notice, aren't here. That's because they were always putting their arms around me and telling me, 'Your father loves you' and 'Let me tell you about a disagreement I once had with my mother over a key lime pie and how we worked it out.'"

Uncle Barry hugged me. "And now, young man, you go live your life. Being miserable to try and make your father happy helped no one. Enough! That man took decades of your life away. He may as well have kidnapped and brainwashed you."

"Like Patty Hearst," I said.

"Sickening!" Aunt Arlene said.

"You've got a lot going in your favor. Great wife. Great kid. Good career," Uncle Barry said.

Aunt Arlene added, "It really is lovely!"

As my uncle began chatting with Kurt and Angie, a woman walked in the front door: Jill Hirshon, who lived two doors down from Nat.

Speak of the devil, and she shall arrive.

I didn't remember inviting her—nor did Joey—but I wasn't in the mood for a fight, so I didn't say anything. She had a mournful face with basset hound eyes, and I had a real fear of people like this who knew Nat.

"Your father loved you, Sandy, " Jill said, walking toward me.

Joey, who'd been retrieving bottled water from the basement, stepped closer, her eyes flashing red.

"He really wished you could have spent more time together, Sandy," Jill continued. "He didn't understand why you couldn't find it in your heart to do that. He was a lost soul without you."

Joey put her palm up to Jill's face and showed her teeth. "From the grave that motherfucker is still working it," Joey said. "Jill, get the hell out of here now and never come back."

"What did I say?" the basset hound whined, as Joey propelled her out the door.

Soon after, Frigging Alex showed up wearing a suit from a thrift shop, gave me an awkward hug, and said he was sorry about Nat. He appeared to have trimmed his hair a bit, too. He was very gentle with Finn, tucking her hair away from her face and holding her hand. After a quick huddle in my study, Joey and I agreed that we would postpone murdering him—but we didn't rule out planting heroin in his car and alerting the Montgomery County Police.

Haddon, holding a glass of wine and wearing a black turtleneck that served as a soft pedestal for her gorgeous head, sweetly approached me and said, "It must be hard for you."

"No," I said. "It's easy. The last half-century was hard."

"You have an interesting way of looking at things, Fuse."

"I'm an interesting guy, Haddon. Did you know I was once a rodeo cowboy?"

"You're terrible."

"You love me."

"I do."

She hugged me, and I thought about the stupid panda. I waved to Joey and gave her a broad, cheesy Dean Martin–style grin.

• • •

After everybody else but Haddon and the Rossiters had gone, Joey implemented her idea to cheer me up—and the Rossiters too. She'd made a lineup of songs that were popular when we all got to be friends, mostly from 1975.

Haddon played around with Joey's iPhone and set it onto a larger device with a speaker. She hit play, and Captain & Tennille's "Love Will Keep Us Together" came on. Haddon persuaded Kurt and me to get off our asses, although I loathed dancing. Kurt was eating a barbecue chicken sandwich as he danced and still managed not to look like a dork. Joey danced close to Haddon, and Angie swayed, moving barely an inch as she stared out the window into the blackness, as if searching for her life.

The mood turned to bedlam when "Ballroom Blitz" came on, and we all just ran in place or around the pool table. Haddon actually remembered how to dance to "The Hustle" and led us in that big hit by Van McCoy and the Soul City Symphony. When Frankie Valli's slow number "My Eyes Adored You" came on, Kurt was standing next to Joey and, perhaps seeing Angie's withdrawn disposition, took Joey's hands and started dancing with her. Yes, I felt a primitive rush of stress hormones, but now was not the occasion for expressing where my mind was going.

Rather than slit my wrists, I did something better: I took Haddon's hands and began slow dancing with her. All I could do was get lost in the fourteen-year-old Haddon of more than four decades ago, and thought for a nanosecond that if Joey ran off with Kurt after Angie divorced him, maybe I could make a go of it with Haddon after all.

I noticed Angie's eyes drifting toward me from the sinking depths of the sofa and I reached out for her. Janis Ian's "At Seventeen" wept through the speakers. Although the song was a declaration of war against girls like the one Angie had been, I realized that for the first time in her bubbled life, as she was catapulting through middle age, Angie had found herself to be life's ugly duckling, like the girl in the song. Clearly, the savaging of Angela Pfeiffer Rossiter was a shock to every cell in her body. She just needed to dance with a man who had not done this to her, and at that moment I was just content to possess a Y chromosome.

• • •

Later, when everyone was truly gone, Finn found me in my study, staring at the crime books I had collected over the years from my research for *Incursion* stories. I thought she was going to ask me about them, but then she said, "Why did your dad hate you so much?"

"He didn't hate me. He hated the world, and for some reason that didn't drain him. It made him stronger."

"It didn't make everyone else stronger."

"No, kiddo, it didn't."

"You should have gotten an iPhone so you could block his calls—not that old flipper thing you have. I could also text you if you had an iPhone."

"If you'll go with me to the mall, I'll get an iPhone. You'll need to teach me how to use it."

Finn's eyes popped, and I wondered if she wanted something from the store, maybe a new phone case or set of earbuds. "Do you think you did the right thing, avoiding your dad as much as you did?" she asked.

This was a very sophisticated question, I thought, even beyond what I saw as her emotional maturity. "Well, I've never regretted one moment of the time I spent with you and Mom. You're everything I've cracked you up to be, and more. I saw Nat as much as I thought I had to, but no more. It was the best of my bad options, but it doesn't mean I feel good about it."

The next morning, Finn and I went to Montgomery Mall and got an iPhone at the Apple store. The place was a total madhouse, which made me more anxious than interviewing terrorists. I didn't understand one thing the kid with the rectangular glasses told me. Finn dealt with him instead.

We practiced texting when we got home. Finn was uncharacteristically delighted with my capacity for growth. She also showed me emojis.

"I like how the poop emoji is smiling," I said. "Like it's happy to be poop. As if it's accepted its role in the world, and it's fine with that."

"You think too much, Dad."

Then I brought up a subject that I was having a hard time finding my way into. "What's Tinder?" I asked.

Finn scrunched up her face. "It's an app people use to hook up."

"So, for sex?" I asked.

"Dad!"

"Am I wrong?"

"People use it to meet, and then what happens is whatever they want to happen."

"I hope everybody can be careful," I said. By *everybody,* I meant Finn.

"Do you think men are animals?" Finn asked.

"Not all men. But I do think both men *and* women have some animal in them. But men are usually stronger . . . bigger, which can make those animals more dangerous. That's why fathers worry about daughters. Sons get their hearts broken, but daughters, you know, can—"

"You don't have to worry about me so much," Finn said.

"Yes, I do." I felt an apple swell in my throat, and tears began to form. "You're so . . . small." I barely got out the word "small."

"You are too," she said, leaning on my shoulder.

"I'm average size," I said. "Maybe an inch shorter than average."

"That's not what I mean. You're more like a girl in some ways. You act goofy and people think you're tough, but it seems like people are always dropping you and breaking you."

I never envisioned those particular words, and in that order, would find a path out of Finn's mouth. I wiped my eyes.

"Dad, do you believe in God?" She bit her upper lip the way she'd done as a small child.

"Where is this coming from?"

"I don't know. I'm just thinking about how hard some people have it, like in these horrible countries that sell children as slaves. Then you look at some of the people around here who have everything and just keep building bigger houses."

"The truth is that I've always believed in God, but I don't claim to know how He works or why He does what He does. Or She. Whatever. I sure don't believe God rewards good and punishes evil."

"Do you ever talk to God? In private?" Finn asked.

"Maybe a few times. I talk to Bob Dylan more."

"Who's he?"

"A songwriter who was big when I was growing up."

"Why do you talk to him?"

"I never thought God was too interested in me. But I had it in my head when I was a teenager that Dylan and I would get along. That maybe he'd hear what I had to say."

"Isn't that a little crazy?"

"What's crazier?" I said. "Trying to talk to a guy I know is real, or to a supreme being I'm not sure really exists?"

"But God can do more than Bob Dylan can."

"Yes, but I can't listen to him whenever I want, and I have no idea what he's thinking."

"Well, maybe I should try to talk to Lady Gaga."

"Better than Kim Kardashian," I said.

I thought about what else I could tell her, but while the words were on shelves in my brain, they couldn't make their way through that apparatus and onto my tongue and out into the world.

I thought about free will and appetite, about how she could do with a boy what she wanted and on her terms. I thought about how Normal was a big region, and she didn't need to define it in the terms of a promiscuous culture. I recalled an interview I once did with an unmarried US senator rumored to be gay, whom I'd known for years. He had come to trust me and asked if he could go off the record on the matter of sex. I agreed. He told me that he was as straight as an arrow but "never had any luck with sex," and long ago he'd concluded that "it simply isn't worth the trouble." I thought that was plausible—and terrific. He had managed to figure out what *for him* was normal and wasn't hurting anyone, and he had made as much peace with himself on the subject as he could.

This is what we should want for our children and ourselves, I thought, but I wasn't smart enough to assemble it in any cogent way.

Instead I just said, "Love you, Cheeks," and chose to believe that Finn knew I cared, which perhaps was the achievement for the day.

45

A FEW DAYS after Nat's funeral, Kate Stark called to let me know I would begin to see promotional spots run in the days leading up to her live AGN Network interview with Pacho Craig.

The first spots concerned me. There were short clips of Pacho making action hero–type statements, and computer models showing how the assailants had entered his townhouse. The viewer saw bullet holes in his walls and shattered plates and glassware throughout his kitchen. There was footage of Pacho and Kate walking in Georgetown—Kate showing her lean runner's legs, and Pacho in his badass bush jacket, appearing to coyly shrug off a compliment.

Had Kate screwed me on this? I had been waiting for Pacho to crash to the ground like the *Hindenburg,* not watch an ode to the creep. I understood that she had no legal obligation to report what I wanted to see, but while I understood she needed to convey balance, I didn't think she'd straight-out betray me.

Joey and I settled in on the couch a few nights later to watch the big interview. At the top of *Kate Stark's USA,* Kate introduced the subjects for the evening broadcast. She led by hitting the highlights of the Pacho Craig saga, which would be the final stand-alone segment, the idea being to torture viewers into watching the initial, less interesting subjects. These topics included an Olympic athlete who had overcome being decapitated by a blender (or something), and people who hire hitmen—usually zit-faced teenagers named Kyle or Wayne who had washboard abs, watched too many mob movies, and worked at a Jiffy Lube in Kingman, Arizona, or an Arby's in Marion, Ohio.

Joey shook her head in disgust at the spectacle and promised to stay quiet during the broadcast of the segment on Pacho.

Kate punched her intro of Pacho's segment with footage similar to what had been shown in the promos. In a wide shot, Kate and Pacho sat across from each other in comfortable chairs. A television flat screen was set up in between the two of them, where both of them could see the display. Pacho was wearing his Indiana Jones hat.

"Asshole," I said. "Check out the hat."

"You wear a fedora," Joey pointed out.

"To protect my scalp from skin cancer and to keep my head warm. And not on TV."

"Oh, okay."

Kate began by asking Pacho about his upbringing and how he got the name Pacho.

Pacho blinked. "I had an uncle on my mother's side—he was quite a guy. He was a guerilla during all the unrest in the Basque region. He was killed there. I never met him, but they say I look like him."

"How long have they been calling you Pacho?"

"As long as I can remember. The resemblance showed from the time I was really little."

They cut to a shot of Pacho walking through Georgetown, being stopped by people on the street and happily engaging with them.

"Did he have the heterochromia too?" Kate asked.

"Oh, my eyes? I think so. It's one of those weird genetic things that comes from that side of the family."

"The guerilla side?" Kate asked with a grin.

"Well, we never called it that. There were some things we weren't supposed to talk about."

"I bet. You've had quite a go of it in the past few weeks."

"You're not kidding," Pacho said, smiling just a little as he tilted his head down and to the side, letting his hair fall in front of his face from beneath his hat—his signature move.

As I watched this, I felt my mouth twist into a sneer, my eyeteeth descending beneath my lips. It was Pacho's shy smile, the way it went off-center—that swindle of predatory vulnerability. God, I wanted to kill him, to strangle that boyish submissiveness that made people want to hear him out and that encrypted his particular evils.

"Take me back to the beginning, Pacho," Kate was saying. "What led up to the recent fireworks?"

"I was very concerned by the murder of the Saudi journalist Adnan Sabbag and had begun digging into it. He was lured to that office in Turkey, where he was suffocated and dismembered. I knew I had to get to the bottom of it. If a man like Sabbag isn't safe, none of us in journalism are safe. We take risks so the people out there don't have to, and they have the right to know what their government and big corporations are up to."

"Sure."

"I came upon some confidential sources who told me that the secretive right-wing billionaire Oliver Shackley was doing a lot of business with the Saudis through his company, General Commodities. He makes products that go into other products for military use, and he had lots of big deals on the table with Saudi Arabia. A source told me that Sabbag was looking into this relationship as he covered the terrible human rights abuses taking place in his home country."

"Of course. Terrible abuses."

"According to my confidential sources, Shackley was very worried about losing those contracts, and the Saudis were very worried about exposure."

"Why?" Kate asked.

Pacho did his confident head-tilt and rubbed his hands together.

"That's a good question, Kate. Saudi Arabia is a country in the Middle East that has ties to 9/11."

I kept expecting him to pat her on the head.

"Most of the terrorists were Saudi nationals. I'm sure you know that. So the question I had to take the risk of asking—at the potential cost of my life—was should a hostile country be doing extensive business with an American company fulfilling military contracts? Do we want a country, that is to some extent an enemy, providing the American military with its supplies? Nobody else was asking, and somebody had to step up to the plate.

Kate was nodding earnestly. She was either inclined to believe him . . . or was playing him quite well.

"According to my sources, Sabbag was onto something, and I came across documents showing that General Commodities indeed had a lot of business with Saudi Arabia. Anyway, after demonstrating a lot of anxiety about the story Sabbag was working on, one day Shackley suddenly stopped worrying—and I think I know why. His key people started telling others that everything would be taken care of. About a week after these discussions, Sabbag was dead."

"Are you saying Shackley ordered Sabbag's murder?"

"He's way too clever for that. There's the old story about one of the British kings, one of the Henrys, who was having trouble with a priest named Thomas à Becket."

I sat in front of the television, amazed that Pacho was about to rip off Elijah's Thomas à Becket analogy. But then again, why should this have surprised me from the King of Shtick?

"One day the king said, 'Who'll rid me of this damned priest?'" Pacho continued. "The next thing you know, Thomas à Becket was dead. I confronted Oliver Shackley about this." He sniffed out a laugh.

Kate chimed in, "That interview didn't go so well." She replayed a segment of the interview with Shackley appearing befuddled, denying any role in Sabbag's death, and swearing legal action against Pacho. "Shackley followed through in his threat to sue you," she said.

"He certainly did."

"For defamation and libel."

"Correct."

"Do you think he has a case?"

"No. I feel very good about what we know. Besides, I never said he gave the order. I simply asked him about it."

"Yes. But Pacho, there's a concept in libel law known as 'false light.'" Kate paused as the camera panned in closer on Pacho's face.

Pacho tilted his head slightly, and his mouth opened about a half inch.

"This applies in the sense that despite not directly saying he killed Sabbag," Kate continued, "your broadcast inaccurately depicted Shackley."

Pacho hesitated for a moment. "False light," he repeated, without inflection.

"Yes," Kate affirmed. "Some cases have been won against the media based on false light, even though the media outlet didn't explicitly say something definitive."

Pacho nodded, clearly out of his depth. "If you look at what happened next, uh, I think it removes doubt about what's going on here."

"We'll jump to that," Kate said, "but in fairness to Mr. Shackley, AGN wants to make clear that *we* are not alleging he played a role in the death of Mr. Sabbag. We're simply reporting on your report. Our attorneys want to underscore that we are not weighing in on his guilt or innocence. We hold no malice toward Mr. Shackley, and as you know, malice is one tenet of libel law."

"I hold no malice toward Mr. Shackley either, Kate."

"Of course. I was making clear *our* position, but it's my duty to ask about false light, as it's likely that—"

"Kate, I'm not an expert on libel law—"

"Neither am I, to be honest, but we need our viewers to know that we will be sensitive to whatever Mr. Shackley's side of the story is. We don't want anyone to suggest that we at AGN are accusing him of anything. We're simply having you on as a guest to tell your story."

It was interesting to see her establish, however obtusely, that Pacho had given very little consideration to defamation in his own broadcast.

"Yes, that's very important," Pacho said.

"So what happened next? There was an attack at your house."

"Yes."

"Tell us about it. It must have been . . . terrifying." She said the last part flatly, with no emotion or excitement in her voice, but Pacho didn't seem to notice. He took a deep breath and took his hat off with a flourish.

Ah, so that was why he had it on. So he could dramatically sweep it off.

"I was at my kitchen table, going over my notes on the Shackley matter. I heard voices outside of my kitchen door. I tiptoed to the door like a cat and peered out through the curtain, but I didn't see anything. I had a bad feeling, a sixth sense that something was wrong. The last time I had that feeling was in Afghanistan, just before the Taliban staged a mortar attack on a convoy I was embedded with. I always keep a golf club near both doors of my house, but if I had known what was coming next, I would have had something more useful than a golf club."

"Do you own a gun?"

"I'd rather not get into that. But, uh, I always figured I could handle any challenge that came my way. To be honest, I never predicted I'd be in a duel with Death . . ." After this last word, Pacho looked straight into the camera. "And Death would be dealing the cards."

Oh, holy jumpin' Jesus.

"Someone knocked and said it was Amazon. I figured it was just a normal delivery. Foolish of me. I won't make that mistake again."

"What happened next?" Kate asked.

"I opened the door. Two men were standing there. They were tall. Muscular. Both were wearing dark sweaters and military-style balaclavas, the kind you see on terrorists. Before I could slam the door, they pushed their way into the house. I tried to grab something . . . anything. I knew the golf club was out of reach, so I dove to the ground. I had an advantage over them—I knew my house layout. Presumably, those ninjas did not."

Oh, now they've gone from terrorists to ninjas.

"Could you tell anything about what they looked like?"

"Just that they had dark skin. Maybe Middle Eastern. I could see where the mask was open around their eyes."

"Then what happened?"

"I cut to my left into my living room. I popped my head up. When I heard footsteps, I dove over my sofa and heard the first shots. I couldn't believe how loud it was. I hadn't seen the guns when I first opened the door, but at some point I saw that one of the revolvers had a silencer. The kind assassins use. More shots rang out. There were lamps exploding and wood splintering as the bullets smashed into my shelves. I crawled along the ground as the shots kept coming. *Bam. Bam. Bam.* I finally made it to my kitchen. I saw only two options. One was to get out the rear kitchen door. The other was to grab the knives on my counter."

"This is unbelievable."

"Except that it happened. It was real." Pacho swept his hand up from his side and pressed his thumb and forefinger to the bridge of his nose. "By God, it was real. Then there was an eerie silence, and one of the men said, 'We don't have long.' Something like that. I knew I had to act fast. I crouched beneath the island's counter line. I saw that there was no way out through the kitchen door. I would have to stand up, and I wasn't about to do that without a weapon. My hands reached up on the counter, and I found the wooden block that holds my knives and knocked it to the floor. I picked up the two biggest knives and sprang up.

"There were two men and I threw one of the knives at them. I didn't know whether I hit one or not, but I heard one of the men curse. The next thing I heard was the sound of shoes squeaking against the floor, and then the front door flew open. I waited a few seconds, and all I heard was silence. I assumed they had gone, and then I snuck out back through the kitchen door. I had my phone in my pocket and called to report the shooting."

When he was done speaking, Pacho leaned back in his chair and studied his hands. He brought them together folded, his eyes not leaving his hands at first. Then his eyes slowly traveled upward and met Kate's. Pacho touched his hand to his heart. "It's racing again. Like when it happened."

Spare me.

Kate leaned forward and patted Pacho's knee. "We're glad you're okay, Pacho."

"I'm glad, too—believe me."

Kate let the drama sit for a moment and said, "I have so many questions for you, and I'm sure some of them will seem dumb, but I have to start somewhere."

"Ask away. There are no stupid questions."

"First off, who did you think the men were? Did you recognize them at all?"

"I did not. My first thoughts turned back to my attempt to interview Oliver Shackley, but I had no proof then."

"Do you have proof now?"

"Well, as the saying goes, 'Sunlight is the best disinfectant.' I'm hoping the investigation will ferret out the assassins once and for all."

"But your suspicions lie with Shackley," Kate said.

"The investigation will find what it finds, but we can't ignore what happened to Adnan Sabbag. We can't ignore the business Shackley had with the Saudis as a motive. That's all I'm going to say."

"You seem like a man who knows guns."

"I've been around them. Yes."

"Did you know that silencers aren't used on revolvers?"

"What?"

"Revolvers have a gap around the barrel that allows the explosion to escape. There's really no point of using a silencer with a revolver, because silencers won't suppress the sound. They're used on semiautomatics."

Pacho took a beat. "It's a b-b-blur, really."

"I'm just saying that professional assassins wouldn't use a suppressor with a revolver. Plus, why use a suppressor with one gun while the other gun is making a huge noise?"

"Like I said, it was a blur." Pacho now wore a puzzled expression, like a child who had unwrapped a present and didn't know exactly what it was. "I may have the details a little off."

"Pacho, I'd like to turn your attention to the television screen between us," Kate said.

Pacho did as he was told. On the screen were two African American men in their late twenties sitting across from Kate in an AGN Network studio.

"Do you recognize these men?" Kate asked.

Pacho leaned toward the screen. "No," he said.

"See if you recognize them after you hear them speak."

The video played. One of the men said, "Pacho Craig hired us to shoot at him in his house."

Kate asked the men, "Why would he do that, do you know?"

The other man said, "Wasn't ours to know, miss. We got a few thousand and didn't have to hurt nobody. That was that."

Pacho didn't appear angry. In fact, he was grinning stupidly, as though not processing what was taking place. "Is this a joke, Kate?"

"No, Pacho, I'm afraid not. You've never seen these men?"

"No, never."

"Take a look at the screen now," Kate said.

On the screen appeared a black-and-white surveillance photograph of the same two men standing outside the rec center where he'd met with Abigail and Elijah. One of them was shaking Pacho's hand. In the photo, Pacho's face was not visible. In the next photo that appeared on the screen, his head was turned so that the camera captured him perfectly, smiling broadly.

"What?" Pacho threw his arms up. "Those were just two guys standing around when I walked out of a random building one day! I don't even know them!"

"The same two guys who claim you hired them to shoot up your house?" Kate cocked an eyebrow, incredulous. "What were you hoping to accomplish? I guess one might say . . . this is your chance. Only a coward wouldn't take it."

Apoplectic rage invaded Pacho Craig's face. His features distorted and became ugly. His long hair made him look like an evil warlock rather than a mellow surfer. "Nothing! I wasn't accomplishing anything. You are making this up!"

"Are you saying this is a doctored photo from a security camera?"

"No! I mean, I don't know . . . Those guys are lying."

"What could they possibly have to gain by volunteering what they did?" Kate asked.

"It's a setup!"

"What else do we think we know about you that may not be real?"

Pacho rose as if he was going to end the interview, but a voice in his head must have told him that would only make it look as if he had something to hide, so he sat back down. "What kind of question is that?"

A glamour shot of Pacho appeared on the television screen.

"So? That's me. What?" Pacho said.

"Look at your eyes."

Pacho went pale despite his makeup.

"One eye blue, one eye green," Kate said. "Heterochromia."

"So?"

The current photo was replaced with one from Pacho's high school yearbook. Then one from college.

Again, Pacho said, "Yes. That's me."

"That's you?" Kate said. "All of them?"

"I know what I look like, Kate."

"Look at your eyes."

Pacho was as still as marble.

"Both of your eyes are blue in the older photos. You're using contact lenses now," Kate said.

Pacho shrugged.

"But you don't have heterochromia, despite extensive discussion about it in your profiles," Kate said.

"We're actually talking about my *eyes*?"

"We asked some of your relatives about your Basque guerrilla uncle, Pacho. No one has ever heard of him. Nor do you have Spanish ancestry. You apparently took Pacho as a nickname from when you tried to pronounce your name when you were little. Paul Charles—"

"Who knows?" Pacho said, his hands up defensively. He was still half sitting, half standing.

"Let's listen to this tape." Kate touched her ear for dramatic effect. "These are two clips from an audio feed of your voice." In the first one Pacho said, *They're just a bunch of f-gs*. In the next one, he said something about *all these n---ers*.

"What the fuck was that?" Pacho said. AGN didn't bleep him.

"Was that your voice?"

"I never use those words. *Ever.*"

"A forensic analysis we did says that was your voice. Or was it faked? Like the shooting? Or your eyes? Or your name? Or your reporting?"

"This is bullshit!"

"Maybe you want more time to prepare? We can do a second interview?"

"Yes! Yes!"

"We'd be happy to have you. And we can talk about some of the women in your life. We may have some interesting guests."

"Ask me anything," Pacho said. "I have nothing to hide."

For the first time in this whole affair, I actually felt sorry for him.

I had seen this with scandalized figures before. They are the last to know how much trouble they are in. When they're in the eye of the hurricane, they cease to see the world beyond the vortex. They think whatever they've convinced themselves of in the elusive quiet of their own faltering mind—the fantasy of themselves—is the only thing that matters. It took me years to realize that people who do bad things rarely see the weight of what they've done. Things others view as essential, they just see as collateral.

I wondered if Stalin ever thought he was a bad person or if, when his alarm clock went off in the morning, he sometimes opened his eyes and said, "Oh, shit! I'm *Stalin*!" Even the most monstrous of people can operate only if they convince themselves they are good. This is why we hear about hardened killers in prison who hate child molesters. *I'm not that!,* they reason, which allows them to rob, cheat, or kill under the protection of some enzyme that sprays their brains with a sense of exemption.

"Thanks for being with us, Pacho," Kate said. She looked at the camera. "I think we're done."

I thought Pacho was done too.

46

AS PACHO CRAIG presumably stood catatonic in the AGN greenroom, still plugged into his microphone, I thought of Eddie Fontaine and hoped his men had gotten the job done in time. That morning, I had given Eddie's cousin Tiger the digits for Bob Woodward's birthday—the punch code to Pacho's house. A few weeks earlier, I had handed Tiger a thumb drive that contained some of the video Abigail and Goblin had taken of Pacho's house, including the pathway up to his bedroom. While Pacho was being interviewed at AGN's studio, Eddie's handpicked team, knowing the terrain, had entered and removed Pacho's watch collection.

When Pacho got back to his house, cops were carrying boxes of material out the front door. Goblin had begun to send printouts of the contents of Pacho's computers to the police and media outlets the moment Pacho's ass had hit the chair in Kate Stark's studio. And the whole world would soon be watching: Deb Diamond of CBA News, speaking on camera with longtime anchor Pete Sloineth at his desk in New York City, was on-site outside of Pacho's place. We'd tipped her off that the police would be raiding the townhouse.

When I watched the news report later, I couldn't believe that the escapade had actually gone down.

"We don't know what's in all the boxes, Pete, but we can see the police have got both laptop and desktop computers," Diamond was saying. "Our sources have told us that some of the items on Pacho Craig's computer include neo-Nazi websites and sadomasochistic pornography, some of the porn involving, um, dwarves . . . pardon me, little people. There are also map searches that prosecutors will argue relate to where Craig was meeting with the conspirators who staged the so-called assassination attempt."

"What's that, Deb? There?" Sloineth asked, pointing.

The camera focused on a cumbersome plastic contraption with tubes and spheres.

"I believe, Pete, that is what is known as a Habitrail. It's, uh, for gerbils and such. But I would prefer not to go down this road further."

As I watched the coverage unfold, I imagined Pacho arriving home to the chaos and opening his watch drawer to put his Omega De Ville Tourbillon away. His eyes would be positively shivved by the hole displayed before him. He would be used to the sudden blinding flash of the bezels when he performed this ritual, but this time—on the velvet pads where his watches had once been—there would be nothing. He would think he was losing his mind. When he pulled out the velvet pads in a frantic search for his watches, all he would find would be a calling card printed with calligraphy typeface, reading:

"Good day, sir. You've been taxed by the Callous Sophisticates."

My house phone rang. When I picked up, I heard Kurt's voice. "Fuse, you did it! Are you watching?"

"No details on the phone, Kurt. But yes, I'm watching. Is Sammy?"

"Yes," Kurt said. "I didn't want her to think I was staring at her, but she definitely gave me the side-eye when it was all going down. The corner of her lip kinda curled up like it did when she was little and had just done something naughty."

"Well, that's a lip curl in the right direction. If she asks you anything, don't do more than tell her you love her."

"Will you be at home in five minutes?"

"Yeah, why—"

"I'll meet you out front."

Kurt's Tesla was in my driveway in four minutes. He left the car running as he skipped toward me. "I love you, man," Kurt said, hugging me so tight I couldn't breathe.

"Love you too," I said. We had never spoken like this to each other.

Kurt returned to his car and drove away.

• • •

Kate published her follow-up story overnight on AGN's website, beating the *Incursion* and everybody else. The story read:

Pacho Craig Arrested for Staging "Assassination" Attempt

By Kate Stark

Washington, DC — MyStream star reporter Paul "Pacho" Craig was arrested tonight at his Georgetown home and charged with crimes associated with staging an attempt on his life.

Mr. Craig has claimed that two masked gunmen burst into his house on November 15 and attempted to kill him. In a broadcast on *Kate Stark's USA,* Mr. Craig wove a dramatic tale of fighting off his assailants. Like much of what viewers have come to know about Mr. Craig, this story has turned out to be a fabrication. He has denied these charges.

Two men identified exclusively by *Kate Stark's USA*, Lamont Rucker, 28, and Michael Thomas, 30, confessed that Mr. Craig paid them $10,000 in cash to enter his home and fire several shots to make it appear as if there had been an assassination attempt. The working theory, according to police sources, is that Mr. Craig staged the hoax as a publicity stunt in order to imply that billionaire Oliver Shackley, CEO of Rockville-based General Commodities, was so threatened by his investigation into Saudi Arabian ties that he sought to silence Mr. Craig.

Mr. Shackley has filed a $1 billion defamation suit against Mr. Craig and MyStream. AGN has found no evidence linking Mr. Shackley to the murder of Saudi Arabian journalist Adnan Sabbag.

While the district attorney has not offered specifics about all the charges being considered against Mr. Craig, the Metropolitan Police Department has removed boxes of evidence from Mr. Craig's house in Georgetown, including computers containing neo-Nazi and white supremacist writings in addition to pornography involving deviant behavior.

The Adnan Sabbag Foundation was presented with the emails that Mr. Craig claimed were exchanges between Sabbag and General Commodities executives. The Foundation denied these emails were authentic, explaining that Sabbag had a different email address and that the writing style depicted in the emails did not resemble Sabbag's. Furthermore, General Commodities legal counsel Carlie Locke similarly claimed that the documents purported to show correspondence about Saudi business dealings were "complete fabrications."

A charged interview on *Kate Stark's USA* probed other fraudulent aspects of Mr. Craig's career and persona, and learned that his purported genetic condition, known as heterochromia, also appears to be of his own making. Photos of Mr. Craig as a younger man and child show him to have two blue eyes rather than one green and one blue. The condition cannot emerge later in life, and the two-color effect can be achieved only through specialized contact lenses.

Mr. Craig had also claimed that the nickname "Pacho" derived from an uncle who was a Basque guerrilla in northern Spain. Our investigation could find no evidence that such an uncle ever existed,

> nor could we find any Craig family ancestry beyond his English and Irish heritage.
>
> "Pacho Craig is an invention of a rich kid from Gibson Island named Paul Charles Craig. He's a fake," said a former schoolmate who asked not to be identified. "But I bet he gives the contact lens industry a real boost."

Hours after Kate Stark's interview ran, Pacho's biggest sponsor, Blue Ridge Summit, dropped him. The company's statement emphasized the alleged racist and homophobic slurs that were picked up in audio recordings. I had encouraged Kate to run a poll asking people whether they thought Blue Ridge should drop Pacho. The answer to these leading polls is always *Hell, yeah!* The result was catalyzed by an internet meme featuring Pacho posing with the company's equipment and the tagline *Blue Ridge Summit: For All Your Concentration Camping Gear.*

The evening after Kate Stark's blockbuster interview, the AGN website led with another scoop Kate had been unable to talk about with me. It was a headline I had only hoped was coming:

Woman Claims Pacho Craig Assault at Debate

The story featured a photograph of a young woman named Christine Josephs who said that Pacho had groped her in the media room at a presidential debate.

I watched the following day as Josephs tearfully recounted her story at a news conference hosted by a feminist attorney, accompanied by two other alleged Pacho victims. One of them alleged an outright rape at a hotel. All these young women were either subordinates or starstruck assistants who conceded some degree of flirtation prior to Pacho getting aggressive—a remarkably similar m.o. to what had happened to Samantha Rossiter.

The son of a bitch has done it before, I kept repeating to myself. I knew it, but I hadn't *known* it. Taking Pacho out had been a damned public service.

There were plenty of tabloid headlines in the following days:

Not So Macho, Pacho!

Pacho Hides Under Poncho
(featuring Craig cowering in the rain in his bush coat)

Nazi Pacho
(in which an opinion writer condemned his racism and supported the end of his Blue Ridge contract)

Watch It, Pacho!
(where a growling plaintiff's lawyer surrounded by his alleged victims vowed to put Pacho in jail)

The photos and memes in the media depicted Pacho with insanely mismatched eyes, including other mutant-eyed memes of goblins, devils, aliens, and murderous lunatics like Charles Manson, Ted Bundy, and John Wayne Gacy.

While standing outside of his townhouse in the days following the AGN interview, Pacho repeatedly denied all the allegations against him, underscoring that he was the victim of an "incomprehensible smear." A #PoorPacho meme sprouted on Twitter almost instantly, featuring a frowny face emoji with razor stubble and an Indiana Jones fedora.

One late-night comedian sniffed, "Pacho may not be in prison yet, but he'll never work again, and he'll never be able to walk into any place of respect without seeing *this.*" And then he made the #PoorPacho frowny face. "That's what this movement needs to do if it can't put these scumbags in jail. We should ostracize them."

"If they find pee-pee porn on Pacho's computer," said another late-night wag, "it'll give a whole new meaning to the name MyStream!"

Another skit featured a comedian dressed up like Pacho, crawling through a human-sized Habitrail. It was idiotic but hilarious.

Within a day, the whole #PoorPacho fuss was replaced by the Next Big Thing: a wave of hysteria involving the president's suggestion that some of the graves at Arlington National Cemetery be exhumed and transferred to Prince George's County, Maryland, in order to build "super-luxurious" housing for the proposed Olympic games.

When my new iPhone vibrated that day, I saw it was a text from an unfamiliar number. I touched the messages icon on the phone and saw a circle with Samantha's photo in it. Her text was just an emoji with two hands held together in prayer. I asked Finn what the emoji meant, without telling her who had sent it.

"It means thanks," Finn said casually.

I sent back an emoji of my own to Samantha: a heart. Love was all I had to give her. The crucible of finding a place for her hardship would be hers alone.

47

"YOU PULLED IT off!" came Abigail's voice over the line later that day.

"*I* did it?" I said. "I was just the conductor. You played all the instruments."

"I can't believe it," she said. "I keep watching the news."

"How are you feeling?"

"I'm in shock, to be honest. But I feel like I just got accepted into a great college or something."

I laughed. "You're a tough customer, Abigail, the way you walked right into that bear cave. Your dad would be proud of you."

"Well, Sandy, I think Dad had other things in mind for me," she said softly.

"And you'll make those things happen. But first you showed your dad, wherever he is, that you're not a victim. Maybe our little game wasn't like winning the Nobel Prize, but you didn't let the world trample on you."

"I know, Sandy. Have you heard anything about how Shackley's doing?"

"Every news report has been careful to show that he was wronged by Pacho's reporting. He's been looking for vindication like this for years. Nobody will ever want to accuse him of anything again."

"That's good. I never thought he was a bad man."

"Just another guy who likes his money. There are plenty of worse guys than Oliver Shackley."

"Thanks for bringing me into this. Maybe next time you'll take me to somewhere other than that deli."

"Change is hard for me, but I'll try to branch out."

It occurred to me that Abigail and Samantha would like each other, but that was a meeting that could never happen. The Callous Sophisticates were best kept in the dark and far apart.

• • •

Pacho Craig was brought to police headquarters, which TV reporters enjoy calling the Daly Building as opposed to simply "police headquarters." It's like how whenever a new royal family member is born in England, they can't just say the kid is at the hospital. They have to juice it up by reminding the world that the royals are at the Lindo Wing—have to wedge that jargon in there, in the same spirit that any structure where a Kennedy is present is referred to as a "compound."

As I watched the CBA News coverage, the TV cut to action footage of Pacho getting out of a Chevy Suburban and walking toward the weathered building, past concrete barriers, and toward the front entrance. He was with his attorney, Alessandra Joyce.

Reporters shoved microphones in Pacho and Joyce's faces. "Did you stage the attack, Pacho?" Deb Diamond asked.

Pacho shot Diamond a look, his lower jaw jutting out and his canine teeth protruding on-screen.

Joyce said, "My client volunteered to come in and answer questions."

Diamond began her broadcast exchange with the New York anchor. "According to our sources, Pete, Craig will be asked questions about his alleged assault on a woman the authorities are calling Jane Doe #1," Diamond said.

"Deb, do we know if the police are talking to Jane Doe?" asked Sloineth, clearly enraptured with his own voice and hair.

"We have not been able to confirm that, Pete. We know that the police are talking to a few women."

"How far away do you think we are, Deb, from an actual arrest?"

"We can't speculate. But there is a groundswell of outrage, with people wondering how many of Pacho's reports have been fraudulent, and sources are saying that MyStream has hired legal counsel to investigate all of Craig's reporting as well as examine his behavior with women.

"'Sources are saying,'" I repeated to Joey as we watched this. "Maybe sources are saying Pacho is the Zodiac Killer."

"He wasn't born during the Zodiac murders," Joey said.

"Right. Actually, Finn's the Zodiac."

"That, we know. You don't believe Diamond has sources?"

"Look," I said, "'sources say' is everything I've come to hate about what's happened to my profession. Most reporters use anonymous sources ethically, but a dirty reporter looking to spice up her coverage could fall back on yahoos who could be anybody and say anything. Some reporters think their targets are so evil, it justifies crossing these lines."

Joey leaned in close to me. "You realize, doofus, I'm well aware who the puppet master was here," she whispered, pointing to the TV screen.

"I am but a humble and passive consumer of the news," I said.

"My little Boy Scout," she said, and kissed me on the ear.

The screen was showing a still frame of Pacho's reaction to Deb Diamond: his jaw jutting forward, his white canines catching the sunlight, his upper lip curled into a snarl. It was impossible to ignore the anger he radiated—anger that Samantha and Abigail had conveyed to me. They had been up against a gargoyle come alive, and I no longer cared about what lines I had to cross to cage him.

• • •

The next day, I was on our elliptical machine downstairs when my new iPhone came alive. It was a text from Finn. Her words flashed up on my screen, bathed in green light. I touched the dialogue bubble. It read:

Dad can u pick me up

I typed back:

Where are you?

Alex

OK

Dont tell mom

Hmm.

I knew where Frigging Alex lived because of the times I had dropped Finn off there, by Walter Johnson High School, before he got his driver's license. I had also staked out his house when contemplating tossing him in a white van and transporting him to Great Falls Park, whereupon I would throw him into the rapids of the Potomac and an inexplicable tragedy would take him from us.

I drove over quickly. As always, I overthought every element of such an excursion. Why didn't Frigging Alex drive Finn home? Why didn't Finn want Joey to know I was picking her up? Was she all right? If it had been a true emergency, why wouldn't she have called rather than texted, knowing my limitations with TICU? And what could the emergency be?

I got there in three minutes. Finn was waiting outside. I'd decided on the drive over to use a light touch rather than pry.

"Hey, Cheeks," I said when she got in beside me. I tried to look at her in the rearview mirror, but I didn't see much. Finn hated when I stared at her. "Working on anything good?" I asked.

"Just stuff."

Had Frigging Alex tried to make a move that she rejected? Or had he already gone too far? Did she choose me to pick her up because I was sufficiently unperceptive?

We drove home in silence. I could hear my own breathing. It sounded like a deafening waterfall in my chest. When we got home, I opened the front door for Finn and let her in. She turned to me before escaping from my view and managed the slightest smile.

"Thanks, Daddy," she said.

That was all I got. But she had called me.

48

EMILY RENI LIVED in a tiny ranch house in Garrett Park, Maryland, which is a charming island of gingerbread residences between Rockville and Kensington. I had found her address months ago, when I was digging around on what had happened to her husband, Guido. I had always hoped to interview her, but my pursuit was spiked before I had the chance.

I wasn't sure what would come of any visit with her, but if nothing else, I felt the need to look into the eyes of a woman who had lost someone to circumstances I found to be disturbing. Sometimes all I got out of visits like this was garden-variety bitterness, but occasionally I saw something that reminded me I wasn't just chasing pixies.

Mrs. Reni was in her mid-sixties and was dressed in faded jeans and a flannel shirt. She wore a wide-brimmed hat as she tied strands of gray rope around a shrub to pull it away from a trellis beside the house.

"Mrs. Reni," I said, "I'm an unemployed but curious journalist. I'm sorry to bother you."

"That's sure a peculiar greeting," she said, unsmiling. She had big blue eyes that had probably once made Guido Reni's heart skip beats, but the lines around them betrayed a desire to take a nap.

"I know. I don't like stalking people at home, so I figured I'd con my way into your good graces with a little humility."

"You haven't yet. I don't like the press much."

"Neither do I. Anymore. That's why I'm here."

"What do you want?"

"I had been researching a story on why my former employer, the

Capitol Incursion, was gunning for Guido. I know a little about ruining people and figure if we can ruin a guilty man so easily, how hard could it be to ruin an innocent one?"

"Bastards. I don't want to be charmed now. I've had my fill of fake-earnest reporters trying to schmooze their way into my good graces only to sever our spines in the end."

"I encourage your skepticism. If you trusted me right now, I'd think you were a goddamned idiot. And to be clear, I'm not working on a story anymore. I can't. I've been put out to pasture at the *Incursion* because I was looking into what happened to Guido."

"You don't look old enough to retire."

"I'm a pain in the ass."

"I can see that. I'll ask you again: What do you want?"

"I think some of my colleagues had it in for your husband—"

"No shit. You're a regular Woodward and Bernstein."

I was liking her more and more. "And I want to know what he was working on that may have made some people feel so nervous."

"Guido loved making enemies," she said. "He really thought there was this big conspiracy to ruin the country with this socialist stuff."

"It's none of my business, but did you agree?"

"I didn't much care. I did tell him he thought it was a big game. He didn't really understand he was screwing with scary people, until it was too late. He thought he was a gadfly. Your people turned him into some kind of Rasputin. What's your name anyhow?"

"Sanford Petty."

"I've seen that byline."

"You won't be seeing it anymore. Why didn't you care about what Guido believed?"

"I just liked seeing him excited. When he was excited, he wasn't depressed."

"He had a problem with that, huh?"

"He blew his brains out. What do you think, Lieutenant Columbo?"

"I assumed so. But there's often a catalyst with these things."

"There was a catalyst, all right. You people."

"Look, Mrs. Reni, I feel badly being here, given everything you've been through. I'll ask you one more question, then leave you alone."

"That's what Columbo said before he nailed the murderer."

That cracked me up. It was true. Peter Falk's Lieutenant Columbo always saved his kill shot for last. "You're absolutely right," I said. "I loved that show."

"Guido and I did too. We used to watch old reruns."

"My wife and I watched it when we were kids in the seventies."

"Together?"

"Yes. We've been together since we were kids."

"That's nice."

"Did Guido ever say anything about why he thought the media was so out to get him?"

"Unions," Mrs. Reni said.

"Excuse me?"

"He knew he made enemies, Mr. Petty, but he thought most of his enemies were a bunch of whiners. He said his biggest mistake was making all that noise about how the unions organize. He was doing interviews in South Carolina when that American Knitting Union was trying to organize that Major Fibers outlet. He traced everything back to that. Kept poring over his notes, especially when the suits from our kids started."

"Notes?"

"Yeah. He kept those drugstore notebooks."

I puffed out my cheeks, trying to think of what to say next.

"Something on your mind, son?" Mrs. Reni asked.

"I wasn't planning to ask you this, but is there any way you'd let me see those notebooks?"

"What for?"

"I'm out of the *Incursion*. I'd like to walk out that door and make some people feel like hell about what they did to Guido. You have no reason to trust me. I get it. But I don't see what you have to lose."

She removed her hat and wiped her brow with a red bandana. She had thick silvery hair that still shone with golden highlights and probably had been blonde once. Joey might have hair like that in ten years. "Aw, hell," she said, "I don't really care anymore."

I followed Mrs. Reni into her cluttered house. There were books and files everywhere. It was the residence of bohemians, not capitalist Running Dogs. There were photos of the Reni children at various ages in tacky old picture frames on mismatched shelves.

"Do you see your kids often?" I asked.

"More now that Guido's gone," she said, leading the way into the dining room. She lifted an accordion file from a chair and set it on the table. "They're trying to come to grips with what happened to their dad, wondering whether they had been wrong to do what they did. Sue him and all."

"I understand there had been trouble with them."

Mrs. Reni put her fist to her mouth and choked back a sob. "What they did to him," she whispered.

I took a step closer. "Who did what?"

"I don't know. The kids started getting letters at home. I have three. One's still in college. People visited them and told them how Guido didn't believe in climate change, how he got a kick out of using animals for medical research. These people started calling the kids' friends and saying this stuff about Guido. Made life hell for the kids until . . ." She sat in the chair where the accordion file had been and completed her thought. "They filed for a divorce from Guido."

"Your kids did? Not you?"

"No."

"Who paid for your kids' legal work?"

"No clue."

"Well, somebody paid."

"I suppose so. I'm not sure they knew."

"Mrs. Reni, may I look at the latest notes Guido made?"

"Might as well."

For the next hour and a half, I read through Guido Reni's drugstore notebooks. It was difficult to follow them, but one thing was clear: Reni had taken extensive notes on the organizing tactics of the American Knitting Union. He had given prolific media interviews and written op-eds on this subject. Not long afterward, AKU's organizing campaign against Major Fibers failed. That's when the lawsuits and media exposés escalated and the "divorce" proceedings from his kids started.

No way was all of this organic.

"So, what do you think?" Mrs. Reni asked, after I had closed the last notebook.

"I think you earned your tears rightly."

"Now what?" she said, which struck me as being oddly profound.

"Mrs. Reni, I'd love to tell you I have a plan to make you whole, but I have no such thing."

"Believe me, I have no expectations from a reporter."

"And you shouldn't. All I can tell you is, I'm going to use what I know, and I'm going to give some of the people involved a lot of heartburn. You probably will never hear about it and won't be able to enjoy it. But if it gives you any solace, somebody's going to have a very bad day."

"A bad day? That's my consolation?"

"Don't look to me for justice." I shrugged. "I can only give you empathy."

49

I MET FRANKIE Waterman outside the *Incursion*'s offices before our showdown with my old bosses. Frankie specifically requested that Gretchen Kramer not be in attendance, citing her belligerent and agenda-driven behavior. This position was, of course, informed not only by her verifiable behavior, but by the illicit review of Kramer's emails performed by Goblin and me. I promised Frankie that I would keep my mouth shut and let her finesse how we knew what we knew.

The objective of this meeting was to lay out our position, with the hope that my suspension would end and we could pave the road for a palatable separation. When we got into the elevator, I asked Frankie to push the appropriate button and tried to explain why the controls didn't work for me. She rolled her eyes but complied.

Joel Mayer and Stuart Gilmore were waiting for us in the *Incursion*'s conference room. There was no videographer this time. I was tense, but the others seemed comparatively relaxed. There was something about meetings that made me wonder if I was going crazy. I'd be in a meeting and look at one particular person and, for no discernible reason, wonder what would happen if I just walked up to the guy and punched him in the face. I assumed today's meeting would leave me with similar impulses.

Once everybody was seated, Frankie asked if there was anything the *Incursion* wanted to say about the state of their inquiry.

"Not really," Mayer said. "It's just plodding along."

"How long will it plod?"

Mayer widened his eyes in a philosophical gesture. "Not much longer, I assure you. How about your inquiry?"

"I'm going to start off on a transparent note," Frankie said. "While we haven't conducted a formal counter-investigation, as you know, my client has a difficult time with investigative impulse control. Ms. Kramer has been stalking him and needling him, and Sandy had no intention of just sitting back and allowing her to lash him with impunity. I counseled him not to do anything that would get him crosswise with the *Incursion*'s inquiry, and I'd like to believe he fulfilled that—for the most part. Nevertheless, some of his investigative work yielded some information that we want to bring to your attention. It is our hope that this will allow both parties here to wrap this up and get on with our lives."

"We're all ears, Frankie," Mayer replied. "Thanks for your candor. We'd like to get things moving along too."

"I'll come to the point," Frankie continued. "This is not an inquiry that either of us wants. Sandy would like to get on with his life. And when I give you the lay of the land, I can only assume that the *Incursion* won't want this to go on ad nauseum. It is our strong preference to conclude this in a peaceful manner, despite what we believe.

"It is our operating theory that the *Incursion* and/or Gretchen Kramer didn't want Sandy investigating the death of Guido Reni because it would reveal that the paper was serving, for quite some time, as an agent of the Sunshine Collective, a PR firm. We believe you did this in part because the *Incursion* agrees with Sunshine ideologically. We believe this because Sunshine has provided you with a steady drumbeat of stories for many years.

"We believe Reni was challenging Sunshine's clients in the media and may have been making headway in getting some other media to look into Sunshine and their handmaidens in the media, including the *Incursion*. We know that a particular union, a Sunshine client, was hell-bent on destroying Reni after he derailed a campaign to organize a plant in South Carolina, and that the union went on a defamation campaign which included turning the man's own children against him and filing baseless lawsuits. The *Incursion* was actively deployed in this effort and embraced its role. We believe this because Gretchen Kramer profited from this arrangement directly via payments for speeches and a book deal, as well as somewhat less directly by helping her and the *Incursion* build its coverage sympathetic to Sunshine's clients, including labor unions, progressive activist groups, short sellers, and plaintiff's lawyers.

"Over the course of eight years, the *Incursion* has run approximately seventy-five stories that took a favorable stance toward Sunshine's clients. There were ten stories alone eviscerating Guido Reni, who was not exactly enough of a public figure to merit such scrutiny. But the *Incursion* covered him with the zeal that you might bring to a story on the Speaker of the House.

"Meanwhile, Ms. Kramer has delivered at least twenty-eight speeches to Sunshine clients and related entities, which has earned her somewhere around three hundred thousand in the speaking market. This doesn't include the advance for a book about the corporate-funded groups that are consistent opponents of Sunshine—that's three hundred and twenty-five thousand dollars more."

Frankie slid the documents across the table to the *Incursion* big shots, who didn't touch them, before continuing.

"It was clearly the feeling among some here—I am not suggesting you, Joel and Stuart—that if Sandy Petty were to publish such a story, it would embarrass the *Incursion* because of its gross and systematic bias and its corrupt links to Sunshine. Your paper basically had become the advertising agency of the Sunshine Collective, a for-profit PR firm. Because the *Incursion*'s coverage is of the correct political pedigree, it probably never even occurred to anyone here that these links were somehow unseemly. Yet the fact that this systematic enterprise resulted in the death of a man—Guido Reni, whom the *Incursion*, Ms. Kramer, and Sunshine all disagreed with—does not acquit you well. Especially since the one reporter who was looking into it, a fifty-something veteran journalist, suddenly found himself in career Siberia."

The room was so silent that the only audible sounds were the ticking of a wall clock and the buzzing of the fluorescent lights. Finally, Mayer raised an eyebrow and said what lawyers all say. "C'mon, Frankie. This proves nothing."

Frankie nodded her head as if in surrender. "In court? Who knows? You guys can take stories from whoever pitches you—and you have. But will this endeavor of the *Incursion* prove to have been worth destroying or impeaching the reputation of one of your best investigative reporters? We don't need to prevail in a false-light lawsuit for discovery to get very unpleasant: The *Incursion* didn't like one of its reporters snooping around on a story, so you got another reporter to spread rumors that he was threatening sources, with the end goal of canning him. And how will all of this play out in front of the Pulitzer Committee? On talk radio? Fox News? In social media? The *Columbia Journalism Review*? In Congress? Before the Federal Communications Commission? Among shareholders? Pension funds? Readers? I think it proves quite a lot."

Everyone in the room knew that we had no intention of going to court. This was a negotiation, and the risk was not legal sanction but an existential threat in the form of a public relations and reputation disaster. Moreover, both Mayer and Gilmore were veterans of an era when striving for balance was a core value, regardless of the deep biases held by ninety-nine percent of the people who worked at the *Incursion*.

"Does Sandy want to come back to work and report this story?" Gilmore asked.

"My client has no interest in returning to the *Incursion*. He would simply like a buyout so that he can pursue other opportunities."

"Would these other opportunities include publishing a story about the *Incursion,* Ms. Kramer, and her agenda in some other outlet?" Mayer asked.

Frankie shook her head. "While my client believes that Kramer and the *Incursion*'s overzealous reporting led to the suicide of Guido Reni, and that this would make for an important story, he would agree not to report on this subject regardless of where he might land, and would cede this reporting responsibility to the *Incursion*. This assumes that the *Incursion* will, in fact, address what happened here and what happened to Mr. Reni, and will take the time to interview his widow—which, by way of disclosure, Sandy already has done. He has also reviewed Mr. Reni's extensive notes."

This, too, was a negotiation. While I would have liked to see the Sunshine Collective phenomenon exposed, I was growing increasingly comfortable with the great American ethic of selling out.

"You're not suggesting that we take responsibility for Mr. Reni's death?"

"Of course not. Cover it as you see fit, perhaps through an ombudsman. That's your call."

Implicit in this position was an understanding that if the *Incursion* engaged in a little self-flagellation—which media outlets do from time to time—it would inoculate the paper against a more savage exposé. But if the *Incursion* didn't address the investigation, someone else would. Badly. Kramer would get smacked around, which would make me happy. Plus, her reputation as a hack—a tool of special interests—would be cemented.

Or they could just fucking pay me.

50

WHEN FRANKIE HUDDLED with Mayer and Gilmore after our meeting concluded, they made no commitments, but signaled that they would halt their inquiry into my conduct and begin talks for a buyout of my contract. Despite not having anything in writing, I felt good about the situation for the first time since the ordeal began.

Frankie and I sat on a bench in Farragut Square. "Did they tell you Gretchen is proper fucked?" I asked.

"They never tell you those things outright. You know that, Sandy," she replied. "But I'll bet you my fee that she will be pursuing other opportunities in journalism within a month."

"Hopefully with an online rag that will go bankrupt soon."

Frankie had been following the adventures of Pacho Craig with interest and warned me that I had better give some thought to how it could boomerang on me. "You're going to have to tell me the basics of the scheme so I can handle it if it comes to that," she said.

I told Frankie about how I had orchestrated the whole scheme—Abigail, Goblin, Eddie, Elijah. Even the two shooters eager to rise in Eddie's organization, who were willing to get nicked on a charge of illegally discharging a firearm within the District of Columbia.

"So Shackley wasn't really screwing around with the Saudis?" Frankie asked.

"Garden-variety boring business. There's no reason to believe he had anything to do with what happened to Sabbag. He's not a guy who kills people. He's a guy who buys people. From what I've heard, he's having the time of his life suing Pacho. It confirms his whole worldview of busybody socialists trying to bring him down."

"Your goal was to get Shackley to sue Pacho?"

"That and whipping up a plausible conspirator who might want Pacho dead and get him talking big. When you're in a dispute with somebody who's bigger than you are, get him to pick a fight with somebody who's bigger than he is. Evil billionaires killing reporters tapped into his sense of grandiosity. It filled both his villain void and his careerism."

Frankie shook her head. "And you figured he wouldn't really do his homework."

"I was counting on it."

"What about all the stuff that was found in his house and on his computer?"

"Once we had access to his house, we planted most of the stuff. Well, except for the kinky porn."

"Charming. Did that give you more insight into what happened with your friend's daughter?"

I nodded. "He's a guy who likes to get rough. He likes the feeling of domination, which is one thing if the woman wants it, but another thing if she doesn't. It's a consent thing. Had he just dumped her after a regular sexual encounter, whatever that is, it would have been chalked up to a heartbreak."

"There's a line . . ."

"I'm not the expert, but yeah, there is. All I know is, this has been Pacho's life. Just not caring about anything other than what makes him feel good in the moment. It's not that he sits and whiteboards evil like a James Bond villain. It's that he just doesn't care and never had to. Reckless disregard, you know. It's why I soured on journalism. After a while, we just didn't care who we ruined."

"And these other women who just came forward?"

"Heh. We sent Pacho a few anonymous emails implying it was

from a woman he abused. He started googling women from his past, searching Facebook and other sites. We blindly messaged these women, telling them Pacho Craig was going to get grilled by Kate Stark. I guess some of them tuned in. When they saw he was blowing up, they joined the fray. There's a reason they call it #MeToo. I'm sure some of them are telling the truth, although others could be scandal tourists."

"Is Samantha going to come forward now?"

"I don't think so. She's trying to move forward with her life. But I like the idea of him knowing she's out there. Forever. And at any moment, without provocation, she might surface and take him down."

"The torture of never-ending anticipation. What about Pacho's homophobic and racist slurs?" Frankie asked.

"I went over all of his videos online with a tech expert. There's a new technology called 'deepfake' that allows you to edit video and audio. We used a process called 'synthesis' to change certain sounds . . . He said 'facts,' which became—"

"I get it. But won't Pacho deny it and prove he didn't say it?"

"Of course he will. But will anybody want to hear it? A huge percentage of people will believe he said it, and his sponsors won't want to even have the debate. The only thing that matters these days is the first round of coverage—that's where all the damage is done. The vortex. Besides, my cyber guy contaminated the original video that we used the deepfake technology on, so it'll be hard to access again and clean up."

"You've been busy."

"My only question, Frankie, is this: with Shackley suing the piss out of Pacho Craig, does the fact of being fed false information give Pacho an out?"

"No. Pacho used that false information and didn't vet it. He chose not to. I imagine he could conduct an investigation of Abigail and the assassins, but if I were his lawyer, I wouldn't like that option very much."

"Why not?" I asked.

"Because, like you said, he's covered in sludge. He's got so much slime on him that anywhere he moves, he'll be slip-sliding into more muck of his own creation. Will he really want to put on the stand the young woman whose father he destroyed? Does he really want to answer questions about dwarf porn—"

"Little people porn."

"—and sexual assaults and neo-Nazi ties, however bogus? I doubt it. My only concern is his pathway to you, Sandy."

"The only way he'd get there would be through Eddie Fontaine, who won't talk, or Abigail, who may talk if she's pressured. But she didn't break the law. Same with another guy—I brought him into the project to pose as a consultant to General Commodities. But there's no law against lying to a reporter."

We both were silent for a minute. Only the sounds of traffic from Connecticut and K could be heard. "Sounds like Pacho was proper fucked from the get-go," Frankie finally said.

"Under the wrong set of circumstances," I said, "we're all proper fucked."

51

HADDON SPENT HER last night in the area staying with Joey and me, and all I could think about was that damn panda bear.

The next morning, I offered to drive Haddon to Reagan National Airport, but she wanted to use a promotion she had received for one of those driving service apps that were beyond my capabilities. Goober or something. Joey had already left to drive Finn to a school event.

"You don't use Uber or Lyft?" Haddon asked with a smirk.

Oh, that was it. Uber. "I could sooner build a space shuttle out of a toothpaste tube and fly to Neptune than use one of those things."

"I was thinking of going there. Neptune."

"I'm sure you will. You're quite a concept, Haddon."

"What's your concept of me these days?" she asked.

Her question made me sad. I always thought of her as invincible like smoke, but asking this made her more human. "It's changed over the years. I used to think you were this hippie kid."

"You don't think that anymore?"

"I honestly don't know. I started out thinking that, and then as I learned more about life, I wondered if your parents really did smoke pot with you and take you to Woodstock when you were little. Then I wondered whether your upbringing was as middle-class pedestrian as mine. Maybe Haddon Seagull was a character you made up along the way to compensate for how ordinary it all was. Who knows?"

Haddon registered no emotion. I walked her outside to wait for the car service. In this light, I could see crow's feet around her eyes. She wore glasses that gave her an uncharacteristically mousy look.

"Haddon, may I say something?"

"Sure."

"I wanted to say I'm sorry. I've put too much on you all these years. It's not your fault," I said, choking nervously on the word "fault."

"What's not?" Haddon said, putting her hand on my shoulder.

"The way I reacted to you. The arguments I probably provoked. The judgments I passed. It wasn't your problem. It was mine."

"I'm not sure I understand," she said, her eyes narrowing.

"I'm not sure I do either. I just feel badly," I said.

"Maybe it's because of losing your dad."

"I don't know. Maybe you came to symbolize something in the part of my brain that registers symbols. All I know is, that fumbled kiss meant a lot more to me than to you. Hell, you didn't even remember."

"I'm sorry."

"At some point it doesn't matter, cause and effect. I just know I care about you and I hate arguing with you. I wanted to apologize."

"You didn't need to, but thanks, Fuse. Maybe whatever it is isn't your fault either. Maybe all this boy-girl stuff going on today started back in '75. Junior high school never ends, like—I dunno, like a lonesome dog barking at a cloud. I don't claim to understand it, but I think you may be confusing your thoughts with your actions. I don't feel like you've ever mistreated me. I just don't understand why I'm always alone."

I understood it perfectly, but I didn't come out and say, *Because some men are the real romantics, and you are a sailboat called* Desperado. *Because I remembered the panda and you didn't.*

Instead I said something gentler. "Even if you've made the right decision with your life, the big challenge is finding a place in your head for the stuff you didn't do." My quasi-silence was wisdom in action, a strategy I undertook in *not* raising with Joey what Kurt had told me about the two of them on the Rehoboth boardwalk decades ago. Not every mental biscuit that gets jammed between our ears merits liberation through conversation.

"By the way," Haddon said, "I borrowed some moisturizer from Joey and noticed she has a panda on her dresser."

"Yeah, I got it for her long ago, when I realized this was it. With her."

"That's sexy."

"No, Haddon, it's not. But I'll tell Joey we made out as soon as she left," I said.

"I'll post the photos on Twitter."

Haddon Seagull kissed me lightly on the lips and flew south.

• • •

With the holidays approaching and winter descending, it was getting too cold to ride my bike. Running had taken a toll on my joints as far as outdoor activity was concerned, so hiking was my default. It gave me a lot of time to think, which I'm not sure was such a good thing.

Guilt covered me like skin. Nat was gone, but he was behind every tree. Every branch was a pointed finger. Guilt was at its root, colossal self-indulgence that had evolved to keep the guardrails on civilization. All you could do was distract yourself by living the best life you could.

In early December, we took Finn to Renato's in Potomac. I made like I was going to put a breadstick up Joey's nose, and even Finn laughed. On the way out of the restaurant, Angie and Kurt and their kids were coming in. They were dressed in Christmas colors. Kurt held Angie's arm, either with affection or for balance. Perhaps he had developed some greater appreciation for her at the expense of his beloved polar ice caps. Steven had his arm on his sister's shoulder. Samantha was planning to head back to the University of Virginia after the new year. Angie looked better than she had at the height of the crisis.

Kurt possessed a hollowness in his eyes and wore a quizzical expression, as if he found himself on another planet, one where consequences blossomed in unfamiliar gravity and everything was tilted on a different axis. We hadn't discussed our big scheme very often. Kurt had come to understand the danger of knowing too many details, especially as Pacho continued to blow up all over the news.

"Hey, Uncle Fuse," Samantha said. She had much better color in her face than when I saw her last. Her hair was down, and she looked remarkably like Angie had looked decades ago. "Do you have a quick second?"

"Sure."

We stepped into a courtyard area just outside the restaurant. "I'm glad you're out and about," I said.

"I'm forcing myself. I still want to sleep all day," she said.

"That's understandable given what happened. Believe me, I know the feeling."

"Not you. You could handle anything," Samantha said, really meaning it.

"You couldn't be more wrong, kiddo. I really do know what it's like to not want to get out of bed."

"*You?* Really? What for?"

"I don't know. Chemistry. A dark view of the world."

Samantha was studying my face, searching for some betrayal of depression. "What do you do about it?" she asked.

"Exercise. Meet people for lunch. Try to do something nice for somebody."

Samantha moved toward me and whispered, "I'm not supposed to say anything about what's been in the news lately."

"What news?" I knew what news.

"About what happened to him."

"Oh, I saw that interview," I said, as if it was about as relevant to me as a traffic report from Croatia.

"He deserved it," she said.

"I think so too. I'm glad somebody took notice."

"Somebody?"

"Somebody."

"I didn't actually say I wanted revenge, you know? My dad wanted revenge. I said I wanted to know why he did it. Whatever you did, it didn't erase what happened, but in a weird way it made me feel like I was loved. Is that terrible? I know I'm loved. That's more than a lot of girls in my spot know. Maybe that's the most you can get."

"You can get more, but it's not a straight or short line."

"I'm not trying to be ungrateful, but it doesn't solve anything. You know, what happened to him. I know I said I wanted to get him when we first talked, and a part of me still feels that way. But it's not like it's all wrapped up. You know, closure bullshit."

"I don't believe in closure."

"What do you believe in?" Samantha asked.

"I believe in learning to live with what you can't cure."

"Then what was this about? Helping me?"

"Doing something to try and balance out the world. I have this all-consuming fear of Finn colliding with the world just as you did, Sammy."

"Why do you think he did it?"

I touched Samantha's nose, as had been my habit for many years with her, and said, "Pacho is somebody who doesn't care. Period. And that's how we got . . . that's what caught up with him."

"He just *doesn't care*? That's the reason?"

"Sammy, there are these rules in journalism law. Malice and reckless disregard. One means you do something bad because you want to hurt someone, and you know you're doing it—that's malice. The other means you really don't care what you do, as long as you get what you want. What Pacho did was malicious to you. But to him, at most, it was the second one: reckless disregard. The thing is, there comes a point when you get tired of hearing about everybody's quirky little illnesses that make them do bad things. Sociopath, narcissist, personality disorder, all that crap." I shrugged. "Sometimes you have to conclude some people are just shitty, regardless of what causes it."

"If you didn't get him, Uncle Fuse, would he have been caught?" Samantha asked.

"I don't believe in cosmic justice. Not even a little. That's one reason why I chose the career I did. For some people, what goes around doesn't come around."

Samantha shook her head. "I just don't get it. Then why should the rest of us bother being good at all?"

"Someday, decades from now, we'll go for a hike and you'll tell me the answer."

"There is an answer?"

"Yes, there is," I said.

"I wonder if Joey and Finn know how lucky they are to have you."

"Joey does, I hope. Finn thinks I'm annoying. I hope that'll change someday. Sometimes I think Finn hates me."

"She doesn't hate you. Girls clash with each parent. I have things with my dad."

This got my attention. "Like what?"

"What he's done. You know what I'm talking about. The women."

"Okay," I said, not wanting to confirm anything.

"Finn just wants to see how far she can push things," Samantha said.

There was something in the sincerity of her presentation that made me accept what she was saying at face value. Yes, she had issues with her father, but they hadn't been of the kind that would push her into fabricating a rape. Maybe Pacho reminded her of her father, but not everything had multiple layers of meaning. Sure, she had been betrayed by both men, but her anger at her father hadn't led her to concoct a sinister, multi layered scheme. And the Rossiters certainly had things they wanted to keep hidden, but didn't we all?

"All I do is worry about Finn," I said.

"You should do more things like what you did for me. Helping somebody who's lost. You're like a good assassin."

"Do you feel lost, Sammy?"

"I feel sorry for people who don't have anybody in their corner like I did. Even with all I have, I don't feel right yet."

"You know what I took too long to figure out? Everybody's trying too hard to overcome their problems," I said. "Sometimes it's more realistic to learn living with a thing and not expecting there will be a day when it'll be over. Trying too hard to make things vanish from your mind is a false goal. When you can't make the thoughts vanish, you'll think you failed, when you really didn't. People are always saying things like 'Don't let it get to you.' Well, sometimes things get to you."

"Uncle Fuse, did you know other women would come forward after the stuff about Pacho came out?"

I kissed Sammy on her forehead and started walking her inside to join her family. "Never occurred to me."

The Rossiters all wore an expression that suggested they just hoped they could eat without being noticed, a sentiment that they had never experienced until Pacho Craig came along and blew up their lives. I had been with Kurt and Angie plenty when they were recognized in public and knew how much they enjoyed it, so this change in the weather system of their existence must have been withering—this thinking that everyone knew their secrets when surely they didn't. My friends would have to learn to live life from the audience and not from the stage.

As I had told Angie, love is your history—and I loved them a lot more than I disapproved of them.

• • •

Back at home, I went into my study, sat at my desk, and gazed at a painting of my mother when she was fifteen. Her eyes were sky blue, and she wore an expression of certainty. This was my way of speaking with her: updating her on my life and my thoughts, through unspoken reflection.

Two minutes into my reverie, my iPhone blinked with a message from Frankie Waterman. She'd attached a tweet from Gretchen Kramer, who was leaving the *Incursion* to finish her book at a cabin in West Virginia, "away from corporate media."

How Walden Pond of her.

I may have been in the midst of a deep empathy fever lately, but my sentiments didn't extend to Kramer.

The *Incursion* had shown no sign of investigating her Sunshine Collective ties, let alone publishing a story about their symbiotic relationship with the outfit. But I had signed an agreement in exchange for money, saying I wouldn't press the matter, and I wouldn't. I had a hard streak, though—one that had earned me my nickname—and I did enjoy knowing that Kramer was stumbling through the cold woods, wondering what the hell had happened to her. I have yet to meet a reporter who admitted, *I fucked up*. We're even worse than the people we go after, in that regard; we're watching them, but there's nobody watching us. It's easier to blame dark external forces rather than oneself.

Anyway, Kramer was too damaged to act, and Lord knows, I was not about to do the Washington Wink—the one where you take another player out to lunch and hint at being the trigger man behind some big hit. The ones who survive in this ripsaw of a town are those who find comfort in the shadows—not the ones who claim credit for unfastening the proverbial parachute while it's being folded into its pack.

I felt just fine about having rid the world of Gretchen Kramer and

Pacho Craig. Now the question was, what did I do for a career when my only skill had become obsolete, and the only way I'd thought to use that skill was taking out people in the very enterprise that taught it to me? I had become a reporter to stop the bastards. My program to wipe Pacho Craig off the board had done more for justice than journalism or the courts ever could, but justice would have to be hunted by other means now.

Perhaps I could try to stop the bastards my own way. Maybe the Callous Sophisticates would return. The world no longer wanted my journalism, but it seemed to have an appetite for my wrath.

• • •

Finn had a holiday party to go to, and I told her that if anybody drank and drove her, I'd blowtorch them.

"Is that why they call you Fuse?" Finn asked.

"Could be."

Joey and I hadn't heard a word about Frigging Alex, and I gently asked my wife if she had gone out and killed him behind my back.

"No," Joey said. "That would have made his allure stronger."

"Do you think we may have gotten rid of him just by being nice to him?" I asked.

"We *were* nice to him, weren't we?"

"Worked better than the blowtorch."

Joey knew I could never personally blowtorch anybody, but she suspected that the man who had once thrown his maniac father off a second story landing probably knew people who did that sort of thing. I think she kind of liked it, too.

Finn left for the party, and I took some comfort in knowing that she was a good kid—and that Patty Hearst had grown up to be a nice person who helped raise money for sick children.

I heard Joey's footfalls going up the stairs, presumably to bed. I wasn't ready to go up yet, so I decided to take a big risk and try to operate the TV myself. I managed to flip through the wilderness of channels and stopped when I heard the opening drums—*Ba Ba Ba BUM*—of *The Rockford Files*. A wave of familiar but rare excitement for life swept through me, just as the scent of burning firewood from a neighbor's house aspirated through a cracked-open window. It was the kind of sensory rush that transported me to a specific time and place where I remembered only the good things, like riding my bike in the dark to Joey's house after dinner in '75, to the torque of "Born to Run" pounding from a passing car.

As I watched *Rockford*'s opening montage, I hadn't heard Joey approaching, but I felt her arms crawl around me from behind.

ACKNOWLEDGMENTS

My editor at Greenleaf, Erin Brown, provided direction that was absolutely essential to what this book became. Without her, I would not have had the insight on my own to redirect certain elements of this story. Her skills brought me to Greenleaf. Thanks also to Lindsay Bohls, Justin Branch, Ava Coibion, Brian Phillips, Amy Dorta McIlwaine, and Kesley Smith at Greenleaf.

My author friends were a great source of support in the writing of this novel. Larry Leamer, Dan Moldea, and Gus Russo encouraged me not to shy away from exploring the grievances of a middle-aged journalist over the demise of his trade. *Mindhunter* author Mark Olshaker gave me consistently valuable insights from his research into sex crimes. Thanks also to some of the other authors in our crew, including Nancy Lubin, Mark Perry, David Stewart, Marty Bell, Joel Swerdlow, and Peter Ross Range.

My friend N., a rape survivor, documentarian, and activist, shared the terrible details of her ordeal and pointed me toward additional sources that could help paint a better picture of what women go through at the hands of sexual predators. N. helped me do my best to avoid stepping on certain landmines and to not even attempt to make this work of fiction a meditation on the #MeToo movement, which this novel surely isn't. Any misconceptions or perceived insensitivities portrayed here are my fault alone.

I found the work of Ken Lanning, who created the FBI's child crimes unit, insightful, both in his publications and in our discussions. My friend L.B. gave me an inside look at how narcotics gangs operate in major cities.

My family—Donna, Stuart, Eliza, Meghan, Lincoln, and Susan—supported me by just being who they are. Thanks also to my four-legged family members: Brick (dog), Berlioz (cat), and alpacas Christo, Heatwave, Helios, Honeybee, Hopper, Ignite, Inola, Isabella, Kala, Khaleesi, Tanqueray, Targaryen, Teja, Twombly, Wildfyre, Zeva, and Zinta, whose puffiness was an inspiration.

I am grateful to my partners at Dezenhall Resources, Ltd.—Maya Shackley, Steven Schlein, Anne Marie Malecha, and Josh Culling—as well as my colleagues at the firm who tolerate my literary indulgences, including Suzi Kindregan, Mike Bova, Maggie McNerney, Fred Brown, Jennifer Hirshon, Reilly McDonnell, Colton Henson, and Riley Althouse. Thanks to Casey Hebert for his help with technology, which is apparently something people are using these days.

Thanks also to Joel Mayer, a childhood friend who allowed me to use his name for a minor character, and Oliver Shackley, whose name I chose for a character only slightly less diabolical than he is. To that end, readers should know that the characters in this book and their actions are completely made up, despite the tendency for people to enjoy speculating about which real people they may be based upon.

I am grateful to Bob Stein, Norm Ornstein, Richard Ben-Veniste, Cary Bernstein, Sean Desmond, Kris Dahl, Sally Satel, Frankie Trull, Tom Clare, and Libby Locke for reasons they know. Finally, I am grateful to my high school English teachers, the late Joseph Truitt (who passed away as this book was being edited), Lorraine Truitt, and Barbara O'Breza of Cherry Hill West, who gave me my initial push into writing.

AUTHOR Q & A

Q: In addition to being an author, you're one of the top crisis management experts in the country. What does that job entail? How did you draw upon that background when writing *False Light?*
A: Crisis management is the business of navigating character assassination, and I really wanted the plot of *False Light,* which is a term from defamation law, to deal with that. I work with companies, institutions, and sometimes individuals under attack. I'm basically a campaign manager specifically focused on stopping reputation attacks, which are sometimes deserved and sometimes not. Much of the plot of *False Light* involves character assassination (and I'm a character-driven writer): potential reputational damage to Samantha, Fuse, Guido Reni, Oliver Shackley, and, of course, Pacho.

Q: Why did you want to include the #metoo movement as a theme in the novel?
A: Character assassination is one of the fault lines of #metoo. One reason why women don't come forward is the fear of their reputations being dragged through the mud. Victims also come to question their own character, wondering if they may be crazy or invited bad behavior. Then there are the reputation concerns of those who are accused. I've found that some of the worst people out there want to be respected even if they don't deserve it. And people who feel they have been wrongly accused have no intention of passively accepting having their lives ruined.

Q: What research did you do to dive into the dynamics of the #metoo movement, from the perspectives of both the victim and the accused?
A: I was extremely anxious about the subject and wanted to acknowledge the phenomenon without editorializing about it. I spoke to a friend who is a rape survivor and activist, and, in addition to telling me her story, she pointed me toward powerful and relevant literature, interviews, and documentaries. She also warned me strongly against my impulse to come to Samantha's rescue in a perfect way; her ordeal could not be neatly solved with everybody living happily ever after. In addition, she said, "Don't try to be the 'cool guy who gets it' because you can't possibly get it."

I interviewed experts including law enforcement officers, sex crime investigators, mental health professionals, and criminal profilers. I've always been lucky to have good female friends whom I could talk to about these kinds of things without them thinking I was crossing a line. I also took into account decades of experience with crisis management during which I've had cases where organizations and individuals have been rightly accused, wrongly accused, and cases where it's been hard to tell.

Q: How did you make the leap from crisis management expert to published author?
A: I can't write down much in my business because of confidentiality and the potential for things to show up in court and in the media. And I can't talk about my clients. Nevertheless, there are so many things I've learned that I want to put out there—lessons on how the world works—without betraying confidences. Most of my non-fiction books deal with my business. My novels incorporate what I've learned along the way about the media, celebrities, and the powerful.

Q: Are any of the characters in *False Light* based on your real-life friends or experiences?
A: I borrowed a little from people I've known and fabricated others. Kurt Rossiter is a guy I made up in college. My mom once asked me whether anything romantic was happening with a girl I knew, and I blurted out, "No, she's going out with Kurt Rossiter." The name just popped out. He didn't exist, but he became my nemesis; an excuse for frustration and dashed hopes. He's the guy who gets away with everything, like Rollo Tomassi in the movie version of James Ellroy's *L.A. Confidential*. It's amazing how over the course of my career, people have thought certain characters were based on other people when, in fact, novelists have *always* been known to make things up.

Q: Throughout the novel, Fuse has serious issues mastering (or even using) technology. He coins an acronym, TICU, for "Things I Can't Use." Is this something you also face, and if so, what do you find the most frustrating aspect about technology and what is the most useful?
A: I'm not quite as bad as Fuse, but I'm pretty bad. A physical therapist once told me that she could sense that my "ions are reversed" and that I could shut down electronic objects by just being near them. I thought that was great, however ridiculous, and I used that in the book. I actually have a "tech nanny" on call because it's so bad. God bless Casey.

I feel that social media has wreaked havoc upon humanity and altered crisis management forever, but it is here to stay. Yes, I use it, but I still handwrite first drafts of my books. I have had to master my iPhone because my kids use it to text and send photos. Plus, I need to see every second of my grandson's development, and technology helps me do that. However, I don't understand how civilization has become dependent on satellites in outer space but can't make a TV remote control that I can use.

Q: You clearly have plenty of knowledge about the realities of media and its "stars" today. What experiences did you draw upon from your own life for that insight?
A: I've been teaming with and doing battle with the media for almost four decades. I believe in the First Amendment and the press' watchdog role. I also believe there is corruption in the media, supported by our laws, that allows them to become assassins and ideological warriors versus reporters of news.

Journalists have threatened me with ruin on several occasions by virtue of the controversial cases I've worked on, and I have seen how the press has free rein legally to take down whomever they don't like. Some of the #metoo cases that have snagged big media figures are a direct consequence of unchecked power on a broader level. There has been a backfire effect in the last few years that has been interesting to watch and participate in.

Q: What was your favorite chapter to write in *False Light* and why?
A: I love the sections when the junior high friends are together in middle age. It's amazing how adolescence—the people, the songs, the humiliations, the mischief—looms large in our lives no matter how old we get. I'm fifty-seven years old and can still hear the jukebox songs, smell the lip gloss, and hear the lockers clanging shut.

Q: Like Fuse, do you also have a great love of history, especially twentieth-century politics? If so, when did this begin for you? Have you always been fascinated by famous yet flawed characters, such as Kennedy and Nixon? Did this influence your initial interest in crisis management?
A: I once thought I wanted to run for office. The first book I ever got was about U.S. presidents. I worked in the Reagan White House in my early twenties and quickly learned I had no idea what politics

really was. I had thought it was about being charismatic and inspirational. I didn't have a clue about policy or the mechanics of advancing in politics. I was ideologically moderate and was unprepared for the meanness of it all.

Crisis management became interesting to me because I saw that it came down to storytelling and the devices to get around the people who wanted to prevent you from telling that story. This happens on both sides of the ideological spectrum. We tend to only support free speech for our side; we want the other side silenced. I took what I learned in politics into the business sector.

Q: Do you have a favorite character in the story? If so, what is it about this character that you most appreciate?
A: I was very intrigued writing about Eddie Fontaine, the gangster. He's loosely based on a friend who was a leader in a violent organized crime ring. He got out of that life; one of the few who did. He's bright, caring, tough, and aspirational, and he just couldn't stand the brutality. He was simply born in a rough environment. In *False Light,* I reflected his anxieties about being in the crime business and the challenges in transitioning out of that life.

Q: What are some of your favorite books and authors?
A: Joan Didion is a favorite. I share her perpetual sense of dread and her ability to turn it into haunting literature. I grew up on Philip Roth, another Jersey boy. When I want to get lost, I go for Daniel Silva, Michael Connelly, or Elmore Leonard. I write a lot about crime and I think Leonard understands the triviality of it. Contrary to what you see in the movies, banal human impulses move the world, not grand conspiracies.

Q: You've also written several successful non-fiction books. Do you enjoy writing novels or non-fiction more, and why?
A: I lean toward fiction because of the liberties I can take. With non-fiction you must verify everything. Also, non-fiction involves real people, and real people tend to see themselves in cinematic terms and often have expectations about how they'll be portrayed that don't pan out in the writing.

QUESTIONS FOR DISCUSSION

1. One theme of the book is the #metoo movement. How does Fuse view the movement?
2. Why do you think Kurt calls Fuse in to help with Samantha/Sammy instead of handling the situation himself? Do you think Kurt feels so guilty about his own extramarital affair(s) that he wasn't in a position to help his daughter?
3. Fuse tells Sammy and her parents that if she calls the police and moves forward with pressing charges, she will be grilled on the stand in court and have her reputation ruined; that it will be a case of he said/she said, and she will be sacrificed in the process. In spite of this, do you think Fuse should have pushed Sammy harder to go to the police? Do you agree with Fuse's perspective?
4. Sammy reacts to Pacho's assault in her own unique way—doubting herself, feeling guilty, and ultimately, not wanting to press charges. Do you feel this is a common reaction for victims of sexual assault? What other responses could she have had? Do you wish she had reacted in another way?
5. There were a few moments when characters questioned whether Sammy was telling the truth and/or if she'd misinterpreted what

had happened with Pacho. Did you ever doubt her version of the events? Did you ever feel that Pacho had been falsely accused?

6. Fuse clearly struggles to understand how men and women should and do interact in the modern workplace, and even in personal relationships. Why does this confuse him so much?

7. Why do you think Fuse uses humor to deal with his father? What other coping skills does he employ to deal with difficult situations and people in his life?

8. How does Fuse's relationship with his father affect other relationships in his life? With his wife, Joey? With his daughter? Does Fuse's struggle to come to terms with his father's abuse also bleed into how he views his work and friendships? How so?

9. Why do you think Joey loves Fuse? What aspects of his personality does she appreciate? What does he provide to her as a loving husband and partner? What does Fuse love about Joey? What does she give to him as a wife?

10. Fuse talks a lot about how media and journalism has changed from the Woodward and Bernstein era to now. How has modern media changed, evolved, or devolved?

11. How would you characterize the relationship between Fuse and Kurt? Does Fuse's resentment of Kurt's wealth and ability to get away with things other men can't prevent a deeper friendship? Does Fuse see a lot of Kurt in Pacho? Does that fuel his resentment of Pacho?

12. Fuse deals with some insecurities—from his abilities with technology to his relationships with the women in his life. How do other people view Fuse? Do other people regard him as intelligent

and capable, or do they view him in the same way he sees himself? Does his self-image change throughout the novel?

13. Why does Fuse still have a crush on Haddon? Does she represent a time in his life that he desperately longs for? A time when the relationships between men and women weren't as complicated?

14. What is Fuse's biggest conflict in the story? Does it get resolved? If so, how?

15. Was Fuse's revenge against Pacho motivated by his desire to help Sammy and her family, or was Fuse more attracted to bringing down the type of modern, young, journalistic media star that he despises?

16. What does Fuse's future look like now that he's not working for a newspaper anymore? What do you think he will do moving forward?

17. Fuse's father, Nat, suffers from a mental illness. Does this information help Fuse come to terms with his father's abuse? Why or why not?

18. Fuse talks a lot about Kurt's ability to get away with things in life without real consequences. If Fuse also had this capability, would he ever cheat on Joey? If so, would it be with Haddon? What other things in life might he try to "get away with?"

ABOUT THE AUTHOR

ERIC DEZENHALL is the author of seven novels and four nonfiction books, many dealing with media-driven scandals. His most recent book (with Gus Russo) is *Best of Enemies: The Last Great Spy Story of the Cold War.* Eric is the CEO of Dezenhall Resources, Ltd., one of the nation's first crisis management firms. He lives near Washington, DC, with his family, some being alpacas. Eric has written for publications including the *New York Times*, the *Wall Street Journal*, and the *Washington Post*. In his spare time, he makes up words such as "nostralgia" (having fond memories of one's nostrils) and "handsomniac" (being so handsome, you can't sleep).